Even the Inspector himself doesn't know—because his secret weapon is as ladylike as she is clever. She's Mrs. Jeffries—the determined, delightful detective who stars in this unique Victorian mystery series. Be sure to read them all . . .

The Inspector and Mrs. Jeffries

A doctor is found dead in his own office—and Mrs. Jeffries must scour the premises to find the prescription for murder.

Mrs. Jeffries Dusts for Clues

One case is solved and another is opened when the Inspector finds a missing brooch—pinned to a dead woman's gown. But Mrs. Jeffries never cleans a room without dusting under the bed—and never gives up on a case before every loose end is tightly tied . . .

The Ghost and Mrs. Jeffries

Death is unpredictable . . . but the murder of Mrs. Hodges was foreseen at a spooky séance. The practical-minded housekeeper may not be able to see the future—but she can look into the past and put things in order to solve this haunting crime.

Mrs. Jeffries Takes Stock

A businessman has been murdered—and it could be because he cheated his stockholders. The housekeeper's interest is piqued . . . and when it comes to catching killers, the smart money's on Mrs. Jeffries.

continued . . .

Mrs. Jeffries on the Ball

A festive Jubilee celebration turns into a fatal affair—and Mrs. Jeffries must find the guilty party . . .

Mrs. Jeffries on the Trail

Why was Annie Shields out selling flowers so late on a foggy night? And more important, who killed her while she was doing it? It's up to Mrs. Jeffries to sniff out the clues . . .

Mrs. Jeffries Plays the Cook

Mrs. Jeffries finds herself doing double duty: cooking for the Inspector's household and trying to cook a killer's goose . . .

Mrs. Jeffries and the Missing Alibi

When Inspector Witherspoon becomes the main suspect in a murder, Scotland Yard refuses to let him investigate. But no one said anything about Mrs. Jeffries . . .

Mrs. Jeffries Stands Corrected

When a local publican is murdered and Inspector Witherspoon botches the investigation, trouble starts to brew for Mrs. Jeffries . . .

Mrs. Jeffries Takes the Stage

After a theatre critic is murdered, Mrs. Jeffries uncovers the victim's secret past: a real-life drama more compelling than any stage play . . .

Mrs. Jeffries Questions the Answer

Hannah Cameron was not well-liked. But were her friends or family the sort to stab her in the back? Mrs. Jeffries must find out . . .

Mrs. Jeffries Reveals Her Art

Mrs. Jeffries has to work double-time to find a missing model *and* a killer. And she'll have to get her whole staff involved—before someone else becomes the next subject . . .

Mrs. Jeffries Takes the Cake

The evidence was all there: a dead body, two dessert plates, and a gun. As if Mr. Ashbury had been sharing cake with his own killer. Now Mrs. Jeffries will have to dish up clues . . .

Mrs. Jeffries Rocks the Boat

Mirabelle had traveled by boat all the way from Australia to visit her sister—only to wind up murdered. Now Mrs. Jeffries must solve the case—and it's sink or swim . . .

Mrs. Jeffries Weeds the Plot

Three attempts have been made on Annabeth Gentry's life. Is it due to her recent inheritance, or was it because her bloodhound dug up the body of a murdered thief? Mrs. Jeffries will have to investigate . . .

Mrs. Jeffries Pinches the Post

Harrison Nye may have been involved in some dubious business dealings, but no one ever expected him to be murdered. Now, Mrs. Jeffries and her staff must root through the sins of his past to discover which one caught up with him . . .

Mrs. Jeffries Pleads Her Case

Harlan Westover's death was deemed a suicide by the magistrate. But Inspector Witherspoon is willing to risk his career treading political waters to prove otherwise. And it's up to Mrs. Jeffries and her staff to ensure the good inspector remains afloat . . .

Mrs. Jeffries Sweeps the Chimney

A dead vicar has been found, propped against a church wall. And Inspector Witherspoon's only prayer is to seek the divine divinations of Mrs. Jeffries . . .

Visit Emily Brightwell's website at
www.emilybrightwell.com

MRS. JEFFRIES LEARNS THE TRADE

MRS. JEFFRIES LEARNS THE TRADE

EMILY BRIGHTWELL

BERKLEY PRIME CRIME BOOKS, NEW YORK

THE BERKLEY PUBLISHING GROUP
Published by the Penguin Group
Penguin Group (USA) Inc.
375 Hudson Street, New York, New York 10014, USA
Penguin Group (Canada), 10 Alcorn Avenue, Toronto, Ontario M4V 3B2, Canada
(a division of Pearson Penguin Canada Inc.)
Penguin Books Ltd., 80 Strand, London WC2R 0RL, England
Penguin Group Ireland, 25 St. Stephen's Green, Dublin 2, Ireland (a division of Penguin Books Ltd.)
Penguin Group (Australia), 250 Camberwell Road, Camberwell, Victoria 3124, Australia
(a division of Pearson Australia Group Pty. Ltd.)
Penguin Books India Pvt. Ltd., 11 Community Centre, Panchsheel Park, New Delhi—110 017, India
Penguin Books (South Africa) (Pty.) Ltd., 24 Sturdee Avenue, Rosebank, Johannesburg 2196, South Africa
Penguin Group (NZ), cnr Airborne and Rosedale Roads, Albany, Auckland 1310, New Zealand
(a division of Pearson New Zealand Ltd.)

Penguin Books Ltd., Registered Offices: 80 Strand, London WC2R 0RL, England

This book is an original publication of The Berkley Publishing Group.

Mrs. Jeffries Learns the Trade

PRINTING HISTORY
Berkley Prime Crime trade paperback edition / April 2005
Berkley trade paperback ISBN: 0-425-28346-8

This book has been catalogued with Library of Congress.

PRINTED IN THE UNITED STATES OF AMERICA

10 9 8 7 6 5 4 3 2 1

CONTENTS

THE INSPECTOR AND MRS. JEFFRIES

CHAPTER 1

Dr. Bartholomew Slocum was definitely dead. Inspector Gerald Witherspoon stared morosely at the body slumped over the huge mahogany desk and fervently wished he were home sitting in front of a roaring fire instead of standing in a gloomy Knightsbridge surgery.

From behind him, he heard Constable Barnes clear his throat. Witherspoon thrust the image of a cozy fire and a glass of port out of his mind and remembered his duty. Straightening his spine, he moved determinedly toward the body.

Aware of the two pairs of eyes staring at his back. Witherspoon leaned forward and examined the dead man. It was not a chore he relished. The fact was, he was rather squeamish about dead people, but as corpses went, this was a rather nice one. At least it wasn't covered in blood.

He heard an impatient shuffle of feet behind him, and that brought him back to the problem at hand. "Hmmm," he muttered thoughtfully, trying to sound both wise and official. "The gentleman is definitely dead."

"Yes, we know," said Dr. Sebastian Hightower somewhat irritably. "That is, of course, why I summoned the police."

"Hmm, yes." Witherspoon turned and smiled faintly at the portly man standing next to Constable Barnes. Hightower didn't return his smile. He gazed impatiently from beneath thick brown eyebrows and pointedly picked up his watch chain.

"The doctor was obviously reading when death occurred," Witherspoon said. "See how his head is resting on that book. Except for the rather peculiar way his arms are flopped out, one on each side, you'd think he was merely taking a nap."

"Well he isn't napping," snapped the doctor, glaring at Witherspoon. "He's dead and the circumstances are very suspicious."

"Suspicious?" Witherspoon echoed. He didn't think there was anything suspicious about a dead person in a doctor's surgery. Mind you there were more dead people in hospitals, but surely; if one couldn't die in a hospital, a surgery was the next best place.

"Look, Inspector, I do wish you'd get on with it. You've been here ten minutes and all you've done is stare at the fellow."

Witherspoon stiffened. He was terribly unsure of what to do, but he wouldn't tolerate the fact that it was starting to show. "Staring at the corpse, as you call it," he said cooly, "is the best way to begin an investigation. We don't even know that Dr. Slocum's death is a matter for the police. Now, Dr. Hightower, could you please describe how you came to find the deceased?"

Hightower sighed. "I've already told all that to your constable here."

"I'm sure you have, but I'd like to hear it myself."

"I came in and saw Dr. Slocum slumped over his desk. At first I thought he was doing exactly as you said, taking a nap. But when he didn't move after I'd called out several times, I realized something was wrong. I examined him quickly and checked for a pulse, then realized he was dead. But it was when I saw what he had clutched in his other hand that I decided to send for the police. Luckily, the butler happened to come in then, so I sent him for the constable on the corner."

"I see," Witherspoon muttered. He was annoyed with himself. He hadn't even realized Dr. Slocum *was* holding something in his fingers. Looking down, he saw a small vial curled in the palm of the dead man's hand.

"Precisely. Uh . . . exactly why did you think this vial warranted such an action? I mean, why did it strike you as suspicious? The gentleman's dead, but there certainly isn't any sign of violence. Perhaps the poor man has had a heart attack."

"Inspector Witherspoon," Hightower began slowly, as though talking to a thick-skulled child, "if you'll trouble yourself to lift Dr. Slocum's head, you'll see why I considered his death suspicious."

Witherspoon swallowed hard and rolled the dead man's head to one side. He tried not to shudder as a pair of open, beady gray eyes gazed up at him. The face surrounding those eyes was puffed up like bread dough, and the flesh was flushed a bright pink. A hideously swollen tongue protruded from between lips that had been stretched in a horrible parody of a smile.

Inspector Witherspoon quickly turned the face away and stepped back.

"As you can see, he's swelled up like a bullfrog," Hightower continued. "He may well have actually died of heart failure, but I assure you, it was brought on by something else. I summoned the constable because of the vial in his hand. That's Syrup of Ipecac, man, it's got one use and one use only. An emetic. Dr. Slocum's been poisoned. Furthermore, I suspect he knew it and was attempting to treat himself when he died."

"Right, right, well, the police surgeon will be here shortly, and I'm sure he'll concur with your opinion."

Hightower snorted and reached up to stroke his full brown beard.

"How did you happen to be here today? Did you have an appointment with the deceased?" Witherspoon was sure that was an appropriate question.

"My being here was merely a matter of chance."

"Chance?"

"Yes." Hightower shifted his walking stick from one hand to the other. "Actually, I had an appointment with a patient who lives around the corner, but as I was early, I thought I'd call in on Dr. Slocum. He didn't see patients on Wednesdays. I decided to pop in and say hello. We hadn't seen each other in a good while—"

"He didn't see patients on Wednesdays?" Witherspoon interjected, sure that was a pertinent point.

"No," Hightower replied, "he did not." He stared at the inspector curiously. Was the man going to repeat everything he said? "His surgery was closed on Wednesdays. But as I was saying before you interrupted, I thought I'd call in, but when I knocked on the door, there was no answer. I thought that was a bit peculiar, but as there was nothing I could do about it, I went on round to my patient's."

"Why did you find it peculiar?"

Hightower, who wasn't the most patient of men, took a deep, calming breath. "Because there was no one home, that's what was peculiar." He lifted his hand in a wide arc. "Look at this place. The house does not run by itself. Dr. Slocum had a full staff. Cook, footmen, a housekeeper, two maids and a butler. There should have been someone here."

"Perhaps he gave them all the afternoon off," suggested the inspector. He too had servants, and if the weather was fine and his house was in tiptop shape, he frequently gave them all the whole day off.

Hightower was shaking his head vigorously. "No, he wouldn't have done that. Slocum was much too worried about thieves to give the entire staff the day out. Why, the man always made sure there were at least two footmen on the premises when he took his servants and went to his farm in Essex."

"You certainly are well versed in how the late Dr. Slocum ran his household," Witherspoon said. "You must have been very close friends. Can you tell me—"

"We certainly weren't close friends," Hightower interrupted. He looked as though he'd been insulted. "The entire neighborhood knew every dull detail of his domestic arrangements. He was always boasting about how efficiently he managed things. Just last Saturday he was out in the gardens at Mrs. Crookshank's afternoon tea bragging to everyone about how clever he was. Bored everyone to tears too. That's why I'm so familiar with the way he ran his household." Hightower paused to take a breath.

"Yes, I can see your point. So you're sure that Dr. Slocum wouldn't have given the servants a day off as a special holiday? Perhaps a treat for a job well done."

"I don't think so," Hightower replied, looking a bit uncertain. "I know for a fact that he split their days out. Said it was more efficient that way."

"More efficient, you say?"

"Yes." Hightower's cheeks began to turn red. "Some of the staff got Wednesday afternoons off and the rest got Saturday afternoons off. Someone should have been here."

Witherspoon nodded. "If no one answered the door, how did you get in?"

Hightower looked annoyed. "I got in through the back door."

"Through the back door? But I thought no one was home?"

"There wasn't anyone home," the doctor snapped. "I told you, I was visiting another patient and she lives around the corner. That means she shares the communal gardens on this block. After I finished examining her, she asked me to take a look at her rose bushes. They've got blight. I do have some small renown for growing exceptional roses myself. While I was checking her plants, I happened to glance up and noticed Dr. Slocum's back door was open. Naturally, I came to investigate. For Heaven's sake, man, I've told all this to the constable."

"Yes, yes, I'm sure you have, but—"

"Look. Inspector," Dr. Hightower pulled his pocket watch out again and scowled, "I really must be off. If you've more questions, you can come see me at my surgery in Harley Street."

There were a lot of questions the inspector knew he should ask, but he couldn't quite remember what they were. Thank goodness he'd be able to go home soon. He could think better on a full stomach, and furthermore, he could always think better after a nice chat with Mrs. Jeffries, his housekeeper.

"That'll be fine, Dr. Hightower," Witherspoon said quickly. "Just leave your address with Constable Barnes."

The inspector decided he'd better do as the doctor suggested and get on with it. The fact that he was totally at a loss as to what to do next didn't deter him. He frowned and tried to remember something his housekeeper had said recently. Oh yes, it was about that dreadful business in the Kensington High Street . . . Now what was it? His face brightened as it suddenly came to him. "If you'd been in charge from the first, Inspector," Mrs. Jeffries had said emphatically, "you wouldn't have made the silly mistakes Inspector Nivens made. Why, you'd have searched the murder scene yourself and not left it up to a constable!"

Of course, of course. That's what he'd do next.

Witherspoon walked the length of the room, his footsteps muffled by the thick Persian carpet. He glanced down, noting the rich, muted colors of the rug, and thought that it was awfully fancy for a surgery. His gaze swept the room. The walls were painted white and the windows covered by tied-back green velvet curtains. Floor-to-ceiling shelves and bookcases filled one wall, and along the opposite wall there was a row of cabinets with a variety of vials and bottles of all different colors and shapes. The doctor's heavy mahogany desk was in the center of the room, and at the far end, there was a dressing screen next to the examination table.

Except for the fact it was a bit more opulent than his own physician's surgery, Witherspoon could see nothing out of the ordinary.

He crossed the hall, went into the dining room and walked quickly to the end of the table where the remains of Dr. Slocum's luncheon were sitting on a silver tray.

Witherspoon stared at the table but could see nothing unusual. A crumpled white linen napkin lay next to an empty wine bottle. He reached down and picked up the crystal goblet the deceased had drunk from, and noticed that there was a bit of wine still in the bottom of the glass.

"Are you ready to see the butler yet?" Constable Barnes called from the doorway.

"In a moment," Witherspoon replied, setting the goblet next to a dirty plate littered with lamb chop bones. He picked up a soup bowl and saw that there was a bit of mushroom soup left in the bottom. Sighing, he glanced up at the constable, who was still waiting in the hall. "You'd better find a box, Constable," he said. "This might be evidence, so we'd better send the whole lot off to the Yard for examination."

"You think he might have been poisoned, then?" Barnes asked.

"There is always the possibility," Witherspoon replied. "I'd better have a word with the butler now."

Wendell Keating, a small mouselike man with a wispy white mustache and watery blue eyes, stood waiting in the drawing room, his fingers clutched together in front of him.

Witherspoon advanced toward the servant. "Good afternoon, I'm Inspector Witherspoon from Scotland Yard and I've a few questions to ask you."

"Yes, sir, I'm sure you do."

"You know of course, that Dr. Slocum was found dead this afternoon in his surgery?"

The butler nodded but said nothing.

"We think he's been poisoned." Witherspoon watched Keating's reaction carefully, but the butler's rigid features didn't change. "What do you think of that?"

"That's terrible, sir." The servant's voice was flat.

"It certainly is." Witherspoon allowed himself a brief smile. "And it's our job to find out how it happened."

"Yes, sir."

"Now, why was the household deserted this afternoon?"

"Dr. Slocum gave us the afternoon off."

"But I have it on good authority that Dr. Slocum's regular habit was to give half the staff Wednesday off and the other half Saturday. Are you saying he gave you all the afternoon off at the same time?"

"Yes."

"Why?"

"I don't know."

Witherspoon began to get annoyed. "Had he ever done it before?"

"Yes."

"Well, when?"

Keating shrugged. "Sometimes. I don't rightly recollect when the last time was. But occasionally, he up and gave everyone the afternoon off at the same time. It didn't do no good to ask him why; he wasn't one for telling his reasons."

Further inquiry continued in the same vein, with Witherspoon asking every question that popped into his head and the butler answering precisely what was asked and volunteering no more. By the time the inspector ran out of questions, his head was starting to ache.

He did remember to ask the butler where he'd been that afternoon, though. But that answer didn't help him very much. Keating had spent the afternoon visiting a sick friend in Kew. Witherspoon duly recorded the information and then dismissed the butler.

The inspector was tired, hungry and confused. Surely the information he'd received meant something, but what? He decided to wait until he received the police surgeon's report before he did anything else. Perhaps Dr. Hightower was wrong. Maybe the doctor hadn't been poisoned after all. Even if he had, Witherspoon told himself as he marched into the hall and reached for his overcoat, that didn't mean he'd been murdered. Accidental poisonings certainly weren't unheard of.

Barnes met him in the hallway. "Do you want me to keep a constable here all night, sir?"

"All night?" Witherspoon frowned, wishing he'd thought of that himself. "Good idea, Constable. The rest of the servants aren't back yet, so you'd best station a man here in the hall to keep an eye on things. Put another man out front as well. I'll be back tomorrow morning." He reached for his hat. "Oh, and as the rest of the servants come in this evening, make sure you take their statements."

"Right, sir," Barnes held open the front door for the inspector. "Any ideas, sir?"

Witherspoon paused. He thought longingly of his former job in the records room at the Yard and wished he were back there. Yet it would never do to let on—everyone, including he himself was amazed by his apparently phenomenonal powers of detection.

He gave Barnes a knowing smile. "Lots of ideas, Constable. But then, any fool can have ideas. I don't believe in ideas; I believe in facts."

"Absolutely, sir," Barnes quickly agreed.

"A rigourous and logical examination of the evidence, Constable, that's what will lead us to the truth. Let's not jump the gun here. No, no, that would never do. If I've said it once, I've said it a hundred times. Ideas are useless unless they're correct."

Mrs. Jeffries walked briskly down the back stairs of the big house in Upper Edmonton Gardens and into the warmth of the kitchen. She paused by the doorway and smiled as she surveyed her cozy kingdom.

Betsy, the housemaid, was sitting at the long trestle table, polishing a tray of silver. Mrs. Goodge, the cook, was pulling a pan of bread out of the oven, and Wiggins, the footman, was standing in front of the cupboard. His hands were raised to his face, and he was poking himself in the cheeks.

"Wiggins, what are you doing?" Mrs. Jeffries asked. "This is the third time today I've seen you standing in front of a glass with your fingers boring into your face."

Betsy giggled. Mrs. Goodge snorted. Wiggins dropped his hands and whirled to face her. "Uh, I was a . . . a . . . ," he stammered.

"He's tryin to poke dimples into his cheeks," Betsy volunteered. "Wiggins is sweet on the new housemaid from down the road. But she told 'im she only likes a feller with dimples. Our Wiggins thinks if he keeps on poking 'imself long enough, he'll sprout a couple."

Mrs. Jeffries rolled her eyes. "Wiggins, that is nonsense. One is either born with dimples or one isn't. No amount of prodding at your flesh is going to produce them. Now look at you," she advanced on the hapless youth, "you've got two huge red scratches on your face. Go put a cool cloth on it before you get infection."

"But I've got the beginnings of 'em," Wiggins protested, "and look 'ere." He picked up a copy of one of Inspector Witherspoon's monthly magazines and thrust it toward the housekeeper. "See, look at this picture 'ere. That African's got ears as big as saucers and 'e wundn't born with 'em. He grew 'em, says so right 'ere."

"Wiggins," said Mrs. Jeffries patiently. "It is possible to distort one's flesh. But obviously you didn't read the article that accompanied the picture. If you had, you'd know that Africans begin changing the contours of their flesh in very early childhood. They certainly don't wait until your advanced age."

Wiggins was nineteen.

"But it's workin'. Look, one's starting right here." He pointed to his right cheek.

Mrs. Jeffries ran out of patience. She wasn't going to stand by and let the silly boy mutilate his face because of his latest infatuation, one of many, with a pretty housemaid. "Don't be ridiculous. Pretty is as pretty does. Any young woman who is more concerned with a man's dimples than a man's character has about as much sense as Lady Afton's cocker spaniel."

Wiggins gasped. Lady Afton's spaniel was notorious. The animal was so stupid it didn't even recognize its mistress. "But, Mrs. Jeffries," the boy said, imploringly, "I really like this un."

"Wiggins, you like them all. Take my word for it, a young man as fine as yourself won't have to settle for an empty-headed little chit like that. You can do better."

"Will dinner be served at the usual time?" Mrs. Goodge interjected. She finished smearing butter on the top of the loaves and moved to the table.

"I'm not sure." Mrs. Jeffries frowned as she noticed the cook limping slightly. "Just keep the inspector's dinner in the oven. He's usually home by now. Is your rheumatism acting up, Mrs. Goodge?"

"Only a bit." The cook heaved herself into a chair.

"Leave the food on the stove and let the staff serve themselves for dinner. If your ankles are hurting, you need to stay off them. After dinner I'll make you a poultice."

"Much obliged."

Mrs. Jeffries cocked her head as footsteps sounded on the pavement outside the kitchen window. "There's the inspector now," she announced, bustling toward the stove. "You rest those ankles, Mrs. Goodge. I'll take his dinner up."

Witherspoon was sitting at the dining table when Mrs. Jeffries brought the tray in. She paused in the doorway and studied her employer. He was a tall, robust man with thinning dark brown hair and a neatly trimmed mustache. He had a long, rather angular face, a sharp, pointed nose and clear blue-gray eyes. He was staring dejectedly at the white lace tablecloth.

She knew what was wrong. She'd seen the signs before. Poor Inspector Witherspoon had been given another baffling case. Mrs. Jeffries's spirits soared.

"Good evening, Inspector," she said cheerfully. She sat the tray on the sideboard, picked up his plate and placed it in front of him. He immediately brightened up.

"Good evening, Mrs. Jeffries. How are things here at Upper Edmonton Gardens?"

It was an evocative question, one he asked when he was desperate for her to ask him how things were at the Yard—a kind of code they used for nosing into each other's business without actually having to come right out and pry.

"The household is running smoothly," she replied, picking up a cup of tea from the tray she'd brought up and taking the chair next to him. At

Witherspoon's insistence, it was her habit to keep the Inspector company for his evening meal. "How are things at the Yard?"

"Not so good, I'm afraid," he sighed. "Crime. The criminal element. There's never any rest for those of us in the service of justice." He took a quick bite of roast beef and chewed hungrily.

Mrs. Jeffries waited patiently.

"Why, just today a highly respected doctor was found dead in his surgery. It could be murder. I tell you, Mrs. Jeffries, I don't know what this world is coming to. Everywhere you look—sin, immorality, vice, lascivious living."

Mrs. Jeffries privately thought these things weren't any better or worse than they had ever been. To her way of thinking, human nature was the one constant in an everchanging world. But she contented herself with muttering a platitude as Witherspoon rambled on about the wickedness of modern life.

She was thinking about murder.

"Which doctor was it?" she finally asked.

The inspector was well into his lecture on immorality, so it took a few moments for him to realize what she was asking him. "Dr. Bartholomew Slocum. He had a practise in Knightsbridge."

"How was the doctor murdered?" Mrs. Jeffries asked softly.

"He may have been poisoned, but I'm not sure one can positively say the man was murdered. A vial of Syrup of Ipecac was found in his hand." Witherspoon shook his head. "But no, that still doesn't prove Dr. Slocum was deliberately murdered, despite the learned doctor's opinion."

"But I thought you said the doctor was dead?"

"Dr. Slocum is dead. It was Dr. Hightower, the man who happened to find the body, who hinted of murder. He's the one that notified us. It's pretty obvious to me that Hightower suspects foul play. I mean, why call the constable unless you think something is amiss? But until I get confirmation from our police surgeon, I'm not jumping to any conclusions."

"So you suspect the death might have been accidental?"

"I hope so," Witherspoon replied fervently. He looked at the kindly face of his housekeeper and said hopefully, "It could have been, couldn't it?"

"Of course." Mrs. Jeffries smiled gently. "I'm sure you're absolutely right, Inspector. It was probably accidental. Mind you, you'd think with him being a trained physician he'd be very careful when handling poison. But, I suppose any of us could get careless."

"Hmmm . . ." Witherspoon's face fell. "I hadn't really considered that," he mumbled. "He would be trained properly. And from the appearance of his surgery, one gets the impression he was a most careful man."

Wisely, Mrs. Jeffries let him finish his dinner before asking him any more questions. It was easier to wheedle information out of the inspector when his stomach was full.

"I'll have to interview the rest of the servants tomorrow," the inspector commented morosely. He hated questioning people. He could never tell whether or not someone was actually lying to him, and he knew, shocking as it was, that there were some people who lied to the police on a regular basis.

He glanced at Mrs. Jeffries. She smiled serenely, as though she thought him capable of moving mountains. The sight bolstered his resolve. Of course he could solve this case, if indeed, there was a case to be solved. Wasn't she always telling him how brilliant he was? Hadn't he solved several "unsolvable" crimes before? He stiffened his spine and smiled happily. He didn't know what had gotten into him today; of course he could do it.

Mrs. Jeffries rose to her feet and picked up the inspector's plate. "Well, of course, sudden death is always upsetting, not to mention suspicious."

"Just so," the inspector agreed. "Yet, frankly, I can't think why anyone would want to murder Dr. Slocum. He appears to be a highly respected and presumably very able medical man, so it's unlikely to have been a disgruntled patient. His butler didn't accuse him of drunkenness or gambling, and he didn't appear to need money." Witherspoon shrugged his shoulders. "So who would want to murder him? No, I'm beginning to think we'll find his death was an accident after all."

"I shouldn't be surprised if you're absolutely correct, as usual," Mrs. Jeffries said cheerfully. "Of course, my late husband always said that a sterling character and a fine reputation did not exempt one from the sins of another. As a matter of fact, he often said the best of men had the worst of enemies."

"Uh, yes, well, he would have been one to know," Witherspoon mused thoughtfully. Mrs. Jeffries's late husband had been a policeman in Yorkshire for over twenty years. Yet the inspector still wasn't sure what his housekeeper was on about. "Er, what did he mean by that?"

"It's quite simple, really. A good man, or woman, could easily make quite ruthless enemies by refusing to lie, or cheat or steal or cover up for wrongdoing, or—" She broke off and smiled. "Why, Inspector, you were teasing me. You knew precisely what I meant."

Witherspoon hadn't been joking, but he wasn't about to let her realize that. "Forgive me, Mrs. Jeffries," he replied, giving her the world-weary and wise smile he often got from his chief inspector. "I apologize for letting my sense of humor overcome my sense of decorum. As you know, I have the very highest regard for your late husband's accomplishments as a policeman."

"No apology is needed," she answered briskly. "When will you know for sure?"

His wise smile evaporated. He stared at her in confusion. "Know what?"

"Whether or not Dr. Slocum was poisoned."

"Ah, that. Yes, I'm hoping the police surgeon will have a report for me tomorrow."

She nodded. "I suppose that will determine whether the gentleman was actually poisoned. But if he was poisoned, how will you find out if it was deliberate or accidental?"

Witherspoon's face fell. Mrs. Jeffries immediately said, "Oh please don't answer that; it's such a silly question. Naturally you'll be able to determine whether or not it was murder by your investigation."

Betsy came in carrying a tray. "Your coffee, sir," she announced. She placed the tray on the sideboard and poured a cup for the inspector. As she turned to go, Mrs. Jeffries stopped her. "Betsy, is Smythe in the kitchen?"

"He's just got back from Howard's," Betsy answered, referring to the stables where the Witherspoon coach and horses were kept. Not that the inspector used them often, but he'd inherited the coach, horses and Smythe from a distant relative, and even though it cost a king's ransom to keep them in the city (hansoms were really so much more convenient), he hadn't the heart to sell them off.

Mrs. Jeffries smiled apologetically at the inspector and followed Betsy. "I must have a word with Smythe before he goes out."

Smythe was sitting at the table, his sleeves rolled up his forearms and his powerful frame hunched over a heaping plate of beef and potatoes, when Mrs. Jeffries came down the stairs. He started to get to his feet.

"Please, don't get up," she said quickly, motioning him back into his chair. "I just needed a quick word with you before you went out. I presume you are going to your usual place tonight?" She gave him a guileless smile.

"Ain't missed a night in seven years, have I?" Smythe said, watching her curiously. She sat down opposite him and glanced quickly around to make sure they weren't being overheard.

When she turned to face him, her eyes were sparkling and her chin was cocked at the determined angle he'd come to know well.

She was up to something, he thought. A right good snoop probably. Smythe's pulse picked up. He loved it when Mrs. J started her poking and prying. Livened things up considerably, it did. He leaned across the table and gave her a conspiratorial grin. "All right, Mrs. J. What you want me to do this time?"

CHAPTER 2

Mrs. Jeffries was less startled by Smythe's statement than she was by the knowing expression on his face. Why, the man looked positively smug.

"*What do you want me to do this time?*" His words echoed in her mind. But surely he didn't realize what she was up to. She'd been so careful to be discreet in her investigations on the inspector's behalf. She always took great care to sound exceedingly casual when she sent Smythe off to find a bit of information on one of Witherspoon's cases. She'd deliberately couched her various requests in the most inconsequential language, as though they were things one did as a matter of course. Things to keep one busy and add a bit of color to one's life.

But perhaps she hadn't been quite as discreet as she'd thought, or perhaps the other servants at Upper Edmonton Gardens were a good deal quicker off the mark than she'd realized. Keeping her placid smile firmly in place, she studied Smythe, trying to get a clue as to how much he had guessed about her activities.

Smythe was a tall, dark-haired, powerfully built man with a face that some would call brutish unless they took the time to notice his kind brown eyes. Mrs. Jeffries sighed softly, suspecting that those eyes saw a great deal more than she'd ever guessed and that the rest of the household, save for the inspector, knew precisely what she was doing. They weren't fools.

Oh well, she told herself firmly, it can't be helped. Besides, her little investigations certainly made their lives more interesting.

"It's more a matter of what I want you to not do," Mrs. Jeffries finally replied.

He stared at her quizzically. "Come again, Mrs. J?"

"I don't want you to go to your usual tonight, Smythe. Wouldn't you like to try a new place? Perhaps one of the pubs in Knightsbridge?"

"Knightsbridge?" He regarded her thoughtfully. "I'm right fond of the ale they serve down at the Blue Boar, but seein' as how it's for you, all right."

"Thank you, Smythe." Mrs. Jeffries smiled gratefully and leaned closer to the coachman. "Now. You might have to try several places, but I want you to find out everything you can about a man named Dr. Bartholomew Slocum."

"What's he done?" Smythe took another bite of roast beef.

"Nothing. He's dead."

Smythe's eyebrows shot up, but he kept silent.

"He might have been murdered," she continued.

"*Might* have been murdered," Smythe repeated. "Can't the police tell for sure?"

"He may have been poisoned," she explained, "but the police won't know for certain until after the postmortem. Inspector Witherspoon should have the surgeon's report by tomorrow."

"Then why do you want me to go out snoopin' tonight?" he asked. "In't that puttin' the cart before the horse?"

"Let's just say this is in the nature of a reconnaissance expedition," she replied. "Besides, I've got a feeling about this case. Don't you want to go to Knightsbridge?"

"I don't mind," he said, shrugging one massive shoulder and giving her a cocky grin. "I always fancied myself a bit of a scout, sneaking off into enemy territory, pokin' about and seein' what I can . . ."

"Good," she interrupted firmly, knowing Smythe's tendency to get carried away. "Dr. Slocum's surgery is on Barret Street. See if you can find any of the servants from his household and find out as much as you can."

"Anything in particular you want to know?"

Mrs. Jeffries frowned as she thought back over everything Witherspoon had told her. He hadn't been very specific. She made a mental note to remedy that situation. But the inspector had said the man might have been poisoned.

"Find out what the household had eaten that day, if you can," she said, "and, of course, anything else."

"Right." Smythe rose to his feet. "I'd best be off then." He headed for the door.

As his hand reached for the knob, Mrs. Jeffries called out. "Smythe."

He half turned and gazed at her curiously.

"You will, of course, be very careful," she said softly, her expression concerned.

"Don't fret, Mrs. J," he replied, grabbing the knob and pulling the door open. "I'm always careful."

Mrs. Jeffries fervently hoped so.

"I do wish you'd eat breakfast with me," Witherspoon said as Mrs. Jeffries poured herself a cup of tea and sat down next to him.

"I had my breakfast hours ago, and it really wouldn't be proper for me to eat formal meals with you, Inspector." She smiled. "You know that."

"I don't believe it would be all that scandalous. With all due respect to Her Majesty, this isn't Buckingham Palace. You are my housekeeper, and it's not as if we're particularly formal here." He sighed, rather dramatically. "Eating every meal by oneself gets a tad lonely, you know."

"But you're not alone," she assured him. "I'm sitting right here keeping you company. Furthermore, if you were *married,* you'd have a wife to eat your meals with." She looked at him expectantly.

Witherspoon shook his head and shoved another forkful of fried egg into his mouth. Mrs. Jeffries gazed at him thoughtfully while he finished his breakfast. She so wished the inspector would find a nice young lady. The dear man was lonely. The fact that a wife might very well inhibit her own passion for investigating didn't concern her in the least.

"You know my work is far too dangerous for me to take on the responsibility of a wife," Witherspoon said. "Why, anything could happen to me. I spend my life investigating heinous crimes, murders . . . I can't risk it. I've got so many enemies."

Mrs. Jeffries refrained from commenting that until rather recently the inspector had spent most of his life in the records room at Scotland Yard. She knew why he wasn't married, why the very idea terrified him. Witherspoon was notoriously shy when it came to women. She decided to try another tactic.

"Really, Inspector," she began earnestly, "you know very well that a man of your intelligence is always half a dozen steps ahead of any criminal that might be lurking about."

The inspector beamed.

"Certainly your work is dangerous," she continued, "but there are many men who have even more frightful occupations, and they have the comfort of wives and children."

Turning a bright pink, Witherspoon lowered his fork and gazed fondly at his housekeeper. The dear woman was always looking out for him. But on this subject, he really rather wished she wouldn't press him. "Mrs. Jeffries."

"Yes," she replied, giving him an innocent smile.

The words lodged in his throat as he gazed at her. He remembered all too well how different his life had been before her arrival. But then so much had been different—he'd been nothing more than a records clerk when his Aunt Euphemia died and everything changed. Before he'd had time to catch his breath, he'd inherited a house, a fortune, Smythe and Wiggins. (Well, he hadn't actually inherited them, but as they'd worked for his Aunt Euphemia and she'd been the one to leave him her entire fortune, he could hardly turn them out.)

Yet his life hadn't really changed until he'd taken up residence here eighteen months ago—which had necessitated hiring a housekeeper. Mrs. Jeffries.

Witherspoon frowned as he realized it was soon after that that he'd discovered his amazing abilities as a detective.

"Inspector," Mrs. Jeffries said softly, seeing that the man was daydreaming again, "there's an absolutely lovely woman staying at Lady Afton's. A Miss Liza Cannonberry. Lady Afton has the very highest regard for you, and I'm sure she'd be happy to arrange an introduction."

"Eh?" Witherspoon blinked, but he had heard Mrs. Jeffries's last few words. "Arrange an introduction," he repeated hastily, trying not to panic. "Oh no, I don't think that would do at all."

Luckily for him, the door opened and Betsy came in. Mrs. Jeffries frowned ever so slightly when she recognized the man following behind the maid. Rising quickly to her feet, she forced a polite smile to her lips.

"Inspector Nivens," she said smoothly. "How very nice to see you. Would you care for some breakfast?"

She sincerely hoped he wouldn't. Of all the people she'd ever met, one of the few she'd disliked on sight was Inspector Nigel Nivens. Further acquaintance with the man hadn't changed her opinion either.

Nivens was a slender man of slightly more than average height with a ferretlike face, slicked back dull blond hair and the coldest gray eyes she'd ever seen. As he crossed the room, she noticed how his gaze swept the table, taking in her empty teacup sitting next to Witherspoon's breakfast dishes.

"Thank you, but no. I had breakfast early, I was at the Yard by seven." Nivens gave her a cool, superior smile before turning his attention to Inspector Witherspoon.

"My goodness, you're an eager fellow," Witherspoon said cheerfully. "Did you hear that, Mrs. Jeffries? Inspector Nivens has been up and working since the crack of dawn."

"How very conscientious of you," she murmured, knowing full well that Nivens's sly dig had sailed completely over Witherspoon's head.

"Would you like a cup of tea, then?" Witherspoon asked.

Mrs. Jeffries stiffened. She hoped Nivens would have the good grace to refuse and be off about his business.

The odious man had made it clear on numerous occasions that he didn't believe for one minute that Gerald Witherspoon was much of a detective. He'd actually had the gall after those notorious Kensington High Street murders to tell the chief inspector that Witherspoon's success in apprehending the murderer had been sheer luck. Either that, or he'd had help.

Inspector Nivens made Mrs. Jeffries very, very nervous.

"I'm afraid I don't have time," Nivens replied, straightening his spine pompously. "There's been a robbery in Holland Park. I'm on my way there now. But as I had to pass by your street, I thought I'd bring this to you." He pulled an envelope from his coat pocket and laid it on the table. "It's the surgeon's report on that Knightsbridge matter."

"Why, that's jolly decent of you."

"It was no trouble." He turned and glanced at Mrs. Jeffries. "Of course, I knew you'd want to see this right away."

Mrs. Jeffries stopped herself from looking at the envelope. Her hands itched to pick it up and tear it open. But she knew that would never do. Nivens would like nothing more than to catch her meddling in the inspector's cases. But Hepzibah Jeffries hadn't lived fifty-seven years on God's green earth without learning a few tricks.

Witherspoon used his breakfast knife to slit open the flap. Mrs. Jeffries would have bet two weeks' housekeeping money that that wasn't the first time this morning that seal had been broken. But naturally, one couldn't say anything.

"I'd best be on my way," Nivens said cheerfully, watching Inspector Witherspoon fumbling around to pull the report out.

"I'll see you to the door," Mrs. Jeffries murmured politely. She followed him out of the dining room and down the hall. As they reached the front door, Nivens turned and smiled slyly.

"This might be a difficult case for the inspector," he said softly. "Poisonings always are. Wouldn't you agree?"

"Actually, I'd have no idea," she said innocently. "And neither would Inspector Witherspoon until after he'd read the surgeon's report."

He flushed a deep red as he realized his mistake. But he recovered quicker than she'd hoped.

"You're a very clever woman, Mrs. Jeffries," he said smoothly. "The inspector is lucky to have you in his employment."

"Oh no, Inspector Nivens," she assured him. "It is I who am fortunate. Not everyone is privileged to work for such a kind and brilliant man as Gerald Witherspoon."

Nivens's eyes narrowed slightly as they gazed at each other in silence. From the drawing room, the clock chimed the hour.

"It's getting late," he finally said. "Must be off. Good day to you, madam."

"Good day, Inspector."

As the door closed behind him, she leaned against the wood and took a few seconds to compose herself. Dealing with Nigel Nivens always had the effect of putting her in a foul mood.

Straightening, she patted the pocket of her skirt and then smiled in satisfaction as she hurried back to the dining room.

She found Witherspoon holding the surgeon's report at arm's length and squinting at the handwriting.

"Mrs. Jeffries," he grumbled, "I can't see a ruddy thing. Do you know where my spectacles are?" He glanced up at her. "It's not that I really need them," he explained, "but the light isn't very good in here and this writing is dreadfully small. I don't know why they can't teach these medical chaps decent penmanship."

"I'm so sorry, Inspector. I have no idea where they are." She sent up a quick, silent prayer for forgiveness as she told the fib. "Would you like me to read the report to you?"

Witherspoon turned quickly to glance at the clock on the sideboard and saw that it had gone eight. "It is getting late, and I do need to know the surgeon's findings before I go back to Knightsbridge. I mean, there's not much point in going back at all if we find the chap had a stroke or something." He handed her the report. "Thank you, Mrs. Jeffries. That's most kind of you to offer."

It took less than five minutes to read, and at the end, both of them were shaking their heads.

"Mushrooms," exclaimed Witherspoon. "I've never heard of such a thing. And in the man's soup! Gracious. Dreadful business," he mumbled. "Absolutely dreadful."

"Some mushrooms are quite poisonous," Mrs. Jeffries said slowly. "According to the surgeon, the mushroom Dr. Slocum ingested was called '*amanite phalloide*'—I think that's what we used to call the death cap. Oh yes, Inspector, those are quite deadly." She frowned slightly as something tugged at the back of her mind.

"Apparently so. Oh well," he said cheerfully, "at least I had the foresight to send Dr. Slocum's luncheon dishes to the Yard for examination. No doubt that'll make the Home Office happy."

"I beg your pardon? What does the Home Office have to do with Dr. Slocum's lunch dishes?"

"Why, everything. Thanks to my quick action, the police surgeon didn't have to do much cutting on the body. It says so in the report; they spotted part of a poison mushroom at the bottom of the soup bowl right away. Most convenient for the surgeon." He leaned toward her and lowered his voice. "Her Majesty doesn't really approve, you know."

Mystified, she stared at him. "Approve of what?"

"Cutting on people. She's not all that keen on the surgeons mucking about with someone's body. The Home Office is far happier when we can spot the cause of death without having to actually do any cutting. Just between you and me and the clock on the sideboard, I'd bet my next hot dinner that once our medical man spotted that mushroom, he didn't do any cutting at all. None of them like to upset the Home Office."

"I see." Mrs. Jeffries glanced down at the report in her lap. No doubt, the inspector was right. But really, not wanting to upset the Home Office seemed an awfully useless excuse for not doing one's job properly.

Witherspoon nodded. "Now the doctor is hardly likely to have gone out and plucked a poisonous mushroom from out beneath a bush and popped it into his soup, is he? So I suppose my next step is to find out how it got there."

"That's true."

"Perhaps it was accidental?" He brightened at the thought. "Yes, I expect that's it. A poisonous mushroom accidentally got mixed into a batch of edible ones and ended up in Dr. Slocum's stomach."

"That's possible." Mrs. Jeffries laid the report next to Witherspoon's plate and gave him a serene smile. "And I'm sure you'll find out precisely what happened."

Witherspoon smiled and sincerely hoped his housekeeper was right.

• • •

"Oh leave off, Wiggins," Betsy teased. "We all know why you're so keen to wash the fence." Both she and Mrs. Goodge laughed as the boy turned a bright red.

"I'm not *keen* to wash the bloomin' thing," he protested, reaching for another bun and glancing furtively at the housekeeper. "But it's my job, now, in't it, and Mrs. Jeffries wants it done."

Mrs. Jeffries was only half-listening. Her mind was on the information she'd wheedled out of Inspector Witherspoon about the late Dr. Slocum. She was thinking about the physical description of the victim's face that the inspector had given her as he was putting on his coat. Something about it disturbed her, but she couldn't quite put her finger on it.

"Get on with you," Betsy chided. "Who do you think you're foolin'? You just want to hang out in front so you can moon over that Miss Cannonberry who's staying at Lady Afton's. You're awfully fickle, Wiggins. Yesterday you were in love with that housemaid down the road, but the minute you laid eyes on Miss Cannonberry, you forgot her quick enough. Admit it, you want to be outside there when they walks that dumb dog."

"That's not true," he protested around a mouthful of bun. "And what about you? You hotfoot it outside quick enough whenever that Constable Griffith's around."

"Ohhh . . ." Betsy gasped indignantly and drew a sharp breath. "Of all the rotten—"

Mrs. Jeffries decided it was time to intervene. "Now, now, you two. That's enough. Stop teasing each other. All it ever does is hurt feelings." The two combatants glowered at each other but kept silent.

The housekeeper rose to her feet. "Tea break's over," she announced briskly. "Betsy, you go finish dusting the drawing room, and Wiggins, if you're going to clean the fence, get on with it."

"I think I'll go have a rest," Mrs. Goodge said, rising stiffly to her feet.

As soon as the kitchen was empty, Mrs. Jeffries glanced at the clock and frowned. Where on earth could Smythe be? Mrs. Goodge said he hadn't come in for breakfast, and neither Betsy nor Wiggins had seen hide nor hair of him this morning.

She began putting the cups on the tray, telling herself he was probably already at Howard's, polishing a harness or exercising the horses.

The kitchen door opened and she whirled around.

"Good gracious, you look awful," she exclaimed, looking at the pale-faced Smythe as he slumped against the doorframe. "Are you ill?"

"It's a bleedin' wonder I'm not dead," he muttered, moving carefully toward the table. "Is there any tea left?"

"What happened?" Mrs. Jeffries asked in alarm. This certainly wasn't the first time she'd seen Smythe looking the worse for wear, especially after a night of pub crawling. But today he looked particularly greenish around the gills. She hurried across to the stove as Smythe stumbled toward the table. Snatching a mug off the wooden drain board, she poured it full of strong, hot tea.

"Gracious, Smythe," she said, plonking the mug next to him. "You look ghastly."

He groaned. "Not so loud, please. Me head feels like they's a team of horses kicking me brains in." He took a long drink, his eyes rolling toward the ceiling as the hot liquid poured down his throat.

"I tell ya, Mrs. J," he said after he'd gulped the entire mugful, "it's no wonder I look like the back end of a cow after what I had to drink last night. The swill they serve in some of those Knightsbridge pubs could choke a pig."

"I'm so sorry, Smythe." Mrs. Jeffries sighed. "I had no idea you'd end up like this when I sent you out." Feeling guilty, she gazed at him sympathetically. "Is there anything I can do?"

"Another cuppa would help." He held the mug out, and she quickly got to her feet and poured him more tea.

"Don't fret so," he continued. "I don't mind makin' a sacrifice for you," he paused and looked her directly in the eyes before adding, "and the inspector."

Mrs. Jeffries knew that he meant what he said. If Inspector Witherspoon hadn't kept both Smythe and Wiggins in his employ, both men would be in dire straits. Wiggins was no more a trained footman than she was the Queen of Sheba, and Smythe, for all his strength and intelligence, would be desolate without Bow and Arrow, the inspector's horses.

Mrs. Jeffries waited patiently while the coachman finished his tea. After he'd drained the mug, he sat back and gave her a cocky grin.

"Were you successful with your inquiries?" she asked.

Smythe nodded. "I found one of the footmen. Not much of a talker at first."

"Oh dear," she said, clearly disappointed. "You mean you didn't get anything out of him?"

"Course I did. Once the feller had a few pints down his gullet, his tongue loosened considerably," the coachman replied. "It seems the good doctor wasn't liked very much by his staff. According to the footman, he was a right ol' tartar."

"He didn't treat them very well?" Mrs. Jeffries said, wondering if that could possibly be a motive for murder. Then she realized it probably wasn't. If servants habitually killed harsh employers, half the gentry would be dead and buried.

"Treated 'em rotten, but he paid 'em good. That's what the footman claimed. Said the only reason the servants put up with the man was because he paid better than most."

"Were you able to find out what they'd had to eat that day?"

"They had porridge and tea for breakfast, not like here, where we get a decent meal of bacon and eggs. Then at lunch they had soup and bread with cheese. When they's all arrived back, the police were there, so they didn't get much for dinner that night." Smythe grinned. "The footman was real niggled about that too, said it wun't right, just because the man was dead shouldna mean the rest of them need starve. But the cook was wailin' and cryin' and not about to stir herself to fix 'em a bite o' supper."

"Did he say what kind of soup they'd eaten?"

"Mushroom." He paused as he saw Mrs. Jeffries eyes widen. "Is that important?"

"It could be," she replied thoughtfully. "Did the doctor eat the same meal?"

"No. He had the soup and cheese, all right, but he had himself a couple of lamb chops too. And a bottle of wine. Seems Dr. Slocum was right fond of the stuff. The footman claimed he sloughed it back like water every time he sat down to a meal."

"I see," she murmured. But if the doctor had been poisoned by the soup, why hadn't the rest of the household died?

"You want me to go back tonight? See what else I can find out?"

Mrs. Jeffries grappled with her conscience for all of two seconds and then gave the coachman a grateful smile. "If you wouldn't mind, Smythe. You might be able to learn something more. Something we can use to help the inspector solve this case."

It was pointless to pretend any longer that Smythe didn't know what she was up to.

"Are you going out then?" Betsy tossed a blond curl off her shoulder and watched as Mrs. Jeffries put on her hat.

"Yes, I'm going over to Bond Street to try and match that material for the dining-room curtains." The housekeeper could hardly announce that she was really going to Dr. Slocum's to search the scene of the crime. Or could she?

She paused, still holding her hatpin. "No, that's not true."

Since her talk with Smythe, Mrs. Jeffries thought it best to clear the air. The other servants had probably guessed the truth too, and it was best to make a clean breast of things. Truth to tell, her conscience was bothering her.

"It's not?" Betsy stared at her curiously.

"Come sit down, please. There's something I need to tell you."

Obediently, Betsy laid down her dust cloth and crossed the room to the settee. Mrs. Jeffries patted the spot beside her, and the girl sat down.

Mrs. Jeffries took a deep breath. "I'm sure you've guessed that occasionally, well . . . I, that is, we, do a few minor things to help the inspector with his cases."

Betsy nodded vigorously. "Oh yes, like that time during them 'orrible Kensington High Street murders when you 'ad me goin' round to talk to all the shop assistants. Or when you send Wiggins out with notes and all, or hide the inspector's spectacles so you can read the police surgeon's report, like this morning."

"Goodness, you saw that?" Mrs. Jeffries was shocked. She hadn't realized she'd been that indiscreet.

"Oh yes. It's like when you're on to something about one of the inspector's cases and you send Smythe off to a pub or get Mrs. Goodge to start gossipin'. Though mind you. I don't see how Mrs. Goodge knows so much about everyone in London, seein' as 'ow she never leaves the kitchen."

Mrs. Jeffries's amazement turned to relief, and she laughed. "So you've known all along. Have the others caught on as well?"

Betsy laughed too. "Well, I wouldna say we've known right from the start. It took us a bit a time to work it all out. But we're all of the same mind. We think what you're doin' is right. Inspector Witherspoon is the kindest man that ever lived. He's been so good to all of us. We'll do anything we can for him. And with the likes of that awful Inspector Nivens always sniffin' around, I reckon our inspector needs all the help he can get."

"I'm glad you feel that way," Mrs. Jeffries said softly.

"He kept me from havin' to walk the streets," Betsy continued earnestly. "And he kept Smythe and Wiggins after his Aunt Euphemia died, when everyone knows he need a coachman and a footman about as much as I need a diamond tiara to do my dustin' in, not that I wouldn't like to 'ave one, mind you."

"So you and the rest of the staff don't mind doing a little, shall we say, detective work, for our dear inspector?"

"Mind? You must be pulling me leg. Course we don't mind. It's interestin', and it's little enough to do for the man after all he's done for us."

"Good. Then you won't mind taking charge of the house this morning while I go to Knightsbridge?"

Betsy shook her head. "What are you going to do there?"

"I'm going to search the scene of the crime." Mrs. Jeffries rose to her feet. "We need to make sure a clue hasn't been overlooked."

She walked out into the pale October sunshine. Wiggins was halfheartedly washing the black wrought-iron fence as he kept an eagle eye out for Miss Cannonberry.

She started down the steps and then paused as she realized it couldn't hurt any to learn as much as possible about mushrooms. Leaving Wiggins happily staring up the street, she turned swiftly, went back inside and into the inspector's study.

A few moments later she came out again, a folded note clutched in her hand. "Wiggins. Come here, please. I need you to run an errand for me."

The boy looked crestfallen. "Now? You want me to leave now? But, Mrs. Jeffries, I'm right in the middle of this."

"It'll still be here when you get back," she assured him.

Reluctantly, Wiggins dropped the washrag back into the pail and trudged over to the housekeeper. He stared at the note in her hand. "Where do you want me to go?"

"To Mudie's," she replied, referring to the circulating library. She handed Wiggins the note. "Give this to Mr. Oliphant, and then wait until he finds a book for you. Bring it back straight away and have Betsy put it in my room."

After he'd gone, Mrs. Jeffries hurried to the corner and turned toward Hyde Park. She decided to walk to Dr. Slocum's—she needed to think.

CHAPTER 3

Mrs. Jeffries stopped across the road and studied the tall yellow-brick house of the late Dr. Slocum. The paint on the front door and around the windows looked new, the earth in the tiny space behind the wrought-iron fence was freshly turned and planted with bulbs, the stone steps were swept clean and the brass plate with Dr. Slocum's name and surgery hours was polished to a dull sheen.

Mrs. Jeffries crossed the road and headed for the police constable standing to one side of the brass door knocker. She was relieved when she recognized Constable Barnes's familiar craggy face.

"Good morning, Constable," she said cheerfully. "Isn't it a beautiful day."

"Why it's Mrs. Jeffries. What are you doing here, ma'am?" Constable Barnes looked both delighted and puzzled.

"The most dreadful thing has happened, Constable," Mrs. Jeffries said, gesturing to the front door. "I really must get inside there. Inspector Witherspoon mislaid his cigar case yesterday, and he hasn't the faintest idea where!"

Courteously, Barnes had already reached for the doorknob when he remembered this was a murder scene. But before he could say anything, Mrs. Jeffries was brushing past him and sailing inside.

"And it's a most valuable case," she continued, giving him a wide smile. "His father gave it to him for his twenty-first birthday. The poor man will be devastated if he's lost it."

"Can't he find it himself?" Barnes asked helplessly.

"I don't think so," she replied, moving briskly down the hall. "You know the inspector; he's far too involved in the case to remember a little detail like where he put his cigar case. But don't worry, I'll be very careful."

"I suppose it's all right, then," Barnes called out when he couldn't quite work up the nerve to stop the woman.

Mrs. Jeffries threw Barnes one last, confident smile as she reached the surgery and quickly stepped inside.

She didn't have much time and she knew it. Turning, she scanned the room, her observant eyes taking in as much as she could with one glance.

She moved to the row of cabinets, stopped by the first one and peered inside. Through the glass, she saw Dr. Slocum's medical instruments. In the cabinet next to that, she saw rows of neatly labeled medicines and chemicals.

Nothing odd here, she thought, turning toward the desk.

Cocking her head, she picked up one side of the large book that was lying open on it and read the title. *Adamson's Medical Comprehensive on Common Poisons and Antidotes.*

Surprised, she stared at the page and wondered how the inspector could have neglected to mention this to her. He probably forgot, she thought. She dropped the edge of the book and turned her attention to the desk. Searching quickly through the drawers, she found nothing out of the ordinary.

Nothing that gave her a clue as to why or who had murdered the doctor . . . if he'd been murdered. But she rather suspected he had, especially after seeing the open book on the desk. And hearing Smythe's report, Dr. Slocum had probably guessed he'd been poisoned as well.

But why? Why would a highly successful member of the British medical establishment think he'd been poisoned? She could think of only one answer. Because he knew someone wanted him dead.

Dropping to her knees, she peered under the desk. Nothing there. She continued searching the floor, tugging her long skirt high to prevent it from slowing her pace. She noticed how clean everything, including the carpet, was.

Beneath the medicine cabinet nearest the door, she spotted a small dark object. She reached into the shadowy space and pulled it out.

Holding it up to the light, she saw that it was a small piece of cork, approximately the size of her little fingernail. Her brown eyes narrowed thoughtfully as she studied it. Then she looked again around the room, noting how there wasn't a speck of dust anywhere, not even in the corners. She stood up and ran her fingers over the top of the cabinet. Her hand stilled. Bending close, she saw a fine layer of particles, not quite dust and not quite grit, scattered in the center of the wood.

From the hall, Mrs. Jeffries heard the sound of footsteps. She straightened and smoothed her long skirt just as the door opened and Inspector Witherspoon appeared.

"Mrs. Jeffries," he said in surprise. "What on earth are you doing here?"

"Finding your cigar case," she replied, pulling the case out of her skirt pocket and handing it to him. "I realized this morning when I handed you your coat that it wasn't in the pocket. I thought you must have lost it when you were here yesterday."

"Gracious me," he exclaimed, taking the case and staring at it with a puzzled frown. "How very clever of you. I didn't even know it was missing."

"No, of course you didn't. Once you're on a case, Inspector, your mind is fully occupied."

Witherspoon smiled modestly. "Well, it's very good of you to come find this for me." His smile faded and the puzzled look came back into his eyes. "But how did you know I'd mislaid it here?"

"Now, now, Inspector, don't be so modest. Why, you know very well I used your own methods of deduction to find it."

"You did?"

"Naturally, one can't be around a mind such as yours for very long without picking up a trick or two." She laughed merrily. "You had it yesterday at lunch. Then you were called here. As I said, it wasn't in your coat pocket when I checked this morning, and it wasn't at home. Obviously I knew there was only one place it could be. Here."

"Why didn't you mention it to me before I left?" he asked. "There was no need to trouble yourself to come all this way—"

"It was no trouble at all," she assured him. "And I don't like to bother you with trifling matters like a missing cigar case when you're so very busy. Besides, I had to come to Knightsbridge anyway. There's a draper's shop on Brompton Road that can match the fabric in the dining-room curtains."

"Well, as long as it was no bother, thank you." Witherspoon sighed happily. He was such a lucky man—how many other housekeepers would go to so much effort to see to his every comfort and need? And he was most fond of his cigar case. Even though he rarely smoked. Tobacco made him ill.

"Do you know, it's the most curious thing," Mrs. Jeffries said.

"What is?"

"I found the case beneath this medicine cabinet. The corner was sticking out. It must have slipped out of your pocket when you were searching the room yesterday. But when I went to pick it up, I found this as well." She handed the piece of cork to him. "Isn't that odd?"

"Looks like a piece of cork," he muttered, squinting at it. "Wonder what it was doing there."

"Yes," she said thoughtfully, "I wondered the same thing myself. Strange, isn't it?"

"How so?"

"Well, this room. It's so clean, and I couldn't help but notice when I was looking for the case that there isn't a speck of dust anywhere. Except for right here." She pointed to the top of the cabinet.

"Hmmm . . ." Witherspoon frowned as he bent over and stared at the spot. "You're right. There's dust on top of the cabinet. But that's probably just a patch the cleaning woman missed."

"Really? Do you think so. In a doctor's surgery?" She shook her head. "I daresay the rest of the room has had a thorough cleaning; there's not even a speck of dirt in the corners. It's peculiar that the maid would miss this. And I'm not all that sure this is dust. Doesn't it look a bit too coarse?"

"Hmmm, yes, actually. It does."

"And, of course, this is a doctor's surgery. The maid would have to insure it wasn't just tidied up, but really cleaned every single day."

"Naturally, naturally," Witherspoon agreed absently. Suddenly his eyes lit up in understanding. "That would mean that, perhaps, if this room was cleaned the morning of Dr. Slocum's death, that this," he held up the piece of cork, "was dropped either by Slocum himself or . . . the murderer."

"Murderer?" she queried softly. "Then you think the victim's death was deliberate and not accidental?"

"I'm afraid so," he said with a sigh. "One of the constables found another poisonous mushroom in the cooling pantry. It was in a bowl with some edible ones, and it couldn't possibly have gotten there accidentally."

"Why not?" Mrs. Jeffries wasn't surprised to find out the doctor had been murdered, but she was a bit puzzled by this new piece of evidence.

"Because the other mushrooms, the edible ones, had been properly cleaned. The poisonous one hadn't. There was dirt on the cap and stem, as if it had just been pulled from the ground and tossed into the bowl." He broke off and stared at the piece of cork again and then walked over to the medicine cabinet, opened the door and pulled out a brown bottle. "Aha, just as I thought."

"What is it?"

"Why, this piece of cork. Look here." He held the bottle toward his housekeeper. "It was obviously dropped by the doctor himself. The top is made of cork." Bending down, he peered inside for a moment and then said, "Half the bottles and vials in here are topped with cork."

Mrs. Jeffries looked over his shoulder at the inside of the cabinet. She reached around him and drew out a dark blue vial. "Yes, but look here. These tops are made from much finer-grained cork, while that one," she pointed to the piece he was still holding, "is very coarse. I think it's from a much larger bottle than the ones Dr. Slocum has here in his medicine cabinet."

Witherspoon's face mirrored his disappointment. He hated clues that didn't make any sense. "Hmmm, yes. I see what you mean." Drat, he thought, now he'd have to try and figure out the significance of the piece of cork. If it had any significance. He didn't relish talking to the maid again, either. She'd told him she didn't much care for policemen.

Confident she'd set her inspector on the correct path of inquiry, Mrs. Jeffries straightened. "I must be off now. Will you be home at your normal time for dinner?"

"Yes," he murmured, still staring dejectedly at the small piece of inscrutable evidence. "After I speak with the maid, the constable and I are going house to house around the garden to see if anyone saw anything unusual yesterday."

"Fine, then. We'll expect you at six." She waved a cheerful good-bye and left.

Mrs. Jeffries left the inspector still standing morosely in the surgery. As soon as she was in the hall, she stopped, listening for sounds of activity within the household. But there was nothing but silence. The servants, no doubt, had taken to their rooms or gone out for the day.

She decided this might be a good opportunity to find out how easy it was to get in and out of the Slocum house. Moving quietly, she went down the hall to the back stairs, past the door leading to the kitchen and out onto the tiny terrace that faced the garden. The first thing she must do was see if the garden gate was kept locked. But she hadn't taken two steps before she was stopped in her tracks.

"You there." The voice was flat, twangy and loud enough to wake the dead.

Mrs. Jeffries turned and saw a wrinkled, white-haired old woman wearing a bright red dress and hobbling toward her at surprising speed. "Were you addressing me, madam?" she asked politely.

"You're the only one out here," the woman replied and Mrs. Jeffries knew from her accent that she was an American.

"I'm Mrs. Archie Crookshank, first name's Luty Belle. Who're you?"

"Hepzibah Jeffries." She was trying to think of a plausible reason for being on Dr. Slocum's terrace, but she found she didn't have to. Mrs. Crookshank kept right on talking.

"Is the old geezer dead, then?" she continued. "I expect he was murdered, what with the constable swarming all over the place. That's not surprising. He wasn't exactly well liked around these parts." She broke off and cackled. "Shouldn't speak ill of dead, I suppose, but land's sake, that man could set a saint to running in the opposite direction." She peered at Mrs. Jeffries suspiciously, her brown eyes narrowing. "You ain't any kin of his, are you?"

"No." She smiled. "I didn't know the deceased. I'm merely here because my employer happens to have business in the house. But why do you think he was mur—"

"Good," Luty Crookshank interrupted, "then I ain't offendin' none." She raised a wrinkled hand and pointed to the house next door. "I live right there. Fancy place, ain't it? But Archie, that's my late husband, he was English, and after he'd made his fortune in the mines back in Colorado, he was determined to come back here. Been here now nigh onto twenty years. Ain't surprised someone finally killed ol' Slocum. He was the kind that always comes to a bad end."

"Did you know Dr. Slocum well, Mrs. Crookshank?" Mrs. Jeffries asked.

"Call me Luty Belle. Yup, I knew him pretty good. Didn't like him much. Too sly for my blood. Always pussyfootin' around trying to butter people up and then slippin' off and trying to listen in to private talks. Why, just last Saturday, when I was havin' my tea party, Slocum practically hid behind a bush so he could hear what Dr. Hightower and Mrs. Leslie were jawin' about."

"You mean the man was eavesdropping?"

Luty Belle snorted. "He did it all the time. I almost didn't invite him, but, well . . . he was a neighbor." She broke off and frowned. "Hey, you there, boy," she bellowed.

Mrs. Jeffries looked up in time to see a young gardener come out from behind a tree. Grinning, he waved and then hurried across the garden toward them.

"Mornin', Garret," Luty Belle shouted. "Did you dig them dead eyes out yet?"

The gardener shook his head. "No, ma'am."

"What are you waiting for, boy?" she said indignantly. "I told you, them things are poisonous. Now, you get over there and get to it."

"What things?" Mrs. Jeffries wasn't above interrupting herself.

"Dead eyes. Mushrooms."

"But, Mrs. Crookshank," the gardener said earnestly, "I can't dig them out. They're gone."

"Gone! What are you talkin' about? They didn't just get up and go for a stroll. There was a whole danged nest of them under that tree. Mrs. Leslie couldn't finish eatin' her cake after she found out what they was. Now, you go have another look, boy, and if'n you find 'em, I'll give you a guinea—"

"Luty Belle," Mrs. Jeffries shouted, and both of them turned to stare at her. "Forgive me, please. But this is very important."

"What is?" Luty Belle asked with a glare.

"Are you saying that during your tea party, which I presume was last Saturday, you saw some poison mushrooms?"

"Yes, there was a whole slew of them, right under that big tree out there where I was having my party. As soon as I saw they was dead eyes, I yelled at Garret here to dig 'em out as soon as he could." Luty Belle cocked her head to one side and stared hard at Mrs. Jeffries. "Why are you so interested?"

She debated about telling the truth and finally decided she had no choice. "Because Dr. Slocum was killed by eating a poison mushroom. Tell me, Luty Belle, did you mention the mushrooms during the party?"

She nodded slowly, her expression somber. " 'Fraid so. Everybody heard me."

"Who is everybody?"

"Let's see, Dr. Slocum was here and Colonel Seaward, he's the gentleman that lives in that mausoleum at the end of the garden." She pointed to her left. "Mrs. Leslie was here and Dr. Hightower. The Wakeman sisters were both here—no, they'd already left by then because they was fixin' to go to visit their niece in Shropshire and had to catch a train. Let me see, who else? The Baxters had gone by then too, but Mr. and Mrs. Eversole were still eating . . . Course, they never leave until the last crumb's gone, not that I mind. That's what it's for—"

"I think, Luty Belle," Mrs. Jeffries interrupted softly, "you'd better talk to my employer." She turned to the boy. "Could you please go inside and ask to see Inspector Witherspoon? Tell him Mrs. Crookshank needs to see him."

A few minutes later, she left a rather bewildered-looking Inspector Witherspoon with Mrs. Crookshank. Luty Belle was still talking when Mrs. Jeffries left the terrace.

• • •

Mrs. Jeffries waited till lunch was over before she began. The little chat she'd had with Betsy that morning, coming on top of Smythe's less-than-subtle hints, had convinced her that her attempts to discreetly help the inspector with his cases weren't fooling anybody.

"I've called you all together," she said, "because I need to . . . shall we say, clarify a situation of which I'm sure you're all already fully aware. It concerns the inspector and, of course, his cases."

Smythe gave her a cocky grin, Betsy giggled, Mrs. Goodge nodded and Wiggins looked confused.

Feeling suddenly very guilty, Mrs. Jeffries cleared her throat. "As some of you may have guessed, sometimes, the inspector . . ." She faltered, not wanting to come right out and say the dear man was a bit slow when it came to crime.

"Don't know what he's doin'," volunteered Betsy.

"Is a bit thick," interjected Smythe.

"Has his head in the clouds," stated Mrs. Goodge.

"Huh?" said Wiggins.

"Really," Mrs. Jeffries said, suddenly defensive of her inspector. "He's not that bad."

"No disrespect intended," Smythe said smoothly.

"Oh no, he's a wonderful gentleman, is our inspector," Betsy said quickly.

"They don't come any finer," Mrs. Goodge agreed.

"Well, yes, I'm delighted all of you feel that way," Mrs. Jeffries continued. "As I was saying, sometimes the inspector has some very difficult cases, and occasionally, he needs our help. It's very gratifying that you've all grasped that so quickly and without my having to come out and ask for your assistance."

"A bit hard to miss, if you ask me," Smythe put in. "Ever since those Kensington High Street murders you've been sending me round to half the pubs in London to pick up bits and pieces for ya."

"And I do so appreciate all your efforts, as I'm sure the inspector would too," Mrs. Jeffries paused and then said meaningfully, "if he knew about it."

"Is that what this is all about, then?" Betsy asked. "You don't want us lettin' on to the inspector that we's helps out." She shook her head. "You don't have to worry none about that. We knows how to keep our traps shut. All of us think the world of him, so we're not likely to say anything."

"Certainly not," Mrs. Goodge seconded.

"Say something about what?" Wiggins looked even more confused.

"About running all over London gettin' information on the inspector's cases, you dunderhead," Smythe exploded. "What do you think Mrs. J has been up to when she sends you running off to Mudie's Circulating Library or following some toff?"

"Oh," Wiggins's face lit up in a smile. "Is that what's been goin' on, then? I was wondering."

Mrs. Goodge mumbled into her teacup, and Mrs. Jeffries could only make out the words "thick as two short planks."

"So we're all agreed, then?" she asked. "We'll continue helping our inspector and we won't say a word about it?" She gazed quizzically around the table.

They all solemnly nodded their agreement. Smythe cocked his chin to one side and asked, "Why'd you not tell us right off? Did ya think we wouldn't be willing to help the man?"

"No," she sighed, "that wasn't it at all. I suppose I was worried that you'd resent it, or feel that I was asking you to do things that weren't part of the normal household tasks."

"Resent it?" exclaimed Betsy. "We love it. Believe me, dashing about findin' clues is a lot more interestin' than polishing the silver."

"That's for sure," Smythe muttered. He looked down at his big hands for a moment and then back up at Mrs. Jeffries. "All right, what's next then? Are we on to something with this Slocum case?"

Mrs. Jeffries swallowed the sudden lump in her throat. Her instincts about them had been right. They all had their own reasons for being devoted to Inspector Witherspoon:

Betsy, an untrained orphan, whom he'd found huddled and sick in a back alley and brought home for Mrs. Jeffries to nurse.

Smythe and Wiggins, whom he'd saved from probable unemployment by keeping them on after his Aunt Euphemia died. And he'd needed them about as much as he needed that odious Inspector Nivens dodging his every footstep.

Mrs. Goodge, who'd become slow and arthritic and destined for who-knew-what, before Witherspoon offered her a job as his cook.

And herself. A lonely widow from Yorkshire with a passion for mysteries and a need to mother the whole world. Yes, she thought happily, they'd all do quite well.

"Mrs. Jeffries." Betsy's voice brought her out of her reveries. The girl sat up straighter in her starched uniform and smoothed a curl off her shoulder. "About Dr. Slocum?"

"Yes. Let's see." She glanced at the coachman. "Smythe, I'm afraid I'll have to ask you to make the supreme sacrifice and go back to that awful pub in Knightsbridge."

He groaned and then nodded agreement. "To find out what?"

"Anything you can about the Slocum household. How many servants were employed there, who they were and what their jobs were. We need to know what's going to happen to them now. And if you can, find out who inherits the Slocum estate."

She also gave him the names of the others who'd been present at Luty Belle Crookshank's tea party on Saturday and told him to see what he could find out about those people. In doing so, she explained about the poisoned mushrooms growing in the communal gardens and that everyone present at the party knew about them.

"That it?" Smythe rose to his feet.

Mrs. Jeffries tapped her finger against her chin. "See if you can find out if anything unusual happened that day. *Anything*, no matter how trivial."

She turned to Wiggins. "I want you to go to Knightsbridge this afternoon," she told him. "See if you can make the acquaintance of any of the servants who are employed by any of the guests at that party on Saturday. But for goodness' sake, be discreet. Inspector Witherspoon is still at Dr. Slocum's, and we don't want him seeing you."

"But that'll take me all afternoon," Wiggins protested.

"Did you have other plans?" she asked archly.

"I wanted to finish cleaning out front," he stammered.

"Humph," Betsy snorted. "You don't care a fig about your cleaning; you just don't want to miss seeing that Miss Cannonberry."

"That's not true."

"Get on with you, boy," Mrs. Goodge said. "There's lots of pretty girls to turn your head in Knightsbridge."

Wiggins sighed but got to his feet.

"What do you want me to do?" Betsy asked. Her eyes were shining with eagerness.

"I want you to go with Wiggins," Mrs. Jeffries said briskly. "But once there, you'll need to start talking to all the clerks and tradesmen in the area—just as you did that time on the Kensington High Street."

"But what should I ask?"

"Just get them talking," she replied. "Right now, we're not sure about what we need to know. Find out if Dr. Slocum paid his bills promptly, if he was well liked; find out anything you can. We'll sort out what's important and what's not later."

A few minutes later they left the kitchen, and Mrs. Jeffries found herself alone with the cook.

Mrs. Goodge was a tall, gray-haired woman with painful arthritis and a somewhat cranky disposition at times. She was also a snob. Yet at the same time, she was also kindhearted and generous—some would say overly generous, as Mrs. Jeffries had several times found her feeding beggars at the back door. Naturally, the housekeeper had pretended to notice nothing—she knew Mrs. Goodge valued her testy reputation. The cook also had another, rather startling, quality.

She knew everything there was to know about everyone worth knowing about. Not a tidbit of gossip, not a breath of scandal ever escaped her eager ear. There was nothing particularly startling in that except for one very important fact. Mrs. Goodge never left the kitchen. Except for retiring to her quarters at the back of the house every night, the woman was never outside her domain. Not even to go to church.

"Can I make you a fresh cup of tea?" Mrs. Jeffries asked. "I saw you limping earlier, and I can see your arthritis is acting up again."

The cook nodded regally. "I'd be much obliged."

"We'll put another poultice on your ankle tonight before you go to bed. Perhaps that'll help ease the pain a bit."

"Thank you. The last one you fixed worked wonders. Better than that stuff old McCromber tried to foist off on me."

Old McCromber was the Witherspoon household physician.

Mrs. Goodge considered him a silly old fool, and Mrs. Jeffries wasn't sure but that she agreed with that assessment. The man was too overly fond of laudanum to her way of thinking.

"Mrs. Goodge," she said as she went to the stove to put the kettle on. "Do you know anything about Dr. Slocum?"

"What's his full name?"

"Bartholomew Slocum."

"Let me think a minute," Mrs. Goodge ordered. She stared into space, her face grave in concentration. Several minutes passed, and the teakettle whistled.

Mrs. Jeffries grabbed the kettle and poured the boiling water into the china pot just as Mrs. Goodge spoke.

"I'm sorry," she said. "Could you repeat what you said? I'm afraid the kettle was making so much noise I didn't hear you."

"It'll keep till the tea's ready."

A few minutes later, Mrs. Jeffries set a steaming cup under the cook's nose and then sat down in the chair beside her with her own cup. "Now, what were you saying about Dr. Slocum?"

Mrs. Goodge took a dainty sip of tea. "Nothing."

"Nothing," Mrs. Jeffries repeated, her astonishment obvious. "Does that mean you don't know anything about the man?"

"Afraid so." Mrs. Goodge reached for a digestive biscuit off the plate in the middle of the table. "He's not really anyone important. He's only a doctor and a common one at that."

"Oh dear," Mrs. Jeffries replied. She was very disappointed. She'd been hoping for something to sink her teeth into, a bit of scandal or old gossip. But if Mrs. Goodge didn't know anything about the man, that could very well mean there wasn't anything worth knowing. Drat.

"No, no. I've never heard a word about Dr. Slocum. But I know a lot about Effie Beals."

"Effie Beals?" Mrs. Jeffries perked up. "Who is that?"

Mrs. Goodge smiled, taking pleasure in showing off her knowledge. "Dr. Slocum's cook."

CHAPTER 4

Mrs. Jeffries breathed a sigh of relief. Anything, no matter how small, might help. She gazed expectantly at Mrs. Goodge. "Why how very clever of you," she said. "But then, you're quite remarkable when it comes to learning about what is going on in this city. Tell me what you know about the cook."

"It's not all that much," Mrs. Goodge said modestly. "But it caused a right ripple when it happened."

"When what happened?" Mrs. Jeffries asked patiently, resisting the urge to hurry the woman along. Mrs. Goodge enjoyed the telling of it far too much. She hoarded her tidbits of gossip like an old miser with a pot of gold.

"Why, Effie Beals leaving the Duke of Bedford and going to work for a common doctor." Mrs. Goodge's delicate snort showed what she thought of such strange behavior. "I never heard of the like before in all my days. Leaving a duke to work for a doctor. Monstrous, that's what it was, absolutely monstrous."

Mrs. Jeffries would hardly have labeled it monstrous, but she kept her opinion to herself. "Perhaps," she ventured, "the duke wasn't a very good employer?"

"Not a good employer!" Mrs. Goodge exclaimed, her eyes widening and her whole body swelling indignantly. "Of course he's a good employer. Look 'ere, my sister's husband's cousin is a footman in his Lordship's London house; there isn't a better master alive than the duke." She shook her head. "No, I tell you, something peculiar must have happened. Nobody in their right mind gives up good wages and a fancy roof over their heads unless something inn't right."

"Perhaps she was asked to leave. Perhaps her culinary skills failed to keep up with the duke's standards."

The cook shook her head. "No, that weren't it. I heard the duke himself tried to talk her out of leaving."

"But, Mrs. Goodge, there could be any number of reasons for changing employment."

"Like what?"

"Improprieties, or perhaps she didn't get along with the rest of the servants. Or perhaps it was simply too much responsibility for the poor woman. Cooking for a lord of the realm must be quite daunting."

"Effie Beals is one of the best cooks in London. She worked there for years before she up and left," Mrs. Goodge countered. "Her own daughter was training for the duke's service. No one ever leaves the duke's household—he's a kind, thoughtful and generous man. I tell you, somethin' peculiar happened to that woman, either that or she isn't right in the head. You don't just up and walks away from a position like that to go work for some nobody doctor in Knightsbridge."

Mrs. Jeffries nodded thoughtfully. She wasn't sure Mrs. Goodge was right, but all the same, it was peculiar. Why had Effie Beals left the Duke of Bedford to go to work for Dr. Slocum? It was an interesting question, but one that probably had no relevance to Slocum's murder.

"People leaves their jobs for two reasons," Mrs. Goodge said. "Rotten wages or rotten treatment. Take my word for it," she said firmly. "Neither of them reasons is the right one for Effie Beals."

Witherspoon's ears were ringing by the time he escaped from the garrulous Luty Belle Crookshank. Taking Constable Barnes, he hurried off to question the neighbors before Mrs. Crookshank could remember anything else to tell him.

Witherspoon didn't relish talking to Colonel Seaward. Rumor had it that the man was being tapped as the next governor to one of those horridly hot little islands out in the West Indies. In the inspector's experience, people like that didn't much care for being questioned in murder investigations.

But it couldn't be helped. Witherspoon sighed heavily as they climbed the stone steps to the front door. Regardless of how unpleasant this might be, he had his duty to do.

The butler opened the door and they stated their business. The servant didn't blink an eye. He sent Barnes with a housemaid off to the servants' hall and then told the inspector that Colonel Seaward was in his study.

A few moments later, Witherspoon stopped just inside the study door and blinked in surprise. The most peculiar objects he'd ever seen filled every available inch of the large room.

There were tables scattered about, covered with exotic fringed cloth and topped by woven baskets, multicolored pottery jars and other knickknacks he didn't even recognize.

On the far wall, the head of a tiger stared at him impassively. Next to that was what looked like some sort of African shield with crossed spears at the top. Slowly, Witherspoon turned his head, surveying the room like a child studying the window of a toy shop.

There were more shields and spears on the walls, as well as four fearsome-looking African masks and a wickedly sharp set of ivory knives. He counted three cases of mounted butterflies and six brightly stuffed birds. Next to the window, he saw a bookcase topped with a row of glass cases.

Squinting, he gulped when he saw what they contained: spiders, snakes, lizards and bugs. Witherspoon suppressed a shudder. He hated creepy crawly things. Without taking his gaze off the window, he moved in the opposite direction and banged his foot against something.

"Egad," Witherspoon shouted as he looked down and then leapt to one side. He'd run into a giant crocodile.

"Don't worry, it's dead," said a voice.

Witherspoon tore his eyes away from the hideous creature and saw a man rising from behind a desk in a shadowy corner of the room. "Colonel Seaward," he croaked. "I'm Inspector Witherspoon of Scotland Yard."

"Sorry about that," the colonel replied, gesturing at the stuffed animal. "I hope it didn't startle you too badly."

Seaward was a tall, impeccably dressed man wearing a black morning coat and vest. He had thinning auburn hair streaked with gray, a pencil-thin mustache and an anxious smile.

"I do keep some live reptiles out at my country house," he continued, his gaze on the inspector's pale face. "But I assure you, sir, that one is definitely dead."

"Of course," Witherspoon replied. "Bit of a shock, but not to worry, I'm fine now."

"I expect you've come to see me about that dreadful business at Dr. Slocum's. Won't you please sit down." Seaward nodded toward a chair and went back behind the desk.

"Yes, I have," the inspector replied breathlessly. "If you don't mind, I'd like to ask you a few questions. All routine, I assure you."

"Certainly. Though I don't think there's much I'll be able to tell you. I wasn't all that well acquainted with Dr. Slocum."

Trying to slow down his racing heart, the inspector took a deep breath and cleared his throat. "Were you a patient of the deceased?"

"Not really," the colonel replied. "I did see him professionally once, but that was years ago, when I left the military."

"I see. So he was just a neighbor, not really a close friend?"

"Yes, but . . ." Seaward smiled slightly, as though he wanted to add something but was too much of a gentleman.

"But?" Witherspoon queried.

"One doesn't like to speak ill of the dead. But I must say, Dr. Slocum wasn't really the sort of person one would wish to spend one's time with, if you know what I mean."

"Hmmm, yes. Yet you were at Mrs. Crookshank's tea party last Saturday and Dr. Slocum was there."

"Of course," Seaward gave him a wide man-to-man smile. "It's impossible to refuse one of Mrs. Crookshank's invitations; she's a rather determined woman. But for the most part, I, and everyone else around here, avoided the man like the plague."

"Mrs. Crookshank happened to mention that you're out in the garden a great deal of the time. Did you happen to notice any strangers lurking about on Wednesday? Or anything else that struck you as unusual?"

"Wednesday? Oh yes, the day Slocum died." Seaward's thin eyebrows drew together. "No, I'm afraid I didn't. But that's to be expected. You see, as soon as I could decently leave Mrs. Crookshank's tea, I left for my country estate in Surrey. I didn't get back until Wednesday. I had guests coming to luncheon, and I only just got here ahead of them." He laughed. "My butler was most annoyed. Poor fellow probably thought he was going to have to entertain Lord and Lady Stanhope on his own."

The inspector smiled faintly. "When did your guests leave?"

"Let me see, we finished luncheon a little after one-thirty, chatted for a bit and then they left at. . . ." He cocked his head to one side. "It must have been just after two. I remember because Mrs. Melton kept looking at the clock. She had an appointment at two-thirty. Would you like the names of my guests?"

"That would be most helpful," the inspector replied. Goodness, he thought, this was turning out to be a most interesting interview. He must remember to tell Mrs. Jeffries about this room. She'd find it fascinating.

And wasn't he lucky that Colonel Seaward was being so cooperative. Not at all like some he'd had to question.

The colonel pulled a sheet of paper out of a drawer and began scribbling names.

"I assure you," Witherspoon said earnestly, "this is all routine. But we will need to contact your guests to see if any of them heard or saw anything on the day of the murder."

Seaward stood up and handed him the list of names. "Of course, I understand; you're doing your duty. We must all do our duty, mustn't we?"

"Yes indeed." The inspector tucked the paper into his pocket and rose to his feet. "I understand congratulations might soon be in order."

"Perhaps," Seaward murmured with a modest smile. "We shall see what happens when Her Majesty returns from Balmoral next week. I have it on good authority that the Palace will be announcing several appointments at that time." He broke off and frowned slightly. "Do you think you'll have this matter sorted out by then?"

"Hmm, I'm not sure. But one certainly hopes so."

Mrs. Jeffries pounced on Witherspoon the moment he came in. "My goodness, Inspector," she said, holding the front door open and ushering him inside, "you're soaked."

"Good evening, Mrs. Jeffries," Witherspoon said brightly. He shook the rain off himself and unbuttoned his coat. "Foul evening out there."

Mrs. Jeffries rushed forward and grabbed the garment as he shrugged out of it. Surreptitiously, she felt his pockets as she hung it on the brass coatrack.

She didn't usually violate a person's privacy by fingering his pockets, but in the inspector's case, she'd long since come to terms with her conscience over the matter. Witherspoon needed all the help he could get. Frequently, what was or was not in his coat gave her the means to assist him without having to hurt the dear man's feelings by being blatant about it.

"Started to rain the instant I left the Brompton Road," Witherspoon continued, "and it hasn't let up since. Naturally, there wasn't a hansom to be found. Amazing how they're never around when you need them."

"Poor man, you must be chilled to the bone," Mrs. Jeffries clucked.

"Not to worry, a little bit of water won't hurt me. What delight is Mrs. Goodge cooking up for dinner tonight?" He rubbed his hands together. "I must say I've quite an appetite."

"It's one of your favorites, Inspector. Roast chicken. But come into the drawing room and have a nice glass of sherry first. We don't want you catching a chill—not in the middle of a case."

Witherspoon followed her into the drawing room, his eyes lighting up with pleasure when he saw the two glasses poured out and sitting atop the mahogany table by his favorite armchair. A fire was burning in the fireplace. "Splendid. You're going to join me then."

"I thought perhaps that would be nice." She handed him a glass and picked up her own. "Dinner will be ready in a few minutes, but why don't you tell me about your day? How is the case going?"

The inspector began telling her about his interview with Colonel Seaward. He described the fantastic room, told her about the glass cases and the mounted butterflies and the African masks. She listened carefully, every now and then asking him a question.

"So he provided you with a list of the guests who were there on Wednesday," she remarked thoughtfully. "I suppose you'll have to question them. Even though it's quite usual in a case like this, I expect it might be a bit embarrassing for the colonel."

"Not if I can help it," Witherspoon vowed. "If the servants verify that the colonel was with his guests until two o'clock, then I won't have to embarrass the man by questioning his guests. I should know tomorrow. Barnes was still over there taking their statements when I left."

"You think Colonel Seaward's innocent because he can account for his time during the period the murder was committed?"

"Not just that." Witherspoon took a sip of sherry. "The man had no reason to kill Dr. Slocum. He barely knew him, and from everything he said, he avoided him as much as possible. Besides, the man is a *gentleman*. Furthermore, we have found someone who did have a motive to murder the doctor. Someone in his own household."

"Who?"

"Dr. Slocum's cook. Effie Beals."

"Really?" She hid her surprise behind a smile. "What leads you to that conclusion?"

"Simple. One of the housemaids told me she overheard the cook having a violent argument with the deceased not ten minutes before lunch. Mrs. Beals could easily have known about the mushrooms because Mrs. Crookshank had told the gardener, in front of several witnesses and goodness knows how many servants, that there were poisoned mushrooms in the garden. In a fit of rage, Effie Beals dashed out to the garden, plucked one and popped it into Slocum's soup."

"How abominable!" Mrs. Jeffries paused for a moment and then said,

"But what about the second mushroom, the one you found in the cooling pantry?"

He dropped his gaze and stared into his glass. "Hmm, yes. Well, that was probably a spare, in case the first one didn't work."

"You think so? But even if Mrs. Beals did have an argument with her employer, it doesn't necessarily follow that she'd murder him."

"Well, she didn't much like him," Witherspoon mused.

"Did the rest of the servants?"

"Not particularly. So far, I haven't found anyone who liked the man."

"If he was so heartily disliked by everyone who knew him," Mrs. Jeffries ventured, "perhaps there's more to this case than you've discovered so far."

"I don't think so," Witherspoon insisted. "It looks very clear to me. Mrs. Beals is the only one who could have done it. Perhaps she had some sort of fit or something. All the other servants were gone and the house was empty. The doors were locked. There weren't any strangers lurking in the neighborhood, and by the time the poisoned mushroom was added to the doctor's soup, the only person in the house was Effie Beals." He shook his head. "No, let's not make this more complicated than it already is. I think we've found our killer. I've left a constable on duty at the Slocum house to make sure our suspect doesn't do a flit in the middle of the night. I'll be questioning her tomorrow."

"No doubt, you're absolutely right." Mrs. Jeffries knew the inspector believed he'd solved the case. But she also knew that no matter how much he wanted to believe it was over and done with, if she kept asking the right questions and nudging him in the right direction, he'd keep right on investigating. She deliberately frowned.

Witherspoon's satisfied air disappeared. "Why are you looking like that?"

"Like what?" she asked innocently.

"Like you've just thought of something."

"I must admit, I'm puzzled. You said the doctor had an emetic clutched in his hand when you got there," she explained, hoping he'd pick up on her reasoning.

"Yes," he said encouragingly, "he did. But what's that got to do with it?"

"Doesn't that imply he knew he'd been poisoned? And if he knew he'd been poisoned, he must have had some inkling as to why." She held her breath.

"I suppose one could make that assumption," he admitted cautiously.

"Well, if his argument with Mrs. Beals was so violent that he felt she was dangerous, why didn't he sack her right then and make her leave the house? Did the housemaid say Mrs. Beals had been let go?"

"Er, no." Witherspoon's shoulders slumped. "But the maid might not have known. He could have sacked the cook and that's why she killed him! Yes, I'm sure that's probably it. He fired her and she decided to kill him."

"Then why did she return to the house that night? If one has been fired and then murdered one's employer, I'd expect the last thing one would do is return to the scene of the crime and wait to be arrested."

"Er, well, look, Mrs. Jeffries. You may have a point there." He sighed and put his glass on the table. "Drat. I was so hoping this would be a nice simple one. But I daresay, unless the cook is a half-wit, you're probably right. Mrs. Beals wouldn't have come back to the house if she'd killed him. I suppose I'll just have to keep on looking. But honestly, she's the only suspect I've got."

"Don't look so glum, Inspector," Mrs. Jeffries said firmly. "You haven't failed yet in the cause of justice. I know you'd rather shoot yourself in the foot than send an innocent person to the gallows. Besides, you've still got all the other neighbors to question. Perhaps one of them saw something useful."

The mantel clock struck six. Witherspoon reached into his pocket, pulled out his watch and checked the time, then absently set it down on the table.

Mrs. Jeffries and the inspector rose at the same time.

"Dinner should be ready now," she said, eyeing the watch. Witherspoon straightened and hurried toward the hall and the dining room. She waited until he was halfway across the room and then quickly snatched the watch and dropped it in the pocket of her dress.

Tomorrow she had to talk to Effie Beals.

"Inspector," she called as she followed him into the dining room. "Did you speak with the maid again?"

Witherspoon paused, his hand on the back of his chair. "Maid?"

"Yes, remember, you mentioned that it might be pertinent to find out when the surgery had been cleaned?"

"Oh yes, I did say that, didn't I? As a matter of fact, I talked to her this afternoon." He frowned, remembering the plain, uncooperative woman who'd stared at him with her unblinking black eyes and her mouth curled up in a permanent sneer. Most uncomfortable. For the life of him, he couldn't understand why some people seemed to hate the police.

"And?"

He pulled the chair out and sat down, his attention focused on the steaming plates of food. "And what?"

"What did she say?" Mrs. Jeffries managed to keep the impatience out of her voice. "When was the room last cleaned?"

"The morning of the murder." Witherspoon helped himself to some roast chicken and managed to splatter gravy on the white lace tablecloth. Mrs. Jeffries glided to the table and deftly picked up his plate. Within seconds she had heaped it full of food, and all without more damage to the tablecloth. She set it under the inspector's nose and then sat down next to him. Honestly, she thought, when he was hungry, it was difficult to get him to concentrate on anything.

She waited until he'd taken several mouthfuls and then said, "So it was cleaned that morning. Was that the usual routine in the household?"

"Oh yes, the woman told me Slocum was a stickler for cleanliness. She said he watched her like a hawk, and if he even found one speck of dust anywhere, he, in her words, 'had a royal fit,' whatever that is." He reached for the potatoes and plonked another one on his plate before Mrs. Jeffries could intervene. The drippings landed halfway between his plate and the bowl. She gave up any hope of saving the tablecloth.

"I showed her the piece of cork," he continued, "and she's sure it wasn't there that morning. She swept the entire room, including underneath all the cabinets and cupboards, and she's certain it wasn't there. Claims the doctor would have noticed."

"Perhaps someone dropped it on the floor after the maid had cleaned," Mrs. Jeffries suggested.

"Not likely. Except for cleaning the surgery, none of the servants were ever allowed to go in there. Slocum was adamant about that. Fired a housemaid once for wandering in and having a peek at his books."

"Perhaps Dr. Slocum himself dropped it or tracked it in on his shoe?"

Witherspoon shook his head. "No. He wasn't seeing patients that day. According to the maid and the butler, he wasn't in his surgery at all. Except for going out briefly that morning, Slocum was in his study." He snorted delicately. "If you ask me, the old boy was a bit of a martinet. But then, one can't really blame him—at least not when it comes to keeping his surgery clean. But I don't like the way he treated his servants. I tell you, Mrs. Jeffries, none of them are in the least bit upset over the man's death. Except, of course, they're all wondering what will happen to them now that he's gone."

"What will happen to them?" she asked idly, her mind still on that small piece of cork. If it hadn't been there that morning, then there were only two people who could have dropped it. Slocum or the murderer.

"Right now, nothing. His solicitor is keeping the servants on until the estate's settled. That won't be for another fortnight."

"Goodness, what's taking so long?"

"The solicitor's been ill—fellow's had the gout for a month now. Dashed nuisance for the heirs, I'd imagine."

"Heirs?" That perked her ears up. "Who inherits?"

For a moment, she was positively furious at her own stupidity. The question of who was going to get all the doctor's worldly goods was the first thing she should have found out! She couldn't believe she'd been so obtuse. "I understood the man didn't have a family."

"He didn't have much of one, just a nephew hanging about somewhere. I'll know more after I've seen the solicitor, I'm seeing him tomorrow. Gout or not, I've got to get the details about Dr. Slocum's will." He frowned and absently stared across the room. "You know how these solicitors are. He may balk at giving me any useful information. Well, I shall just have to impress upon him that in a murder investigation, it's rather important that we know who's going to get the estate. Motive, you know. Yes, that's what I'll do. I'll simply insist, if necessary." He gazed at Mrs. Jeffries anxiously. "Gout's not catching, is it?"

"No, Inspector. It isn't."

Relieved, he reached for his wine, took a sip and leaned back in his chair. "I say, this is a jolly good dinner. Mrs. Goodge has really outdone herself, hasn't she?"

Mrs. Jeffries sat up late that night, reading the book on mushrooms that Wiggins had gotten from Mudie's Circulating Library. But it wasn't much help. There was practically nothing in it about "Death Caps" or, as Mrs. Crookshank called them, "dead eyes."

Holding the open book in her lap, Mrs. Jeffries closed her eyes and let her mind wander over what few facts she had about the case. Somehow, she didn't think Mrs. Effie Beals was the culprit. If the cook had done it, she would have to be a half-wit to come back to the house that evening and wait to be arrested, especially with that second mushroom sitting in the midst of the cook's domain—the cooling pantry. No one was that stupid.

Her mind drifted back and forth over everything the inspector had told her. But there was still so much she and the other servants needed to find out. Except for her fortuitous meeting with Mrs. Crookshank, none of them had learned all that much today.

Betsy had popped in after dinner to report that she hadn't had any luck getting anyone to talk about Slocum, but she was determined to go back the next day and have another go at it.

Smythe showed up, and he too had nothing to report. Wiggins probably hadn't fared any better than the other two, Mrs. Jeffries thought, but she'd have to wait until tomorrow to find out. The boy had declared himself dead tired and trotted off to bed directly after dinner.

Opening her eyes, Mrs. Jeffries straightened her spine and took a deep breath. She needed to get to sleep. Tomorrow was going to be a busy day.

It was mid-morning before Mrs. Jeffries was able to track Wiggins down. Sometimes she rather thought she'd become a bit too lax in the household management. No doubt some would say her methods were the sad result of too liberal an education for a female, but she didn't bother herself overly much with others' opinions. Yet she did often wonder what she would have been like had she not been exposed to the philosophical writings of John Locke and the poetry of the American Mr. Walt Whitman. (Many, were, of course, scandalized by Mr. Whitman's poems, but she found them thought-provoking and rather charming.)

And as to her household management, well, she always hated having anyone looking over her shoulder as she worked.

So when she first came to the inspector, she had devised a revolutionary, at least in her opinion, system to keep the household running smoothly. She'd sat down with everyone and made a list of all their duties and responsibilities. She'd then told them it was up to them to see that everything got done.

Along with that, she'd also encouraged free expression, personal liberty and a respect for everyone's privacy. Unlike in most households, she didn't think it her business to inquire as to what the servants did on their days off, what their religious preferences were or how they spent their wages.

But as she spied Wiggins heading down the hall with a bucket of water, intent upon cleaning the fence again, she wondered if she'd gone too far. Perhaps some people simply weren't ready for unsupervised responsibility. That fence didn't need another cleaning.

"Wiggins," she called from the top of the staircase. "Where are you going with that bucket? The fence has already been done."

He flushed guiltily. "Uh, uh, I was going to clean the front steps."

"They don't need to be cleaned either," she said calmly, coming down the staircase and pinning him with her steely gaze. "You did them the day before yesterday."

"I did?" he said innocently. "I must have forgotten."

"Wiggins," she sighed, "I know you like to perch out front in the hopes of seeing one of your lady love's walk past. But there isn't anything out there that needs doing. So far this week, you've cleaned the stairs, washed the fence and swept the walkway. Twice. You've also polished the brass door knocker and the lamps to such a brightness it's a miracle we haven't blinded people. But, dear boy, you have many other duties. The rugs need to be beaten."

"But, Mrs. Jeffries," he protested, "them rugs have to be done out back, and I ain't seen her for the longest time."

Mrs. Jeffries wondered which "her" he was referring to, but wasn't sure she wanted to ask.

"Yesterday you had me running all over ha'f o' London getting the goods on them tea party guests."

"Speaking of which," she interjected cheerfully, "what did you find out?"

He snorted. "Not much. If you ask me, it was a right waste of time. But I did find out that Mrs. Leslie has a French maid, right stuck-up one too, and that Dr. Hightower hangs around that neighborhood like he lives there, an' he don't."

"Anything else?"

"I'eard all about that Colonel Seaward," Wiggins replied wearily. "Right boring ol' toff too, if you ask me."

"Well done, Wiggins," Mrs. Jeffries said. "How clever of you. How did you manage that and, more importantly, what precisely did you find out?"

The boy grinned as she praised him. He straightened and puffed his chest out importantly. "I hung around the side of Seaward's house until I saw one of the maids come out, then I follows her to the butcher."

"Excellent," Mrs. Jeffries murmured.

"Anyways, this maid, her name was Sophie, she wan't much to look at, but she was a nice enough girl and a real chatterbox. I asked if I could carry her basket back to the house. Clever, huh?"

"Very," she replied dryly. She did wish he would get to the point, but she also realized that, like Mrs. Goodge, he needed to feel his contribution to the inspector's case was important.

"Sophie says the colonel's an old army officer, but he's not in the army now. I asked Sophie if the colonel was acquainted with the doctor, if they was friends like, and she said no. Said Colonel Seaward didn't like the man much."

"From what I've heard, no one liked the doctor very much."

"That's the truth," he agreed, nodding his head. "Sophie says no one round there had much to do with 'im, even if he was always droppin' them fancy little callin' cards at people's houses."

"Calling cards?" Mrs. Jeffries's brows drew together. "Are you saying that Dr. Slocum dropped off his calling card at Colonel Seaward's and at other homes in the neighborhood?"

"That's what Sophie says. But no one round there liked 'im much. She said Dr. Slocum could clear the neighbors out the garden faster than a bad smell. But that didn't stop him from going round and tryin'. It's funny, inn't? Even on the day he was murdered he'd dropped one o' them fancy little cards by Colonel Seaward's. Sophie says she thought ol' Slocum wanted to be invited to lunch."

"What?" Mrs. Jeffries said sharply. "You mean he sent his calling card around on the day he was killed?"

"That's what Sophie says, and she ought to know. She's the one he give it to when he came round that morning."

CHAPTER 5

Witherspoon stood impatiently next to the settee in Catherine Leslie's drawing room and waited. He'd been waiting a good ten minutes now, he thought irritably as he glanced at the clock on the marble mantelpiece. What on earth was taking that blasted maid so long? He didn't have all day. There was so much to do this morning. Effie Beals had to be questioned again and then he had to go see Dr. Slocum's solicitor, and if there was time, he wanted another word with Dr. Hightower.

Oh dear, he was never going to get it all done. He began to pace back and forth. Thank goodness he'd had the foresight to have a quick word with that boy that did the gardening. At least he had some information now, even if he wasn't quite sure what it meant.

"Inspector Witherspoon?"

The sound of the soft, feminine voice startled him. He whirled around and stumbled over his own feet. Witherspoon's eyes widened as he saw Catherine Leslie standing in the doorway.

Tall and slender, she was past the bloom of first youth, yet she was one of the loveliest women he'd ever seen. Her upswept hair was jet black and pulled straight back to frame a perfectly smooth oval face. She had high cheekbones, an aristocratic nose and a full, generous mouth. But it was her eyes that drew one's attention. Deeply set and the color of violets, they watched him warily from across the room.

"Inspector Witherspoon," she repeated softly.

Realizing he was staring, he blushed. "Yes, I'm Inspector Witherspoon. You must be Mrs. Leslie."

She inclined her head and moved gracefully to the settee. "My maid said you wished to ask me some questions. Please sit down."

"Thank you. I'm sorry to have to intrude upon you like this, but as you've no doubt heard, your neighbor, Dr. Slocum, was murdered a few days ago."

"Yes. I know. He was poisoned, wasn't he?"

"Unfortunately, yes."

"I don't really see what it has to do with me," she said. "I'm sorry he's dead, but I hardly knew the man."

"Rest assured, madam," the inspector explained, "we haven't singled you out. We're talking with everyone who lives round these gardens. It's very much the normal course of events in an investigation of this kind."

She glanced at the clock and then gave him a nervous smile. Witherspoon had the feeling she was waiting for something.

"Now," he began briskly, "could you tell me how long you've been acquainted with the deceased?"

"I met Dr. Slocum shortly after I moved here from Birmingham. That was three years ago, after my husband died." She bit her lip and looked toward the mantel again.

"So you've known the deceased for three years." Witherspoon repeated. "Yet you weren't particularly friendly with him, is that correct?"

"That's correct."

"Were you in the garden this last Saturday—at Mrs. Crookshank's tea party?"

"Yes."

"And wasn't Dr. Slocum there as well?"

"Yes, he was, but so were a lot of other people." Mrs. Leslie sighed softly. "Inspector Witherspoon," she began in a tone of clarification, "you must understand. No one around here liked that odious little man. Everyone avoided him as much as possible, but Mrs. Crookshank is an American and somewhat of an eccentric as well. She has rather peculiar notions about hospitality, and she invited everyone who lives on the gardens to her party."

"Yes, I see." Witherspoon paused. "Mrs. Leslie, did you happen to see any strangers in the gardens on Wednesday, just before noon?"

"I don't think so," she answered vaguely. "I spent most of the morning lying down. I wasn't feeling well."

"I'm so sorry to hear that. So you saw or heard nothing out of the ordinary that morning?"

They paused as the maid came in carrying a silver tea tray. "Your tea, madam," she said in a pronounced French accent.

"Thank you, Nanette. Would you care for tea, Inspector?"

"Why, that's very good of you," he replied enthusiastically. "I wouldn't mind a cup."

The maid, a pretty blond-haired girl, gazed speculatively at the inspector for a moment and then picked up the silver pot.

Witherspoon took no notice of the maid, he was watching Catherine Leslie. "So you're saying you didn't know the doctor well at all and had no wish to, is that it?"

She accepted a cup of tea and nodded.

"And Dr. Slocum knew you had no wish to further your acquaintance with him?"

"Yes, I'd made that clear on several occasions."

"Then why, Mrs. Leslie, did Dr. Slocum persist?"

Her brows rose. "I'm afraid I don't know what you mean?"

"I think perhaps you do, madam," Witherspoon insisted. Really, did these people think all policemen were fools? "The gardener told me that on the day Dr. Slocum was murdered he accidentally dropped two calling cards on the path. The boy picked them up, caught up with Slocum and gave them back to him. He then watched him come to this house."

There was a loud crash as the maid dropped the cup of tea she'd just poured for Witherspoon. The steaming liquid spilled directly onto Catherine Leslie's skirt.

"Oh, madam," the maid cried, dropping to her knees and brushing at the material with a linen napkin she'd grabbed off the tray. "I am so clumsy, forgive me. I am so sorry. *Mon dieu*, thees will leave a terrible stain."

"It's all right, Nanette," she answered, motioning her away. "It's only a dress." She looked at Witherspoon and took a deep breath. "Inspector, I don't know what you're talking about. Dr. Slocum did not call here on Wednesday morning."

Nanette gasped, and they both turned to look at her.

"But, madam," the girl said, staring at her mistress out of wide, frightened eyes. "Surely you remember, zee awful man, he came here that morning and he left those two cards. One for you, and one for Dr. Hightower."

"That's enough, Nanette," Mrs. Leslie cried.

"No, madam, I can't let you do eet. I can't let you harm yourself to help *Monsieur le Docteur* Hightower. You must not lie to thees policeman, you must tell zee truth. If you do not, he will think you murdered Dr. Slocum and you are innocent."

"Now, now," Witherspoon interjected, but both women ignored him.

"Nanette, please be quiet. You don't know what you're saying."

"I do know what I am saying," the girl cried. "You must tell thees man zee truth. You must tell him everything."

"Nanette, silence."

"*Mais non*, I will not be silent. I will tell everything, I will tell everything, I will tell about zee nasty *docteur* waving his ugly lettle key in your face, threatening you with lies and—"

"Noooo," Mrs. Leslie screamed, and then she stumbled backward.

Inspector Witherspoon reached out to steady her and then made a grab for her as she collapsed, catching her before she hit the floor. "Oh, dear," he said.

Catherine Leslie had fainted.

Mrs. Jeffries once again made her way to Dr. Slocum's. As she climbed the stairs, she noticed that there was no longer a constable on duty. That was a bit of luck. She didn't think she could pull the wool over Barnes's eyes again. He wasn't a fool.

Clutching Inspector Witherspoon's pocket watch in her hand, she knocked on the door.

A few minutes later, the door opened and a white-haired butler with watery blue eyes peered out. "Good morning, madam."

"Good morning. I'm terribly sorry to disturb you," she said, easing closer to the door. "But I must speak with Inspector Witherspoon."

"Who?"

"Inspector Witherspoon, of Scotland Yard," she repeated patiently, not at all surprised by the butler's reaction. Witherspoon sometimes had that effect on people. Unless he was right under their noses, they tended to forget he was in the house. "I believe he's here this morning."

"Oh, him." The butler's eyes narrowed suspiciously. "Are you from Scotland Yard too? Never heard of a woman peeler before. What da ya want? Are you a neighbor? Some nosy parker that thinks she knows something? If you've come around here to start stirring things up and tellin' tales—"

"No, no, no," Mrs. Jeffries said quickly. She leaned closer and caught the distinct smell of brandy on the man's breath. Holding up the pocket watch, she said, "I've only come to return the inspector's watch. I'm his housekeeper. He left this morning without it, and if I don't get it to him, he'll miss some very important appointments."

The butler made a noise that sounded like a grunt and moved to one side. "Come on in, then," he muttered grudgingly. "Take one of them chairs by the surgery door. I'll go see if I can find the copper. He only arrived a minute ago himself. I'll ask the maid where he's got to."

"Thank you," Mrs. Jeffries said sweetly. How very curious, she thought. The butler was obviously in his cups, and he seemed to be under the impression she was coming in to tell tales. I wonder what kind of tales he's worried about, she thought as she watched him weave slowly down the long hallway. As soon as he'd turned the corner, she leapt quickly to her feet and hurried off to examine the layout of the first floor of the house.

Ignoring the surgery, she stopped at a set of double doors just opposite. Peeking inside, she saw that they led to a large library or study cluttered with bookcases, sofas, tables and reading lamps. There was green-and-white wallpaper on the walls, but every inch seemed to be covered with objects. There were oil paintings of country scenes and horses, gilt mirrors and corner shelves crammed with china figures. Probably Dresden, she decided. There was an ugly bright-red velvet settee and two matching chairs at one end of the room and, directly behind them, a grand piano covered by a garish gold fringed shawl. The room was so overly stuffed with bric-a-brac, it was positively gaudy.

Closing the doors, Mrs. Jeffries went next to the room just off the bottom of the staircase. Inside was a dining room fitted out with an oval rosewood table large enough to seat twelve, a matching sideboard and a huge crystal chandelier.

She heard a shuffle of footsteps from behind the staircase and deduced that the butler had located Inspector Witherspoon. She hurried back to the chair outside the surgery and sat down just in time.

"Sorry that took so long, madam," the butler announced, "but one of the maids said the gentleman was upstairs in the parlor. If you'll follow me, madam. It's this way."

Nodding, she followed him upstairs. He'd obviously regained some of his composure, though he did sway slightly when they reached the top. Perhaps the maid he'd spoken to had reminded him that this was a murder investigation.

They stopped outside a partially open door. There was a chair there too. Mrs. Jeffries sat down. "Thank you so much," she said, keeping her voice low. "I think perhaps I'll wait out here for just a few moments. I don't wish to interrupt the inspector."

"As you wish, madam."

"What is your name?" she asked kindly.

He looked surprised. "Keating, ma'am."

"And have you worked here long?" She kept her voice soft and sympathetic.

"Six years, ma'am," he sighed wearily, "but it seems more than that, seems like I've been here a ruddy lifetime."

After having Catherine Leslie faint and then coping with her hysterical maid, Witherspoon had been sure his day couldn't get any worse. But he'd been wrong. He was getting absolutely nothing useful out of Effie Beals.

He stifled a heavy sigh. He knew Constable Barnes was watching him expectantly, waiting, no doubt, for him to pounce upon the woman with a series of devastatingly clever questions.

He glanced over at his only suspect. She was sitting primly, wearing a neatly pressed white apron over a gray dress and watching him with frightened brown eyes.

Mrs. Beals was a heavy-set woman, well into middle age, with dark brown hair, a round face and a pale complexion. She didn't look like a murderess. Not that Witherspoon knew precisely how a murderess should look, but she was so precisely what a cook should look like that it made him jolly uncomfortable.

Mrs. Jeffries's comments the night before had pricked his conscience. There really was no reason to believe Effie Beals had wanted her employer dead.

Witherspoon cleared his throat. When all else failed, try surprise. "Mrs. Beals, did you poison Dr. Slocum?"

"I never," the woman protested with a vehement shake of her head. "Why would I want to kill 'im?"

"Because you'd had a violent quarrel with him and he was going to sack you."

"Who says? He never sacked me," she insisted. "And I didn't kill 'im. You got no right to accuse me—"

"No one is accusing you of murdering Dr. Slocum," Witherspoon interrupted. "We're merely asking the question." Drat, this was going to be far more difficult than he'd hoped. "All right, once again, could you describe your movements on the day of the murder?"

She sniffed. "How come you don't have everyone else in here, answering your questions? I weren't the only one that had a set-to with him, you know."

"We've spoken to all the other servants, Mrs. Beals. They all said the same thing. You were the last one in the house the day Dr. Slocum was poisoned."

"I've already told you about that—I stayed on because I was goin' to visit me daughter out at Chelmsford and the train didn't leave till two o'clock." Her bosom swelled with indignation. "Why should I hang about some drafty old train station when I can stay right here in the comfort of me own room?"

"Did you see Dr. Slocum after the others had left?"

She shook her head. "No, I left his lunch on the dining table, just like he asked me to."

"What did he have for luncheon?"

"Mushroom soup, lamb chops and some bread and cheese. He told me not to bother with a puddin' and so I didn't."

Witherspoon nodded wisely. "Was there anything else? Something to drink, perhaps?"

"Well, he had his bottle of wine. He was a real stickler for that, made Keating bring up a fresh bottle every day. But that weren't my business, that was Keating's. He was in charge of supplyin' the wine. It was sitting on the sideboard when I brung up the lunch tray. So I knows he had it."

"And how long were you at your daughter's?" Witherspoon asked.

"All afternoon." Mrs. Beals brushed at a stray lock of hair that had slipped from beneath her cap. "I didn't even know the man was dead until I got back that night and the police was here."

Mrs. Jeffries ignored the crick in her neck as she cocked her head closer to the door and strained to catch every word. Keating had disappeared again, and she'd overheard most of the inspector's questions. She sighed as she heard him mumbling softly to Constable Barnes, and then she heard him ask Mrs. Beals for her daughter's address in Chelmsford.

Her hands balled into fists of frustration as his deep voice began asking the same questions all over again. Mrs. Jeffries had to restrain herself from flying into the room and ordering Witherspoon to ask the cook why she'd argued with Dr. Slocum. She straightened suddenly as the butler's laborious footsteps sounded on the stairs again.

"Would you care to come into the kitchen for a cup of tea?" Keating asked politely.

Casting one quick glance at the door, Mrs. Jeffries rose and gave him her most charming smile. "Why thank you, Keating, that's most thoughtful of you."

She followed him down two sets of stairs, through a hall and into the kitchen. Her eyes widened in surprise as she gazed at the room. A long table dominated the center. On the far wall were the usual two sets of sinks the scullery maids must use to do the washing up. Next to that was the largest wooden plate rack Mrs. Jeffries had ever seen. Across from the table, there was a brand new Livingstone iron range, so new the plating still shone, and even more, there was one of those new fangled "gas kitchener's" she'd seen in a Charing Cross shop window.

Keating moved to the range and pulled open the hot box. "I've taken the liberty of warming some buns, ma'am," he announced as he lifted a plate out and set them on the table.

"Thank you," she said again. "I didn't want to disturb the inspector, and I daresay he'll be a bit longer speaking with your cook."

Keating put the buns on the table next to a teapot and cups and sat down next to Mrs. Jeffries. "He must be a good employer, ma'am, if you've come all this way just to return his watch."

She nodded and smiled as the butler poured them each a cup of tea. Satisfaction poured through her. Her little scheme was working. Mrs. Jeffries often marveled at the different talents the good Lord had chosen to bestow on people. Some were blessed with great beauty or tremendous artistic or musical talent, and some, like herself, were blessed with subtler gifts. Why, it was her own special gift that had first got her involved with solving crimes, back when her dear late husband had his first employment with the constabulary in Yorkshire.

People talked to her. They told her things they'd often never revealed to another soul. A bit of interest, a kind smile and before you knew it, they were talking their heads off. With her plump, material figure, gray-streaked auburn hair and sympathetic brown eyes, she knew she probably reminded people of a kindly aunt or a spinster sister.

"Humph," the butler sniffed. "You're right lucky, then. If you've got a good master." He cast a quick glance over his shoulder, presumably to make sure no one was sneaking up on him.

"I take it Dr. Slocum wasn't an easy man to work for," she ventured gently.

"Easy! He was a right old tartar."

Mrs. Jeffries didn't know if it was her unique gift or the brandy the man had consumed earlier that was loosening his tongue, but either way, she didn't want him shutting up now.

"Oh dear," she clucked sympathetically. "That does make one's life difficult, doesn't it? And these days, respectable employment is so hard to find."

He nodded vigorously. "That's the truth. None of us would've stayed if we didn't have to."

"Yes, I quite understand."

"And he wasn't much of a doctor, neither, if you asks me," Keating exclaimed. His face was turning red. "He was mean to his patients too. If they couldn't pay his price, he wouldn't treat 'em."

Another disapproving cluck. "That's dreadful."

"He was a dreadful man. About six months ago one of his old patients from when he was over in Hammersmith came in—it was an elderly gentleman, someone who looked like he'd seen better days. He begged the doctor to attend his wife, but he couldn't pay, so Slocum threw him out."

"How monstrous." Mrs. Jeffries did indeed think it was monstrous, but she also knew it was actually quite a common practice. There were many physicians in London who hardened their hearts to the poor and needy.

"It was, ma'am. He was a pathetic old gentleman, I can tell you that. And he'd once been a good patient of the doctor."

"You knew him?"

"Oh no. I've only been here six years. Slocum had his practice in Hammersmith long before that. But I heards this gentleman remind the doctor of all the patients he'd referred to him when he was just starting out." Keating snorted again. "But it didn't do no good. Dr. Slocum tossed him out anyway."

"Hammersmith," Mrs. Jeffries murmured thoughtfully. "That's not a very nice area. Makes quite a change, doesn't it, from Hammersmith to Knightsbridge?"

"Yes. And he didn't get here because his doctoring skills improved any. Half of his patients still ended up dying," Keating stated flatly. "He got this house an' all because he inherited a packet of money from a relative."

"Really? That's interesting."

"And there's more to that story than meets the eye too, 'cause the old uncle who left it all to him didn't even like him."

"How do you know that?" Mrs. Jeffries asked quickly.

Too quickly, because the butler drew back and gazed at her suspiciously.

"Forgive me," she said softly, giving him an understanding smile. "I forget myself, but well, you're such an interesting person to talk with and one can't help being curious, can one?"

Some, but not all, of the suspicion left Keating's eyes. "I suppose so," he said cautiously. But he didn't answer her question.

She decided to change tactics. "I'm so sorry. You must have had a dreadful few days, and here I am bending your ear with my curiosity. And Dr. Slocum not even buried yet." She clucked sympathetically and shook her head. "Even if he wasn't the kindest of employers, I'm sure you're upset."

"Well," he agreed slowly, "I wouldn't exactly call it upset. More like I'm wondering what's going to happen next."

"No doubt you are, and that, of course, is such a worry."

"Course it is," he echoed, "I'm sixty this next spring, and where am I going to get another position? People wants young men they can train, not old men like me, working for them."

"But surely Dr. Slocum made some provision for you? He must not have been completely heartless—after all, he did give you a day off for no apparent reason."

"How do you know about that?"

"The inspector happened to mention it."

"Oh." Keating smiled cynically. "But don't go thinking he was giving us time off out of the goodness of his heart. He had a reason, all right. He was up to something on those days. We just never figured out what it was. The old tartar didn't do anything unless there was something in it for him."

"You mean this wasn't the first time the doctor had given the staff the day off?"

"He'd done it before, several times. But none of us ever knew why."

One of the maids entered the kitchen and then stopped dead. "You're needed upstairs, Mr. Keating," she said, staring at Mrs. Jeffries. "Constable Barnes wants you to show them the attic."

"I'd better go find Inspector Witherspoon," Mrs. Jeffries interjected as she headed for the stairs herself. She wanted to nab the inspector before he disappeared. "Thank you so much for the tea," she called over her shoulder. "We must do it again sometime."

Inspector Witherspoon was pacing the drawing room when Mrs. Jeffries entered. He didn't look surprised to see her.

"Hello, Mrs. Jeffries," he muttered absently, massaging the sides of his head as he paced. "I've had the most dreadful day."

"Good day, sir," she said. "I'm so sorry to hear that. I've brought you your pocket watch. You left it on the table, and I was sure you'd need it."

Witherspoon stopped pacing and stared at the watch with a puzzled frown. "I left it on the table," he muttered, "but I could have sworn I checked there before I left this morning."

Her conscience gave Mrs. Jeffries a nasty nudge. He had left it on the table, but she'd determined she had to be here today and now she was glad she'd come. She'd learned several interesting facts.

"Well, sir," she said cheerfully, "I shouldn't worry about a trifling thing like that. My, my, isn't this an opulent room."

"Uhmm . . . yes." Witherspoon gave up trying to think. It was giving him a pounding headache. "It is very nice."

"Amazing, isn't it? Dr. Slocum has certainly done well for himself. You know, the butler happened to mention that a mere ten years ago he only had a rather small practice in Hammersmith."

"Really?" Witherspoon looked genuinely surprised by that bit of news. Even he understood the economic differences between the elegance of Knightsbridge and the working-class grit of Hammersmith.

"How is the investigation going?" Mrs. Jeffries drifted to the window and peeked through the white lace curtains to the street below.

Witherspoon sighed deeply. "I'm afraid it's not going well at all," he admitted, giving in to the urge to confide in his understanding housekeeper. "The cook, Effie Beals, doesn't look in the least insane, and she's got absolutely no real motive to want to kill Dr. Slocum. But as there was no one else who had touched his food or was even in the house, I don't know where else to look."

"How distressing." She kept her gaze fixed out the window. "But I'm sure you'll come up with the true culprit. You always do."

"And on top of that, Mrs. Leslie fainted when I was trying to get her to tell me about the calling cards, and then the maid had hysterics, and now I've got to go back and interview them all over again."

"Calling cards?"

"Yes, I don't think they've a thing to do with the murder, but they're one of those niggly little details I've got to try and sort out." He went on to describe his talk with the gardener and his subsequent visit to the Leslie household.

Mrs. Jeffries listened carefully. There was a whole heap of questions the inspector should be asking. But she knew she had to be subtle. "Do you think, perhaps, the doctor left calling cards anywhere else?"

"Hmm, I don't know. It's possible, I suppose. Drat, another thing to do. And I've still got to try and see that solicitor today. Not to mention sending Barnes round to the Yard to check the personal effects of the deceased and see if we can find that wretched key."

"What key?" Mrs. Jeffries asked sharply.

"I don't really know," Witherspoon said. "But the maid mentioned a key just before Mrs. Leslie fainted. I don't recall seeing a key on the body. It might be important, so I'm duty-bound to follow it up." He sighed melodramatically. "Oh dear, where will I find the time?"

"Don't upset yourself, Inspector," Mrs. Jeffries said soothingly. "You'll get to the bottom of this case. You always do."

Her mind was on the key. She went over everything she'd learned so far today, and none of it made sense. There were so many questions she needed to answer. Why did Keating think Dr. Slocum was up to something when he gave the servants the day off? And why had he accused her of telling tales when she'd arrived this morning? What kind of tales? About whom? Why had Catherine Leslie fainted? Where was the key and what did it unlock?

She drew in a sharp breath as her gaze caught a familiar figure walking briskly down the pavement on the other side of the street.

It was Inspector Nivens. If he found her here, he'd start nosing around again, trying to prove that Witherspoon wasn't worth a fig as a detective. He'd like nothing better than to catch her snooping into one of Witherspoon's cases. Nivens wasn't brilliant by any means. But he wasn't stupid either. He reminded her of a fox sniffing around the henhouse. If she weren't careful, he'd find a way in.

Yet there was one more important point she needed to make. Mrs. Jeffries moved away from the window and toward the door. "Well, I hope the solicitor will be helpful. Perhaps you'll find that he's left his entire estate to his servants."

Witherspoon laughed. "I don't think so, Mrs. Jeffries. From what I've found out, he didn't like his servants much and they certainly didn't like him."

"Yes. I daresay you're right. Of course, that makes his behavior on the day of his death even more puzzling."

"Pardon?" he said. He'd lost track of the conversation.

"Why, his giving the servants the day off," she reached the door, pulled it open and turned to face the inspector. If she hurried, she could get down the back stairs and out the kitchen door before Nivens realized she'd been in the house. She only hoped that Witherspoon had enough sense to be discreet about the matter.

"I'm sorry. I don't follow you." Witherspoon looked more puzzled than ever. "What's so strange about his giving his people the day out? I've done it myself on more than one occasion."

"But you're a wonderful employer, Inspector. Dr. Slocum wasn't, and it's peculiar for precisely that reason. It sounds to me as if the man gave his servants time off not to be kind, but to insure that he was here all alone."

She heard voices in the front hall and knew she was running out of time. "Perhaps he wanted to be alone because he didn't want any witnesses to know how he spent his afternoon."

CHAPTER 6

Mrs. Jeffries managed to evade the odious Inspector Nivens by ducking into a doorway and then beating a hasty retreat down the stairs after he'd gone past. She paused by the front door, trying to decide whether to go home and pry more information out of Mrs. Goodge, or duck into the back garden and have a look around. She needed to talk with Effie Beals as well, but this wasn't the best time. Not with Inspector Nivens hanging about.

Decision made, Mrs. Jeffries pulled open the heavy front door and hurried down the stairs.

There was still no sign of Smythe when she arrived back in Upper Edmonton Gardens, but she refused to let it worry her anymore. Smythe was a law unto himself—he'd turn up eventually, and when he did, he'd no doubt have something useful to tell her.

She quickly took off her hat and started for the back stairs. But she hadn't taken two steps when the drawing-room door opened and Betsy's excited voice stopped her.

"Oh, good, you're back. I've been waitin' for you," Betsy announced as she rushed forward, a dust cloth hanging limply in her right hand. Her eyes were sparkling, and her cheeks were flushed with excitement. "Mrs. Jeffries, I've learned ever so much."

"Can it wait for a few moments?" Mrs. Jeffries asked, edging closer to the back stairs. "I really must have a word with Mrs. Goodge."

"But, Mrs. Jeffries," Betsy protested, "you won't believe what all I've found out. I did just like you told me—I chatted up every shopkeeper and clerk I could find. There wasn't much to learn about Dr. Slocum, but I got me an earful about everyone else livin' round that garden, I can tell you. Just goes to show, you shouldn't give up. Yesterday was a bit of a waste o' time, but today I got right lucky. I asked about everyone who was at that tea party on Saturday." She smiled shyly, her face lighting up with pride.

"Let's sit in the drawing room then," Mrs. Jeffries said. Mrs. Goodge would have to wait.

She turned and led the way toward two velvet-covered chairs next to the window. "All right, Betsy," she said as she settled herself, "what did you find out?"

"Well, like I said, Mrs. Jeffries, none of the tradespeople knew much about Dr. Slocum, except that he haggles over their bills . . ."

"Haggles? You mean he doesn't pay what he owes?"

Betsy nodded. "The butcher says he was always nippin' off a few pence here or a half a shilling there. And the fishmonger told me he'd stopped supplying him last year when Dr. Slocum claimed some kippers he'd sent over was rotten and refused to pay for 'em."

"From what we've learned about the man, that doesn't surprise me." The picture of the murder victim Mrs. Jeffries had been forming in her mind became clearer, more defined. Dr. Bartholomew Slocum seemed to go out of his way to make enemies.

"I also found out that he's not the only one round that ways that people gossips about," Betsy continued excitedly. "Colonel Seaward, the one that lives round the corner, he's got a taste for fine wine, buys it by the caseload and all of it from France too, not at all like Dr. Slocum. The wine merchant's assistant was braggin' that you could sell the doctor any old slog as long as it had a fancy label on the bottle. That's one place old Slocum didn't haggle with. They says he paid his bill every month and in full too." She laughed. "Funny, inn't it? What people seems to think is important. Oh yes, I almost forgot. Colonel Seaward, he's some sort of an . . ." Frowning, she paused. "I can't remember the exact word, but he's one of them people that's always fussin' with strange animals and growing exotic plants in his conservatory. He's an amateur . . . oh something or other."

"Naturalist?" Mrs. Jeffries supplied helpfully. She wondered if Colonel Seaward's exotic plants included mushrooms, and then realized it didn't matter. The mushroom that poisoned Dr. Slocum hadn't come from a conservatory or greenhouse, it had come from the communal garden.

"That's it," Betsy agreed. "The colonel's a bit of an odd one too, if you ask me. Donald Roper, he's the grocer's delivery boy, he told me that the colonel actually tried to hire 'im to catch mice and rats. Said he needed them to feed his snakes. Got a whole slew o' them out at his country house. Well, Donald says he weren't havin' none o' that. He's ever such a nice boy, is Donald. Quite handsome too, not that he's really a boy, he's only a year or two younger than me and—"

"Betsy," Mrs. Jeffries interrupted. "Please, let's not digress. You can tell me all about Donald some other time."

"Oh, sorry," she said with a blush. "Now let me see, where was I? Now I remember. That Catherine Leslie, seems she's carrying on with that Dr. Hightower and he's the one that found the body. That's pretty suspicious, if you ask me."

"Are you sure about that?"

Betsy nodded vigorously. "I heard it from the girl in that fancy dress shop on the corner of Brompton Road. Mrs. Leslie's one of their customers, and Tillie, that's who told me, she sometimes goes to the Leslie house to help with dress fittin's. Tillie reckons that Mrs. Leslie is seeing the doctor on the sly, though why she should have to be doin' it on the sly is a wonder to me. She bein' a widow and all. But then, I guess, the doctor would have to be careful, seein' as he's a married man." She sighed melodramatically. "It's such a waste, inn't it? The poor man, I feel so sorry for 'im. It's a romantic tragedy, that's what it is."

"Whom do you feel sorry for?" Mrs. Jeffries asked with a puzzled frown.

"Dr. Hightower." Betsy's voice dropped to a whisper. "His wife is a lunatic. He keeps her at home. Tillie says he's round Mrs. Leslie's house all the time, but theys have to be discreet about bein' in love with each other. Course everyone knows what's goin' on."

"Yes, I expect they do," Mrs. Jeffries murmured thoughtfully. She was silent for a long moment, thinking of everything the girl had told her. Finally, she asked, "Anything else?"

Betsy pursed her lips. "No, I think that's it. Do you want me to keep at it?"

There were several things that Mrs. Jeffries needed to know, but she wasn't sure that Betsy was the one to send.

She had a feeling that the case was becoming more complicated. More dangerous. And she didn't know why.

"Yes, but not just yet," she answered slowly as she rose to her feet. "You've done an excellent job, Betsy. I'm very proud of you. Give me a day or two to decide what we need to do next."

The girl blushed a becoming pink. "You just lets me know when you're ready for me to go out again. This detectin's excitin' work. I do think I'm startin' to get it right, aren't I?"

"That you are, my dear," Mrs. Jeffries muttered as she walked to the door. "That you are."

Mrs. Goodge was rolling pastry when Mrs. Jeffries came into the kitchen. The cook's face was a mask of concentration as her arthritic hands worked the rolling pin slowly back and forth over the dough.

"What are you making?" the housekeeper asked, stepping up to the table. Unlike in most households, she didn't bother going over the menus with the cook; there was no need. They ran things simply here, and Mrs. Goodge was the queen of this kitchen.

"Steak and kidney pudding," she replied without taking her eyes off her dough.

"Lovely. I'm sure it will be delicious." Mrs. Jeffries decided not to waste any time in preliminaries. She needed to get this case moving a bit faster; Inspector Nivens showing up at the Slocum household was a bad sign.

"Mrs. Goodge," she began firmly, "I need some information."

"About who?"

"Several people. Catherine Leslie, Dr. Sebastian Hightower and a Colonel Clayton Seaward. They're all neighbors sharing the same communal gardens as Dr. Slocum. Do you know anything about any of them?"

Mrs. Goodge put the rolling pin down, dusted off her hands and looked up. "Hmmm . . . ," she mumbled. "Seaward, Leslie and Hightower. Wait a minute, wait a minute, something's coming to me."

"Take your time."

"Seaward, Seaward." Suddenly, the cook's eyes lit up. "I remember now. I've heard of *him*. Oh yes, yes indeed. I know all about Colonel Seaward."

"Excellent."

"He's quite a famous man, you know."

"Really?"

"In some circles, that is," Mrs. Goodge said with a sniff. "But he couldn't possibly have anything to do with that murder. Why he's been decorated by the Queen herself. For bravery."

"How interesting." Mrs. Jeffries tried to mask her impatience. Goodness, how the woman liked dragging out the pertinent details in bits and pieces. "Do go on."

"He was in charge of a military outpost in one of them heathen African countries." She wrinkled her brow. "I can't remember which, though. But he was defending the crown when it happened."

Mrs. Jeffries privately thought he was probably defending English commercial and agricultural interests, but she kept that opinion to herself. She'd noticed that her unorthodox views regarding the British Empire were less than popular with most people. "When what happened?"

"Why, him defending the British garrison almost single-handedly. He was half-dead by the time reinforcements got through." Mrs. Goodge shook her head. "There was a native uprising against us, and Colonel Seaward, he was in charge. He managed to hang on, even after most of his men had been slaughtered, till more troops arrived. He was still at his post, fighting off the savages, when the reinforcements broke through."

"I would hardly refer to the native peoples of another country as savages," Mrs. Jeffries said quietly. Regardless of how badly she needed information, her conscience could not let Mrs. Goodge's last remark pass without comment.

"But that's what they was, a savage mob," the cook argued. "And Colonel Seaward was badly wounded. He left the army and came back to England. That's when he was decorated by Her Majesty."

"When did this happen?"

"About ten or twelve years ago." Mrs. Goodge picked up the rolling pin. "But he's not one of those idle do-nothings. He's worked for the government ever since. I hear he's in line for a very important appointment."

"Indeed? What kind of an appointment?"

"Governor to one of them islands out in the Caribbean." She shook her head. "Sounds like one of them right nasty places. Hot, miserable and the people running around half-undressed. Makes a body wonder why anyone would want to go to such a place. But that's the kind of man Colonel Seaward is, a real gentleman. Knows his duty. Never any scandal attached to his name, I can tell you that."

Mrs. Jeffries had no doubt that she could. "Is he married?"

"No. He's given his whole life to public service. If you ask me, I think the country needs more like him."

"Yes," Mrs. Jeffries replied softly, "I'm sure you do. Do you know anything about Catherine Leslie or Dr. Hightower?"

The cook's brows drew together. "I'm not sure. The names sound a bit familiar, but I can't think of anything right off. I'll let you know if I remember anything."

"Thank you, Mrs. Goodge. That'll be fine." Deep in thought, Mrs. Jeffries walked away. At the door, she stopped. "When is the announcement of Colonel Seaward's appointment expected to be made?"

"Why, I believe it's to be this week sometime. When Her Majesty returns from Balmoral."

"Good heavens, man. You've upset Mrs. Leslie terribly and I won't stand for it, do you hear? I don't care if you are the police, that doesn't give you the right to come barging in here and making ridiculous accusations." Dr. Sebastian Hightower paused to take a breath. "Furthermore—"

"Dr. Hightower," Inspector Witherspoon interrupted, "I assure you, sir, I did not mean to upset the lady, but this is a murder investigation. I've no idea why Mrs. Leslie became so distraught over a few simple questions. Questions, I might add, that everyone living on these gardens has had to answer."

He was getting annoyed. But drat it all, nothing had gone right today. He'd been on his way out to try and get to the Slocum solicitor when Mrs. Leslie's maid, Nanette, had popped up like a rabbit out of a hat and imperiously demanded that he return to the Leslie house.

He would have gone back there in any case, he thought defensively. But he certainly didn't like being summoned as if he were an errant schoolboy, and by none other than the arrogant Dr. Hightower. "And if you'll recall, sir, I didn't barge in here, you sent the maid over to ask me to come."

"Right, well." Hightower had the good grace to flush. "I thought it was important to get to the heart of this matter as soon as possible. Nanette told me that Mrs. Leslie fainted while you were questioning her this morning."

"That's correct. As I said, she became most distraught, as did the maid."

"Yes, well, that's the point I'm trying to make. Mrs. Leslie has a very high-strung and nervous disposition. She upsets easily. The least little thing sets her off, and I wouldn't want the police to place undue importance on a minor fainting spell."

"I see." Witherspoon didn't see in the least. What on earth was the man trying to tell him? That he wasn't supposed to question people in a murder case because they might faint! Ridiculous. "Dr. Hightower, I've placed no importance whatsoever on Mrs. Leslie's behavior this morning. Why it's a well-known fact that females frequently swoon."

"Good. I'm glad you understand."

"However," Witherspoon continued as though Hightower hadn't spoken. "Though I've no wish to distress either Mrs. Leslie or her maid any further, I will be asking them more questions. There are several unusual facts to this matter that must be clarified."

Dr. Hightower stared at him incredulously. "If you must ask your blasted questions, sir," he snapped, "then I suggest you direct them to me. I can assure you, Mrs. Leslie had absolutely nothing to do with Dr. Slocum's murder."

Witherspoon gazed at him thoughtfully. "You couldn't, by any chance, shed any light on what the maid was on about? She kept saying that Mrs. Leslie shouldn't lie to the police. That she must tell the truth. Do you know what she was talking about?"

"*Non!* 'E does not."

The inspector whirled around at the sound of the girl's voice and saw her standing by the door. "Then perhaps you'd care to tell me what you were talking about," he said.

She shrugged. "As I told you when we were walking over here, there ees nothing to say. I was upset. I thought you were going to arrest my mistress. The English polees, they are always arresting innocent people."

Witherspoon gazed at her pityingly. Poor child, she didn't know what she was talking about. But then what could one expect from the French? Why it was a well-known fact that anarchists, revolutionaries and even worse walked the streets of Paris without so much as a by-your-leave.

"But you said this morning," he continued, getting back to the matter at hand, "that Dr. Slocum threatened to tell lies about your mistress. Isn't that true?"

"You misunderstood me, Monsieur Inspector. I meant that I was afraid the polees would believe lies about my mistress. The British, they are always gossiping and making up tales."

"But you said . . ." Witherspoon broke off in confusion. Blast it, what all had the girl said? Something about a key, and yes, calling cards. "You stated that Dr. Slocum dropped two calling cards here on the day he died."

The girl glanced quickly at Hightower and then back at the inspector. But it was the doctor who answered.

"He did. But there was nothing unusual in that. Dr. Slocum was constantly trying to push himself upon his neighbors." He turned to the maid. "That'll be all, Nanette. Please go and sit with Mrs. Leslie. We'll call you if we need you."

Witherspoon waited until the girl had left. "So Dr. Slocum wasn't a welcome guest here?"

"No. Mrs. Leslie didn't like the man. Nor did anyone else."

Witherspoon racked his brain for another question. "You were, I believe, at Mrs. Crookshank's party this past Saturday?"

"Yes. Mrs. Crookshank is quite a forceful person. It's difficult to refuse her invitations. Besides, I like the lady. Despite her rather colorful way with words, she's a most charming and kindhearted woman."

"And why were you invited? You don't live on the gardens."

Hightower looked surprised by the question. "I was invited because I'm Mrs. Crookshank's physician as well as her friend."

"So you and Mrs. Leslie were both present when Mrs. Crookshank told the gardener to get rid of the poisonous mushrooms?" Witherspoon was sure he was on to something here.

"Yes. But the way Mrs. Crookshank bellows, I shouldn't be surprised if half of London heard her ranting and raving about those mushrooms." Hightower's eyes narrowed. "What are you trying to imply?"

"Why, nothing. I'm merely trying to ascertain how many people knew the mushrooms were there. That was how he was killed, you know."

Dr. Hightower stared at him incredulously for a moment. "Mushroom poisoning? Good Lord, man, you must be joking."

"I assure you, I'm not. How did you think he'd been killed?"

"I knew Slocum had been poisoned." Hightower's brows drew together. "But I didn't know it had anything to do with mushrooms. Are you sure?"

"Quite sure," Witherspoon said defensively. "Our police surgeon confirmed it."

"Did he do a postmortem examination? Was he absolutely sure about the cause of death?"

The inspector felt his hackles rising. "Really, Doctor. Of course I'm sure. We are very thorough at Scotland Yard, certainly capable of ascertaining the correct cause of death."

Dr. Hightower stared at him silently.

After a few moments, Witherspoon pulled out his watch and checked the time. "I really must be off," he said. "I'll have to come back and finish questioning Mrs. Leslie tomorrow."

"As her physician, I'd like to be present when you do."

Witherspoon wasn't sure he liked that, but he couldn't think of any legal grounds upon which to object. "As you wish, sir. Until tomorrow."

It started to rain right after lunch, and Mrs. Jeffries decided to put off her return to the Slocum house till the next morning. Trudging about in the wet would only hamper her search for clues.

After tea, she went up to her sitting room at the top of the house and started to think in earnest about the murder of Bartholomew Slocum.

He was a nasty little man, she decided, taking a seat by the window and staring down at the street below. Slocum was miserly with tradespeople, miserable to his servants and refused to treat patients who couldn't pay. But none of that added up to a reasonably good motive for murder. Or did it? She leaned back in the chair, closed her eyes and let her mind wander.

If Slocum had been murdered in a fit of rage, perhaps what she'd learned of his character could be of some use. But he hadn't been killed on the spur of the moment. He hadn't been stabbed by a servant driven to his or her limit of endurance, and he hadn't been attacked suddenly by a shopkeeper or a rejected patient because of his mean and miserly ways.

No, she thought, this crime had been carefully and meticulously planned. Someone had deliberately slipped a poisoned mushroom into his soup bowl. Someone had known he was going to be alone in the house and unable to summon help. Someone had known his habits and his customs. Someone who wanted him dead had known the servants were going to be gone and that his surgery would be closed. And that someone had then seized the opportunity to kill him. She didn't for a minute think that person was a middle-aged, frightened cook either.

No. Whoever had done the deed was cool, calculating and desperate.

"Good evening, sir," Mrs. Jeffries reached for Inspector Witherspoon's bowler hat. "I hope you've had a successful day."

"Well, it's actually been quite a dreadful day," he answered with a weary smile. "But I think I've learned some important facts about the case, so I suppose it's been worth it. Shall we have a glass of sherry before dinner? I daresay I could use a bit of warming up."

"I've got you a glass poured," she said, following him down the hall and into the drawing room. She handed him a glass and picked up the one she'd poured for herself.

He took a sip of his drink. "I questioned the solicitor today. Chap was as you'd expect, tight-lipped and well . . . not very accommodating. Naturally, when I impressed upon him how grave the situation was, he was a bit more forthcoming."

"I presume he told you the terms of Dr. Slocum's will?"

"Yes, and very interesting it was too. Slocum was going to leave his estate to his nephew, Joshua Slocum. But a few weeks ago, he suddenly changed his mind."

Her eyes widened in surprise. "Really?"

"Oh yes. According to Mr. Carp, the solicitor. Slocum asked him to come round because he wanted to alter his will. This was two weeks ago. Mr. Carp told us that Slocum gave him instructions to change the will completely. Instead of leaving the bulk of his estate to his nephew, he'd decided to use his money in quite a different manner."

"He was leaving everything to someone else?" Mrs. Jeffries asked.

Witherspoon smiled slightly. "Not quite. You see Slocum had a decidedly high opinion of himself. He was going to build a memorial to himself after he was dead. Every penny was to be used to endow a wing in his name at the hospital in Chelmsford. Oh yes, and he also left instructions that they had to put up a statue to him as well. So you see, there's absolutely no doubt about it now. The new will is the key to the murder. Effie Beals killed him for the hundred pounds he left her in his old will."

"So he had left bequests to the servants in his old will," Mrs. Jeffries mused. "But if he made a new will, why would the cook murder him now?"

Witherspoon smiled. "Simple. Mr. Carp came down with gout and that delayed the drafting of the new will. Until it was signed and properly witnessed, the old will was still the legal document for the dispersion of the Slocum estate. Joshua Slocum is still the heir and Mrs. Effie Beals will get her hundred pounds—well, she would if she wasn't going to be arrested for Dr. Slocum's murder, that is."

"But how did she know Slocum had left her any money?" Mrs. Jeffries asked. "Surely he didn't tell her."

"Of course he didn't. But unfortunately one of the witnesses did," Witherspoon explained. "I'm afraid Mrs. Melcher called in for a sleeping potion and Slocum made the mistake of asking her to sign as witness to the will. She obliged and then promptly told the whole neighborhood what she'd seen."

"And what did she see?" Mrs. Jeffries asked. She could see the hangman's noose edging closer to Effie Beal's neck, and she didn't like it one bit.

"The bequests to the servants." Witherspoon said sadly. "The woman could read, and those particular items were on the last page. Her signature was just below it."

"I see. Did he leave the other servants the same amount?"

The inspector shook his head. "Only the butler. He got a hundred too, the maids and the footmen were each given twenty-five. But Effie Beals is the only one with the motive and the opportunity. All the rest of the household had already gone when she served his lunch to him."

As a motive, Mrs. Jeffries thought it was fairly weak.

"But surely, killing Dr. Slocum would be a bit like killing the goose that laid the golden egg," she said. "After all, he was her employer—once he was dead, she'd be out of work."

"Well, yes," the inspector mumbled with a puzzled frown, "but a hundred pounds is a lot of money to someone like her. She doesn't strike me as being an overly intelligent woman. I suspect she acted on the spur of the moment without thinking of the possible future consequences of her actions. So many of that class of people live only for today. They don't stop to consider what might happen tomorrow."

Mrs. Jeffries let that ridiculous statement pass without comment. Witherspoon, despite his good heart, wasn't immune to the prejudices and beliefs of his class. But she would hardly think that killing someone with a poisoned mushroom was a spur-of-the-moment act. They had to be picked and probably pressed or pulped as well. She'd just have to work harder to prove that Effie Beals hadn't done it.

"Yes, Inspector," she replied, "I expect you're correct. By the way, I thought I saw Inspector Nivens come in as I left."

"How observant you are," Witherspoon exclaimed. "The fellow dropped by to ask if he could lend a hand in the Slocum matter. He's already solved that robbery in Holland Park. Generous of him, wasn't it? He even offered to escort the maid back to the Leslie house and question Dr. Hightower for me, but naturally, I told him I'd have to do that. And I'm jolly glad I did too. Do you know, that Hightower fellow actually had the gall to hint that our police surgeon was mistaken about the cause of death?" Witherspoon set his glass down with a loud thunk. "Can't imagine what Nivens would have made of that. He'd have probably lost his temper. Yes, yes, it's a good thing I took care of that matter—"

"Inspector, please," Mrs. Jeffries interrupted. "You're getting ahead of yourself." She paused and gave him a guileless smile. "Now, why don't you tell me all about your visit to the Leslie house?"

She listened patiently as Witherspoon gave her the details of both his first and second visits to the Leslie household.

"But you know, Mrs. Jeffries," he said as he concluded the narrative, "going over it again leads me to believe there's something deucedly strange going on there. Don't you think so? I mean, I know I couldn't have been mistaken about the maid's statement this morning. Yet this afternoon, she'd completely changed her story. Makes one think, doesn't it?"

"Then you're not absolutely convinced Effie Beals is guilty?" she asked cautiously. "Do you think perhaps you ought to investigate just a bit more? Especially about the matter of the calling cards."

"That's the puzzle," he muttered. "Perhaps I should. The evidence points to the cook, but somehow, I get the feeling there's more to this case than meets the eye. Too many loose ends, that's what it is. And you know how I hate loose ends."

"Then you'll continue the investigation?"

"Oh yes," he exclaimed. "My conscience would torment me horribly if I arrested the woman now. I'm almost positive she did it, but until a few other questions are settled to my satisfaction, I won't rest."

"I'm delighted to hear you say that," Mrs. Jeffries said earnestly. "And what other loose ends are troubling you?"

"The house being empty was one worry, but I think I've solved that to my satisfaction."

"Do tell," she coaxed. "You know I so love hearing how you've arrived at your conclusions."

His chest swelled and he sat straighter. "Ah yes, my conclusions. First of all, the house was empty because he'd given the staff the day off. That in and of itself was unusual, but upon serious questioning of the servants, I found it wasn't the first time it had happened."

She bit her tongue to keep from telling him they already knew that.

"But the important question," he continued, "was determining whether or not the house being empty had any connection with the doctor's death. It didn't."

Mrs. Jeffries stared at him in amazement. "How did you deduce that?"

"The calling cards. Dr. Slocum had sent his calling card to several of his neighbors the day before. Well, it's perfectly obvious."

"What is?" Her jaw was beginning to ache with the effort it took to keep a pleasant smile on her face.

"Dr. Slocum," he explained, smiling at her benevolently, "was not a very popular man. But he never stopped trying to become better acquainted with his neighbors. From what we've learned of his actions in the twenty-four hours before he died, I've concluded that he took his calling card around hoping one of his neighbors would return the favor and drop by on the afternoon of his death. Not only did he go round with his card, but he also ordered the butler to bring up a case of his best French wine. Naturally, if a guest dropped by, he wanted to be able to offer them refreshment."

"But if he were expecting *guests*," she said, deliberately stressing the last word, "wouldn't he have made sure that at least the maid and butler were on hand to serve them?"

"Not necessarily. If he were expecting a gentleman to come, he could easily pour a glass of wine."

"But you know that he sent a card to Mrs. Leslie," Mrs. Jeffries said. "She's a lady. He'd have kept at least a maid in attendance if he were expecting her."

"I think not, Mrs. Jeffries," Witherspoon said, shifting uncomfortably. "Slocum was a man of the world . . ." He paused and coughed lightly as a blush crept up his cheeks. "Mrs. Leslie is a very beautiful woman. I suspect he deliberately got rid of the servants so he could be alone with her."

CHAPTER 7

Betsy popped her head into the drawing room and announced that dinner was served, so Mrs. Jeffries had to wait until the inspector was settled at the dining table before she could continue her questions.

"Are you suggesting Dr. Slocum was arranging an assignation of a romantic nature, then?" Mrs. Jeffries asked briskly as the inspector picked up his fork.

The fork halted halfway to Witherspoon's mouth. He'd just remembered the second card, the one for Dr. Hightower.

"Well, not exactly," he hedged. "You see, when he dropped the card off for Mrs. Leslie, he also left one for Dr. Hightower." He looked down at his steak and kidney pudding to hide his confusion. "But I'm sure his taking the cards around hadn't anything to do with his murder. Dr. Slocum was merely trying to become better acquainted with his neighbors. Yes, that's what the fellow was doing. I'm sure of it. The cards are nothing more than a coincidence. Nothing to do with the case at all."

Mrs. Jeffries stared at him, debating whether or not to tell him about the calling card left at Colonel Seaward's. Seeing the confusion in the inspector's eyes, she decided to say nothing for the moment. Those cards were important, but she wasn't sure precisely what they meant. But she would find out, and she thought she knew exactly how to do it.

"It's rather sad, isn't it?" she remarked with a theatrical sigh.

"What is?"

"The way the poor man was continually trying to establish friendships with his neighbors. I suppose he wasn't particularly gifted at getting others to like him all that much." She turned her head and sniffed. "And then he was murdered. It's heartbreaking."

"Dear, dear, Mrs. Jeffries," the inspector said, leaning forward and patting her hand. "Don't distress yourself so. Dr. Slocum wasn't in the habit of going around with his hat in hand begging for friendship. Why, Keating's told us he only went out to call once every quarter or so."

She turned and gave him a brilliant smile. "I'm so glad to hear that. It's dreadful thinking of that poor man all alone, friendless and desperate for companionship."

"You're much too kindhearted, Mrs. Jeffries. Don't waste your sympathy on Dr. Slocum. By all accounts, he was a perfectly happy man living his life entirely as he wished."

"That is good to hear." For effect, she paused momentarily and piously gazed down at her folded hands. Then she suddenly straightened and lifted her chin to meet Witherspoon's gaze. "Inspector," she said breathlessly, "you really are a sly one, aren't you?"

Witherspoon gaped at her from behind a forkful of mashed potato he was trying to get to his mouth. "Pardon?"

"Why, of course you are," she exclaimed. "But that's all right, you can play the innocent with me. I know precisely how that mind of yours works, and I know you won't be so cruel as to keep me in the dark. I shall expect a full accounting tomorrow at dinner." She laughed merrily. "Oh my, you are a clever man."

Witherspoon put the bite of potato back on his plate. "Yes, I suppose I am." He gave a deprecatory laugh. "But then it's no use trying to hide my methods from you, is it?" He paused and cleared his throat. "Just for the sake of argument, Mrs. Jeffries, what do you think I'm going to do tomorrow?" He leaned forward, eyeing her the way a dog does a meaty bone.

Mrs. Jeffries didn't like tormenting her kindly employer. She'd hoped he'd grasp her meaning without her having actually to come right out and say it, but he obviously wasn't going to. She cocked her head to one side and smiled conspiratorially. "You're going to find out if Dr. Slocum's calling upon his neighbors ever coincided with his unexpectedly giving the servants the day off."

Witherspoon blinked several times and then sat back, a bemused expression on his face. "What a good idea," he murmured. He sat up taller in his chair. "Of course it's a good idea," he exclaimed in a stronger tone of voice, "and that's precisely what I was planning on doing."

Satisfied, Mrs. Jeffries nodded. She heard the rustle of a starched apron and glanced at the door. Betsy was standing in the hall, directly behind the inspector and jerking her chin frantically toward the kitchen.

"If you'll excuse me, Inspector," she said, rising quickly and hurrying toward the door. "I must see to your coffee."

Betsy motioned her down to the end of the hallway.

"We've got a message from Smythe," she whispered excitedly. "A rag and bone man just brung it—he says Smythe says to say he's hot on the trail, but he don't say on whose trail or why. He says not to worry, he'll be back in a day or so."

"Thank goodness we've finally heard from him," Mrs. Jeffries replied. "I don't mind admitting I was getting alarmed. Smythe is an admirable man and well able to take care of himself, but even so, it's been two days."

"But what does it mean? That old rag and bone man won't tell us anything else. He didn't say where Smythe was or anythin' useful. He's just sittin' downstairs stuffin' in the last of Mrs. Goodge's treacle tarts."

Most housemaids would rather die than admit to their employer or their employer's representative that the cook was feeding someone other than a member of the family or a guest. But Betsy knew that she was safe in telling the housekeeper. Their household wasn't like anyone else's, and that was all there was to it. Mrs. Jeffries practically encouraged such behavior. And after watching the way Mrs. Goodge got the old man to talking, Betsy was beginning to suspect she knew why too. But she'd keep that little tidbit to herself. It was too good to pass on now. Yet someday, when Mrs. Jeffries really needed proof of how good her detectin' skills was gettin', she'd reveal exactly how their snobbish old cook knew what was going on in this town without ever leaving the kitchen.

"Don't fret about Smythe, Betsy," Mrs. Jeffries soothed, "I think I know what he's doing. But I do wish he'd come back soon. There's a matter or two I'd like him to look into."

Betsy's blue eyes sparkled like dewdrops in the sun. "I can look into it for ya," she blurted. "I can find out anything Smythe can. Just give us a chance. 'E's not 'ere and I am, and there's no tellin' when 'e'll be back. Come on, Mrs. J, please. Let me 'ave a go at it."

She drops her h's completely when she's excited, Mrs. Jeffries thought idly as she stared into the girl's eager face. "But you don't even know what it is I want you to do."

"That's all right; whatever it is, I'm willin'."

Mrs. Jeffries silently debated the issue and then made her decision. Betsy was right; she was here and Smythe wasn't. "All right. Here's what I want you to do. Tomorrow, you'll have to go back to Knightsbridge. We need to know several things. One, find out anything you can about the butler. When I spoke to him yesterday, he seemed to think I was there to 'tell tales' of some sort or another. See if you can pick up any gossip about his activities. Also, try and make the acquaintance of someone from the Slocum household—a housemaid or a footman, if you can. The Leslie maid was going on about a key the doctor always carried. See if you can get any information about that."

Betsy nodded gravely. "That shouldn't be too hard. I think I can do it."

"I know you can," Mrs. Jeffries said earnestly. She'd often observed that people generally lived up to whatever expectations they had of themselves. Building someone's self-confidence did a lot more good in getting the best results out of people than making them feel as if they couldn't do anything right. "I have complete faith in you, Betsy. But for goodness' sakes, be careful."

The next morning, Mrs. Jeffries waited until Inspector Witherspoon had left before donning her hat and cloak. She caught a hansom on Holland Park Road because she was in a hurry to get to Knightsbridge. If she were lucky, one of the side gates leading into the communal garden would still be unlocked. Frequently, lazy groundskeepers unlocked the gates early in the mornings so they wouldn't be bothered having to let tradespeople and delivery men in and out.

As the hansom clopped briskly toward Dr. Slocum's residence, Mrs. Jeffries thought carefully of how to approach Effie Beals. By the time the horses had stopped on the side street, near the gate, she'd made up her mind.

Mrs. Jeffries paid the driver, tipped him handsomely and then slipped through the unlocked (just as she'd thought) gate. She stopped inside and slowly looked around. The gardens were an elongated octagon. Along the center strip was a spacious expanse of grass dotted here and there with tall, sheltering oak trees. Beside the grass and circling the perimeter of the octagon was a ten-foot strip of space filled with a variety of plants, flowers and greenery, Obviously, each household had the right to plant whatever they liked in the space adjacent to their property. Behind some houses there were high shrubs, while others had neatly laid rows of flowers and shrubs. She noticed that the Seaward house occupied all the room at the far end of the octagon and that the strip of garden there was virtually a jungle. The shrubs and plants were so thick and high one could probably get lost in them. The foliage extended virtually all the way to the Slocum house.

She raised her hand to shade her eyes against the sunlight as she studied the area. Each house had one thing in common, she thought. A path leading from a recessed area behind the houses through their bits of private garden onto the main garden. As she walked toward the Slocum house, she noticed that each individual path went down a set of stone stairs onto a flat terrace about ten feet by ten feet.

Intent upon reaching her goal, she didn't hear the shuffle of footsteps coming up behind her.

"Yoo-hoo," screeched a familiar flat twang.

Mrs. Jeffries started and whirled. Luty Belle Crookshank, dressed in a garish green dress, trimmed with gold on the cuffs and collars, stood grinning at her.

"It's Mrs. Jeffries, ain't it?" said Luty Belle. "Well, I sure am glad to see you. Ever since ol' Slocum went and got himself done in, this place has been like a ghost town. You'd think the man died of the pox, the way folks has been avoiding coming out here."

Mrs. Jeffries edged closer to the Slocum terrace. She had a feeling that if she started a conversation with Luty Belle, she'd be there half the day. And she had so much to do. "Good morning, Mrs. Crookshank," she said politely, as she continued moving toward the Slocum house.

"Told you to call me Luty Belle. Purty day, ain't it?" Luty Belle came after her. "Would you like to have a cuppa tea?"

"Er, no thank you, Luty Belle. I'm in rather a hurry this morning."

"That's the problem with folks these days," Luty Belle complained. "Always in a dang-blasted hurry to get somewhere. Where you headed? Over to the Slocum house?"

"Yes, as a matter of fact, I am."

"Good, then you can take a message to them fatheaded lawmen for me. Been trying to git one of them to stand still so's I could tell for the past two days now, but every time they see me coming, they take off like the hounds of hell was chasin' 'em."

Mrs. Jeffries stopped dead. "Do you have some information about Dr. Slocum's murder?"

"Murder? If'n what I heard is true there might not even have been a murder." Luty Belle cackled.

"What are you talking about?"

"Dead eyes. That's what they're saying killed him, inn't that so?"

"Yes," Mrs. Jeffries replied. "That's correct. Do you have a reason to believe otherwise?"

Luty Belle cocked her head to one side. "Sure do. You see, I knows how dead eyes kill, and the only ways Slocum could have died from eatin' one was if he ate it a good four days earlier than the day he died. Dead eyes don't kill you quick, you see. They makes you real sick and then it looks like you're gittin' well, but then you take a turn for the worse and finally go a few days later. But it takes at least four days and if'n what I heard was right, they're saying the doctor ate the danged thing for lunch and then keeled over right away." Luty Belle shook her head. "But that weren't the way it happened. Couldn't be, and I should know."

Mrs. Jeffries was utterly stunned. Surely the police surgeon couldn't make a mistake. Surely this old woman was wrong. "How do you know?" she finally asked.

"'Cause I've seen folks die that way," she said impatiently. "What do you think I'm doin', making up tales just for my own entertainment? Back in '53 I nursed two miners who'd eated dead eyes. It was a bad year; people was starvin' 'cause the snow was so bad no supplies could get through. As soon as some of the snow melted, these two miners went mushroomin'; they was that hungry. My Archie and I we took 'em in when they got sick, and I nursed 'em. Nells Bells," Luty Belle banged her cane against the ground. "It took one of them four days to go and the other one almost a week. So take my word for it, Slocum didn't die in two hours from eatin' no poisoned mushroom."

Mrs. Jeffries studied the old woman's face. She could see from the determined glint in Luty Belle's eyes that she was telling the truth. Maybe the police surgeon had made a mistake. "Luty Belle," she said slowly. "If you're right . . ."

"Course I'm right." Luty Belle snorted. "And from what I hears, they're gittin' ready to arrest Slocum's cook. Stupid lawmen, same the world over, always taking the easy way out—"

"Would you like to prevent a gross miscarriage of justice?" Mrs. Jeffries interrupted.

Luty Belle stared at her warily. "I reckon. Don't want to see someone that's innocent strung up like a side of beef. What do you think I should do?"

Suddenly inspired, Mrs. Jeffries said, "You've got to find Inspector Witherspoon and tell him everything you've told me." She paused, trying to remember precisely where Witherspoon said he might be this morning. There were several places. Quickly, she rattled the list off to Luty Belle.

"And don't let one of his underlings put you off," she finished. "You've got to make sure Inspector Witherspoon understands everything you've told me."

"Reckons traipsin' round London lookin' for this copper beats sittin' in that empty old mausoleum of a house o' mine," Luty said cheerfully as she turned to go.

"Oh and Luty Belle," Mrs. Jeffries called. The woman stopped and gazed at her inquiringly. "It would be best if you didn't mention our little chat to the inspector."

The Slocum terrace was put to practical use. Outside the kitchen door there was a long table with several baskets of vegetables sitting on it. Mrs. Jeffries hurried past them and marched boldly up to the kitchen door. She rapped her knuckles imperiously against the wood.

The door opened about two inches, and a pair of worried eyes glared at her suspiciously from within. "Yes, what do you want?"

"Mrs. Effie Beals?"

The door closed to an inch. "Who wants to know?"

"Mrs. Beals, I've come to help you." Mrs. Jeffries surreptiously wedged her toe close to the door.

"Help," snorted the woman. "We don't need no help here. The solicitor didn't say he was sending anyone round, so you've got no business here." She jerked the door open wider as a forerunner to slamming it shut, but Mrs. Jeffries was too quick for her and managed to get her heavily booted foot inside.

"You don't understand," Mrs. Jeffries said firmly. "I haven't come to help you in the kitchen, I've come to help you keep from being arrested for a murder you didn't commit."

The suspicious eyes widened in fright, and Effie Beals stared at her as if she'd seen a ghost. For a long moment, the two women took each other's measure. Finally, the door opened fully and the cook jerked her chin once in the direction of the house. Mrs. Jeffries took that to mean she was welcome to come inside.

"Thank you, Mrs. Beals," she said politely as she stepped inside. "I realize this is most irregular, but I assure you, you've nothing to fear from me."

"Are you from the police?" Effie asked as she moved slowly down the hallway.

"No."

"Then why are you here?"

They came into the servants' hall. "If it's no trouble, I could do with a cup of tea," she said matter-of-factly. People always spoke more easily over a nice hot cuppa, she thought.

The cook stared at her for a moment. "I've just made a pot; nothing much else to do now, but drink tea. Now that he's dead, we just have simple meals down here. Between the ruddy police and that ferret of a solicitor, we're all stuck here until this misery's done."

By that, Mrs. Jeffries assumed she was referring to the investigation of Slocum's murder. She took a seat at the table and waited while Effie Beals poured two cups of tea, found a tin of sugar and a pitcher of cream, placed the whole lot on a tray and came to join her.

The cook's apron was wrinkled, her eyes were red, and as she poured the tea, Mrs. Jeffries saw her hands shaking.

"Mrs. Beals," she said softly, "I really have come to help you."

"How can you help me?" the woman wailed. Tears slipped down her cheeks, and she hung her head. "No one can help me. He's dead and they think I killed him. Besides, why should you care? And you never told me what you was doing here, neither."

"My name is Hepzibah Jeffries and I'm Inspector Witherspoon's housekeeper." There was a strangled gasp from Effie Beals, but Mrs. Jeffries resolutely ignored it. "I've come here because, well, I'm quite astute at solving mysteries and I've realized you couldn't possibly have killed Bartholomew Slocum."

Another strangled gasp, and Effie Beal's mouth gaped open like a flounder's. Mrs. Jeffries held up her hand for silence.

"Like you, I'm in domestic service. However, I'm reasonably intelligent, very observant, and more importantly, I can think. If you will answer my questions honestly and quickly, we may just be able to keep a hangman from stretching your neck."

She'd deliberately used the brutal words to shock the woman and gain her cooperation. Time was running out. She didn't have the luxury of winning Effie Beal's confidence with her usual patience and tact.

Effie sniffed and brushed at an escaping tear. "You think I'm innocent?"

"I'm certain of it." After meeting the cook face-to-face, Mrs. Jeffries was positive she wasn't guilty. After what Luty Belle had told her, she didn't know precisely what to think. But she did know that Slocum's murder, if it had been murder, was carefully and meticulously planned. Effie Beals was an emotional woman. Only a great actress could fake this level of distress. If this weeping woman were going to kill someone, she'd do it in a frenzy of rage and quite probably in front of a dozen witnesses!

Effie bowed her head and sobbed quietly into her apron. Mrs. Jeffries waited patiently, knowing the woman needed a few moments to work the fear out of her system.

With a final shudder, she brought herself under control, wiped her cheeks and lifted her head. "Let's get on with them questions of yours," she said, giving Mrs. Jeffries a watery smile. "Do you want me to tell what happened that day?"

"No, that won't be necessary. I know the sequence of events. You've got to tell me *why* someone would want to murder Bartholomew Slocum."

"Why? That's simple enough," she replied with a snort. "He's a blackmailer."

"How do you know that?" Mrs. Jeffries found that she wasn't in the least surprised.

"Because he was blackmailin' me." Effie lifted her chin. "You don't think I'm workin 'ere by choice, do you? The old bastard forced me to come here. And it's such a bleedin' waste too. He didn't appreciate fine cooking. The man had a palate like a billy goat, wouldn't know good food if he was buried in it up to his arse."

"His palate, or lack of it, isn't pertinent right now," Mrs. Jeffries said firmly, excusing the vulgarity. "But you must tell me why he was blackmailing you."

Effie dropped her eyes and stared at the toe of her scuffed black shoe. "Do you have to know that?"

"Yes, I'm afraid I do."

The cook raised her chin, and her eyes were awash with fresh tears. "All right then, I'm trustin' that what I'm going to tell you will go no farther. It's not myself I'm worryin' about," she said quickly, "it's someone else, someone very dear to me."

Mrs. Jeffries reached over and patted her arm. "Believe me, Mrs. Beals," she said softly, "I'll do everything in my power to insure that innocent people aren't ruined because of this murder. But I can't give you any promises. If the information you're going to give me will save you from the gallows, I'll certainly use it."

"Fair enough." She took a deep breath and focused her gaze on the far wall. "Ten years ago I was the cook at the country house of a very important family, aristocrats. I was a widow and it was a fine position because they let me keep my daughter with me." She broke off and smiled sadly. "Abigail was fourteen and the prettiest child you ever saw. But it seems that the young master of the house thought she was pretty too, because he seduced her, and him a grown man who should have known better. He got her . . . ," her voice faltered and she bit her lip, "with child."

"I'm so very sorry," Mrs. Jeffries said quietly.

Effie nodded, and her hands balled into fists. "I confronted the family and told them what their son had done. I expected them to own up to it, to help me daughter. For goodness' sakes, she weren't but a child." She gave a bitter laugh. Mrs. Jeffries was fairly certain she could guess the rest of the tale. "But they sacked me and threw us both out. But I weren't too scared. I'd saved me wages, and I knew I could get another position. I took me girl to London. The son, maybe having a bit more of a conscience than his father, gave me a reference to the London house of the Duke of Bedford. So I had me employment, but I couldn't keep me girl with me, not in her condition. I got her rooms with a respectable woman in Hammersmith and paid the lady to keep an eye on her."

"And Dr. Slocum delivered the baby?" Mrs. Jeffries asked.

"No, when she was five months along, she lost it. She were bleedin' so bad I thought for sure she'd die, so I sent the landlady for the doctor. It was Slocum."

"And he managed to save your daughter's life."

"Yes, he saved her, but he charged us a pretty penny, I can tell you that, not that I minded payin'," Effie explained earnestly, "but I didn't like his manner. He was wicked, he was. Filled her with some damned potion that made her ramble on and on. And he was askin' her questions, gettin' her to own up to who the father was and pokin' his nose in where it didn't belong. I soon put a stop to that bit o' meanness, I did. Paid the man an extra guinea to shut his mouth." She laughed harshly. "The old miser took it and left. I'd hope that we was shut of him, then. But we wasn't."

"Is that when he started the blackmail?"

"No, that didn't start for another five years."

"Five years?" Mrs. Jeffries stared at her curiously.

"When my daughter was nineteen she got engaged to a right nice young gentleman. His family owned a draper's shop here in London, and they was going to open another one in Chelmsford." She shook her head sadly. "I don't know how that old goat found out, it weren't in the papers or anything. But one day I got a note telling me to come round here to see him on my day off. Well, what could I do? I came round, and old Slocum told me if I wanted my daughter to marry, I'd better give in my notice to the duke and come work for him. If I didn't, he threatened to tell Abigail's fiancé about what had happened."

"I take it your daughter didn't share that confidence with her intended?"

"Would you?"

"No," Mrs. Jeffries said thoughtfully, "I probably wouldn't." It was her experience that men were exceedingly narrow-minded about some things. "So Slocum didn't blackmail you for money, he wanted you to work here, is that right?"

"That's right. You see, I'd begun to make a real name for meself with me cooking. Slocum didn't care none about the food, though, he just wanted the appearance of having one of the best cooks in London in his household. And not only that, the old miser cut my wages when I came here. I was making a full wage with the duke, seventy pounds a quarter. Slocum cut me to sixty pounds a quarter."

"Did your daughter know you were being blackmailed?"

Effie's eyes narrowed suspiciously at this question. "Abigail didn't have anything to do with Slocum's death," she said quickly. "She was at home the day he was killed."

"I'm not accusing your daughter of murder," Mrs. Jeffries replied patiently. "I merely want to know if she knew you were being blackmailed. Surely she asked you why you left the Duke of Bedford to come to work for a common doctor."

Effie glanced down at her hands. "She didn't know until a few weeks ago," she muttered sullenly. "When I left the Bedford house, I'd told her I was tired of working so hard and that all those fancy dinners were gettin' to be too much for me. I told her I needed a quieter life. She believed me for a while, but finally, I think she guessed I weren't here by choice."

"What prompted you to tell her the truth?"

"Last month Abigail told me she and Neville, that's her husband, were emigrating to Australia. She wanted me to come with 'em. I told her I couldn't—that Slocum probably wouldn't let me. If I left his employment, he'd tell Nev about her."

"What was her reaction?"

Effie smiled broadly. "She said she'd already told Nev everything and he didn't care. Told her he loved her no matter what, that she was his wife and they could have a good life in Australia. I was right proud of her. Nev's a good lad, and I know he loves her."

"So Dr. Slocum wouldn't have been able to blackmail you anymore," Mrs. Jeffries said thoughtfully.

"That's right. It done me heart good to tell that old bastard I was leavin'. That's why I stayed after the others had already gone—I give him my notice, told him I was going to Australia with my daughter and her husband and there weren't nothing he could do about it."

"How did Dr. Slocum take that news?" Mrs. Jeffries was genuinely curious.

"He was furious. That's what we had the row about. He ranted and raved and had a right fit over it."

"Did you know the doctor had left you a hundred pounds in his will?" Mrs. Jeffries watched the cook carefully, but Effie met her gaze squarely.

"Yes, I knew. But that didn't make no difference; he was changin' his will anyway. Keating told us that. And I didn't want the old bastard's blood money anyways. Why should I? I've saved me wages for years."

"Keating told everyone in the household that Slocum was changing his will?" Mrs. Jeffries asked.

The cook nodded. "Yes, but it don't make no difference, they still think I done it." She began wringing her hands together as a fresh batch of tears rolled down her cheeks. "And now look at me. They's goin' to arrest me for murder. I'm not goin' to Australia, I'm goin' to hang."

Mrs. Jeffries grasped her firmly by the shoulders and shook her lightly. "Nonsense. You aren't going to hang. Mark my words, you'll be sailing with your daughter and son-in-law to a new life in Australia. But you'll have to help me save you."

Effied sniffed. "How? What can I do?"

"The first thing is to tell Inspector Witherspoon the truth. Once he knows that Slocum was blackmailing you, he'll start looking for other victims of the man's greed."

"Oh no," Effie wailed, "I couldn't do that. Maybe he won't find anyone but me."

"But you said that Slocum was a blackmailer. I presume that means he was blackmailing others as well."

"He was. But he was careful. I don't know who else he had his hooks into. I can't help you there. If the police find out he was blackmailin' me and they don't find no one else, that'll put the noose around my neck as sure as the sun rises on Monday morning."

Mrs. Jeffries realized that the woman had a point. The key to finding the murderer was in finding the other victims. But that might not be easy.

"All right," she agreed, "for right now, we'll keep this between us."

"Thank you, ma'am."

"Now, I want you to think. On the day of the murder, did you see anyone hanging about outside in the garden?" Mrs. Jeffries was fishing for any and all information she could find.

Effie's brows knotted in concentration. "Well, I saw that French maid of Mrs. Leslie's walking past with one of the gardeners when I was out getting the vegetables from the table. And Colonel Seaward went past right after that. But there weren't nothing strange about either of them. The maid was always making eyes at the gardener, and the colonel took a walk every morning."

"You saw Colonel Seaward that morning? Are you sure?"

"Yes, course I'm sure. I was just gettin' the mushrooms for the soup. It were about ten o'clock that mornin'. I saw him and that maid about the same time, but they was goin' in different directions."

Mrs. Jeffries frowned. "Was there anything else odd about that day? Anything, anything at all? Think, Mrs. Beals. Think hard."

"Well," she answered slowly, "there was one thing that puzzled me. But when I tried to tell the police, they weren't interested."

"What was that?"

"It was that Dr. Hightower findin' the body. He said he was callin' round to visit Dr. Slocum, but I don't think that's true."

"Really? Why?"

"Because he'd never have called around here by choice. He and Slocum hated each other."

CHAPTER 8

"Gracious, how on earth do you know that?" Mrs. Jeffries asked.

"Because I heard them fighting. Dr. Hightower claimed if he had anything to do with it, he'd see to it that Dr. Slocum never touched another patient for the rest of his life." Effie smiled smugly. "Now that don't sound like they was good friends, does it?"

"Apparently not."

"Mind you, I'm not surprised, despite this fancy house and all his rich patients, I don't think old Slocum was much of a doctor."

"Yet he saved your daughter," Mrs. Jeffries reminded her.

"He saved her all right," Effie said thoughtfully, "but I think any doctor could have done the same."

This was the second time Mrs. Jeffries had heard that Slocum wasn't a particularly good physician. She wondered if it were true. It hadn't really seemed likely to her the murderer could be a disgruntled patient, but perhaps she should reconsider.

"Mrs. Beals. Tell me how you came to overhear Dr. Slocum having words with Dr. Hightower."

"Well, it was one of them times when he'd unexpectedly given us the day off. I couldn't go to Abigail's because she and Nev had gone up to Yorkshire to see his Gran."

"How long ago was this?"

"I think it was about six months ago. It were one of them cold, wet, nasty days, and Slocum came trottin' in, ordering us out o' the house like he were doin' us a big favor. But who wants to leave a nice warm house on a day like that? I didn't. But he insisted we leave, so I didn't have much choice. I waited till the others had gone off and then nipped back through the garden. There weren't no one around, and I was thinking I'd just slip into my room and have a rest."

Her voice dropped dramatically. "That was when I heard 'em. They was upstairs, having a right go at each other."

"Slocum and Hightower? You're sure of that?"

"Yes." She nodded eagerly. "Hightower was shouting that Slocum weren't fit to doctor a horse and that if he ever touched her again, he'd have his license."

"Her? Did you hear the name of the lady they were arguing about?"

"I didn't hear him say it, but I reckon it must have been that Mrs. Leslie from across the garden. She used to be one of Dr. Slocum's patients. She quit coming to him when she and Dr. Hightower became friendly like."

"She was one of Slocum's patients? Are you sure?"

"I'm sure. He was treatin' her for some kind of nerve sickness."

"When did she stop seeing Slocum?"

"About two years ago," Effie said cautiously. "But anyways, it had to be her. Hightower's always hanging about over there. And that day, he and Slocum was arguin' loud enough to wake the dead. Just before Hightower left. I heard him threaten Dr. Slocum."

Mrs. Jeffries said nothing for a moment. She stared into space, her hands neatly folded in her lap and her eyes narrowed in concentration. She was sure that Inspector Witherspoon had told her that Mrs. Leslie denied ever being one of Slocum's patients.

"Mrs. Beals," she said slowly, "I want you to think carefully before you answer. Did you actually hear Dr. Hightower threaten to kill Dr. Slocum? Did you actually hear him say so in the Queen's English—did you hear the words?"

Effie shifted nervously in her chair, her eyes darting furtively around the room. "Not exactly," she admitted, "but I'm sure that's what he meant."

"What were the exact words?" Mrs. Jeffries asked softly.

"He said, 'If you go near her again, I'll see to it that you're sorry.' But that could only mean he was threatenin' him. Hightower already told him he'd have his license, so what else was left?"

Mrs. Jeffries sighed. Really, people were so good at hearing what they wanted to hear. "Did you tell Inspector Witherspoon about this?"

"No. I didn't want him thinking I was the kind to sneak around behind my employer's back," she replied defensively. "It'd make me look awful bad. Make me look like if I'd sneak back here one time, I'd do it again. Do you know what I mean?"

"Yes, I think I do, but you've got to tell him what you overheard as soon as possible. There's no time to lose. Will you do it?"

Effie chewed nervously on her lower lip as she thought about it. "If you think I should."

"Good." Mrs. Jeffries rose to her feet. Her mind was frantically trying to put together all these new pieces of the puzzle. Luty Belle Crookshank was convinced that Dr. Slocum hadn't died of mushroom poisoning. Mrs. Beals claimed that Catherine Leslie had once been a patient of Slocum's and that Hightower had threatened the man. Keating was frightened of people telling tales, and on top of everything, the victim was going to change his will. And then there was the matter of the calling cards and the key.

"Mrs. Beals, did Dr. Slocum have a key?"

"He had lots of keys. But Keating would know more about that than I would. He's the butler. Hangin' on to keys is his job."

"Yes, but did he have one particular key that he kept on his person? One that he didn't give to the butler?"

Effie's brows drew together in concentration. Suddenly, she smiled. "Oh yes, that's right. He did have a key, a little gold one he wore on his watch chain. But I never seen him use it."

"Meaning you don't know what the key unlocked?" Mrs. Jeffries stared at her in disappointment as the cook shook her head. "Oh dear, that's a shame. I suspect that key may be important."

"Sorry, but like I said, I never seen him use it. Tell you what. Why don't I have a snoop around and see if I can find out what it went to? It were just a small key, so maybe whatever it opened is still around here somewherc."

"That's a good idea," Mrs. Jeffries said. "Let me know if you're successful. I've got to be going now, but if you think of anything else that may be helpful, send a footman around with a note and I'll come right away."

She gave the cook her address and then turned toward the hall, intending to leave the way she'd come.

She stopped near the door and gazed around the large kitchen. "Are you sure that the back door was locked on the day that Dr. Slocum was murdered?"

"Positive. I locked it myself."

"But someone got into this house that day? How?"

"Could have come in through the window." Effie pointed to the sink.

Above it was a large open window. "That was unlocked. I told the police that, but they didn't think it was important. But I reckon that's how the murderer got in."

"Why was the window open? I thought Dr. Slocum was terribly concerned about burglars?"

"He was, but I'd cooked fish the night before and the smell was awful, so Keating told me to leave the window open and he'd make sure it was shut before he left. But he didn't. It was still open when I got back from Chelmsford that evening."

Mrs. Jeffries added this new piece of information to everything else she'd found out this morning. "Keating told you to keep it open?" she repeated. "Are you certain of that?"

"Absolutely. It's not the sort of thing I'm likely to be mistaken about."

Mrs. Jeffries had arranged to meet Betsy on Brompton Road, where they would board an omnibus together and return to Upper Edmonton Gardens.

Betsy was fairly dancing with excitement when she spotted Mrs. Jeffries walking briskly up the road. She picked up her long skirts and raced toward her.

"Oh, Mrs. Jeffries," she gasped. "I've found out ever so much. You'll be ever so pleased."

"I'm sure I will," the housekeeper said calmly. "But let's wait until we're on board the omnibus before you begin."

She took the girl's arm, and they dodged between hansoms, carriages and various other traffic to cross the busy thoroughfare.

The omnibus pulled up just as they reached the other side. They climbed aboard and went up top, where they found two seats in relative privacy near the back.

"Now, tell me what you've found out," Mrs. Jeffries demanded softly.

Betsy giggled. "This detectin's hard work, I can tell you that. I must have walked two miles this morning gettin' that boy from Colonel Seaward's to chat."

"You made the acquaintance of someone from the Seaward household?" Mrs. Jeffries exclaimed.

"Yes, but that's not important. What is, is that I run into Rosie Scrimmons—we knows each other from back when I used to live over Whitechapel way. But she was with this woman called Maisie Logan, and Maisie's a special friend of that butler, Keating. Inn't that a bit of luck?"

"Yes, it certainly is," Mrs. Jeffries replied. "Go on, Betsy. What did this Miss Logan tell you?"

"Well, this 'ere Keating, he drinks like a fish."

"I suspected that might be the case."

"And not only that, he's been flashin' a lot o' money about." Betsy broke off and blushed. "Maisie's not exactly respectable, but she's a right talker. When I said she was Keating's 'special friend,' I meant that he's keepin' her."

Mrs. Jeffries stared incredulously at the maid. "Precisely what do you mean by that?" She saw Betsy's blush turned a bright crimson. "Oh dear, are you implying she's a . . ."

"Lady of the evening," Betsy finished lamely. "Look 'ere, I know I shouldn't be consortin' with the likes o' Maisie Logan, but she's not a bad sort, and she don't have any other way to make a livin'. Besides, I knows how to talk to 'er. It's not all that long ago that I was livin' in the slums meself."

"It's all right, Betsy," Mrs. Jeffries assured her, reaching over to pat her hand. "I wasn't passing judgment. I'm merely surprised that a person in that particular profession would be up so early. Now what did Maisie tell you?"

"She told me that Keating was one of 'er regulars like, but that about six months ago, he began wanting 'er all to hisself. Didn't want her walkin' the streets no more. Well, Maisie soon told 'im that was no good. A girl's got to make a livin', so Keating started takin' care of her. Payin' her rent and buyin' her things. She says she thinks he suddenly come into a bit o' money, and that he's always boastin' he's got lots more squirreled away." She broke off and snorted. "Mind you, Rosie told me that Maisie still works a bit on the side."

"Goodness, Betsy," Mrs. Jeffries said earnestly. "You've done very well. Fancy getting so much information in such a short time."

Betsy giggled. "Well, like I said, I knows how to get 'em to start talkin'."

"Did you get any information about the key?"

She shook her head. "No, nobody knew anythin' about a key. I'm afraid I didn't get any new information about any of the others either."

"Nothing at all?"

"Just what we've already heard. That Dr. Hightower was carryin' on with Mrs. Leslie and the whole neighborhood knew about it."

Mrs. Jeffries frowned. If it was common knowledge that Catherine Leslie and Dr. Hightower were carrying on an illicit relationship, there wouldn't be any point in Slocum trying to blackmail them. Therefore, neither of them would have a motive to murder him.

"Frankly, I'm not certain how to interpret any of this. We've obtained an enormous amount of information this morning. I've learned quite a bit myself." She quickly filled Betsy in on her meeting with Mrs. Crookshank and her conversation with Effie Beals.

"I don't suppose you learned anything more about Colonel Seaward?" Mrs. Jeffries asked as she ended her narrative.

"Nothing important," Betsy admitted. "The footman I talked to said the same thing as the inspector. Colonel Seaward was with his guests from eleven until two."

"The whole time?" Mrs. Jeffries asked the question halfheartedly. Seaward was the only person on the gardens who didn't have a reason for wanting to murder Dr. Slocum.

Betsy shrugged. "More or less. David did say he left the room for a bit whilst he nipped down to the cellar to get a special bottle of wine. But he weren't gone for more than a few minutes. He said that Seaward's a right good employer, treats the servants properly and all." She shook her head. "It's as plain as the spots on Wiggins's face that the colonel couldn't have done it. And if'n what that Mrs. Crookshank says is true, maybe no one done it! Could be Slocum wasn't even murdered."

"I doubt that's true," Mrs. Jeffries said softly. "We may find out he wasn't poisoned by a mushroom, but I think we can safely assume he didn't die of natural causes."

"What makes you think so?" Betsy stared at her quizzically.

"Because of Dr. Hightower. He wouldn't have sent for the police if he thought Dr. Slocum's death wasn't suspicious."

Mrs. Jeffries lapsed into concentration, trusting that Betsy would nudge her when they reached their destination.

The trouble with this affair, she thought, was there were too many loose ends. Catherine Leslie, Effie Beals, Keating, Colonel Seaward and Dr. Hightower. Even Luty Belle Crookshank—they were all connected in some way with the victim. But was one of them his murderer?

Mrs. Jeffries sighed sadly, hoping that the hangman's noose wasn't tightening around Effie Beals's thick neck.

Mrs. Jeffries brightened somewhat when they returned home. Smythe was back. She found him in the kitchen being fussed over by Mrs. Goodge.

He looked up from a plate of currant buns and gave her a cocky grin. "Hello, Mrs. J. I bet you're wondering where I've been the past couple o' days."

"How very astute of you, Smythe," she replied, taking the seat across from him and pouring herself a cup of tea from the pot on the table. "Your whereabouts have crossed my mind a time or two, but knowing how resourceful and clever you are, I realized you probably had a good reason for staying away so long."

He threw back his head and laughed. Mrs. Goodge walked up behind him and nudged him in the shoulder. "Get on with you, Smythe," she said testily. "We all know you've been snooping round on the murder, so stop keepin' us on the edge of our chairs and tell us what you've been up to."

"Give a body time to have some tea," he protested. "I only got here two minutes ago."

"You've got your tea," Betsy interjected, taking the seat next to the housekeeper. "And we're all dyin' of curiosity, so don't be playin' with us like a cat tormentin' a mouse. We know you've been up to somethin'."

He ignored Betsy and turned his attention to Mrs. Jeffries. "The last time we was all here, you told me to go out and find someone from the Slocum household. Well, I struck gold and ran into that butler, Keating."

"Very good, Smythe," Mrs. Jeffries murmured.

"He's quite a talker when 'e's in 'is cups too," the coachman continued. "And it don't take much to get 'im there neither."

"So what did you learn?" Betsy interrupted impatiently. "We 'aven't got all day, you know. The inspector's going to be here soon."

Smythe shot her a quick frown but continued. "Like I was tryin' to say before I was so rudely interrupted, Keating's a right talker. He was rantin' and ravin' about what a miserable old man Dr. Slocum was. I'd just got him to jabberin' about the murder, when all of a sudden, he glances up and then he snaps his mouth shut. So I looks too. There was a gentleman standin' by the door, a-noddin' to Keating."

He paused and took a sip of tea. "Then Keating hightails it out like a fox runnin' from the hounds. I knew you'd want me to keep an eye on 'im, so I give 'im a minute or two and follows 'im out. You'll never guess what I saw, neither."

Betsy rolled her eyes. Mrs. Goodge snorted, and even Mrs. Jeffries sighed impatiently. "I'm sure we won't, Smythe, so why don't you tell us?"

"Well, I crept up as close as I could and then ducked into a doorway. Keating was standing in the middle of the mews with this 'ere man. They talked for a minute or two, then I saw Keating slip something from his pocket and give it to the other bloke."

"Could you see what it was?" Betsy asked.

"No. It was wrapped in paper. Then they left, but they each went in a different direction and I wasn't sure who to follow, but I reckoned I knew where the butler lived so decided to follow the other un."

Mrs. Jeffries nodded approvingly. "Excellent."

Warmed by the praise, Smythe's chest expanded another inch or two. "Glad I did too, 'cause it worked out right nice. You'll not believe this, but he goes to Howard's livery and rents a carriage. I waited till he was on his way, then I hitched up the horses to the inspector's carriage and took off after 'im. Bow and Arrow is good horses too, caught up with him straightaway, but I stayed far enough back so that he didn't know he was bein' followed."

"You took the carriage out after dark." Mrs. Goodge was outraged. "How foolish. You could have been killed, man. That's not at all safe."

"Don't fret, Mrs. Goodge," Smythe said kindly, used to her fussing. "There was a full moon that night and I lit the lamps. Besides, I've done it before. Miss Euphemia used to love going out in the carriage at night—"

"Yes, yes, we know." Mrs. Jeffries said impatiently. She didn't want Smythe sidetracked by tales about Inspector Witherspoon's rather eccentric late aunt. "Please get on with it. What happened after you left London?"

"Not much until we got to Essex. A few miles outside of Colchester, he pulls into a lane and stops at a cottage. I couldn't follow him any further so I went on past, found a layby to pull off the road and nipped back. I waited long enough to see him light the lamps and figured he must live there, so I knew he wasn't goin' nowhere. I couldn't leave the carriage in the road, so I went on into Colchester and stabled the horses. Then I slipped back and waited." He grinned again. "This is the good part. The next morning, he goes into Colchester and stops at one of them fancy shops."

"What kind of fancy shop?" Mrs. Jeffries asked.

"The kind that sells rich peoples' whatnots. Silly stuff like—broaches and music boxes, china birds and silver bits and pieces. You know what I mean." He waved his hands for emphasis. "I managed to hang about outside, and I watched him through the window. He pulls whatever Keating had given him out of his pocket, takes the paper off and hands it to the shopkeeper. A few minutes later, he's gettin' a fistful of pound notes in return."

"Were you able to see what it was?" Betsy asked.

Smythe shrugged. "I couldn't really see from that distance, but it was small and it was silver."

"Pity you didn't have a chance to go inside and find out," Mrs. Jeffries murmured.

"Couldn't. He came back out, and I didn't want to let him out of my sight."

The sound of footsteps on the pavement outside the kitchen window had Mrs. Jeffries leaping to her feet. "Oh dear, that's the inspector. He's home early."

"How can you tell that's him?" Betsy asked. She was always looking for ways to improve her detecting skills.

Mrs. Jeffries was already heading for the stairs. "His footsteps," she called over her shoulder. "They're quite distinctive."

"Footsteps," murmured Betsy with a puzzled frown.

Mrs. Jeffries opened the front door with a welcoming smile just as Inspector Witherspoon was fishing for his keys. "Good afternoon, sir. How delightful. You've come home early for a change."

"Good afternoon, Mrs. Jeffries," he answered, stepping inside and automatically shedding his coat and hat. "I was close by and decided to come home. It's been quite a day. I haven't even had lunch."

"Then we'll have Mrs. Goodge fix you a nice, substantial tea." Mrs. Jeffries nodded to Betsy, who'd followed her up the stairs.

As soon as the maid hurried in the direction of the kitchen, she turned to the inspector and said, "Why don't you come into the drawing room and have a rest? Betsy will bring the tea when it's ready."

She was eager to hear what he'd learned today.

"I knew you'd be dying of curiosity, Mrs. Jeffries," he said as he settled into his favorite chair. "So as you requested yesterday, I'm going to give you a full accounting."

"Inspector, how kind of you. Please begin. I'm all ears." She took her chair across from him and smiled encouragingly.

Witherspoon gave her a weak half-grin in return and quickly lowered his gaze. She noticed how apprehensive the poor man was. He sat as rigid as a post, his fingers nervously fiddling with his watch chain. But it would do no good to rush him. She could guess what was wrong with the dear man, but he'd tell her about it in his own good time.

"It was just as I thought," he began. "Keating has confirmed my suspicion. Slocum did give the servants the afternoon off directly following his going out and passing out his calling cards. Mind you, finding that out took a bit of doing. I had to question the butler and the other servants for half and hour before we were able to discover that one simple fact."

"Gracious," said Mrs. Jeffries. "That must cast considerable doubt on Mrs. Beals's guilt."

"I'm not sure," he replied glumly. "Nothing in this case is what it seems to be. As to the cook's guilt or innocence, I'm still looking into that. Naturally, though, the more complex the situation becomes, the deeper I dig."

"And what has your digging uncovered?" She gave him another encouraging smile.

"Quite a bit, actually. Today I sent Constable Barnes around to every house in the square. I wanted to know who the doctor had called upon the morning of the murder." He frowned slightly. "It's really quite peculiar. He only left calling cards at Colonel Seaward's and Mrs. Leslie's, but, of course, he left Dr. Hightower's there as well, so I suppose that counts as three."

Mrs. Jeffries didn't find it in the least peculiar. She already knew it. "Really? Isn't that rather outrageous, leaving a calling card at a woman's house for a man who isn't her husband? What a revolting thing to do. By the way, how long has Mrs. Leslie been widowed?"

"Three years. Her husband was a wealthy manufacturer in Birmingham. When he died, Mrs. Leslie sold his factory and moved to London." Witherspoon shook his head. "Rather sad, really. The late Mr. Leslie was only in his forties when he popped off with a rather sudden stomach ailment."

"Yes, one never knows when the good Lord will call one home, does one?" She wondered if she should start hinting that Slocum was a blackmailer. But she decided against it. She wanted to hear the rest of Smythe's story before she steered the inspector in a new direction. Who knew what she'd learn next? So far there was blackmail and theft.

"No, one doesn't." Witherspoon sighed. "Bit strange, though. I wonder why Colonel Seaward didn't mention the calling card when I was questioning him. Oh well, perhaps the gentleman merely forgot."

"Yes, I expect you're right," Mrs. Jeffries murmured. There were moments when she really had to bite her tongue. Colonel Seaward hadn't forgotten; he just hadn't wanted to admit any closer acquaintance with the murder victim than necessary. But then again, she thought, Mrs. Leslie and Dr. Hightower hadn't admitted that Slocum had dropped his cards there either. The inspector would never have found out if the gardener hadn't told him.

"I'm afraid my day got progressively worse after talking with Keating," Witherspoon admitted morosely.

"I'm sorry to hear that," Mrs. Jeffries said sympathetically. "What happened?"

"Oh, you'll never believe it. After I'd gone back to the Yard, who should pop in but that Mrs. Crookshank. You remember, I told you about her. She's that rather forceful American woman who lives in the house next door to Slocum's."

"Really? And what did she want?"

His eyes narrowed as he leaned forward. "I don't know what to make of what she said. She had some sort of outlandish notion that Dr. Slocum hadn't died of mushroom poisoning."

"No!" Mrs. Jeffries surreptitiously crossed her fingers.

"Yes," the inspector exclaimed. "And on top of that, she made this accusation just as the chief inspector happened to come in. Of course he asked her to explain herself. She claimed she'd seen several cases of mushroom poisoning in her native country and that Dr. Slocum didn't die from it." Witherspoon looked thoroughly confused now. "So you can see, it's very difficult now. The whole matter's got horribly muddled. Mrs. Crookshank freely admits that 'death caps,' or 'dead eyes' as she persists in calling them, are very lethal. But she also insists it takes several days before one actually dies."

"Gracious!" Could it possibly be true? Do you think she knows what she's talking about?"

"Unfortunately, what I think doesn't matter. The chief inspector called the police surgeon in and started questioning him." He snorted. "And that Mrs. Crookshank wasn't shy about putting her oar in either. She had the gall to ask Dr. Bainbridge, that's Sir Reginald's son, by the way, exactly how many cases of mushroom poisoning he'd treated. Well, it was most embarrassing."

"How many had he treated?"

"To be precise, none. But that doesn't give Mrs. Crookshank the right to laugh in Dr. Bainbridge's face. Nor does it mean that he was mistaken," Witherspoon explained defensively. Suddenly, he broke off and stared glumly into space for a moment before adding, "But I rather think he was mistaken. Even worse, so does the chief inspector. The poor man practically admitted he barely touched the body. He based his entire diagnosis on finding that mushroom piece at the bottom of the soup bowl. Well, one can understand that. You've got a corpse and you've got a bowl with a poisoned mushroom in it—the conclusion is obvious."

"What is going to happen now? Will the investigation continue?"

"Most definitely. Dr. Bainbridge is still certain the deceased was poisoned. We should know more tomorrow—they're doing another post-mortem tonight." Witherspoon grimaced. "Won't be a very nice task, I should think. After all, Slocum's been dead now a good few days."

"Won't you have to . . ." She wrinkled her nose. "Exhume the body?"

"No, actually we've got lucky on that. Slocum's remains were sent to the mortuary, but they haven't been buried yet. His solictor is still ill and hasn't had time to make the funeral arrangements. Lucky for us the man had the gout. Otherwise, we'd have had to dig the old boy up."

Betsy brought in the tea tray. "Tea is ready," she announced. She caught Mrs. Jeffries's eyes and jerked her chin meaningfully toward the kitchen.

Mrs. Jeffries waited until the inspector had tucked into a plate of sandwiches, excused herself and then dashed back to the kitchen.

Everyone was sitting at the table. Smythe had obviously not said another word, because Betsy and Mrs. Goodge were glaring at him and Wiggins was watching them all warily.

"Smythe, go ahead and finish your report," she commanded softly as she took a chair.

"What report?" Wiggins asked.

"Later, Wiggins," Betsy promised. "Right now we want him to finish up."

"There's not much more to tell," Smythe replied. "I spent the rest of the time keepin' my eye on him, but he didn't do much. It wasn't until last night that he went out again and that was to a pub."

"So you've spent the past few days skulkin' round Colchester and that's all you've found out," Betsy said accusingly.

"What was 'e doin' in Colchester?" Wiggins asked. Everyone ignored him.

"I didn't say that, now, did I? If you must know, I've found out quite a bit about this gentleman," Smythe answered testily. "And I wasn't skulking about. I was standing in the cold and wind and doing my duty so our inspector won't end up with egg on his face."

"Now, now, no one's accusing you of dereliction of duty, Smythe," Mrs. Jeffries interjected hastily. "And we are very curious about what you've learned."

That soothed his ruffled feather's some. "Well, like I was saying before I was interrupted." He glared at Betsy. "I waited until after the toff left, then I started asking questions about him. It seems he's been living above his means for the past few years and owed everyone in town. But recently, he's come into a bit and is payin' off his creditors. It's my opinion he's payin' 'em off by sellin' the stuff Keating's been slipping him."

"That's a reasonable assumption," Mrs. Jeffries said calmly. "Go on."

"And the man can't hold his liquor neither. Spends most nights drinking in his local pub. But lately, he hasn't been around much." Smythe paused and then said dramatically, "He wasn't at his local or his home the day that Dr. Slocum was murdered, neither. He was in London."

"Very good, Smythe." Mrs. Jeffries beamed like a school-teacher at an especially gifted student. "And now why don't you give us the most important news of all."

"I thought I was doing just that," he protested, but he was breaking into another one of his cocky grins. "All right, Mrs. J, I reckon I should have known better than to try and keep you guessing."

"What's he talking about?" Mrs. Goodge scowled at the both of them.

"I'm talking about the name of the man I've been watchin' for the past few days. The man I followed this morning to a squalid little 'otel off the Brompton Road. It's the dead man's nephew. Joshua Slocum."

CHAPTER 9

"You could have told us that before," Betsy protested.

"Does that mean the old man's nephew murdered him?" Wiggins asked. He glanced around the table in confusion.

"Humph." Mrs. Goodge snorted. "You just like to play about, don't you, Smythe? Well, I tell you this 'ere is murder we're talking about—"

"Now, now," Mrs. Jeffries said soothingly. "Let's all keep calm. I'm sure Smythe wasn't deliberately withholding the name of the gentleman for purely dramatic effect. He's far too sensible for nonsense like that." She looked at the coachman.

"Certainly not," he said innocently, trying to keep from breaking out in a grin. "But that's not important now. What is important is that I figures Joshua Slocum only comes into London when he's wanting to meet that crooked butler and pick up a few more goodies. This is our chance, Mrs. Jeffries. I reckons there's a bit o' theft to be going on tonight."

"Get on with you, Smythe," Betsy burst out. "Why should Joshua Slocum keep stealing from the house? He's the heir. He owns everything now."

"The heir! How do you know that?" he shot back irritably.

"Mrs. Jeffries told us," Betsy said smugly. "While you was off diddling about in the country, we wasn't sittin' 'ere twiddling our thumbs. You're not the only one who can find things out."

His face fell and he looked at Mrs. Jeffries. "Is it true?"

"Yes it is," she admitted. "Joshua Slocum is Bartholomew Slocum's heir. But we don't know that he knew that very important fact. Remember, Keating had told Mrs. Beals that the doctor was changing his will. No doubt, he told Joshua as well."

"How'd ya find out all that?" Smythe asked.

Mrs. Jeffries quickly filled the coachman in on all the information they'd learned to date. She finished her narrative by telling everyone about Witherspoon's unfortunate encounter with Mrs. Crookshank and the second postmortem.

"So you see," she concluded, "many of our previous assumptions about the manner of Dr. Slocum's death may now have been proven false. Therefore, we can't afford to overlook anything. Joshua Slocum may have had every reason to keep right on stealing from the house—as far as he knows, he's already been disinherited. There's no evidence that Keating or any of the household knew the new will had been delayed."

"And even if he did know he was the heir," Betsy pointed out. "He still won't get a penny till this 'ere murder is solved. If'n what Smythe says is true and he was in London on the day of the murder, he's bound to be a suspect and I knows you can't profit from a crime. Inn't that right, Mrs. Jeffries?"

"That's absolutely correct." She smiled proudly at Betsy. "How on earth did you know that?"

"From them 'orrible Kensington High Street murders. I overheard you and the inspector discussin' it."

"Hmm. Very good, Betsy." She glanced at the clock on the mantel. "However, back to our immediate problem. I suspect that Smythe is absolutely correct. There is going to be another theft tonight. Hurry. Smythe. You and Wiggins dash upstairs and put some warm clothes on."

"Warm clothes?" Wiggins complained. "What do we need warm clothes for?"

Smythe was already getting to his feet. "Whaddaya think, you knothead?" he snapped. He was still a bit put out over Betsy's superior knowledge of British law. " 'Cause tonight we're goin' to catch a thief."

Tendrils of fog floated through the darkness of the mews behind the pub. Betsy huddled closer to Mrs. Jeffries and pulled her cloak tighter. " 'Ow much longer? My feet are gettin' cold."

"You didn't have to come," Smythe shot back before the housekeeper could reply. "You and Mrs. Jeffries should 'ave stayed 'ome with Mrs. Goodge. This 'ere is men's work—"

"Ha, you and Wiggins? Don't be daft."

"What do you mean by that?" Wiggins hissed indignantly.

"Hush, all of you," Mrs. Jeffries interjected. "If you don't keep still, someone's going to get the constable."

They were standing behind the pub, waiting for Joshua Slocum to show up. Keating was already inside. They'd followed him from the Slocum house and that hadn't been easy, considering there were four of them. Betsy, when she'd realized that Mrs. Jeffries meant to go, wouldn't hear of being left behind herself.

Suddenly the door of the pub opened. In the brief light, Mrs. Jeffries recognized the butler. He stepped into the mews and turned his head.

Smythe, Wiggins, Betsy and Mrs. Jeffries all crowded closer in the passageway where they were hiding. A few moments later, they heard the sound of boot steps approaching from the opposite end of the mews.

Smythe leaned his head out of the passageway. "It's him."

"I've got ta sneeze," Wiggins moaned.

"Nell's bells." The coachman shot the boy a disgusted look. "This is the last time I take you anywhere."

Wiggins grasped his chin and made a squeaky, keening noise.

"Hold your nose," Mrs. Jeffries advised softly. "We can't risk being seen."

From the mews, they heard the murmur of voices, and she raised her hand for silence. They cocked their heads toward the sound, except for Wiggins, who was holding onto his nose and lolling his head from side to side.

"What's he doing?" Betsy whispered. "I can't see. Wiggins's fat ol' 'ead's in me way."

"E's not doing nuthin'," Smythe answered, crouching low and peering out the passage. "They's just standin' there. Talking. You want me to grab 'em?"

His last statement was directed at Mrs. Jeffries.

She shook her head negatively.

A moment later, both men started walking in the direction of Brompton Road.

Smythe stood up and started to follow. Mrs. Jeffries laid a restraining hand on his arm. "Not yet," she murmured. "Let's give them time to get to the end of the mews."

Wiggins lost the battle. He sneezed loudly. "Sorry," he muttered defensively, as three heads turned and three pairs of eyes glared at him accusingly.

A moment later, Mrs. Jeffries judged that the men had had time to reach the road. She jerked her head, and they started off.

The quartet followed the two men through Knightsbridge, dodging back and forth across the quiet streets to avoid gas lamps and patrolling constables.

When they arrived at their destination, Mrs. Jeffries wasn't surprised to see the two men disappear inside Dr. Slocum's house.

"What'll we do now?" Smythe asked.

"It's quite simple," she replied, heading up the stairs. "We go inside."

Smythe grabbed her elbow. "Look, Mrs. J. I think I'd better 'andle this." He leapt ahead of her, raced up the stairs and banged the knocker before she could protest.

Keating opened the door. "What do you want, knocking this time of the night?" he demanded. "If you've come to see the doctor, you're too late, he's dead."

"Oh, we've come about the doctor, all right," Smythe replied hotly, not liking being addressed so rudely. "And if you knows what's good for ya, ya'd best be lettin' us in before I goes to call the constable. He'd like to hear about that nice bit o' thievin' you and Mr. Slocum's got for yourselves."

The butler's jaw dropped. Mrs. Jeffries quickly stepped in front of the coachman. "Keating, it's me, Hepzibah Jeffries, Inspector Witherspoon's housekeeper. Please let us in. We must talk to you and to Mr. Slocum."

"What's going on?" The thin, pale face of Joshua Slocum appeared behind the butler. "Who are these people? What do they want?"

Keating didn't answer. He was still gaping at the burly, threatening Smythe.

"May we please come in?" Mrs. Jeffries said in her most imperious tone. She wasn't overly concerned about their safety. Mrs. Goodge had been left with strict instructions that if they weren't back by midnight, she was to awaken the inspector and tell him everything. And she also knew that despite her objections, Smythe had stuck a rather wicked-looking hunting knife in his boot. She had a feeling he knew how to use it too.

Joshua Slocum scowled at them. "Who the devil are you?"

"It's that police inspector's housekeeper." Keating moaned. He started wringing his hands together.

"I fail to see how that's of any consequence," the young man blustered, but he stared at them uncertainly.

"I'm afraid our presence here is very consequential, sir," Mrs. Jeffries said. "Unless you'd rather speak with Inspector Witherspoon himself about the murder of your late uncle, I suggest you let us inside."

Without waiting for permission, Keating pulled the door open wide. "We'd better do as she says. They knows about us."

Slocum glared at them sullenly as they filed past and followed the butler into the drawing room. Mrs. Jeffries watched Slocum as they settled themselves into chairs.

He continued to stand. His mouth was compressed into a thin, flat line, his pale face had gone a ghastly white, and beneath the bluster and arrogance in his eyes, she could see he was afraid. He lifted his chin and met her gaze.

She heard him take a deep breath.

"Now what the devil do you people want?" he said.

"Mr. Slocum," Mrs. Jeffries replied. "We want the truth. A woman's life may depend on it."

"If you're talking about the old boy's murder, I don't know anything about that—"

She raised her hand for silence. "We know all about your and Keating's thefts."

"You can't prove anything," Slocum blustered, "and furthermore, a man can't be arrested for selling his own property."

"Yes, but it wasn't your property until very recently was it? These thefts have been going on for a long time, haven't they? At least six months."

Slocum stared at her in amazement for a moment and then slumped against the wall. "Just tell us what you want and get out of here."

"Watch your manners, boy," Smythe snarled.

"I want you to answer some questions," Mrs. Jeffries stated firmly. "And please, don't try to lie to us. We know you were in London on the day your uncle was murdered. But what I want to know now is where were you exactly?"

Keating moaned.

Slocum shot him a quick, open glance of disgust. "I was at my hotel all day." He sneered.

"Really? That's not what the porter says," Mrs. Jeffries replied. She ignored the fact that Betsy, Smythe and Wiggins were staring at her curiously. She only hoped that Joshua Slocum hadn't noticed. She had no more spoken to the porter than she'd had tea with the Queen.

"According to the porter, you left your room quite early that morning and didn't return until late that afternoon." She tilted her chin to one side and gazed at him speculatively. "Come now, why don't you save yourself a lot of pain and grief? Tell us the truth. Where were you?"

"For God's sakes, tell her," Keating shouted. "Can't you see, she already knows."

"Shut up, you fool," Slocum blazed.

"You were here that day, weren't you?" Mrs. Jeffries asked calmly. She silently breathed a sigh of relief that her gamble had worked.

All the bluster left Slocum then. He stared at her for a long moment, then sighed and buried his face in his hands. "Yes. I was here," he muttered softly.

"Did you see your uncle?" Betsy interjected.

Slocum laughed bitterly. "No, that was the last thing I wanted to do. I was hiding in the attic."

Mrs. Jeffries gazed at him thoughtfully. "Did you poison Bartholomew Slocum?"

He lifted his head and shook it slowly. "No, I hated the old man, but I didn't kill him."

"Then why were you hiding in the attic?"

"Because that's where Uncle Bartholomew kept the things he'd lost interest in. I was looking for something to steal." He sighed. "But I don't rightly think of it as stealing. More like reclaiming my own property."

Smythe snorted.

"It's true," Slocum protested. He gestured around the room with his hand. "All of this, by rights, should belong to me. If that miserable old blackguard hadn't blackmailed our Uncle Thaddeus, it would be mine."

"Dr. Slocum blackmailed your uncle?" Mrs. Jeffries asked.

"Yes. That's how he got started in his evil ways, not that he was ever a particularly good man."

"When did this happen?"

"It was eleven years ago. I remember because it was the year I left school," Slocum explained. "Uncle Bartholomew had come out to Colchester to try and make up with our Uncle Thaddeus. Uncle Thaddeus was my guardian, and I lived with him, of course. But Thaddeus stupidly broke his leg. While he was in Bartholomew's care, he admitted he'd embezzled his partners in a business venture."

"You mean he just came out and confessed bein' an embezzler to a nephew he didn't even like?" Smythe asked with disbelief in his voice.

"No, no, that wasn't Bartholomew's way. He used some sort of medicine to get Thaddeus to talk. Some awful kind of potion that kills the pain. I don't know what it was called." He looked up defensively. "But I do know that if you pump someone full of this stuff and then start asking questions, he'll talk his fool head off."

"Hmm," murmured Mrs. Jeffries. "I wonder if he was using opium on his patients."

"I don't know." Slocum shrugged and looked down at the floor. "But whatever kind of brew he used, it worked. At least on Uncle Thaddeus, and before you could say Bob's your uncle, Bartholomew was the new heir and I was left out in the cold. Then Thaddeus up and died the next year, and I've been living hand-to-mouth ever since."

"So that was probably Dr. Slocum's first successful attempt at blackmail," Mrs. Jeffries said. She watched to see if Slocum would react. But he didn't, and she knew then that he was fully aware of how his late uncle's nefarious activities began.

Slocum shrugged. "What does it matter, first or not. It worked and he ended up with my fortune."

"So you decided to steal it back from 'im?" Betsy said.

The butler moaned again, but everyone ignored him. They were all staring at Joshua.

He cleared his throat. "Yes, I did decide to steal it back from him. Why shouldn't I? It should have been mine. But that doesn't make me a murderer."

"Why should we believe you?" Mrs. Jeffries said softly.

"Why should I want him dead?"

"You were his heir."

"But I didn't know that till a couple of days ago." Slocum grinned triumphantly. "I thought dear Uncle Bartholomew had changed his will. I didn't know the will had been delayed until Keating told me the other night when I met him behind the pub."

"That was the night I followed 'im to Colchester," Smythe said.

"You followed me?" Slocum stared at him curiously. "Really? I had no idea."

"Course not. I'm bleedin' good at it."

"Gentlemen, please," Mrs. Jeffries interjected sharply. "We don't have time to digress. Mr. Slocum, will you please continue."

"Like I said, I was in the house to find something else to take," he admitted honestly. "But I didn't kill him. Keating and I were going through the attic. No one ever goes up there." He smiled slyly. "And the place is crammed full of expensive trinkets that Bartholomew had lost interest in."

Mrs. Jeffries frowned slightly. "Why did you pick that particular day?"

"I always came on a Wednesday. Bartholomew's surgery was closed and half the servants were gone. It was perfect. If by chance my dear uncle stayed home, whoever was in the house generally had to wait on him hand and foot."

"But that day, your uncle gave everyone the day off," Smythe said. "That must have put a spoke in your wheels."

"It did."

Mrs. Jeffries leaned forward eagerly. Betsy straightened her spine, and Wiggins almost fell off the edge of his seat in his eagerness to hear the rest. Smythe reached out a hand and pulled him back as he slid toward the floor.

"I'd been up there less than ten minutes when Keating came dashing in and told me all the servants were being given the day off," Slocum continued. "We knew our plan was ruined then, because that meant Keating had to leave too and I didn't want to actually leave the house with anything on my person. It was too risky if Bartholomew happened to catch me."

Puzzled, Betsy asked, "If you didn't carry the goods away, why did you risk coming here in the first place?"

"Because I knew what would fetch the most money. Keating couldn't tell a piece of Dresden from a cheap china cat."

Keating's mouth flattened to a thin line, but he kept silent.

"Did you see or hear anything as you were leaving the house?" Mrs. Jeffries asked impatiently. Really, she thought, if he didn't hurry up, they'd be here all night.

He nodded. "I was halfway down the stairs, just outside of Bartholomew's bedroom, when some of the servants came up to get their coats. I ducked into the bedroom, thinking I'd wait till everyone left and then get out by the servants' steps."

"What time was this?" Betsy asked.

"About five minutes to twelve or thereabouts. That's a guess, as I didn't bother to check my watch. So I waited for a few minutes, and then I peeked over the stairs and saw the cook walking down the hall with Bartholomew's lunch tray. Well, I thought it would be prudent to wait a few more minutes before leaving—I didn't want to run into any last-minute stragglers in the kitchen. But just as I decided to risk it, I heard another set of footsteps."

"And who was that?" Smythe asked, not wanting to be outshone by Betsy.

"I don't know, but it wasn't any of the servants."

"How can you be sure of that?" Mrs. Jeffries asked.

"Because whoever it was went into the surgery, and the servants would never do that. Bartholomew had strict rules about the surgery. Even the maid wasn't allowed in except for early in the morning when she did the cleaning."

"Could it have been Dr. Slocum?" Mrs. Jeffries asked.

"No, Keating had told me he was in his study, and you can see the study door from the top of the stairs. The door was still closed when I came out of the attic." He shook his head. "I knew he was in there. But as you can imagine, by this time I was beginning to get nervous. Keating had left the house right after he spoke to me, so I was on my own. I waited for a few minutes, and then the footsteps came out of the surgery and down the hall."

"Could you tell if the footsteps went into the dining room?" Surprisingly enough, it was Wiggins who asked this question.

Betsy, Mrs. Jeffries and Smythe all turned and stared at him in amazement.

"No. I couldn't. But Bartholomew was still holed up in his study. Probably scribbling nasty secrets about one of his patients in that ugly little black book of his."

Mrs. Jeffries straightened. "Black book? Do you mean his medical notes?"

"Hardly," Slocum answered with a sneer. "He wasn't that conscientious a doctor. I don't think the man ever recorded a word about what was actually ailing a person. But he did keep records about people's secrets, things they'd tell him in the course of treatment. Or even worse, things he'd get out of them when he was dosing them with one of his evil potions."

"How do you know? Did you ever see this book?" Mrs. Jeffries wasn't sure but that the man was lying. It was a bit too convenient, a written record of other blackmail victims and therefore other murder suspects. She knew it wasn't the need for confession that had loosened Joshua Slocum's tongue tonight. It was fear and shock. No doubt he wanted to throw as much suspicion as possible somewhere else.

"Once. I'd come to ask my beloved uncle for a loan. He was sitting at his desk, scribbling away, a malicious smile on his face as he told me to seek honest employment. That's a laugh, him telling me to find *honest employment*. But he got called downstairs to see a patient, and when he was gone, I took a look at it."

"You mean he just left it sitting on his desk?" Smythe asked cynically.

"Of course not. He locked it in the top drawer. But he was in a hurry and the lock didn't quite catch. It was easy to open the drawer. I took the notebook out and read it."

"What was in the notebook?" Mrs. Jeffries asked cautiously. She wasn't sure she believed any of it.

"Just letters and numbers. I think it might have been a code."

Mrs. Jeffries looked over at the butler. Keating was slumped against the wall, staring morosely at the floor. "Keating."

There was no response. She wondered if he'd been drinking.

"Keating," she repeated loudly.

His head snapped up and he blinked. He stared at her blankly for a moment before his eyes focused. "Yes, ma'am."

"Where is the notebook?"

"Notebook?"

"Yes," she said impatiently, "the notebook. Dr. Slocum's notebook."

"The little black one he usually kept in his study desk," Slocum interjected by way of explanation.

"Oh, that one," Keating said. "I don't know. Don't the police have it? Wasn't it in his desk?"

Mrs. Jeffries started to inform him in no uncertain terms that the police certainly did not have it. Then she clamped her mouth shut, thinking that perhaps the fewer people who knew the notebook wasn't in the possession of Scotland Yard, the better.

But where was it? Witherspoon certainly didn't have it. He would have told her if he'd come across anything as remotely mysterious as a book inscribed in code.

"They may," she lied. She turned to Joshua Slocum. "Did he always keep it locked in his study desk?"

Slocum shrugged. "I have no idea."

"I do," Keating said, pushing away from the door frame and straightening his spine. Gazing at Mrs. Jeffries, he drew himself up to his full height, and for a moment, he grasped an old and possibly forgotten shred of dignity. "Dr. Slocum did not keep the notebook in his desk. It was most valuable to him. He locked it away somewhere known only to himself."

Mrs. Jeffries knew then what the key unlocked. "I suppose," she said to Slocum, "that on the day you saw the book, Dr. Slocum wasn't expecting to see you?"

"That's right. He wasn't expecting me. He wasn't expecting anyone. I walked in unannounced and found him working at his desk."

"How very fortuitous for you. You don't, by any chance, happen to have any idea who your uncle was blackmailing, do you?"

Again she watched Slocum carefully, and again he showed no reaction.

"No. But it wouldn't surprise me to find out he had half of London under his control. He was a grasping man. Nothing was ever good enough for Bartholomew. He always wanted more, more, more. More money, more power, more everything." Slocum broke off and laughed bitterly. "You'd have thought a decent practice and one fortune would have been enough for any man. But it wasn't, not for him. I'm glad he's dead. I'm glad someone's finally given that cur what he deserves."

"No doubt," Mrs. Jeffries said briskly as she rose to her feet. Betsy, Smythe and Wiggins got up too. She realized that it was imperative to find that notebook before Joshua Slocum could get his hands on it. She wasn't sure but that he was as capable of blackmail as his late uncle had been. "You've benefited very nicely, haven't you?"

Slocum's face darkened as he flushed. "And why not? It should have been mine by rights anyway."

Mrs. Jeffries turned suddenly to Keating. "Did you leave the house immediately after you'd warned Mr. Slocum?" she asked.

"No, ma'am. Dr. Slocum rang for me just as I was leaving. When I went to the study, he asked me to make sure I'd brought up the right bottle of wine."

"Is there a wrong kind of wine?" Smythe asked sarcastically.

"Yes," Keating replied testily. "Not that I'd expect someone like you to know the difference—"

"From what we 'ear, Slocum wasn't one to know good wine from bad either," Betsy said testily, leaping to Smythe's defense. "The wine merchant was braggin' you could sell 'im any old kind of slog, as long as it 'ad a fancy label on it."

"Unfortunately, that is true." The butler looked embarrassed. "But he did want to make sure I'd brought up a red wine and not a white. He was having lamb for his lunch."

Mrs. Jeffries frowned at Betsy and Smythe before giving Keating a sympathetic smile. "And had you brought a red wine?"

"No. So I had to rush out to the cooling pantry and get one."

"Is the cooling pantry off the kitchen?"

"It's off the kitchen, but you have to go outside and across the terrace to the side of the house. There's no connecting door from inside."

"So you were out on the terrace between . . ." Mrs. Jeffries cocked her head to one side and calculated back. "Quarter to twelve and ten to. Would that be a reasonable assumption?"

Keating nodded.

"Did you see anyone in the gardens?"

"The police have already asked that," he protested. "And I'll give you the same answer I gave them. I was in a hurry; I didn't want to hang about in case the doctor happened on Joshua somehow, so I didn't have time to look at the ruddy flowers. Even if I had, you can't see very much from that end of the terrace. The only bloomin' thing I saw was a . . ." He faltered and then stopped completely, his face bewildered.

"Keating?" Mrs. Jeffries prompted. "Have you remembered something?"

"Blimey," he exclaimed, "I have. It just now come back to me. When I was rushing across the terrace, I saw something out of the corner of my eye."

Smythe sighed impatiently. "Well, what was it?"

"It was a bit of skirt, a woman's skirt. There was a patch of bright green sticking out from behind the tree across the way."

Betsy's eyes narrowed suspiciously. "Are you trying to tell us someone was hiding behind a tree?"

That was precisely what the butler was trying to tell them. An hour later they were all gathered around the kitchen table back at Upper Edmonton Gardens. Mrs. Goodge was clucking over them like a broody hen and pouring out cups of steaming hot cocoa.

After discussing every aspect of the case thoroughly, they still hadn't decided whether or not the butler was lying. Smythe was sure he was, Betsy was sure he wasn't, and Wiggins couldn't make up his mind.

"How did you know that Slocum had been in the house on the day of the murder?" Smythe finally asked.

Mrs. Jeffries delicately took a sip before answering. "I didn't. That was a lucky guess."

"Cor, blimey," Wiggins exclaimed.

"Who do you think was behind the tree?" asked Betsy. "You know it could 'ave been the cook, Effie Beals."

"No, the one person who wouldn't have had to skulk about in the gardens is Mrs. Beals. Remember, she had a right to be in the house."

"Maybe it was that Mrs. Crookshank," Smythe suggested.

"Perhaps," Mrs. Jeffries said thoughtfully. "Or perhaps it was Catherine Leslie."

"But didn't her maid claim she was lying down that whole morning." Betsy said.

Mrs. Jeffries was pleased that all of them remembered the details of the case so clearly. "The maid could have been lying to protect her mistress, or Mrs. Leslie might have slipped out unbeknownst to the girl."

"I don't know." Smythe shook his head. "I still don't think those two we was talkin' to tonight would know the truth if it walked up and bit 'em in the ars—arm," he amended quickly. "I stills thinks they's lying their 'eads off and there weren't no one hiding behind any tree."

"But why?" Mrs. Jeffries put her cup down and stared at the coachman. He was a very intelligent man, and she had a great deal of respect for his reasoning ability.

"To throw suspicion elsewhere in case one of them gets charged with murder." Smythe jabbed a finger at Betsy. "I was thinkin' on what she said—about not profitin' from a crime. Well, what if Slocum caught 'em that day and they killed him? From what you said, the old boy didn't die from eatin' no mushrooms, but there must have been all kinds of nasty stuff lurkin' about in his surgery. After they'd poisoned his food or even his wine, Keating remembers Mrs. Crookshank goin' on about them mushrooms growin' outside, so he nips out and plants them in the soup bowl and the kitchen so the cook will get the blame."

As a scenario, Mrs. Jeffries had to admit it might be possible. And if Slocum had caught his nephew stealing, she had no doubt that he'd prosecute. "You might be right."

"And I really think you oughts to tell the inspector what we've found out tonight," Smythe continued. "Tellin' Slocum and Keating you're gonna give 'em a chance to go to 'im themselves! If you wants my opinion, and I'm sure you do, that's a bit dicey. We already know they're theives and probably killers too."

"Smythe, you know why I can't tell the inspector anything," Mrs. Jeffries said gently. "He'd be dreadfully hurt if he knew we were assisting him with his cases. He'd think we had no confidence in him. Besides, you will recall that I also told Mr. Slocum and Keating that if they did not voluntarily make a statement to the inspector, I'd see to it myself."

"All right," he replied grudgingly. "But I didn't like 'em and I don't trust them neither."

"Speaking of the inspector," Mrs. Goodge said as she sat another pot of hot chocolate on the table, "he asked me to tell you he'd be leaving especially early for the Yard. So if you want to ask him any questions, you'd best be up early yourself."

Mrs. Jeffries frowned slightly. "Did he say why?"

"He got a message from the Yard this evening. The doctor that did the postmortem, he wants to see him first thing tomorrow morning."

CHAPTER 10

Mrs. Goodge's announcement caused another stir. Everyone had a different idea about what it meant, so another half hour passed before Mrs. Jeffries escaped to her quarters for a good think.

She sat in the soothing darkness of her room, going over and over every scrap of information she had about the murder of Dr. Bartholomew Slocum. For, indeed, she knew now he had been poisoned, and the lethal dose hadn't been in a mushroom either.

If the original diagnosis of Slocum's death had been correct, the message from the Yard for Inspector Witherspoon would have said exactly that. But it hadn't, and that could mean only one thing. They now knew what had killed the man.

She pulled her wrapper tighter against the chill as she tried to think what the next step should be. For several minutes, she was uncharacteristically unsure of how best to proceed in the investigation. Suddenly, she realized the reason for her uncertainty. She stopped thinking and let her mind wander. Closing her eyes, she took a deep, calming breath. A tendril of an idea nudged at the edge of her mind. She didn't force the thought to come; she let the vague images flow and ebb in their own good time. Before long, the images began to swirl and take shape, forming a nebulous chain of thought.

Her breathing slowed. She was close to the answer. Very close.

Slowly, Mrs. Jeffries opened her eyes as the ideas coalesced into a hard certainty. There was so much to do tomorrow. She had to talk to Catherine Leslie and to Effie Beals. She made a mental note to make sure she took Wiggins and Smythe with her. She'd need them both.

If her suspicions were correct, tomorrow the case would be solved.

• • •

Seeing Catherine Leslie was impossible. A petite blond-haired French maid hautily informed Mrs. Jeffries that Mrs. Leslie "wasn't receiving." Upon further questioning, the girl reluctantly admitted she wasn't even at home.

"You will forgive me, madam," the maid said in delicately accented English, "but I fail to see what business you have with my mistress." She cast a rather disparaging glance at Mrs. Jeffries's plain but respectable brown bombazine dress and plain topknot of hair. "You are not a friend of hers, no?"

Mrs. Jeffries studied the girl, wondering whether to try charm and diplomacy or bluntness and threats. The maid cocked her chin regally and started to close the door. There was no time for charm. "No, I'm not a friend, but I could be the person who helps keep your mistress from facing a hangman. So if I were you, Miss Nanette Lanier, I'd cease playing the lady of the manor and allow me in."

"How do you know my name?" Nanette exclaimed. "Who are you?"

"Who I am isn't important. Why Mrs. Leslie was hiding behind a tree in the gardens right before Dr. Bartholomew Slocum was murdered, is."

The maid cast a quick, frightened glance up the street. "You'd better step inside," she said hastily. "I theenk we need to speak together."

Nanette's accent was considerably more noticeable when she was rattled. From the pallor in her cheeks and the wariness in her blue eyes, Mrs. Jeffries knew she was indeed shaken.

She followed the maid down a hall to a small sitting room. Going inside, Nanette hurriedly closed the door and nodded toward a chair. "Please sit down." she invited. "We aren't likely to be disturbed in here. Madam Leslie is the only one who uses this room, and she's not here." She advanced toward Mrs. Jeffries and sat down on the couch opposite her. "Now, please, tell me who you are and what you want."

"My name is Hepzibah Jeffries, and I'm the housekeeper for the police inspector that questioned you and Mrs. Leslie after Dr. Slocum's murder." She ignored Nanette's gasp of surprise. "You're very loyal to Mrs. Leslie, aren't you?"

"But of course," Nanette replied. "She eez an angel. I would do anything for her. But—"

"You and your mistress both stated that on the day of the murder Mrs. Leslie hadn't left the house all day except to go onto the terrace with Dr. Hightower," Mrs. Jeffries continued, interrupting the girl. "I know for a fact that's not true. Mrs. Leslie was seen outside the Slocum house just before noon, only a few moments before the doctor was poisoned."

"But she didn't kill him," Nanette claimed passionately. "She only went over there to try and reason with him."

"Reason with a blackmailer?" Mrs. Jeffries queried softly, with a shake of her head. "Oh no, I'm afraid that was a rather foolish thing to do."

The maid's eyes widened. "How do you know she was being blackmailed?"

Mrs. Jeffries hadn't been sure until that very moment. She crossed her fingers in her lap and hoped her luck would continue.

"Dr. Slocum," she said softly, "seemed to make a habit of blackmailing his neighbors. Mrs. Leslie was only one of his victims."

"He was a terrible man and I'm glad he's dead," Nanette cried passionately. "But Mrs. Leslie didn't kill him. She eez a saint. She wouldn't hurt anyone."

"Why was he blackmailing her?"

"He wasn't," Nanette replied. "At least, he hadn't gotten any money out of her yet."

"But he was trying to."

Her shoulders slumped. "Yes. But I don't know why I should tell you about this. What business eez eet of yours?"

"Because if you don't, you'll have to tell Inspector Witherspoon, and I'm far more likely to believe you than he is. So I suggest that you trust me. If Mrs. Leslie is innocent, she has no reason to fear me."

For a few moments, the maid stared at her in silence. Finally, she spoke. "A few days before the murder, we were out in the garden and Dr. Slocum came outside." She gave a derisive laugh. "He hurried over as soon as he saw us, despite the fact that Mrs. Leslie had made it very plain she did not like him. The man had a hide like the rhinoceros. Very thick. But this time, he refused to be put off, he was very . . . how you say, forward. He insisted Madam walk with him along the path. I tried to follow, but he waved me away. I watched them walk across the garden, the doctor murmuring low in her ear and waving a little key under her nose. Suddenly, I hear her cry out. Naturally, I ran to her, but she told me to go back to the house."

"Did you?" Mrs. Jeffries asked.

Nanette shrugged. "But of course. I 'ad no choice in the matter. When Madam Leslie came inside, she was so pale I was frightened she would faint. I asked her what was wrong." She leaned forward. "You must understand, I am not just Madam Leslie's maid, I am her only confidante. She told me that Dr. Slocum threatened her. If Madam didn't give him money, he'd tell everyone that she and Dr. Hightower had murdered her husband."

Mrs. Jeffries was careful to keep her surprise from showing. "Had they?"

"*Mais non!* Excuse me, I mean, certainly not."

"Then why was Madam Leslie so worried? To be sure, it's a vicious, ugly thing to say, but if the doctor had no proof, then Mrs. Leslie or Dr. Hightower could certainly have had him up on a charge of slander. English courts do not take such matters lightly."

"That's what I told her," Nanette said earnestly. "But she claimed the doctor did have proof."

"How?" Mrs. Jeffries asked with a shake of her head. "If she and Dr. Hightower were innocent, there couldn't be any evidence."

"Oh, there was not proof of murder, but there was proof of suspicion."

"I'm afraid I don't quite follow you," Mrs. Jeffries admitted.

Nanette waved her hands in the air. "Oh, I'm explaining it so badly! This Dr. Slocum had somehow managed to obtain the medical . . . how you say . . . history, notes . . ."

"Medical records?"

"Ah yes, that eez it, medical records of Madam's late husband. This was very bad, because his own doctor, the one that wasn't there when he died, made some kind of note on these papers that Monsieur's death was odd. You see, he'd examined the man only a week earlier and found him to be in perfect health." Nanette scowled. "Bah, that only means the doctor was an idiot. But it looks very bad for Madam. It eez not the proof, but eet eez very suspicious. There eez already gossip about my dear Madam and Dr. Hightower. If something like this was spread around, especially by someone as respectable as Dr. Slocum, they would both be ruined."

Mrs. Jeffries frowned, trying to recall everything she'd heard about Mrs. Leslie. Then she remembered. "But didn't Mrs. Leslie and her husband live in Birmingham?"

"That makes no difference. Dr. Hightower happened to be there for a medical meeting. Monsieur Leslie was taken ill and his own doctor was gone. Dr. Hightower came instead. Then poor Monsieur Leslie died suddenly." She sighed and gave a Gallic shrug. "Eet was no one's fault. Eet was the will of God. But the English, they do not understand that."

"So Slocum threatened to spread the rumor that they'd murdered her husband so they could be together," Mrs. Jeffries mused. "Yes, I can see, it all makes a nasty sort of pattern, doesn't it? But why now?"

"That eez easy to answer," Nanette said. "Madam Leslie's husband left her enough money to be comfortable, but she was not rich until now. She's an heiress. Her mama passed away recently, and she inherited everything."

"Did she tell Dr. Hightower about the blackmail attempt?"

"*Mais non*, she was too frightened. She is desperately in love with *Monsieur le Docteur*, but he has a quick temper. She was going to talk to Dr. Slocum and if that didn't work, I think she was going to pay him to keep silent."

"I see." Mrs. Jeffries's brows drew together in a puzzled frown. "But if she was just going to talk with him, why didn't she come to the front door and ask to see him? Why was she skulking around in the gardens?"

"She didn't want anyone to see her and mention it to Dr. Hightower. It is common knowledge that he loathes Dr. Slocum. So she was going to try and slip in the back door. But when she got outside his house, the butler was crossing the terrace and she didn't want him to see her. She hid behind the tree and then when the butler was gone, she couldn't go in because she heard someone in the bushes."

"Which bushes? Where?"

Nanette waved her hands toward the window. "The ones at the end of the garden, near the Seaward house. Madam was terrified by this time; she lost her nerve. So she rushed back here and told me she'd wait until her appointment to see the doctor."

"She had an appointment with him?"

"Yes, he brought his calling card around that morning. She was to see him at three o'clock that afternoon."

"Then why did she try to go over before noon?"

"Because Dr. Hightower had gotten a calling card from the doctor too," Nanette said indignantly. "He had the bad taste to actually leave it *here* when he dropped off Madam's. Dr. Hightower's appointment was for two o'clock. Madam wanted to see Dr. Slocum and try and reason with him before Dr. Hightower saw him. She was afraid of what would happen."

"Did she see who was in the bushes?"

"No, she was frightened. She fled before they came out."

Mrs. Jeffries studied the maid carefully. "You haven't told the police this, have you?"

"*Mais non!* Why would I put my mistress's neck in a noose? If I tell the police, they will think she killed him to keep him silent about her husband."

"But you must tell them, mademoiselle, you must," Mrs. Jeffries said as she rose to her feet. "And you must do it right away. I'm not the only one who knows Mrs. Leslie was in the garden right before the doctor was murdered. Inspector Witherspoon is far more likely to believe your story if you tell it voluntarily than if he finds out you've been lying."

Without waiting for an answer, she walked to the door. She turned suddenly. "Oh, and this time, I wouldn't bother with any fake hysterics."

Nanette's eyebrows rose.

Mrs. Jeffries smiled. "As a ploy, it worked once to keep the inspector from questioning your mistress too closely, but I don't think it would work twice."

Nanette looked startled for a moment, and then she laughed. "You think not, madam?" She tilted her chin to one side and regarded her out of suddenly shrewd eyes. "I thought it was rather clever of me. Especially as I was able to slip in my tidbits about Dr. Slocum's key and calling cards."

"Yes, I suspected you might have done that deliberately. Actually, it *was* rather clever. It certainly got the inspector looking elsewhere."

Nanette shrugged. "Thank you. I knew the police would find out about the cards anyway. And I hoped if they knew about the key, they would suspect someone else. Tell me, why are you here? Why are you so concerned with who killed that odious leetle man?"

Surprised by the question, Mrs. Jeffries replied without hesitation. "Because I like to help the inspector. You see, loyalty to one's employer isn't a character trait reserved solely for the French." Realizing she'd said more than she should, she quickly clamped her mouth shut.

Nanette broke into a knowing smile. "But your employer, he does not know you help him, eez that not true?"

"Well, not exactly."

The girl stared at her thoughtfully. "You can tell much about a person by his or her face. I think, madam, you have a passion for justice. You will not let them hang my mistress. Don't worry, Madam Jeffries. I will tell the inspector everything." She grinned impudently. "Except, of course, your leetle secret."

Mrs. Jeffries left by the terrace door. Nanette Lanier had sent a footman to Scotland Yard, and she knew the inspector would be along soon.

Moving quickly, she made her way to the far end and stood for a moment examining the tall, dense shrubs that composed the border on this side of the garden. Glad that she'd had the foresight to wear a sturdy pair of boots, she stepped off the path and ducked beneath a hanging branch and into the greenery.

Once inside, she stopped to get her bearings. Though the strip between the path and the border was less than ten feet wide, once you were in, you couldn't see out because of the density of the foliage. There was a good chance that whoever had been in here on the day of the murder, hadn't seen Catherine Leslie hiding behind the tree.

Slowly, her eyes on the ground, Mrs. Jeffries made her way toward Dr. Slocum's house.

As she walked, she noticed that some of the grass was bent and many of the twigs and branches had been broken off, as though someone had been there. But that could have been the police, she reminded herself. The garden had been thoroughly searched.

The dense foliage ended at the house next to the Slocum residence. Mrs. Jeffries steeped onto the path, turned and looked back at where she'd come from. She calculated it had taken her approximately two minutes to work her way from the upper end to this spot. Interesting information, she decided reluctantly, turning toward the Slocum house, but hardly useful unless she could find that key.

Effie Beals answered the door on her first knock. "Morning, Mrs. Jeffries," the cook said with a cheery smile. "Your men's been keepin' me company till you got here."

"Good morning, Mrs. Beals," Mrs. Jeffries replied, following the woman down the passageway to the kitchen. "I hope Wiggins and Smythe haven't been a bother, but I fear that before the day is out, we'll need them."

"Course we 'aven't been a bother, Mrs. J," Smythe answered. He lifted a cup of tea in a salute. "We knows our manners."

"Been sittin' here twiddlin' our thumbs, that's what we've been doin'," Wiggins interjected mournfully. He was still put out because he hadn't had a glimpse of Miss Cannonberry in two days.

"Would you like tea?" Effie asked.

"Yes, thank you." She pulled off her gloves and took a chair at the table. "As soon as we've all had a nice cuppa, we've got to get busy."

"Doing what?" the cook asked, placing a cup of tea in front of Mrs. Jeffries.

She took a delicate sip and waited until Effie had sat down. "Is Mr. Joshua Slocum in? How many servants are here today?"

Effie snorted. "There's no one 'ere but me. Mr. Slocum's taken Keating and gone back to Colchester for his things. Once he left, the other servants decided to scarper off. While the cat's away the mice will play."

Smythe leaned forward. "What are we lookin' for?"

"A key. I think I know what it unlocks—a strongbox. Even better, I'm fairly sure I know where it is."

They all stared at her in astonishment. Mrs. Jeffries held up her hand to belay the spate of questions she was sure was hovering on the tips of three tongues. "Time is running short. The inspector will be here soon, and we've got to find that key before he gets here." She got to her feet and turned to Wiggins. "You take the dining room, Wiggins. The key is quite small, so you've got to be sure and check inside every single object. Look under the rugs and along the curtain rails too."

Smythe leapt up. "Where do you want me to search?"

"The study. Make sure you go over the desk thoroughly; there might be a secret compartment."

"And me?" Effie stared at her uncertainly. "D'ya want me to help?"

"Yes," Mrs. Jeffries said. "Search the drawing room. Search every nook and cranny."

They searched the first floor in vain. Mrs. Jeffries pulled up carpets, peeked into oversized vases and knocked on desk drawers, looking for hidden cubbyholes until she was covered with dust.

"I don't think it's 'ere," Effie exclaimed breathlessly, as she and Smythe and Wiggins joined Mrs. Jeffries in the front hall. "We've been over this whole floor—if we didn't find it and the police didn't find it, it just ain't 'ere."

"It's got to be here," Mrs. Jeffries said firmly. "Come on, let's try a different strategy."

She led them into the dining room. "Smythe, go and sit at the head of the table and pretend to be Dr. Slocum."

Smythe raised an eyebrow and then walked to the table, pulled out a chair and sat down. "Now what?"

"Pretend you're eating lunch."

Mrs. Jeffries studied the coachman, mentally casting him as Dr. Slocum. "All right," she murmured. "Here he is sitting, eating his lunch."

"He'd have drunk his glass of wine first," the cook interjected. "He always did. Real pig swill it was too, despite all them fancy labels."

Dutifully, Smythe pretended to drink a glass of wine.

"Yes, yes," Mrs. Jeffries murmured. "He'd have drunk the wine and then started eating the soup." Smythe pantomimed the actions as she spoke.

"Then he'd have gone on to the main course." She paused. "A few moments later, he'd have felt ill. Very ill."

She cocked her head to one side and then turned toward the door. "But he was expecting guests."

"He weren't expectin' nobody," Effie cried. "He'd given us all the day off. You don't invite a house full of people around when you don't have none 'ere to wait on 'em."

"He was expecting guests, or rather, blackmail victims. That's why he'd given the servants the day off, that's why he'd taken his calling cards around the neighborhood. That was his way of telling his victims to come along and pay up," Mrs. Jeffries said patiently.

Wiggins looked shocked. "Cor, blimey. That's a mean thing ta do ta someone."

"So here he is, feeling dreadfully ill," Mrs. Jeffries continued.

Smythe stood up and clutched his stomach. "And he had to make sure that none of them got their hands on his key." She whirled around and stared toward the hall. "So what does a doctor who's desperately and suddenly ill do?"

Before she could move, Smythe shot across the room and staggered toward the surgery. Mrs. Jeffries, Wiggins and Effie were hot on his heels.

" 'E 'eads for his surgery," Smythe yelled triumphantly.

Inside the surgery, Mrs. Jeffries stopped suddenly to avoid running into the coachman. He turned, still clutching his stomach, and looked at Mrs. Jeffries. "This is as far as I can figure it," he admitted reluctantly.

"You've done very well, Smythe," she said quickly.

"Now what?" Wiggins asked.

Mrs. Jeffries studied the room. "Slocum couldn't risk anyone getting their hands on that key, so he has to hide it, and quickly."

"But we've already searched in 'ere a dozen times," Effie protested.

Mrs. Jeffries ignored her and slowly turned. The key was in here. It had to be. She stared at the neat rows of books, the medicine cabinets and supply cupboards. Frowning, she glanced at the floor. Nothing there but a Persian carpet and the doctor's medical bag leaning against the leg of a coatrack.

The medical bag. It had been sitting there since before Dr. Slocum's death.

"That's it!" she cried, dashing across the room and snatching up the bag.

"How comes the police didn't look in there?" Effie asked curiously. "They's searched the whole house."

"Because this looks like part of the furniture," Smythe answered, squatting down on his haunches. "It's been sittin' 'ere right under our noses, but because it were never mentioned and it belongs 'ere, nobody probably bothered to give it more than a quick look. Right, Mrs. J?"

"Right," she muttered. She snapped the latch and the bag popped open. "Lets see what's inside."

Bottles, pills and vials were jumbled haphazardly together in a heap beside a stack of mangled bandages. Mrs. Jeffries leaned back so Effie Beals could see the inside of the case.

"Was this normally the way the doctor kept his case?" she asked.

Effie shook her head. "I don't rightly know, but I shouldn't think so. He was generally a very particular person, didn't like a mess."

Mrs. Jeffries reached inside and began taking the contents out, one by one. Soon there was a pile of bottles, bandages and vials, but no key. Disappointment flooded her as she peered inside and saw the last object, a small flat box. She yanked it out and flipped the lid up.

"Drat," she murmured. "It's only his scalpel case." Keeping the lid open, she gently shook the case. From beneath the leather of the scalpel bed she heard a faint, but distinct thud.

"There's somethin' inside the case," Wiggins said excitedly.

Handing the case to Smythe, Mrs. Jeffries said, "Will you do the honors?"

He grinned, opened it, lifted up the instruments and the false bottom and pulled out a thin chain. At the end of the chain was a small gold key.

Wiggins shook his head. "I still can't suss out how you knew that that there key would be 'ere."

"The key had to be here," Mrs. Jeffries explained with a relieved smile. She gazed at the three puzzled faces surrounding her. "Or at least, I hoped it would be. Dr. Slocum was obsessed with money and power. Yet he had time to make his way into the surgery, get to one of his medical cupboards and try to dose himself with an emetic. But from what we know of his character, it occurred to me that before he did any of that, before he even tried to save his own life, he'd protect this key. It's not just a key to a strongbox, it's the key to his wealth and power."

Smythe shook his head admiringly, and Wiggins stared at the instrument case as if he expected it to disappear any moment.

"Where's this 'ere strongbox then?" Effie asked. "And what are we going to do when the police arrive? You said that inspector would be here any minute."

"We haven't time to worry about the strongbox now," Mrs. Jeffries said quickly. "Besides, it will be better if the inspector finds that himself." She got to her feet and turned to the cook. "Here's what I want you to say when the police arrive."

Less than half an hour later a rather puzzled-looking Inspector Witherspoon followed Effie Beals into the kitchen. As instructed, the cook had told him everything, including the fact that Dr. Slocum was a blackmailer.

"So you see, sir," Effie continued, glancing covertly out of the corner of her eye at the three people sitting around the table. "When I found that key, I knew I should let you know as quick as I could. But I were just a bit nervous, so I sent a footman round to your house to fetch your Mrs. Jeffries. We met the day she come here to bring you your cigar case, and she's a right nice lady. I felt easier talkin' with you and tellin' you about the blackmail with her 'ere."

"Yes, yes," Witherspoon replied. "I can well understand why you'd want Mrs. Jeffries, but what on earth are Wiggins and Smythe doing here?"

"That's my doing, Inspector," Mrs. Jeffries said calmly as she rose from her chair.

Smythe and Wiggins got up too. "No it's not," Smythe countered. "It's my doin'. We insisted on coming. For protection like."

"We couldn't let her come to a 'ouse where theys been a murder," Wiggins pointed out. "Not all alone. So we's tagged along."

"They insisted on escorting me, Inspector, and after we got here and heard Mrs. Beals's story, I thought you might need them to stay. It looks as if this case of yours might be . . . uh, taking a turn for the better."

As she spoke, she neatly maneuvered the inspector back a step so that Smythe, Wiggins and Effie Beals could get past him and into the hall. As she'd instructed them, they were going up the stairs to wait for her and the inspector outside the door of the surgery.

"Hadn't you better start searching, sir? Mrs. Beals is almost sure that key goes to a strongbox." Mrs. Jeffries smiled innocently.

Witherspoon sighed. "Yes, I suppose I should, and of course, I will. But I must confess," he lowered his voice, "I'm really dreadfully tired. It's been such a day. First, the police surgeon was in a terrible state when he had to admit he'd made a mistake in the initial postmortem. Dr. Slocum didn't die from eating a poisoned mushroom, and Bainbridge is most annoyed about that. Not that I much blame him. I mean if you find a poison mushroom tidbit lying at the bottom of a chap's soup bowl, it's reasonable to assume that's how the chap died. Well, I think it's quite reasonable, but the chief inspector was livid, absolutely livid—"

Mrs. Jeffries deemed it prudent to interrupt. "I take it Dr. Slocum was poisoned?"

"Oh yes. Of course. Mrs. Beals is no longer a suspect. The woman could hardly have got hold of venom. It's not the sort of thing one finds in a kitchen."

"Venom," Mrs. Jeffries exclaimed. "What kind of venom?"

Witherspoon's footsteps slowed as they mounted the stairs. The others were already at the top. "That's another reason the doctor was upset. He couldn't tell. The body was a bit too . . . well," he grimaced, "far gone."

"I see."

"Yes, and then I got this frantic message from the Leslie household, and I had to go along there and talk to that rather snippy French maid."

Mrs. Jeffries smiled sympathetically. "Did she say anything that sheds any light on this new development?"

"I'm not sure. On the one hand, she insists that Catherine Leslie is innocent, while on the other, she tells me Mrs. Leslie was out hiding behind a tree right before Dr. Slocum was murdered. On top of that, Mrs. Leslie claims someone was hiding or walking in the bushes." He sighed dramatically as they reached the top of the stairs. "I don't know what to believe anymore."

"There, there, Inspector." Mrs. Jeffries reached over and patted his arm. "Not to worry. You'll sort it all out. You always do."

Witherspoon brightened somewhat. "Yes, I suppose I will."

They walked to the surgery and joined the trio standing in front of the door.

"I thought we might help you with your search, Inspector," Mrs. Jeffries volunteered. She smiled at Effie Beals as she threw open the doors of the surgery and led the way inside. "Wasn't it clever of Mrs. Beals to find that key?"

"What? Oh yes." The inspector looked confused. "Uh, Mrs. Jeffries, why are we here?"

"Why, Inspector, you must be jesting. Surely you know why we're here." She broke off and laughed. "Oh now, stop being so modest. This was all your idea. You told me all about it yourself."

Behind Witherspoon, she saw Smythe roll his eyes and Wiggins grin. Even Effie Beals had to turn her head to hide her smile.

"I did?" Witherspoon said. "When?"

"Don't you remember, sir? It was only a few days ago." She took his arm and steered him toward the bookcases on the other side of the surgery. "You told me that Dr. Slocum had once fired a housemaid for going near his bookcases." She pointed to the key that Witherspoon had been holding between his fingers since he'd come into the kitchen. "Mrs. Beals says that key unlocks a strongbox." She broke off and waited for him to get her point.

It took a good few minutes, but suddenly his eyes lit up like a couple of shooting stars. "By golly, I think I'm on to something here. Quick, Smythe, Wiggins, get a footstool and help me search behind the books on those top shelves. Mrs. Jeffries, you and Mrs. Beals take the lower ones."

In the end, it took less than ten minutes to find Dr. Bartholomew Slocum's strongbox. The heavy metal chest was secreted behind a set of the complete works of Mr. William Shakespeare.

CHAPTER 11

"This must be the notebook," Witherspoon said as he reached inside the strongbox and pulled out a small leather book. He flipped it open, scanned the first page and frowned. "Can't make hide nor hair of this. It's all numbers and initials."

"But Sir, this is just as you surmised. Slocum was a blackmailer. Wouldn't this be a record of payments?" Mrs. Jeffries explained. She reached over the inspector's shoulders and pointed to the top entry. "Look, DLS and right beside it, the figure 500 PQ and then the date. That's probably the initials of someone blackmailed into paying Dr. Slocum five hundred pounds every quarter."

"Egad, I believe you're right. My goodness, there's a rather lot of initials in this little book." Witherspoon ran his finger down the column, muttering to himself.

"DDI-100 PQ; LBD-225 PQ; CCS-350 PQ. Gracious, Slocum must have been blackmailing half the city."

"Wouldn't surprise me none," Effie said earnestly. "He blackmailed me into workin' for 'im. The man was capable of anythin'."

"He sounds like a right blackguard." Smythe sneered. "It's a wonder someone didn't kill 'im before now."

Witherspoon smiled wearily. "Dr. Slocum may have been a very bad man, perhaps even evil, but that doesn't give someone the right to take his life."

"Inspector, what are those?" Mrs. Jeffries pointed to the remaining papers in the strongbox.

The inspector glanced up. Effie, Smythe, Wiggins, Mrs. Jeffries and even Constable Barnes, who'd arrived just as they'd found the strongbox, were staring at the open box with avid curiosity.

Cautiously, the inspector reached inside and pulled out the stack. They were neatly folded sheets of plain white paper. On the outside of each one a name was written in precise blue ink.

He unfolded the first one, which was marked "Bradshaw". Witherspoon's expression turned grim as he read. When he'd finished, he took a deep breath; folded the paper again and placed it carefully to one side.

"What was it, sir?" Mrs. Jeffries prodded gently.

"Oh dear, I'm afraid it's the very worst. These papers are what Dr. Slocum was using to blackmail his victims. They are written records. This one," he jabbed a finger at the one he'd just put down, "is signed in the victim's own hand. It's a statement, admitting to a . . . well, youthful indiscretion."

As the inspector had turned a bright pink, Mrs. Jeffries didn't press him further. "How dreadful. Are you going to go through the rest and see if any of your suspects have one of those wretched things?"

"Hmm, yes, I expect that's exactly what I should do."

She watched as he went through the stack. Most of the names were meaningless to her. But one of them she recognized as belonging to a member of the House of Lords. Witherspoon recognized the name too, because he carefully slipped it under the bottom of the pile so the others couldn't see it.

Finally, he came to another name that was familiar to them both. Mrs. Jeffries reached over his shoulder and tapped the sheet gently. "I think that's the one you're looking for."

His hand stilled, and he glanced up and met her eye.

"Yes, Mrs. Jeffries," he agreed sadly. "I rather think it is. After all, the murder was committed by someone who knew those wretched mushrooms were out in the garden."

Mrs. Jeffries didn't remind him that several of the blackmail victims had this information.

Inspector Witherspoon's eyes narrowed as he flipped the sheet open and began to read. Ignoring discretion, Mrs. Jeffries crowded closer to the inspector and read over his shoulder.

Witherspoon clucked his tongue softly and shook his head. "Well, what do you make of that," he muttered softly.

"A great deal," she replied briskly. "And I suspect every word of it is true. His initials were in the notebook, so we can assume he was paying."

"Hmm, yes, and he was foolish enough to sign this statement in his own hand." Witherspoon put the page facedown on the desk. "But I don't see how he could have murdered Dr. Slocum. He was with his guests."

"Who are you talking about?" Constable Barnes asked. He hadn't been close enough to the desk to see the name.

"Colonel Seaward," the inspector answered glumly.

The constable cleared his throat. "I'm not so sure he was with his guests the whole time, sir." He reached into his pocket and drew out his own small notepad. Flipping the pages, he said, "If I recall, I believe one of the footmen mentioned that the gentleman left the dining room for a few minutes. Ah yes, here it is. The lad's name is David Packard."

No longer able to contain his curiosity, Smythe asked, "Why was the colonel bein' blackmailed?"

The question galvanized Witherspoon into action. He stood up. "Colonel Seaward wasn't a hero back in that African campaign he's so famous for." He held up the paper. "This is a statement he signed admitting that he hid in a secret cellar in his quarters while his men died fighting for Queen and Country. When the reinforcements arrived, Seaward crawled out, grabbed a gun and pretended he'd been there fighting all along."

"Why would the colonel be daft enough to admit to cowardice? Especially if all the rest of 'em was dead and there weren't no one left to tell?" Wiggins asked.

"Perhaps he signed it under the influence of opium," Mrs. Jeffries answered. She turned to the inspector and smiled. "Perhaps that's how Dr. Slocum learned most of his victims' secrets. You did tell me that Slocum once treated Colonel Seaward. Don't you think it's likely he drugged the information out of him?"

"No doubt you're right," Witherspoon replied, staring at the page. "See, the signature's very wobbly. I imagine the poor man talked his head off while he was under the influence of the drug, and then Slocum made him sign this before he'd regained the use of his wits. Then he started blackmailing him."

"But sir," Constable Barnes said, "how do you know he's the murderer?" He nodded toward the desk. "Looks to me like there's a whole heap of suspects now."

Witherspoon clasped his hands together and frowned. He was thinking.

Mrs. Jeffries decided it was time to intervene. "Well, of course he's the one, and Inspector Witherspoon can prove it."

The inspector gave her a puzzled frown. "Eh?"

"Oh sir, don't be so self-effacing. Why, you were the one that pointed out the significance of that piece of cork we stumbled onto here in the surgery."

"Yes, I suppose I did." He looked very confused now.

She gave him a confident smile. "Now, don't tell me, let me guess. Your next step will be to send Constable Barnes over to bring that footman here. Once the lad is here, you'll confirm precisely how long the colonel was actually gone. Am I right, sir?"

"Of course," Witherspoon gave himself a slight shake. "Of course," he repeated more forcefully, "that's exactly what I was going to do. Barnes, go get the lad."

She waited till the constable left before continuing. "And then you'll send Smythe along to the Yard to get the bottle Dr. Slocum drank from on the day he died. Correct?"

Witherspoon smiled uncertainly. "Uh, yes." He turned to the coachman. "Smythe, would you pop along to the Yard for me? It's just as Mrs. Jeffries says; I want you to get that wine bottle. It's in the evidence box."

Smythe nodded. "Do you want me to bring it here?"

"Yes." The inspector broke off as he suddenly realized what to do. "I mean, no. Before you come back, stop at the wine merchant's, the big one on the corner. Give the bottle to Constable Barnes. He'll question the proprietor to see if they have a record of who they sold that bottle to." Pausing, he reached into his pocket for his notebook, scribbled a quick note and handed it to Smythe. "Use this to get the Yard to release the bottle into your custody. Barnes will be waiting for you at the corner."

Relief swept over Mrs. Jeffries as she realized that the inspector was finally seeing the probable sequence of events. There was only one way the murder could have been committed. She'd known that since last night. Now, she knew why.

"Come on, boy," Effie said to Wiggins. "Let's go down to the kitchen for a cuppa. There's nothin' we can do here but get in the way."

"Do I have to?" Wiggins complained, looking at Mrs. Jeffries. "It's just now gettin' interestin'."

"I think so," she replied softly. "We'll call you when we need you."

After they'd gone, Mrs. Jeffries turned to the inspector. "I suppose it was learning that the doctor had died of venom poisoning that made you realize the murderer could only be Colonel Seaward."

Actually, the inspector hadn't even thought of the cause of death until Mrs. Jeffries mentioned it. But now that she had, he quickly saw the connection.

"Naturally. As soon as the police surgeon said the word 'venom,' I understood everything."

"You're so very clever, sir."

"Not really," He laughed modestly. "There's only one person in this case who has access to any kind of venom at all. Colonel Seaward. I think I must have begun to suspect he was the killer when Nanette Lanier claimed that Mrs. Leslie had heard someone in the bushes right before the doctor was murdered. After seeing that," he nodded at the paper on the desk, "I knew for certain. In case you didn't know it, Mrs. Jeffries, Colonel Seaward is quite a well-known amateur naturalist. He's the only suspect who not only had access to venom, but would have had the skill to extract it as well."

Mrs. Jeffries was quite impressed. Though the inspector often appeared baffled by his cases, he was quite capable when it came right down to it. "What led you to the conclusion that the poison was snake venom? I thought the police surgeon wasn't sure."

"He isn't. But it could hardly have been bee venom, not this time of year, and I don't think it was a scorpion or a poisonous spider. Contrary to what most people think, those poisons aren't always lethal, but some snake venom is."

The door opened. Constable Barnes and a dark-haired young man wearing the livery of a footman entered. "Here's the lad, sir."

The boy nodded nervously as the introductions were completed.

After the preliminary questions concerning the day of the murder were done with, Witherspoon got right to the point. "Now, I know you've stated that Colonel Seaward was with his guests from eleven till two, but wasn't there a period where he left for a few minutes?"

"No," the boy replied hesitantly. "I don't think so, sir."

"Now, lad," Constable Barnes cautioned, "we're talkin' about a murder here. Don't you remember tellin' me that the colonel nipped out for a bit to fetch a bottle of wine?"

"Oh, that. But he was only gone a few minutes."

Witherspoon began pacing the floor. "How many minutes?"

"Well, I wasn't watching the clock, sir," the footman protested. "So I don't know exactly."

"Yes, yes," the inspector said soothingly. "I can understand that, but surely you can estimate how long he was gone."

The boy chewed on his lower lip. "It was perhaps five, maybe six minutes."

"But it could have been as long as seven or eight minutes? Is that possible?" Witherspoon stopped in front of the footman and fixed him with a hard stare.

"I suppose so," he admitted reluctantly.

"Good." Witherspoon turned toward Barnes. "That'll be all. Take the lad back and then pop over to the wine merchant's. My coachman will meet you there—he'll have the wine bottle the victim drank from. Check the records and get a confirmation as to whom that bottle of wine was actually sold to."

"Right, sir." Barnes and the footman started to walk to the door.

"Just a moment," Witherspoon called. They both turned. "Does Colonel Seaward have any poisonous snakes in his collection?"

"Several, sir," the boy said, looking surprised. "But he keeps them in Surrey. He's got two cobras from Africa and a great big rattler from the United States."

"Fine. Thank you. Carry on, Constable."

As soon as they'd left, Mrs. Jeffries said, "I must admit it's so exciting to watch you work. What will you do next?"

She wondered if she should tell him about her own excursion into the foliage at the end of the garden. Going slowly, it had taken her two minutes to get from the Seaward house to Dr. Slocum's.

"What will I be doing next?" he repeated. He gazed around the surgery, his expression mirroring his uncertainty.

Mrs. Jeffries decided he needed a few more nudges.

"Why don't you take Wiggins, sir?" she suggested cheerfully. "I think he feels left out."

Witherspoon cocked his chin to one side. "Take Wiggins where?"

"Why, to the gardens." She gave a disappointed sigh. "Oh dear, don't tell me I've guessed wrong. I felt sure you'd go out into all that dense foliage at the far end and time how long it took to get from here to the Seaward house."

Witherspoon stared at her for a moment and then blinked.

"Now, now," he said, reaching over and patting her hand. "Don't look so disappointed. Your guess was most accurate. That's precisely what I intend to do. And taking Wiggins is a good idea. He can hold my watch."

While Wiggins and Witherspoon were in the garden, Mrs. Jeffries tried to decide whether or not to tell the inspector about Joshua Slocum and Keating. He hadn't mentioned speaking with either man.

A few minutes later, she heard footsteps in the hall and decided to say nothing. What good would it do? Joshua Slocum had really only stolen from himself. Scotland Yard had more important matters to concern themselves with.

"One minute and forty seconds," Witherspoon announced as he and Wiggins came into the surgery.

"How interesting," Mrs. Jeffries said. "Then it's entirely possible for Seaward to have gone through the bushes unseen, climbed into the open window in the kitchen, rushed up here," she paused and walked to the cabinet they'd found the piece of cork under, "and propped the wine bottle he'd taken from his own cellar up here." She pantomined the gestures as she spoke. "Wiggins, watch the time. But in his rush, he pushed too hard on the corkscrew, which I suspect he had hidden in his coat. When he pulled the cork out, it disintegrated and he didn't notice. Then he added the poison, which he'd also secreted somewhere on his person . . ." She turned suddenly and dashed for the dining room. Witherspoon and Wiggins were right behind her.

"He snatched the wine Keating had put here for the doctor's lunch," she continued as she walked to the table. "And then added the poison mushroom bits he'd taken from the garden to the soup bowl. On his way out, he dropped the other poison mushroom into the bowl of edible mushrooms so that it would look like an accident or as if someone else had done the murder." She turned to Wiggins. "How long did that take?"

"Two minutes."

"So he had more than enough time," Witherspoon mused. "And now we know what his motive was."

"I reckon he got tired of payin' up," Wiggins said helpfully.

"Oh no, Wiggins," Witherspoon replied. "His motive was far more complex than that. No doubt Slocum knew about the upcoming appointment. I believe I mentioned it to you, Mrs. Jeffries. Seaward was in line for a very high position in the service of the Crown . . ."

She pretended to look confused for a moment. "Why, yes. How astute of you to make the connection."

Wiggins scratched his chin. "Make what connection?"

Before the inspector could answer, the door flew open and Smythe and Constable Barnes burst in. Barnes held up the wine bottle.

"You were right, sir. This bottle wasn't sold to Dr. Slocum; it was sold to Colonel Clayton Seaward. The proprietor keeps excellent records, he does. Likes to make sure he has what his customers want on hand. This here is fine wine, much better than the swill he sold Dr. Slocum."

"Right, then." Witherspoon started for the door. "We'd better go and ask the colonel a few questions. Constable, bring the bottle. The sight of it may loosen the gentleman's tongue."

"But, Inspector," Barnes cried, "Colonel Seaward isn't there anymore. When I took the lad back, the butler told me the colonel had left for his estate in Surrey right. He scarpered right off as soon as we brought young David over for questioning."

"Damn—oh, excuse me, Mrs. Jeffries," he said apologetically. "That kind of language is unpardonable, especially in front of a lady."

"Please, sir, it's quite all right. Believe me, I do understand. What will you do now?"

Witherspoon started pacing. "Oh dear, oh dear. I wonder if he suspects we're on to him?" Suddenly he stopped and looked at the coachman. "Smythe, there's no time to lose. How quickly can those horses of ours get us to Surrey?"

"With me driving, Bow and Arrow can beat about any set of nags on the road," Smythe said proudly. "But the colonel's got a good 'ead start."

Witherspoon nodded and turned to his housekeeper. "Mrs. Jeffries, I hate to burden you with this, but would you be kind enough to take the strongbox and its contents back to Upper Edmonton Gardens?" He smiled gently. "I'll feel better knowing it's in safe hands."

She was touched by his trust. "Of course, Inspector."

"Come on then," he said to Barnes and Smythe as he raced to the door. "Let's get cracking. Oh, and Wiggins, you're to escort Mrs. Jeffries home. Guard her and that box with your life."

"Yes, sir," Wiggins shouted as they disappeared out the door.

Despite a hair-raising ride to Seaward's estate, by the time they found the open gates leading to the house, they were a good hour behind their suspect.

Smythe slapped the reins as the horses raced up the curved driveway and the carriage took the bend on two wheels.

"Egad, do try and get us there in one piece," Witherspoon shouted as the carriage bounced hard back onto the ground.

"Yes, sir." Smythe pulled powerfully on the brake as the house came into view. When they'd jolted to a sharp stop, he jumped down off the seat and flung open the carriage door. "Do you want me to come in, Inspector?"

Witherspoon's bowler was askew, and Barnes's ruddy complexion was pale.

"There's only the two of us, sir," the constable pointed out. "Perhaps it would be a good idea for your coachman to accompany us."

"Yes, I expect you're right."

They crossed the porch, and Barnes, still holding the wine bottle clutched to his chest, used his other hand to bang the knocker hard.

A tall, white-haired butler answered the door. "Yes?"

"We'd like to see Colonel Seaward," Witherspoon began.

"Are you the police?"

Puzzled, the inspector nodded. The butler opened the door wider and ushered them inside.

"Colonel Seaward is expecting you," he said, leading the way down the hall. "It's right this way."

Confused, they looked at one another as they followed the butler through a set of double doors and into the study.

"Ah, Inspector Witherspoon, good to see you, sir. I've been waiting for you." Colonel Seaward, holding a glass of what looked like whiskey in his hand, rose from behind a desk as the three men advanced across the polished hardwood floors.

Witherspoon swallowed nervously. Now that he was here, he wasn't precisely sure how he should approach the matter.

"Good day, sir. I'm dreadfully sorry to disturb you, but I've some rather pertinent questions to ask you." He nodded to his companions. "This is Constable Barnes, whom I believe you've met, and this is . . . 'er . . . my coachman."

Seaward gazed at them blankly; then his attention focused on the bottle in Barnes's hands. For a moment, he simply stared at it; then he sucked in a long breath of air and expelled it in a sharp hiss.

"I shouldn't worry about asking me any questions, Inspector," Seaward said sadly. He smiled slightly, lifted the glass to his lips and drained it in one long gulp.

"I'm not worried, sir . . . ," Witherspoon said hesitantly. This was the most confusing situation. The man was acting decidedly odd.

Seaward put down the glass, picked up a paper from the desk and handed it to Witherspoon. "Everything you need to know is right here."

Startled, he took the sheet. As he read the small, neat handwriting, the inspector's eyes widened. When he finished, he looked up and met the other man's eyes.

Witherspoon was so stunned he found it difficult to speak. When he could find his voice, he said, "Good Lord, man. Do you know what you've done? This is a confession."

Seaward laughed harshly. "Naturally. I'm not a fool. I knew as soon as your constable came for the footman that you were on to me. So I decided to save Her Majesty's Police Force a great deal of time and trouble. Thoughtful of me, isn't it?"

Witherspoon straightened his spine and cleared his throat. "Colonel Clayton Seaward, I'm arresting you for the murder of Dr. Bartholomew Slocum. This confession will be used in evidence against you at your trial. Do you understand that?"

"Trial?" Seaward laughed again. "There won't be a trial," he said. "That was rather thoughtful of me too."

And then he doubled over.

Witherspoon, Barnes and Smythe all moved at once. They scrambled around the desk, trying to grab the stricken man.

Smythe reached him first and gently lowered him into the chair. "Cor, guv', take it easy. Let's get ya into this chair."

"Barnes, call for a doctor," Witherspoon ordered. But before the constable could move, Seaward held up his hand.

"It's too late for that," he murmured. "I've meted out my own punishment. I'll die the way I killed him."

"Go on, man," the inspector shouted as the constable hesitated. "Take the coach and get the nearest doctor." Barnes ran for the door.

Seaward moaned and shook his head. "It won't do any good. I'll be dead before he gets here. I made sure of that. The venom of the cape cobra is the most toxic of all." He groaned and let out a strangled gasp.

"My God," Smythe muttered, as he stared at the colonel's face. "Poor, stupid bastard."

Seaward's body was starting to swell, and his skin was whitening as the seconds ticked past. "The cobra's in the conservatory," he rasped. "Seven feet long, nasty little creature. Have your men take care when they . . ." He broke off, clutched his chest and slumped forward onto the desk.

But it was another hour before he died. Witherspoon was glad the man had, mercifully, been unconscious.

"So you see," the inspector said proudly. "Once the footman told us that Seaward kept poisonous snakes out at his country place, well, the solution was as clear as the nose on your face."

"But I still don't understand what them mushrooms had to do with it," Betsy said.

Mrs. Goodge, Wiggins, Betsy, Smythe and Mrs. Jeffries were all sitting around the kitchen table listening to Inspector Witherspoon's brilliant resolution of the case.

The inspector and Smythe had arrived back late in the evening, so late that Mrs. Jeffries had almost worn a hole in the floor with her pacing. But when they finally arrived, shocked but unharmed, she'd insisted everyone sit down to a nice cup of hot chocolate.

Witherspoon had been talking nonstop ever since.

"Well, you see, Betsy," he continued, reaching for another currant bun, "the mushrooms were really the key to the whole mystery. I expect it was when Colonel Seaward heard Mrs. Crookshank shouting about those poisonous mushrooms that he came up with his plan."

Wiggins wrinkled his nose. "Why didn't he use one of them to kill the doctor? Why go to all the trouble of gettin' snake venom?" He shuddered.

"Because mushrooms aren't nearly as reliable as venom," Witherspoon explained. "Furthermore, Colonel Seaward was an avid naturalist. His butler admitted he was very skilled at milking snakes. But when he knew about the mushrooms, he saw his opportunity. If the doctor died of mushroom poisoning, there was a good chance the death would be ruled accidental. Snake venom without a snake is rarely considered accidental."

"So let me see if I've got this right," Mrs. Goodge said. "Colonel Seaward heard about them mushrooms on Saturday at Mrs. Crookshank's tea party."

"That's right," Witherspoon agreed. "Then he went to Surrey. On Wednesday morning, he milked the snake and brought the venom back."

Smythe leaned forward. "But 'ow did he know Slocum would be alone that day?"

"Well," Witherspoon hesitated, "he didn't know for certain until Slocum dropped his calling card by. That was Slocum's way of notifying his victims to come along and pay up. That's why none of the servants were ever present."

"How come Seaward didn't just pay up?" Betsy asked. " 'E's a rich man and he'd been paying for a bloomin' long time. Why risk committin' a murder?"

"I knows that one," Wiggins interjected proudly. "He was gettin' that appointment from the Queen. He didn't want nuthin' interferin' with that, right?" He looked at the inspector.

"Yes, that's it exactly. In the confession, he admitted that he'd been paying Slocum blackmail money. He also said he feared that money wasn't going to be enough. Slocum didn't just want cash anymore; he wanted acceptance and access into Colonel Seaward's circle of friends and acquaintances. Seaward, of course, couldn't risk that. Not only did Slocum know about the African incident, but he was disreputable enough that I'm sure the colonel feared he'd try his nasty blackmailing tricks on others. No true gentleman would want to expose his friends to a person like that."

Mrs. Jeffries thought that a "true gentleman" wouldn't commit a murder either. "Do you honestly think that's why Seaward killed him?" she asked softly. "To save his friends?"

Witherspoon looked thoughtful. "I don't really know. I'd like to think so."

Betsy frowned. "But why'd he kill himself? You told us when you first come in that the case against him was pretty circum . . ."

"Circumstantial?" the inspector supplied helpfully. "It was, but we could have made a case and Seaward knew that. Once we knew what to look for, Dr. Bainbridge would have found evidence that Slocum had died of cape cobra venom. We already had the statement from the wine merchant confirming that the bottle of wine found in the Slocum house was one that Seaward had purchased, and we would have had the footman's testimony that the colonel was away from his guests long enough to have committed the murder." He shrugged. "But as to why he took his own life, I expect he couldn't face the disgrace. It would have all come out. Blackmail, Africa, being a coward."

"I reckon it's all for the best," Mrs. Goodge said. "Even with all that evidence, he still might 'ave gotten off, and that wouldn'a been right."

"I don't think so," Mrs. Jeffries countered. "He was the only one with a truly compelling motive. Effie Beals didn't have to kill the doctor; she was getting ready to leave for Australia. Dr. Hightower couldn't have done it, because he hadn't heard about Slocum's attempt to blackmail Mrs. Leslie. Slocum was already dead when Hightower arrived and found the body."

"What about Mrs. Leslie?" Mrs. Goodge protested. "She 'ad a right good motive."

"She also has the backbone of a spineless chicken," Mrs. Jeffries argued. "I don't think that woman would have the gumption to say boo to a goose, let alone kill a man."

Everyone laughed, and the impromptu little gathering broke up. As soon as Witherspoon had disappeared up the stairs, Mrs. Jeffries turned to the others.

"Well, we've done it. We've helped our inspector solve another case." She smiled broadly. "You should all be very proud of yourselves. Each and every one of you made an extremely valuable contribution. Because of your efforts, an innocent woman will be able to leave these shores for a new life."

Wiggins yawned. Betsy stood up and stretched. Smythe checked the time to see if the pub was still open, and Mrs. Goodge stuffed the last of the currant buns into her mouth.

"Well, really," Mrs. Jeffries protested. "Here I am trying to hand round compliments and you lot can't be bothered to listen."

"Don't take it wrong, Mrs. J," Smythe said as he headed for the door. "But time's a-wastin', and I ain't been for a quick one in two days."

"Oh no," Betsy said soothingly, "we're just a tad tired tonight. You can compliment us all you want tomorrow. We just can't take it all in tonight." She gave another mighty stretch. "*I'm* all in. I'm for bed."

"Frettin' and worryin' is hard work," Mrs. Goodge pointed out. "And we've done our fair share this afternoon and tonight. Why don't you save that pretty little speech till tomorrow when we can all appreciate it like?"

Mrs. Jeffries shook her head and went up to the drawing room. She understood what they were trying to tell her. They were tired, both emotionally and physically. And so was she.

As she passed the drawing room, she saw the inspector kneeling in front of the fireplace. He was building a fire. She hesitated just inside the door and watched as the match flared and the flames caught.

"Inspector Witherspoon," she called softly.

He turned slightly, and she saw what he was doing. "Mrs. Jeffries, do come in."

Dr. Slocum's strongbox was opened. Witherspoon began feeding in the papers, one by one. Slowly, Mrs. Jeffries walked to the hearth.

She stopped beside him.

"I won't burn Colonel Seaward's statement," he said, as he tossed another paper into the flames. "That's evidence. But I really didn't think it was *right* for the indiscretions of many innocent people to be in the possession of the Metropolitan Police."

"I see."

He looked up at her, his eyes pleading for her to understand. “Do you think I’m doing the right thing, Mrs. Jeffries?”

“Oh yes,” she answered with a smile. “I think you’re doing exactly the right thing.”

Epilogue

Mrs. Jeffries put the last of the clean sheets in the linen closet, tucked in a few dewberry-scented wood chips and closed the door. She stood in the hallway for a few moments, wishing she had something to do next more interesting than going over the shopping lists with Mrs. Goodge.

But she didn't have anything particularly interesting to do. She hadn't had anything particularly interesting to do since they'd discovered Dr. Slocum's murderer over three weeks ago. Mrs. Jeffries thought that was a miserable state of affairs.

And from the way the rest of the household has been acting, she mused as she trudged down the stairs, they all agreed with that sentiment.

Not that the case hadn't ended satisfactorily, she told herself as she paused on the third-floor landing. It had.

The Home Office had quietly congratulated the inspector on another brilliant investigation, while at the same time they buried any news reports regarding the matter so deep a mole couldn't find them. That annoyed Mrs. Jeffries. She thought that possible embarrassment to Her Majesty was a decidedly stupid reason for manipulating an alledgely free press. But there was little she could do about it.

As she reached the bottom of the steps, she decided she was being foolish. She and the rest of the household had to get back into their routine. Everyone at Upper Edmonton Gardens was suffering from a bad case of the doldrums, and it had to stop.

Betsy was so bored she'd taken to reading the obituaries every day on the off chance that she'd come across something suspicious. Mrs. Goodge's cooking had deteriorated, Smythe had stopped going to the pub, and even Wiggins couldn't be bothered to hang about out front and watch for Miss Cannonberry.

They were all being far too self-indulgent. Why, one couldn't expect always to have a nice little mystery to sink one's teeth in.

As she passed the drawing room, Mrs Jeffries popped her head in and checked the time. She smiled. They'd all be in the kitchen having tea. This was as good a time as any to tell them to stop feeling sorry for themselves.

Well . . . She paused and decided that maybe she'd wait till tomorrow to deliver her lecture. Perhaps today they'd all go out for a nice treat somewhere. That would cheer everyone up.

Mrs. Jeffries was halfway down the back stairs when she heard the laughter. She hurried into the kitchen and then came to a full stop.

The table was set for an elaborate tea. Mrs. Goodge had used the good china and a linen tablecloth. She'd put out cakes and buns and plates of dainty sandwiches.

But that wasn't what made Mrs. Jeffries blink with surprise.

Luty Belle Crookshank was sitting at the head of the table as if she were the Queen of Sheba. She'd just made some comment that had Smythe roaring with laughter, Betsy giggling and Wiggins grinning from ear to ear. Even Mrs. Goodge was smiling.

"Hello there, Hepzibah," Luty shouted as she caught sight of her. "I was wonderin', if you was of a mind to join us."

"Luty Belle," Mrs. Jeffries exclaimed as she came to the table. "This is certainly a delightful surprise. I'm so happy to see you."

Luty cackled. "I'm mighty glad to be here. I was just tellin' everybody about how I was watchin' them gardens during the Slocum trouble."

"Really," Mrs. Jeffries said cautiously.

Luty cackled again. "Now, Hepzibah. Don't go gettin' stiff on me. But a body'd have to be blind not to notice you lot out there prancin' about and askin' questions."

Everyone at the table went utterly still. Betsy's eyes were as wide as saucers, Smythe was watching the elderly lady the way a fox eyes a chicken, Wiggins had ceased chewing on a slice of Battenburg cake, and Mrs. Goodge's hand had stopped halfway to the teapot.

Mrs. Jeffries decided to brazen it out. "Why, Luty Belle, I haven't the faintest notion what you're talking about."

"Good bluff," Luty said admiringly. "Did ya ever play poker? I bet you'd have been doggone good at it. But that's not why I'm here."

Mrs. Jeffries smiled politely. "I thought this was a social call."

Luty Belle shook her head. "Nope. Mind ya, now that I've been and had a good time, I'll be sure to come again. But I really came because I thought you—" She broke off and looked around the table. "And the rest of ya—could give me a little help."

"If'n you're offerin' us a job," Smythe said, "we're sorry, but we's happy here."

"It's a job all right," Luty replied with a vigorous shake of her head. "But it's not what you're a thinkin'. You see, I saw the ways all of you helped solve ol' Slocum's murder. Got sharp eyes, I have. You lot were all over that neighborhood, asking questions, and even better, you was gettin' answers."

"Luty Belle," Mrs. Jeffries interrupted. "What is this all about?" Her spirits were lifting by the second, but she didn't want to get her hopes too high.

Luty sighed, and all traces of amusement left her face.

"Well," she said softly, "I've got me this problem and I think I need some help. I was hoping you all could give me a hand."

MRS. JEFFRIES DUSTS FOR CLUES

CHAPTER 1

"Most folks is too wrapped up in themselves to pay attention to what's goin' on right under their noses," Luty Belle Crookshank insisted. "But I ain't most people. And I know Scotland Yard would still be lookin' for Slocum's murderer if it weren't for you lot. That's why I need your help."

Mrs. Jeffries, the housekeeper for Inspector Gerald Witherspoon of Scotland Yard, wasn't sure she should let Luty's statement pass unchallenged. To be sure, if not for herself and the other servants at Upper Edmonton Gardens, Inspector Witherspoon probably couldn't have solved the Slocum case as quickly as he had, but she had no doubt he would have solved it eventually.

"Now, Luty Belle," Mrs. Jeffries chided. "That's not precisely true. Inspector Witherspoon had matters well in hand." She broke off and gestured toward the other servants around the kitchen table. "We merely helped out a bit."

"Course you did." Luty gave them a wide, conspiratorial grin. "I ain't asking you to admit anything, I'm just wantin' a little help."

Mrs. Jeffries glanced at the others. For the first time in three weeks, they didn't look bored. Betsy, the maid, was hanging on Luty Belle's every word. Smythe, the coachman, was grinning from ear to ear. Wiggins, the footman, was leaning forward in his chair so far that Mrs. Jeffries was sure if he wasn't careful he'd knock it out from under himself, and Mrs. Goodge, the cook, was nodding her head vigorously up and down.

Mrs. Jeffries had the distinct impression she'd have a mutiny on her hands if she refused Luty Belle Crookshank a hearing. Whatever was bothering the elderly American woman, the others wanted to help.

For that matter, so did she. "All right, Luty Belle. Why don't you tell us what this is all about?"

"Like I said," Luty began. "I've got me a problem."

"What kind of problem?" Betsy asked. She cocked her chin to one side so that one of her blond curls spilled coquettishly onto her shoulder.

Luty put her teacup on the table. Beneath the fabric of the bright blue-and-lavender-striped dress she wore, her shoulders slumped. "A real bad one," she replied slowly, her white head shaking sadly. "A friend of mine is missing."

"Someone's missing? Have you reported it to the police?" Mrs. Jeffries queried softly.

"Nah, I didn't git worried over the girl until a couple of days ago. Besides, I ain't one to go runnin' to the law about every least little thing. Not that I think that Mary's disappearin' ain't important; it is. But I reckoned you all could do a better job of findin' out what happened to her than the police could. If'n I went to them, they'd just say that Mary's probably run off with some man, and I knows that ain't true."

"Very wise," mumbled Mrs. Goodge.

"You're right to come ta us," Smythe added. "We can find out what happened to yer friend faster than the police." He flicked a quick glance at Mrs. Jeffries. "No disrespect intended to our inspector," he explained quickly. "He's a good copper."

"Smythe's right," Betsy interjected. "You just tell us all about it; we can find her for ya. We're right good at solvin' mysteries."

"What mystery?" Wiggins asked. He gazed in confusion around the table.

"Haven't you been listenin', boy?" Mrs. Goodge admonished. "Luty's friend 'as disappeared."

"Oh, sorry." Wiggins grinned sheepishly. "I thought she said her friend went *visitin'*. Guess my mind wandered a bit."

Luty gave him a sharp look, Smythe and Betsy rolled their eyes, and even Mrs. Jeffries had to stifle an impatient sigh. The footman, no doubt, had been daydreaming about his newest infatuation.

"Yes, well perhaps you'd better pay a bit more attention to the conversation, Wiggins," Mrs. Jeffries said firmly. "And the rest of us had better not make Mrs. Crookshank any rash promises. We'd better find out exactly what this is all about before we decide we can resolve the matter." She turned to Luty Belle. "Now, who, exactly, is missing?"

"Mary Sparks. She used to be a housemaid at the Lutterbank house. They're my neighbors. They live down at the other end of the gardens. Mary's just a girl, only nineteen, and I'm real worried about her."

"We can see that." Mrs. Jeffries nodded. "How long has she been gone?"

Luty sighed. "Two months."

"And you're just now startin' to look fer her?" Smythe asked in disbelief. "Cor, anythin' could have 'appened to 'er by now."

"That's a long time for a body to be lost," Wiggins added thoughtfully.

"If it's been two months," Betsy put in somberly, "she in't missing, she's dead."

"For goodness' sakes," Mrs. Jeffries exclaimed as she saw the elderly woman turn pale, "will you all please stop scaring Luty? We can't make any assumptions about what has or has not happened to Mary Sparks until we hear the rest of the story."

Luty Belle smiled gratefully and took a deep breath. "I reckon I'd better start at the beginning. About two months ago, I was fixin' to go to Venice. As it turned out, I shouldn'a bothered. Smelly place. Waste of money, but that's neither here nor there. But you need to know what took me so long to start frettin' over the girl." She paused. "Anyhows, a few days before I was leavin', Mary come over and she was cryin' and carryin' on like she'd just lost her best friend. When I got her calmed down, she told me the Lutterbanks had let her go. Seems they accused her of stealing a silver brooch."

"Had she stolen the brooch?" Mrs. Jeffries asked quickly.

Luty shook her head. "Nah. The girl's no thief. I know that for a fact."

Smythe raised an eyebrow. "What makes ya so sure?"

" 'Cause that's how me and Mary became friends," Luty replied tartly. "I got acquainted with the girl when she returned my fur muff. I'd dropped it in the gardens, and furthermore, young man, that muff was stuffed with money. Now if'n Mary Sparks was a thief, she wouldn't have bothered to give the danged thing back to me, would she?"

"Nah, if'n she were a thief, she'd 'ave kept it," he agreed.

"What happened then?" Betsy said hastily.

"I told Mary she could stay at my place until I got back and then we'd sort everything out. But Mary wasn't one for acceptin' charity. All she wanted me to do was to write her a letter of reference to one of them domestic employment agencies. She'd heard about a position with some preacher's family over in Putney. So that's what I did." Luty grasped her hands together. "The next day, the agency give her the job. She come back to my place, picked up her carpetbag and said good-bye. I went on to Venice. It wasn't until a few days ago, when I realized that I hadn't received any letters from her, that I got worried."

"Mary could read and write?" Betsy asked.

"Yup, that's one of the reasons we became friends. Mary and I both liked to read. I used to loan her some of my books." The harsh set of Luty's jaw softened as she smiled. Then the moment passed and she continued. "But that's neither here nor there. As I was sayin', I started to fret over not hearin' from Mary, so I sent my butler to the Everdene house, that's the place where Mary was goin' to work, to check on the girl. But when Hatchet got back, he told me the Everdenes claim Mary up and quit the day after she arrived."

"Could she have gone back to her family?" Mrs. Goodge asked. She pushed another plate of buns toward Luty Belle.

"Nah. Mary didn't have no family. She'd been on her own since she was fourteen." Luty Belle picked up a currant bun and put it on her plate.

Mrs. Jeffries nodded thoughtfully. "Did the Everdenes say where she'd gone?"

"Hatchet didn't think to ask," Luty replied in disgust. "I was thinkin' of going there myself and seein' what I could find out."

"I think you'd better let one o' us do that," Smythe said quickly.

"Why?" Luty's black eyes narrowed dangerously. "You think I couldn't get that toffee-nosed bunch to answer my questions?"

"Of course you could," Mrs. Jeffries said soothingly. "But I'm afraid I must agree with Smythe. You should leave the task to us. If they've lied to your butler, they'll probably lie to you as well. We've got better ways of finding out the truth."

"Yeah, I reckon you're right at that. There's no tellin' what kind of tales that preacher might make up." Luty snorted. "Never did much trust preachers."

"Have you asked the Lutterbanks if they've heard from her?" Mrs. Jeffries asked.

"Nah," Luty said grimly. "I knows that bunch too well to bother talkin' to them. Old Mrs. Lutterbank is as crazy as a bedbug, Mr. Lutterbank is a pompous windbag, Fiona wouldn't know the truth if'n it walked up and pinched her on the cheek, and Andrew is such a slippery varmint, I wouldn't trust him to tell me the sun rose in the east and set in the west."

"Gracious, you certainly don't sound as though you care for them overly much." Mrs. Jeffries cocked her head to one side. "Do you think they may have had something to do with Mary's disappearance?"

"I'm not sure. But I've seen the likes of Andrew Lutterbank before. He's a mean, vicious bastard, and I know he had a right yen for Mary. But she weren't havin' none of that. Mary's a good girl, and she was too smart to risk her employment by prettyin' up to a no-count varmint like him." Luty shrugged. "But much as I dislike that bunch, I don't think they had anythin' to do with Mary bein' missin'. From what I've heard, Andrew's walkin' a fine line these days. The last time he got a housemaid in trouble, it cost him five hundred pounds and a trip to Australia. Nah, he might have had his eye on Mary, but I reckon he left her alone."

Betsy gazed at Luty Belle sympathetically. "Did Mary have any other friends? Did she go out on her day off with any of the other housemaids?"

"Well," Luty Belle replied thoughtfully, "she was friendly with Garrett, the grounds keeper's assistant. But he's three years younger than her, and she's practically engaged to his older brother, Mark. But Mark's away at sea, so I knows she didn't go to him. Sometimes, I'd see her walkin' about in the gardens with Cassie Yates."

"Where could we find this Cassie Yates?" Smythe asked. He leaned forward on his elbows and clasped his big hands together under his chin.

"Cassie's a shop assistant at MacLeod's. They're on the King's Road. I reckon you can find her there." Luty Belle shook her head. "Other than those two and myself, Mary kept pretty much to herself. She's a quiet little thing." She fixed her gaze on the far wall, and her lower lip started to tremble. "I'm so scared somethin' awful's happened to Mary." Luty blinked furiously and got ahold of herself when she realized they were all staring at her sympathetically.

"Perhaps," Mrs. Jeffries suggested gently, "she's found a . . . well, sweetheart, and eloped?"

"She'd have let me know," Luty Belle insisted. "Don't you git it? Mary and me was friends. She promised to write, to keep in touch. But I ain't heard a peep from her. And even if'n she decided she didn't love Mark McGraw and had gone off with some smooth-talkin' man, she'd have written me."

Betsy reached over and touched the old lady's arm. "Mrs. Crookshank."

"I told ya to call me Luty Belle."

"Sorry, Luty Belle, Mary may have gone off with someone and, well, been ashamed to let you know about it. Especially, if'n he didn't marry 'er. It 'appens, you know."

Mrs. Goodge nodded wisely and Wiggins blushed.

"Nah. Mary wouldn't have been ashamed. Not with me."

"On the day that Mary came to you, did you give her any money?" Mrs. Jeffries asked briskly.

"I tried to, but she wouldn't take a penny. All she wanted was one night's lodgin' and a letter of reference." Luty Belle suddenly stood up. "Are you goin' to help me or not?" she demanded. "Causin' if you ain't, I reckon I'll have to start lookin' myself or hire me one of them private inquiry agents. But come hell or high water, I'm goin' to find out what happened to Mary Sparks."

Mrs. Jeffries gazed around the table. Each time her eyes met one of the others', there was a barely perceptible nod to show accord. They all wanted her to say yes.

"Of course we're going to help you," Mrs. Jeffries stated calmly.

"I ain't askin' any of you to do it fer free," Luty Belle announced. When they all started to protest, she held up her hand. "Quit your caterwaulin'. I ain't goin' to insult anyone by offering you *money*. Agreed?"

Betsy's eyebrows lifted, Smythe looked amused, Mrs. Goodge pursed her lips, and Wiggins grinned happily. Mrs. Jeffries cleared her throat. They all turned and stared at her expectantly, waiting for her to speak for them. Mrs. Jeffries wasn't quite sure what to say. She opened her mouth and then closed it. She could hardly refuse Luty's offer. If she did, she was sure the American woman wouldn't let them help. Luty Belle was too proud for that. And she knew that if the household lost this chance to do a bit of detective work, they'd all be utterly miserable.

"Um, Luty," she began, trying to think of a delicate way to tell her payment of any kind would be rather uncomfortable.

"You look like a gaping fish, Hepzibah." Luty put her hands on her hips. "Now, I knows you're all proud as pikestaffs, and I told you I ain't offerin' you money. Let's just say that no matter what you find out, I'll do what's right and we'll leave it at that.

Mrs. Jeffries smiled. "That will be just fine, Luty."

They got a few more details about Mary Sparks out of Luty Belle, and then she left. As soon as the kitchen door had closed behind her, they all started talking at once.

"The girl's probably run off with some man," Mrs. Goodge said darkly as she began to gather up the tea things.

"Or she could have been sold into white slavery," Betsy said.

"If the girl's been missin' for two months," Smythe added, "she's probably at the bottom of the Thames."

"Maybe she's gone to America," Wiggins said cheerfully.

"Really," Mrs. Jeffries said. "You all have most appalling ideas. I'm glad you managed to keep some of those rather depressing opinions to yourself. Poor Luty Belle's worried enough."

"What do you think 'appened to her, then?" Betsy stuffed the last bite of currant bun into her mouth and then nimbly got to her feet and took the plate to the sink.

"That's impossible to say right now," Mrs. Jeffries replied. "But we'll do our best to find out. Wiggins, I want you to get over to Knightsbridge and talk to Garrett McGraw."

Wiggins's round face creased in worry as he pursed his lips. "What should I ask?"

"Find out everything you can about Mary Sparks and about the Lutterbank family." Mrs. Jeffries turned to Betsy. "Would you like to go shopping?"

"Want me to question Cassie Yates, do ya?" Betsy grinned from ear to ear, her blue eyes sparkling with the thrill of the hunt. "I'll find out anythin' I can."

Smythe cleared his throat and crossed his arms over his massive chest. His big brutal face was set in an expression of feigned boredom, but his dark brown eyes were sparkling as brightly as Betsy's. "I suppose you want me to go back to them miserable pubs in Knightsbridge."

"If you wouldn't mind," Mrs. Jeffries replied sweetly. She knew Smythe was teasing her a little. He'd gotten an enormous amount of information on the murder of Dr. Slocum from hanging about those Knightsbridge pubs. For all his complaints, Mrs. Jeffries knew he enjoyed his forays.

She turned to Mrs. Goodge. The cook gazed back at her knowingly. "I expect I can remember a bit of gossip about the Lutterbanks," she said calmly. "But you'd better give me a few hours. The name hasn't rung any bells yet."

Mrs. Jeffries nodded. Mrs. Goodge knew every morsel of gossip about every important family in London. Like Smythe, she too had come up with some invaluable bits and pieces during the Slocum investigation.

"Are we goin' to mention the girl to the inspector?" Betsy asked as she pulled on her gloves.

"Not right away," Mrs. Jeffries replied. "We may have to eventually, but for right now, we'll see what we can come up with on our own. We don't want to bother him unless it becomes absolutely necessary."

The inspector was kept completely in the dark about their activities. None of them wanted the dear man to think they lacked confidence in his skills as a dectective. "But I will ask him some discreet questions when he gets home," she continued. "He should be able to tell us if any young female bodies have turned up in the last two months."

Betsy made a face. She was turning into an excellent detective, but she was really quite squeamish.

Mrs. Jeffries waited until everyone had left and then she sighed in satisfaction. There was nothing like a mystery to lift one's spirits.

Magpie Lane had been almost obliterated. Where there had once been a row of tiny redbrick houses, there were now only piles of rubble and debris. The one house that hadn't been torn down stood alone at the end of the street, a forlorn shell with no windows and the doors haphazardly boarded over. On the other side of the road was an abandoned brewery enclosed by a twelve-foot wall.

Inspector Gerald Witherspoon slowed his steps as he followed Constable Barnes to the far end of the street. Three workmen and two uniformed police constables were standing over an open trench. "She's in there, sir," the taller of two constables called. He pointed down into what had once been the cellar of a house. "We sent for CID as soon as we realized the remains were human, sir."

"Thank you, Constable." Witherspoon gulped and studiously avoided looking down. "Constable Barnes," he ordered, "you'd best see to it."

Barnes hurried down the ladder someone had stuck at the side. A moment later, Witherspoon's worst fears were confirmed.

"It's a body, all right, Inspector," Barnes called cheerfully. "You'd best come down and see for yourself."

There was no hope for it, he had to look at the corpse. Witherspoon didn't like dead bodies. Despite his being a police officer, his stomach was really quite delicate. As he descended the ladder, he found himself hoping that this body would be as tidy as his last one, but considering it had been in the ground, he thought that was rather a faint hope. He was right.

He stopped at the bottom of the ladder, took a deep breath and then walked over to stand next to Barnes. Keeping his gaze level with the top of the trench, he silently prayed he wouldn't be sick or, even worse, that he wouldn't disgrace himself by fainting. He took another deep breath and then immediately wished he hadn't. Now that the remains had been exposed, the smell was awful. The air in the confined space was filled with the sickeningly sweet stench of decaying flesh.

Witherspoon's stomach turned over.

"Looks like it's a woman," Barnes said. He stepped back to give his inspector room. Witherspoon was trapped now. He had to look.

The corpse was lying on its side, the face turned into the flat dirt of the trench. He could see that she was wearing a dark blue dress and that her hair, which had once been blond, was tangled with matted earth.

"Yes," the inspector mumbled, "so it appears." He knelt down and held his breath.

"Shouldn't we turn 'er over?" Barnes asked.

Witherspoon shuddered as he forced his hands to touch the dead shoulders. Keeping his head down so no one would see that his eyes were closed, he pulled the body onto its back.

Barnes made a funny choking noise. "Cor, this one's bad."

A wave of nausea washed through the inspector, but he grimly reminded himself of his duty. "Get out your notebook, Constable," Witherspoon ordered. Perhaps, he thought, it would be best to get this over with as quickly as possible.

"Right, sir."

"Uhmm, well. The body is that of a woman." He forced himself to open his eyes and then almost gagged. "The face is blacked and bloated. Virtually unrecognizable."

"Blimey, don't you want to put a handkerchief over your nose?" Barnes asked the inspector. "She's gettin' riper by the minute."

"No, no, I'm quite all right," Witherspoon lied. He knew if he didn't get this done quickly, he'd never be able to force himself back into this hole. "The deceased is wearing a heavy . . . ," he broke off and tentatively touched the material of the dress, ". . . wool dress. It's a dark blue."

"Any sign of what killed her, sir?" Barnes glanced down at the body, and his lips curled in disgust. "Cor, that's obvious, isn't it? Looks like there's a great big gapin' hole in her chest. Think she's been stabbed, sir?"

"Yes, Constable," the inspector replied faintly, "it certainly seems so." He quickly averted his gaze from the wound. "We must be sure and have our lads do more digging to see if the weapon is here as well."

"What kind of knife do you think it was, sir?" the Constable asked cheerfully.

"I really shouldn't like to say at this point in the investigation."

"Right, sir. She got a weddin' ring on?"

Witherspoon glanced at what was left of her hands, then quickly looked away. "Difficult to tell, Constable. But we must make sure we instruct the searchers to look for one. It could have slipped off when the flesh was . . ." He broke off, wondering just how to phrase the truly horrendous thought. When the flesh was eaten by rats or decomposed or whatever wretched force of nature had caused the poor girl's hands to be nothing but bones.

"She must have had money," Barnes said. "Look, that brooch on her dress looks like silver."

Witherspoon hadn't even noticed the jewelry. He glanced at the horseshoe-shaped silver pin, saw that it was so encrusted with dirt and mud that it was impossible to identify the small stones set along the top of the curve, and then looked away. "Not necessarily, Constable. Someone may have given it to her. For all we know, the poor woman may have been as poor as a church mouse. It's a bit too early to start making assumptions."

Barnes knelt down and pointed at the feet. "You're probably right, sir," he said. "But them shoes look like good quality." He leaned to one side, stared at the corpse's foot and then reached over and began brushing the dirt away from the sole. "Inspector, these shoes are new."

"Really?" Witherspoon answered curiously. "How can you tell?"

The constable continued his assault on the shoes. "Because this dirt here is from being buried, but when you brush it away, these soles look like new. See, look 'ere, there isn't even a scuff mark."

"Yes," Witherspoon replied weakly, after one fast look at the shoes, "I see what you mean. Good observation, Constable." Actually, he didn't have any idea whether it was a good observation or not, but he felt he must say something.

"Cor, she's got right big feet for someone her size, doesn't she?"

"Someone her size," Witherspoon mumbled. Oh dear, if he didn't get out of this pit, he really would faint.

"Sure, she's a little thing. Doesn't look more than a bit over five foot."

Abruptly, Witherspoon stood up and headed for the ladder. "See to the body, Constable," he called as he climbed out into the blessed fresh air. "I'm going to talk to the man who found her."

Witherspoon took a few moments to catch his breath before advancing on the three workmen who stood a few feet away, their shovels and picks sticking straight up out of the soft ground.

"Which of you gentlemen found the er . . . body?" he asked.

"It were me," the largest of the three said. He took off his cap and stepped forward. "I be the leadman. Jack Cawley."

"Er . . . yes. Could you tell me precisely how you happened upon the er . . . deceased."

"Well, I were diggin', weren't I. Mind you, I wouldn't have been diggin' if them fools hadn't flooded out that trench over on Ormond Street. We'd a never been here if them stupid engineers knew what they was doing." Cawley snorted in disgust.

"Inspector," Barnes called excitedly as he came out of the pit. "I found this around her neck. It's a necklace of some kind." He held the dirt-encrusted object out to the inspector. "And it's got a ring on it. Maybe she was married after all."

Wrinkling his nose, Witherspoon took the necklace and examined the ring. "A married woman wouldn't wear her wedding ring around her neck," he said. He flaked a bit more dirt off the ring and held it up to the light. "I don't think this is a wedding ring."

Through the layers of grime, he could see the dull yellow glint of gold. Scraping more dirt off, he saw three dark blue stones set between filigreed patterns on the metal. The ring was valuable. He suspected the stones might be sapphires. Drat, whoever had murdered the girl hadn't robbed her. Witherspoon sighed deeply. A dead girl and an expensive ring usually meant trouble. Complications. A nasty case. Perhaps even a crime of passion.

"Could it be a betrothal ring?" Barnes asked.

"A what?"

"A betrothal ring. Engaged couples wear 'em. Though I don't know why. Seems to me a good plain weddin' band should be enough for most folks. But that don't seem to be good enough for young people these days," the constable said as he shook his head.

"Yes, I suppose it could be." Witherspoon turned back to the workman he'd been talking with. "Now, as you were saying."

"I were saying if it hadn't been for them fool engineers, we'd never have found 'er."

"I'm sorry," Witherspoon said. "I don't really follow you. What do the engineers have to do with your finding the body?"

Cawley's bushy eyebrows rose. "It's got everythin' to do with it. We wouldn't have been diggin' up Magpie Lane if they hadn't flooded the other trench." He pointed toward the body. "We wouldn't have been here fer another six months if they hadn't flooded out Ormond Street. With all the damp and the vermin down where she's been layin', she'd've been dust by the time we'd got here—if we'd stuck to our schedule. Probably wouldn't have even been the shoes left."

"Exactly what are you digging?" Witherspoon asked. He wasn't sure that was a particularly pertinent question, but he felt he should ask.

"A new Underground line. The Underground were supposed to be under Ormond Street and a new road here on Magpie Lane. But them fools made a mistake 'cause Ormond Street sits on a bleedin' buried stream." Cawley shook his head. "So at the last minute, they change their bloomin' minds and send us over here to start hacking up Magpie Lane. This here's the first trench—this time, they decided they wanted to make sure there weren't no water before they brought in the heavy diggers."

"I see." Witherspoon nodded. "And you're the one that actually found the er . . . remains?"

Cawley grunted. "Not very pretty either. 'Ere I was, diggin' away and me shovel all of a sudden hits her foot. Well, I weren't sure what it was when I first hit it, so me and the blokes just kept on going diggin'. You can see what we found. As soon as we realized it were a body, we sent for the coppers."

"Inspector," Barnes called again. "How deep should I have the lads dig? Whoever killed her may have buried the weapon under the body."

Witherspoon had no idea. He took a wild guess. "Oh, have them go down another foot or so. And be sure to do a house-to-house as soon as you're finished searching the trench."

"House-to-house?" Barnes asked in confusion.

Witherspoon remembered there weren't any houses. "I meant, a house-to-house up on the main road."

"And what will they be asking, sir?"

"On second thought, Constable, I think we'd better delay that part of the investigation until after we've identified the victim." He hurriedly turned back to Cawley. "You don't, by any chance, happen to know when the houses on this street were demolished, do you?"

" 'Fraid not," the workman replied. "I don't live around these parts. But Fred might know. He lives 'round 'ere." Turning, he called to one of the two workmen standing a few yards away. "Get over here, Fred. The copper wants to ask you some questions."

The small, wiry man didn't look pleased, but he pushed away from the shovel he was leaning on and walked toward the inspector.

"What is your name?" the inspector asked.

"Fred Tompkins."

"And I understand you live nearby. Could you please tell me when these houses were torn down?"

"About a month ago," he replied sullenly. "Everyone who lived here was evicted, thrown out on the streets just so they could tear down some perfectly good 'omes. It were a crime, that's what it was. A crime. Throwing people out of their 'omes just so some toff could tear 'em down and sell the land to build a bloody road."

Witherspoon watched the man sympathetically. "I take it the locals weren't too pleased," he said softly.

"We hated it. Me own sister lost her 'ome." He turned and pointed toward the one remaining house. "She used to live right next to that one. Nice little place it was. Good solid redbrick, plenty of space in the back for her vegetable plot, and she gets tossed out, without so much as a by-your-leave. They only give her a few days to pack up her belongings. She had to move to a grotty set of rooms in Lambeth. And her with three kids and a sick 'usband."

"I'm sorry," Witherspoon said sincerely. "So the residents were suddenly told they had to leave. Do you happen to know who owns these properties?"

Tompkins's lips curled in disgust. "Weren't no owners, leastways, not like real landlords. This whole street was owned by a property company, so there weren't even someone to complain to." He kicked at a loose stone and sent it flying. "Hard-hearted bastards."

"Do you know the name of the company?" Witherspoon wished the police surgeon would get there. The smell of the corpse was getting stronger.

"No. But I can ask my sister. She got a letter from 'em and the name were written right at the top."

"Thank you. That would be most helpful." He pulled out his notebook and took down the man's address. "I'll send a constable around tomorrow for the information."

There was a tap on Witherspoon's shoulder. Startled, he whirled around and found himself staring into the familiar face of Inspector Nigel Nivens.

"Goodness, Inspector Nivens, you gave me such a shock. What are you doing down here?"

Nigel Nivens was a sharp-nosed, pale-faced man with cool gray eyes, slicked back dark blond hair and a thin mouth. He gave Witherspoon a weak smile. "I thought I'd come down and see if you needed any assistance. I understand you've been given another murder."

"I'd hardly put it in those terms, Inspector," Witherspoon said lightly, "I really don't feel like I've been given anything." Then he silently chided himself. Inspector Nivens's turn of phrase was no doubt unintentional. Perhaps he was even being sympathetic. But dear, he did make it sound so odd. Witherspoon knew he was being given another wretched murder to solve, not a nice present for Christmas.

Inspector Nivens looked toward the open trench. "Is it in there?"

"Yes, I'm afraid so. It's a woman."

"Definitely murdered?"

"Yes. She's been stabbed." Witherspoon sighed. "It's jolly kind of you to offer your assistance, but I'm afraid I can't allow you to help. You know how the Chief Inspector feels, one senior officer to a case. Gracious, if two inspectors are tied up on one case, he'd be most annoyed."

"Humph, I suppose you're right." Nivens looked longingly toward the trench. "But it doesn't really seem fair. After all, this is your second murder in a row. I should think, Witherspoon, that it would be only sporting to give someone else a chance." He mumbled something under his breath. Inspector Witherspoon couldn't quite make out what he said, but he did hear the word "competent."

"It really isn't my decision, now, is it?" Witherspoon said soothingly. "Perhaps if you had a word with the Chief Inspector . . ."

"Wouldn't do any good. For some reason, he thinks you're a genius when it comes to murder." Nivens smiled coolly. "It'll be interesting to see how you do with this one. Perhaps it won't be as simple as the Slocum murder."

Witherspoon was slightly offended. Finding the murderer of Dr. Bartholomew Slocum had been anything but simple. And he didn't really understand what Inspector Nivens was complaining about. The fellow always got good, clean burglaries. Lucky man.

CHAPTER 2

Mrs. Jeffries was waiting in the hallway when Inspector Witherspoon arrived home. "Good evening, sir," she said cheerfully as she took his bowler hat and coat. "Have you had a good day?"

She knew he hadn't had a particularly good day. One look at his long face had told her that much. But she wasn't deterred, certain a cozy chat and a nice glass of sherry would no doubt fix him right up.

"Good evening, Mrs. Jeffries," Witherspoon replied. "As a matter of fact, it's been a very dreadful sort of day."

"Oh dear, I'm so sorry to hear that." She turned toward the drawing room. "But not to worry, you'll feel much better after you've had a chance to relax."

The inspector dutifully followed her into the drawing room and sat down in his favorite wing chair. A fire blazed in the hearth, a glass of amber liquid was sitting on the table next to his chair, and Mrs. Jeffries was gazing at him sympathetically. He felt much better already.

"What delight is Mrs. Goodge cooking up for our dinner tonight?" he asked as he reached for his glass.

Mrs. Jeffries desperately wanted to know whether the inspector knew of any unidentifed female bodies turning up in the last two months. But she didn't want to arouse her employer's curiosity. Not just yet. There would be time enough for that after she and the others had done more investigating into Mary's disappearance. She curbed her impatience and decided to wait until he had some sherry in him before she brought up the subject. Besides, the inspector was always far more willing to talk on a full stomach.

"Roast pork and poached apples," she replied with a smile. "Now, Inspector, tell me all about it."

"About what?"

"Why your dreadful day, of course." She gazed at him earnestly. "I know you never like to complain, but really, sir, sometimes it helps to get things off one's chest. As soon as you walked into the house this evening, I knew something utterly appalling must have happened."

"You're so very perceptive, Mrs. Jeffries," he murmured with a relieved sigh. "And you're absolutely right, as usual. There's been a murder. A very difficult one, I'm afraid."

"How terrible." Mrs. Jeffries tried to sound appropriately subdued, but it was difficult. Not that she condoned murder, naturally. But she couldn't help but be elated by the fact that she and the rest of the household would now have two cases to work on. Not only would they find the missing Mary Sparks, but they could help their dear inspector as well. "Why do you think this one's going to be difficult?"

"Because the body was only found today." Witherspoon paused and took a deep breath. "And the murder was committed several months ago."

"Several months ago!" Mrs. Jeffries was scandalized. The trail would be colder than a February frost.

"Perhaps even more. The police surgeon was only guessing when he made that estimate." The inspector drained the rest of his drink. "I tell you, Mrs. Jeffries, the world has become an evil place. Imagine, this poor girl dead, stabbed right through the heart and buried in the bottom of some cellar and no one even notices she's missing. You'd think that when a person didn't appear as usual, that someone would take the time and trouble to notify the police."

Mrs. Jeffries refused to jump to a conclusion. Just because Inspector Witherspoon had found the body of a woman didn't mean that the body was Mary Sparks. Despite what the good inspector said, she knew dozens of people disappeared all the time in the city and no one bothered to tell the police. "That's appalling. I take it the deceased is a young woman?"

"Yes. Dreadful, isn't it."

"How old was the victim?"

"We're not absolutely sure. The best the police surgeon could do is give us an estimate. He thinks she couldn't have been more than twenty-five, but naturally, we'll know more after the postmortem."

Mrs. Jeffries asked, "Do you know who she is?"

"No, I'm afraid not." Remembering the state of the body, he shuddered. "Unfortunately, she'd been in the ground so long her face is unrecognizable. But she was smallish, only an inch or so over five feet tall and she had blond hair."

Mrs. Jeffries didn't like the sound of that. "Oh dear, however are you going to find out who the poor girl was?" She reminded herself that there were hundreds of women who had blond hair.

"We're comparing her description to those we have of missing women. Hopefully, we'll turn up something soon. It'll be very hard to find out who murdered her if we don't know who she is, er, was." He shook his head. "But we don't really have much to go on."

"Not to worry, Inspector," Mrs. Jeffries said briskly. "I'm sure you'll find out everything you need to know and solve this case just as you've solved all the others. Was there anything unusual about the way she was dressed? Anything that would give you a clue?"

"Not really. She was wearing a good-quality blue dress and she had several pieces of jewelry on her person. But it's the sort of dress one sees everywhere. You know, very much like the one that Betsy wears on her day out." He shrugged. "I don't see that her clothing will be of much use, more's the pity."

"Perhaps you'll have better luck with the jewelry. What kind was it?" Mrs. Jeffries asked cautiously. "A wedding ring, perhaps."

She sincerely hoped it was. If the victim had been married, it almost definitely wasn't Mary Sparks who had been found. But Mrs. Jeffries's hopes were quickly dashed.

"Oh no," the inspector said. "Not quite. I believe the object we found is more properly called a 'betrothal ring,' " Witherspoon explained. "But the odd thing was she didn't have the ring on her finger, as one would expect. She wore it round her neck on a small gold chain. There was a silver brooch on the lapel of her dress as well. Both pieces looked quite valuable."

"That should help you determine her identity," Mrs. Jeffries replied slowly. Her mind was working frantically. She wished she'd asked Luty Belle if the brooch Mary Sparks had been accused of stealing had ever turned up at the Lutterbank house. She made a mental note to talk to Luty tomorrow morning.

"I certainly hope so. I mean the girl was well dressed and had expensive jewelry on her person. She must be someone important. You'd think someone, somewhere would have reported her missing."

"One would think so," Mrs. Jeffries agreed. "Obviously the murder wasn't committed as part of a robbery."

"Uhmm, that was a bit of hard luck. After all, a robber would hardly have left a valuable ring and brooch on his victim." Witherspoon sighed dramatically. "A simple robbery would have been most helpful. It would certainly make this case easier to solve."

Mrs. Jeffries stared at him curiously. "Do you really think so?"

"But of course." Witherspoon put his glass down. "Thieves have to sell their ill-gotten gains somewhere," he explained, "and we've got quite good connections into the criminal classes these days. Why, Inspector Nivens has several sources of information he regularly taps when it comes to robberies. Now if we'd been lucky on this case, the poor girl would have been robbed before she was murdered. I could then have quite legitimately taken Inspector Nivens up on his kind offer of assistance."

"Inspector Nivens offered to help you with this case?" Mrs. Jeffries asked carefully, striving to remain calm.

"Oh, yes," Witherspoon answered as he glanced at the clock on the mantelpiece. "He came round Magpie Lane today as soon as he'd heard a body was discovered. Most thoughtful of him. But naturally, I couldn't accept. You know the Chief Inspector's views on having more than one senior officer on a case."

By sheer willpower, Mrs. Jeffries managed to restrain herself from blurting out precisely what she thought of Inspector Nigel Nivens. Her dear inspector was far too innocent about some things. But it was obvious to her that Nigel Nivens was just waiting for his chance to ruin Gerald Witherspoon. Why the man had once had the audacity to complain to the Chief Inspector that Inspector Witherspoon must be getting outside help on the cases he'd solved. If Nivens was going to be snooping around on this murder, and she had no doubt that he was, they'd have to be very careful. Very careful, indeed.

"Do you think Mrs. Goodge has dinner ready yet?" Witherspoon asked.

Mrs. Jeffries deliberately kept the conversation away from bodies and murder as she ushered the inspector into the dining room. She waited until he was well tucked into his supper before mentioning the subject again.

Witherspoon, who really wanted to get the horrid experience off his chest, soon told her every little detail about finding the body and questioning the workman. He particularly enjoyed repeating Jack Cawley's remarks about the stupidity of engineers and local officials.

"And really, Mrs. Jeffries," he continued as he helped himself to another serving of poached apples, managing to edge a slice of apple onto the rim of the plate, "I'm amazed at how callous some people are."

Mrs. Jeffries snatched a spoon and shoved the apple back into the dish before it landed on the white linen tablecloth. "People aren't really callous, sir," she said soothingly. "I expect they merely say whatever pops into their heads as a way of dealing with the horror of it. Finding a body when one is digging a trench must come as a bit of a shock."

The inspector raised his eyebrows. "I wasn't referring to the workman who found the body, I was referring to Constable Barnes. No doubt, there's much truth to what you say, but really, I thought it most ungallant of the man to mention what big feet the victim had." He paused, remembering what else Barnes had said. "But then again, if he hadn't commented on her feet, we might not have noticed she was wearing new shoes."

"New shoes?" Mrs. Jeffries cocked her chin to one side. "But if the body had been in the ground for two months, how could you tell? Weren't the feet encrusted with dirt?"

"Scuff marks." He smiled triumphantly. "There weren't any scuff marks on the soles. Once the dirt was brushed away, it was very obvious the lady had put on a pair of brand-new shoes. Good leather too, good quality."

"I suppose you've already got the constable out looking for the shop that sold them."

Witherspoon frowned. "Do you think that's necessary? We're hoping to identify the victim by tracking down the jewelry. Both the brooch and the ring are somewhat unusual. It should be easy enough to find the shop that sold them."

"But what if the victim didn't purchase either of them? Perhaps they were gifts. Women don't often buy jewelry for themselves."

"Oh, that doesn't matter," Witherspoon replied airily. "I've already thought of that possibility. A girl hardly buys her own betrothal ring. Once we find where the jewelry was purchased, it'll be quite easy to obtain the name of the person who bought the items. When we know that name, we'll soon know the name of our victim. I suspect the betrothal ring, at least, was bought by a man for his young lady. He's bound to know who she is, er, was."

"I take it you're assuming that whoever bought it was engaged to the victim?"

"Well, that had crossed my mind."

"Then why hasn't he reported her missing?" Mrs. Jeffries asked blandly.

"Er, perhaps he doesn't know she's gone," Witherspoon mumbled. But even to his own ears, that sounded like nonsense. Drat! Why hadn't the man reported his fiancée missing? If, indeed, she was someone's fiancée. But perhaps she wasn't. Perhaps she was something else, something else entirely.

Witherspoon's face fell as he realized just how many problems he might be facing. Perhaps he would have Constable Barnes try to trace the shoes as well. "You know, I do believe I will have Barnes see if he can find out who sold our victim her shoes. Can't afford to ignore any line of inquiry, can I?"

"Why, you've never done that, sir," Mrs. Jeffries said hastily as she saw his gloomy expression. "You're a most efficient policeman. You never leave any stone unturned. Why you've foiled the most diabolically clever murderers, and I'm sure you'll do the same for this last unfortunate victim."

Her words cheered him instantly. "Oh, please, Mrs. Jeffries." Witherspoon flushed with pleasure at her praise. "You're being far too kind. I'm merely a simple man. I do my duty to God, Queen and Country and hope that my small, insignificant contribution makes the world a better place."

The sun was shining brightly as Mrs. Jeffries came into the kitchen the next morning. Betsy, Smythe, Wiggins and Mrs. Goodge were already sitting around the table, waiting for her.

"Good morning, everyone," she said as she took her seat. "I trust that everyone was successful yesterday?"

"Absolutely, Mrs. J." Smythe grinned. "As a matter of fact, you'd best let me talk first today. I thinks you'll be right interested in what I've come across."

" 'Ow come you get ta go first?" Betsy asked.

" 'Cause as soon as Mrs. J hears what I've found out, I expect she'll be wantin' me to go out agin."

Betsy started to protest, thought better of it, and contented herself with a sniff.

"Please proceed, Smythe," Mrs. Jeffries said quickly.

"Well, it's all right mysterious. One of the Lutterbanks' footman told me he saw Mary Sparks back in the communal gardens on the evenin' of September 10th. That's two days after she quit workin' for 'em."

"Two days? Are you sure?" Mrs. Jeffries frowned. "Luty Belle said Mary only stayed the one night. What would she have been doing back in Knightsbridge the following evening? She was supposed to have been working for the Everdenes by then."

Smythe nodded. "I'm sure. The footman was definite about the dates. He remembers because the tenth was always the day that Andrew Lutterbank got his quarterly allowance from his father. But on September 10th, the old man refused to give it out. Instead, he and Andrew had a right old shoutin' match. Every servant in the bloomin' 'ouse 'eard the two of 'em goin' at it. Wesley, that's the footman, finally couldn't stand it anymore so he took himself out to the garden to get away from the screamin'. While he was out there, he saw Mary Sparks."

"What time was this?" Mrs. Jeffries asked.

"He weren't sure, but he said it had just gone dark when he seen her. Spotted her hangin' about at the gate near the far end. He's a right nosey 'un. Wondered what she were doin', her havin' left and all."

"How long did she hang about by the gate?" Mrs. Goodge asked curiously.

Smythe grinned. "Long enough to watch Andrew Lutterbank leavin' in a huff. Wesley thought that was right peculiar too, said Mary were just hoverin' down the far end when all of a sudden his nibs trots out the back door and flies down the path like the 'ounds of 'ades was on his 'eels. Well, Mary looked right surprised, and she jumped into that tangle of brush down at that end of the garden, waited till Lutterbank had stormed out the gate, and then a few minutes later, she and Garrett McGraw scarper off as well. Wesley says he watched Garrett put the girl in a cab."

"Perhaps that's when she went to the Everdenes," Betsy suggested. "Maybe she didn't go right away, like she told Luty. Maybe when they give Mary the position, they told her not to come back till that evenin'."

"No." Mrs. Jeffries shook her head, her expression thoughtful. "I don't think so. Why would Mary lie to Luty about such a trivial matter? If the Everdenes had instructed her not to come till the evening, why not simply ask Luty for permission to spend the afternoon in Luty's home? And we know she never asked. She told Luty as soon as she returned from the agency that she had the position, and then she left immediately. But obviously, despite what the Everdenes claim, Mary was not in their home that night, but back in Knightsbridge. How very curious."

"Maybe she was too proud to ask Luty to let her stay for the rest of the day," Betsy continued doggedly. "Luty did say that she was ever so proud."

"I suppose that's possible," Mrs. Jeffries agreed reluctantly. She noticed that Betsy's chin was tilted in a determined angle as the girl glared at the grinning coachman. She had the distinct impression that Betsy was arguing more in an attempt to wipe that smug expression off Smythe's face than for any other reason.

"But it's not bloomin' likely," Smythe retorted. "Look, why should she fib to Luty about a piddlin' little matter like what time she were expected at the Everdenes? Besides, we've only got their word for it that she even turned up at all."

"Are you suggestin' she never went to the Everdene house?" Betsy snapped.

"I'm sayin' it's possible," Smythe argued. "We've only got their word fer it that she showed up, and then they claimed she up and quit the very next day. If you ask me, that story sounds like a load of codswallop. The truth of the fact is the last time anyone really saw Mary Sparks was the evening of the tenth."

"That's the silliest . . ." Betsy sputtered.

"It's not silly, it's a ruddy fact," Smythe interrupted huffily.

"Yes, of course it is." Mrs. Jeffries said quickly. She smiled at Betsy. "Now let's not argue among ourselves. Smythe does, indeed, have a point. Until we get assurances from someone other than the Everdenes that Mary was at their home on the tenth, we must assume that the last time she was seen was in the gardens on the afternoon of the tenth."

Betsy gave Smythe one final glare. "Oh, all right," she muttered ungraciously.

Mrs. Jeffries turned to the coachman. "I expect you know what I want you to do next."

He nodded. "You want me to find that hansom driver and see if he took her to the Everdenes' or to some place else?"

"That's correct." Mrs. Jeffries turned back to Betsy. "Now, what did Cassie Yates tell you about Mary?"

"Not much o' anythin'," Betsy admitted sheepishly.

Smythe smiled and said caustically, "Couldn't get her ta talk, huh?"

"Fat lot you knows about it," she retorted. "I can git anyone to talk. But you can't get someone to chattin' if'n theys disappeared, can you?"

"Cassie Yates has disappeared too?" Mrs. Jeffries asked in alarm. "Oh dear, this is getting most complicated . . ."

"Don't fret yourself, Mrs. J," Betsy said soothingly. "From what I heard about Cassie Yates, she can take care of herself. I talked to one of the girls that works in the shop with 'er, and she reckons Cassie's run off with some man. Says the girl had a couple of gentlemen friends and that she was goin' around braggin' about how both of 'em wanted to marry her. One of 'em had even posted the banns and bought the license."

Mrs. Jeffries nodded. "Did you find out where Miss Yates lives?"

"No. But I did find out she used to work for the Lutterbanks too. That's how her and Mary become friends."

"Did they sack her?" Mrs. Goodge asked.

"She quit about two weeks before Mary disappeared." Betsy gave Mrs. Jeffries a puzzled frown. "Why'd you want to know where Cassie lives?"

"Because this case seems to be getting complicated," Mrs. Jeffries replied. She was hedging. Betsy was no doubt right and Cassie Yates was probably a respectable married woman by now. But she couldn't get the thought of Inspector Witherspoon's body out of her mind. She wasn't certain the dead girl was Mary Sparks or Cassie Yates. A coincidence like that would be odd, but not unheard of. However, until both young women were accounted for, she wanted as much information as she could get.

"What about me?" Wiggins scratched his chin. "I found out quite a bit meself yesterday."

Mrs. Jeffries smiled at his enthusiasm. "Were you able to find Garrett?"

"I found 'im all right, but I didn't have a lot of luck gettin' much out of the lad," Wiggins reported sadly. " 'E was right friendly-like until I mentioned Mary's name. Then 'e got all nervous and twitchy, kept lookin' over his shoulder like he was expectin' someone to be sneakin' up behind 'im and listenin'. It were right peculiar if you ask me." He broke off and glanced toward the cupboard. "Is there any of them currant buns left? I could fancy a bite or two."

"The buns is all gone. When we've finished here, I'll get you a roll." Mrs. Goodge rolled her eyes. "Now get on with it, boy. What did Garrett say?"

"Give us a minute. I'm gettin' to that." He stopped and took a deep breath. " 'E says he don't know Mary very well, just enough to speak to her every now and again in the garden, and that 'e ain't seen her since she left the Lutterbanks. But 'e also told me the Lutterbanks were a right nasty bunch, too. Fiona, that's the daughter, likes to tell tales, and Andrew, that's the son, is a bit o' a bully. Mrs. Lutterbank, who used to be just a little on the barmy side, is now completely round the bend, and Mr. Lutterbanks has a bad temper. Anyways, as soon as Garrett started talkin' about them, I asked him about Mary stealin' the brooch." Wiggins paused dramatically. "That's when 'e got angry. Claimed Mary Sparks wouldn't steal nothin' if her life depended on it, claimed the Lutterbanks were makin' up tales and they ought to be horsewhipped. He got right worked up, went on and on about it."

"For someone who claimed not to know Mary very well," Mrs. Jeffries said thoughtfully, "he certainly leapt to her defense quick enough."

"That's what I thought," Wiggins exclaimed.

"I think we need to keep our eyes on Garrett," she continued. "Wiggins, why don't you try and follow him this evening when he leaves work? See where he goes, find out where he lives and find out where his older brother lives."

"Huh? Older brother?" Wiggins looked thoroughly confused. "What's he got to do with it?"

Mrs. Jeffries shrugged. "Possibly nothing. But Luty Belle mentioned that Mary was almost engaged to Mark McGraw. He's away at sea. However, if he doesn't live with his family, he may have rooms somewhere and Mary may have taken refuge there. Especially if she could convince Mark's landlady she was his intended bride. It's a tad farfetched, I'll admit, but it's worth looking into."

Smythe and Betsy started to get up, each of them eager to get on with their investigating. The housekeeper waved them back into their chairs. "Don't go just yet. I'm afraid there's another matter we need to discuss."

She then proceeded to tell them about Inspector Witherspoon's newest case. As was her custom, she told them every little detail she'd managed to wheedle out of the inspector.

"You don't think the body they found is Mary, do you?" Betsy's eyes were as big as saucers.

"It's possible. But whoever the victim is, I hope you understand what this means."

"It means we've got two mysteries to solve." Smythe grinned wickedly. "Blimey, it's either feast or famine around 'ere. When are we going to 'ave time to get our work done? I can't neglect them horses forever." Smythe was absolutely devoted to the inspector's two horses, Bow and Arrow.

"Leave off with you, Smythe," Betsy said. "We'll have plenty of time for everythin'." She grinned at the footman. "Except for poor Wiggins here. He might have to cut back on his courtin' some."

"I'm not courtin'," Wiggins said indignantly.

"Course he's not courtin'," Mrs. Goodge teased. "He's pinin'. There's a difference, you know. That pretty little maid from up the road hasn't looked his way once. She struts by with her nose in the air while the poor lad worships her from behind the drawing-room curtains."

"I never," Wiggins yelped. He blushed a bright pink. "I was washin' them windows. Besides, Sarah Trippet isn't my sort of girl at all. She's too short."

"Maybe that's why she's always walkin' about with her nose in the air," Smythe suggested. "She wants to look taller."

Betsy and Mrs. Goodge both laughed. Wiggins's infatuations were legendary.

• • •

Inspector Witherspoon's day was going from bad to worse. He stood over the trench where the body had been buried and shook his head. "Are you absolutely certain, Barnes?"

"Absolutely, sir," Constable Barnes said. "These houses were vacant for months before they got around to tearing them down. The family that lived here was long gone before that body was buried. And you heard the police surgeon. He's fairly sure that with the amount of decomposition, the girl'd only been here for no more than two months. The folks that lived here has been gone for four." He turned his head, frowning at the high wall on the other side of Magpie Lane. "For that matter, so's everyone else. That brewery's been abandoned for almost a year now. We'll not be having any witnesses on this one, sir."

"Drat." Witherspoon glared at the one remaining house on the road. "Why haven't they torn that one down yet?"

"They forgot."

"They what!"

"They forgot it," Barnes explained. "According to the clerk at Wildworth's, that's the property company that owns this land, they forgot there was one house left to be demolished. But that's a bit of luck for us, sir. Mr. Raines, the shopkeeper on the main road, claims there's an old man who dosses down in that house. If we can find him, he might be able to help us with our inquiries."

"Excellent, Barnes. Get some men on it right away." Witherspoon started toward the house.

"Yes, sir. Where are you going, sir?" Barnes called.

"To search that house," Witherspoon replied. "We've already searched this area, and we haven't come up with a thing."

"But, sir. The men have already gone through it. They found nothing but the usual rubbish. Why are you going to do it again?"

Witherspoon hated to admit it was because he couldn't think of anything else to do. "One never knows, Barnes," he called out briskly. "Perhaps I'll spot something the chaps have overlooked."

Mrs. Jeffries waited patiently at the top of the stairs for the rag-and-bone man to finish his tea. She didn't want to intrude on Mrs. Goodge when she was pumping one of her prime sources for information. There was a regular stream of visitors to the kitchen at Upper Edmonton Gardens. Delivery boys, chimney sweeps, carpenters, and last week, there'd even been a man from the gas works chatting with Mrs. Goodge as if they were old friends. But Mrs. Jeffries didn't mind. Mrs. Goodge was quite good at prying every tidbit of gossip out of those that passed through her kitchen.

Mrs. Jeffries had no doubt that right at this very moment, the cook was working furiously to find out anything she could about the Lutterbanks and the Everdenes. She sighed and leaned against the banister. Such a pity, really. So many in the upper classes failed to notice that many servants were diligent, perceptive and oftentimes highly intelligent human beings. Sad really, but so many of the wealthy were most indiscreet in both word and deed in front of those they considered beneath them. But then again, Mrs. Jeffries concluded, if they actually treated servants and working people like human beings, no doubt she and the household would find helping the inspector a great deal more difficult. Mrs. Jeffries supposed one could see that as the silver lining around the dark cloud that society cast on most of the city's population. It wasn't much of a comfort, but she decided it would have to do. The world was changing, that was for sure. But a fair and equitable way of life for all people certainly wouldn't happen in her lifetime. Still, she had great hopes that it would happen eventually.

She heard Mrs. Goodge say "Cheerio, ducks" to the rag-and-bone man and then the sound of the kitchen door closing. Mrs. Jeffries flew down the stairs and into the kitchen.

Neither of the women wasted any time on preliminaries.

"I've gotten an interesting bit of gossip about the Everdenes." Mrs. Goodge smiled triumphantly.

Mrs. Jeffries knew better than to ask the cook for her source. It could have been the rag-and-bone man that had just left, or it could have been any one of half a dozen other people. Mrs. Goodge was nothing if not thorough. But the housekeeper was disappointed. She'd been hoping for a bit of information about the Lutterbanks. "Indeed. How very enterprising of you, Mrs. Goodge."

"There's tea on the table, Mrs. Jeffries." Mrs. Goodge waved a hand at the pot and moved her large bulk toward a chair. "If you'll pour us a cup, I'll tell you everything."

"It will be my pleasure." She sat down and poured out two cups of the steaming brew. Handing one to the cook, she gazed at her expectantly.

"Well, it seems the Everdenes are from an old Yorkshire family. But there's only the reverend and his daughter left. Their branch never had much money until recently, when the girl inherited a packet from a distant relative. And a good thing it was too. But that's not the interestin' bit." Mrs. Goodge paused and took a quick sip of tea.

Mrs. Jeffries curbed her impatience. It did no good to try and hurry the woman along. She would have her moment of glory.

"The Reverend Everdene left his last congregation under a cloud." The cook smiled knowingly. "And us bein' a bit more worldly than most, I reckon's you can guess just what kind of a cloud I'm referrin' to."

Mrs. Jeffries could. "Choirboys or young women?"

Mrs. Goodge pretended to look scandalized. Then her broad face broke into a grin. "Young women. According to what I've heard, he used to limit his attentions to servants. But he made a mistake with the last one, and his hands got a bit too free with the daughter of the local magistrate. Naturally the church tried to hush up the scandal. But it ended with the Reverend Everdene out of Yorkshire and supposedly retired." She broke off and cackled with laughter. "It's a nice piece of luck his daughter inherited all that money. He didn't get another parish."

"Hmm," Mrs. Jeffries said thoughtfully. "That may explain why Mary Sparks left the Everdene house so precipitously. If the reverend tried . . . well, anything, she may have felt justified in leaving her post without notice. If, of course, she was there in the first place."

"Humph. The old goat should be locked up. And him with a daughter too. He ought to know better." Mrs. Goodge pursed her lips. "Disgusting. I feel sorry for the daughter, but at least she'll be gone soon. She's engaged to be married."

"But that still leaves us in the dark," Mrs. Jeffries said thoughtfully. "We still don't know for sure if Mary was ever at the Everdene house."

"True. But if she was, we've at least got an idea of what made her leave so quickly. The old fool probably tried to start pawin' at her the minute she got there."

"That's possible. I suppose the next step is to find out if Mary did or did not arrive at the Everdene house at all." Mrs. Jeffries cocked her head to one side. "Mrs. Goodge," she said thoughtfully. "If you were a young woman in genuine fear of being ravished, what would you do?"

"Do?" The cook snorted. "I'd pack me things and get out of that house. And I'd be quick about it too."

"But we know Mary hadn't much money. If she were frightened and desperate, where would she go?"

"I'd go to the one person who'd shown me a bit of kindness," Mrs. Goodge said promptly.

"Luty Belle Crookshank." Mrs. Jeffries shook her head. "But Luty Belle was in Venice and the house was locked up."

"There's ways of gettin' into locked houses. There's ways of gettin' into locked gardens too. Remember, it were still early September. Even if Mary couldn't get into Luty's house for shelter, she'd probably feel safer sleepin' in the communal gardens than she would walkin' the streets. And the Everdene house is in Putney. It's not close, but it inn't that far neither."

"Do you think she would have walked?" Mrs. Jeffries sipped her tea.

"No. London streets are dangerous. If she'd had any money at all, she'd have taken a hansom."

"I think you're right. And I think I'd better go have a nice little chat with Garrett McGraw."

"The gardening boy?" Mrs. Goodge looked puzzled. "Why?"

"Because Mary knew that Luty was already gone. The only other friend she had was Garrett. If she crept back to Knightsbridge and hid in those gardens, it was for one reason and one reason only. She thought she could get help from someone."

"But we don't know that she did any of that."

"No, but I've got to start somewhere." Mrs. Jeffries rose to her feet. "And in all fairness, I must tell Luty Belle about the body in Magpie Lane."

CHAPTER 3

Luty Belle was pacing the drawing room when Mrs. Jeffries arrived. "Mornin', Hepzibah," she said. She gestured toward the settee, indicating that her guest was to sit down. "I've been expectin' you."

"But you only came to see us yesterday," Mrs. Jeffries exclaimed as she settled herself comfortably on the plush velvet cushions. "Surely you don't imagine we've found Mary so quickly."

"Course not. But I knowed you'd have found somethin' out by now." Luty sank wearily into a seat next to the settee, her bright orange skirts clashing horribly with the deep red of the overstuffed wing chair. "And you bein' the kind of woman you are, I knowed you wouldn't waste any time tellin' me what you've learned."

Mrs. Jeffries could see she was very worried. There was a decided slump to her shoulders and deepening lines of worry around her black eyes and thin lips.

"We've learned several interesting things," Mrs. Jeffries began briskly.

Luty's face brightened. "I knowed I could count on you," she said earnestly. "I knowed you'd come up with something!"

"First of all, we've learned that Mary came back here the day she was supposed to have gone to the Everdenes. She was seen in the gardens on the evening of the tenth. A witness saw her get into a hansom cab."

"But that don't make no sense," Luty said. "Why'd she come back here after she'd gone to all that trouble to git that danged job?"

"We're not sure. Are you sure that your butler's information is correct? Are you absolutely certain he actually went to the Everdenes' home and inquired after Mary?"

"Course I'm sure. Hatchet's got no reason to lie. He might be an old stuffed shirt, but he does what I tells him. If he says he went to there, then he did." Luty shook her head. "And they told him that Mary had come that day, worked the one evenin' and then left."

"Hmm, yes. Then obviously, either we have a case of mistaken identity here or someone is not telling the truth."

"Well, I know it ain't Hatchet," Luty said. "Why'd you think Mary come back? She was mighty anxious to git away from here. Kinda give me the idea she wanted to put plenty of distance between herself and the Lutterbanks."

"She may have had equally good reason for wanting to put some distance between herself and the Everdenes," Mrs. Jeffries said. "We don't know that she didn't go there and then decide to leave. There are some that say that the Reverend Everdene isn't an honorable man."

Luty's lips curled in disgust. "Couldn't keep his hands to himself, eh? Mary wouldn't put up with bein' pawed by the likes of Andrew Lutterbank, I don't reckon she'd put up with it from some preacher either. That might explain why she hightailed it back here. Maybe she was hopin' I hadn't left yet."

"Did she know what time you were leaving?"

"Yup. All the servants except Hatchet left right after breakfast. Mary was still here then, but she knew I were fixin' to be on the noon train. She left at nine o'clock, after she'd helped me do a bit o' packin', and Hatchet and I left for the station about eleven-fifteen."

"Is it possible she came back, hoping to get into the house and stay here until you returned?" Mrs. Jeffries asked.

"Don't reckon so," Luty said slowly. "Mary helped Hatchet and me lock this place up tighter than a floozie's corset early that mornin'. She'd a had to break out a window or knock down a door to git in, and I knowed she wouldn't do somethin' like that no matter how desperate she was."

"Do you think she came back to get help from Garrett McGraw?"

"Maybe," Luty said doubtfully. "Like I told ya yesterday, Garrett was right sweet on Mary. But I'm purty sure that Mary has an understandin' with Mark McGraw. Too bad Mark's at sea. He'd a made danged sure that no one was botherin' the girl. But he ain't even due back in the country for another week or two, so he couldn't a taken Mary in. And I don't rightly see why she'd come to git help from Garrett. Ain't nothin' he could do."

"Perhaps he sent her to his home?" Mrs. Jeffries suggested. "The witness said Garrett put her into a hansom cab."

"Nah," Luty said. "The McGraws are as poor as church mice. Mark sends money home whenever he can, but it don't go very far when you've got seven mouths to feed. Mr. McGraw was hurt in a bad accident a couple of years ago and ain't worked since, so they's in a bad way. Garrett knows how hard life is for his family. He wouldn't be sendin' Mary there for them to feed and house." She broke off and stared morosely at the far wall for a few seconds. Then she added, "It don't look good, does it, Hepzibah?"

"It looks better than it did yesterday," Mrs. Jeffries replied. "At least we're beginning to put together Mary's movements. Smythe is trying to track down the driver of the hansom that picked Mary up, and Betsy is trying to trace her friend, Cassie Yates."

"Why you lookin' for her?" Luty snorted. "Cassie ain't the kind to be takin' someone in."

"Yes, but you did say she and Mary were friends. We're hoping Cassie Yates may have some idea of where Mary could have gone."

"I don't think so. The only reason they was friends was because Mary felt sorry for her. Cassie was such a cat the other girls couldn't stand her."

"But we're assuming that Mary was desperate," Mrs. Jeffries explained. "We've heard that Cassie may have gotten married recently. If she's a respectable married woman, there's a chance that Mary may have gone to her to stay until you returned from Venice."

"Cassie Yates a respectable married woman!" Luty laughed. "That's danged unlikely."

"Whyever not?"

"I don't know what kinda tales you been hearin', but Cassie Yates ain't the type o' woman to tie herself down to jest one man. Why at least twice, I've seen the little tart with men, and they wasn't jest talkin' neither, if'n you take my meanin'. One time she was letting Andrew Lutterbank kiss her, and the other time she was behind that big old oak tree with a blond-haired young feller, and they wasn't havin' tea together. Besides, if'n Mary went to Cassie, then why ain't I heard from her?" Luty jumped to her feet and began to pace the room. "Even if'n Cassie'd take her in, and that's a big if'n, believe me, that don't explain why she didn't contact me when I come back. Mary knew when I was comin' home."

Mrs. Jeffries lowered her gaze and stared at the scrolling pattern of acanthus leaves in the Brussels-weave carpet beneath her feet. She had no choice. She had to tell Luty about the body. Despite her assurances to Betsy and the others, there was a chance that the corpse was the remains of Mary Sparks. Luty had a right to know.

"Luty," she said softly, "there's something else I must tell you."

Luty stopped pacing. "What?"

"There's been a murder. They've found the body of a young woman. She was wearing a dark blue dress. Inspector Witherspoon says the girl's been dead several months."

The elderly woman stiffened and seemed to brace herself. "Do you think it's Mary?"

"No. But I had to tell you. The possibility does exist. The timing is too coincidental to ignore. Besides that, the deceased had dark blond hair and a silver brooch was pinned on the lapel of her dress."

For a moment, Mrs. Jeffries thought Luty might faint. She watched her close her eyes, sway gently to one side, clutch the back of the chair and then take one deep, shuddering breath. "Are you all right?" she asked in alarm.

Luty's eyes flew open and she straightened her spine. Ignoring Mrs. Jeffries's question, she hurried to the door and flung it open. "Hatchet," she bellowed. "Bring me my hat and cane."

Puzzled, Mrs. Jeffries leapt to her feet. "What are you doing?"

"What does it look like? I'm gittin' ready to go out." Luty took her hat and cane from the tall, white-haired butler, nodded her thanks and jammed the hat on her head. "They've got the body somewhere, don't they?"

"Yes, of course they do," Mrs. Jeffries replied. "Oh, no. You're not going to . . ."

"Yup. I wanta see it. I wanta see with my own eyes if it's Mary."

"But, Luty," Mrs. Jeffries protested. "According to Inspector Witherspoon, the body is so . . . so . . ."

"Rotten."

"Decomposed." She smiled gently, trying to think of a way to dissaude her friend from such a gruesome undertaking. There was no point in going to identify the remains if they were in no state to be identified. Luty would only upset herself. "The inspector says it's impossible to tell who the woman was. You won't be able to tell whether that unfortunate young girl was Mary or not. For goodness' sakes, Luty, you'll only distress yourself."

"Fiddlesticks, Hepzibah." Luty scurried to the door. "I've seen plenty o' corpses in my time, and ain't none of them ever sent me into a faint or caused a hissy fit. Now, come on, let's git this done. The sooner's we git there, the quicker we'll know that it ain't Mary."

Mrs. Jeffries hurried after her.

Hatchet, who Mrs. Jeffries assumed was used to his employer's eccentricities, had already hailed them a passing hansom by the time they stepped outside.

Mrs. Jeffries instructed the driver to take them to Scotland Yard.

"You will be careful, madam," the butler said as he helped them into the cab.

"Ain't I always, Hatchet."

"Not that I've noticed, madam," he informed her as he slammed the door shut and nodded to the driver.

Luty settled back in the seat and grabbed the handhold to steady herself as the driver cracked the whip and the horses trotted forward. "Where'd they find the body?"

"In the cellar of a torn-down house," Mrs. Jeffries answered. "On Magpie Lane. That's in Clapham. All the houses had been torn down to make way for a new road, but then they changed their minds. They ended up digging instead, supposedly for one of those new underground railway lines."

Luty made a face. "Horrid things. Trains is bad enough. Fancy those fools thinkin' that anyone would want to ride one that went underground." She faltered and her brows came together. "Magpie Lane. Now, where have I heard that name before?"

"You've heard of it?" Mrs. Jeffries asked. "When? Where?"

"Offhand, I don't rightly remember. Give me a minute now."

"Think, Luty. It may be important."

"Why? I've heard of lots of places."

"Because this street wasn't occupied by gentry or anyone else you're likely to have met. The homes that were torn down were all small houses let by the month. If you've heard the name before, there's a good chance that Mary had too."

"Nells bells," Luty said disgustedly. "It went plum out of my head." She held up her hand. "Don't worry, Hepzibah, it'll come back to me. Just give me a few minutes to clear my mind." She turned and stared out the open window. Luty remained silent as the cab rumbled up Knightsbridge and past Hyde Park. Mrs. Jeffries was deep in thought as well. The hansom rolled on through the busy streets, and she jumped when Luty finally spoke.

"It were at that silly garden party last August."

"What was?"

"Magpie Lane. That's where I heard the name. Emery Clements was complainin' about it." She gave another inelegant snort. "He kept goin' on about how his solicitors had evicted the tenants too early. Said the houses was all sittin' empty when they could have been collectin' rent."

"Who gave the party? Who was there?" Mrs. Jeffries noticed they were drawing close to Charing Cross. They'd be at the Yard soon.

Luty rubbed her chin. "The Lutterbanks. They was the one's giving it. That caused some talk too, seeing as how they was all supposed to still be in mourning for old Angus Lutterbank. He'd only died the month before. Not that I blame them fer not wastin' too much time grievin' for Angus—he was a nasty ol' fool. Had so few friends and neighbors willin' to come to his funeral service that the Lutterbanks made all their servants go jest to fill up the pews." She snorted. "But the place still looked half-empty."

"Please, Luty," Mrs. Jeffries interrupted. "About the party?"

"Oh, sorry. Anyways, like I was sayin', they had this here party and invited most of us that lives round the gardens, but they're such miserable people, most folks didn't come. Let's see. The Lutterbanks were all there, including Andrew and his sister, Fiona. I remember because Andrew kept gabbing at the maid serving the sandwiches. And they had two of their friends with them. Emery Clements, he was the one doin' all the braggin', and another young feller named Malcolm Farnsworth. There was others there too, but I'll have to think awhile to remember their names."

"Was Mary there?"

"No. Mary was never anywhere near Andrew if she could help it."

Mrs. Jeffries leaned forward as the cab drew to a halt. "Was anyone else nearby? Any other neighbors or servants?"

The cab stopped, and the driver leapt down and helped the ladies out. Luty handed the man a few coins, ignored his effusive thanks for the generous tip she'd included and grabbed Mrs. Jeffries's arm.

"Garrett was weeding one of the flower beds," Luty continued thoughtfully. "And one of the other gardeners was plantin' some early bulbs. I recall that because Mrs. Lutterbank come out of her stupor long enough to yell at the boys to go work somewhere else. Well, I can tell you I told her quick enough that those boys were workin' where they'd been told to work and if'n she didn't like it, to take it up with the head gardener and not be shoutin' at them like they was dirt under her feet."

"Yes, yes, I'm sure you did. Quickly, before we reach the inspector's office, tell me everything you heard about Magpie Lane."

"All I heard Clements talk about was them houses bein' empty and him losin' his precious rent," Luty replied as they climbed the steps and went inside.

"So every one of the people at the party knew that there were empty houses on Magpie Lane."

"Yup. A body would've had to be deaf not to hear Clements's voice. He's louder than a mule with a burr under its blanket."

Mrs. Jeffries nodded and suddenly remembered something else. "Why would Garrett be nervous to talk about Mary Sparks?"

Luty stopped abruptly. The uniformed constable behind the counter at the far end of the room stared at them curiously.

"I don't rightly know," Luty replied slowly. "There shouldn't be any reason for him to shy away from talking about Mary. I could see him not wanting to talk about Cassie Yates, but exceptin' for him bein' a bit sweet on Mary, there ain't no reason for him to not want to talk about her."

The constable came out from behind his desk and headed in their direction. Mrs. Jeffries ignored him. "Why would Garrett not want to talk about Cassie Yates?"

"Because that time she was bein' pawed behind the oak tree, well, Garrett happened to see it. He blushed so hard I was scared he was goin' to pass out from it." She cackled. "And we weren't the only ones to see her carryin' on either. Andrew Lutterbank was watching the whole thing from one of the upstairs windows. Come to think of it, it was right after that that Cassie left the Lutterbanks and went to work in that shop."

Mrs. Jeffries turned to the approaching constable and gave him a dazzling smile. "Good morning, Constable. Could you direct us to Inspector Witherspoon?"

The mortuary at St. Thomas's Hospital was one of Inspector Witherspoon's least favorite places. As he escorted the two ladies into the huge room, he tried not to wince. He loathed the peculiar trick of lighting that cast a faint, greenish glow on everything. Every time he set foot in this horrid place, he could feel the blood rushing from his head to his toes. He hoped he wouldn't become ill. It would simply be too embarrassing if he were to disgrace himself in front of Mrs. Crookshank and his own housekeeper. He glanced at them out of the corner of his eye.

Both women were looking around the room with avid curiosity.

Dr. Potter, who'd done the postmortem on the body found in Magpie Lane, came forward to greet them. He was holding in his hand a dark red, wet object the size of a potato. Witherspoon cringed as the man paused next to a table and dropped the ominous-looking thing in a jar of liquid.

"What are you doing here, Inspector?" Dr. Potter asked, smiling politely at the two ladies. "I didn't expect to see you until the coroner's inquest."

"Good day, Doctor." Witherspoon tried not to breathe too deeply. The smell was appalling. "I know the inquest isn't until day after tomorrow.

But as we already know we're dealing with a murder, we're not waiting until it's official before we start investigating."

Potter's bushy black eyebrows rose. He was a heavyset man of medium height, with thick black hair and a florid complexion.

"Allow me to introduce you to these ladies." The inspector gestured to Luty. "This is Mrs. Crookshank, and this is my housekeeper, Mrs. Jeffries."

Dr. Potter nodded politely.

"Mrs. Crookshank would like to view the er . . . deceased," Witherspoon explained hastily. "She may be able to help in the identification."

The doctor looked surprised. He turned to Luty Belle. "You want to view the body, madam?"

"Unless you know of any other way I kin tell if'n it's Mary Sparks, I reckon I'll have to." Luty gave him a long, hard stare.

"Mary Sparks?" the doctor repeated.

"That's a young friend of Mrs. Crookshank's," the inspector said. "She'd like to insure that the body isn't that of Miss Sparks."

"But, madam," Potter protested, "I doubt you'll be able to tell. The remains are in an advanced state of decomposition."

"Why don't you let me be the judge of that? If'n it's Mary, I'll be able to tell, all right."

Dr. Potter wasn't used to having his judgment questioned. He drew himself up to his full height and fixed Luty with an intimidating glare. "In my opinion, madam, I hardly think that's likely. The girl's own mother wouldn't be able to identify her. If you'd like, you may look at the victim's clothing. That may help tell who she was."

"Dang and blast, man," Luty cried in exasperation. "This is no time for social niceties. I want to look at that corpse. It may be someone I know. I ain't squeamish and I ain't gonna faint, if'n that's what you're frettin' on."

"Well, really," Dr. Potter said huffily. He turned and gestured toward one of his assistants, and the young man had to hastily wipe a wide smile off his face. "If you insist, Dr. Bosworth will take you into the morgue. Good day to you."

"Oh, dear," Witherspoon murmured. "I believe he's offended."

"Stupid fool," Luty muttered. She marched behind the assistant like the Queen of Sheba. "Men! What did the man expect me to do, faint or have a fit? It's a wonder the police ever git anyone identified. I've seen worse than anything they have here."

As they walked down a long hallway, Luty kept up a long litany of various horrors and dead people she'd dealt with in her long life. By the time

Bosworth ushered them through the door and into the morgue, the poor young man's eyes were bulging. Mrs. Jeffries noticed that Inspector Witherspoon had gone pale. Wanting to spare the doctor and the inspector further assaults on their sensibilities, she tugged on Luty's arm. "Luty, please. You're making me quite ill."

Luty broke off and stared at her suspiciously. She knew Hepzibah Jeffries wouldn't turn a hair over some of the things she'd been tellin'. Then she glanced at the inspector and the young physician. Seeing they were both pale, she nodded.

Bosworth gestured for them to come inside. They stepped into the dim, eerily quiet room. There were three tables, and on the center one a shroud-draped corpse rested in silent dignity. As they walked farther into the room, Mrs. Jeffries realized that the temperature was very low. She wondered how the hospital kept this room so cold.

"It's not a very pretty sight," Bosworth warned as he drew back the covering. Mrs. Jeffries steeled herself, Luty took a deep breath, and Inspector Witherspoon stepped back a pace.

The face was unrecognizable. Black, bloated and without color, it could be identified as female only by the long blond hair.

"Humph," Luty snorted. "The hair is the right color, but I can't tell anything from looking at the face."

Mrs. Jeffries nodded. "Did Mary have any distinguishing marks or scars upon her person?"

"Not that I know of." Luty gestured for Bosworth to lower the covering. She turned to the inspector. "Where's her clothes?"

Witherspoon, who was trying not to look at anything except the floor, didn't realize that Mrs. Crookshank was addressing him.

"He gone deaf or something?" Luty asked irritably when the inspector didn't reply.

"Inspector Witherspoon," Mrs. Jeffries said gently, "Luty would like to see the victim's clothing."

"Huh. Oh. Certainly. Uh, I believe they're . . ." He broke off because he didn't quite remember where they were.

Bosworth finally spoke up. "They're still here. The police haven't taken them into evidence yet. We don't like to let them go until after the coroner's verdict."

Witherspoon, who'd never heard of such nonsense, shook his head. "All right, then. Go and get them. We'll wait, uh, well, out in the hallway."

They moved into the corridor, and Witherspoon took several long, deep breaths of air. After a few seconds he began to feel better.

"How come they took her clothes off anyways?" Luty wanted to know. "Seems downright disrespectful if you ask me."

"Dear lady, nothing could be further from the truth," Witherspoon assured her quickly. "But the doctors can hardly determine causes of death if they can't examine the victims, and the only way to do that is to undress them."

"Here's the victim's things, sir," Bosworth said, handing a cloth bag to Inspector Witherspoon.

Gritting his teeth, the inspector put the bag on the floor and reached inside. He pulled out a tattered, dark blue dress with a silver brooch pinned to the lapel.

Luty Belle gasped. Then she reached over and lifted the right sleeve. A small moan of distress escaped her as she studied the inside lining of the wrist.

"I take it the dress is familiar to you?" Mrs. Jeffries said gently. Her heart went out to Luty. One look at the woman's face was enough to assure her that the dress had, indeed, belonged to Mary Sparks.

Numbly, Luty nodded her head.

"But how can you be sure?" Mrs. Jeffries persisted.

Luty didn't answer right away. Her throat worked convulsively for a moment, and her breathing was harsh. "Because I told her to sew this here little pocket into the lining." She held the sleeve toward Mrs. Jeffries. "Mary didn't like to get out and about much. She was always scared of pickpockets and the like. Last summer, I showed her this old trick from when me and Archie used to hang about the Barbary Coast." She blinked furiously to hold back the tears. "See, the pocket's just big enough to hold a few coins. But Mary never carried more than a shilling or two."

Witherspoon knew he should be relieved now that the body had been positively identified. But he felt awful. Poor Mrs. Crookshank, despite her eccentricities, was dreadfully upset.

"There, there," he said. "Don't distress yourself, madam. You have my assurances that Scotland Yard will find the evil perpetrator that foully ended this young woman's life."

Luty gave him an incredulous stare. Mrs. Jeffries quickly said, "Of course, Inspector. We have every confidence in the police."

Witherspoon's chest expanded. Luty snorted.

"Now," the inspector said. "Why don't you take Mrs. Crookshank outside for a bit of fresh air? I wouldn't want to question her until she's quite recovered herself."

"I ain't lost," Luty interrupted, "and you can ask me any questions you want. There's only one thing that's important now and that's findin' Mary's killer."

"Are you going to keep the bag of clothes?" Bosworth asked. He was staring at Luty Belle in morbid fascination.

"Yes, yes. Of course I'm going to keep the clothes. This is evidence, man." Witherspoon made a mental note to speak to Constable Barnes. The deceased's effects should have been taken into evidence at once.

"Luty," Mrs. Jeffries said. "Can you identify the pin?" She pointed to the silver brooch.

"Yup. It's Fiona Lutterbank's all right, but I can't figure how it comes to be on Mary's dress." She pursed her lips. "I knows Mary didn't steal it."

"Are you saying this brooch is stolen property?" Witherspoon asked curiously.

"According to Fiona Lutterbank it is." Luty shrugged her shoulders. "But I wouldn't believe her if she told me that dogs have fleas and cows eat grass. Girl's a god-awful liar. She probably gave Mary the pin and then told her father Mary stole it."

"Oh, dear," Witherspoon said. He didn't much like the way this was going. Mrs. Crookshank didn't seem the type of lady who would stand back and let the police handle this murder in a tactful and diplomatic manner. He certainly hoped she wouldn't go about making wild accusations and calling people liars. That could make things most awkward. Most awkward, indeed.

"Are you absolutely certain that Mary didn't steal that brooch?" Mrs. Jeffries wasn't sure why she was pressing the point, but her instincts were telling her it was important.

"Hepzibah. I'm a very old woman, and I've spent my life learning to judge a person's character. That's the only way you survive in a wild place like Colorado." Luty crossed her arms over her chest. "And I'm tellin' you, that girl was no thief. She'd have starved to death before she ever took something that didn't belong to her. I don't know whys that danged pin is on her dress, but I do know that however it got there, Mary Sparks didn't steal it."

"But nonetheless, the pin is there."

"Bosworth," Dr. Potter shouted from the other end of the corrider. "Would you mind getting back to work?"

Bosworth started and then reluctantly excused himself. He continued to look longingly at the three of them as he trudged off.

"Now, now, Mrs. Crookshank," Witherspoon said. "I don't question that you're an excellent judge of character, but sometimes even the best of us are fooled."

The inspector refused to let go of the idea that Mary Sparks was a thief. Well, it would explain so very much. Yes, yes, he could see it now. No doubt Mary Sparks was part of a ring of thieves. Masquerading as a housemaid, she obtained positions in fine homes and took to stealing. There was probably a man in the situation as well, he decided. Someone she passed the goods on to. No doubt he'd stabbed her when she demanded a bigger share of the booty.

Luty glared at him. "Speak for yurself, Inspector. I ain't wrong about Mary. And if'n you're fixin' to pass her murder off as a fallin' out among thieves, you'd best just think agin."

For one horrid moment, Witherspoon thought she'd read his mind. "No, no," he assured her quickly. "I'm sure Miss Sparks was of the very finest character. You have my solemn word, madam. Regardless of the circumstances under which the unfortunate young woman was slain, I won't rest until her killer is brought to justice."

"Humph."

While Inspector Witherspoon and Luty Belle were sparring with each other, Mrs. Jeffries was thinking hard. Her mind went over and over every scrap of information she and the other servants had come across. Luty was certain Mary wasn't a thief. So why was a stolen brooch pinned on the lapel of her dress? But perhaps Luty wasn't such a good judge of character after all. She slanted the woman a quick, assessing glance.

Luty had launched into a recitation of some of Scotland Yard's more spectacular failures. The inspector, much to his credit, was vigorously trying to defend the police force without offending his opponent.

Mrs. Jeffries studied Luty's sharp, shrewd eyes. The American woman hadn't carved out a fortune in the ruthless wilds of the American West by being a fool. Therefore, she was inclined to accept Luty's assertion that Mary wasn't a thief. But if Mary hadn't stolen the brooch, who had? The murderer? And why pin it on her dress after she'd been killed?

"Inspector," she said quickly, interrupting Luty's tirade about the lack of gas-lighting fixtures in the poorer sections of London. "Why don't you show Mrs. Crookshank the betrothal ring? Perhaps she'll know something about it."

"Huh." Witherspoon blinked in surprise. "Oh, yes." He reached into the bag and fumbled for a moment before withdrawing the gold chain and the ring dangling on its end. "Have you ever seen this, madam?"

Luty reached for the ring. She frowned as she studied it.

"Do you think Mark McGraw gave it to her?" Mrs. Jeffries asked. "You did say you thought the two of them had an understanding."

"I've never seen it before," Luty replied, handing it back to the inspector. "But it don't look like anything Mark would have given her. It's awfully fancy."

"What about the shoes?" Mrs. Jeffries said. "Perhaps you'd better show them to Luty as well. She may be able to tell you where Mary is likely to have bought them."

Witherspoon dutifully dug into the bag once again and lifted out a pair of black high-topped shoes. Luty snatched them from his hand.

For several long minutes she stared at them. Then all of a sudden she started to smile. The smile turned into a chuckle, and the chuckle soon turned into a laugh. Within seconds, Luty was laughing so hard her whole body shook.

Witherspoon, thinking the woman had become so overwrought by the sight of Mary's shoes that she'd lost her mind, began to wring his hands. "Oh, dear. Please, Mrs. Crookshank. Do calm yourself."

He turned to Mrs. Jeffries. "I knew this would be too much for her. Please, can't you do something? She's having hysterics."

"She's not having hysterics, sir," Mrs. Jeffries replied. "She's laughing."

"I ain't never had hysterics in my life," Luty protested as she brought herself under control. "I was laughin' because this here pair of shoes is about the happiest news I've had in a month of Sundays."

"What are you saying, Luty?" Mrs. Jeffries stared at her friend curiously.

"I'm sayin' that that corpse I just looked at ain't who I thought it was."

"You mean, now you're saying that the deceased isn't Mary Sparks?" If Witherspoon hadn't been so confused, he'd have been depressed.

"It sure as shootin' ain't." Luty grinned. "I don't know who that poor woman is, but I know who she isn't. She ain't Mary Sparks."

Mrs. Jeffries tilted her chin to one side. "What leads you to that conclusion?"

Luty waved the pair of shoes under Witherspoon's nose. "These shoes. They ain't Mary's. These clodhoppers are big enough to fit a bear. Mary's feet are small and dainty. They ain't much bigger than a child's. I knows because I was going to give her a pair of my old slippers last year when Mark was home. He was plannin' on takin' her on an outin' to Richmond

Park. Now I've got right small feet for a woman my size, and my shoes looked like they was a couple of rowboats on Mary's tiny feet." She cackled with glee. "So that mean's that Mary's still alive."

"Well, if Mary Sparks isn't the woman in there," Witherspoon gestured toward the room they'd left earlier, "who is?"

CHAPTER 4

Luty was in high spirits all the way home. Mrs. Jeffries dropped her off in Knightsbridge and then proceeded on to Upper Edmonton Gardens. She'd changed her mind about having a talk with Garrett McGraw—there were a few more facts she needed before she tackled that duty.

As she'd expected, the household was gathered in the kitchen for the noon meal. Mrs. Jeffries decided to wait until she heard their various reports before telling them that Luty Belle was certain the body discovered in Magpie Lane wasn't Mary Sparks.

She paused in the doorway and studied their faces. Smythe was hunched over his plate like a disgraced dog, Wiggins was shoveling rolls into his mouth as if he hadn't eaten in days, Betsy was smirking, and Mrs. Goodge was staring out the window with the intense concentration of a cat watching a sparrow.

Calling out a cheerful greeting, Mrs. Jeffries crossed the room and took her seat at the head of the table. "And how is everyone today?" she asked kindly, feeling that no matter how important the case, the amenities should be observed. Wiggins, Mrs. Goodge and Betsy assured her they were all just fine. Smythe grunted.

Betsy tossed her blond curls over her shoulder and shot the coachman a triumphant glance. "Best let me go first this time," she chirped happily. "I expect I've got a bit more to tell than the others."

Smythe gave her a quick glare but said nothing.

Obviously Betsy's inquiries had gone better than anyone elses, Mrs. Jeffries thought as she filled up her plate. And the pretty maid wasn't being tactful about the fact either. But then she really didn't blame her. Smythe was hardly reticent about lording it over Betsy when he stumbled onto a particularly good bit of information.

"All right, Betsy," she agreed. "Do tell us what you've learned."

"It was ever so interestin'," the girl responded eagerly. "I went back to the shop and found out where Cassie Yates used to live."

"Used to live?" Mrs. Goodge interrupted. "You mean she's not there now?"

Betsy shook her head. "Her landlady told me she left two months ago. She had rooms in Morton Street, off the Brompton Road." She wrinkled her nose. "It wasn't a very nice place, but it's respectable. The landlady, Mrs. Rose, claimed she didn't allow men up in the rooms or any other carryin's on. Said that Cassie didn't cause any trouble. She paid her rent on time and kept a civil tongue in her head."

Mrs. Jeffries was delighted that Betsy was taking care to pronounce her *h*s properly today. "Did the landlady say where Cassie had gone?"

"She doesn't know."

"Oh, dear," Mrs. Jeffries murmured. There was a sinking sensation in the pit of her stomach. She'd been so hoping that Betsy would report that Cassie Yates was alive and well. An image of the body she'd seen that morning lying in the mortuary flashed through her mind. "That's rather bad news. I was hoping to hear that Miss Yates was now a respectable married woman." Or even an unrespectable one living in sin, she silently added.

"But she is," Betsy exclaimed. "That's why Mrs. Rose don't know where she's livin' now. She got married. Cassie weren't just braggin' when she claimed one of the men she'd been seein' actually wanted to wed her."

Wiggins reached for another bread roll. "Did you find out 'is name?"

"No, more's the pity. The only thing Mrs. Rose could tell me was that he was tall and fair-haired. She claims she didn't get much of a look at his face—he 'ad on a top 'at and a scarf. She thought it were right funny, but the feller claimed he 'ad a bad cold and needed to keep the chill out." She broke off and laughed. "But Mrs. Rose says he was a real gentleman. He dressed nice and carried himself well. He come and got all Cassie's things the day after they got married. Took 'em away in a hired carriage."

"I don't suppose you managed to find out what day the gentleman came for his wife's belongings, did you?" Mrs. Jeffries asked.

"Now, that's where I had a right bit of luck." Betsy said with a grin. "Mrs. Rose remembered because he come on her daughter's birthday. It were September 11th. She was right irritated with 'im because she had to leave off in the middle of the noon meal and let 'im into Cassie's room. He tipped her a 'alf a crown."

"Very good, Betsy," Mrs. Jeffries said. The more excited the girl became, the worse her pronunciation. But that was understandable. She'd learned a great deal in a very short time. "It's a pity Mrs. Rose wasn't able to give you a better description of the man."

"Yes, but like I said, all the woman saw of 'im was a bit of his 'air stickin' out from under his top hat . . . Oh yes, he had a funny hand too."

"Funny hand?" Mrs. Goodge repeated with relish. "What'd you mean by that? Did he have webbed fingers? I knew a girl that had a hand like that. Worked for Sir Richard Morton out Richmond way."

"It weren't webbed fingers," Betsy replied impatiently. "It might not be much of anythin' really. Mrs. Rose said she thinks the man had a crooked little finger, only she in't certain. She only had a quick look when he was handin' her the coin."

"Well, that's something at least." Mrs. Jeffries started to turn her attention to Smythe.

"But that's not all I've found out," Betsy protested. "The girls at the shop had plenty to say about Cassie too. Ellen Wickes, that's the one that seemed to be the best acquainted with her, says that Cassie quit her position a few days before she got married. Well, the manager was livid because Cassie was leavin' without givin' notice. He threw her out of the shop and told her never to come back. But Ellen claims she did come back."

Smythe finally looked up from his potatoes and beef. "Why?"

"To get the five shillings Ellen owed her. Ellen had been hopin' that Cassie had forgotten about the loan," Betsy explained quickly. "But she 'adn't, of course. Anyways, Ellen claims that Cassie showed up the day after she got her pay packet—that was on the mornin' of the tenth and demanded her money."

"What's so interestin' about that?" Smythe demanded. "All it tells us is that Cassie Yates wasn't one to forget who owed her money."

"If you'd just let me finish, you'd know." Betsy straightened her spine. "The money wasn't important. What's important is what happened when Ellen was tryin' to pay the woman. Ellen says she'd had to nip into the back room to get the coins, and when she come out, Cassie was runnin' out of the shop like the devil 'imself was on 'er heels. Ellen went to the door and saw Cassie chasing another girl around the corner. Well, whoever this girl was, she made Cassie forget all about the money. Ellen waited all day, but Cassie never come back."

Mrs. Jeffries frowned thoughtfully. "Did Ellen see the other girl? Would she be able to tell us what she looked like?"

"No." Betsy sighed. "I asked her. All she could remember was seeing a bit of dark blue skirt disappearin' around the buildin'. She said it looked right funny. Cassie was wearing a fancy pink dress that had a bustle as big as a bread basket. The skirt was so tight she could barely walk, let alone run. Ellen had a right good giggle over that, watching Cassie tryin' to chase this girl without lifting her skirts too high. Not that Cassie wasn't the type to lift her skirts now and again, according to what Ellen was tellin' me . . ." Betsy broke off and blushed as she realized everyone was leaning forward and hanging on her every word.

Mrs. Jeffries cleared her throat. "Yes. Thank you, Betsy. Smythe, would you like to speak next?"

"Not much to tell," the coachman muttered.

"I take it you weren't successful in tracking down the driver of the hansom?" Mrs. Jeffries suggested. Really, she thought, Smythe was being awfully childish today.

He raised his dark brown eyes and gave her a long, level stare. Then he grinned. "Successful? Well, I reckon that depends on 'ow ya look at it. I got a right earful of gossip about that funeral the Lutterbanks had a few months back. The blokes I was talkin' to had done the funeral drivin'. But none of them had picked up Mary Sparks on the night she disappeared."

"What'd you hear, then?" Mrs. Goodge leaned forward with an expression of avid interest on her broad face.

"Just that the family insisted all the drivers come inta the church for the service, paid 'em extra to do it, and the funny thing was, the only one doin' any cryin' at the funeral was one of the housemaids."

"Yes, yes," Mrs. Jeffries interrupted impatiently. "I'm quite certain that's all very interesting. However, we really must keep our minds on our current problem."

Smythe flushed guiltily. "Sorry. Like I was sayin', I ain't found the one that picked Mary up yet, but I will. One of the other drivers gave me the names of three men who were working the streets around the gardens that night. I've done talked to one of 'em, and he don't remember the lass, but I'm hopin' one of the other two will." He rubbed his chin. "Do you happen to know if Mary was pretty?"

Wiggins's eyes lit up.

"I'm assuming she must be," Mrs. Jeffries replied. "Garrett McGraw's infatuation and the fact that Luty has implied that Mary had to fight off the unwanted attentions of Andrew Lutterbank lead me to assume she must be a most attractive young woman."

"Good." Smythe leaned back in his chair and fixed Betsy with a cocky grin. "I like lookin' for pretty girls."

"Me too," Wiggins added.

Betsy and Mrs. Goodge both snorted, and even Mrs. Jeffries smiled before turning to the footman. "All right, Wiggins, it's your turn. Did you follow Garrett McGraw after he left the gardens yesterday evening?"

"Course I did. But it didn't do no good. He just went home."

"He didn't stop off anywhere?" Mrs. Jeffries prodded. She'd rather hoped that young Garrett would lead them to Mary. He was the last person known to have seen her and therefore their only real clue.

"He didn't stop," Wiggins answered. "He went 'ome. I hung around outside a bit, but the only one who come out was one of Garrett's little brothers."

Mrs. Jeffries nodded. She looked expectantly at Mrs. Goodge.

"Sorry," the cook said, "I ain't remembered anything about the Lutterbanks, but I've got me feelers out. Give me another day or two—I'll have a few bits and pieces by then."

"Very well," Mrs. Jeffries said. "I believe it's my turn now."

The others sensed the change in her tone. Everyone's expression sobered as they gave her their full attention.

"This morning I told Luty Belle about the murdered girl," Mrs. Jeffries began solemnly. "She insisted on going to the mortuary and viewing the body. It wasn't a chore I relished, but once Luty Belle Crookshank makes up her mind, there's no stopping her."

"Ugh, how awful," Betsy said sympathetically.

"Indeed, it wasn't very pleasant," Mrs. Jeffries agreed. "But you'll all be pleased to know that despite the distastefulness of the task, we learned something very important. Luty's sure the body isn't Mary Sparks."

"Thank the good Lord for that," Mrs. Goodge said.

"However, there is something else you should know." Mrs. Jeffries paused. "Whoever the girl was, she was wearing Mary's dress, and the brooch that Mary had been accused of stealing from the Lutterbanks was pinned on the lapel."

"Cor! Blimey, this is getting more confused by the minute." Smythe scowled. " 'Ow did this girl come to be wearin' Mary's clothes?"

"I don't know," Mrs. Jeffries replied earnestly. "But obviously the two cases are now connected."

Betsy grimaced. "Did you see the body?"

"Yes. It wasn't a pretty sight. Frankly, it was unrecognizable. Luty Belle only realized it couldn't be Mary when she looked at the shoes. They were much too large to have belonged to her."

"And didn't the inspector say they were new shoes?" Mrs. Goodge said thoughtfully, remembering the details the housekeeper had shared with them earlier.

Mrs. Jeffries gave her an approving smile. "Yes. And Mary Sparks had just lost her position. She'd hardly have gone out and bought a pair of new shoes. But Cassie Yates, on the other hand, was apparently not in the least concerned about making a living. She'd quit her position."

Wiggins looked up from his now-empty plate and said, "Do you think the dead girl is Cassie Yates?"

"I'm not sure. If Betsy's information is correct and Cassie got married, then it's highly unlikely she's the victim."

"Now, why would the dead girl be wearin' Mary's clothes?" Betsy mused. "And 'ow did she get them?"

"I don't know," Mrs. Jeffries said. "But we're going to find out."

"Hmmm? That's gonna be a bit 'ard. We'll need more luck than most is given to find out what 'appened to this one." Smythe crossed his massive arms over his chest. "Seems to me that all we know so far is that Mary Sparks got into a 'ansom and disappeared on the evening of the tenth. Supposedly, Cassie Yates got married that very same day, and an unknown woman wearin' Mary's clothes gets herself done in and buried in a cellar around at about this same time."

"What are you getting at, Smythe?" Mrs. Jeffries asked.

"I ain't sure. I just don't like the way this is startin' to look."

Betsy leaned forward on her elbows. "Course we don't know that the dead girl's got anythin' to do with either Mary or Cassie, but it's a bit too . . . too . . ." Searching for the correct word, she broke off.

"Coincidental," Smythe supplied. Betsy gave him an irritated frown.

Seeing another tiff brewing, Mrs. Jeffries hastily stepped into the discussion. "You're absolutely right, Smythe, it is too coincidental. The first order of business is for you to find that cab driver. It's imperative that we trace Mary's movements."

"Mary's movements?" Mrs. Goodge echoed. "Shouldn't we be lookin' for Cassie Yates too?"

"Of course," Mrs. Jeffries answered smoothly. "But finding Mary is our most important task. That's why Wiggins is going to keep Garrett McGraw under observation from the time he leaves the gardens tonight until he returns there in the morning."

"All night?" Wiggins wailed. "But it's cold at night."

"Stop frettin', boy," Smythe interjected. "I'll be along after the pubs close to relieve you."

"The pubs!" Betsy screeched. "You can't be goin' off for a drink when you're supposed to be findin' that driver."

"Of course he isn't going out to drink, Betsy," Mrs. Jeffries said. "I have no doubt that Smythe will find the driver we seek well before the pubs open." She looked at Smythe. "Right?"

"As usual, Mrs. J." He gave her a lazy grin and rose to his feet. "I'm goin' to the stables now." He started walking to the door and then suddenly stopped. "Do you want me to see if I can find out where the carriage that took Cassie Yates's things was hired from?"

Smythe knew every stable and livery in the city. Mrs. Jeffries was annoyed at herself for neglecting to think of that.

"Excellent idea." She beamed her approval. "Perhaps we'll get lucky. Perhaps the carriage was hired from Howards. That would certainly save you some time."

Looking decidedly skeptical, he left. Howards was the stable where the inspector's carriage and horses were kept.

"What do you want me to do next?" Betsy asked eagerly.

Mrs. Jeffries thought for a few moments. "We need to concentrate on finding Cassie Yates. If she married, the marriage would be recorded in the parish church. Go back and talk to Ellen Wickes. If the wedding was held at any of the churches around here, she might know which is the most likely."

Betsy nodded and stood up. "But what if the banns were read at the groom's church?"

"That's a possibility. I tell you what, if you can't get any more information out of Ellen Wickes, why don't you see if you can make the acquaintance of anyone else who knew Cassie? Try her lodging house, and you might want to see if any of the other maids at the Lutterbank household would be able to give you any help. They may not have liked Cassie, but one of them may have known the name of her young man. Sometimes one's enemies are more inclined to talk than one's friends. Let's hope so anyway. As a matter of fact," Mrs. Jeffries added, "try and get the names of any young men Cassie might have been involved with."

Betsy arched an eyebrow. "From what I've 'eard of 'er, that might be quite a list."

"Just get the most recent ones," Mrs. Jeffries advised, refusing to be offended by Betsy's bluntness. When one was investigating a murder and a disappearance, one didn't cling to outdated and ridiculous notions about whether or not innocent young housemaids should be so knowledgeable about the more unsavory aspects of the human condition. "Concentrate on the men Cassie is likely to have known this past year."

"I expect you want me to put a bit of a fire under some of my sources," Mrs. Goodge asked as she heaved herself out of the chair. "The butcher's boy is due in a few minutes. I'll have him snoop around some . . . and ol' Horace, the fruit vendor, is due on the corner this afternoon. I 'aven't had a chat with 'im in a long time . . ." She picked up the teapot and wandered toward the pantry, muttering to herself as she walked.

Mrs. Jeffries had no doubt that by this time tomorrow, Mrs. Goodge would know every morsel of gossip or scandal about the Lutterbank family. She only hoped that there'd be something genuinely useful in the information.

As the housekeeper went about her duties, she went over and over the few facts they'd obtained concerning the missing girl and the body buried in Magpie Lane. By some bizarre twist of fate, the two cases were now linked. It couldn't be a coincidence that Emery Clements was the owner of the property company that owned those houses, and it would be equally unlikely that after he'd publicly complained about the houses standing vacant, a girl would be murdered and buried there by chance. Not when so many of the principals were directly connected to the Lutterbank house, and it was at a Lutterbank party that Mr. Clements had voiced his displeasure over the vacant property and the lost rent.

After she'd checked the linen cupboards, Mrs. Jeffries came downstairs. On the bottom step she stopped suddenly. Gracious, she thought, I'm overlooking one of the obvious courses of action. No one had gone back to the Everdene house. She pursed her lips as she remembered the rather ugly gossip Mrs. Goodge had shared with her. Mary Sparks was a lovely young girl. Reverend Everdene had an unsavory reputation.

Mrs. Jeffries yanked off her apron and hurried to the hall closet for her cloak and hat. Taking time only to stick her head into the stairwell and tell Mrs. Goodge she'd be back later, she snatched her reticule from the hall table and raced out the door.

The Everdene house was a large gray monstrosity squatting at the end of a row of newer semidetached redbrick villas. An expanse of shrubs, lawn and trees separated the house from its smaller neighbors. Mrs. Jeffries, who'd walked from the Putney High Street, took a deep, calming breath and boldly marched up the broad stone steps.

She banged the knocker and waited, hoping that the door would be answered by a nice, motherly-looking housekeeper. She'd considered her strategy on the way there and had decided things would go far more smoothly if she could gain the confidence of another woman. Preferably an older woman. Hopefully the housekeeper.

But the door wasn't opened by a nice friendly female. It was opened by an unsmiling, bald-headed butler. Mrs. Jeffries immediately discarded her first plan and went to her second one.

"Good day," she said firmly, drawing herself up to her full height of five foot three. "I would like to speak to Miss Everdene."

"Who shall I say is calling, madam?"

"I fear my name will mean nothing to your mistress," Mrs. Jeffries said. "But my business is of the utmost importance. Please tell Miss Everdene I'm here concerning a missing girl."

He looked faintly surprised. "Wait here, please," he said, stepping aside and gesturing for her to enter. "I'll see if Miss Everdene is receiving."

Mrs. Jeffries was fairly sure Antonia Everdene would be willing to speak with her. Her assumption was correct, for a few moments later, the butler returned. "Miss Everdene will see you." He led the way down an oak-paneled hall to a set of double doors and nodded for her to enter.

Mrs. Jeffries stepped inside. The drawing room was paneled in the same dark oak as the hall, and the windows were covered with heavy royal-blue curtains. Sitting on the settee next to the fireplace was a young woman. "Miss Everdene?" Mrs. Jeffries said politely.

"I'm Antonia Everdene," the woman replied. She didn't smile or rise in greeting. She had mousy brown hair worn parted in the middle and drawn back in an unbecoming bun. Her features were narrow and sharp, her mouth a thin, disapproving line. Deeply set hazel eyes regarded Mrs. Jeffries suspiciously for a few seconds; then Antonia lifted a hand and impatiently gestured for her to come forward. "Who are you and what do you want?"

Mrs. Jeffries smiled coolly. "My name is Hepzibah Jeffries," she said as she sat down opposite the woman. "And as I told your butler, I'm here seeking information about a missing woman."

Beneath Antonia Everdene's sallow complexion, she paled. "I've no idea what you're talking about. I don't know why I told Piper I'd see you. You'd better leave."

"I think not," Mrs. Jeffries said firmly. "If you didn't have some idea as to why I was here, you'd have had your butler show me the door immediately. But you didn't. Therefore, I must assume you have some knowledge of her whom I seek. Please, Miss Everdene, let us speak plainly. I'm here to ask you some questions about a Miss Mary Sparks. And I'm not the first person to come and inquire about her either."

"How dare you!"

"I dare because I must," Mrs. Jeffries explained patiently. "Your home is the last place that Mary Sparks was seen." She paused dramatically and added, "Alive."

"This is an outrage. We know nothing about a missing girl."

Mrs. Jeffries could see that the woman was on the verge of panic. She decided to try another tactic. Smiling kindly, she said, "Miss Everdene, I assure you, I haven't come here seeking anything but your help. A young woman is missing. We fear she may have come to some harm."

Antonia Everdene's beady hazel eyes watched her warily for a moment before she nodded. "All right," she said grudgingly. "I don't see why I should speak with you, but as you're here, I may as well find out what this nonsense is all about."

"As I said, it's about a young woman named Mary Sparks," Mrs. Jeffries answered, watching the other woman closely. Beneath her haughty demeanor, she could see the fear in Antonia's eyes. "She came here about two months ago. On September the tenth."

"I don't know anything about that. Mrs. Griffith, my housekeeper, takes care of hiring the servants." She gave a patently false shrug of her shoulders.

"You mean you never saw Miss Sparks," Mrs. Jeffries persisted, deliberately using the girl's name again. She wanted to impress upon Miss Everdene that a human being was missing, not an object or a piece of furniture. "But surely that's impossible. Mary was here for at least one night. Someone in your household, possibly your housekeeper, has already admitted that much."

"I didn't say I never saw the girl," she snapped. "But who pays attention to servants?"

"Didn't you see her when you interviewed her for the position?"

"All interviewing is done by either a domestic agency or my housekeeper. I don't like to be bothered." Antonia Everdene's hands balled into fists. "However, I did catch a glimpse of the girl the day I dropped into the agency to see how much longer it would take them to find me a maid. Miss Hedley pointed to a young woman who was just leaving and said she'd found someone for me and that the girl would be at the house later that morning. The only other time I saw this person was in the early evening, when she escorted my dinner guests into the parlor."

She rose imperiously to her feet. "The girl was gone before I awakened the next morning. For all I know, she may have left in the middle of night. So you see, Mrs. Jeffries, neither I nor my servants can help you find this person."

Mrs. Jeffries stayed seated. "What was the girl you saw at the employment agency wearing?"

"Wearing?" she repeated, obviously surprised by the question. "I don't know. It was two months ago, I hardly make it my business to remember what kind of dress a housemaid was wearing."

"I suggest, Miss Everdene," Mrs. Jeffries said smoothly, "that you try. I should hate to have to tell the police a vital clue in their inquiries couldn't be obtained because of your lack of recollection."

The veiled threat hit its mark, and Antonia Everdene blanched and sat down again. "Police? Who said anything about the police?"

"I did. You see, I'm afraid if I'm unable to obtain a little more information from you, I'll have to go to my employer and ask for his help."

"Your employer? But you're not from the police. They don't have women police persons . . ."

"My employer is Inspector Gerald Witherspoon of Scotland Yard," Mrs. Jeffries said calmly. "Mary Sparks is, shall we say, a friend of a friend. She's disappeared. We want to find her. If you can be of any help in finding this young woman, then I shan't have to bother Inspector Witherspoon. Otherwise . . ." She trailed off, letting the implication hover in the air.

"The girl was wearing a dark blue dress," Miss Everdene said quickly. Her composure was slipping rapidly. She twisted her hands together in her lap, and the movement caused Mrs. Jeffries to note the small gold ring she wore on her left hand. "Naturally, once she was here, she changed into the proper housemaid's dress. But she was only here for one night." Her voice rose. "I don't see why you or anyone else should be worried about one such as her . . . Bold little baggage, she couldn't keep her eyes off my fiancé. Not that he would ever take notice of the impudent chit."

Mrs. Jeffries looked at her sharply. That hardly sounded like Mary Sparks. "Are you saying that she flirted with your intended?"

"Flirted!" she replied in disgust. "It was worse than that, she was positively shameless in her behavior. When she helped him off with his coat, her hands were all over him. The brazen hussy simpered and smiled and coiled around him like a cat. She was so bold that even when she tore her eyes away and saw me standing in the doorway, she didn't stop. She just kept smiling and patting her hair and swaying her hips. It was disgusting."

"I presume your fiancé was shocked by her behavior?"

"Of course he was," Antonia snapped. "But Malcolm is a gentleman. He pretended not to notice that anything was wrong."

"And what did you do about her behavior?" Mrs. Jeffries asked.

"Do?" Antonia's chin rose. "I waited until Malcolm was talking with Father, and then I hurried into the pantry and told the little beast her behavior was intolerable." The words tumbled out quickly now. "I told her I wasn't going to put up with that kind of insolence and for her to pack her things and be out of the house by morning—" She caught herself, and her hand flew to her mouth as she realized what she'd said.

"So Mary didn't leave unexpectedly. You sacked her."

"Yes," she hissed. "Of course I sacked her. Her behavior almost ruined what should have been the most important evening of my life. I was furious at her. I knew Malcolm was going to ask Father for his permission to marry me. I was right too, because as soon as I went back into the drawing room, Father announced that he'd give us his blessing."

"Exactly when did your fiancé propose?"

"Why do you ask? What difference does it make?" Miss Everdene's eyes narrowed suspiciously.

"I was merely curious," Mrs. Jeffries said blandly.

"Well, if you must know, Malcolm had proposed to me the evening before. We were at the opera."

"Malcolm? Is that your fiancé's name?"

"That's none of your concern," Antonia snapped. "My fiancé has nothing to do with that girl being missing."

"Really?" Mrs. Jeffries replied. "I'd hardly say it had nothing to do with him. He was, after all, the reason you sacked Mary."

"He can hardly be at fault because some silly maid took it into her head to flirt with him."

Mrs. Jeffries decided not to press the point. There were other ways to find out the man's name. "True," she agreed. "What did Miss Sparks do when you told her her services were no longer needed?"

"The impudent girl laughed in my face." Antonia Everdene's expression hardened.

"Did she say anything?" From the look on Antonia's face, Mrs. Jeffries was sure the girl had said plenty.

Antonia bit her lip and stared at the carpet. "No. She said nothing. She just turned and stalked off. I never saw her again. The next morning, she was gone."

"Did she take her things with her?" Again, Mrs. Jeffries decided not to press the point. She could easily find out what had passed between Miss Everdene and Mary Sparks another way. Knowing servants as she did, she was sure someone had overheard the exchange.

"Yes. She only brought one small carpetbag with her. It was gone the next morning as well, so I presume she must have taken it with her."

"Did anyone see the girl leave?"

Miss Everdene shrugged. "No, she obviously left the house before the rest of the servants had gotten up."

"How did she get out, then?" Mrs. Jeffries asked. She knew most households were locked up tighter than a bank vault.

"The key to the back door is kept on a nail in the kitchen. When the housekeeper and cook went in, they found the back door standing wide open and the key in the lock. Obviously, she got up early, let herself out and didn't bother to close the door."

"I see." Mrs. Jeffries started to get up and then stopped. "Did your father meet Mary Sparks?"

"No," she replied quickly. Too quickly. "No. Father was gone all afternoon. He might have caught a glimpse of her when she was answering the door, but he didn't really see her. When he came in that evening, he stayed in the study until Malcolm arrived. By the time we went into dinner, the girl was in her room."

Mrs. Jeffries suspected this was a lie. But like the full name of the mysterious fiancé, she knew she could get the truth from easier sources. She made a mental note to send Smythe over to try the pubs in Putney.

Antonia Everdene got to her feet. Lifting her chin, she said, "I believe I've told you everything I know. If you'll excuse me, I've got an appointment with the dressmaker."

The interview was clearly over. Mrs. Jeffries smiled and rose as well. She said a polite farewell and turned on her heel. She could feel the other woman's gaze boring into her back as she left the drawing room and let herself out. She breathed a sigh of relief as the front door closed behind her, and then she hurried off down the road toward Putney High Street.

Mrs. Jeffries caught an omnibus on the High Street. The interview with Miss Everdene had given her the most unexpected results.

As the omnibus trundled over the newly built Putney Bridge, which had only been completed two years earlier, in 1884, she gazed at the dark water of the Thames.

Antonia Everdene was frightened. But why? Sacking a servant, even if the servant did come up missing later, wouldn't explain the depth of fear she'd sensed in the woman. Unless, she thought, Miss Everdene knew a great deal more than she was willing to tell about Mary's disappearance. Or unless the lady suspected that someone else knew something they weren't telling. Someone, perhaps, that Miss Everdene was trying to protect.

CHAPTER 5

It was mid-afternoon when Mrs. Jeffries arrived back at Upper Edmonton Gardens. Deep in thought, she climbed the stairs. She felt sure she'd learned something vitally important from Antonia Everdene, but she wasn't sure what. She gave herself a small shake as she opened the door and stepped into the hall. There would be time enough to put all the pieces together later, she told herself firmly. As her dear late husband, who'd been a constable in Yorkshire for over twenty years, had always said, during the first days of an investigation, gathering as many facts as possible was the most important task. Making sense and drawing the correct conclusions about those facts should then follow as a matter of course. She mustn't try to rush things. Justice would be served in its own good time.

The house, save for Mrs. Goodge, was deserted. Mrs. Jeffries took off her cloak and hat and hurried down the hall and into the cupboard under the kitchen stairs. Arming herself with a feather duster and broom, she retraced her steps and started dusting the furniture and knickknacks in the drawing rooms. When the other servants were out on the hunt, she frequently took it upon herself to do their work. Menial labor helped her think. Today she had much to think about.

A half an hour later the mindless, repetitive chores had worked their magic, and she'd decided what the next likely course in their inquiries should be. She put the duster and broom away, took off her apron and went in search of Mrs. Goodge.

The fruit vendor and the butcher's boy were leaving by the back door as she came into the kitchen.

Mrs. Goodge gave her a triumphant smile and said good-bye to her guests. As soon as the back door closed, she turned. "Good afternoon, Mrs. Jeffries. I'm glad you're back."

"I take it your inquiries have been successful?"

"Very." She nodded toward the white china teapot on the table. "Do you have time for tea?" At Mrs. Jeffries's nod, she picked up a cup and saucer from the sideboard.

"I'm not all that sure that I've learned anything useful about Mary's disappearance," Mrs. Goodge said honestly as she set the tea in front of the housekeeper. "But you did tell me to find out what I could about the Lutterbank family, and that's what I've done."

"We don't know yet what will or will not be useful," Mrs. Jeffries replied. "So please don't worry about that. Just tell me what you've found out since I've been gone."

"The Lutterbanks have lived in Knightsbridge for about five years," Mrs. Goodge began. "They's originally from Leicestershire. The money comes from shoes. They own a factory up around Market Harborough way, so I wasn't able to find out what they was up to before they come to London."

"But you were able to find out something?"

"Well, I had to dig long and hard to get the few bits and pieces I got today," she said slowly. "But I did learn one interestin' tidbit. Last year, there were some right nasty rumors about the son, Andrew."

"What kind of rumors?"

"The usual ugly ones," Mrs. Goodge said in disgust. "Seems he was havin' his way with a young housemaid. Course when the girl gets in trouble, Andrew didn't want to know. Not at first, that is."

"Oh, dear. I suppose the poor girl lost her position." Mrs. Jeffries wasn't surprised. It was an age-old story.

Mrs. Goodge nodded. "The girl's the one that always suffers, isn't she? Especially them that's all alone, like this girl was. But it didn't work out too badly for the lass. She weren't tossed out in the streets. The butcher's boy heard the story from the tweeny that lived in the house next door to the Lutterbanks. There was quite a to-do about it all, because the girl went running to old man Lutterbank and claimed that Andrew had forced himself on her. Claimed she could prove it too." She broke off and grinned. "She must have been pretty convincing, or maybe the Lutterbanks wanted to avoid a scandal, because they paid the girl off and the next thing you know, she's gone to Australia."

Mrs. Jeffries looked surprised. "By herself?"

"I'm not rightly certain." Mrs. Goodge pursed her lips. "I reckon she must have gone on her own if she didn't have a family. Why?"

"Well," Mrs. Jeffries replied thoughtfully, "I think that it's very odd for a pregnant young woman to just up and sail off to a foreign country all by herself, don't you? If they gave her a settlement, why did she leave? Why not just go to another part of England? The trip to Australia is long and difficult under the best of circumstances, let alone for someone expecting a child."

"Hmm, I hadn't thought of it like that," Mrs. Goodge admitted. "It is a bit strange, unless she's got people there. Maybe some of her relatives had emigrated? There's been a lot that's gone, you know."

"That could be the answer, I suppose," Mrs. Jeffries said. "Did you find out the girl's name?"

"Hello, hello. Anyone home?" Witherspoon called cheerfully from the top of the stairs.

Mrs. Jeffries leapt to her feet. "Gracious, what's he doing home so early?"

"I hope he's not here to eat," the cook mumbled darkly as the housekeeper raced out of the kitchen and up the stairs.

"Good afternoon, Inspector," Mrs. Jeffries said brightly. "What are you doing home at this hour, not that it isn't a pleasure to have you here."

"How good of you to say so," Witherspoon replied with a broad smile. "I do hope it isn't a nuisance, my popping in in the middle of the day, but I was just over on Holland Park Road and as I was so close by, I thought I'd come in for tea."

"Why not at all, sir," she assured him. "What were you doing on Holland Park Road? Anything interesting?"

"Oh, yes. Yes, indeed. We've finally had a spot of luck on this wretched murder case. I was at Broghan's, the jewelers at the top of the hill. They're the ones that made the betrothal ring."

"Goodness, sir, you certainly found that out quick enough."

Witherspoon shrugged modestly. "Just doing my duty, Mrs. Jeffries, no more, no less." He broke off and frowned. "I say, the house is awfully quiet today . . ."

"Why don't you have your tea out in the gardens?" Mrs. Jeffries said hastily.

"But won't it be a bit chilly . . ."

"Not at all, sir." She raised her voice, hoping that Mrs. Goodge would hear. "I know it's November, but it's a lovely day outside. Pity to waste it." She glanced over her shoulder and saw the cook's round face peeking up from the top of the stairwell. Mrs. Goodge nodded, indicating she'd bring the tea outside.

"I say," Witherspoon said as they seated themselves at one of the small wooden tables, "this is a jolly good idea. It's most pleasant out here."

"I thought you'd enjoy the view," Mrs. Jeffries replied. "You've been working so very hard on this latest murder case, I thought perhaps a breath of fresh air might be just the thing."

The garden was still lovely. The leaves on the huge oaks were turning to gold and crimson, the grass of the lawn was still a lush, deep green, and there were even patches of vivid red and yellow in a few late-blooming roses.

"How very considerate you are, Mrs. Jeffries," the inspector said. "And you're right, of course. Murder cases always take so very much out of me. But I think this one might be different. I think we'll be able to ascertain the identity of the victim very, very soon."

"I'm certain of it, sir."

"Well, as I said, we've had a spot of luck in tracing that betrothal ring. Naturally, we started the inquiries on Bond Street. That's only reasonable, of course, considering that that is where the greatest number of jewelers are concentrated. But wouldn't you know it, the very first place Barnes tried told him that the piece had been made at Broghan's."

"I wonder how they knew."

"Something to do with the technique or the style or, oh, I can't remember exactly how they knew, but they did. When we got to Broghan's, the proprietor recognized the piece straight away. One of his goldsmiths had made it, and even better, he'd only sold the one." He leaned back and beamed at her. "And you'll never guess who he sold it to."

"Oh, do tell, Inspector."

"A gentleman named Emery Clements."

Mrs. Jeffries forced her expression to remain blank. As far as the inspector was concerned, she'd never heard of Emery Clements. "I see. I presume now, that since you know who purchased the ring, you'll ask him for whom he purchased it. Correct?"

"Correct," he confirmed. "More importantly, we've found another very interesting connection between Mr. Clements and the victim." Witherspoon smiled smugly. "The gentleman is also one of the major shareholders in Wildwoods Property Company."

"Oh, don't tell me, let me guess. Wildwoods is the property company that owned the houses on Magpie Lane."

"Right you are. Well, I'm naturally going to call around and have a chat with him as soon as possible."

Mrs. Jeffries rose to her feet as she saw Mrs. Goodge waddling toward them with a crowded tea tray. "Excuse me, sir," she said apologetically as she rushed toward the cook. "But I'd best take that tray from Mrs. Goodge. Her rheumatism's been acting up again, and that tray looks heavy."

"Do you want me to tell the others about Andrew Lutterbank?" Mrs. Goodge whispered as she handed the tray to Mrs. Jeffries.

"That's a good idea. We might not have much time this evening." She hurried back to the inspector and set the tray on the table.

"Now, as you were saying, sir." She poured him a cup of tea.

"Saying?" Witherspoon looked at her blankly. He'd become so engrossed in watching the sparrows chasing off an invading group of starlings that he'd forgotten what he'd just said.

"About having a chat with Mr. Clements." Mrs. Jeffries finished pouring her own cup and sat down. She was rather full of tea at the moment, so she put her cup aside and gazed inquiringly at the inspector. "You said you were going to speak with him as soon as possible."

"Oh, yes." Witherspoon reached for a ham sandwich. "Unfortunately, he's out of London at the moment, but his clerk told Constable Barnes he's due back tomorrow. I'll see him then."

Mrs. Jeffries wondered where Emery Clements was and precisely what, if any, connection he had to the dead girl. She also found it suspicious that he was conveniently out of town.

"Don't you find that rather . . . odd?" she asked.

"In what way?" Witherspoon popped a huge bite into his mouth and chewed hungrily.

"I don't know," she replied hesitantly, hoping he'd catch her meaning. "But isn't it rather strange that only yesterday the story of finding the body was in the papers, and today you can't find the most important link to the girl?"

Most important link? Witherspoon frowned uncertainly. "I'm not sure I understand what you mean."

"The ring, sir. Wasn't it mentioned in the papers?" Mrs. Jeffries wished she'd taken the time to read them herself this morning.

"Oh, that." Witherspoon smiled. "We were very cautious in what we said to the press. There was no mention of a betrothal ring. So even if Mr. Clements had given the deceased the ring, he'd have no way of knowing she was the murder victim."

He would if he killed her and buried her body in Magpie Lane, Mrs. Jeffries thought. As much as she liked and admired her employer, there were moments when his naïveté was annoying. Her dear late husband always used to say that when one found a murder victim, the most likely place to look for the killer was among the nearest and dearest. "But the papers did say where the body was found," she ventured cautiously. "And surely the name of the road should have meant something to Mr. Clements. I'm rather surprised he didn't get in touch with the police himself."

"But why should he?" Witherspoon reached for a bun. "Wildwoods is a huge company. They own property all over the south of England. Magpie Lane probably meant nothing to him."

"Yes, I'm sure you're right," she replied. She wondered if she should tell him that that particular road did mean something to Emery Clements. But if she told him about the party in the garden and about Emery Clements's complaining about losing the rents on the abandoned houses, she'd have to tell him about their involvement in finding the missing Mary Sparks. So far, Witherspoon only knew the girl was missing and that Luty was concerned. He didn't know she and the other servants were actively searching for the girl. She decided to say nothing. Until she and the rest of the household had more information about the girl's whereabouts, her feeling was to keep silent. Mrs. Jeffries had always trusted her feelings.

"We must be very delicate in the handling of this matter," the inspector continued. "After all, if the victim was wearing a betrothal ring given to her by Mr. Clements, then that means they were engaged."

"But didn't you mention the girl was wearing the ring on a chain around her neck?"

"Yes. But what does that have to do with it?" Witherspoon asked quizzically.

"If they were officially engaged, sir," she pointed out, "the victim would probably have worn the ring on her finger."

"Oh, dear, I forgot."

"Not to worry, sir," she reassured him. "You're a man. That's the sort of detail a woman remembers. Of course, she may have been wearing the ring around her neck because it was a bit too large and she didn't want to lose it. But generally, if that were the case, when the man presented it to her, he'd have noticed it didn't fit and taken it back to the jeweler for proper sizing right away."

"Really?" Witherspoon said. He wished he'd thought of that possibility.

"Or perhaps," Mrs. Jeffries said softly, "she had the ring around her neck because she didn't want her engagement made public."

"Goodness, you mean people do such things?" The inspector looked thoroughly shocked. "But why would someone get engaged and then not want anyone else to know about it?"

"For a good many reasons, sir. Parental disapproval. An inheritance, a prior engagement. Oh yes, indeed, there could be dozens of reasons why a couple would become engaged and then want it kept secret." Satisfied that she'd made her point and that the inspector would ask Mr. Clements the right questions, she broke off and smiled cheerfully.

Witherspoon stared at her dolefully. "There are moments, Mrs. Jeffries," he said slowly, "when I wonder if it wouldn't be a good idea to have female police officers. There are simply so many details in this world that a man just doesn't understand."

Wiggins helped himself to another cup of cocoa. "Garrett McGraw's safe at 'ome," he said defensively, "and I don't think he'll be goin' anywhere in this weather."

A hard rain beat steadily against the kitchen windows. Betsy glanced anxiously at the door. "Don't you think Smythe should be 'ere by now?"

"Stop worrying, Betsy," Mrs. Jeffries said soothingly. "I'm sure he'll be along any minute." She turned her attention back to Wiggins. "No one is suggesting you spend the night watching the house," she explained gently. "We're not criticizing your decision to come home. After all, it is very late and it's pouring with rain. Betsy merely asked if Garrett did anything suspicious on his way home this evening."

"I weren't havin' a go at you," Betsy said. "I only asked ya if you left the boy's street before or after the rain started."

"After, of course. I knows me duty. I wouldn't 'ave left if'n I thought the boy was daft enough to be goin' out, and he didn't do nothing suspicious neither." Wiggins shook his head. "Today was the same as yesterday. The boy went straight 'ome and stayed there. No one come out but one of the little 'uns."

"You mean Garrett's younger brother?" Mrs. Goodge asked.

"That's right," Wiggins said. "And he did the same thing he done yesterday, scarpered off to play."

"Obviously, we'll have to do a bit more than just keep an eye on Garrett McGraw," Mrs. Jeffries said thoughtfully.

Wiggins brightened appreciably. "Does that mean I don't 'ave to spend every minute keepin' an eye on 'im? I can tell you, it's downright dull, and I'm gettin' awful tired of 'idin' in those bushes too. I don't care 'ow fancy that garden in Knightsbridge is, them bushes got the same bugs and briars as any other place. I almost got set on by that awful bulldog of Major Parkinson's. He's a real vicious brute, and he woulda 'ad me if'n I 'adn't jumped the fence." He looked down in despair at his torn trousers.

"Yes, I'm sure your experience was dreadful," Mrs. Jeffries said quickly. "You won't have to spend all of your time watching Garrett McGraw." They'd heard the bulldog story several times already. She didn't relish listening to it again. She glanced at the clock. "Perhaps tomorrow, I'll try my luck with the boy. Gracious, it is getting late. We can't wait any longer for Smythe."

They'd deliberately waited until after Inspector Witherspoon had gone to bed before convening around the kitchen table to compare notes. Smythe was the only one who wasn't here, but Mrs. Jeffries knew from experience that the coachman could take care of himself, so she wasn't too concerned. They'd have to start without him.

Mrs. Goodge had already told Wiggins and Betsy the gossip she'd heard about Andrew Lutterbank.

"Betsy." Mrs. Jeffries said, "would you like to tell us what you've found out today?"

"I don't know, Mrs. Jeffries." Betsy gave the back door another worried glance. "It don't feel right startin' without Smythe."

"Your feelings are very understandable, but this isn't the first time we've had a meeting without him." Considering the rivalry between the coachman and the maid, Betsy's insistence was rather surprising. But perhaps not, Mrs. Jeffries thought, as she studied the girl. They all shared a sense of camaraderie and fair play in their little adventures. Yet as she saw the girl flick another anxious glance at the back door, another idea struck her.

Betsy's china-blue eyes had gone to the door half a dozen times in the last few minutes. She was genuinely worried about the coachman. No. It couldn't be, Mrs. Jeffries told herself. Smythe and Betsy were as different as chalk and cheese. Surely this lovely, fair-haired girl hadn't developed an infatuation for their big, almost brutal-looking coachman. She was instantly ashamed of herself for thinking of Smythe in those terms. He might be large and cursed with prominent features and a swarthy countenance, but he was one of nature's true gentlemen. Mrs. Jeffries couldn't think of anyone she'd rather have by her side when trouble came.

She was being silly. Of course Betsy and Smythe weren't interested in each other—why, what an odd idea. The maid was merely a bit jittery because the wind was howling and the night was black as sin.

"Remember when we were investigaing the Slocum murder," Mrs. Jeffries reminded her gently. "Smythe disappeared for several days. When he finally appeared, he was perfectly all right and downright full of himself to boot."

"True," Betsy agreed. "He was right proud of himself that time, wasn't he?"

" 'E 'ad reason to be," Wiggins said in defense of his friend. " 'E did find out a lot about old Slocum's nephew being a thief."

"Yes, yes, of course he did," Mrs. Jeffries said impatiently. "Now, it's getting very late, and we really must get on with the business at hand."

Betsy nodded reluctantly. "All right, then. I did like you said and I went back to the shop. 'Ad a bit of luck there too. The manager was busy in the back, so I got a chance to get Ellen Wickes a talkin'." She grinned. "Ellen was right jealous of Cassie Yates. She told me that Cassie was always braggin' about the men 'angin' round and wantin' to marry her. Course, Ellen claims at first she didn't believe her. Thought Cassie were tellin' tales and makin' up stories to make 'erself look important."

"What happened to change her mind?" Mrs. Goodge asked.

"The men started comin' round the shop. That changed Ellen's tune fast enough." Betsy leaned forward on her elbows. "Three of 'em."

"Three!" Wiggins looked positively scandalized. "That's disgustin'."

The footman was a hopeless romantic. Mrs. Jeffries made a mental note to give him back the love poem she'd found lying on the pantry table this afternoon. Perhaps she'd gently encourage him to try another method of expressing his feelings about the housemaid from up the road. "Your cheeks as round as the moon in June," might be a bit offensive. Sarah Trippet could feel he was saying she had a fat face.

Betsy shrugged. "Disgustin' or not, that's what Ellen told me. And she said all three of the men were real sweet on Cassie."

Mrs. Jeffries asked, "Did she say how she knew that?"

"Of course she did. I tell you, Mrs. Jeffries, the girl was dishin' out the dirt on Cassie Yates faster than a dog digs a bone. She said she seen the first bloke, a great big tall blond feller, call for Cassie in a fancy carriage at least twice. Cassie claimed 'e was takin' her to one of them posh restaurants over on the Strand both times." Betsy stroked her chin. "Ellen saw the second man a couple of days after the first one took Cassie out to supper. He was a heavyset bloke, with dark hair and chin whiskers. Cassie claims he took her to the opera and then to supper afterward. Ellen said he looked like a real gent—'ad on expensive clothes and all."

"And the third man?" Mrs. Jeffries prompted. Betsy did tend to get carried away.

"Now, that's the interestin' one—Cassie was right cagey about the third bloke," Betsy said meaningfully. "She didn't say much about him to Ellen."

Mrs. Jeffries looked disappointed. "Oh, dear. So you don't know much about him, then?"

Betsy grinned. "I knows plenty about 'im. Cassie wouldn't talk much about the feller, but that didn't stop Ellen from doin' a bit of snooping. Seems he only called around the shop twice. Both times on foot too. When Cassie wouldn't say much, Ellen got curious. So the second time he come around, Ellen claimed she just 'appened to be leavin' just after them. She claims she just 'appened to follow them up the street. They stopped at a park and the man pulls her behind a tree. Ellen says she saw him give Cassie something. Something small."

Mrs. Goodge snorted. "Ellen Wickes saw all this, did she?"

Betsy shrugged. "She says she just happened to catch it out of the corner of her eye, but I reckon she was following them and spyin' on them."

"Did Ellen ask Cassie about him?" Mrs. Jeffries asked. She was glad to hear Betsy restoring her *h*s to their proper place. She wished she could get the girl to concentrate as easily on the final *g* of her words, but she didn't like to correct her in front of the others, and in all fairness, except when she was terribly excited, Betsy was very careful with her pronunciation.

"No. Ellen were dyin' to know who the man was, but she told me she wouldn't lower herself to ask. Besides, Cassie talked free enough about her men. Ellen figured it were just a matter of time before she said somethin'."

"I don't suppose Ellen was able to give you any names?"

"No. But one of the other maids at the Lutterbanks' house did," Betsy said proudly. "After I finished talkin' to Ellen, I went to Knightsbridge. Honestly, Mrs. Jeffries, it was too easy. I 'adn't been there more than three minutes when one of the parlormaids come out and hotfoots it down the street. She was takin' a note to the butcher, and I caught her when she come out of the shop. She 'ad even more to say about Cassie than Ellen did."

" 'Ow do ya get them to talk so fast?" Wiggins asked curiously.

"Oh, that's easy," Betsy explained loftily. "I just start askin' questions. When they ask me why I'm a askin', I tell 'em that Cassie Yates told a pack of lies about me and I lost me position because of it. I tell them I want to get a bit of me own back."

The footman gazed at her in open admiration. "Cor, that's a good 'un. I'll have to try that sometime meself."

"You've got to play your story a bit by ear," Betsy explained earnestly, "dependin' on who you're tryin' to get information on, but I figured that with someone like Cassie Yates . . ."

"Speaking of which," Mrs. Jeffries interrupted firmly, "could we please stop digressing and get back to the matter at hand? I believe Betsy was going to give us the names of the men who'd been seen with Cassie."

"Malcolm Farnsworth and Emery Clements," Betsy stated hurriedly. She blushed and leaned back in the chair. "Accordin' to the parlormaid, Cassie was seein' both of them."

Mrs. Goodge frowned heavily. "What about the third one, then?"

"She didn't know his name. But she knew there was someone else. She seen her with him. Cassie weren't one to keep conquests to 'erself."

Emery Clements was certainly a familiar name, Mrs. Jeffries thought. For that matter, so was the name Malcolm. "Malcolm Farnsworth," she said thoughtfully. "I wonder if that's Antonia Everdene's fiancé. I know his Christian name is Malcolm."

Betsy gaped at her. "How'd you find that out?"

"I went to the Everdene house today," Mrs. Jeffries admitted. "I'll tell you all about it in a minute. First, though, I want to hear the rest of what you've found out. Did you question the parlormaid about Mary Sparks?"

"Didn't have much luck there . . ." Betsy paused. "But you know, it's right strange. When I asked Abby, that's the parlormaid, if there'd been any stealin' goin' on, the girl said there hadn't. Don't you think if an expensive brooch was stolen, she'd a known about it?"

Mrs. Jeffries frowned. "Yes, one would think so."

"I think so too. But even when I were hintin' that maybe that's why Mary Sparks left the Lutterbanks, Abby just shook her head and said no. Claimed Mary just up and left one day. There weren't no fuss made about a stolen brooch or anything else. Abby were right surprised too. She thought Mary and Mark McGraw had an understandin'—Mary had been sayin' she was goin' to keep on workin' for the Lutterbanks until Mark come home."

Mrs. Jeffries drew a sharp breath. "So the household didn't know about the alleged theft."

"Not a word. And, if you ask me, it's downright impossible," Betsy said flatly. "There in'n a 'ouse in London that can keep that kind of gossip out of the servants' 'all. Oh, I did think to ask her what Mary was wearin' the day she left."

"What's that got to do with anythin'?" Wiggins asked.

Betsy ignored him. "She 'ad on her blue dress and a pair of dark shoes.

But they wasn't new shoes. I asked Abby about that too. She said Mary was still wearin' a pair of old brown ones."

Mrs. Jeffries beamed in approval. "Very good, Betsy. Now, as we've already heard what Mrs. Goodge and Wiggins learned today, it's my turn."

Just then, they heard the screech of the hinges as the back door opened and Smythe stepped inside. He was soaked. Water dripped from his coat onto the floor, his shoes squeaked with every step, and his dark hair was plastered flat against his skin.

Betsy leapt to her feet. "You're soaked, man. Get that wet coat off before you catch yer death." She dashed behind him and tugged at the wet garment.

"Stop yer fussin'," he said with a lazy grin. "A bit of water never hurt anyone. I see ya started without me."

While he was stripping off his coat and drying off before the stove, Mrs. Jeffries told him everything the others had discovered that day.

"I was just starting to tell everyone what I'd learned today when you came in," she finished. "So I may as well continue. As I said before. I went to the Everdene house today, and I must say, I think Antonia Everdene knows something about Mary Sparks's disappearance."

"I should bloomin' well 'ope so," Smythe muttered as he settled gratefully into a chair.

Mrs. Jeffries looked at him sharply. "Why?"

"You'd best finish first," he said somberly. "When you 'ear what I've found out, it'll become clear enough."

She stared at him for a moment and then went ahead and told them everything. Naturally, she gave them every little detail of the visit. "All right, Smythe," she commanded softly as soon as she finished with her story. "It's your turn now."

He took his time answering, his big, dark eyes staring blankly into space for a few moments. "I've spent most of today lookin' for the livery that hired the carriage that come to take away Cassie Yates's belongin's," he finally said. He glanced at the housekeeper. "It weren't Howards. It were Steptons over near the Wandsworth Bridge. One of the blokes there remembers a toff comin' in on September 11th and hirin' the carriage, but he weren't the one that did the drivin', and he wouldn't sneak a peek at the logbook for me. He did give me the name of the feller that drove the carriage that day, but the man's gone to Bristol to visit his relations and in't due back for a few days."

"So we'll have to wait until he comes back to find out just who it was that took away Cassie Yates's belongings," Mrs. Jeffries said. Her apprehension mounted. Smythe was certainly taking a long time to get to the point. If it had been Mrs. Goodge talking, she'd have thought nothing of it, but he never beat around the bush.

"Right." Smythe began drumming his fingers against the top of the table.

Mrs. Jeffries cleared her throat, and when Smythe looked up at her, she gave him a long, level stare. "What else did you learn today?" she asked quietly.

His mouth flattened into a grim line. "I found the driver that picked Mary Sparks up the night she left Knightsbridge."

"Where'd he take her?" Betsy asked.

"This was the day after she'd supposedly gone to the Everdene house, right?" Mrs. Goodge said. Her eyes were narrowed in concentration.

"Yeah. It took me a long time to track the bloke, I chased him over 'alf of London today . . ."

"Smythe," Mrs. Jeffries interrupted. "Please tell us what you've learned."

He took a deep breath, and his big body slumped against the back of the chair. "The driver picked Mary up just after it got dark. But you're not goin' to like where he took 'er." He paused and rubbed one hand over his face. "He drove her to Magpie Lane."

There was a horrid, stunned silence. Mrs. Jeffries was the first to find her voice. "But Luty Belle was sure the body wasn't Mary . . ."

"Cor, I know that," Smythe exclaimed. "But she must've been wrong."

Wiggins's chubby round face twisted into a scowl. "I don't understand what you're all on about. Why's everyone gettin' in such a state?"

"Because if'n he took Mary to Magpie Lane that night," Mrs. Goodge explained irritably, "no matter what Luty Belle Crookshank says, the dead girl is probably Mary Sparks."

"But Mary had small feet," Wiggins protested.

"That don't mean nuthin'," Betsy interjected. "If'n you're poor and you come across a brand new pair of shoes, you go ahead and grab 'em."

"How could she keep 'em on her feet?" he argued. "If'n they's too big, they'd have come off."

"They were high-button shoes," Mrs. Jeffries said quickly. "Mary could have stuffed the toes with newspapers."

"I don't believe it," Wiggins insisted.

Mrs. Jeffries wished she didn't have to believe it either. No wonder

Smythe wasn't crowing like the cock of the walk tonight. He'd probably dreaded having to share this particular bit of news. Luty Belle was going to be dreadfully upset.

"Wiggins," Mrs. Jeffries said gently. "None of us want to believe it. But the facts do speak for themselves. Mary has been missing for two months. A body that's been dead for approximately the same amount of time has been found in Magpie Lane. If Smythe's information is correct, and we've no reason to think it isn't, the last time anyone saw Mary alive was the night she was taken to Magpie Lane."

CHAPTER 6

Inspector Witherspoon knew it wasn't going be a good day. He glanced at the clerk working in the corner of the outer office of Wildwoods and stifled a sigh. Outside the narrow windows the sky loomed cloudy and ominous. He could hear the clatter of the omnibuses and the clip-clop of horses' hooves blending with the raucous cries of the street vendors.

He frowned at the closed door of Emery Clements's office and wished the man would hurry up so he could get this uncomfortable interview over. Witherspoon hated asking questions of a personal nature. He much preferred the nice, easy straightforward inquiries such as what is your name, what is your address and where were you at such and such a time. Yet now he had to go into that office and ask Mr. Clements about a betrothal ring and possibly even a fiancée. Goodness, he thought, this could turn out to be a crime of passion. The idea made Witherspoon shudder. No, he decided, it definitely wasn't going to be a good day. But much as he dreaded the coming interview, he still found himself hoping that Emery Clements could give them some useful information. The Chief Inspector was beginning to make pointed remarks. So far they hadn't identified the victim, located the murder weapon or found any witnesses. None of his police constables were getting anywhere with their door-to-door inquiries around Magpie Lane, nor had they had any success in locating the shop that had sold the victim her shoes. If he didn't find something useful soon, he simply wouldn't know what to do next. Even his household had been glum and morose this morning.

The door opened, and a thin-faced clerk stuck his head out. "Inspector Witherspoon, Mr. Clements can see you now."

Witherspoon straightened his spine and trailed the clerk into the inner office. Constable Barnes, who'd been hovering by the front door, followed.

A tall, heavyset gentleman dressed in a beautifully tailored black frock coat, gray vest and white shirt, with a narrow tie under a wing-tipped collar, rose from behind a mahogany desk. He had brown hair, a neat beard topped with a handlebar mustache and a florid complexion.

"Good morning, Inspector. I'm Emery Clements. My clerk says you'd like to talk to me. I must say I'm a bit mystified," he began, not bothering to hide his irritation at the interruption. "I can't imagine what interest the police could possibly have in me."

"Good morning, sir," Witherspoon replied. "I'm Inspector Gerald Witherspoon and this is Constable Barnes."

Clements acknowledged the constable with a barely perceptible nod and then turned his attention back to Inspector Witherspoon.

"Please sit down." Clements motioned to the one chair in front of the desk. The inspector sat. "Now, sir, why don't you tell me what this is all about?"

"I understand, Mr. Clements, that you've an account at Broghan's on Holland Park Road. Is that correct?" Witherspoon tried to infuse his voice with authority. He hadn't liked the way his constable had been treated. Surely it wouldn't have been too much trouble to find a chair for Barnes as well.

Clements arched one bushy eyebrow. "That's correct, but I can't see why that's any concern of Scotland Yard."

"I assure you, sir, it is our concern." The inspector reached into his pocket, drew out a small cloth bag, opened it, lifted out the betrothal ring and laid it on the top of the desk. "The manager at Broghan's said this ring was charged to your account. That was on September ninth. Would you mind telling us the name of the lady you gave it to? It is, as you can see, a betrothal ring."

For a moment, Clements stared at the ring. When he lifted his chin and gazed at the inspector, he looked genuinely puzzled. "There's obviously been some sort of a mistake here. I've no idea what you're talking about. I've never seen this ring in my life."

Witherspoon's heart sank. The Chief Inspector wasn't going to be pleased. "But it was charged to your account. The manager was quite sure about that."

"Yes, well, I'll have to have a word with the manager about his shoddy record-keeping practices, won't I? I certainly would remember if I purchased something like this." He tapped his finger at the ring. "An engagement is generally a rather important event in one's life, Inspector. I assure you, it isn't the sort of occasion I'd forget."

"So you can tell us nothing about it?" Witherspoon asked.

"I'm afraid not. Now, if you'll excuse me, I've a rather busy day planned . . ." Clements broke off and then suddenly smiled. "Wait a moment. Now I know what happened. Of course, how stupid of me not to remember."

"Remember what?" Witherspoon glanced at Barnes to make sure he was taking notes. He was.

"Inspector, you're quite right, that ring was charged to my account." Clements gave a hearty laugh. "But I wasn't the one who actually purchased it. I allowed a friend of mine who'd just become engaged to a lovely lady to use my account. He was in a, shall we say, somewhat embarrassing financial position."

The inspector thought it odd that one could forget allowing a friend to use one's account at a very expensive jeweler's. He wondered if there were anything else Emery Clements had forgotten. Perhaps the man had forgotten any number of important facts. "What's this friend's name?" Witherspoon asked.

Clements's smile disappeared. "Would you mind telling me what this is all about? I've no wish to appear uncooperative, but really, sir, you have started asking what I consider most impertinent questions. Who I allow to use my accounts is my concern and my concern only."

Witherspoon felt a blush creep up his cheeks. By all rights, Mr. Clements did deserve an explanation. Generally, he always told people straight off why he'd come to see them, but with this particular gentleman, he'd had a strong feeling that keeping silent would net some results. He'd been hoping for some sort of reaction when he produced the ring, yet all he'd seen was genuine puzzlement. Drat.

"We've no wish to intrude upon your privacy, Mr. Clements," Witherspoon explained. "But unfortunately, we've no choice in this case. We must find out who owned this ring. It was found on the body of a murdered woman."

Clements jerked back as if he'd been shot. "Good Lord. Murder? I take it this isn't a joke." His brows drew together into one line across his face. "I do believe, sir, you should have informed me you were investigating a murder before I began answering any of your questions."

"Why?" the inspector asked honestly, briefly wondering if there'd been some new judges' rules issued lately that he'd missed.

"Why?" Clements was incredulous. "Why, you ask. My dear sir, I'd no idea when you popped in here asking questions that you were investigating a murder."

"Would you have answered differently if you had known?" Witherspoon asked. He wondered why the man was making such a fuss. He either knew something about the ring or he didn't. But perhaps, he thought craftily, Mr. Clements knew something after all. Something he didn't want the police to know.

"Of course not." Clements clamped his mouth shut and took a deep breath. "I'm not sure but that I shouldn't have my solicitor present before I answer any more questions."

"That is your right," Witherspoon answered. He watched him carefully for a few seconds, looking for signs of distress or guilt. But the man didn't look in the least guilty. He merely appeared annoyed. But why should he be angry if he hadn't bought the wretched ring? Oh, dear. The inspector felt another one of those nasty headaches coming on. He thought longingly of his former job in the records room. Then he remembered his duty and the poor young woman who'd had her life so brutally ended. He also remembered where her body had been found. Witherspoon stopped worrying about whether or not he was irritating Emery Clements. There were a few more questions that needed to be answered here. "We'll be happy to wait while you send one of your clerks for your solicitor."

Clements gazed at Witherspoon uncertainly. Then he held up his hand. "Actually, there's no need to bother him. My solicitor and I are both very busy men. Frankly, I don't want to take any more time on this matter than is absolutely necessary. I've no idea how that ring ended up on the hand of a murdered woman, but I can assure you, it's nothing to do with me or the gentleman I allowed to use my account."

"Good. Then we'll carry on, shall we?" The inspector smiled politely.

Clements nodded stiffly. He took a long, deep breath and asked, "Who was the victim?"

"We're not sure," Witherspoon replied.

"You're not sure?" Clements repeated. "What does that mean?"

"It means, sir, that when the body was found, it was decomposed to the point where it was impossible to make any identification whatsoever." He watched Clements' face go pale.

"My God." Clements looked down at his desk. "Decomposed," he mumbled. "How dreadful. How awful."

The inspector noticed that the man's hands, which had been lying flat on the desk, were now balled into tight fists. The inspector cleared his throat. "I know this is rather shocking news," he said softly, "but you can see why it's rather important we trace the ring."

"Yes, yes. Of course I can." Clements took another deep breath and seemed to get ahold of himself. "I'm afraid what I've got to tell you won't be of much use."

"Why don't you let us be the judge of that? We'd still like that name."

Clements ignored him and instead asked a question of his own. "Could you tell me, when was this unfortunate woman murdered?"

Witherspoon saw no reason not to answer. "Approximately two months ago."

Clements's mouth turned down in disgust. "Two months ago? That doesn't sound very nice."

"Yes, well, that's why the victim was decomposed, you see. The murderer buried her in a cellar, and the body was only found two days ago," Witherspoon explained.

"Then obviously, there has been a mistake. I've seen the young woman my friend purchased the betrothal ring for, and I can assure you, that as of yesterday she was alive and well. So quite obviously, there's been some sort of muddle in the identification of the ring."

Witherspoon knew there hadn't been any mistakes. The jeweler who'd made the ring had been positive. But he saw no reason to share that information with Emery Clements. "May I please have their names?" he asked patiently.

"Malcolm Farnsworth is the person I allowed to use my account," Clements admitted grudgingly. "He's engaged to a Miss Antonia Everdene."

"The engagement was recent?" The inspector decided to ask any question that popped into his head. It seemed as good a way as any to get the man talking . . .

"No," Clements answered quickly. "They became engaged in September. But I've already told you. There's obviously been a terrible mistake. Malcolm's fiancée is alive and well. I've told you, I saw the lady myself."

Witherspoon regarded him thoughtfully. "I understand you own the property on Magpie Lane."

"My company does. Why?" His eyes narrowed suspiciously. "What's that got to do with it?"

"The body was found buried in the cellar of one of those houses. Your own clerk has confirmed the houses were sitting empty for several months without tenants before they were demolished." Witherspoon leaned forward. "Tell me, sir, have you any idea what that young woman was doing wearing a ring bought on your account and in one of the properties your company owns?"

"Certainly not," Clements exclaimed, "and I must say, I don't like your attitude or the implications of your questions."

Witherspoon caught himself. "My question wasn't meant to imply anything. I was merely wondering if perhaps you knew of any reason a young woman would ensconce herself in an abandoned house."

"How should I know?" Clements leaned on his elbows and twined his fingers together. "As you said, those houses had been sitting empty for a long time. There was a dispute between the local authority and the underground rail builders. The land was originally cleared for the purpose of widening the road. But there was some kind of argument, and at the last minute everything changed and it was decided to build the underground."

"I see," Witherspoon said slowly. He gazed steadily at Emery Clements. "You know, sir, that's how the body was found. She was buried in the cellar. The workers digging the exploratory trench found her."

Clements closed his eyes briefly. Witherspoon began to revise his first impression of the man. He actually seemed genuinely moved by this poor woman's murder. Perhaps Mr. Clements hadn't invited Constable Barnes to sit down because he didn't think police constables were supposed to be seated while they took notes.

"How was she killed?" Clements asked softly.

As that information had already been ferreted out by the press, the inspector could see no reason not to answer. "She was stabbed."

"Appalling."

"Very." The inspector got to his feet. "Could you please give me Malcolm Farnsworth's address? Naturally, we'll need to talk with him."

"He lives with me," Clements replied. "We've been friends since our school days together. When he came to London a few years ago, I invited him to stay with my mother and me." He started to write the address on a piece of paper.

"We have your address," Witherspoon told him. "Is Mr. Farnsworth at home now?"

"I've no idea."

Witherspoon smiled slightly. "Can you tell us where he works?"

"Mr. Farnsworth has a private income," Clements said. "His job is managing his investments. Naturally, he works at home. If he isn't there, you can try his club."

"And which club would that be, sir?" Constable Barnes interjected softly.

Clements appeared to be surprised that the constable could speak. "Picketts. It's near Regent's Park."

"We know where it is, sir," Witherspoon said quickly.

They left the office shortly after that. Barnes waited till they'd turned the corner onto Wellington Street before he began asking questions. "What did you think of him, sir?" he asked with a half smile.

"I'm not sure, Barnes," Witherspoon replied. He frowned at the heavy traffic and then turned and walked toward Waterloo Bridge and the river. A tram on its way to Temple Station momentarily obscured his view of the river. Sighing, he said, "Not a likable fellow, but he did seem genuinely distressed by the murder. Still, I don't suppose the man has any reason to lie to us . . ."

"He does if he's the killer," Barnes muttered. He was still smarting over having to stand and take notes. "And his acting all concerned about the poor girl bein' done in and buried in that cellar could be an act."

"Hmmm. Well, yes, but we've no evidence he is the killer, do we? But still, there's something decidedly peculiar about his story," Witherspoon said.

"Like what, sir?"

"I didn't like the way he hedged over giving us those names.

Surely, when a man hears there's been a murder committed, he immediately wants to tell the police everything he knows." Witherspoon increased his pace. "But that wasn't how Mr. Clements reacted at all. Even after he knew why we were there, he didn't want to tell us who had used his account at Broghan's to buy that ring."

"And then, of course, there's the body bein' found on his property," Barnes added.

"Right, Constable. I don't like it. I don't like it at all." Witherspoon jabbed his finger in the air for emphasis. "There's more to this case than meets the eye, I can tell you that."

"Where to now, sir?" Barnes was practically having to run to keep up with the inspector.

"To the tramway," the inspector replied. "I want to stop in at the Yard and go over those workmen's statements before we pay a call on Mr. Malcolm Farnsworth."

Mrs. Jeffries, Betsy, Smythe and Mrs. Goodge were halfheartedly tending to their chores. Betsy was polishing the silver, Mrs. Goodge was leafing through her recipe book, Smythe was filling the coal bins and Mrs. Jeffries was counting sheets.

After they'd heard Smythe's depressing news of the night before, the only one who'd faced the day with any enthusiasm was Wiggins.

At breakfast, he'd bounced into the room and announced he was going back to Knightsbridge for "another go at Garrett McGraw." No matter how they all protested it was useless, he wouldn't be deterred. Mrs. Jeffries wasn't sure what to make of such behavior. But the boy was so convinced that Mary was still alive, she didn't have the heart to try and stop him. Truth to tell, she wasn't sure she wanted to either. He'd soon enough come to the same conclusion the rest of them had arrived at last night.

Mary was dead.

Mrs. Jeffries shoved the linen basket into the corner and then stood there staring at the wall. Her conscience bothered her. She should have gone to Luty Belle's as soon as she got up that morning, but she'd deliberately been putting it off. Well, she told herself, stop dithering and get to it. The sooner she got this uncomfortable duty over with, the better.

The gloom of the overcast day matched Mrs. Jeffries's mood as she walked with Luty Belle in the communal gardens behind the row of tall townhouses. The elderly woman was not taking the news very well. She didn't, in fact, appear to have heard a word Mrs. Jeffries had said.

"I tell you, that corpse weren't Mary Sparks." Luty shook her head vehemently. "I knows it. I kin feel it."

"Now, Luty," Mrs. Jeffries said gently. "None of us want to believe that Mary is dead, but the facts speak for themselves." She stopped by the gate and pointed toward the street beyond. "Mary left the gardens from right here. She walked out that gate, got in a hansom and was taken to Magpie Lane. She hasn't been seen or heard from since."

"That don't mean she's dead," Luty said stubbornly.

"The body of a young woman wearing Mary's clothes was found buried in the cellar of a house in Magpie Lane," Mrs. Jeffries continued doggedly. "As dreadfully awful as it is, we've got to face facts."

"An' the one fact you seem to be forgettin', missy, is that them shoes on that body weren't Mary's." Luty banged her cane against the ground for emphasis.

Mrs. Jeffries gazed helplessly at the stubborn old woman and wondered how to convince her of the truth. "But as Betsy pointed out," she began, "Mary had very little money. Perhaps she found those shoes, and they were in such good condition, she decided to wear them despite the fact they were too large."

"Horse patties," Luty cried. "Mary wouldn't have happened to find a pair of brand-new shoes, and I know fer a fact she wouldna wasted what little money she had buyin' 'em. Besides, she didn't steal that danged brooch, and you said it were pinned to the dress when they found her."

"I'm not accusing her of theft," Mrs. Jeffries explained. "But there's another solution to that particular mystery."

Luty cocked her head to one side. "An jus' what's that?"

"The murderer could have pinned that brooch on Mary's dress after she was killed."

"She's alive," Luty insisted stubbornly. "I know it. I kin feel it."

Mrs. Jeffries took her arm and led her to one of the wooden benches under an elm tree. When they were sitting, she said, "I know exactly how you feel. I don't want to believe the girl's dead either. But the facts speak for themselves." She held up her hand for silence when Luty opened her mouth to protest. "Furthermore, you're not doing Mary any good by letting her murderer get away with this foul deed."

"But I ain't doin' that!"

"Yes, you are," Mrs. Jeffries said firmly. "Every minute we waste our time and energy looking for the girl, in the mistaken belief that she is alive, is one more minute for the killer to cover his tracks. If we're not careful, if we don't start concentrating on who actually took her life, he'll get away with it." She paused and gave Luty a long, hard stare. "Is that what you want?"

Luty glared at her for a few seconds and then she quickly turned away. Her thin shoulders slumped as she gazed at a pile of fallen leaves. "No," she whispered in a trembling voice. "If'n Mary is dead, I want the one that did it to hang."

They sat in silence for a few moments before Luty straightened and turned to Mrs. Jeffries. "All right, we'll have it yur way. Mary's dead. I don't like it, but I never was one to hide my head in hole when the truth of the matter was smacking me in the face."

"I know it's hard, Luty. But the only thing we can do for the girl now is to find her killer."

"What do you want me to do?" Luty asked, staring at Mrs. Jeffries shrewdly.

"I want you to tell Inspector Witherspoon everything you know." She reached over and patted the wrinkled hand that held the top of the cane in a death grip.

"What good'll that do?" Luty snorted.

"Well, for one thing, it will put him on the right track. Once he knows the victim is definitely Mary Sparks, he can start questioning everyone she had contact with prior to her death. We know that Mary must have been killed after she left here on the tenth. With that date as a starting point and all the other information we've managed to learn about the Everdenes, the Lutterbanks and Cassie Yates, he's bound to come up with something."

"You reckon one of that bunch is the killer?" Luty asked softly.

"It's possible."

"Are you and the others still goin' to be sniffin' around too? No offense meant to yur inspector, but I won't feel right if'n you all just hand everythin' over to the police."

"Don't worry, Luty," Mrs. Jeffries assured her. "We'll most definitely be sniffing around. Now, I think I'd better bring you up to date on our investigation. You'll need to pass this information along to the inspector."

For the next half hour, Mrs. Jeffries gave Luty every little detail. She told her about her visit to the Everdene house, Betsy's investigation of Cassie Yates, about Wiggins's perpetual watch on Garrett McGraw and about Smythe's finding the hansom driver who took Mary to Magpie Lane. Luty snorted in disgust as Mrs. Jeffries related Mrs. Goodge's gossip about Andrew Lutterbank and the girl he'd gotten pregnant. "I remember the girl," Luty said. "Real sweet, used to like to talk every now and agin when she could git away from the house. Sally Comstock was her name. She used to like to do embroidery. Some of the other girls laughed at her, said she were givin' herself airs. Always embroidering her initials on everythin' she owned. Reckon they was probably jealous—she were a right purty girl."

"You mean you knew about the scandal? Why didn't you tell us this before?"

" 'Cause I didn't remember until you just now reminded me." Luty shrugged. "And it weren't all that much of a scandal at the time. The family was purty good at hushin' everythin' up. Even I wouldna known if'n Mrs. Devlin, the Lutterbank housekeeper, hadna happened to mention it . . . but that was several weeks after the family had got rid of the girl." She shrugged. "That scandal don't have nuthin' to do with Mary anyhows. Sally Comstock was gone before Mary started workin' for the Lutterbanks. Matter of fact, last time I even saw poor Sally was at old Angus's funeral."

"Is there anything else you know about Andrew Lutterbank?"

"Just what I told you before. Don't reckon he's much count. The women like him fine, what with all his dandy clothes and smooth manners. But he's got a mean streak a mile wide. Holds a bad grudge too."

"How do you know that?" Mrs. Jeffries asked curiously.

"Hatchet told me. Don't let that poker face of his fool ya, the man's as nosy as a curious cat. Hears more gossip around these parts than I do." Luty sighed. "Come to think of it, I reckon I should have remembered all this before now, but that's what comes of gittin' old. Sometimes things slip your mind."

"You're not old, Luty," Mrs. Jeffries assured her. "And how does your butler know that Andrew Lutterbank holds a grudge?"

"One of the Lutterbank footmen told him. When Andrew was away at school, one of the other boys got him into some kind of trouble," Luty explained. "Lutterbank waited for years to get even—Hatchet didn't know all the details, but it seems Andrew managed to squeeze whoever it was that wronged him out of a real good investment deal. The footman knew about it because Andrew was braggin' to his friends about how he never forgot an enemy. He once tried to whip his coachman too, but the man was bigger than him." Luty broke off and shook her head. "But I don't reckon he murdered Mary. She didn't like him much, but she weren't scared of him. Besides, he ain't got no reason to have killed her."

"None that we know of anyway," Mrs. Jeffries added. Until they knew more about the murder, she was prepared to consider anyone who'd known Mary a suspect.

Luty pursed her lips. "How am I supposed to tell the inspector I come by all this information?" she asked. "I knows none of you want me lettin' on that you're helpin'."

"Oh, that's quite simple." Mrs. Jeffries smiled. "Come by the house this evening and tell him everything I've told you. If he asks, and there is always the chance that he won't, tell him you were so concerned you hired a private inquiry agent—an American inquiry agent who has since left."

"You don't expect he'd be dumb enough to believe that?" Luty said incredulously. "Come on now, Hepzibah, that kind of yarn wouldn't fool a child, let alone an inspector from Scotland Yard."

For a moment Mrs. Jeffries was at a loss. "Oh, dear, I do hope I haven't given you the wrong impression. Inspector Witherspoon isn't stupid," she explained. "But he is very, well, trusting. Actually, that particular trait is the reason he's so successful as a detective. People are constantly underestimating him; consequently they don't guard their tongues and they inevitably give themselves away." It was a very thin explanation, and Mrs. Jeffries knew it. From Luty's caustic expression Mrs. Jeffries suspected that she knew it too.

"All right, I'll be by around eight." Luty kicked her cane to the ground and leapt to her feet.

Mrs. Jeffries hid her smile. She'd suspected that Luty didn't need a cane any more than Betsy did. She also suspected that the only reason the woman carried it was that she couldn't carry a gun in the streets of London. Luty had once confessed to her that when she and her husband had moved here after years of living in the Wild West of America, giving up her six-shooter had almost killed her. Any weapon, even a stick, was better than none. "I think that'll work perfectly, Luty."

Mrs. Jeffries's spirits were better when she arrived back in Upper Edmonton Gardens. She took off her coat and hat and hurried down to the kitchen.

Betsy looked up from the silver serving spoon she had been slowly polishing, Mrs. Goodge grunted a hello and Smythe nodded and then hunched back over his cup of tea.

"Luty took the news as well as can be expected," she announced quickly, "and apparently she and Wiggins are the only ones who realize we've still got a murder to solve."

"Give us a bit o' time, Mrs. Jeffries," Betsy whined. "We all know there's a killer out there somewhere, but it'll take a day or two to get over the upset. Even though none of us knew Mary, we'd all got right fond of 'er just listening to Luty Belle talk about the girl."

"I'm aware of that," Mrs. Jeffries said firmly. "But we don't have a day or two to play about."

"Mary's not in no 'urry," Smythe complained. "She's been dead two months now."

Mrs. Goodge sighed. "Rotten luck."

Mrs. Jeffries felt like shaking the lot of them. "I know how you all feel," she said. "But we're not going to find Mary's murderer by sitting around here and moaning. Come on, now. Get up. There's work to be done."

Smythe arched one heavy black brow. "And exactly what do ya wan' us to do?"

"First of all, I want you to find that driver who came and collected Cassie Yates's belongings from the lodging house."

"But why?" Betsy asked in confusion. "Cassie don't have nuthin' to do with Mary's murder. She weren't the one buried in Magpie Lane."

"I'm not sure why," Mrs. Jeffries replied honestly. "But Ellen Wickes said that Cassie ran out of the shop and chased a young woman around the corner—all she saw was the skirt of the woman's dress, but remember, it was a dark blue dress."

"I get it. It might 'ave been Mary that Cassie was chasin' after." Smythe jumped to his feet. "Is that what yur sayin'?"

"That's it exactly."

The kitchen was suddenly filled with suppressed excitement. Betsy's eyes began to sparkle, Mrs. Goodge shoved her recipe book into a drawer and Smythe dashed to the back door, eager to be off on the hunt.

"What do you want me to do?" Betsy began to tumble the silver back into the box.

Mrs. Jeffries thought for a few moments. There were so many loose ends, so many tiny clues that might or might not be worth pursuing. Suddenly Antonia Everdene's pinched face flashed into her mind. "I want you to go to the Everdene house in Putney. See if you can find a housemaid or a footman and find out every little detail about the time Mary spent there."

Betsy nodded eagerly, picked up the silver box and jammed it into the cupboard. She was dashing toward the kitchen stairs when Mrs. Jeffries called her back.

"Betsy, be sure and find out if any of the servants overheard what Antonia Everdene said to Mary when she sacked her."

"What if none of them was listenin'?"

"Oh, really, Betsy," Mrs. Jeffries admonished. "Do you think that's likely?"

The maid grinned and tossed her blond curls. "No, but on behalf of the servin' classes, I felt I ought to say it."

Mrs. Goodge turned toward the teakettle. "I'd best get ready, then. The boy'll be here in a few minutes to pick up the laundry, and there's a chimney sweep comin' into Mrs. Gaines's house next door. We've got a delivery of fish expected as well, and ol' Thomas, the rag-and-bone man, is usually around these parts late in the day." She glanced up at Mrs. Jeffries as she filled the kettle. "Is there anything in particular you want me to be diggin' for?"

Again Mrs. Jeffries had to stop and think. This case was getting so complicated, she wasn't sure what was important and what wasn't. But she certainly didn't want the cook wasting any precious gossip opportunities just because she couldn't determine the next course of action. She decided to err on the side of caution. One could never learn too much about the people involved in a victim's life. "See if you can learn anything else about the Lutterbanks. Concentrate your efforts on Andrew Lutterbank, and see if you can ferret out any more details about that scandal with that young girl who was sent off to Australia."

"What about the Everdenes?"

"Find out what you can about Antonia Everdene's engagement," Mrs. Jeffries replied. "See if anyone knows how Miss Everdene met her fiancé and more importantly where she met him. And see if anyone knows anything about Cassie Yates."

"Her?" Mrs. Goodge said in surprise. "What are we wastin' our time on her for?"

Mrs. Jeffries hesitated. "I'm not really sure, Mrs. Goodge. But I've a feeling she might be important. She may have seen or heard something that will give us a clue to who killed Mary. Anyway, it's worth trying."

"What do you want me to find out?"

"Oh, let's see now. Why don't you ask about the facts? Find out where she's from, what her background is, whether or not she ever left any of her other employers and under what circumstances. That sort of thing."

Mrs. Goodge nodded, and Mrs. Jeffries headed up to her rooms. She needed to sit down and think.

CHAPTER 7

Inspector Witherspoon wished he'd gone home for lunch. A nice, calm meal with his housekeeper would have been just the sort of activity he needed to get rid of this pounding headache. Instead, he'd gone back to Scotland Yard and heard another unsettling bit of information about this wretched case. Beside him, Constable Barnes shuffled his feet. Witherspoon gave him a weary smile. "It shouldn't be much longer, Constable. I daresay this house isn't that large. The butler should be back any moment with Malcolm Farnsworth."

They were standing in the opulent drawing room of Emery Clements's home in Kensington.

"Do you think that young Dr. Bosworth knows what he's talking about?" Barnes asked. He kept his gaze on the open doorway. "After all, he did admit he wasn't sure."

"I don't really know, Constable," Witherspoon admitted. "But I'm inclined to take the view that it's possible. Medical science is advancing further every day, and if Dr. Bosworth thinks the girl might have been pregnant, then we'll assume he's correct."

"But even he said he couldn't say for certain," Barnes argued.

"True. The internal organs were badly decomposed, but Bosworth strikes me as an intelligent young fellow." Witherspoon didn't need to add that he thought Dr. Potter was a pompous fool—his constable already knew that.

"But coming to the conclusion the girl had a bun in her oven just from lookin' at a few bits and pieces of her insides under that . . . that . . . What was the name of that thing he was going on about?"

"A microscope."

"That's it. Well, I tell you, it ain't right." Barnes shook his head. "How could he see if she was expectin' or not just from looking at her innards?"

"Bosworth merely said that when he examined her internal organs under the microscope, there was some indication that she might have been with child." Witherspoon shrugged. "It's not the sort of evidence we could ever use in court, of course. But let's face it, Barnes, we're at the point in this investigation when any little bit helps. At the very least, perhaps the pregnancy was a motive for murder."

"That's true." Barnes agreed grudgingly. "It wouldn't be the first time a man's got rid of an unwanted burden by killin' it. But the whole idea gives me the willies. It's bad enough to think of some poor pregnant girl gettin' murdered, but then to have her insides poked and prodded about by some fool doctor, and all in the name of science too."

"Now, now, Constable." Witherspoon glanced at the door again. "Dr. Bosworth was only doing what he thought was right. He didn't have to come to us at all and took a substantial risk by telling us his suspicions. We both know that Dr. Potter certainly wouldn't have appreciated Dr. Bosworth's interference. Potter's notoriously territorial about postmortems."

"Humph. Not that it does us much good, even if Bosworth's right. Pregnant or not, we still don't know who she is."

They both turned at the sound of footsteps. Witherspoon stared at the tall, fair-haired young man entering the room. He was somewhat overdressed for the afternoon, in a pristine white shirt, dark blue coat, fashionable vest and brilliant crimson cravat. His handsome features were composed in an expression of cautious interest, but the bright blue eyes beneath his long, dark lashes were wary.

"Good afternoon, gentlemen," he said forcefully as he advanced across the room. "I'm Malcolm Farnsworth. My butler said you wanted to have a word with me."

"Good afternoon, sir." Witherspoon inclined his head in acknowledgment of the introduction. "I'm Inspector Witherspoon of Scotland Yard, and this is Constable Barnes."

Farnsworth smiled slightly. "May I ask what this is all about?"

"My constable and I have had a hard morning, sir," the inspector replied, knowing that Barnes's feet were probably hurting him. "May we sit down?"

"Certainly." Farnsworth waved a hand toward a settee, and the matching wing chairs. Everyone sat down. "Now, could you please tell me why you're here?"

Witherspoon reached into his pocket and fished out the ring. He handed it to Farnsworth. "Can you identify this betrothal ring as one you purchased?"

"Egad. Where on earth did you find this?" Farnsworth smiled in delight. "I must say, I'm very impressed. It never occurred to me that Scotland Yard would trouble themselves over such a trifle. Not that it wasn't expensive, mind you. It jolly well was, but I hardly thought a lost ring would be of much concern to the police. I say, how did you know it was mine? I never reported losing it."

The inspector shot a quick glance at Barnes, who peered up from his notebook with an expression of surprise.

"Are you saying you lost this object?"

"By heavens, yes. You chaps must be frightfully clever to find it." Farnsworth chuckled. "I must say, it put me in a decidedly awkward position."

Witherspoon was disappointed. "In what way, Mr. Farnsworth?"

"Well, here I was, getting ready to ask my fiancée for her hand in marriage, and when I reached into my pocket for the ring, the wretched thing was gone." He leaned forward and smiled conspiratorially. "You know how the ladies are, Inspector. It was dreadfully embarrassing. Of course, Antonia pretended not to notice anything was wrong, and I hardly felt like admitting that I'd done something so silly as to lose her engagement ring."

Witherspoon hadn't the least idea how the ladies were, but he refrained from saying so. Instead, he forced himself to concentrate. "When did all this happen? I mean, when did you realize it was gone?"

"As I've just said," Farnsworth replied huffily, "I realized the ring was gone when I went to put it on my fiancée's finger."

"And exactly when would that have been?"

"Do you want the date?" Farnsworth asked. At the inspector's nod, he lifted one long, elegant hand to his chin and his eyes narrowed in concentration. "I believe it was sometime in early September," he answered slowly. "Perhaps the tenth or the eleventh, but I can't be certain."

"You can't remember the date you got engaged, sir?" Barnes asked.

"Well, no." Farnsworth gave the constable a puzzled frown. "That's the sort of thing a woman remembers, not a man. I say, Inspector. What's this all about?"

Witherspoon waited a moment before answering. "Murder."

"Murder! My God, how dreadful. But what does it have to do with this ring?" Farnsworth gulped and looked down at his hand. As he stared at the tiny band, a wave of color washed over his cheeks and he shuddered slightly. Witherspoon coughed softly, and Farnsworth quickly handed him the ring.

"It was found on the body of the victim," the inspector replied. He slipped the ring back into his pocket. "She'd been stabbed and then buried in the cellar of a house on Magpie Lane. Do you know the place?"

Farnsworth clamped his hands together. "No."

"Strange. The property is owned by Mr. Emery Clements. There was considerable controversy over those houses, some sort of dispute about whether a road would be built or a new underground line dug. As you live with Mr. Clements, I'm surprised you never heard him mention Magpie Lane."

"Mr. Clements's company has property all over England," Farnsworth replied, but his voice was noticeably less strong than before. "I can hardly be expected to recall every little detail of those properties which are causing him difficulties. It happens all the time."

"I see." Witherspoon studied the man carefully. The mention of murder had shaken him to his core. Gone was the confident voice and the ready smile. Farnsworth was white as a sheet and was having to twine his fingers together to keep them from shaking. He was hiding something, but what? "Do you have any idea who the young lady was?"

"What young lady?"

"The victim."

"Don't be absurd, man." Farnsworth swelled with indignation. "How on earth would I know such a thing? I've told you, I lost that wretched ring on the day I asked my fiancée to marry me. For all I know, my pocket might have been picked! It's not as if you fellows are much good at protecting innocent citizens from thieves and pickpockets."

"Exactly where did you go on that day?" Barnes asked softly. "It would be helpful if we knew exactly where you lost it."

The question appeared to startle Farnsworth for a moment. "Lord. I've no idea. Could you remember what you did on any particular day two months ago?"

"I could if I'd just asked a young lady to be my wife," Barnes replied firmly. "And if I'd lost the expensive engagement ring I'd bought to put on her finger."

"Well, obviously, I'm not as romantic as you appear to be, Constable. Except for asking Antonia to marry me, it was a day like any other." Farnsworth leapt to his feet and began pacing in front of the marble fireplace.

"Perhaps if you'd tell us how you generally spend your days," Witherspoon said, trying to be helpful. "Perhaps that would nudge your memory a tad."

Farnsworth stopped pacing and turned to stare at the inspector, his expression skeptical. After a moment, he shrugged. "Oh, all right, but I think it's useless. Normally, I get up and breakfast with Emery. I spend an hour or two after that in my rooms; then I frequently accompany Mrs. Clements on a walk. After luncheon, I generally go to my club or to visit friends. I spend my evenings in much the same way."

"When do you see your fiancée, sir?" Barnes asked.

Farnsworth looked offended. "That's hardly any of Scotland Yard's concern. But if you must know, I see Antonia quite frequently. And I'm afraid this little exercise has been pointless. The only thing I can remember about the day I lost the ring is just as I've told you. It wasn't there when I reached into my pocket."

"Your fiancée is a Miss Antonia Everdene," Witherspoon said. It was a statement, not a question.

"How do you know that?"

"Mr. Clements told us," the inspector replied. "We saw him earlier today. That's how we traced the ring to you. Mr. Clements identified it as one you'd purchased on his account at Broghan's. Is that correct?"

"Yes." Farnsworth flushed a dull red and looked away.

Witherspoon gazed at him sympathetically. It must be terribly humiliating to have to obtain a loan to buy one's fiancée a ring. And then to have that fact become public knowledge. Well, the inspector could understand the gentleman's embarrassment. He got up, and so did Constable Barnes. "I'd like to have a word with Mrs. Clements, if I may," he said.

"That's impossible," Farnsworth replied. He looked quickly toward the open door. "She can tell you nothing. Mrs. Clements is a very elderly lady, and she's resting. You'll have to come back tomorrow. If I were you, I should do it when Mr. Clements is here."

Barnes and Witherspoon exchanged glances.

"Yes, perhaps you're right," Witherspoon said. "Could you give us Miss Everdene's address?"

"Why do you want her address?" Farnsworth asked in alarm. "I tell you Antonia knows nothing of this murder. I won't have you bothering her with such nonsense!"

"Murder is hardly nonsense," the inspector replied softly. "And I assure you, sir, we will do our best not to upset Miss Everdene."

Farnsworth sighed. "All right, if it's absolutely necessary. But I must warn you, Antonia's very delicate. She lives at number Three Harcourt Lane, in Putney."

The inspector thought of the young woman who'd lain buried in a dark, dirty cellar for two months. Perhaps she'd been a delicate woman too, yet no one seemed overly concerned with her.

"Perhaps Miss Everdene can recall the exact date you proposed to her," Barnes interjected with a sly smile. "As you said, Mr. Farnsworth, that's the sort of thing a woman remembers."

The inspector had just finished telling Mrs. Jeffries the details of his day when she hastily excused herself to answer the front door.

A few moments later, he stifled a groan as his housekeeper returned, followed by Luty Belle Crookshank. He'd been so looking forward to eating his dinner in peace.

"Howdy, Inspector," Luty said. "Now don't you be fretting that I'm gonna take a lot of your time. I jes needs to have quick word about that body you found in Magpie Lane."

"Please sit down, Mrs. Crookshank," Witherspoon responded as he leapt up and ushered the elderly lady to his favorite chair. "It's always a pleasure to see you," he lied gallantly, not wanting to hurt the dear lady's feelings. "And don't worry about taking my time—I'm not in the least concerned about how much of my time you need. Now, what's all this about?"

"Well," Luty spread the skirts of her scarlet satin dress more comfortably around her feet. "I've been thinkin' I mighta been wrong the other day."

"Wrong? In what way?"

"People see what's they want to see, Inspector." Luty glanced at Mrs. Jeffries, who gave her a reassuring smile. "And I'm thinkin' when I told you that body weren't Mary, I mighta made a mistake."

"Now you think it is Mary?" Witherspoon didn't know whether to be elated or depressed.

"Well, it's like this. I've learned a few things . . . No offense meant, Inspector, but when Mary plum disappeared the way she did, I went out and hired me an inquiry agent."

"An inquiry agent?"

Luty nodded her head. "Yup. An American inquiry feller, used to know him in San Francisco. Name's Braxton Paxton. Silly name but a smart man. He's a mighty fine snoop too. Well, it only took him a few days of pryin' around to find out all sorts of interestin' things."

"Really? Gracious, what did this Mr. Baxton learn?"

"Paxton," Luty corrected. "And he learned enough to make me think I mighta made a mistake about that body you showed me."

For the next half hour, Luty told the inspector every detail the servants of Upper Edmonton Gardens had learned in the course of their investigations.

She told him about Mary's disappearance, the missing brooch, the Lutterbanks, the Everdenes and even the odd bits of gossip about Sally Comstock and Andrew Lutterbank. Finally, she told him about Cassie Yates.

Witherspoon listened attentively, occasionally asking a question. If he wasn't asking the right questions, Mrs. Jeffries would interject one, just to make sure he was getting the point.

"My word," Witherspoon finally said, when Luty Belle had finished. "You've found out an enormous amount of detail. I say, I'd really like to have a word with this Mr. Caxton."

"His name's Paxton, but you can't talk to him." Luty smiled innocently. "He's gone to France to work on a problem for some winemaker. Don't know why. The French are about the snootiest bodies on the face of the earth. But that's Paxton for ya. He goes anywhere there's trouble. Why, back in sixty-eight he single-handedly stopped the biggest shanghai operation on the coast. Had half the scum of San Francisco on his tail that time, and he didn't turn a hair."

Mrs. Jeffries shot Luty a warning glance, but the elderly woman just gave her a guileless smile and got up. "I've got to be goin' now," she said. "It's gettin' late and I want to git home." Witherspoon started to get up too, but she waved him back in his chair. "Don't trouble yerself to see me to the door. I kin find my own way."

"I'll see you to the door," Mrs. Jeffries announced. She took Luty firmly by the arm, and when they reached the hall, she leaned over and hissed in her ear, "Now really, Luty. Don't you think you were overdoing it a bit in there? The inspector's no fool. Gone to France, indeed. And where did you come up with that peculiar name?"

"I didn't make that name up," Luty said defensively. "There really is a Braxton Paxton. Course I wouldn't exactly call him a detective, more like a fix-it man, if you ask me. He used to do a lot of jobs for some of the cattle ranchers and shipping companies back in San Francisco."

"Not to worry then," Mrs. Jeffries said soothingly. "You were quite right. If the inspector does do any checking on Mr. Paxton, he'll find he exists." She stopped by the front door and smiled. "You did well, Luty. I know it couldn't have been easy for you. But we'll find whoever killed Mary. I promise you."

Luty stared at her for a moment, her black eyes unreadable in the glow of the gas lamps. "I'm still not so sure that Mary is the one that's dead." She held up her hand when she saw Mrs. Jeffries open her mouth to protest. "Don't go gettin' all het up, Hepzibah. I ain't askin' you to waste any more time lookin' for the girl, not when there's a murderer runnin' around out there. But I got me this feelin' . . ." She broke off. "Leastways, I won't really believe she's dead until we catch whoever done it and they admit it from their own lips. But until then, I ain't givin' up hope."

Over dinner, Mrs. Jeffries wondered whether she should have told Luty about the possibility of Mary having been pregnant. But as the inspector himself hadn't been sure of that particular fact, she decided she'd done the right thing.

The inspector discussed the case freely. Mrs. Jeffries made sure that everything he'd heard from Luty Belle was planted firmly in his mind. In turn, she deftly managed to make him repeat everything he'd learned from Emery Clements and Malcolm Farnsworth. She made it a point to emphasize the fact that both Clements and Farnsworth were frequent visitors to the Lutterbank house and therefore had to have known Mary Sparks.

By the time dinner was finished, she was eager to get down to the kitchen. Betsy, Smythe and Wiggins should be back by now. She flushed guiltily as she remembered the tiny white lie she'd told to explain the maid's absence. Inspector Witherspoon thought Betsy was at a Methodist Ladies Temperance meeting. She must remember to share that fact with Betsy too.

She was the only one who'd returned. She and Mrs. Goodge were just finishing their own dinner when Mrs. Jeffries came into the kitchen.

"There weren't no one home at the Everdenes'," Betsy said as Mrs. Jeffries stepped up to the table. "So I went back to Knightsbridge to see if I could learn a bit more about Mary or Cassie. Was that all right?"

"Of course it was," Mrs. Jeffries replied. She frowned at the two empty places where Smythe and Wiggins should have been sitting.

Betsy caught the housekeeper's anxious expression. "It's past nine o'clock and they're not back yet," she burst out. "And I'm startin' to get real fidgety over it."

So was Mrs. Jeffries. She didn't worry all that much about the coachman—he could take care of himself. But it certainly wasn't like Wiggins to be late. "Now Betsy," she said calmly, "I'm sure they'll be here any moment. Worrying won't do any of us any good."

"It's not like Wiggins to be late," Mrs. Goodge said darkly. "Something's wrong. He'd sooner give up mooning over one of those silly girls than miss his dinner."

"We don't know that anything is wrong," Mrs. Jeffries said firmly. She hesitated, not sure what to do next. "But it would be pointless to start discussing the case now and then have to repeat ourselves when those two finally show up. Why don't we give them an hour or two? We can meet back here later for cocoa. Is that agreeable to everyone?"

Betsy sighed and nodded. "I don't feel much like talkin' now, that's for certain. Without the others 'ere, it wouldn't seem right."

"I agree." Mrs. Goodge heaved herself out of her chair and reached for her empty plate. "I don't much like havin' to repeat myself."

"All right, then. We'll meet here at ten o'clock." Mrs. Jeffries forced herself to smile. "I'm sure both Smythe and Wiggins will be here by then, and they'll have all sorts of interesting facts to report."

"But what if they're not?" Betsy asked anxiously. "What'll we do?"

"If they're not back," Mrs. Jeffries said firmly, "we'll start looking for them."

"What? Us? Start lookin'?" Mrs. Goodge said incredulously, clearly appalled at the thought of leaving her kitchen.

"Yes, us. If we have to, we'll wake the inspector and we'll get some of Luty Belle's servants to help." Mrs. Jeffries lifted her chin. "But I'm sure it won't come to that. Nothing has happened to either of them. Smythe's more than capable of taking care of himself, and Wiggins, despite occasional actions to the contrary, isn't a fool."

For the next hour, Mrs. Jeffries paced her room. She tried to concentrate on the facts she had about the murder, but it was so hard to think. She was too worried about the missing men. Especially about Wiggins.

Stopping in front of her window, she stared out at the night sky and tried to put her finger on precisely what was bothering her. But the task was hopeless. There was no reason for her to be so anxious. No doubt Wiggins would turn up safe and sound and with a perfectly good explanation for his absence. It wasn't as if this case were peopled with desperate killers brandishing knives and pistols. Then she realized what she'd just thought and remembered that Mary Sparks had been stabbed.

Perhaps whoever had killed Mary had found out Wiggins was investigating the crime. But how could that be? The only place Wiggins went was Knightsbridge and from there to Garrett McGraw's home. So how could anyone know he what he was up to?

But maybe someone had seen him lurking about the gardens? But who? Andrew Lutterbank? He was a definite possibility—he lived there. Or Emery Clements and Malcolm Farnsworth? They were friends of Andrew's. Or perhaps even one of the other servants, someone who had a grudge against Mary and then realized that Wiggins was following the one lead they had to the girl . . . Oh, drat, Mrs. Jeffries thought disgustedly, this is getting me nowhere.

With sheer willpower, she went to her desk and pulled out a piece of paper. Taking up her pen, she began writing down the details of the case she'd learned so far.

As soon as she'd finished, she picked the paper up and read it through. Her spirits sank. All she had was a useless list of facts, dates and rumors. There was no murder weapon; there were no witnesses—no nothing. There wasn't a clue as to who the killer was, and even more disheartening, there wasn't a thing on the paper that gave her any idea of why Mary had been murdered. And until they understood the why of it, she had a feeling they'd never discover the who.

They met in the kitchen at exactly ten o'clock. The two men still weren't home. Mrs. Goodge had made cocoa and put out a plate of buns. "Right," she said briskly as she slammed a mug down in front of her. "Who wants to get the inspector?"

"I expect I'd better," Mrs. Jeffries said. She was interrupted by a soft knock on the back door. Betsy jumped to her feet so quickly her chair fell over with a crash, but she ignored it and raced for the door.

"Ask who it is," the housekeeper warned, but she was too late. Betsy had already pulled the door wide.

"Well, good evenin', darlin'." A smiling redheaded giant of a man stepped into the kitchen. "Wiggins didn't say I'd be meetin' one so fair as you, now. But then, I'm not surprised. 'E's no doubt keepin' you all to himself, and who could blame a man for that?"

Startled, Betsy stared at the man as if he had two heads. "'Ho are you?" she exclaimed, so surprised she reverted back to her old way of speaking.

Mrs. Jeffries stood up. "Yes, I believe introductions are in order."

The man swept off a rather grimy flat cap and bowed to the ladies. "Pardon me, madam. My name is Fletcher Beaks. I'm a friend of Wiggins's. I've brought a message from him. He was afraid you'd be a bit worried, now."

Mrs. Goodge eyed the smiling giant warily. "We have been a mite anxious," she mumbled.

Fletcher Beaks stood a good six and a half feet tall, with shoulder-length carrot-red hair, a ruddy complexion and pale blue eyes. He was dressed in dark trousers, a white shirt with full sleeves and a pin-striped vest. Over one of his large arms, he carried a brown cloak.

"Well, we're glad Wiggins finally decided to get in touch with us," Mrs. Jeffries said. Knowing she was being rude, she tried hard not to stare. "Please come in and sit down, Mr. Beaks."

Betsy finally gathered her wits and rushed back to the table, stopping to pick up the chair she'd overturned. Fletcher Beaks, his eyes following the maid's every movement, trailed behind her. He took the chair Mrs. Jeffries indicated.

"Thank you, ma'am," he said with a wide grin, his eyes riveted on Betsy.

Mrs. Goodge cleared her throat. "Would you care for some cocoa?" she asked.

"No, thank you." Reluctantly, he tore his gaze away from the maid. "Much as I'd love to stay and revel in your charmin' company," he said to the table at large, "I've only got a minute or two. I'll just deliver my message and be on my way. But perhaps you'll take pity on a poor lonely fellow like myself and invite me round another time."

"Yes, I'm sure we will," Mrs. Jeffries said hastily. "Now, what is the message?"

"Wiggins told me to tell you that he's hot on the trail and not to worry," Fletcher Beaks said. "By tomorrow morning, he should find what he's looking for."

Mrs. Jeffries smiled. "Where is Wiggins?"

"As to that, I can't say." He shrugged. "The last time I saw the lad, he was running down Dunsany Road."

"Where's that?" Betsy asked.

"Hammersmith." Fletcher's smile widened as he turned and gazed at Betsy.

"Hammersmith?" Mrs. Goodge frowned. "What's he doin' in that part of town?"

"I really don't know." Keeping his gaze on Betsy, who was now blushing a furious red, Fletcher got up. "But as I owe the boy a favor or two, I was delighted to bring his message. Now, much as I'd like to stay and talk with you lovely ladies, I really must be off. I've got to get to work."

He bowed formally, put on his hat and left.

"Well, at least we know that Wiggins is all right," Mrs. Jeffries said as the back door closed behind their mysterious visitor.

"But what about Smythe?" Betsy said. " 'Ow come he's not 'ere?"

"Perhaps he too is 'hot on the trail,' " Mrs. Jeffries suggested hopefully. "Besides, as we've said before, Smythe can take care of himself."

"Not if some killer's stuck a knife in 'im!" Betsy protested.

"Oh, get on with you, girl," Mrs. Goodge snapped. "No one's gonna be stickin' nothing in Smythe except a pint of bitter, and he'll be gettin' that from some barman. Stop yer frettin', and let's get on with this. I've found out somethin'."

"Excellent," Mrs. Jeffries said.

"But I thought we were going to wait for the others," Betsy wailed.

"We don't have time," Mrs. Jeffries replied. She turned to Mrs. Goodge. "Go on."

"I've found out that Andrew Lutterbank's been virtually cut off." Mrs. Goodge crossed her arms in front of her and rested them on the table. "He still lives at the house in Knightsbridge, but his father won't have much to do with him. Exceptin' for spendin' an occasional weekend at some little cottage he's got out in the country somewhere, he's practically a prisoner."

"But why?" Betsy asked. "If he's been disinherited, 'ow come he's still livin' at 'ome?"

" 'Cause he don't have nowhere else to go nor any money." The cook reached for a bun. "And he can't get employment. Seems his reputation is too unsavory for them that employs gentlemen."

"Why was he disinherited," Mrs. Jeffries asked eagerly, "and more importantly, do you know when?"

"The best I could find out was that his father was finally fed up with 'im seducin' housemaids and leavin' his bastards everywhere. The last time it happened was with that girl," she broke off, trying to remember the name.

"Sally Comstock?" Mrs. Jeffries supplied.

"That's her. Anyway, it seems that when he got her in trouble, his father paid the girl off with a big wad of money. Money that was Andrew's quarterly allowance. Then he told young Andrew he was tired of such behavior and that the boy couldn't expect to inherit anything from him." Mrs. Goodge laughed cynically. "But blood's thicker than water, and I reckon one of the reasons the boy's still livin' at home is in hopes of softening the old man up."

"That's right strange, you know," Betsy said thoughtfully.

"What is?" Mrs. Jeffries poured out a cup of chocolate.

"Well, I 'appened to find out that Cassie Yates, when she was workin' at the Lutterbanks, shared a room with Sally Comstock." She broke off and laughed. "As a matter of fact, the only nice thing I've heard about Cassie at all was that she'd snuck out the night Sally left—she told everyone she wanted to say good-bye to her friend." Betsy shrugged. "Jus' goes to show that everyone's got some little bit of good in 'em, don't it?"

"Indeed it does, Betsy." Mrs. Jeffries turned back to the cook. "Did you find out when the Comstock girl left?"

"No, but it should be easy enough to check. She left right after old Angus Lutterbank's funeral. Mr. Lutterbank was so angry with Andrew that as soon as the service was over, he made the boy take the girl straight down to the docks and put her on the ship to Australia himself. We can check at St. Matthew's for the date of the funeral."

"Why are you so interested in Sally Comstock?" Betsy asked curiously. "Mary weren't even workin' at the Lutterbanks' when Sally was there."

"I'm not sure," Mrs. Jeffries confessed. "Curiosity, I suppose. Now, what all did you find out?"

"Not much really," Betsy admitted. "But I did find out the name of the man who was Cassie Yates's third admirer. It were Andrew Lutterbank himself. But he must have learned his lesson 'cause the girl I was talkin' to told me that Andrew took care only to meet with Cassie away from the house."

"Then how did she find out?" Mrs. Goodge asked.

"She saw Cassie and Andrew together twice. They met in the park. Oh, and there's no record of Cassie gettin' married at any of the local churches, and none of the girls I talked to 'ad any idea where it could have taken place." Betsy turned to Mrs. Jeffries. "Do you want me to keep lookin'?"

"I'm not sure, Betsy," Mrs. Jeffries confessed. "Wait until you hear what I've learned today, and then we'll decide what to do next."

She told them all about Emery Clements and Malcolm Farnsworth. She gave them the details of Luty Belle's visit and said that Witherspoon had mentioned he was going to the Everdene house tomorrow. She then told them about Dr. Bosworth's theory that the victim had been pregnant.

"Pregnant?" Betsy gasped. "But that doesn't sound like Mary at all."

"The behavior Antonia Everdene described to me didn't sound like Mary either," Mrs. Jeffries said earnestly. "Yet we know she went there that day and started work. But nothing makes sense in this case so far.

However, we won't give up until we uncover the truth." For a moment she was tempted to quote Mr. Walt Whitman, the American poet. She couldn't quite remember the verse, but it was something about looking until one really saw. And that's just what they'd keep doing too. She turned to Betsy and said, "Will you be able to get to Putney tomorrow? I think it's rather important that we find out what happened between Antonia Everdene and Mary."

"I'll go first thing in the morning."

"Be careful that you don't run into the inspector," Mrs. Jeffries warned. The back door slammed and startled her so that she jumped.

"Cor, it's about time you got 'ere," Betsy shouted.

Turning, Mrs. Jeffries saw Smythe. He gave her a cocky smile and swaggered to the table like the king of the mountain.

CHAPTER 8

"Good evening, Smythe," Mrs. Jeffries said pleasantly. "We've been a bit concerned about you."

"There was no need for that," he replied, giving Mrs. Goodge a wink and pulling out a chair. "You knows I can take care of myself."

"Not when there's a murderer runnin' around stickin' knives in people's 'earts," Betsy snapped. "Worryin' us to death was right inconsiderate."

The coachman looked startled. "Now, now, lass," he began soothingly. "I weren't doin' it a purpose, but I was in the thick o' things and couldn't get back."

Mrs. Goodge snorted and Betsy narrowed her eyes. Mrs. Jeffries quickly intervened. "Well, now that you are back, perhaps you'd be so kind as to tell us what you've been up to."

Smythe reached for the pot of cocoa, poured himself some and leaned back in his chair. "Where's Wiggins?"

"He's hot on the trail," Betsy said sarcastically, taking care to enunciate every word. "Like you, I guess he can't be bothered with comin' 'ome either."

"Look I've done told ya—" he began defensively, but Mrs. Jeffries cut him off.

"Yes, we know what you've told us," she said. "Now we're wasting time here. We've learned a lot since you've been gone, and we need to know what you've found out."

"I finally found the bloke that drove the hired coach from Cassie Yates's lodgin's. That's why I've been gone so long." He smiled smugly and took a long, leisurely sip from his mug.

Betsy sighed, Mrs. Goodge rolled her eyes and even Mrs. Jeffries was tempted to give him a swift kick in the leg; instead she gave him what he wanted to hear. "We knew you'd catch up with the fellow sooner or later. You're very clever, Smythe."

He leaned forward on his elbows, his dark brown eyes shining. "The man that come for Cassie's belongin's were a tall, well-dressed feller who paid double the regular 'irin' price—seems he were in a 'urry that mornin' and didn't want to wait around for one of the other coaches to come back. He paid twice what was needed to take a coach and driver out that were already promised to someone else."

"Who was the man?" Mrs. Jeffries asked.

"He never give a name, and he took some pains to disguise 'imself. Mitchell, that's the man that drove the coach that day, said 'e wore a fancy top hat and a scarf around 'is neck to cover his face."

"We already know that," Betsy said waspishly, letting them know, less than tactfully, that she'd already reported this particular fact two days ago.

Smythe frowned impatiently. "Yes, but what you don't know is 'ow strange the feller acted. On the mornin' of the eleventh, he ordered the driver to go to the girl's room. 'E tipped the landlady nice and then went inside. 'Alf an hour later, he come out loaded down with a carpetbag and boxes and the like. Now this is where it starts to get interestin'. Mitchell 'urried over to give the man a bit o' 'elp, but the bloke was 'avin' none of that. He ordered the driver back onto the coach, loaded Cassie's things inside 'imself and then told the man to drive on."

"What's so interestin' about that?" Betsy asked archly.

Instead of taking offense at her sneering tone, Smythe turned and gave her a long, thoughtful stare.

"It's interesting because by rights, the man who 'ired the coach shouldn't have lifted a finger to do any of the work," Mrs. Goodge explained.

"True," Mrs. Jeffries added. "Generally, the driver does all the carting and loading, but in this case, whoever hired that coach didn't want the driver anywhere near either Cassie's rooms or Cassie's things."

"Oh." Betsy flushed slightly.

Smythe grinned. "But that's not all that's odd 'ere," he continued. "Once the bloke was back in the coach, 'e ordered the driver to take 'im out of London, to a small village in Essex. Once they got there, the same thing 'appened. The driver just sat there while the man unloaded Cassie's belongin's."

"Was Cassie there?"

"Not 'ide nor 'air of 'er," Smythe said firmly. "The reason I were so late gettin' in tonight were because I been out to the place."

"Did you manage to get inside?" Mrs. Jeffries asked.

"Couldn't," he admitted with a shake of his head. "The place were locked up tighter than a bank vault, but I got a good gander in the windows, and no one's been there in months. The man just left 'er belongin's piled in a 'eap in the parlor, but there's dust and cobwebs everywhere."

Mrs. Goodge poured Smythe more cocoa. "Who does the place belong to?"

"It don't rightly belong to any one person," the coachman confessed. "The cottage sits on less than an acre of its own ground. Accordin' to one of the neighbors, it were sold last year to a London property company."

Mrs. Jeffries's eyes met Smythe's. "Wildwoods." It was a statement, not a question. She wasn't surprised when he slowly nodded.

"Yes. I found that out from one of the neighbors. But no one can figure out what they want with a piddly bit o' land and a tumbledown cottage."

"What did the man do after he'd taken in Cassie's things?" Betsy asked. She seemed eager to redeem herself.

" 'E got back in the coach, and they drove back to town. The driver left 'im off at Hyde Park, and that were the last 'e saw of 'im. Except the man give 'im 'alf a crown."

"You've done very well, Smythe," Mrs. Jeffries said. "Now I do believe we'd better bring you up to date on what we've learned in your absence."

She gave him the information, leaving nothing out and stressing Betsy's contribution. She also told him about the missing Wiggins and the mysterious message. When she'd finished, the coachman's normally cheeky expression had been replaced with a heavy frown.

"Good gracious, you look like you've just bitten into a sour apple," Mrs. Jeffries exclaimed. "What's wrong?"

"I'm not sure," he said slowly, "but I'm not likin' the feel o' this case. And I don't much like the fact that Wiggins is off by 'imself gettin' into mischief. The lad's good-hearted, but let's be blunt, Mrs. J, sometimes 'e's got about as much sense as a lump of Mrs. Goodge's bread dough."

"That's not true," the cook snapped. "Wiggins might moon about a bit every now and again over some girl, but the boy's no fool."

"I'm not sayin' 'e's a fool," Smythe argued. "I'm sayin' I'm worried. There's too many 'orses in this stable, too many bits and pieces we don't know."

Smythe's attitude began to affect them all. Mrs. Goodge bit her lip, Betsy began twisting one of her long blond curls, and even Mrs. Jeffries had to fight the urge to get up and start pacing. Smythe wasn't an alarmist.

"What particularly worries you so much?" Mrs. Jeffries finally asked.

"Everythin'. Don't you see, the driver didn't get a look at the man . . . He were deliberately 'idin' his face."

"But Cassie isn't the one that's dead. Mary is," Betsy pointed out.

"Aye, Mary's dead and Cassie's missing, and there's at least three men who had something to do with both girls."

Mrs. Jeffries stifled a surge of panic as she grasped precisely what Smythe meant. "You're right," she said quietly, forcing herself to keep calm. "But that doesn't mean we're dealing with a madman. The only thing we know for certain is that Mary is dead. We're only assuming that Cassie is missing because we haven't located her yet."

"Madman?" Mrs. Goodge yelped. "Who said anythin' about a madman?"

Across the table, Smythe and Mrs. Jeffries gazed at each other, their eyes grave, their expressions somber.

"Are you two sayin' you think theys a lunatic killer runnin' about murderin' 'ousemaids?" Betsy glanced from the housekeeper to the coachman, then looked quizzically at the cook.

"Aye," Smythe said slowly. "That's exactly what I'm sayin', and I want you to start bein' a bit more careful . . ."

"Let's not jump to any conclusions," Mrs. Jeffries said firmly. "We could easily be wrong. Mary is dead, but we don't know that there's anything in the least diabolical about Cassie Yates's disappearance. From what we've learned of that young lady's character, she could be off with some man."

"Then 'ow come 'er belongin's is in that cottage and she ain't?" Smythe asked belligerently.

"Simple. The man might be married, and Cassie could have agreed to be his mistress," Mrs. Jeffries explained. "She could have insisted he buy her new clothes. Oh, I don't know, but there are any one of a thousand reasons that could explain why he took her things to that cottage. But it's now imperative that we find out more." She turned to Betsy. "Don't bother with any of your chores tomorrow. I'll take care of dusting and cleaning the drawing room. Get over to Putney as early as you can and see if you can find out more about Mary's stay in the Everdene house."

"I don't think that's a good idea," Smythe said quickly. "Shouldn't she stay 'ere and keep an eye out for Wiggins?"

"Don't be daft, man," Betsy said with a sneer. "I knows how to take care of meself too, and Mrs. Goodge'll be 'ere when Wiggins finally sees fit to come 'ome."

Smythe scowled at the girl but didn't bother to argue the point. He turned to Mrs. Jeffries. "I suppose you want me to see if I can find out what everyone was doin' on September eleventh?"

Mrs. Goodge slapped her hands flat against the table. "Excuse me if I seem a bit slow," she said sarcastically, "but would someone mind tellin' me which three men we're talkin' about here?"

"Emery Clements, Malcolm Farnsworth and Andrew Lutterbank," Mrs. Jeffries said. "Whoever took Cassie's things that day was probably one of those three, but we don't know which."

"And why is that so important?" the cook inquired sourly, "Mary's the one that's dead."

Smythe sighed heavily, and Mrs. Goodge glared at him.

"Because," Mrs. Jeffries intervened hastily, "once we know who moved Cassie's things, we can find out once and for all if Cassie's all right."

"You mean once we know that she's off livin' in sin, we can rest easier because we'll know we ain't dealin' with a lunatic," Mrs. Goodge finished smugly. "Seems to me that's a waste of time. We'd be better concentratin' on what happened to Mary Sparks after she left the Everdene house."

"That's precisely what Betsy is going to do." Mrs. Jeffries rose to her feet. "And if you would be so kind, Mrs. Goodge, do you think you could possibly find out the exact date of Angus Lutterbank's funeral? I'd like to know when Sally Comstock left for Australia. Supposedly, Andrew Lutterbank took her to the ship that night himself."

"Why don't ya let me do that?" Smythe said as he rose to his feet. "I can nip by St. Matthew's tomorrow and have a word with the vicar. Then if you're really wantin' to find out if the girl left, I can pop down to the docks and nose around there. See if her name was on any passenger lists."

Mrs. Jeffries thought for a moment. "Yes, that's a very good idea."

"What'll I be doin' then?" the cook asked.

"Carry on as before," Mrs. Jeffries replied. "Just keep asking your questions. You've turned up a great deal of useful information so far, and there's no reason to think the well's run dry at this point." She paused and smiled kindly at Mrs. Goodge, hoping the woman's feelings hadn't been hurt by the abrupt change in plans.

Mrs. Goodge nodded. "What are you goin' to be doin' next?"

"I've got the most difficult task of all," Mrs. Jeffries replied with a sigh. "I'm going to have to think of a way to let the inspector know everything all of you have learned. That's not going to be easy." She broke off and stared intently at the wall. "But I think I might be able to drop a few hints at breakfast."

"Do you want me to go out and 'ave a quick look round for Wiggins?" Smythe asked. He was staring at Betsy, who was gazing at the toe of her black shoe, barely visible beneath the hem of her gray housemaid's dress.

Betsy's head came up, and she smiled gratefully at the coachman. "I think that's a right good notion," she began excitedly. "Even with gettin' a message from 'im, I don't think I'll sleep much knowin' he's not 'ome."

Mrs. Jeffries stared curiously at her two friends. She had the oddest feeling that Smythe had made the offer to keep Betsy from worrying. She watched as his broad, harsh face softened when he gazed down into the maid's eyes. But then she decided she must be mistaken as she heard his next words.

"Maybe I'll try a few of the pubs round Knightsbridge way," he said, giving Betsy a cocky grin.

Betsy leapt to her feet. "Pubs. Wiggins wouldn't go ta no pubs," she exclaimed angrily. "And 'ere I was thinkin' you was concerned, and all you want to do is go 'ave a few pints."

"Give it a rest, lass." He laughed and headed for the back door. "I'm as concerned as the rest of you. And believe me, I'll come closer to findin' the boy by makin' me rounds than I would by skulkin' about in the streets."

"Men." Betsy gave an unladylike snort. "They're all alike. If they ain't thinkin' of their stomachs, they're thinkin' of their drink. Disgustin'."

There was nothing remotely spiritual or comforting about the Reverend Wendell Everdene, Witherspoon thought. He was a tall, barrel-chested bull of a man with a sallow complexion, a hawk's beak of a nose and a booming voice that reminded the inspector of a braying donkey. And from the way poor Barnes cringed slightly every time the reverend opened his mouth, Witherspoon imagined the constable's ears were probably ringing by now.

"Of all the impertinence, man," Everdene bellowed. "The girl was here for less than a day. I'm not surprised she's come to a bad end. That kind of creature always does. God will not be mocked. Sinful little chit, wouldn't allow her to sully the place."

Constable Barnes winced. "Are you saying, sir, that it was you who asked the girl to leave?"

Everdene's beady hazel eyes narrowed. "What kind of a question is that? I'm the master of this house. The girl was a harlot. She had to go."

"So you're confirming that you were, indeed, the one who actually asked her to leave?" Inspector Witherspoon wasn't terribly sure this was an important point, but he hadn't liked the way the man evaded answering Constable Barnes. In his experience, people who didn't give you a straight answer frequently had something to hide.

"I don't see that I need confirm anything." Everdene glanced at his daughter. She was sitting rigidly in front of the fireplace, her thin lips pursed together and her hands neatly folded in her lap, the very picture of filial devotion.

"But we have it on good authority that it was Miss Everdene who fired Mary Sparks." The inspector nodded politely to the lady. "We understand that Miss Sparks was behaving rather badly when Miss Everdene's fiancé arrived that evening and that Miss Everdene witnessed this behavior. Shortly afterward, she fired the girl. Isn't this true?"

"Absolutely not," thundered the reverend. "Who told you such wicked lies? My daughter was in the parlor when Malcolm arrived. I was the one who saw the disgraceful way the harlot behaved. I was the one that told her to get out. Antonia knew nothing about the matter till the next morning."

" 'E's lyin' 'is bleedin' 'ead off," the girl scoffed as she gently eased the door shut and turned to grin at Betsy.

Betsy smiled back at her and then glanced worriedly at the door the parlormaid had just shut. She sincerely hoped that Inspector Witherspoon wouldn't take it into his head to search the house. There was no possible way she could explain being in the small pantry between the drawing room and dining room with Essie Tuttle.

Betsy couldn't believe her luck when she'd arrived at the Everdene house this morning and found most of the servants gone and a talkative parlormaid who was more than willing to chat. But within minutes of her own arrival, Inspector Witherspoon and Constable Barnes had shown up.

Essie Tuttle, who didn't appear at all concerned about losing her position, had obligingly hurried the both of them into the pantry, opened the door a crack and then settled down to eavesdrop.

"How do you know 'e's lying?" Betsy whispered.

"Cause he were the one that was in the parlor," Essie replied. "He was so soused he could barely walk. Mary coulda danced rings around 'im that night and he wouldna noticed."

From the drawing room, Betsy heard Inspector Witherspoon point out that the betrothal ring found on Mary Sparks had been purchased for Antonia Everdene.

"Don't be absurd," the reverend sneered. "Malcolm knew Antonia wouldn't want a gaudy piece of jewelry like that. Not for something as sacred as marriage. He very rightly gave my daughter a small, plain band inscribed with the cross of our Lord. He showed it to me when he asked for my permission to wed the girl."

Betsy stared in surprise. If she remembered correctly, Malcolm Farnsworth had claimed that when he showed up at the Everdenes' house, he didn't have a ring with him at all.

"He's lyin' again," Essie giggled. "Cor, for a preacher, it's a wonder his tongue ain't dropped off from all them lies."

"What do you mean?" Betsy strained to listen but she didn't want the flow from Essie to dry up either.

"He's seen that ring afore this. I know 'cause I saw him kissin' Mary's hand and lookin' at it the day she come 'ere."

"He was kissin' her hand?"

Essie laughed cynically. "And everythin' else he could grab. She hadn't been in the 'ouse 'alf an 'our before the old lech was pawin' at 'er."

Betsy opened her mouth to ask the maid how Mary had handled the reverend's advances, but before she could get the question out, she heard Inspector Witherspoon ask Antonia Everdene if she'd ever seen the betrothal ring. Betsy cocked her ear in the direction of the drawing room.

"No, I've never seen it," Antonia replied in a firm voice.

"She's a bloomin' liar too," Essie said with a sneer. "She's ruddy well seen that ring. Mary Sparks had it on her finger the night she was 'ere. When the mistress sacked 'er, she was holdin' her 'and up and laughin'."

"You mean Mary showed the betrothal ring to Miss Everdene?"

"And that ain't all," Essie said eagerly, bobbing her head. "She laughed at the mistress, told her it would be a cold day in the pits o' 'ell before she ever married Malcolm Farnsworth. Said he was weak and greedy, but he'd do right by her when she told 'im the truth."

There was another bellow of rage from the drawing room. Essie quickly eased the door open a crack.

"The girl went to her room. She didn't leave that night." Everdene's heavy footsteps echoed through the house as he began to stomp up and down the room. "She was a jezebel, but as a good Christian man, I would not throw her out in the cold of night," he shouted.

Betsy winced in sympathy for her inspector and Constable Barnes. Their heads must be spinning by now. The man's voice was loud enough to wake the dead.

" 'Ere goes another one." Essie hunched her thin shoulders and eased the door shut again. "She was tossed out that night all right, right after the mistress slapped her."

"Miss Everdene slapped Mary?" Betsy gave up all pretense of trying to listen to what was going on in the drawing room. She'd finally decided she could only concentrate on one conversation at a time, and she was having much better luck getting the truth than the inspector was.

Essie grinned, her buck teeth making her look like a spiteful ferret. "Oh yes, I 'eard the whole thing." The girl's reedy voice dropped to an excited whisper. "As soon as Miss Everdene got her drunken old father settled into the study, she come chargin' into the kitchen. But she were already too late."

"Too late for what?"

"Too late to stop Mr. Farnsworth. He'd already slipped me a note to give to Mary. He done it as soon as Miss Everdene were busy lookin' after 'er father. Ya see, she'd had the old fool propped up in the drawin' room, awaitin' for Mr. Farnsworth to come in and ask for her 'and in marriage. But the reverend got restless and come out. He were weavin' all over the 'ouse when Mr. Farnsworth got here. By that time, Mr. Farnsworth had had plenty of time to slip me the note for Mary. He'd already gone into the study. He even used Miss Everdene's notepaper to write on."

"So Miss Everdene didn't see Mr. Farnsworth's note?" Betsy wanted to be sure she understood.

"Her? Nah, she didn't know nuthin' about that. She were just mad at the way Mary 'ad been all over Mr. Farnsworth when Mary'd answered the door. Miss Everdene come chargin' into the kitchen like a mad dog huntin' a fox. She told the girl off right and proper for the way she'd been 'angin' onto Mr. Farnsworth, but Mary weren't the least sorry. She'd already got what she wanted. Mr. Farnsworth had noticed her. She just let Miss Everdene rant and rave for a few moments, and then she lifted her 'and and pointed to her finger. That's 'ow come I knows the mistress is in there lyin' to that peeler. She got a good gander at that ring."

"Go on," Betsy hissed. "What happened then?"

"But I've already told ya." Essie frowned. "Mary jus' laughed and said Malcolm Farnsworth was no more goin' to be marryin' Miss Everdene than he was goin' to marry the Queen 'erself. Said that though he were a weak, greedy man, once Mary told him the truth about the baby, Malcolm would be marryin' 'er. Then she laughed again and rubbed her belly. That's when Miss Everdene 'it 'er. Slapped her right across the face and ordered 'er out o' the 'ouse."

"Did Mary go?" Betsy couldn't believe her luck. She watched Essie's thin, plain face and excited eyes and wondered if the girl were telling the truth.

"She left all right, flounced right into our room, snatched up her carpetbag and waltzed out the front door with 'er nose in the air."

Betsy cocked her ear toward the drawing room, just in case. "And that was the last time you saw 'er?"

"Course not," Essie said peevishly. "I followed her out. This was the most excitin' thing that ever 'appened around 'ere. I didn't like to see Mary go. She weren't very nice, but she'd only been in the 'ouse a few hours and the fur was already flyin'. Besides, Mr. Farnsworth give me a shillin' to deliver 'is note to her, and I were hopin' maybe Mary'd give me a bit as well."

There was silence from the drawing room. "How far did you follow her?" Betsy asked carefully. Essie's colorful speech patterns had made her very aware of her own tendency to lapse.

"Just to the corner. I could see she was 'eadin' for the 'igh Street. I started to call out to 'er, to say good-bye, but then I saw a feller step out of the trees on the other side of the road, so I turned around and come 'ome."

"Was the man following Mary?" Betsy's heart began to beat faster.

Essie shrugged. "I don't know. For a minute I thought it might be Mr. Farnsworth—the bloke was dressed like a gent. But it weren't 'im. When I got back to the 'ouse, Mr. Farnsworth was still here."

"Did you read the note?" Betsy asked hopefully.

"Read!" Essie laughed incredulously. "I can't read."

"Well, did you listen in on Mr. Farnsworth and Miss Everdene then?"

Essie gazed at her for a few moments before answering. "I'm not rightly sure that I remember," she said slyly.

"But just a moment ago, you remembered every little detail about that evening," Betsy protested. Then she realized what the girl wanted. Obviously remembering that Malcolm Farnsworth had given her a shilling to deliver that note had reminded the girl that sometimes you could make a bit of money.

Sighing, Betsy reached into her cloak and pulled out some coins. Making sure she had enough for her fare home, she handed the rest over to Essie. She didn't begrudge the girl the money, for in truth Betsy could well remember what it was like to be poor and desperate.

Essie greedily snatched the coins. "Course I listened in. Nothing else to do around 'ere, is there?"

"Did Miss Everdene mention anything about Mary Sparks to Mr. Farnsworth?"

"Nah, she just talked sweet to 'im, pretended everything was fine. She didn't say a word about what 'appened in the kitchen. Stupid cow, 'e's only marryin' 'er fer 'er money." Essie's lip curled up in a sneer. "You'd think she'd figure that much out every time she looked in 'er mirror. Why would a 'andsome man like 'im want someone like 'er if'n she hadn't inherited a packet from her old grandmother?"

"So Miss Everdene inherited a rather large sum of money?" Betsy frowned thoughtfully.

Essie shook her head. "Believe me, Mr. Farnsworth couldn't see the woman for dust until 'e found out 'ow much she had. It's got the reverend's nose out of joint too. 'E'd been hopin' to keep Antonia at 'ome. But she put her foot down and said she was marryin' Malcolm Farnsworth whether 'e liked it or not. Two of 'em 'ad a right good row about it. But as she's the one that gets the money, she's the one that makes the rules now. She's of age. The old man can't keep 'er from marryin', and 'e knows it."

"I don't care where that woman's body was found," Everdene's voice boomed, "it's nothing to do with us."

Essie eased the door open again, and both women put their ears near the crack. Betsy heard the inspector say, "But, sir, we're not insinuating it does have anything to do with either you or your daughter. I'm only asking if either of you knew the houses were sitting empty. After all, both of you are shareholders in Wildwoods. It's not inconceivable that the fact the houses were empty might have been mentioned here, and that Miss Sparks overheard the remark and decided to take refuge there for the night."

"She didn't leave here until the next morning," Antonia Everdene insisted.

"Now she's lyin' again," Essie said in disgust. "Cor, acts so holy and then lies 'er bleedin' 'ead off to the coppers. Probably thinkin' by lyin' she's protectin' Malcolm Farnsworth."

"Why would she need to do that? I thought you said he was still here after Mary left." Betsy reluctantly pulled away from the door.

" 'E was, but 'e didn't stay long. 'E didn't even stay to eat, and he certainly didn't take Miss Everdene for a walk by the river like 'e did most times 'e come." Essie smiled maliciously. " 'E only stayed long enough to talk a bit, and then 'e claimed 'e had to get back to Knightsbridge. Said 'is friend's mother was feelin' poorly and 'e 'ad to get back to sit with her a spell." She broke off and laughed. "The only woman he were goin' to sit with was Mary Sparks. You could tell 'e couldn't wait to git out of 'ere and go to her."

"So what time did he leave?"

Essie shrugged. "Couldna been more than 'alf an 'our after 'e arrived. Miss Everdene was madder than a wet 'en. 'Ated to see all that fancy food she'd bought for the occasion wasted on her drunk of a father and 'erself. Right tightfisted, she is. I wonder if she'll be so mean once she's married. Probably so, stingy is stingy if'n you ask me."

Betsy gazed at the thin, plain girl and felt both pity and revulsion. Essie couldn't read or write, probably didn't have any parents and certainly didn't know the meaning of loyalty. But Betsy refused to judge her. There but for the grace of God go I, she thought humbly. If not for Inspector Witherspoon taking her in when she was sick, desperate and at her wit's end, she could well have ended up like this girl: illiterate, ignorant, ill-treated and ignored. Essie had been so hungry for someone to talk to that Betsy hadn't even had to come up with a reasonable story to get into the house and start asking questions.

"I expect you're leavin' now," Essie said sadly.

"Yes, I'd better be goin'. They'll be getting worried if I don't get back soon." She broke off and hesitated, wondering if she had the right to say what she couldn't suppress any longer.

"All right, then." Essie squared her thin shoulders beneath the cheap fabric of her dress. "I'll make sure there's no one 'angin' about, and you can slip out the back way."

"Wait a minute." Betsy couldn't help herself. There was something about this girl. "Look, if you ever decide to leave here . . ."

"Leave 'ere? Where could I go? I'm not really trained. The only reason the Everdenes keep me on is because no one else will put up with 'em. They're 'orrible to work for, but at least it's a roof over me 'ead." Essie gazed at her suspiciously. "What are you on about?"

"Nothing," Betsy said quickly. "But if you ever do decide to leave here, come see me." She started to offer to write Inspector Witherspoon's address down, but then she remembered that Essie couldn't read. "You've a good memory, well, you must 'ave." She quickly rattled off the address and then left before she could say anything more.

• • •

Witherspoon's ears ached by the time he and Constable Barnes were out of the Everdene house and safely into a hansom.

From out his window the inspector spotted the figure of a heavily cloaked woman hurrying toward the High Street. Though he couldn't see the face, there was something very familiar about the way the woman moved.

"I'll wager that no one ever slept through one of his sermons," Constable Barnes said with a groan. He rubbed his ears and winced.

"Only if they were deaf, Constable, only if they were deaf." Witherspoon sighed and wished he could go home for a nice soothing cup of tea, but he couldn't. He still had to sort out this wretched murder case. And as if that weren't bad enough, his Chief Inspector was dropping hints that things weren't progressing fast enough to suit him. Well, really, the inspector thought, what do they expect me to do? It's not as though this were a simple case. Even identifying the victim had taken a dreadfully long time.

"We know that Mr. Farnsworth is lying now," Constable Barnes said in satisfaction. "Wonder why he told us he didn't discover the ring were missing until he reached into his pocket to give it to Miss Everdene?"

"Perhaps, Constable, because it's true."

"You mean you think the reverend's lyin'?" Barnes sounded scandalized.

"Well, we know that someone is, Constable," Witherspoon said morosely. He didn't have a clue as to which of the prinicipals in this case wasn't telling the truth. But he was hardly going to admit that.

"Perhaps the Lutterbanks won't be as bad as this lot," Barnes said hopefully as the hansom clip-clopped across the bridge.

"Hopefully," the inspector muttered. "But I highly doubt it. You know, Barnes, I never realized . . ."

"Realized what, sir?"

"That the rich were just as prone to lying as the poor."

CHAPTER 9

Mrs. Jeffries paid the hansom driver and then paused to look around the busy corner. She glanced at the crumpled note in her hand and double-checked the address. Yes, this was the place where Wiggins had told her to meet him. Shepherd's Bush. Craning her neck, she stared across the heavy traffic on Goldhawk Road, to the Green, looking for the familiar face of their errant footman.

From behind, someone grabbed her elbow and spun her around, and she found herself face-to-face with a disheveled Wiggins. "Good gracious, Wiggins. You startled me. Now, where on earth have you been and what in heaven's name have you been up to?"

A smear of dirt was on his chin, his clothes were wrinkled, and there were dark circles under his eyes. "Thank goodness you've come in time," he gasped, ignoring her question. " 'Urry. We've no time to lose. She'll be 'ere soon." He tugged her round the corner onto Shepherd's Bush Road. "I was scared she'd slip back into the 'ouse before you got a gander at 'er."

"Just a moment," Mrs. Jeffries panted as the footman pulled her around handcarts and dodged in and out of clusters of pedestrians. "What are you talking about? Who are we looking for?"

" 'Urry," he urged, ignoring her questions. "She'll be 'ere any second."

"Who?"

"There she is!" Wiggins said triumphantly as he pointed to a young woman crossing the road.

The girl was dressed in a pale lavender housedress covered by an apron. She was slender, blond and very pretty. She wore a short cloak of brown wool over her dress and carried a large shopping basket.

They watched as she went into the grocer's shop.

"Is that who I think it is?" Mrs. Jeffries asked.

"It's her, all right."

She was so relieved. They weren't dealing with a madman! Cassie Yates had done precisely as she'd said she'd do. She'd gotten married. Wiggins pushed a lock of hair off his rather dirty forehead and nodded. But before he could explain further, Cassie came out of the shop and headed purposefully back the way she'd just come. The footman grabbed Mrs. Jeffries's elbow again.

"Blimey," he yelped. "She's given the grocer her list. That means she'll be comin' back this afternoon to collect the basket. But we can't risk losin' her now. I think she knows she's bein' followed. She might 'ave spotted me yesterday."

They dodged through the busy streets, keeping the brown cloak in sight. Mrs. Jeffries was too winded to ask where they were going or how Wiggins had managed to find Cassie Yates so quickly. She was only glad that he had.

The chase ended at a tall brick house at the bottom of Dunsay Road. They had to duck behind a bush as the girl paused at the end of the small front garden and turned to have a quick, suspicious look around before she slipped into the house.

As soon as the door closed, Mrs. Jeffries turned to the footman. "Excellent, Wiggins, you've done a remarkable job. But the next time, do please let us know what you're up to. Despite that rather mysterious message from Mr. Beaks, we've all been rather worried."

Wiggins picked a blade of grass off his rumpled shirt. "Sorry, Mrs. Jeffries. But I were 'ot on the trail, and I 'ad to make sure she was the right one." He brushed more dirt off his sleeve. "Sorry about this too," he mumbled, as the housekeeper glanced anxiously at his soiled clothes, "but I've been sleepin' rough."

"Oh dear, I do hope you won't take a chill."

"Not to worry, I'm right as rain. Anyways, like I were sayin', it couldn't be helped."

"However did you manage to find her?" Mrs. Jeffries asked. "Did she come back to Knightsbridge?"

"I found 'er by keepin' a sharp eye out on the McGraw 'ouse. Sure enough, once I'd figured out that Garrett's little nip of a brother come out to play the instant Garrett got 'ome every day, it were as plain as the nose on yer face," Wiggins explained proudly. " 'E were sending the lad to keep an eye on 'er. So instead of keepin' my eye on Garrett, I followed the little 'un, and he lead me straight to 'er."

Mrs. Jeffries stared at the footman incredulously. "Garrett McGraw's little brother? But what does that have to do with Cassie Yates?"

Now it was Wiggins's turn to look surprised. "Cassie Yates? Who said anythin' about 'er? That girl that just went into that 'ouse inn't Cassie Yates. She's Mary Sparks."

Edgar Lutterbank glared at the inspector for a moment before shifting his hard gaze to Constable Barnes. "I presume you've a good reason for this inconvenience?"

Inspector Witherspoon stifled a sigh. The Lutterbank family was being every bit as uncooperative as he'd feared. He and Constable Barnes had been kept waiting for half an hour before Mr. Lutterbank would even condescend to see them.

"We're not trying to inconvenience you or your family." Witherspoon smiled tightly at the four people staring at him with enmity. No, he corrected silently, only three of them were hostile. Mrs. Lutterbank was pretending they weren't there. The pale, mousy woman had been gazing blankly at the wall since he and Constable Barnes had been shown into the drawing room.

"However," he continued, trying to infuse some authority into his tone, "this is a murder investigation. Mary Sparks was in your employ directly prior to her death. She spent less than twenty-four hours at the Everdene household. So if you don't mind, it would be most helpful if you can answer a few questions."

"Of course we mind," Edgar Lutterbank charged. "But I don't see that we've any choice in the matter." He pulled a watch out of his exquisitely tailored coat and frowned. "But do get on with it, man, I've a meeting in the city in an hour."

Witherspoon turned to Mrs. Lutterbank. He might as well start with the least aggressive member of this household. "As the mistress of the house," he asked, "could you explain your reasons for asking Mary Sparks to leave?"

Mrs. Lutterbank ignored him. She continued to study the wallpaper.

"She didn't ask Mary to leave," Mr. Lutterbank cut in quickly. "The girl left of her own accord and, I might add, without giving notice."

Fiona Lutterbank, a plump, brown-haired girl who reminded Witherspoon of a pigeon, gave a short, high-pitched bark of laughter. It was not a pleasant sound.

"Oh, yes," Fiona said as they all looked at her. "Mary left without giving notice. Mama was so upset."

The inspector suspected that might be a fabrication. He couldn't see that anything short of a blast of fireworks would upset Mrs. Lutterbank. Why, the woman had barely blinked since he'd been there. "But our information is that Miss Sparks left because she'd been let go." The inspector addressed his question to Edgar Lutterbank. Out of the corner of his eye he saw Fiona turn her head sharply. He quickly shifted his gaze to the other side of the room and saw Fiona openly smirking at her brother, Andrew.

"Nonsense," Mr. Lutterbank snapped. "I don't care what kind of ridiculous tales you've heard, it isn't true. Mary was a good worker. Why would we let her go? She just up and took it into her head to leave."

"And you've no idea why?" the inspector asked.

"I think I know why," Fiona said slyly. She giggled again. "Mary must have overheard Mama and me talking about the Everdenes needing a parlormaid. They're acquaintances of ours because Papa does business with them. I suppose the girl must have thought she wouldn't have to work so hard at a minister's house. Don't you think so, Andrew?"

Again she smirked at her brother. He gave her a tight smile, then looked at Witherspoon. Like his father, he was impeccably, if somewhat foppishly, dressed. He was a tall, thin man with a sharp aristocratic nose and weak chin. He smiled coolly at the inspector and said, "I've really no idea. I don't make it a habit to concern myself with the servants' business."

Despite his calm voice and the arrogant tilt to his head, Witherspoon had the impression Andrew Lutterbank was nervous. The chap was trying a bit too hard. His lazy posture seemed posed, his face too carefully blank. And the inspector had noticed that when the young man thought no one was looking, he nervously rubbed his chin.

"I'm sure you don't, Mr. Lutterbank. But surely, you must have some idea why Miss Sparks would simply leave? According to witnesses, you were seen having a rather prolonged discussion with the girl on the day she left." Witherspoon hoped he remembered that tidbit of gossip correctly, but he wasn't quite sure. Perhaps it had been someone else Andrew Lutterbank had been talking to that day. Drat, there were times when it was so difficult to keep facts straight in one's head.

"I don't care what you've been told," Andrew said loudly. Too loudly. "Mary was a servant here. If I was seen talking with her, it was probably because I wanted her to take better care in dusting my things. Except for giving her an occasional reprimand about shoddy work, I had nothing to do with her."

Witherspoon noticed that he didn't deny he'd been speaking to the girl. "Then why did you give her a brooch?"

Edgar Lutterbank leapt from his chair. "Now, see here, Inspector."

But Witherspoon ignored the outburst. He was too busy watching Andrew Lutterbank's face go utterly white. He had no idea if the young man had given Mary Sparks that brooch, but from his reaction, Witherspoon knew his shot in the dark had hit the target. His spirits soared. At last he was on the right track. Now perhaps they'd get somewhere in this case.

But the inspector's hopes were immediately dashed. For it wasn't Andrew Lutterbank who answered his question; it was his sister.

"Andrew didn't give Mary that brooch," Fiona yelped. "I gave it to her."

"Really?" Witherspoon was terribly disappointed. "Why?"

Fiona stared at him like a stricken rabbit. She swallowed convulsively. "Because I felt sorry for her," she mumbled.

"You felt sorry for the young lady?" The inspector had found that repeating an answer as a question often got results, and he was desperate enough to try anything.

Fiona's head bobbed up and down. "Yes, her fiancé was away at sea, but he was due home in a couple of months. Mary didn't have anything nice, no trinkets or jewelry. She wanted to look pretty for Mark, and I didn't particularly like that old pin anyway, so I gave it to her."

"Let me see now. You gave an expensive silver brooch to a servant because she didn't have any jewelry to wear for her sweetheart." Inspector Witherspoon's brows rose. "Is that what you're telling me?"

"My daughter speaks perfect English, Inspector," Edgar Lutterbank said testily. "If she says she gave the girl the trinket, then she did. Besides, what's this pin got to do with anything?"

"As the victim had the brooch pinned to her dress," the inspector replied, "we'd like to know precisely how a rather impoverished young woman went about acquiring it." He turned back to Fiona. "You didn't by any chance happen to give the girl a betrothal ring as well?"

Fiona blinked in surprise and shook her head. Mrs. Lutterbank continued to stare at the wall, and Andrew slumped back against the settee.

"Really, Inspector." Edgar Lutterbank's gaze narrowed suspiciously. "Isn't that a rather ridiculous question? Come now, do ask something that makes sense. You're wasting all our time. Out of the kindness of her heart, my daughter gave the girl a trinket, and that's all. Why should any of us know anything about some betrothal ring?"

"The betrothal ring in question was purchased by a Mr. Malcolm Farnsworth to give to his fiancée," Witherspoon explained. "The gentleman is, I believe, acquainted with the family."

"Certainly. Both young Malcolm and Emery Clements are frequently guests of my son. But I assure you, sir, we're not in the habit of relieving them of their valuables and passing them on to the servants."

"I certainly didn't mean to imply any such thing." The inspector wasn't sure what he had meant to imply, but he did think this line of questioning was producing some interesting results. He glanced at Constable Barnes and found the man gazing at him in admiration. "So you've no idea how Mary Sparks happened to be wearing an expensive pin and betrothal ring when she was murdered?" He slowly turned his head, gazing expectantly at the four Lutterbanks.

"I believe I can solve that particular mystery," Andrew Lutterbank drawled. "Malcolm happened to lose the ring the very day he bought it. We'd been out in the gardens having tea. Mary obviously found it and picked it up."

Inspector Witherspoon deliberately kept his expression blank. How on earth did Andrew Lutterbank know the ring had been lost when Malcolm Farnsworth didn't? But he wasn't going to show his hand now. Oh no, the inspector thought craftily. Before he pursued any more questions about that ring he'd have another word with Mr. Farnsworth. Nodding to the young man, he turned to Edgar Lutterbank. "Are you a shareholder in Wildwoods?"

One of Mr. Lutterbank's heavy gray eyebrows rose. "Yes. Not that it's any business of the Metropolitan Police."

Witherspoon looked at Fiona and quickly asked, "Other than her fiancé, was Mary Sparks seeing any other men?"

Fiona's mouth gaped in surprise for a split second before she recovered. "Well, yes," she said, giving the inspector a knowing smile. "Actually, Mary was a flirt. I believe there were several young men who were smitten with her. And she encouraged them all."

Mrs. Lutterbank suddenly straightened. "Oh yes," she chirped brightly. "Oh yes, there were always men. She was a tart. Men all the time. Why in this very house, I've had to speak harshly . . ."

As Mrs. Lutterbank rambled on about harlots and tarts, Edgar Lutterbank's face darkened to crimson. Suddenly he leapt to his feet. "That's enough," he roared, and Mrs. Lutterbank jumped and ceased her muttering. He turned to the inspector. "My wife's not well, sir. These questions have upset her terribly. Fiona, take your mother to her room."

A swell of sympathy filled Witherspoon as he watched Fiona lead the poor woman away. He realized now that the reason she'd been sitting quietly and staring at the wall was probably that she was a tad touched in the head. Really, it was such a shame.

He waited until the two women had gone and then turned to Mr. Lutterbank. "About Wildwoods, sir. I'm afraid your association with that company is very much the business of the police. Mary Sparks's body was discovered in one of Wildwoods's properties." He looked quickly at Andrew. "Would you mind telling me, sir, where you were on the night of September 10th?"

Edgar Lutterbank quickly stepped between the inspector and his son, blocking the policeman's view of Andrew's expression.

"He was at home," Edgar supplied hastily.

Witherspoon studied the older man for a moment. "You must have a remarkable memory, sir."

"Not at all, Inspector." Lutterbank retorted. "I don't need a remarkable memory to know where my son was on that particular evening. He was at home every evening in September."

"Surely that's unusual." Witherspoon tilted his head to one side and tried to give Andrew a disbelieving smile. "A wealthy bachelor spending all of his free time at home . . ." He let his voice trail off meaningfully.

"There's nothing in the least peculiar about my staying home," Andrew said, getting up from the settee and coming to stand beside his father. "My mother wasn't well in September. I wanted to be close by in case she took a turn for the worse."

"I see." The inspector tried to think of something else to ask. Unfortunately, nothing occurred to him. "Well, if you can think of anything else which might shed some light on this matter," he said, "do please contact me at the Yard. I take it none of you have any plans to leave London? We may need to ask a few more questions."

"Now, see here, Inspector," Edgar Lutterbank protested. "Don't you think you're being unreasonable? Are you telling us we can't leave the city?"

"No, no, of course not," Witherspoon answered.

"Well it's a jolly good thing. Leave London, indeed!" Lutterbank snorted. "I'm going to the continent in a few days, and I'm taking my son with me. Business trip. Now, if you've an objection to that, perhaps I'll have a word with your superiors."

"That won't be necessary," the inspector replied wearily. "You're free to go where you please."

He signaled Constable Barnes to put away his notebook and took his leave of the Lutterbank family. He couldn't wait to get home and have a nice, quiet cup of tea. Thank goodness this tiresome day was almost over.

• • •

Mrs. Jeffries listened carefully to the details of Inspector Witherspoon's day. She clucked her tongue sympathetically, ladled more potatoes onto his plate and gently asked a few questions. Tense herself because of what she and the others would be doing later, she barely listened as he repeated the facts of the interview he'd had with the Everdenes. Mrs. Jeffries wasn't worried overmuch by missing any of that tale—she'd already heard the entire story from Betsy.

"I believe I'll turn in early, Mrs. Jeffries," Witherspoon announced as he pushed his plate aside and stood up. "Perhaps a good night's sleep will help rid me of this dreadful headache."

She quickly assured him that that was precisely what he needed. As soon as he disappeared up the stairs, she hurried to the hall closet, grabbed her hat and cloak and raced to the kitchen.

Betsy and Mrs. Goodge were waiting at the kitchen table.

"Smythe should be back any minute now," the maid told her. "He'll have had time to get to Luty's and back."

"Good. Did Smythe have time to tell you what he'd learned today?" She looked expectantly at the two women. They both shook their heads.

"He only had time to snatch a bite to eat," Mrs. Goodge explained. "Before he left to get the carriage and Luty Belle."

As they waited for the coachman to return, she told them everything she'd learned from the inspector over dinner. "We must be sure and tell Smythe everything too," she finished, cocking her head toward the street as her sharp ears picked up the distinctive sound of a carriage turning the corner.

"I'll ride up front with 'im and let 'im know," Betsy volunteered eagerly. As the coach drew up out front, she picked up her cloak. "Hope the inspector stays abed tonight. Wouldn't look right for 'im to ring for something and find us all gone."

"Not to worry," Mrs. Goodge said calmly. "I can hear his bell from me room. I'll take care of the dining room too. Give me somethin' to do while I'm waiting for you to get back. If'n the inspector wants something, I can fetch it. Besides, all I have to do is 'int that you and Mrs. J are feelin' poorly, and he wouldn't think of askin' where you be. He'll think you're abed."

"Thank you, Mrs. Goodge," Mrs. Jeffries said to the cook. "I don't know how we'd manage without you. We don't like leaving you to cope, but it's vitally important we confront Mary Sparks."

• • •

By the time they arrived outside the brick house on Dunsany Road, Luty Belle was quivering with excitement. "I still can't understand why Mary didn't come to me," she said, pulling her bright purple cloak tighter against the cool chill of the night.

"Yes, that's very curious, isn't it?" Mrs. Jeffries reached for the door latch as soon as the horses stopped. "And that's why we want you with us when we talk to her. I've a feeling that whatever it is she's hiding, she'll be more apt to tell the truth if you're there."

"Stop frettin', Hepzibah," Luty ordered as she spritely leapt from the carriage. "Mary will tell the truth."

"It's about time you got 'ere," Wiggins whispered. He'd come from his hiding place in the bushes when he'd seen the coach round the corner.

"Is she still there?" Mrs. Jeffries asked.

"Yeah. No one's gone in or out since the last lodger got home at half past six."

"Come on." Luty headed for the house. "Let's git this over with."

With Luty Belle in the lead, they marched up the walkway and banged the knocker. A moment later the door opened and a tall middle-aged woman with black hair peered out.

"Yes, what is it?" she asked sharply. "I've no rooms to let now—" She broke off as she became aware of the small crowd littering her stoop. "Here now, what's all this? What do you lot want?"

Luty Belle stepped forward. "We've come to see Mary Sparks. We knows she's here, and we're not leavin' until we see her."

The woman looked taken aback for an instant, and then her bony face hardened. Mrs. Jeffries quickly shoved Luty to one side.

"Please forgive my friend's rather bold manner," she began pleasantly. She ignored Luty's snort of derision. "But it's terribly important that we speak to Mary Sparks. One could almost say it was a matter of life and death. This is Mrs. Luty Belle Crookshank, and she's a dear friend of Mary's. We've been so very worried about the girl. We must see her."

The woman regarded her suspiciously for a moment and then stepped back and opened the door wider. "I'm Agnes Finch. Go on through to the parlor. I'll see if Mary wants to see you."

They trooped into the parlor, and a few moments later Mary Sparks appeared. Puzzled, she stopped in the doorway and gazed at the unfamiliar faces. When she reached Luty Belle's, she gasped and rushed forward. "Oh, Mrs. Crookshank, it's you. I'm so glad you've come."

"Well, I reckon I had to come," Luty exclaimed as she rose and gave the girl a hug. "You weren't exactly bustin' your horses to come see me, was ya?"

"I'm so sorry," Mary pleaded. She bit her lower lip. "But I've been so scared. Everythin's so mixed up. Garrett said I should just wait here until Mark come home before I did anything." She paused and cast a quick, curious glance at the others.

"These are my friends," Luty hastily explained. "If'n you didn't murder Cassie Yates, then they've come to help."

Mary's eyes widened, and she paled. "Then she really is dead. I knew somethin' had happened to her," she whispered.

"You knew Cassie had been murdered?" Mrs. Jeffries interjected softly.

"No." Mary shook her head. "I mean, I thought somethin' bad might have happened to her, but I didn't know it were murder."

"Why'd ya think somethin' had happened to Cassie?" Luty asked. "Dang and blast, this ain't makin' no sense at all. How'd you come to get mixed up with Cassie Yates and her troubles?"

"I didn't want to get mixed up with her," Mary said earnestly. "But I didn't have no choice about it. Then, after she didn't show up to collect her pouch, I knew somethin' was wrong."

Luty's gaze sharpened. "What pouch?"

"The one she gave me to keep for her . . ."

Mrs. Jeffries stepped forward again. "I think it would be best if Mary sat down and told us what happened in her own good time."

Mary looked at Luty for guidance, and when the elderly woman nodded, she sat down on the settee.

Betsy and Smythe leaned forward, Wiggins balanced on the edge of his chair and even Mrs. Jeffries was excited. She forced herself to calm down. "Now," she said, sitting down across from Mary and Luty Belle. "Why don't you tell us what happened?"

The girl chewed her lower lip and twisted her hands together in her lap. "I'm not right sure where to begin."

"Why don't you start with the event that led you to decide to leave the Lutterbank house?" Mrs. Jeffries suggested smoothly.

Mary nodded. "Well, it were the day before I went to Mrs. Crookshank. I were upstairs dusting the landin' when all of a sudden, Andrew Lutterbank slinks up behind me and tried to put his arms around me waist." She wrinkled her nose in disgust. "He's done that before, but this time it were different."

"Different how?" Mrs. Jeffries asked.

"Bolder. Like he didn't care if I said somethin' to his father. I slapped his hands and told him to leave me be, but he just laughed and lunged at me again. This time I stepped back far enough to run if I had to, and that made him stop. I told him if he didn't leave me be, I'd tell his father, and he just laughed and said he didn't care." Mary shook her head. "Said he didn't need to worry anymore, that he had a bit of money comin' to him. But I knew that were a lie. He'd been lickin' his father's boots for weeks tryin' to get Mr. Lutterbank to give him back his allowance. Andrew hadn't had as much as a farthing from Mr. Lutterbank since he got Sally Comstock in the family way, and they used Andrew's allowance to pay her off and ship her to Australia."

"So you know about that," Mrs. Jeffries said. She remembered that Mary wasn't at the Lutterbank house when that incident had occurred. "Who told you?"

"Cassie told me," Mary replied. "But it weren't a secret. Everyone in the house knew what had happened. Oh yes, everyone knows. Especially with Cassie goin' on about it all the time. You'd have had to been deaf as a post not to have heard the story."

"Then what happened?" Luty asked impatiently.

"Well, after I told him to leave me be, he flounced out of the house and into the garden. Mr. Farnsworth and Mr. Clements were waitin' for him. I watched from the window. I didn't want to run into him, and I were hopin' he'd be goin' out with the other gentleman. They often went to their club and played cards—gamblin' and the like."

"But how could Andrew gamble?" Mrs. Jeffries asked. "You said he didn't have any money." She frowned as she remembered the gossip Mrs. Goodge had told her.

"He didn't use money. Least he hadn't been. He used the belongin's he had in his room," Mary explained. "He had a lot of nice things some old relative who'd died out in India had left him. Strange kinds of objects, gold candlesticks, jewels, a pair of ivory-handled daggers. His friends were quite willing to let him play with that instead of money. He'd already lost most of them because Sarah, the upstairs maid, weren't complainin' so much about how long it took her to dust."

"All right, so we know that Lutterbank had a yen to gamble every now and agin," Luty said impatiently. "But time's awastin'. Git on with the story, girl. What happened next?"

"Well, after he went into the garden, I decided I had to leave. It were one thing to stay when Andrew was behavin' himself, but after what he'd just told me about not carin' what his father thought no more and not needin' his allowance, I knew I'd best get out and find myself another position." Mary paused and took a deep breath. "There was somethin' not right goin' on in that house. Somethin' I couldn't quite put my finger on, and I just wanted to go. I'd heard about another position, over in Putney, at a minister's house."

"Who told you about the position?" It was Betsy who asked that question.

"Cassie Yates. Miss Fiona had sent me out that day to get her a box of chocolates. I met Cassie when she was comin' out the side gate of the garden."

"Who'd Cassie been visiting?" Betsy interrupted.

"I don't know. I never asked," Mary admitted. "But anyways, she saw that I were upset and asked me what was wrong. I told her I'd decided to leave, and she told me about the Everdenes needin' a new maid. She give me the name of the domestic agency that was doin' the hirin' as well."

"Did Cassie ask you why you wanted to leave?" Mrs. Jeffries asked.

"No, she didn't have to. I think she knew." Mary made a wry face. "Not that she were ever scared of Andrew; she weren't. But that's neither here nor there. Early the next mornin' I give Fiona Lutterbank the news that I were leavin' and I wouldn't be back. Then I went to Mrs. Crookshank."

"Why'd ya lie to me about that brooch?" Luty asked sharply.

"But I didn't." Mary turned earnest eyes to her friend. "You see, when I told Miss Lutterbank I were leavin' she accused me of stealin' her silver brooch. But I never took no brooch. I never took nothin' from her. So I told her she were wrong and I left."

Luty stared at the girl's pleading face for a few seconds and then grinned. "Reckon you're tellin' the truth, child." She reached over and patted Mary's hand. "Git on with your tale."

Relieved, Mary nodded. "Mrs. Crookshank wrote me a letter of reference and let me spend the night. The next day, I put on my best dress and went to the domestic agency that hired for the Everdenes. I got the job. They told me to get over to Putney as soon as I could. I went back and said goodbye to Mrs. Crookshank, picked up my carpetbag and started for the Everdene house. On my way I happened to pass by the shop where Cassie Yates used to be employed. Well, she'd already give that position up, so I were right surprised when I heard her calling me to stop." Mary swallowed and dropped her gaze to her lap. "I didn't want to, but she said she had to talk to me, said it were important. We went to her rooms, and then she started askin' me a lot o' questions."

"What kind of questions?" Mrs. Jeffries interjected.

"She started off by askin' if I'd got the job and had anyone from Everdene house seen me. I told her I was to start that day and that the only person I'd seen except for the lady that did the interviewin' was a well-dressed woman who come into the office just as I were leavin'." Mary broke off and shuddered. "I didn't know it then, but she had somethin' in mind with all them questions. Before I could say Bob's-your-uncle, she ordered me to change clothes with her."

"Change clothes with her?" Wiggins looked positively scandalized.

"Yes. Then she told me I weren't goin' to be workin' for the Everdenes; she was. She were goin' to pretend she were me and take the post."

"Why did you go along with this?" Luty asked indignantly.

"I didn't have no choice," Mary explained. "When I tried to tell her I wouldn't do it, she pulled that silver broach out of her reticule and dangled it under me nose; then she reached into her pocket and pulled out a handful of pound notes. She said she'd taken the money and pin from Fiona Lutterbank, and she'd done it wearin' my old gray cloak. She said she'd made sure several people saw her leavin' the house wearin' my cloak. If I didn't do as she asked, she'd tell the Lutterbanks where I was goin' and they'd have me put in jail." Her voice trembled, and she broke off for a moment and turned to Luty Belle. "You were already gone to Venice, Mark was still at sea and I didn't know what to do. I changed clothes with her and she left."

"You poor girl," Wiggins murmured. "All alone and frightened. It's a cryin' shame, that's what it is . . ."

"Wiggins, please," Mrs. Jeffries said. "Go on, Mary. What did you do then?"

"Well, I waited until it were evening and I went back to Knightsbridge. I were hopin' that Garrett could help me. But he couldn't do anythin' until the next day. He couldn't take me home with him—there's not a spare bed at their house, and he couldn't bring me here because Mrs. Finch weren't home. So he told me to go to Magpie Lane. He said he overheard Mr. Clements tell Mr. Andrew and Mr. Farnsworth about the houses bein' empty. Garrett said for me to go to the back of one of the houses and break a window. Said the whole street were deserted and no one would hear. So we waited a bit, and then I got a hansom and left."

"Why did you delay going to Magpie Lane?" Mrs. Jeffries asked.

"I didn't want Mr. Andrew to see me on the street. Garrett and I had to hide in some bushes until Mr. Andrew got his own hansom and went off. It took a bit of time. Hansoms were hard to come by that night. It were pouring with rain."

"When you were there that night, did you hear any other cabs go up the road?"

Mary nodded. "Oh yes. For a deserted street it had a bit of traffic that evening. I were trying to sleep when I heard the first one, then right after that the second one, and then, a good hour later, the third cab come around the corner. After midnight, I was able to finally doze off."

"When did you realize that Cassie Yates was missing?" Mrs. Jeffries asked softly. She watched Mary's face closely, but the girl continued to gaze at her openly.

"The next day," she replied in low voice. "I knew something was bad wrong the next day. Cassie had told me to meet her at a tea shop, but she never showed. I knew something had happened then."

Betsy leaned forward. "What made you so certain?"

"Because Cassie had given me a pouch for safekeepin'. I was to bring it to her the next day. But she never came."

"What was in the pouch?" Mrs. Jeffries asked.

Mary bit her lip again, and her eyes flooded with tears. "Money. Lots of it."

CHAPTER 10

Mrs. Jeffries ignored the gasps from the other occupants of the room. "Money," she repeated softly. "Are you sure?"

Mary brushed at her cheeks. "I'm sure. It liked to frightened me to death, walkin' about London with a pouch full of pound notes."

"How much money are we talkin' 'ere?" Smythe asked.

Mary turned to took at him and shrugged her shoulders. "Well, I didn't count it, so I don't rightly know. But it were a lot, more than I've ever seen before."

"When Cassie didn't show up," Mrs. Jeffries asked softly, "what did you do with the pouch?"

"I took it to Knightsbridge," Mary replied, giving Luty Belle an anxious glance. "I hid it in one of them tubs on Mrs. Crookshank's terrace."

"One of my tubs," Luty repeated. "You mean one of them big fancy urns I've been plantin' my orange trees in?"

"Yes. Garrett had told me he'd dug them out that day," Mary explained hastily. "And I couldn't think of any other place where the money would be safe. You know, in case Cassie showed up and wanted it back. So when I went to the gardens that day, I waited till there was no one around, then I shoved the pouch in the bottom o' the tub and piled a bit o' dirt on top to hide it. I didn't know what else to do," she wailed. "I couldn't even tell Garrett about the money. I didn't want him involved any more than he was. But I didn't want to keep it. Cassie's money didn't belong to me! I weren't rightly sure that money even belonged to her. I don't know how she got it, but when she didn't show up, I knew I didn't want to hang on to it."

Mrs. Jeffries tilted her head to one side and studied the girl's earnest expression. "Why did you feel so strongly about it? Cassie had blackmailed you out of a position, and you hadn't much money of your own.

Under those circumstances, I should think you'd have been very tempted to hang on to that pouch."

"Tempted to steal?" Mary cried. "I'm no thief, Mrs. Jeffries, and it's a right good thing too. I reckon Cassie were murdered for that money. If I'd a kept it, the same thing would have happened to me."

"Why do you think the money caused Cassie's murder?" Luty Belle asked bluntly. "Are you sayin' you know who wanted the money, you know who wanted her dead?"

Mary hesitated. "I'm not sure. But I know she didn't come by that money honestly. She had ways of gettin' things from people, usually men. And I know that she was plannin' on causin' a lot of trouble, and I didn't want any part o' it."

Luty's black eyes narrowed. "Trouble fer who?"

"Malcolm Farnsworth, for one," Mary replied. "I knew about him because she told me when we was a-changin' clothes so she could take my place at the Everdene house. She went on and on about him, almost like she didn't know what she were sayin'. She said she wasn't lettin' him get away with it, that he'd do right by her if it was the last thing he ever did, and that if he thought payin' her off with a few quid would get rid of her, he had another think comin'."

"Cor," Smythe exclaimed. "She said all that?" He looked at Mrs. Jeffries. "It wouldn't be the first time a man's done killin' to keep his secrets from showin'. Looks to me like we might 'ave a motive for murder 'ere."

"So it would appear." Mrs. Jeffries turned to Mary. "Did Cassie say what she planned to do when she got to the Everdene house?"

"No, she just rambled on about how Malcolm would see that she didn't mean to be trifled with. That he'd have to marry her or she'd cause a scandal." Mary shrugged. "When I asked her how she could do that, she told me that if she had to, she'd stand right up in church if Malcolm tried to marry Antonia Everdene. Said she'd tell the whole world she was going to have Malcolm's bastard." Mary broke off as a blush crept up her cheeks. "It weren't very nice language, I know. But that's what she said."

Betsy pursed her lips. "So you're sayin' that Cassie went to the Everdenes' just to show Malcolm he couldn't get rid of her?"

"That's what she said," Mary answered. "But I thought she was talkin' crazy. She'd already taken money from him."

"You mean she claimed the money in the pouch was definitely from Malcolm Farnsworth?" Mrs. Jeffries felt this was an important point.

"Well, she didn't exactly say he give her the money," Mary admitted, "but who else was there? And I know she saw Malcolm that day, 'cause she showed me a ring he give her. It were a pretty one too. She had it on a chain round her neck."

"But if'n he give Cassie a ring," Wiggins put in, confused, "wouldn't that mean he meant to marry 'er?"

Betsy snorted. "Not always. If Cassie were raisin' a fuss, he might 'ave given her the ring to keep her quiet. He probably lied through his teeth and told Cassie he'd marry her. Then, when she found out he were really fixin' to propose to Antonia Everdene, she might have been mad enough to want to get a bit of her own back."

"But 'ow would Cassie know that Malcolm Farnsworth was goin' to ask Miss Everdene for her 'and?" Wiggins asked curiously.

It was Mary who answered. "She could have found out easy enough. Cassie was always hangin' about . . . She might have seen Andrew Lutterbank that day, and he might have told her. Like I said before, Cassie weren't scared of Mr. Andrew. She used to brag that she knew how to handle him. She were half-mad that day, rantin' and ravin' about Malcolm and Emery Clements and Andrew Lutterbank. She might have seen any of them, and any of them could have told her about Malcolm plannin' on proposin' to Miss Everdene."

"Did she specifically state she'd seen any of those gentlemen?" Mrs. Jeffries asked. She watched the girl carefully.

"Not exactly," Mary replied slowly. "I don't recall evrythin' she said that mornin', but I do remember I had a . . . a . . ."

"Impression," Betsy supplied helpfully.

"That's right, a impression she'd seen them all. But I couldn't say for certain." Mary sighed. "All I know is I was ever so glad when she left and I could get away."

"So the last time you saw Cassie Yates was the morning she made you change clothes and took your place at the Everdene house, is that correct?" Mrs. Jeffries asked briskly.

"That's right."

"Why have you been hiding yurself?" Luty asked. She tilted her chin and stared hard at the girl.

Mrs. Jeffries saw Mary's throat muscles move as the girl swallowed. Finally, she said, "Because I was scared of Malcolm. Garrett told me that no one had seen Cassie about since that day she went to the Everdenes'. Malcolm was still engaged to Antonia Everdene, and I knew Cassie wouldn't have stood for that. I knew somethin' bad must have happened, but I didn't have no real proof that he'd done anythin'. What could I say? Who'd believe me? I didn't even know for sure she was dead until tonight."

"But didn't you see the story of the body being discovered in the newspapers?" Mrs. Jeffries asked.

Mary shook her head. "No, I don't have money to waste on newspapers. I knew I should do somethin' about Cassie, but I weren't sure what. So I decided to stay here until Mark come back. He'd know the best thing to do."

Mrs. Jeffries nodded and asked, "And when is your fiancé due back?"

"At the end of the week," Mary replied with a shy smile.

"Good," Luty said firmly. "But afore then, you'd best come with me to see Inspector Witherspoon. We'll go tomorrow morning. Cassie Yates mightn't a been much good, but she didn't deserve to be murdered and stashed in some dark hole of a cellar like she was nothin'."

"You want me to go to the police?" Mary's voice squeaked in alarm.

"But of course, my dear," Mrs. Jeffries said firmly. "You must tell Inspector Witherspoon everything you've told us."

"But what about Mr. Malcolm? I don't want him comin' after me."

"You needn't fear Malcolm Farnsworth," Mrs. Jeffries said soothingly. "I'm sure that once the inspector hears what you have to say, Mr. Farnsworth will no longer be a problem."

As soon as she said the words, something tugged at the back of her mind. She tried to grasp what it was, but she couldn't.

"Don't you worry none," Luty said as she stamped her cane. "You jus' go pack yer things and come with me. You can stay at my house till yer man gets back, and don't be frettin' none about a no-good polecat like Farnsworth. I keep a six-shooter under my bed, and Hatchet's purty danged good with a rifle. We ain't scared a him. Tomorrow mornin' we'll go see the inspector, and by tomorrow night Mr. Malcolm Murderin' Farnsworth will be locked up tighter than the crown jewels."

Inspector Witherspoon allowed himself a smug smile as Mrs. Jeffries took his hat and coat. He couldn't help it. For once, the day had gone exceedingly well. Perfectly, in fact. This wretched murder was virtually solved. By tomorrow morning, they'd have the rest of the evidence they needed to arrest the murderer.

"You're looking very happy, sir," Mrs. Jeffries said as she hung his hat on the rack and then turned and led the way to the drawing room. "Have you had a good day?"

"An excellent day, Mrs. Jeffries," the inspector said as he settled into his favorite chair. "We've made monumental progress in this case. Why, it's practically solved. I must say, your comments this morning at breakfast helped enormously. You were quite right, you know. The only way to truly determine if Antonia Everdene was telling the truth was to question her servants." He broke off and accepted a glass of sherry. "I must say, we had a spot of luck there." He broke off and frowned slightly. "Er, I hope you don't mind, but when it became clear that Essie Tuttle wouldn't tell us the truth because she was afraid of losing her position, I did make a rather, a well . . . a rash promise."

"Oh?"

"Yes, I'm afraid I had to assure the girl that I'd find her another post," Witherspoon confessed. "Well, I thought that if worse came to worst, perhaps you could find a spot for her here. I know you're in charge of the household, Mrs. Jeffries, and I certainly wouldn't be presumptuous enough to interfere in any way, but do you possibly think we could find something for Essie to do here at Upper Edmonton Gardens?" He leaned forward, his expression earnest. "I know that's not a particularly usual method of getting the truth from a witness, but honestly, Mrs. Jeffries, the poor girl was utterly terrified. I couldn't get a word out of her until I'd told her I'd find her another place. If you don't think she'd fit in here, do you suppose Mrs. Crookshank might be able to use another housemaid? Her house is rather enormous, and despite dear Mrs. Crookshank being rather eccentric, she strikes one as being a most kindhearted soul."

"Not to worry, sir," Mrs. Jeffries said quickly, wanting to get the inspector back to the case. "I'm sure that between Luty and me we can work something out for the girl. Now, do go on, sir. I'm burning with curiosity."

The inspector sighed with relief. "Oh, gracious," he cried, "I'm forgetting to give you the best news of all."

Mrs. Jeffries prepared to took surprised.

"Luty Belle came to see me this morning, and you'll never guess who she brought with her."

"Who?"

"Mary Sparks." Witherspoon answered smugly. "She isn't dead. The body we found in Magpie Lane is Cassie Yates."

"Goodness, really?"

For the next ten minutes, Witherspoon related how Luty Belle Crookshank had shown up at the Yard with Mary Sparks in tow. He repeated Mary's story almost verbatim. "Of course," he concluded, "we realized Miss Sparks must be telling the truth when we accompanied them back to Mrs. Crookshank's and dug up that pouch. It had over five hundred pounds inside!"

"Goodness, that's a lot of money." There was another faint tug at the back of Mrs. Jeffries's mind. But it disappeared as quickly as it had come.

"It was a piece of luck that I'd already decided to go to the Everdene house again," the inspector continued happily. "Hearing Mary's story gave us precisely the information we needed to ask the right questions."

"Nonsense, Inspector," Mrs. Jeffries said briskly. "Luck had nothing to do with it. As usual, you're being far too modest. It was your own brilliant detective work that made you realize that the Everdenes were trying to hide something. You've an instinct for such things, sir. Tell me," she continued when he beamed with pleasure, "what did Mr. Farnsworth say when you confronted him this afternoon?"

"At first he tried to deny everything," Witherspoon said. "But when the chap realized that we had a witness to the fact that he'd left the Everdene house shortly after Cassie Yates did, and that we knew all about his relationship with her, he caved in and admitted the truth."

"He admitted he killed her?" Mrs. Jeffries asked in astonishment.

"Oh no, no. He admitted they'd been . . . ," he broke off, blushed a deep pink and lowered his eyes to his glass, "intimate. He also admitted he'd seen her earlier that day and told her it was all over between them. He gave her fifty pounds."

"Did he give her anything else, sir?" She hoped the inspector had discovered how Cassie Yates had ended up with Antonia Everdene's betrothal ring around her neck.

"No, just the money. Mind you, he claimed not to know anything about the five hundred pounds we'd found in that pouch. Claimed he didn't have any idea where that had come from."

Mrs. Jeffries thought that was odd. Why would he lie about how much he'd given Cassie to get out of his life? "That's a silly thing to lie about."

"Yes, I thought so too," the inspector agreed. "Mind you, Farnsworth claims that once he gave Cassie the fifty pounds, she agreed to let him alone. But obviously she changed her mind and threatened to tell Miss Everdene about the child. Farnsworth killed her to make sure his marriage to an heiress wasn't in jeopardy."

"How did she get the betrothal ring?" she asked.

Witherspoon raised his eyebrows. "Farnsworth claims she stole it from him on the morning he asked Miss Everdene to marry him. That's probably how Cassie realized Farnsworth was going to wed Miss Everdene. She saw the betrothal ring. He admits he saw her that day before he went to the Lutterbanks. That's how he met Cassie, you know. They began their association when she was still working there." He sighed. "Poor silly woman, if she'd stayed away from that greedy monster, she'd still be alive. Sad, isn't it? There's so very much tragedy about."

Mrs. Jeffries didn't want the inspector to get started on one of his philosophical discourses. Frequently they had a number of quite interesting chats about the world, the cosmos and the nature of life, but this evening she needed information.

"Of course there is, sir," she said quickly. "But you and men like yourself are certainly doing your very best to make the world a better place. Speaking of which, did Mr. Farnsworth say what happened when he arrived at Magpie Lane?"

"He did indeed." Witherspoon clucked his tongue. "I say, I do so hate it when people lie. The man actually expected us to believe that when he got there, the house was empty. He said there wasn't hide nor hair of Cassie Yates anywhere. Naturally, he claimed he never looked in the cellar, said he didn't even know the house had a cellar. Well, he'd hardly admit he dragged her down there and stabbed her, would he?"

"Certainly not. Have you found the weapon yet?"

"Not yet, but we will. We've started looking for the hansom drivers that took him to and from Magpie Lane. Oh, by the way, Farnsworth confessed that he and Cassie had been meeting secretly there for weeks. That's why he told her to meet him there in the note."

"Yes, sir," Mrs. Jeffries agreed. "Now, you were saying?"

The inspector gave her a blank look.

"We were talking about the murder weapon," she reminded him.

"Of course, of course. What I was getting at is now that we know they were meeting in Magpie Lane, we'll start looking for witnesses. There'll be the hansom driver from that night and, I daresy, many others. If we get really lucky, we may even find someone who saw Mr. Farnsworth tossing something in the Thames River."

Mrs. Jeffries felt the inspector would hardly be that lucky, but she didn't like to say so.

"I wanted to search his rooms today," Witherspoon continued, "but Mr. Clements raised such a fuss I decided it would be better to wait until after we'd made an arrest."

"Emery Clements didn't want you to search Mr. Farnsworth's rooms? Why ever not?" Mrs. Jeffries thought of all the gossip she'd heard about Cassie. The girl hadn't been involved only with Malcolm Farnsworth and Andrew Lutterbank. She'd also been seeing Clements. Then she caught herself. This case was solved. There was no need for her to keep prying about for additional suspects.

"He kept muttering about us being on a fishing expedition and not bringing a warrant. Said that as we weren't actually arresting Mr. Farnsworth right then, we'd no right to search his home. Sent for his solicitor. But don't worry, Mrs. Jeffries." Witherspoon set his empty glass down on the table. "I've got several men watching the Clements' house. They'll make sure nothing is taken out of the place before I get a chance to have a good look round. We'll have both a warrant and an arrest by tomorrow morning."

"Are you going to ask Cassie's landlady to try and identify Mr. Farnsworth?"

"Well, er, no." Witherspoon stared at her in surprise. "Farnsworth admitted he and Cassie used to meet in Magpie Lane. I don't think her landlady would be of much help, do you?"

"Of course, you're right," Mrs. Jeffries replied hastily. She sighed. "But you know, it might be helpful if you searched Cassie's belongings."

"Really?"

She gave an embarrassed laugh. "It's silly of me, sir, but I couldn't help but think that sometimes women keep little keepsakes of their sweethearts."

"Do they indeed?" The inspector looked genuinely surprised by this information. "And what would a keepsake, assuming that she kept something Malcolm had given her, prove?"

"Why, sir, it would prove they'd been together . . ." She broke off and laughed merrily. "Now, Inspector, you're teasing me. You know very well what I'm getting at."

Witherspoon smiled uncertainly. He hadn't a clue what his housekeeper was trying to say, but he decided it would probably be a good idea to send Barnes around to search Cassie Yates's belongings. "Not to worry, Mrs. Jeffries," he said. "You know how I love my little joke, and come to think of it, you're right. I'll send Barnes around tomorrow to go through the girl's belongings."

Mrs. Jeffries sighed softly. "Poor girl, how sad that the man she loved ended up being the one who took her life."

"Yes, tragic," Witherspoon commented. "But there is so very much wickedness in this world, it's quite appalling. Why even with all the evidence we've got against this chap, he still insists he didn't do the deed."

"It's hardly likely that he would confess," Mrs. Jeffries said dryly.

Witherspoon's eyebrows shot up. "I'm not so sure, Mrs. Jeffries. You'd be amazed at how often people do. But Farnsworth isn't one of them. He claims he had a change of heart. He says he spent the rest of the night walking the streets and thinking. Though he has no money, he'd decided that if Cassie was indeed going to bear his child, he'd marry her."

"And what were they going to live on? Neither of them was employed, nor had they much money."

Witherspoon shrugged. "I asked him that. He claimed he was going to sell all his belongings, take the money and Cassie and emigrate to America. Said he wanted to go somewhere where he and Cassie could start over."

As Witherspoon spoke, Mrs. Jeffries could see a rather puzzled expression forming in his eyes. "What are you thinking, sir?"

"It's quite silly, really," he admitted with an embarrassed laugh. "But somehow I almost believed Farnsworth. There was something about him that led me to believe he was telling the truth. Yet he's the only one with the motive and the opportunity. Andrew Lutterbank was home with his family, Emery Clements was visiting his club, and as far as we know, Farnsworth was the only person who knew that Cassie Yates would be at Magpie Lane."

"What about Antonia Everdene? Or for that matter, the Reverend Everdene? Either of them could have slipped out of the house and followed Cassie." Mrs. Jeffries didn't think this was very likely, but she wanted to make sure they didn't leave any lines of inquiry untouched.

"I don't think so," the inspector murmured. He suddenly smiled at Mrs. Jeffries. "And it's not because I don't like to believe a woman is as capable of murder as a man. Your stories about some of your late husband's cases have certainly opened my eyes about that particular prejudice."

Mrs. Jeffries was inordinately pleased. Sometimes she wondered if her dear inspector would ever see the world as it really was rather than as what he wished it to be. "Then why couldn't either of them have done it?"

"I suppose Miss Everdene could have. She certainly had the motive. She's desperately in love with Farnsworth. But after Farnsworth left, she went into her room and wasn't seen by the servants until the next morning. And she didn't know where Cassie had gone. The reverend couldn't have done the murder—he was indisposed."

"Oh, I see. He was still drunk."

"Quite."

"Will you definitely be arresting Mr. Farnsworth tomorrow?"

Witherspoon closed his eyes. "Yes. The case is circumstantial, but nonetheless it's quite strong."

• • •

Mrs. Jeffries didn't sleep well that night. Her mind simply wouldn't stop working. She went over and over every detail of the case and knew that something was wrong, something didn't make sense.

At three in the morning she awoke with two facts pounding in her head. Five hundred pounds . . . She remembered now where she'd heard that figure mentioned before. And Essie Tuttle had told Betsy that she'd seen someone step out of the shadows and follow Cassie Yates on the last night of her life. Malcolm Farnsworth was still with his financée then.

Mrs. Jeffries threw off her bedclothes, grabbed her robe and hurried out of her room. Almost running, she dashed up the steps to the top floor and tapped on Smythe's door.

"What is it?" Smythe stuck his head out and peered at her out of sleepy eyes. "Cor, Mrs. J, it's the middle of the night."

"Yes, I know. But there's something I must know. When you went down to the docks, were you able to find out if Sally Comstock got on a ship for Australia?"

He yawned and pushed a lock of hair off his forehead. "I checked at the Pacific East Line and Merritor's Shipping, they's the two that carries the most passengers from the London docks. They both had sailings on the day Angus Lutterbank was buried, but there weren't no one named Comstock on the passenger manifest."

"Oh dear," Mrs. Jeffries whispered. For a moment she was terribly afraid. But despite the fear, she knew what she had to do. There was no other way. For she knew who the killer was. If she were wrong, she'd take full responsibility. She could not ask anyone else to do what had to be done. If she were wrong, she would not only be violating man's law, but God's as well.

"What's goin' on, Mrs. J?" Smythe gazed at her quizzically.

"Smythe, is there a shovel anywhere about the place?" she asked, ignoring his question.

"There's one in the cooling pantry," he replied. " 'Ere now, what are you up to?"

"Don't ask," she replied firmly as she turned and started for the stairs. "It's not the sort of thing I could ever ask anyone else to do. I don't want you involved."

"Now just a minute 'ere. If'n you think I'm lettin' you toddle off in the middle of the night with a bleedin' shovel all by yerself," he yelped softly, "you've got another think comin'."

She stopped and turned. The coachman was watching her with a hard, determined expression. "Smythe," she said gently, "I'm going to break the law. I'm going to do something I couldn't in good conscience involve anyone else in. I think I know what happened, but I'm not absolutely certain. However, what I propose to do is the only way I can know for sure. I simply must do it alone. There's too much risk involved—"

"I don't care 'ow much risk there is," he interrupted. "I ain't lettin' you go off on your own at this time o' night. You ain't goin' without me," he said flatly.

"Smythe—"

"No, Mrs. J. You jus' give me a minute to get dressed, and don't try leavin' on yer own. Whatever you're up to, I'm goin' with ya."

She started to argue the point, then realized it was useless. From the fierce expression on his face, she knew Smythe meant to come with her. "All right, meet me downstairs in five minutes. But I'm warning you, you won't like it one bit."

Mrs. Jeffries was absolutely right. Smythe grimaced as he, Mrs. Jeffries and a very jittery Wiggins stopped inside the gate of St. Matthew's churchyard.

"Blimey, this is a miserable place," Wiggins moaned. He gave a quick, terrified glance behind him at the first row of graves. "Are you sure we ought to be 'ere? It don't seem right."

"Well no one invited ya to come along," Smythe snarled.

Wiggins had heard Smythe moving about in his rooms and taken it into his head to go with them, and after a good ten minutes of arguing he had finally convinced Mrs. Jeffries and the coachman that he could be of some use. But now, viewing the ghostly churchyard with its eerie tombs and old misshapen headstones, he sincerely wished he'd stayed in bed.

"Which is Angus Lutterbank's grave?" Mrs. Jeffries asked briskly. She held the lantern up.

"Over there." Smythe pointed to the darkest spot in the churchyard. Wiggins groaned.

"Come on, let's get this over with." Squaring his shoulders and taking a firm grip on the shovel, Smythe headed toward the other side of the graveyard.

Mrs. Jeffries held the lantern as the grim trio made their way to Angus Lutterbank's final place of rest. The night was silent. The churchyard, which held generations of London's dead, was so quiet the sound of their footsteps seemed as loud as drumbeats. In the bushes behind the Lutterbank grave, a night scavenger scuttled noisily away from the approaching humans.

"Blimey." Wiggins jumped and banged into Smythe's broad back. "What was that?"

"Cor, get off me, ya silly twit. It's just an animal," Smythe snapped. He put his lantern down, gave Mrs. Jeffries a long, level stare and then stuck his shovel deep into the grave. " 'Ow deep do you reckon we'll have to go?"

"Not more than a couple of feet," she murmured, wondering again if she were doing the right thing. But she couldn't think of what else to do, and if she did nothing, Cassie Yates's murderer would get away scot-free. Surely God was more concerned with bringing a killer to justice than a bit of digging about in a spot of hallowed ground. Mrs. Jeffries truly hoped so.

For the next twenty minutes the two men dug steadily as Mrs. Jeffries held the lamp and watched.

" 'Ere now," Smythe mumbled as his shovel dug into something that wasn't soft earth. "I think we've found what we're lookin' for." He tossed the shovel onto the small hill of dirt at the side of the shallow pit and dropped to his knees. Using his bare hands, he continued to dig.

A moment later he gasped and straightened. "You were right, Mrs. J. Angus in't the only one buried in this grave."

"Oh no," Wiggins moaned. Clenching his teeth and keeping his eyes closed, he dropped to his knees beside the coachman and began to dig too.

They had her uncovered in minutes. Taking a deep breath, Mrs. Jeffries stepped closer and held the lantern directly over the body. An ivory-handled knife still protruded from the corpse's ribs. Smythe, his face a mask of horror and revulsion, was breathing raggedly. Wiggins had gone pale. Even Mrs. Jeffries felt a shakiness in her knees.

"Who is she?" Wiggins whispered.

Before Mrs. Jeffries could answer, Smythe reached down and pulled a bit of tattered cloth from the dead hand. He swallowed and held it close to the lantern.

The cloth had once been a delicate white handkerchief. But in the glow of the light they could see it was badly torn and covered with dark stains. There were embroidered letters in the bottom corner.

"S C," Smythe said softly. He looked up at Mrs. Jeffries, and their gazes met. "Looks like Sally Comstock never even made it to the docks."

Their plan was quite simple. As dawn broke, Mrs. Jeffries, accompanied by Wiggins, went to Luty Belle's. Smythe kept watch in the churchyard.

Luty listened to them without comment, then ordered Hatchet, who'd been standing in the corner clucking his tongue, over to St. Matthews. The butler didn't look particularly happy about the fact that he was part of their plan. However, he contented himself with a brief speech about grave-robbing, amateur detectives and lunatic Americans before leaving to carry out his part of the scheme.

"Don't pay him no mind," Luty said as she watched Hatchet's stiff back disappear through the door. "He's devoted to me. He'll never let on that it was you who dug the girl up."

"We didn't dig 'er up," Wiggins protested. "We didn't even know she were there. It was more like we discovered 'er."

"Are you absolutely sure about the finger, Luty?" Mrs. Jeffries asked anxiously.

"Yes. I'm sure." Luty grabbed Mrs. Jeffries by the arms and ushered her to the front door. "Now stop yer frettin' and git on home, Hepzibah. None of this is goin' to work if'n the inspector wakes up and finds you gone. You've got to be there when Hatchet shows up with that cockamamie excuse and drags the inspector out to the churchyard. And besides, come this evenin', the killer will be locked up good and tight. I reckon a bit of grave diggin' is a purty small price to pay for justice."

CHAPTER 11

"Now, let me see if I have this right," Witherspoon said as he stared at Luty Belle Crookshank. "You sent your butler over to check the date of Angus Lutterbank's death herc at St. Matthew's, and when he got to the churchyard, he noticed someone had . . . er . . . dug it up? Is that correct?" He glanced from the stern features of Hatchet to Mrs. Crookshank.

"Yup, that's right." Luty grinned. "Wanted to do some snoopin' on my own afore I told ya what I suspected."

"And the grave just happened to be open?" The inspector's brows rose. "That is a remarkable coincidence, wouldn't you say?" He avoided looking down at the exposed body. Starting his day off by examining another corpse was simply too much. He'd delay that unpleasant chore as long as possible.

Hatchet snorted delicately, and Luty Belle threw him a quick glare before she answered the inspector. "No, I wouldn't say it were a coincidence at all. But if'n you're accusing me of sneakin' over here in the middle of the danged night and diggin' that girl up, you're plum crazy. Take a look at me, Inspector. I'm an old woman, and if'n you think that stiff-necked stuffed shirt of a butler of mine," she broke off and jabbed her cane in Hatchet's direction, "would have the stomach for minin' bodies in the middle of the night, you've got another think coming."

Witherspoon glanced at the impeccably dressed, white-haired servant and sighed. Unfortunately, this eccentric woman was right. He couldn't see either of them doing a spot of grave digging in the middle of the night. But if they hadn't, then who had? Drat. And he'd thought this miserable case was over and done with. Now he had another body, another murder and the whole horrid business was going to start all over again.

"Besides," Mrs. Crookshank continued earnestly when the inspector remained silent. "What's it matter who dug the girl up? She's dead, ain't she? Looks to me like it's murder too. There's an ivory-handled dagger sticking outa her rib cage. Now, there's only one person that I know of who'd had a reason to murder the girl, and it sure as shootin' ain't Malcolm Farnsworth, neither."

"I'm sorry," Witherspoon said curiously. "But I don't really see what it is you're getting at. How can you possibly know anything about who took this person's life? We don't even know the identity of the victim."

"Nells bells, man." She stamped her cane in frustration. "Can't you see what's right under yer danged nose? Of course we know who that girl was. Didn't you see them initials embroidered on that hanky? It's Sally Comstock. And the only one who had a reason for wantin' her dead is Andrew Lutterbank. Farnsworth didn't even know the woman. And if'n you don't make tracks, that no-good polecat is gonna get clean outa the country. He and his daddy is fixin' to go to the continent this morning."

"Gracious, are you certain?" Witherspoon asked in alarm.

"Course I'm certain," Luty snorted. "Why do ya think I had Hatchet over here at the crack of dawn checkin' the dates on this tombstone?"

"I beg your pardon?" Witherspoon wished the woman would explain herself a bit more clearly. He was having a most difficult time following her reasoning. "I'm afraid I don't quite understand."

"Well, it's simple enough," she explained. To Luty this part of the plan was the weakest, but as it had been the only idea she and Mrs. Jeffries had been able to come up with early this morning, it would have to do. "Yesterday, when I heard that you was sniffin' around Farnsworth and peggin' him as the killer, I suddenly thoughta something."

"How on earth did you hear that we were asking Mr. Farnsworth to help us with our inquiries?" Witherspoon asked.

"Oh, that don't matter." Mrs. Crookshank waved the question aside and started talking faster. "Anyhows, I remembered that when they paid Sally Comstock off, they'd supposedly give the girl five hundred pounds. It was the money in the pouch that reminded me o' that. Now, I knew Farnsworth didn't have that kind of cash, so I asked myself how on earth he could have given it to Cassie Yates. Well, he couldn't, could he?"

"Hmmm . . . I'm still not quite sure I follow you," Witherspoon said hesitantly.

"Then stop interruptin' and listen," Luty snapped. She'd decided the best defense now was a fast and furious offense. "Then I recalled that my inquiry agent had told me about a bit of gossip he'd picked up about Cassie Yates. Seems on the day that old Angus was buried, Cassie had snuck out that evenin' and supposedly followed Sally and Andrew down to the docks. Claimed she wanted to say good-bye to her friend." She laughed cynically. "Knowin' what I know about that girl, I sure as blazes didn't believe she were sneakin' out to say good-bye. Cassie Yates weren't the kind to git mushy. So I figured that Cassie must have seen somethin' that night she weren't supposed to. I reckon she followed Lutterbank and Sally, saw him kill her with one of those fancy knives of his and then probably sat back and had a good chuckle while Andrew buried the poor girl in Angus's grave."

"Good gracious, you deduced all that merely from hearing that Cassie Yates had five hundred pounds in her possession?" The inspector gazed at her in awe. Peculiar as the story sounded, it had the ring of truth about it.

"Well." Luty shrugged modestly. Hatchet sniffed delicately and then turned it into a cough when his employer's eyes narrowed. "It weren't just that," she admitted. "It were the crooked finger too."

"Crooked finger?" Witherspoon repeated.

"Yup. Braxton Paxton told me that when he went round to Cassie Yates's rooms, the landlady said the man who collected her things the day after she was murdered had a crooked finger." She shook her head in disgust. "I don't know why it took so long for me to put it all together. But yesterday, when we come home from talking to you, Mary Sparks said something that reminded me that Andrew Lutterbank's little finger is bent. Course, then I knew. The man who collected Cassie's belongin's had to be Andrew, and then it were clear that he was the one that killed her. But it took me a spell to figure out why. At first I figured he musta done her in 'cause he's crazy, well—you've seen his mother. Reckon madness runs purty deep in that family. But I couldn't get that five hundred pounds outa my head. I knew it had somethin' to do with it."

"Yes," Witherspoon muttered dazedly. "I see."

"Inspector," a familiar voice called.

"Oh, good." The inspector turned and saw Constable Barnes and three other uniformed police officers picking their way carefully through the churchyard. "The lads have arrived. I suppose I'd better take Barnes and perhaps another one and get on over to Mr. Lutterbank."

"You'd best hurry, Inspector," Luty warned. "They'll be leavin' the country if you don't git over there and put a stop to it. And once Andrew is out of England, it'll be a cold day in the pits of hell before you can git your hands on him agin."

• • •

"Now, stop that pacin', Hepzibah," Luty Belle said calmly as she sat in the kitchen of Upper Edmonton Gardens. "Everythin' went just like we planned. The inspector is probably arrestin' Andrew Lutterbank right now."

"Are you sure he wasn't suspicious about our story?" Mrs. Jeffries asked anxiously.

Luty shrugged. "He did seem a mite concerned about that grave being conveniently opened. It's a purty shady story, but I think I convinced him that it didn't matter all that much how the girl got found."

"And did he understand the significance of the money?"

"Yep, after I explained it, he did." Luty took a sip of her tea. "Course gettin' that part in about the crooked finger weren't easy. I ain't sure he really understood what I was tryin' to tell him. But by that time, I had him convinced that if he didn't git over to the Lutterbank house and get his paws on Andrew, the boy was goin' to be gone fer good. The inspector took the dagger with him too. Maybe once Lutterbank sees that the murder weapon can be traced directly to him, he'll git so rattled he'll confess." Luty suddenly looked around at the empty kitchen. "Where in tarnation is everybody? I'd think with all the excitement they'd all be here."

"Mrs. Goodge is in the pantry. Wiggins and Smythe are upstairs taking a rest," Mrs. Jeffries replied. "Remember we did leave poor Smythe to stand guard while I fetched you and Hatchet. Both of them are exhaused. Poor Smythe barely made it in the kitchen door as Hatchet was coming in the front this morning. And oh yes, Betsy's gone over to Putney to get Essie Tuttle. She'll be staying here for a few days while I try and find her another position." She paused and gave Luty a wide smile. "Speaking of Miss Tuttle . . ."

Luty raised her hand. "All right, Hepzibah, you can save your breath. I owe ya. I'll hire the girl. Have Betsy bring her on over to my house this afternoon."

"Thank you, Luty," Mrs. Jeffries said. Upstairs the front door slammed, and both women jumped.

"Gracious, what was that?" Mrs. Jeffries exclaimed as she leapt to her feet. But before she even reached the kitchen steps, a white-faced Inspector Witherspoon stumbled down them and into the kitchen. He threw himself into a chair.

"Inspector, what on earth is the matter?" Mrs. Jeffries hurried over to the stove and reached for the teakettle. "You're as pale as a ghost. Let me make you a cup of tea."

"I'd rather have something a bit stronger, if you don't mind," Witherspoon croaked. "I've had a rather unsettling morning. Actually, I'd like a whiskey."

Shocked, Mrs. Jeffries whirled around and stared at him. His hair was disheveled, his lips faintly greenish around the rim, and his hands were shaking.

"Sit still, Inspector," Luty said as she nimbly leapt to her feet and headed for the stairs. "I'll git the whiskey. Is it in that sideboard in the dining room?"

At Mrs. Jeffries's affirmative nod, she disappeared upstairs.

A few moments later she returned, holding the bottle in her arms like a child. "Hepzibah, you git us some glasses."

They waited until after the inspector had taken a few good swallows of the liquid before asking any questions.

Finally, when some of the color had returned to his cheeks, Mrs. Jeffries said, "Now, why don't you tell us what happened?"

Witherspoon took a long, deep breath. "I suppose I really shouldn't be so upset," he said slowly. "I am, after all, a policeman. But honestly, I've never seen anyone shot before my very eyes before."

"Good gracious," Mrs. Jeffries murmured. "How utterly dreadful. Oh, you poor man, no wonder you came in here looking as though you'd seen something unspeakable. You had."

"Who got shot?" Luty asked softly.

The inspector took another quick sip of whiskey. "Andrew Lutterbank. Emery Clements killed him."

"What!" Mrs. Jeffries was stunned. She glanced at Luty and saw the same surprise on her face. "But why?"

"I suppose I'd better start at the beginning," Witherspoon said. He was beginning to feel better. But then he'd known he would once he saw his housekeeper and got this horrible experience off his chest. That's why he'd made his excuses and slipped home, telling the Chief Inspector he'd be back directly after lunch.

"I think that's probably wise, sir," Mrs. Jeffries agreed.

"After leaving Mrs. Crookshank in the churchyard, I took the dagger and . . ." He paused. "I assume Mrs. Crookshank has told you what happened this morning?"

"Yes, sir." Mrs. Jeffries smiled sympathetically. "I know all about your adventure. You see, I'd already sent Luty a message that I wanted to see her. I was hoping she'd be able to give Miss Tuttle a position, you see. She very kindly came round and told me about the body in Angus Lutterbank's grave." She clucked her tongue. "Really, sir, you've had a terrible day."

"Yes," Witherspoon sighed. "It's been awful. But anyway, let me get on with it. I took the dagger we'd found in Sally Comstock's ribs and, along with Constable Barnes and another officer, went to the Lutterbanks'. It was the most amazing thing, Mrs. Jeffries. Remember how I once told you that murderers often confess?"

"I do, indeed, sir."

"Right, well, Andrew took one look at the dagger and admitted everything." He flung his arms out in a gesture of disbelief. "I hadn't even started to ask any questions before he started confessing to two murders. Naturally, I cautioned him that anything he said could be used in a court of law against him but that still didn't shut him up. Andrew wouldn't even listen to his own father. Mr. Lutterbank tried to intervene, but he just went on and on. He finally shut up when the butler interrupted him long enough to announce Emery Clements."

"Is that when Clements shot him?" Luty asked.

Witherspoon shook his head. "No, that didn't happen till later, till after we'd arrested Lutterbank and taken him into custody. And the irony of it is it was pure chance that Clements happened to come to the Lutterbank home at all. He'd come to give Andrew a bank draft. It seems Clements was the one who'd actually bought Andrew's cottage in Essex."

"Clements had bought the cottage," Mrs. Jeffries repeated. "But why?"

"He bought it for Cassie Yates," the inspector said softly. "Unfortunately for Andrew Lutterbank, Clements was in the hall long enough to overhear Andrew confessing to murder. I expect the whole household heard the man—he was screaming at the top of his lungs. But right after the butler announced Clements, he suddenly left, and naturally, I thought he was going because, well . . . it's not precisely gentlemanly to hang about and watch a friend get arrested for murder."

"What happened then, sir?" Mrs. Jeffries asked. She took a small sip from her own glass, grimacing as the whiskey burned the back of her throat.

"We arrested Andrew and took him to the police station so he could make a formal statement." Witherspoon lowered his head and stared at the table. "While we were taking his statement, the door suddenly flew open and Emery Clements charged in. Before I could do anything, before any of us could make a move, Clements pulled out a revolver and fired twice." He shuddered and drew a long, deep breath. "Both shots hit Lutterbank right between the eyes."

"Lord, sir," Mrs. Jeffries whispered. "How perfectly awful."

"It was," the inspector agreed with feeling. "Then Clements put the gun down, pushed Andrew out of the chair he'd been sitting in and sat down in his place. That was the worst of it, Clements sitting there talking quite calmly with Lutterbank's corpse at his feet. He confessed to killing Andrew Lutterbank. He said he was avenging Cassie Yates's murder."

"Good gad almighty," Luty exclaimed in disbelief. "You mean that man was stupid enough to walk into a police station and murder someone right under yer nose because of a woman like Cassie Yates? I tell ya, if that don't beat all. The man's ruined his life."

"Yes, I'm afraid he has," Witherspoon said. "But he didn't seem to mind. Said that with her gone his life wasn't worth living anyway. Obviously, he was in love with her. They'd been meeting secretly for months. When he found out for certain that Andrew was responsible for Cassie's murder, he decided to take the law into his own hands."

"But he defended Farnsworth," Mrs. Jeffries said. "Clements wouldn't let you search his house yesterday and was going to get a solicitor on his friend's behalf. Why?"

Witherspoon gave her a weary smile. "I don't think he was defending Malcolm Farnsworth. I think he was planning on killing him. At least, I think he'd have killed him as soon as he knew for sure that Farnsworth was responsible for her murder."

"You mean he was only pretending to help Malcolm?" Luty asked. "What makes you think so?"

"Because of the way he spoke about Cassie Yates." The inspector frowned thoughtfully. "He was desperately in love with her. He told us he'd arranged to buy Andrew's cottage because he was going to give the place to her as a gift. A lure. He wanted her more than anything in the world."

"Then why in tarnation didn't he do something about her the past two months?" Luty leaned forward on one elbow. "Where'd he think the girl was all this time?"

"He said he thought she was abroad." Witherspoon looked at his almost empty glass of whiskey and then shoved it away from him. "On the day she died, Cassie had led both Clements and Farnsworth to believe she was leaving the country. That's why Farnsworth was so stunned when he found her at the Everdenes'. He fully expected that she was on her way to France."

"Why did she want everyone to believe she was leaving?" Mrs. Jeffries asked. That was one of the few things she hadn't been able to piece together on her own.

"I'm not sure," the inspector murmured. "But Lutterbank told us she'd come to him that morning demanding the five hundred pounds he'd murdered Sally Comstock to keep. Cassie had followed them that night he'd supposedly put Miss Comstock on a ship for Australia, and she'd witnessed the murder. But Cassie bided her time before actually trying to blackmail Lutterbank. She told Andrew and Clements she was going abroad. She'd probably planned to use the money as an added inducement in her campaign to force Malcolm to marry her. Clements told us that when he'd seen Cassie on the morning of the tenth, he'd been the one who told her Farnsworth was going to propose to Antonia Everdene. She wasn't having that. She took the money, forced Miss Sparks to change clothes with her and then confronted Malcolm. Unfortunately, when she left the Everdenes', Andrew followed her. He waited until she was inside the house at Magpie Lane, stabbed her and buried her body in the cellar." The inspector paused and smiled sadly. "He committed murder to keep that money and to silence her forever. Imagine how he must have felt when he realized she didn't have it with her. That's why he went to get her things the next day. He wanted to look for the money and make it appear that she'd actually left." Witherspoon took a deep breath and stood up. "I'm going back to the station," he said firmly. "Much as I'd like to stay here and forget this dreadful day, I've still my duty to perform."

It was very late that evening before Mrs. Jeffries and the others could gather round the kitchen table.

" 'Ere I was hanging on to that silly Essie Tuttle and helpin' her pack with that awful Miss Everdene screechin' at both of us, and all the time, the case were comin' to a close." Betsy scowled heavily. "It don't seem right. I missed everythin'."

"I don't think you really missed all that much, Betsy," Mrs. Jeffries said kindly. "Watching one man shoot another certainly isn't a very nice sight."

"I still don't understand." Wiggins yawned. " 'Ow did you know that Sally Comstock would be buried in Angus's grave?"

"She's already explained that twice," Mrs. Goodge complained. "Haven't you been listenin'?"

"That's quite all right, Mrs. Goodge. It's no wonder Wiggins can't concentrate. He didn't get much sleep last night." Mrs. Jeffries smiled at her two fellow conspirators. "I suspected Sally was in the grave because of the amount of money that was found in the pouch Cassie gave Mary Sparks for safe-keeping. If you'll recall, the first time Luty Belle came to ask for our help, she made a very casual comment to the effect that Andrew Lutterbank's indiscretions had cost him five hundred pounds and a trip to Australia. When Smythe confirmed that there was no record of Sally ever having been a passenger to Australia, I decided that Andrew had probably killed her and buried her body in a convenient place. In this case, Angus's grave. The earth was still nice and soft; it wouldn't have been very difficult for a healthy young man to reopen it and put her inside."

"You were takin' a chance there, Mrs. J," Smythe said. "I only checked with two lines that goes to Australia. What if she'd left from another port?"

"I was hoping the Lutterbanks were in such a hurry to get rid of the girl, they booked her passage on a vessel leaving that very day," Mrs. Jeffries answered.

"'Ow come a rich man like 'im did 'er in for a piddlin' little amount like five hundred quid?" Wiggins asked.

"Five hundred pounds is a lot of money," Mrs. Goodge said. "Eat some more of them cakes, boy. You've missed too many meals lately." She shoved the plate closer to the footman.

"It wasn't just the money," Mrs. Jeffries said softly. "I think that perhaps Luty was right. There is madness in that family. Andrew was tainted with it. I think he enjoyed killing those women."

"Well," Betsy said, "I still don't quite see 'ow you knew it were 'im that did the killin'. Were it just the money that gave you the hint?"

"No, it was also the fact that you reported that Essie Tuttle had said that when Cassie left the Everdene house, a man stepped out of the shadows and followed her." Mrs. Jeffries explained. "I knew that man couldn't have been Malcolm Farnsworth. Essie said he was still in the house when she went back inside. So I decided that the murderer was most likely the man who'd followed Cassie and not Malcolm. For one thing, if Farnsworth had murdered her, he wouldn't have buried her body in the cellar. He knew that Magpie Lane wasn't going to be widened for a road. Why would he have buried the girl when he knew perfectly well the property along there was going to be dug up for an underground railway? Clements knew the same thing. So I suspected that neither of them were the killers. That left Andrew Lutterbank."

"But he was supposed to have been home that night," Mrs. Goodge put in.

"That's another reason I suspected him." She smiled wryly. "How many of us know exactly where we were on any particular night from several months ago? Yet when the inspector asked where he'd been, his father immediately stated he was home. I knew that was a lie."

"You think his father might have suspected Andrew of bein' the killer?" Smythe asked as he poured himself another cup of tea.

"I'm certain of it." Mrs. Jeffries yawned. "I think he knew all too well what kind of evil his son was capable of doing. That's probably why he suddenly decided to take young Andrew on a business trip. He wanted him out of the country, out of the reach of Scotland Yard."

Betsy sighed. "Well, it's over now, at least for us."

"Too bad it ain't over for the inspector," Smythe said. "Looks like there's goin' to be a bit of a ruckus on this one." He scowled and lifted his chin to meet Mrs. Jeffries's eyes. "You think 'e'll be all right?"

"He'll be just fine," she announced. "As soon as this case is officially closed, he's going off to the country for a few days to visit friends. It'll do him the world of good."

Betsy suddenly giggled. "Speakin' of the country, you should 'ave seen Hatchet's face when I took Essie to Luty Belle's. 'E didn't spend two minutes with her before he looked like 'e'd like to put her on a train and send 'er to parts unknown."

They all laughed.

"Speaking of Luty," Mrs. Jeffries said when the merriment had died down, "she sent me a note this afternoon. When the inspector leaves for the country, she wants to take us all on a nice outing."

"Maybe she'll take us to one of them posh restaurants over on the strand," Betsy said excitedly.

"I could fancy a day at the races meself," Smythe muttered.

"Nah, let's hope she takes us to the circus," Wiggins countered.

"An outing on the river would be nice," Mrs. Goodge said thoughtfully.

"I was rather hoping for a concert or perhaps the ballet," Mrs. Jeffries interjected. "Mozart would be very nice."

Epilogue

She took them to a music hall. Mrs. Jeffries felt she really ought to protest, but when she saw how excited the others were, she simply didn't have the heart. And she was rather curious herself. She'd never been to a music hall.

Dressed in their best and accompanied by Luty and Hatchet, they drove off in high spirits.

The place was warm, garish and hazed with smoke from dozens of cigars. The noise level was so loud, Mrs. Jeffries couldn't hear herself think.

Luty tapped her cane in time to the tinny music from the piano, Smythe and Wiggins almost got cricks in their necks from stretching to get a better view of the can-can dancers, and Betsy and Mrs. Goodge laughed themselves silly at the bawdy jokes from the vaudeville comic.

All in all, everyone had a wonderful time. Even Hatchet unbent far enough to join in the raucous sing-along.

The evening ended far too quickly. As Luty's coach drew up outside the front door of Upper Edmonton Gardens, Mrs. Jeffries leaned forward and said, "How's Essie Tuttle getting along, Luty?"

Luty cackled with laughter. "Oh, she's gettin' along just fine. It's Hatchet I'm worried about. The girl's givin' 'im fits. Silly old fool took it into his head to teach her to read. Now he's complainin' that that's all she wants to do."

Betsy giggled. "Honestly, men. They think they own you just because they gives you a little 'elp now and again."

Smythe snorted. "Yeah, and you females spend all yer time runnin' a poor man ragged."

"What's that supposed to mean?" Betsy demanded indignantly.

"You know very well what it means." The coachman glared at her.

"You was runnin' that poor lad ragged tonight. He musta fetched you three glasses of lemonade."

" 'E offered," she sniffed, "and besides, I didn't invite 'im to sit next to me."

"You didn't discourage 'im, neither," Smythe snapped. "And I don't think it's right you agreein' to see 'im again."

"I didn't agree to see him again," Betsy defended herself. "He just asked me if I were interested in spiritualism, and I said I was. It's an interestin' subject."

"Spiritualism," Mrs. Jeffries exclaimed. "Good gracious, you're not thinking of going to visit a spiritualist with this young man, are you?"

"I'd like ta go too," Luty put in. "I've always wanted to go to one of them there séances. Used to be a fortune teller in San Francisco I'd go see. She were right good too."

Mrs. Jeffries and Smythe both scowled at Luty, who ignored them.

Betsy tossed her blond curls and frowned at the coachman. "Oh, I don't see why you're gettin' so miserable all of a sudden. I'm not goin' to see Edmund again."

"Good," Smythe mumbled. He reached for the door latch. "I don't want you gettin' into trouble."

"Don't be silly," Betsy replied airily as she stepped out of the coach behind Luty and Mrs. Jeffries. "What kind of trouble could I possibly get into by going to a séance?"

THE GHOST AND MRS. JEFFRIES

CHAPTER 1

Abigail Hodges slammed the door so hard the gold-leafed mirror rattled dangerously against the foyer wall. She paused long enough to fling the door key and her silver beaded purse onto a mahogany table before stalking across the polished oak floor to the bottom of the curving stairway.

"Mrs. Trotter," she bellowed for her housekeeper. "Come here at once. At once, do you hear me!"

There was no answer.

"Mrs. Trotter," she shouted again. "Thomasina? Thomasina! Where are you? What's going on here? Whcre is everybody?"

Impatiently her toe tapped against the floor. Where was the confounded woman? They'd pay for this! Abigail fumed. She'd teach the servants to ignore her summons. She'd teach them to play about while the mistress of the house stood waiting for service.

Her toe stopped tapping against the floor as she realized how very silent the house was. Ominously silent, almost as though it was empty.

A slow chill climbed her spine as she remembered the medium's parting words. "Darkness, death, despair," the woman had intoned portentously.

Abigail took a deep breath and resolutely brushed Esme Popejoy's warning aside. What nonsense the woman had spouted. She'd been absolutely right to tell that so-called medium precisely what she thought of such silly twaddle. She'd certainly had the last word on that matter.

It was a deeply held principle that Abigail Hodges always had the last word.

But where was everybody? The house was deathly quiet. Too quiet, Abigail thought. She listened for the faint noises that indicated the presence of those well-trained servants whose duty it was to wait up for the mistress of the house. But she heard nothing. "Hello. Is anyone here?"

After a moment she snorted indelicately. She wasn't going to stand here all night like some frightened ninny. "Could that wretched husband of mine possibly have given the servants the night off?" she finally muttered, pushing the medium's theatrical warning to the back of her mind. She started slowly up the stairs, her steps encumbered by the heavy skirts of her evening dress. "No doubt he thinks it was wrong of me to keep them all in last Sunday. Well," she continued muttering under her breath, "we'll just see about that. Coddling servants! When Leonard finally decides to bring himself home, I'll give him the task of sacking everyone. That'll put him in his place. That'll teach him, to try to undermine my authority."

Abigail reached the top of the stairs and paused to take a deep breath. She glanced back over her shoulder, hoping to hear the tapping footsteps of a running maid or Mrs. Trotter's breathless apologies for not being on duty to receive her.

She heard nothing.

Despite her brave words and utter fury, Abigail was frightened. She didn't like the feeling. It was unfamiliar to her and it made her even angrier than she'd been when Leonard had announced his intention of escorting that silly Mrs. Popejoy to the train station. And after everything that had happened! Oh, she'd make him pay for this. She'd make him really pay.

Esme Popejoy. That stupid woman! She'd never go to *her* for a reading again. Just because Mrs. Popejoy was the current rage and supposedly the best medium in the city didn't mean she had any genuine talent. Why just look at tonight's fiasco. Seven people had paid good money to try to contact their dear departed loved ones and they'd gotten nothing but some melodramatic claptrap! Darkness, death and despair, indeed.

Abigail's temper flared again. Why was *she* the one to have been singled out for a warning? she asked herself. Absolute rubbish. And that despicable Leonard! Instead of bringing *her* home and giving *her* comfort, her own husband had cavalierly agreed to escort that charlatan of a medium to the station!

Tonight was the first time Leonard had ever openly defied her wishes. The experience left a nasty taste in her mouth. Abigail wasn't used to anyone defying her wishes. She wasn't about to let it go unpunished either. She smiled slightly, thinking of the conversation she'd have when her husband finally had the good sense to come home. She'd have the last word about that too, she promised herself.

From below, she heard a loud creak. It sounded like a footstep. Abigail's heavy brows drew together. "Who's there?"

But no one answered her.

Instead of calling out again, she stomped down the hall to her room. Bravado desperately trying to ward off an unwelcome curl of fear, Abigail frowned thoughtfully as she noticed all the lamps in the hallway had been lighted. They'd been on in the drawing room as well, she remembered. Flinging open the door, she marched inside, noticing that every lamp in her room was blazing too. She wondered if Mrs. Trotter had done that before she'd taken herself off tonight. Usually, that kind of wastefulness annoyed Abigail, but tonight she was almost grateful for the brightness. It helped keep the fear away.

There was another creak. Abigail froze. The sound had come from the staircase. For some reason, though, she couldn't bring herself to call out again.

Tilting her head towards the door, she listened hard for the noise to repeat itself. But there was nothing but silence.

After a few moments had passed, she decided she was merely being fanciful. Imagining things. This was an old house. Old houses groaned and creaked all the time, she had just never noticed it before. Abigail walked over and stood in front of her dressing table. Lifting her arm, she started undoing the buttons on the sleeve of her dress.

There is nothing outside the door, she told herself firmly. She finished the buttons on the sleeves and then reached behind her. Her fingers couldn't quite reach the tiny ornate buttons on the back of the dress.

Suddenly the bedroom door crashed open. Abigail whirled around. Her mouth opened in shocked surprise, her eyes widened in sheer terror.

A shot rang out and then another.

She was dead before she hit the floor.

For once, Abigail Hodges didn't get the last word.

It was a miserable way to start the new year, Inspector Gerald Witherspoon thought as he trudged up the staircase of the opulent residence. Only the fifth of January and already there was a murder. Witherspoon sighed. He'd so hoped that 1887 would be a good year, one that didn't have people murdering one another every time one turned around.

He paused at the top of the landing and took a long, deep breath before turning to Constable Barnes. "Now tell me again, Constable, who found the body?"

Actually he had no need to ask Barnes to repeat any information, he was merely trying to delay the moment when he had to examine the body. Nasty things, corpses. Witherspoon didn't much care for them.

"Her husband, sir," Barnes replied. "He found her early this morning when she didn't appear for breakfast. Looks like the poor woman walked in on a thief and he shot her. Twice. Once in the head and once in the chest."

The inspector swallowed heavily. Oh dear, this was going to be a bad one. Gunshot wounds were so terribly messy. Then he realized exactly what Barnes had said. "You mean the victim was murdered in the course of a burglary?" he exclaimed. The constable hadn't mentioned that fact before.

"So the lad that sent in the report seems to think."

"But if it was a burglary." Witherspoon argued, "then what are we doing here? Why wasn't this case given to Inspector Nivens? Gracious, he's the Yard's expert on robbery. Furthermore, Nivens has been complaining for months that I'm getting all the homicides, practically accused me of 'hogging' them. Seems to me it's only fair he should get a crack at one."

Barnes cleared his throat. "Now, sir," he said cautiously, "the gossip I got at the station was that the orders for you gettin' this one came down from Munro himself. Seems the victim is a bit of an important person. They want the case solved quickly. Besides, Nivens has got the measles."

"Oh dear," the inspector muttered. One didn't ignore or even dare to argue with orders that came from James Munro, the head of the Criminal Investigation Division himself. But drat, it wasn't fair. Why should he be the one who was always having to look at dead bodies? "I expect we'd better get on with it then."

Witherspoon and Barnes marched down the wide hallway, their footsteps muffled thumps against the thick carpet. The young police constable who'd been assigned to stand guard outside the door of the victim's room was sitting slumped in a chair, his eyes closed in a light sleep.

"Sleeping on duty, are you, lad?" Barnes called, startling the young man.

"Sorry, sir," the young constable replied, leaping up so fast he tripped over his feet. "But I wasn't really asleep."

"Could have fooled me," Barnes said sternly.

"I was merely resting, sir," he explained as his pale cheeks turned a bright pink. "I was on duty all night, sir. We're a bit shorthanded at the moment."

"The police are always shorthanded," Barnes replied. "That's no excuse for falling asleep at your post."

"Now don't be too hard on the lad," Witherspoon interrupted. "We've all had to catch a catnap a time or two when we're on duty and I expect the constable won't do it again."

"No, sir," the young man replied gratefully. He quickly opened the door and stepped aside. "Absolutely not, sir."

Barnes let the inspector enter first. Witherspoon gathered his resolve and determined not to make a fool of himself. However distasteful it might be, he knew his duty.

Once inside, the inspector stepped away from the door so the constable could step around him. He stood where he was and slowly surveyed the victim's room.

The bedroom was large, with a high ceiling, and curved in a bow shape at one end. The walls were covered with a dark-green-and-gold-flowered wallpaper, heavy gold velvet curtains covered the windows and a brilliant emerald-green-and-gold-patterned carpet was on the floor. A bed with a carved mahogany headboard and a gold satin spread was in the center of the room. Opposite the bed was a matching dressing table and tallboy. The drawers had been pulled out. He glanced at the bed again and saw that a jewelry case was lying upside down, propped against the footboard.

On the side of the bed where he stood was a round table covered with a gold-fringed shawl. The top was cluttered with a lamp, porcelain figurines and a silver bowl. The room also contained an ornate dressing screen done in the Chinese style, a gold velvet settee and a footstool.

"Uh, sir," Barnes said. "The body's over there."

"I know, Constable, I know. But it's important to take in the details of a place before one begins investigating." Witherspoon thought that sounded quite good. He really didn't like the idea that others might catch on to his sqeamishness about corpses. That would be most embarrassing.

But he could delay no longer and he knew it. Steeling himself, he walked to the opposite side of the bed and reluctantly knelt beside the dead woman.

She'd been a tall, heavyset middle-aged woman with gray-streaked dark brown hair, thick eyebrows, a jutting nose and a thin flat mouth. She lay on her back, with her hands behind her neck, her arms at sharp angles on each side. She was dressed in a pale lavender evening dress with long, tight sleeves and a high lace neck. He deliberately didn't look at the gaping hole in her chest. He flicked his gaze to her arms and saw that the cuffs of her dress were hanging open, revealing the pale white flesh of the inside of her arms. Witherspoon felt a wave of pity wash over him. Poor woman. Murder was dreadfully undignified.

"Did you notice her feet, sir?" Barnes asked.

"Er, yes," the inspector replied hastily. He hoped he wasn't blushing. But he'd deliberately looked away from the dead woman's limbs when he'd seen that her ankles were exposed. Still, Witherspoon knew that his duty required him to examine the victim with all due care. Why, even the smallest detail could help him solve this terrible crime.

"Looks like she were killed instantly, don't it, sir?" Barnes continued chattily.

Witherspoon hadn't the foggiest idea how the constable had come to that conclusion, but he wasn't going to admit it. He stared quizzically at the victim's feet. Her long voluminous skirts had ridden up, probably as she fell, and the inspector could see her feet, still clad in evening shoes, were crossed at the ankles. Suddenly it came to him. "Why yes, Constable. That's my conclusion exactly. From the angle of her arms, we can conclude she was probably trying to unbutton her dress." He forced himself not to stammer over those words. "And if the killer came in and she whirled about quickly, then from the way her feet are crossed we can conclude that death must have been almost instantaneous." He sincerely hoped he hadn't just made a fool out of himself and knew a tremendous relief when Barnes nodded.

"I'm not surprised she died quick, sir," the constable continued. "It were probably a double-fast shot. One to the head and one to the heart."

Witherspoon nodded weakly and forced his gaze to the victim's wounds. There was a small dark hole in the center of the forehead. But the worst was the woman's chest—it was covered in a round swell of dried blood with a crimson blackened pit at the center. It was only duty that made the inspector bend closer and examine each of them in turn. He held his breath and tried not to get dizzy.

"We had a bit of luck with this one, sir," Barnes said cheerily. "The husband saw right off what had happened. He had the good sense not to touch anything."

"Not even his wife's body?" Witherspoon was rather surprised by that.

"Not even her, sir. He said he could see she was dead as soon as he saw her lying there. And when he saw the jewelry case on the bed and them drawers pulled out, he figured it was probably a robbery. He thought it best just to close the door and send for the police. No one's been in the room since he found her."

"That is a bit of luck," Witherspoon agreed. "Usually the relatives muck the body about so much that what little evidence there is in cases like this gets horribly muddled."

"What do you make of it, sir?" Barnes asked.

"Too early to tell, Constable, too early to tell. When is the divisional surgeon arriving?"

"Dr. Potter should be here any moment now."

"Potter?" Witherspoon moaned. "Oh dear, hasn't he retired yet? I'm sure I heard someone say he was going off to Bournemouth to grow roses."

The constable sighed. "Not yet, sir."

Neither man held the divisional surgeon in high esteem.

"I suppose I'd better go talk with the husband," the inspector said. He'd learned what he could from staring at this poor woman. There was no point in prolonging this distasteful task. For the life of him, Witherspoon couldn't understand what one was supposed to learn from studying a corpse. It wasn't like they were ever going to speak up and tell you who'd done the foul deed. "What's his name?"

"Hodges, sir. Leonard Hodges. The victim is Abigail Hodges."

Drat, Witherspoon thought, I should have asked the identity of the victim before I examined the body. He wasn't sure why he should have done that, but he felt like he'd missed the boat. "How many others are there in the household?"

"The victim's niece, Felicity Marsden, lives here and then of course there's the servants, sir. A housekeeper by the name of Thomasina Trotter, a cook, several maids and a footman. Considering the size of the house and the kind of neighborhood hereabouts, it's a fairly small staff."

"No butler?"

"No, sir."

Leonard Hodges waited for them in the drawing room. He was a tall, distinguished gentleman with deep-set hazel eyes, dark brown hair worn straight back from a high forehead, an aquiline nose and prominent cheekbones. He would have been a handsome man save for the expression of utter despair and grief on his face. Dressed in an elegantly tailored black morning coat with gray trousers and a matching waistcoat, Leonard Hodges paced nervously in front of the wide marble fireplace. He also, the inspector noted, appeared to be a good deal younger than the late Mrs. Hodges. But naturally one couldn't comment about such a thing.

"Mr. Leonard Hodges," the inspector began politely as he and Barnes advanced into the room.

"Yes." Hodges started violently. Seeing the constable's uniform, he smiled weakly. "I take it you're the police?"

"I'm Inspector Witherspoon and this is Constable Barnes." They nodded courteously at one another. "I'm sorry, sir, we didn't mean to startle you when we came in just now. Let me say I'm dreadfully sorry for your loss," the inspector said sincerely. "It must have been a terrible shock. I understand you're the one who found your wife?"

Hodges closed his eyes for a moment before answering. "That's correct."

"Could you tell us the circumstances, please," Witherspoon asked. His heart swelled with sympathy for the poor man.

"The circumstances," Hodges repeated blankly. "Oh yes. Of course, you'll need to know the details. Forgive me, please, I'm not thinking too clearly."

"That's understandable, Mr. Hodges," Witherspoon replied kindly. "Please take your time and begin at the beginning. When did you find your wife's body?"

"When she didn't appear at breakfast this morning, I became concerned. I thought perhaps she'd taken ill during the night," Hodges began softly. "I went upstairs to her room and saw her lying there. I knew right away she was dead." He paused and took a deep breath. "So I sent Peter for the police."

"And what time was that, sir?" the inspector asked.

"Just after seven-thirty this morning. We always breakfast at half past seven." His voice broke.

The inspector gazed at him in dismay. "I'm dreadfully sorry to have to put you through this, Mr. Hodges," he said gently, "but the more you can tell us now, the faster we can catch the villains that perpetrated this evil deed."

"Of course." Hodges got hold of himself. "I understand. Please, go on. Ask me anything you like."

"May we sit down, sir?" Witherspoon inquired.

"Oh please," Hodges said quickly, gesturing towards the wing chairs opposite the settee. "I've forgotten my manners. Forgive me. Would you care for a cup of tea, or coffee, perhaps?"

"No, thank you," the inspector said as he sat down. He waited until Barnes was settled in the wing chair and had taken out his notebook. Then he turned back to Mr. Hodges. "When was the last time you saw your wife alive?"

"Last night, about nine-fifteen."

"Is that the time Mrs. Hodges usually retires for the evening?" the inspector asked.

"No, no. But she didn't retire then," Hodges explained. "We weren't here when I last saw her. We'd been out for the evening. The last time I saw my wife alive was when I put her in a hansom cab outside Mrs. Popejoy's home." He dropped his face into his hands. "Oh, this is all my fault."

Witherspoon straightened. Egads, was the man going to confess? He couldn't believe his luck. "Your fault, sir?"

"Yes," Hodges cried passionately, lifting his head and gazing at the inspector with tear-filled eyes. "If only I'd come home instead of going to my club to stay, this wouldn't have happened. But I was so angry. I stupidly indulged in foolish pride and my poor wife paid the price for my stubbornness. If I'd been with her, I could have protected her. If I'd only come home, she might still be alive, she might have been saved."

"I doubt that, sir," Barnes put in dryly. "The way I see it, your missus was probably dead before she hit the floor."

Witherspoon shot Barnes a frown. Really, sometimes his constable was so tactless.

"That's no comfort," Hodges moaned. "I'll never forgive myself. Never. I should have come straight home from the station and checked on her."

"Could you explain that a bit further, sir?" Witherspoon asked.

"We'd gone to see a medium, a Mrs. Esme Popejoy." He shrugged. "I know that sounds rather absurd. I'm not a believer, but my wife is, or was. Mrs. Popejoy is quite well known, at least in some circles. When the séance was over, she asked me to escort her to the train station. She was going to visit a sick friend in Southend and she was rather frightened of going to the station by herself at that time of night. It was a decidedly awkward position. Well, I could hardly refuse the woman, and I thought Abigail would be perfectly safe coming home in a hansom. I didn't really feel I could say no to Mrs. Popejoy's request. At the time I thought it the only decent thing to do." He frowned uneasily and looked away. "Abigail wasn't pleased. We had words when I put her in the cab. That's why I went to my club."

"And what club might that be, sir?" Witherspoon asked.

Something that sounded very much like a sniffle accompanied Hodges's reply. "Truscott's, near St. James Park."

Before Witherspoon could ask another question, Barnes stuck his oar in. "And what time did you arrive at your club, sir?"

Hodges sniffled again. "It was ten-thirty. I remember because the clock was chiming the half hour when I entered the lounge." Suddenly his shoulders slumped and he lifted his hands to cover his face. Soft, quiet sobs racked him.

Witherspoon and Barnes stared helplessly at one another. Obviously the poor man was so overcome by grief he couldn't answer any more questions.

Rising to his feet, the inspector said, "Perhaps, sir, it would be best if we continued the questioning at a later time."

He and Constable Barnes quietly left the room. When they were in the hall, Witherspoon said, "Is someone taking a statement from the niece and the servants?"

"Miss Marsden isn't here, sir. One of the housemaids told me that the girl had gone to the ballet with a friend and was spending the night there. We've sent a constable 'round to fetch her. And as for the servants"—Barnes snorted—"one of the lads has already told me we won't get much out of them today. The housekeeper is the only one on the premises that isn't havin' hysterics. Do you want to talk to her now?"

The inspector sighed. "I suppose we'd better."

"Should I have the lads start a house-to-house?"

"Wait until after Potter's seen the body," Witherspoon replied. "Perhaps he'll be able to at least estimate the time of death. Asking questions is always so much easier when you can pinpoint the likely time the crime took place."

Barnes looked doubtful. "But what if Potter can't or won't estimate the time? You know how he is, he won't want to say a word before he does the autopsy. And you know as well as I, sir, that the longer we wait before questionin' the neighbors, the worse everyone's memory gets."

"True," Witherspoon admitted. "Then go ahead with the house-to-house now, have our lads ask the neighbors if they saw anything suspicious last night. Anything at all."

"Do you think the inspector will be home on time for his dinner?" Mrs. Goodge asked. The cook cast a worried glance at the oven, where a nice bit of lamb was roasting.

"I expect so," Mrs. Jeffries, the housekeeper, replied. The servants at Upper Edmonton Gardens, home of Inspector Gerald Witherspoon, had just finished their evening meal. "He's not involved in any important cases now, so I don't see why he shouldn't be here at his usual time."

"More's the pity," the maid, Betsy, added. "He hasn't had a good case since November. I tell ya, it's right borin'."

"I don't think it's borin'," Wiggins the footman said. A wide, cheerful grin spread across his round face. "I think it's nice. Restful like, gives a body time for other things in life."

"Hmmph," Betsy said. "You're just happy the inspector's not on a murder, so ya don't have to give up none of your courtin' time. Not that it's done ya much good. That Sarah Trippett still ain't givin' you the time of day."

"Now, now, Betsy," Mrs. Jeffries admonished. "Let's not tease Wiggins. He's got a right to privacy." She smiled to take the sting out of the words. "I wonder where Smythe is this evening? He's late."

Smythe, the inspector's coachman, for all his independent ways, might be late for a meal, but he rarely missed one completely.

" 'E didn't say nothin' about bein' late this evenin'," the cook muttered. She shoved her empty plate to one side, rested her plump arms on the table and gazed thoughtfully at Betsy. "But then again, he were a bit miffed when he left this mornin'. I could hear the two of you havin' a go at each other. What were that all about?"

Everyone looked at Betsy. She stared fixedly at her lap as a bright blush spread over her cheeks. Mrs. Jeffries sighed. Really, this was becoming tiresome. For the past few months Betsy and Smythe seemed to be at odds every time one turned around. "Oh dear. Did you and Smythe have words again this morning?"

Betsy raised her chin and tossed her head, sending one long blond curl over her shoulder. Her blue eyes flashed defiantly. "It weren't my fault this time," she said. "I don't know what's got into that man. He walks around 'ere with a long face, snarlin' and snappin' at people and stickin' 'is nose into where it don't belong. Well, this mornin' I got fed up and told him to mind his own bloomin' business."

"Admittedly Smythe hasn't been in the best of moods lately," Mrs. Jeffries agreed thoughtfully. She'd assumed that Smythe, like the rest of them, had a bad case of the winter doldrums. The weather hadn't been very good, the excitement of Christmas was over and, even worse, the inspector hadn't had a good case for them to snoop about in since November. But as she gazed at Betsy's stubborn expression she wondered if perhaps there might be more to Smythe's bad temper than a prolonged case of boredom. "But I am surprised he actually missed his meal. He must be very annoyed with you, Betsy. Would you like to tell us why? Perhaps we can help."

Betsy sighed. "Oh, all right. Smythe's got a flea in 'is ear over me goin' to that spiritualist tomorrow night with Luty Belle."

Mrs. Goodge snorted. "I don't think it's Luty Belle that he objects to," she said. "More like that young man who's escortin' the two of you."

"And who might that be?" Mrs. Jeffries was curious. Though most households made young female servants account for every moment of their free time, she'd always made it a policy not to interfere.

Betsy went back to staring at her lap. "Edmund Kessler," she mumbled. She raised her chin. "But it's all quite respectable. Luty's goin' too. It's not like I'm goin' out and about with 'im on my own. Edmund's just a friend."

Wiggins snickered. Mrs. Goodge snorted again and even Mrs. Jeffries raised an eyebrow. Edmund Kessler had been hanging about now for two months. No wonder Smythe was annoyed, the housekeeper thought. Every time one turned around, Edmund was underfoot—ever since they'd met the young man two months ago at a music hall. Luty Belle Crookshank, a rather elderly, wealthy and eccentric American, had taken them all on the outing in gratitude for the help they'd given her in finding a young friend of hers who'd turned up missing. During the course of that investigation, the servants of Upper Edmonton Gardens had also helped solve a rather nasty double murder, not that one ever let on to anyone that one did such things, Mrs. Jeffries thought.

Save for a few trusted friends who were privy to their investigations on the inspector's behalf, it was a decidedly well-kept secret. Their dear employer, whom they all liked and admired tremendously, was completely in the dark about their activities. And they were committed to keeping him in the dark as well.

But unfortunately one of the results of their lovely outing to the music hall had been that Mr. Edmund Kessler, bank clerk, had become smitten with their Betsy. He'd also become a bit of a nuisance.

Edmund had contrived excuse after excuse for seeing the girl. He brought Mrs. Goodge recipes, he kept them apprised of where the best bargains for household linens were to be had and he'd even gone so far as to help Wiggins wash the front windows. But Mrs. Jeffries knew that the girl wasn't really interested in the poor lad. Why, she was actually quite surprised that Betsy had even agreed to go to a séance with him. It wasn't like the maid to lead the boy on. Betsy must really want to go to that séance.

"Well," Mrs. Jeffries said, "I expect Smythe is over his bad temper by now. He'll come home in his own good time."

The words were no sooner out of her mouth than they heard the backdoor opening and the subject of their conversation stepped inside.

Smythe was a tall, powerfully built, dark-haired man with heavy, almost brutal features usually softened by a generous smile and a pair of twinkling deep brown eyes fringed with long lashes.

He was not smiling tonight, nor was there a cocky grin on his face.

"It's bloomin' cold out there," he said, shrugging off his overcoat and hanging it on the oak coat tree. "Almost as bad as last year."

He walked to the table, his big body moving almost silently despite his being such a large man. Under his arm he carried a folded-up newspaper. Smythe's heavy dark brows came together in a scowl when his gaze fell on Betsy. She refrained from looking at him. Instead, as he tossed the evening paper down at his place at the table, she snatched it up and opened it.

"Sorry I'm late," he mumbled, easing himself into a chair and ignoring the fact that Betsy had pinched his newspaper.

"That's quite all right, Smythe," Mrs. Jeffries assured him, "we've already eaten, but Mrs. Goodge has your supper warming in the oven."

The cook started to heave her considerable bulk to her feet, but the coachman stopped her. "Don't trouble yerself gettin' up," he told her. "I can wait a bit fer me dinner and I can get it myself."

"We were having a nice natter about Betsy goin' to that spiritualist," Wiggins said innocently.

Smythe's scowl deepened, but he said nothing. The footman didn't appear to notice.

"I'm only goin' 'cause it might be interestin,' " Betsy said. She put the paper down. "Not like we've got much else to do."

"I don't see what's so excitin' about wantin' to talk to a lot of dead people." Wiggins helped himself to another currant bun. "Let the dead rest in peace, that's what I always say. I mean, how do they know what's goin' to 'appen in the future?"

"You don't go to a spiritualist to find out about the future," Betsy argued.

"Then why do you go?" Smythe asked quietly. He reached for the pot of tea and poured some into his mug.

"Lots of reasons," Betsy replied. "It's interestin'; it's different."

"It's silly," Smythe said, and smiled at Betsy's outraged gasp. "For once, the lad is right. Spiritualism and séances are a right old load of rubbish. The only people who take notice of such stupid carryin's-on are gullible old ladies and stupid twits."

"Are you calling me a twit and Luty Belle stupid!"

"If the shoe fits, wear it."

Mrs. Jeffries knew she really should intervene. This was getting out of hand. "Now really, this must stop. Calling one another names is vulgar. And I do believe that however the rest of us feel about spiritualism, Betsy and Luty Belle have a perfect right to investigate any . . . er . . . philosophical avenue they choose."

"I don't reckon it's the girl that's so eager to go as it is Luty Belle," Mrs. Goodge commented. "Frightening though it is, I'm forced to agree with Wiggins. Let the dead stay dead and buried. Seems to me if you keep botherin' 'em with a lot of tomfool questions, they'll get right annoyed! Probably tell a packet of lies just so you'll leave 'em be."

"Leave off it," Smythe snapped. "You're all talkin' about it like it were real. Spiritualists are nothin' but a bunch of thieves takin' hard-earned money off the likes of gullible girls like Betsy and old women like Luty."

Mrs. Jeffries gave up. She might as well let them argue.

"A fat lot you know about it," Betsy responded. "You've never been to one."

"And I've got too much sense to go to one too."

Oh well, Mrs. Jeffries thought as the debate raged around the table, there was nothing wrong with a free exchange of ideas and opinions. Her gaze fell on the newspaper. She scanned the page quickly, and a small article at the bottom of the front page caught her eye. She snatched the paper up and hurriedly read it.

"You've just got a closed mind," she heard Betsy snap.

"And I intend to keep it closed to bloomin' rubbish like that," Smythe shot back.

"Why does anyone think the dead wants anyone talkin' to 'em?" Wiggins asked.

"This is quite an interesting article," Mrs. Jeffries began. Everyone ignored her.

"You can get advice from 'em." Betsy said heatedly. "They're on the other side, they can keep you from makin' terrible mistakes, help you with your investments and such."

"Investments!" Mrs. Goodge was outraged. "What do they know about investments? That's a bit risky, if you ask me. I don't see that just 'cause someone dies he gets any smarter. Just look at old Mr. Trundle, he was the half-wit that lived over on Faverhill Road. Could you imagine the likes of him telling you what to do or where to invest your money?"

"I really think you ought to listen to this." Mrs. Jeffries tried again. "It may be very important."

They took no notice of her.

Exasperated, she shouted, "There's been a murder."

The word was magic. Silence descended as everyone stopped talking and turned to her.

"A murder?" Mrs. Goodge took her elbows off the table and sat straight up. "Where?"

Betsy's blue eyes widened. "Who?"

Smythe leaned forward, his expression serious and intense. "Is it in the inspector's district?"

Wiggins's mouth turned down in a dismal frown. "Oh no," he moaned. "Not again."

CHAPTER 2

"Get on with you, boy," Mrs. Goodge snapped. "Quit your moanin'. What does it say, then?" She nodded at the newspaper in Mrs. Jeffries's hand.

The housekeeper cleared her throat. "Woman Found Murdered," she began. "This morning the body of Mrs. Abigail Hodges of number eight Camden Street was discovered by her husband, Mr. Leonard Hodges. The police were notified and the deceased was taken to a mortuary. The police would only confirm that the victim had died of gunshot wounds. Reliable sources, however, have said the deceased may have been murdered in the course of a robbery. An inquest will be held tomorrow."

"Is Camden Street on our inspector's patch, then?" Betsy asked hopefully.

"Should be. I think it's one of them posh streets near the Royal Crescent," Smythe replied. He grinned slowly. "Looks like the inspector's got himself another one!"

"Not necessarily," Mrs. Jeffries said. She shook her head, dislodging a dark auburn tendril from her well-kept bun. "This case could very well be given to Inspector Nivens."

"Inspector Nivens!" Smythe yelped. His grin disappeared. "That ferret-faced little toff. Bloomin' Ada, that one couldn't find a horse at a racecourse let alone a murderer."

Mrs. Jeffries smiled at the coachman's colorful description of Inspector Nivens's ability. She didn't think highly of the man herself.

"I couldn't agree more," she said. "The odious man is constantly interfering in Inspector Witherspoon's cases, or at least trying to, but disliking him won't change the facts. If this article is correct and the murder was committed during a robbery, I expect the case will go to him. Inspector

Nivens is the Yard's resident expert on burglary. He's far more experienced with that sort of crime than our own Inspector Witherspoon."

"Well isn' that just the worst luck," Betsy complained. "We finally comes across a decent murder and we're not goin' to get it. It's not fair."

"What's so unfair about it?" Wiggins asked. He brushed a lock of light brown hair off his forehead. "Seems to me our inspector gets more than his share of murders. Maybe this Inspector Nivens wants a turn too."

Mrs. Jeffries gazed down the length of the table. Except for Wiggins, everyone else looked as glum as an undertaker. She raised her eyes and stared blankly at the opposite end of the kitchen to the set of windows that faced onto the street. This floor of the house was built below ground level, so the melancholy music of the drizzling rain was louder, more intense. The miserable weather now matched their moods. Mrs. Jeffries sighed. She wished she had kept quiet about that article. There was nothing worse than raising false hopes. And there was nothing she could say to cheer anyone up. It would be terribly wrong to wish for another murder merely because the household of Upper Edmonton Gardens was bored.

She turned her head slightly as she heard the clip-clop of horses' hooves stop on the pavement outside the house. A moment later there were pounding footsteps. "There's the inspector now," she said, getting to her feet. "Not to worry, then. There's always the chance that this case has been given to him. And if so, I shall find out all the details I can."

"Should we meet back here for cocoa after he's gone up?" the cook called. She gazed at the housekeeper hopefully. "Just on the off chance he did get it?"

"That'll be fine, Mrs. Goodge," Mrs. Jeffries said as she hurried up the stairs. "Cocoa at ten o'clock."

"Good evening, sir," Mrs. Jeffries called out cheerfully as the inspector stepped through the front door and into the hall. A gust of cold January rain came in with him, sprinkling water on the brand-new Oriental rug. The housekeeper hurried forward. "Gracious, sir, what a dreadful evening."

"Yes, it is rather," Witherspoon replied morosely as he took off his hat and coat. A cascade of water dripped off the rim of his bowler. The inspector didn't seem to notice.

Mrs. Jeffries watched him carefully as he hung up his wet things. His bony, angular face was set in lines of despair, there were deep creases around his clear gray-blue eyes, and when he'd taken his hat off, the thinning dark brown hair on the top of his head was standing on end, as though he'd spent hours running his fingers through it.

"It may be wet outside, sir," she said, "but we'll soon have you warm and dry." She hid her delight behind a sympathetic smile as she turned and led the way to the dining room. From his expression, she'd bet six months' housekeeping money that he'd gotten the Camden Street murder. "Mrs. Goodge has a lovely dinner waiting for you. That'll soon fix you right up."

"Er, I say." The inspector hesitated at the door of the drawing room. "I've no wish to inconvenience the cook, but do we have time for a spot of sherry? I daresay, on a day like this that'll warm me up even faster than one of Mrs. Goodge's superb meals."

"Of course, sir," Mrs. Jeffries agreed, stepping back smoothly and entering the drawing room. She walked to the walnut table upon which the sherry decanter and a set of glasses rested and poured two glasses of amber liquid.

They frequently had a glass of sherry together before Witherspoon's evening meal. The inspector had started the custom soon after Mrs. Jeffries had arrived in his household. He'd claimed that drinking alone wasn't a healthy habit. Mrs. Jeffries agreed, but she also knew that he really liked these little chats together so he could unburden himself. People had been unburdening themselves to her for as long as she could remember. She was not only used to it, she encouraged it. For she knew that one of her greatest assets in life was her ability to listen.

With her plump motherly face and dark brown eyes, she inspired confidence in those who desperately needed someone to confide in. This ability had stood her in good stead over the years and she'd developed a sixth sense, an almost uncanny talent for getting information out of people. Even when they didn't want to say a word.

"Here you are, sir," she said, placing his glass on the table next to the inspector's favorite chair and then sitting down on the settee. "Now, why don't you tell me all about it, sir."

"About what?" Witherspoon asked.

"About whatever it is that's making you so morose this evening, sir. You're not your normal, cheerful self. Come, come, I know you, sir. You're far too hardy a man to let a spot of bad weather take the spring out of your step."

The inspector sighed and settled himself more comfortably in his chair. The fire crackled merrily in the hearth, the air was tinged with the agreeable scent of lemon polish and his wonderfully understanding housekeeper was inviting him to share his cares with her. Perhaps this wasn't going to be such a bad day after all, he thought. "Naturally one doesn't like to complain, of course, but there is something troubling me." He sighed deeply. "It has been a terrible day."

"You never complain, sir," she assured him quickly.

Witherspoon smiled faintly. "To put it bluntly, Mrs. Jeffries, I'm feeling rather put-upon at the moment."

"Oh dear." She clucked sympathetically. "How so, sir?"

"There's been a murder."

"How very dreadful." Mrs. Jeffries waited patiently for him to continue.

"Well, you see, I've been given the case and I don't really think it's fair."

"Not fair?" She took a dainty sip of sherry. "In what way?"

"Because, by rights, this one really shouldn't have been given to me, it should have been given to Inspector Nivens."

"Why would you say that, sir? Surely you don't believe that Inspector Nivens is anywhere near as good as you are at solving homicides." Mrs. Jeffries knew precisely why Witherspoon was feeling put-upon. Obviously he'd been handed the Camden Street murder and he wasn't happy about it. She decided to use this opportunity to bolster his confidence. "Why you're a positive genius when it comes to catching killers."

The inspector smiled self-consciously and sat just a bit straighter in his chair. "That's most kind of you to say, but be that as it may, this particular homicide isn't really a homicide at all. At least not in the sense I usually deal with. The victim was shot during a burglary. By rights, it should be Nivens who gets this one." He gestured impatiently. "Dash it all, Mrs. Jeffries. This is a most awkward situation. Nivens is always going about saying I'm hogging all the murders, and now that there's finally one that should be his, he has the audacity to have measles."

"Measles." The housekeeper quickly lowered her chin to prevent the inspector from seeing the laughter on her face. "Not a bad case of them, I hope."

"I shouldn't think so. But nonetheless his being covered in spots is causing me no end of trouble. I'm stuck with this wretched case," Witherspoon complained. "And I don't mind telling you, I don't think it's at all right. No, not at all right."

Mrs. Jeffries stared at him in some alarm. Complaining and shirking his duty were definitely not in his normal character. Obviously it was going to take more than a few words to bolster his self-confidence, for she had no doubt that he was feeling less than equal to the task ahead of him. Inspector Witherspoon was having a bad case of nerves.

"Perhaps it isn't right, sir, but you're the best man for the task." She smiled gently. "And I think you know it, sir."

"If only I could believe that was true." Witherspoon's own smile was wistful. "The chief inspector said much the same thing when I brought the matter to his attention," he admitted slowly. "But honestly I'm not terribly sure I'm up to it. You know, sometimes when I look back on the cases I've solved, I can't quite recall how I actually did them. And today, when I was standing over that poor woman's body, I kept thinking that perhaps I'd only been lucky in the past, perhaps I'd fail this time and never catch the beast that had taken her life. It was a most depressing thought, Mrs. Jeffries. Most depressing."

Mrs. Jeffries's heart went out to him. Of course he couldn't recall how he'd solved those cases, she thought. If he could, it would be obvious he'd had help and that would never do. "Now, sir, don't be absurd. Why you know very well how you've tackled each and every case."

"I do?" Witherspoon looked genuinely surprised.

"Now stop teasing me, sir." She laughed. "You know you always do a superb background check on the victim and you know good and well that unlike most police officers, you're willing to go beyond what's right under your nose and keep digging until you find the truth. Just look at how you solved that last case. You kept asking questions and picking up small bits and pieces of gossip, which, as we all know, turned out to be vital clues. Then your brilliant mind came to the only possible conclusion. The results were, as they nearly always are when you're on the case, justice for those poor unfortunate victims who without you would have gone unavenged by their own society."

Witherspoon sat straight up in the chair. By golly, Mrs. Jeffries was right. But of course, one couldn't come right out and say so, modesty prevented such disclosures. He felt ever so much better.

"Really, Mrs. Jeffries. You mustn't keep saying I've a brilliant mind," he murmured, his lips quirking in a smile he couldn't quite hide.

"I can see that I've embarrassed you," she said briskly. "So I'll speak no more about the subject. Why don't you tell me all about this latest murder?"

Betsy stuck her head into the drawing room. "Should I serve dinner now?"

"Not just yet, Betsy," the housekeeper replied. "The inspector needs to dry off a little before he goes into the dining room. It's a bit drafty in there."

The maid nodded. "I'll ask Mrs. Goodge to hold it for fifteen minutes, will that do you?"

"That'll be fine." Mrs. Jeffries turned back to the inspector and gave him an encouraging smile. "Do go on, sir."

His confidence restored, Witherspoon cleared his throat. "The victim was one Abigail Hodges, aged fifty-two. She was married and lived in one of those big houses in Camden Street, that's just off the Queens Road. Very wealthy neighborhood, but not one that's had many housebreakings lately. Unfortunately it looks as if the poor woman came home after an evening out and walked in on a thief. He shot her once in the head and once in the chest."

"How appalling." Mrs. Jeffries clucked her tongue appropriately. "Who found the body?"

"Her husband, Leonard Hodges."

Mrs. Jeffries regarded him curiously. "I take it Mr. Hodges came home later than his wife? Or was he in the house when the shooting happened?"

"He wasn't there. The house was empty when Mrs. Hodges came home. Poor Mr. Hodges didn't find the body until the next morning when his wife didn't come down to breakfast on time."

"Surely that's unusual," Mrs. Jeffries said. "The house being empty, I mean. Where were the servants?"

"They'd been given the evening off." Witherspoon shrugged. "Mr. Hodges hadn't a clue there was anything wrong until this morning. Poor fellow, blames himself, you know. Suspects that one of the servants let it be known the house was going to be empty and the robbers found out about it and came in."

"Hmmm," Mrs. Jeffries said thoughtfully. "I presume you've reasons for the assumption of murder committed during the course of a burglary."

She knew this was a very important point.

"There's absolutely no doubt about that. Even Mr. Hodges realized what must have happened. Mrs. Hodges's jewelry box was upside down and emptied on the bed, all the drawers in the bedroom had been rifled and several expensive pieces of jewelry are now missing." He took another sip of sherry. "Mrs. Hodges obviously surprised the thieves and she was shot to keep her from identifying them. We found a broken window in the kitchen where the thief or thieves had gained entry to the house."

"I see," Mrs. Jeffries replied. She still needed to know exactly where

Mr. Hodges had been while his wife was being murdered, but she'd get back to that point later. She wanted to get the actual murder scene set in her mind first. "Where was the body found?"

"At her house in Camden Street," Witherspoon replied, giving her a doubtful look. "Haven't I already mentioned that?"

"I mean where precisely in her house was the body found?"

"Why, her bedroom." He cocked his head to one side. "I thought I'd said that too."

"Perhaps you did, sir," Mrs. Jeffries assured him. "What I meant was, was the body in the doorway, or behind a dressing screen or lying on the bed?"

"Oh, the body was lying in front of her dressing table. The sleeves on her dress were undone, and from the position of her arms it looks as if she were starting to, er"—he broke off and coughed delicately, his pale cheeks turning a bright pink—"undress herself."

Mrs. Jeffries's eyebrows drew together. "Really, sir? Now, that is peculiar. Let me make sure that I understand. Mrs. Hodges was standing in front of her dressing table getting ready for bed. Correct?"

"Er, yes."

"Presumably the bedroom door was closed? Right?"

Witherspoon's face puckered into a puzzled frown. "Yes, that's correct."

"So the thieves opened a closed door in an empty house and walked in and shot her? Is that how you think it happened?"

"That's certainly how it appeared." Witherspoon peered at her closely. "I mean, I don't think the woman would have begun disrobing with the door open. Do you? Come now, Mrs. Jeffries, you obviously find something amiss here, what is it?"

"It's really nothing, sir. It's just that my late husband always maintained that most housebreakers go unarmed." She smiled sweetly while that bit of information sank in. The late Mr. Jeffries had been a constable with the Yorkshire police for over twenty years.

"Well, yes, I quite understand that, but what's that got to do with the bedroom door being closed?"

"Simple, sir. If Mrs. Hodges were inside her bedroom, why didn't the burglars leave? Why commit murder when they could have slunk out the front door? Even if Mrs. Hodges had become aware of their presence, surely any burglar worth his salt could move faster than a fifty-two-year-old woman."

"But if they'd done that, they wouldn't have gotten the jewelry," he explained. "And that obviously was why they were in the Hodges house in the first place. Now, even I know it's unusual for burglars to carry firearms, but these villains are obviously more ruthless than most. They came to steal and they were willing to murder anyone who got in their way."

For the moment the inspector's mind was made up. Mrs. Jeffries knew that at this stage of the investigation it would be useless to attempt to get him to consider another point of view. But she knew how to bide her time. He was only sticking like a burr to this burglary notion because he was still unsure of his own abilities.

"How are you going to approach this case, sir?" she asked.

"Naturally we're going to try to trace the jewelry."

"What jewels were actually stolen?"

"A string of pearls, an opal ring and a garnet brooch."

Mrs. Jeffries stared at him in surprise. "That's all? Pearls, an opal ring and a garnet pin? None of that sounds particularly valuable, not valuable enough to commit murder over, anyway."

Witherspoon gave her a pitying look. "Dear Mrs. Jeffries, you're so very innocent. Why, there are places in this city where a thief would cut your throat for two shillings."

"But surely a wealthy house off Queens Road isn't one of them." She smiled briefly. "Did the thief empty the jewelry box?"

"Er, no." Witherspoon had been puzzled over that himself. "There were several pieces he didn't take. A gold necklace and a couple of rings, but Mr. Hodges assured us those things were merely baubles. Most of Mrs. Hodges's really good jewelry is kept in a bank vault."

"Hmmm," Mrs. Jeffries replied. "Where did you say the husband was last night?"

"He was at his club." Witherspoon didn't like the doubts Mrs. Jeffries had raised about the subject of burglars. But he comforted himself with the knowledge that there was a first time for everything, including a housebreaker arming himself.

"And where had Mr. and Mrs. Hodges gone before the murder?"

"To visit a medium, a Mrs. Esme Popejoy." Witherspoon gave her his man-of-the-world smile. "It seems Mrs. Hodges was a devotee of spiritualism and séances. I daresay it's quite shocking what nonsense otherwise respectable people get up to, isn't it?"

Mrs. Jeffries didn't think that spending one's money on a séance was any more ridiculous than most entertainments, but for the moment she'd keep her opinion to herself. She didn't want the inspector's mind to wander. "Quite. And after visiting this Mrs. Popejoy, Mr. Hodges went to his club, is that correct?"

"Not entirely. You see, Mrs. Popejoy had put poor Mr. Hodges in a bit of a spot." The inspector dropped his voice to a conspiratorial whisper. "She'd asked Mr. Hodges to escort her to the train station. Mrs. Hodges was not pleased. That's why Mr. Hodges went off to his club afterward instead of going home. He didn't want to have to face Mrs. Hodges when her temper was up."

"I see," Mrs. Jeffries replied. She saw that this "burglary" had more holes than a sieve and that the husband seemed to have an alibi. Mrs. Jeffries was very suspicious of people who had alibis. "I take it you've checked Mr. Hodges's whereabouts at the time of the murder?"

"Of course, we did that right after we spoke to the poor man. He was at Truscott's, all right. The club manager confirms that he arrived there by half past ten. Several other club members also saw Mr. Hodges arrive. We've also spoken to the other guests who were at Mrs. Popejoy's last night. Everyone agrees that the séance was over by nine-thirty. Taking into account the time it would have taken Mr. Hodges to escort Mrs. Popejoy to the station, he'd hardly have had time to nip home, shoot his wife and get to Truscott's by half past ten."

"And you've confirmed with Mrs. Popejoy that Mr. Hodges actually escorted her to the station?" Mrs. Jeffries asked innocently.

"Well, er, no. As a matter of fact we haven't. Mrs. Popejoy is still at her friend's, in Southend. But the servants and one of the other guests told us they saw Mr. Hodges get into a hansom with Mrs. Popejoy." He broke off and laughed. "Really, Mrs. Jeffries, you've a most suspicious mind. Why, anyone would think you didn't believe this was a simple, straightforward burglary."

"Of course it's not a simple burglary," Mrs. Jeffries insisted. She gazed at the faces staring at her from around the table. Mrs. Goodge's head was nodding up and down in vigorous agreement, Betsy's eyes were narrowed in concentration as she tried to take in every word Mrs. Jeffries had said and Smythe's lips were curved in approval. Only Wiggins looked doubtful.

"But how can you be sure it weren't just a thief?" he asked plaintively. "If the inspector says they was after jewels and the poor lady just 'appened to walk in on 'em, how can you know for certain that ain't what really 'appened?"

"Because she didn't just happen to walk in on the thieves," Mrs. Jeffries answered. "From what the inspector told me, she was standing in front of her dressing mirror getting ready for bed. That means the door to the bedroom was closed. Now, if you walk innocently into your own home, you're not particularly quiet about it. Doors slam, dresses rustle, one doesn't tiptoe up a staircase because one is alone. Therefore we can assume that Mrs. Hodges made a reasonable amount of noise when she entered the house."

"All right, so the poor lady weren't bein' quiet," Wiggins argued. "I still don't see what you're gettin' at."

"It's very simple. She went into her room without spotting the burglars. Therefore we can assume she didn't know they were there. But they probably knew she was home—she wasn't being quiet, so why wouldn't they have heard her come into the house? Now, why would a couple of housebreakers, who rarely go armed, hotfoot it into Mrs. Hodges's room and murder the woman when they could just as easily have slunk out the front door with no one being the wiser? Burglars just don't take those kinds of risks."

"Maybe they was in the bedroom when she walked in," Mrs. Goodge put in helpfully.

Mrs. Jeffries shook her head. "No. She'd already undone the buttons on the sleeves of her dress. She was getting ready for bed. That means the room was empty and the drawers and jewelry box were still untouched when she entered. She'd have hardly begun undressing if she'd found her room in disarray. Furthermore, there are several other odd aspects to this murder." She paused for breath and then plunged into telling them the rest of the information she'd wormed out of the inspector over dinner. "The servants weren't just given a few hours off last night, they were given the whole night off. The two housemaids, Ethel and Hilda Brown, went to visit their grandmother in the Whitechapel district and didn't arrive home until early this morning. The footman, Peter, spent the night in Brixton with his father, and the housekeeper, Thomasina Trotter, visited her old nanny who lives in Fulham. And Mrs. Hodges's niece, Felicity Marsden, who lives there too, was out at the ballet with some friends. She wasn't home last night either."

"Did the inspector check up on 'em?" Betsy asked.

Mrs. Jeffries nodded. "This afternoon. Mr. Hodges was supposedly too grief-stricken to answer many questions, so Constable Barnes and the inspector questioned the servants and then confirmed their whereabouts when the murder took place. None of the Hodges servants appear to be lying."

"And Miss Marsden," Smythe asked, "did he check on 'er?"

"Not yet." Mrs. Jeffries shook her head. "The inspector's planning on interviewing her tomorrow morning. But you know, it's quite strange. It was Mr. Hodges who gave the servants the night off, not Mrs. Hodges."

"What's so strange about that?" Mrs. Goodge asked. "The inspector gives us plenty of free time, maybe Mr. Hodges is as good a master as our inspector."

"I don't think so," Mrs. Jeffries replied slowly. "Inspector Witherspoon mentioned he'd asked the housekeeper if it was usual for Mr. Hodges to give them additional free time. She said this was the first time it had ever happened. Furthermore, it was generally Mrs. Hodges who directed the servants and not her husband."

Smythe leaned forward and planted his elbows on the table. "So where do we start?"

"Where we always start," Mrs. Jeffries said with a smile. "With the victim." She turned to the cook. "I think you know what to do, Mrs. Goodge."

"Do you just want me to find out about Mrs. Hodges?" The cook pushed a lock of iron-gray hair off her plump face.

"Not just her. Find out anything you can about Mr. Leonard Hodges and Felicity Marsden. Miss Marsden was supposedly with a family named Plimpton last night. She spent the night at their house after the ballet." Mrs. Jeffries started to turn to Betsy and then remembered something else. "And see what you can learn about the medium, Mrs. Esme Popejoy."

"You know," Betsy said thoughtfully, "Edmund may be able to help there."

"Oh, it's Edmund now, is it?" Smythe said sarcastically.

Betsy glared at the coachman and Mrs. Jeffries quickly raised a hand, effectively silencing them before they could start to bicker.

"Mr. Kessler probably could help," she said to the maid, "but please be careful about how you ask. As you all realize, it's imperative we keep any knowledge of our activities about the inspector's cases confined to a few trusted individuals."

"What else do you want me to do, then?" Betsy asked eagerly.

"Start with the shopkeepers around Queens Road," Mrs. Jeffries said. "Do the usual, find out everything you can about Mr. and Mrs. Hodges and Felicity Marsden. Keep on the alert for any interesting gossip concerning anyone in the Hodges household."

"What about me?" Wiggins asked grudgingly, his tone less than enthusiastic. Another murder meant that his courting time would be seriously limited. And just when he was makin' some progress with Sarah too. Cor, he thought, it just in't fair.

Mrs. Jeffries patted his arm. "It's good of you to ask. Believe me, Wiggins, we all must make sacrifices in the interests of justice. I want you to try to make contact with the footman from the Hodges household. The inspector said young Peter has been in service there for several years. He'll probably know many useful things about the Hodgeses. Try to find him. See if you can loosen his tongue a bit." She sat back in her chair. "Also, keep in mind that the inspector said that Mr. Hodges appeared to be a good deal younger than his wife."

Mrs. Goodge snorted. "Hmmph, he's probably married her for her money, then."

"That's rather a cynical attitude," Mrs. Jeffries said. "But possibly true. Inspector Witherspoon didn't actually say so, but I got the impression that it's Mrs. Hodges who had the money and not Mr. Hodges. Additionally—and getting this tidbit out of the inspector took some doing, believe me—I also got the impression that Mrs. Hodges wasn't a particularly attractive woman either in appearance or character."

"Is there anythin' else?" Betsy stifled a yawn.

"Let me see." Mrs. Jeffries frowned thoughtfully. She'd given them all the information she'd gotten out of the inspector at dinner. It wasn't much in the way of facts, but it was a start.

She lifted her chin until she met Smythe's gaze. But before she could give him any instructions, he rose to his feet and gave them all a cheeky grin. "No need to tell me, Mrs. J, I'm on me way. Lots of good pubs 'round the Queens Road. I should be able to come up with somethin' for ya by tomorrow mornin'."

"Tomorrow mornin'," Betsy yelped. "That's not fair, I can't even get to them shopkeepers till half past nine."

"What are you carpin' about?" Mrs. Goodge snapped. "We're not gettin' any deliveries tomorrow at all. I'll have to sit at the back window all day and snatch whoever walks by before I can start askin' my questions."

Mrs. Goodge was the only one of the household who managed to obtain her information without even leaving the kitchen.

The cook had a well-developed network of delivery people, rag-and-bone men, chimney sweeps, washerwomen, and tramps whom she regularly paraded through the Witherspoon kitchen. With this ragtag band, whom she fed and plied with dozens of cups of hot tea, she obtained every single morsel of gossip about everyone of importance in London.

"Now, now, this isn't a competition," Mrs. Jeffries interjected. Really, a bit of healthy competitiveness was fine, but they were beginning to carry things a bit far. "Remember why we're doing this. It's to help the inspector." And also because they were all born snoops. Solving murders was far more exciting than counting bed linen and polishing silver.

"We're not forgettin' the inspector," Betsy said, her expression sober. "We all owe 'im too much."

Immediately Mrs. Jeffries's annoyance faded as she looked at the somber expressions surrounding her. She knew that despite their natural love for detecting, the real reason they all worked so hard on the inspector's cases was because they all wanted to. It was a way of paying him back, without his knowledge, of course, for what he'd done for each and every one of them.

Betsy had been a half-starved waif on the inspector's doorstep when he hired her. Wiggins and Smythe had both worked for the inspector's late aunt Euphemia. But Wiggins was no more trained as a real footman than a dancing bear and the inspector needed a coachman and horses about as much as he needed a hole in his head. But rather than toss them both out onto the street to fend for themselves as best they could, he'd kept them on. And her. She sighed deeply.

Mrs. Jeffries knew that she'd been in need of a brood to mother and an outlet for her own intellectual curiosity when he'd hired her as his housekeeper. When she'd realized that he could and did need someone to talk his cases over with, she'd been so delighted she'd almost convinced herself that fate had deliberately brought the two of them together. The only fly in the ointment, as far as she could tell, was that Inspector Witherspoon wasn't married. She knew the dear man was lonely. He was also notoriously shy—why, one could almost call him backward—with the fair sex. But Mrs. Jeffries wasn't giving up. She knew that with a bit of help and a few gentle nudges, she could eventually find her inspector just the right woman.

Betsy's voice broke into her thoughts.

"But it in'n fair that 'e"—the maid pointed at the grinning coachman—"should get such a 'ead start."

Mrs. Jeffries noticed that Betsy was so annoyed she was dropping her *h*s again.

"Smythe is not getting a head start," she repeated firmly. "It's merely that it is easier for him to pursue his inquiries at night than it is during the day. . . ." Her voice trailed off as she suddenly remembered something else the inspector had told her. She turned from Betsy to look at the coachman. "Smythe, Mrs. Hodges was sent home in a hansom, and from what the inspector said, Mr. Hodges and Mrs. Popejoy took a hansom to the train station as well. It might be a good idea to try to track the drivers down."

Smythe's cocky grin faded. He'd much rather hang about in pubs than pound the streets looking for cabdrivers. "Bloomin' Ada, Mrs. J. That's a tall order. Remember the last time you 'ad me trackin' down cabdrivers? It might take days."

"I remember the last time quite well," she replied calmly. "And if you'll recall, we learned a substantial amount of information about that case from all your hard work." She smiled softly. "I know it's asking a lot. But I really think it might be useful."

"All right," he said, his tone filled with grudging respect. "Where does this Mrs. Popejoy live? I might as well start checkin' the cabbies in that area first. And what station was she leavin' from?"

"Number seven, Edinger Place. It's less than half a mile from the Strand. The inspector hasn't been there yet. He was merely repeating what Constable Barnes had found out. Mrs. Popejoy's friend lives in Southend—"

"Southend!" Smythe yelped. "Blimey, that's the T and S Line. Them stations is clear over to the East End. It'll take me 'alf the night to track down that cabbie."

"Yes, I know it's inconvenient, but the sooner we get started, the sooner we'll have some real facts to sink our teeth into."

"Is this Mrs. Popejoy still in Southend?" Mrs. Goodge asked.

"As far as I know," Mrs. Jeffries replied. "Inspector Witherspoon is planning on speaking with the lady tomorrow afternoon."

"Why not tomorrow morning?" Smythe asked, his dark eyes narrowed thoughtfully.

"Tomorrow morning is the inquest. The inspector says he wants to hear Mrs. Popejoy's evidence at the inquest before he questions her."

CHAPTER 3

"What did you think of Mrs. Popejoy, sir?" Constable Barnes asked as he and the inspector hurried down Camden Street to the Hodges house. "Not one for hidin' her light under a bushel, is she?"

"No," the inspector agreed, "she isn't." He was only half listening to the constable. His mind was preoccupied with other matters.

They'd just come from the inquest. Witherspoon knew he should be feeling far happier than he was. The ruling had been as expected. Mrs. Abigail Hodges had been murdered. Dr. Potter's evidence along with the evidence of the burglary left no doubt that the death had occurred during the commission of a crime.

Well, obviously, the woman was killed during a robbery, the inspector told himself sternly as they approached the victim's house. Everything pointed to that. He absolutely refused to allow himself to be sidetracked into thinking this crime was a complicated murder plot when everything, including the coroner's inquest, clearly showed it to be a simple robbery with very tragic results.

Yet despite his resolve, he couldn't quite shake the suspicion that there might be more to this case than he'd first anticipated.

He kept remembering his housekeeper's comments. "Housebreakers rarely go armed," she'd said. And then she'd pointed out the matter of the bedroom door being closed and why didn't the thieves simply slip out the front door. Witherspoon sighed. Something else was bothering him as well, something Constable Barnes had mentioned yesterday when they'd been examining the broken window in the Hodges kitchen. The window the thief or thieves had used to gain entry to the house.

The inspector came to a dead stop and turned to face Barnes. "What did you say about all that glass yesterday?"

The constable's craggy face went blank for a moment and then cleared. "You mean the broken window in the kitchen?"

The inspector nodded.

"All I said was the glass fragments looked a mite peculiar."

"I remember that," Witherspoon said earnestly, "but we were interrupted and I never got a chance to ask you what you meant by that remark. How did it look peculiar?"

"The glass was on the wrong side," Barnes explained. "If the window had been broken from the outside, then most of the glass pieces should have been on the kitchen floor. The force of the blow, so to speak. But I happened to notice there were more glass on the outside of the house than on the kitchen floor. The ground outside the window was covered with fragments." He smiled self-consciously.

"Then you're suggesting that the window was broken from the inside of the house and not the outside, is that correct?" Witherspoon asked.

"Well, sir, I'm not exactly suggesting anything, I'm only saying that in my experience, finding the window glass the way it was, was downright odd."

"Are you sure about this, Constable?" Witherspoon persisted. His spirits were sinking by the minute. If that ruddy window had been broken from inside the kitchen, then this crime wasn't a simple, straightforward robbery at all. Drat. "I mean, surely, one can't tell from which direction a window was broken by the way the glass is arranged."

"I didn't say I could, Inspector," Barnes replied with a lift to his chin. "But I've done a number of housebreakin's and it's been my experience that when someone's breakin' a window to get inside a house, there's usually more broken glass on the inside of the room than on the outside. That's all I'm saying."

"Hmmm." Witherspoon started walking again. "I daresay, this case is getting more muddled by the minute."

"Certainly looks that way, sir. Are we goin' to be speakin' with Mrs. Popejoy today?" Barnes asked. They'd reached the stairs of number eight. "You know, I've met her kind before. I wouldn't put it past the woman to know a bit more than she let on at the inquest."

"Why, Constable," Witherspoon said in surprise, "whatever do you mean? I know Mrs. Popejoy's, er, activities are a tad unusual, but she seemed a nice enough woman to me."

"She calls herself a spiritualist, sir," Barnes exclaimed. "Why, in my day we used to call 'em charlatans! And the way she was cozying up to them reporters, hmmph. Ought to be a law against such things. And the way she was muckin' about with our case, trying to tell everyone at the inquest that she'd warned Mrs. Hodges on the night of the murder." He snorted derisively. "Whoever heard of such nonsense."

"Mrs. Popejoy claimed she'd had a message from beyond. She certainly never claimed to have told Mrs. Hodges not to go home that night. I expect the lady was merely trying to gain a bit of notoriety." The inspector smiled wryly. "In her, er, occupation, I expect one needs to get one's name in the paper occasionally. She certainly appeared to enjoy all the attention she received at the inquest."

"She were positively reveling in it, sir," Barnes said in disgust. "Hangin' all over the press, makin' sure they spelled her name right." He clucked his tongue as he banged the brass door knocker. "Blimey, you'd think she were a bloomin' politician or somethin'."

"I must admit, I didn't think speaking with the press was a good idea. But, of course, it would hardly be our place to try to stop her. She's a right to talk to them if she likes, though I can't imagine anyone wanting to actually *speak* to a journalist." He shuddered delicately.

The door opened and a plump red-haired maid stuck her head out. "Oh, it's you," she said with a cheerful grin as she opened the door wide and ushered them inside. "Mr. Hodges said you'd be 'round again. He's in the study with Miss Marsden. If you'll wait here, sir, I'll announce you."

Witherspoon nodded absently and stepped into the hall. He fixed his gaze at the floor, a frown creasing his face. He really didn't know how to approach this case anymore. Much as he wanted to believe this had been a simple robbery with most tragic results, he wasn't sure he could any longer. Mrs. Jeffries had been right when she'd mentioned that housebreakers didn't generally go armed. And now that Barnes had told him about the broken glass being on the wrong side of the window, well, he just wasn't certain how to proceed. Much as Witherspoon wanted to ignore this new evidence, his conscience wouldn't let him.

He heard the approaching footsteps of the maid as she returned, and lifted his chin and straightened his shoulders. He'd investigate this foul crime precisely as he'd investigated his other cases. With resolve, determination and perseverance.

They followed the girl down a long hallway and into the study. The room was dismal despite the fire blazing in the hearth. The heavy bronze curtains were drawn against the pale light from the overcast day, the ticking of a mantel clock seemed overly loud in the gloomy silence and the massive, dark furniture lent an air of depression to the whole room.

Leonard Hodges rose from the settee as they were ushered inside.

"Inspector Witherspoon," he said politely. He gestured to the young woman sitting in a chair next to the fire. "Please allow me to present my late wife's niece, Felicity Marsden."

"Good day, Miss Marsden," the inspector replied. He introduced Constable Barnes.

Felicity Marsden smiled nervously. "Good day, gentlemen," she murmured.

The inspector gazed at the young woman, seeing in her a distinct resemblance to her late aunt. She had the same dark hair, but in her case the curls were soft and drawn back with a ribbon at the nape of her neck. Her skin was a pale ivory and her nose strong without being large. Her face was more refined, more delicate than Abigail Hodges's, her cheekbones high and her brows perfectly arched black wings over the darkest, biggest brown eyes the inspector had ever seen. Beside him, he heard Barnes cough lightly.

Witherspoon realized he was staring. "I'm dreadfully sorry to have to intrude upon you," he began.

"That's quite all right," she replied. "I realize it's necessary."

"We've a few questions that need to be asked"—the inspector deliberately tried to make his tone kind and gentle—"and I assure you, we'll do our very best to make them as brief as possible."

"Thank you." She clasped her hands together in her lap. "I expect you want to know where I was on the night my aunt was . . ." She faltered and then quickly recovered. "On the night it happened."

The maid who'd announced them suddenly appeared in the doorway. "Would you like tea, ma'am," the girl asked.

Though the maid had directed the question to Miss Marsden, it was Leonard Hodges who answered. "That won't be necessary, Hilda," he replied. "This is hardly a social call. I don't expect these gentlemen will be here very long." He smiled briefly at the inspector. "That's correct, isn't it?"

Taken aback, Witherspoon blinked. "Er, yes."

"Inspector." Miss Marsden's husky voice drew his attention. "I was at the ballet. I was with my friends the Plimptons. We had supper together and then went to the theatre. Afterward, I spent the night there." She unclasped her hands and drew a deep breath. "I'm afraid there's nothing else to tell you. The first I heard of the . . . tragedy was when a police constable fetched me from the Plimpton house."

"Yes, I'm quite sure it was a dreadful shock for you, Miss Marsden," Witherspoon said sympathetically. "But even though you weren't here, you may be able to help us."

"I don't see how." She began to fidget with the buttons on the sleeve of her black mourning dress. "My aunt was killed by burglars. How could I possibly know anything about that? I really don't understand why you're here. Surely you don't think any of us had anything to do with Abigail's death? Why aren't you trying to catch the thieves?" Her voice rose. "I don't understand this, I don't understand why you're asking us all these questions."

Witherspoon stared at her in alarm. He hoped she wouldn't become hysterical. Certainly she was still in somewhat of a state of shock and no doubt very upset, but really she was decidedly overreacting here. He didn't think he had asked all that many questions in the first place.

"Please, Felicity," Leonard Hodges said firmly, "the inspector is only trying to do his job. Naturally this tragedy has deeply distressed you, it's deeply upset everyone in the household, but we must cooperate in any way we can." He paused and gave her a slow, sad smile. "Now please, get a hold of yourself. You do want your aunt's murderers brought to justice, don't you?"

She bit her lip and nodded. Hodges turned to the inspector. "By all means, sir. Ask anything you like."

"My apologies, Inspector Witherspoon," Miss Marsden murmured. "Please continue with your questions."

From the corner of his eye, Witherspoon saw Barnes whip out his notebook. "It would be most helpful if you could tell us exactly what time you left the house," the inspector said.

"It was early," Felicity answered slowly. "I wanted to have time to visit with Ada's mother before we had supper, so I expect it was about five."

"You went alone?" Witherspoon wasn't sure that was useful information, but he felt compelled to ask anyway. He wasn't certain whether or not it was common for young women to travel out and about on their own at that time of the day. His housekeeper did, but then she wasn't a young woman.

She nodded. "Peter went to the corner and got a hansom cab."

"And you took the cab directly to the Plimptons' home?"

Again Felicity nodded. "Yes. It had just gone half past five when I arrived."

"Did you happen to mention to anyone at the Plimpton residence that this house was going to be empty that evening?" Witherspoon asked quickly.

"How could I?" Felicity said earnestly. "I didn't know that Uncle

Leonard had given the servants the night out until I arrived home the next day." She tilted her chin and looked directly at Leonard Hodges. "I must say, I was surprised by that."

Leonard arched one eyebrow. "Surprised; why? I felt that after what had happened last Sunday, the servants deserved some free time."

"What happened last Sunday?" Witherspoon blurted.

Hodges stared at him coldly. "It has nothing to do with this, Inspector. Nothing whatsoever."

The inspector suddenly didn't know what to do. He didn't wish to interfere in anyone's domestic affairs, but on the other hand, he felt he really should be in possession of any facts relating to servants and their time away from the house. Servants were notorious gossips. One of them could easily have let it slip that the house was empty. He was saved from having to argue with Mr. Hodges by the intervention of Constable Barnes.

"Begging your pardon, sir," the constable said calmly. "But you really should answer the question. The inspector needs to know if any of your servants might have had a reason to be angry with Mrs. Hodges."

His implication was obvious.

"Oh, all right," Hodges replied grudgingly. "Last Sunday my wife didn't let the servants have their usual afternoon off. She was annoyed with them. A few minor tasks had been left undone and Abigail got very angry. I felt badly for the staff and so I gave them all the evening off. That's all there is to it."

Witherspoon stared at him incredulously. "Why didn't you tell us this earlier?" he asked. "Gracious, if the servants were angry with your wife, then any one of them could have deliberately passed the information that your home was going to be empty that night."

"Surely that's a bit farfetched," Hodges muttered. He looked embarrassed. "And I didn't mention this before because I didn't want anyone thinking less of Abigail. She occasionally lost her temper, but she was a good woman. I won't have anyone saying any different."

"We wouldn't think of it, sir," Witherspoon assured him. He glanced at Felicity Marsden. She was watching her uncle with an unreadable expression on her exquisite face. He suddenly remembered he'd been in the process of questioning her when he'd become distracted.

"Now, Miss Marsden," he began briskly. "You went to the ballet with your friends, correct?"

"Yes."

"And what theatre would that have been?" Barnes asked softly.

"Sadler's Wells Theatre," she replied.

"And you were with the Plimpton family the whole time?" Witherspoon asked. He saw a blotchy red color bloom in the woman's cheeks.

"Of course I was," she replied. "They've a box at the theatre. We were together the whole time."

"Oh, come now, Felicity," Leonard Hodges interjected, "surely you're mistaken. Why, I saw Horace Plimpton at Truscott's. He'd been there the whole evening."

"I meant, Mrs. Georgianna Plimpton and Ada and I were together."

"Mrs. Georgianna Plimpton is Ada Plimpton's grandmother," Hodges explained to the policemen. "So it was only the three of you ladies who went to the ballet? Ada didn't have a gentleman in tow to act as escort?"

"Mr. Plimpton sent the footman with the carriage," Felicity replied defensively. "Don't be so old-fashioned, Uncle. The evening was quite respectable."

Witherspoon was getting confused, but he struggled not to let it show. Clearing his throat, he said, "May I have the Plimptons' address?"

"Number fourteen Tavistock Street," Felicity replied. She suddenly got to her feet. She was small and slim and very delicate looking in the heavy black mourning dress. The inspector felt such pity for the poor girl. Her aunt's death had been a terrible shock. Why, merely talking about the night it had happened had caused her to go completely pale. He noticed her hands were trembling as well.

She looked at him with a dazed, stricken expression of pain. "Inspector, if you don't mind, I must retire. This has all been a dreadful experience. I must go rest. If you've any more questions, you'll have to ask them later." With that, she hurried to the door and disappeared.

"I say," Hodges said, "I'm most dreadfully sorry. Felicity isn't herself today."

"No apologies are needed," the inspector said quickly. "I can see that your niece is terribly upset. Sometimes one forgets what delicate creatures women are."

"Thank you for being so understanding," Hodges said. "Now, if you've no more questions for me, I really must be going. The vicar is waiting for me."

"Ah yes, the funeral arrangements." Witherspoon knew there were one or two more questions he should ask, but he couldn't think just what they were. Something that Mrs. Jeffries had mentioned this morning at breakfast. Something to do with . . . He sighed, he simply couldn't remember what it was. Perhaps it would come to him later. Aware that the man was watching him expectantly, he said, "Is it possible for us to have a word with the housekeeper now?"

Hodges looked surprised. "Of course, but I thought you spoke with Mrs. Trotter yesterday."

"We've a few more questions, sir," Barnes said firmly. "Mrs. Trotter wasn't in the best of states yesterday."

Thomasina Trotter had completely recovered. Tall, grimfaced, gray-haired and ramrod thin, she walked imperiously into the servants' hall and stared at the two policemen with the same suspicious expression she reserved for tradesmen and shopkeepers trying to cheat her. "You wanted to see me?"

The inspector swallowed. This woman definitely didn't have the deferential manner one associated with a servant. As a matter of fact, with her regal bearing and distinct upper-class accent, he found her somewhat intimidating. "Yes, Mrs. Trotter, we did. We're hoping you can help us."

"If you're referring to the robbery and murder of Mrs. Hodges, then I'm afraid you're wasting both of our time. As I told your man yesterday, I wasn't even here. As you know, Mr. Hodges gave us the night off. From six o'clock onward, I was in Fulham."

Witherspoon refused to be cowed. He was serving the interests of justice here. "Visiting your old nanny, I understand. A Miss Adelaide Bush. Is that correct?"

"As I told the police yesterday, that is correct."

"Did you, by any chance, happen to mention to anyone that the house was going to be empty?" Witherspoon asked. "Perhaps you may have mentioned it to someone on your way to Fulham, someone on the tram or the train?"

"I'm hardly in the habit of confiding in complete strangers," Mrs. Trotter said. "Furthermore, though I may be forced by circumstances to use common public conveyances, I certainly don't speak to anyone."

Witherspoon was suddenly curious. Thomasina Trotter had definitely known better days. "How long have you worked for Mr. and Mrs. Hodges?"

Mrs. Trotter's thin eyebrows rose. "The terms and conditions of my employment in the Hodges household haven't anything to do with this crime. Therefore it is hardly the business of the police."

The inspector tried to think of a reasonable reply. He was saved again by Constable Barnes.

"We're askin', ma'am." Barnes said quietly, "because if you've been here awhile and you know the neighborhood, you just might be able to tell us if you saw any strangers hangin' about afore you left?"

"I see." She smiled slightly. "Well, in that case, I shall answer the question. I've worked for Mrs. Hodges for twenty years, and as it happens, I did see a stranger in the neighborhood on the night she died."

"Before you go into that," Witherspoon interrupted. He'd suddenly remembered there were several basic questions concerning this household that he hadn't asked. "Could you please tell us precisely what everyone in the household was doing prior to being given the evening off?" He was quite proud of himself for thinking of that line of inquiry.

Surprised, Mrs. Trotter stared at him. "How on earth is knowing our movements going to help?" She shrugged. "But I assume you should know your business." She made it clear from her tone that she didn't believe this for one minute.

"Just tell us what everyone in the house was doing from," he said slowly, "er, five o'clock onward."

"Everyone with the exception of myself was eating their supper here in the servants' hall. We'd already been told Mr. and Mrs. Hodges were going out for the evening."

"They weren't planning on dining at home?" Witherspoon asked.

"No. They were dining with Mrs. Hodges's nephew, Jonathan Felcher. He'd offered to take them out to dinner and they'd accepted." She laughed harshly. "They were so stunned to actually receive an invitation from him! He's usually around here cadging meals off them. But that's neither here nor there. At half past five, the maids cleared up the dishes and cleaned the hall. Cook left to go visit her half sister in Notting Hill."

"So you knew by this time that Mr. Hodges was giving you the evening free?" the inspector said quickly.

"Oh no. Cook always went to her half sister's on Wednesday evening," Mrs. Trotter replied. "Mr. Hodges didn't tell us we had the evening free until well after cook had left. It was probably close to six o'clock. The maids—they're sisters—immediately left to catch the late train. Peter, the footman, disappeared, probably to go to his father's, and I gathered my things and went to visit my old nanny in Fulham."

The inspector's head was spinning. He took a deep breath and tried to think of the next reasonable question. "May we have the lady's name and address?"

"Wouldn't you rather I tell you about the strange person I saw hanging about?"

"Er, uh, yes." Witherspoon decided he could wait a few moments for the nanny's address. He hated being rude.

"It was a woman. She was standing just at the corner and I happened to notice her because she was completely veiled."

"Perhaps she was in mourning," Witherspoon suggested.

"In a red veil?" Mrs. Trotter replied. "No, this woman was standing at the end of the street. Just standing there. It didn't strike me as odd at the time; I thought perhaps she was waiting for someone. But given what happened, it seems to me she was watching the house."

Beside him, Witherspoon heard Constable Barnes sigh softly and he knew what that meant. This evidence, if evidence it even was, was utterly useless. *After* a crime had been committed, people could always remember a suspicious character or two in the neighborhood. However, none of these people were ever suspicious enough *before* a crime was committed to warrant anyone even mentioning them to a policeman! And finding a lone woman who'd happened to be standing on the same street as the Hodges home on the day of the murder would be an impossible task. And on top of that, the woman probably had absolutely nothing to do with the crime.

Mrs. Jeffries paused at the corner and gazed at her surroundings, looking for a likely hiding place in the event that Inspector Witherspoon or one of his constables happened to come out of the Hodges house. She could hardly claim she'd come to return his glasses or his watch. The inspector had slipped out this morning before she'd had an opportunity to appropriate either item from his coat pockets. But she wasn't going to let that stop her. It was imperative she see the house and, if possible, the scene of the crime itself.

Camden Street came off the busy thoroughfare of the Queens Road. The Hodges house was a large red-brick Georgian at the end of the street. It was separated from its neighbor by a large stretch of garden on one side and enclosed by a six-foot stone wall on the other side.

She hurried to the corner and came alongside the ivy-covered stone wall. Her footsteps seemed inordinately loud as she walked along the pavement stones searching for a gate. When she found the gate, it was locked. She glanced up and saw the tradesmen's bell and, for one long moment, seriously considered giving it a good yank. But she immediately discarded that idea. It was far too likely that a policeman might answer that summons.

Thinking hard, she continued walking, her hand trailing idly against the wall, her fingers skimming over the leaves and brushing lightly against the stone. Suddenly her fingers stilled and she stopped. Leaning close, she saw that there was another, smaller, wooden gate set in the wall. Because of the heavy foliage, it wasn't noticeable. She pushed slightly against the wood and smiled as it silently swung open a few inches. Peeking inside, she saw that the latch was gone and the gate had been held shut merely by the connecting strands of ivy. She shoved again and managed to open up a space big enough to squeeze through.

Once inside, she stood stock-still and examined the area.

The ivy extended for a distance of about eight feet. Mrs. Jeffries could see that only inches from where she stood, the plants had been trampled. A vague but direct line of trampled vines led from the gate to the grass. She suspected she knew now how the killer had made his escape. Turning, she looked at the gate again and shook her head. If her fingers hadn't been brushing that wall as she passed, she'd have missed it completely.

Mrs. Jeffries didn't usually leap to conclusions. However, in this case she made an exception. If, indeed, the killer was the one who'd made those faint tracks through the ivy to get away, then that person was someone who knew this garden well. That gate was too well hidden to be discovered by a casual thief.

Mrs. Jeffries wasted no time. Keeping her head down and dodging from one low-lying clump of bush to another, she was making her way to the Hodges house when the backdoor opened and a man and woman came outside.

The woman was dressed in an elegant, long-sleeved mourning dress and the man was wearing a well-cut suit. She didn't think they were servants.

Praying they were too preoccupied with one another to notice her, she treaded softly across the grass to the only available hiding place, a giant oak tree. In front of the tree was a bench. Mrs. Jeffries made it to the other side of the trunk only seconds before the two stepped off the path and onto the grass verge leading to the bench.

"Well, my dear cousin," the man said as soon as the woman had seated herself. "Don't you think wearing mourning is a mite hypocritical or did you and dear Aunt Abigail manage to settle your differences?"

"We had no differences," the woman replied. "Furthermore, I'm of age. Aunt Abigail couldn't stop me from doing as I chose."

He laughed. "Come, come now. This is Cousin Jonathan you're talking to, remember. We both know you'd never risk your comfortable life here by offending our late, sainted aunt."

"Don't be disgusting, Jon," she snapped. "Abigail's dead. Can't you let her rest in peace."

"My, my, little cousin," he said. "Have we had a change of heart now that she's gone? Or could it be that now that you're set to inherit half of everything, you're inclined to be generous?"

Mrs. Jeffries held her breath and flattened herself closer to the tree. She prayed that neither of them suddenly got the urge to get up.

"I'm not interested in Abigail's money," the woman cried passionately.

"Aren't you?" he replied, his voice so low that Mrs. Jeffries had to strain to hear. "Aren't you in the least interested in money, my dear cousin? Now that she's gone, you can marry that poor clerk you're in love with. Isn't it fortunate how things work out."

"I'm not in love with anyone," she cried. "And if you're implying I had anything to do with Abigail's death, you're wrong. You've more reason to want her dead than me. You hated her, remember?"

"I remember," he replied grimly. "And unlike you, I won't play the hypocrite. I'm glad she's dead. With her gone, I shall have control over my father's estate."

"What makes you think so?" she said cattily. "You've no reason to think that Leonard will instruct the solicitors any differently than she did for all those years."

He sighed. "Oh Felicity, you're so very naive. Dear Uncle Leonard doesn't give a toss about my piddly little trust. He's getting the other half of Abigail's estate. Other than money, Leonard's only interested in one thing, and it isn't business."

"You're being revolting again."

"I'm being truthful. Now that Abigail's out of the way, he'll have even less reason for being discreet. I'm sure with the proper persuasion I can convince Leonard to let me have control of my trust. Why not? I'm thirty years old." He laughed again. "You're the one with the problem, my dear. Last I heard, that clerk of yours had other fish to fry. Even with half of Abigail's money, it may be too late."

She jumped to her feet. "You really are revolting. Benjamin loves me, and if it hadn't been for Abigail's wretched interference, we'd have been married by now."

"Calm down, calm down," the man said soothingly. "You're right, I'm being dreadfully rude. Forgive me, despite my cavalier attitude, hearing about Abigail's murder has upset me. After all, I was one of the last people to see her before she died."

"Don't be so melodramatic," the woman replied. "Leonard told me that after they left you at the restaurant, they went on to the stupid séance. There were at least seven other guests. By the way, how did you come up with the money to take them out for a meal?"

"I had a spot of luck on a horse and decided to repay my dear aunt's many kindnesses to me," he said, his voice dripping with sarcasm.

"You mean you wanted to trap her long enough so she'd have to listen to another one of your silly business schemes."

"They aren't silly," Jonathan snapped vehemently. "If the old witch had given me my money when I wanted it last year, I'd be a rich man now. Do you have any idea how much silver that mine has produced?"

Mrs. Jeffries straightened nervously as she heard the sound of footsteps pounding across the grass.

"Excuse me, sir," an excited female voice exclaimed, "but the inspector from Scotland Yard would like to have a word with you now."

As soon as the twosome had followed the maid back into the house, Mrs. Jeffries peered out from behind the tree to make sure the coast was clear.

Keeping her head low, she crept closer. A series of steps led from the edge of the garden onto a low-walled terrace that opened from what looked like the drawing room. Ducking down, Mrs. Jeffries made her way to the other side of the terrace and the small backdoor that led off the flat, rough-stone service porch.

She studied the area carefully. The first thing she noticed was the service door didn't have a keyhole, which meant that it latched from the inside. Next to the door was a long, rectangular pane of glass, and beside that, the broken shell of a larger window that had had all its glass knocked out. Mrs. Jeffries frowned. Why hadn't the burglar knocked out the small window and then reached inside and unlatched the door? Why take the risk of someone hearing the shattering of a large pane of glass when one could just as easily have knocked out the small one and gained entry through the door?

Suddenly she heard the inspector's voice from deep inside the house. She quickly crept back behind the wall surrounding the terrace and hurried back the way she'd come.

As she walked towards the Queens Road Mrs. Jeffries realized she'd learned an enormous amount of information. Now she had to think of a way to ensure that Inspector Witherspoon learned it as well.

But there were two very important facts that were uppermost in her mind. First, Abigail Hodges had not been much loved, and second, whoever killed her was either the worst kind of bungling burglar or a very clever murderer.

CHAPTER 4

Inspector Witherspoon waited patiently for Jonathan Felcher to sit down. He'd been waiting now for a good two minutes. The fellow couldn't seem to find a place to settle. He'd paced between the fireplace and the settee half a dozen times. Finally the young man stopped in front of a leather wing chair, smiled at the inspector and sat. He gazed at Witherspoon out of a pair of wary hazel eyes and casually flicked a lock of wavy brown hair off his forehead.

"All right, Inspector," Felcher said as he began stroking his beard, "go ahead and ask your questions. Though, I must say, I don't think you're going to learn anything useful. I certainly don't know a thing about who robbed and murdered Abigail."

"I understand you took your aunt and uncle out to dinner on the night of the murder," Witherspoon began. The moment the words were out of his mouth, he wanted to bite his tongue. He really must refer to this crime as a robbery. Blast it, this wasn't a murder plot. Was it? He wasn't sure anymore, just as he wasn't sure what this fidgety young man could possibly tell him.

But dash it all, he had to keep trying. Nothing else about this case was going right. Despite a massive effort by the uniformed lads, they hadn't heard hide nor hair about the missing jewelry. It hadn't turned up in any pawnshops or any of the usual places stolen goods frequently appeared.

"That's true. They've had me 'round for meals so many times I felt I really ought to return their hospitality." Felcher smiled slightly. "It's difficult, though. I live in lodgings, so I had to take them to a restaurant. We went to Clutter's. It's a nice little place near Covent Garden. Do you know it?"

"Er, no. What time did you finish your meal?" the inspector asked. He knew this line of inquiry would probably lead nowhere, but he felt he must do a thorough job of interviewing everyone.

Felcher plucked a piece of lint off the lapel of his brown jacket. "It was rather early, actually. Abigail and Leonard had another appointment. So it must have been half past seven or so when I saw them off in a hansom."

"Did your aunt tell you where they were going?" Really, the inspector thought, the man acted as if he were bored. Wasn't he in the least concerned with helping to catch his aunt's killer?

Felcher gave a condescending smile. "No, but Leonard did. Abigail had the good sense to be embarrassed by her foolishness. But her dear husband isn't anywhere near as discreet! He let the cat out of the bag." He broke off and laughed. "I don't know who she thought she was fooling. Everyone knew she was always trotting off to mediums and spiritualists or whatever it is those people call themselves."

"So you knew she had an appointment with Mrs. Popejoy?"

"But of course. Madame Esme Popejoy is the newest rage in some circles. Once Abigail heard of her, she didn't rest until she'd badgered Leonard into wangling an introduction."

"Why did your aunt have such an interest in spiritualism?" Witherspoon asked curiously.

"My late aunt was obsessed with communicating with the spirit of her son." He yawned exaggeratedly. "A rather pointless exercise if you ask me. The boy died when he was five. The lad could hardly be expected to have much to say."

Witherspoon stifled a sigh. This was getting him nowhere. What could Mrs. Hodges's interest in spiritualism have to do with her murder?

"Yes, yes, I'm sure that's probably quite true," the inspector muttered. He searched his mind for another pertinent question. "Did Mr. Hodges happen to mention to you that he'd given the servants the evening off?"

Felcher's eyebrows shot up. "Certainly not. Why would he tell me? I'm hardly likely to care one way or another."

"That is as it may be," the inspector replied, refusing to give up, "but there is always the possibility he did mention it to you and you inadvertently mentioned that fact to the wrong person."

"The wrong person?" Felcher snapped, half rising from his chair. "Now, see here, I'm not sure I like your implication, sir."

"I'm implying nothing, Mr. Felcher. I'm merely trying to determine how the miscreants that robbed and murdered your aunt could have known the house was going to be unattended that evening."

Felcher relaxed back into his seat, his bluster dying as quickly as it had come. "Well, no one heard that information from me! I didn't even know about it. I'm hardly privy to my aunt's domestic arrangements."

"After you and the Hodgeses had finished your meal," Witherspoon asked, "what did you do for the rest of the evening?"

"What did I do?" Felcher stared at Witherspoon incredulously. "That's hardly any of the police's concern. Look here, I thought my aunt was murdered by a burglar. What's that got to do with me? What's that got to do with how I spent my evening?"

"Calm yourself, Mr. Felcher," Witherspoon said firmly. "Our questions are merely routine. You mustn't read anything sinister into them. We're asking everyone who saw Mrs. Hodges on the evening of her death the same thing."

Felcher didn't look convinced. But he answered the question. "As soon as I put Abigail and Leonard into the cab, I went back to my lodgings. I stayed there for the rest of the evening. My landlady can confirm that."

It was midafternoon when Mrs. Jeffries arrived back at Upper Edmonton Gardens. The house was very quiet. Wiggins, Smythe and Betsy were still out.

Mrs. Jeffries paused at the top of the backstairs. She heard the low murmur of voices. Quietly she tiptoed downstairs and peeked into the kitchen. She saw the cook sipping tea and chatting with the butcher's boy and a man from the gasworks. Obviously Mrs. Goodge had gotten busy.

She went back upstairs and pulled a feather duster out of the cupboard. As she dusted the drawing room Mrs. Jeffries thought about what she'd learned so far. She no longer had any doubts about this crime. It certainly hadn't been a burglary gone bad.

From what she'd overheard about Abigail Hodges she'd wager a year's wages that the woman had been the victim of a well-planned murder. The robbery was merely a trick. A rather clumsy attempt to divert the police's attention from the real motive for the crime. Someone wanted Abigail Hodges dead. But who?

Mrs. Jeffries hovered in the hallway near the backstairs. She'd finished dusting a rather ugly portrait of one of the inspector's ancestors when she heard the backdoor slam.

Tossing the duster into the cupboard, she dashed for the kitchen.

"Good afternoon, Mrs. Goodge," she said cheerfully, taking the chair next to the cook, "you certainly look like you've been busy today."

Mrs. Goodge smiled widely. "Haven't done much cooking, but I've heard a thing or two." She sat back and crossed her arms over her massive bosom. "Let's hope the inspector's not too particular about what he eats tonight."

"Don't fret about that. The inspector enjoys everything you cook. Now, what have you found out?"

"Well, I didn't learn all that much about Abigail Hodges, but I heard a bit about her husband. He was married before."

"He was a widower when he married Mrs. Hodges?"

"Right. He married Mrs. Hodges almost a year to the day after his first wife died. Interestin', isn't it?" Mrs. Goodge smiled smugly. "And his first wife died in a funny way too."

Mrs. Jeffries leaned forward. "A robbery?"

The cook shook her head. "A drowning. Her name was Dorothy. She were a Throgmorton before she married Leonard Hodges." She gazed at the housekeeper expectantly. Mrs. Jeffries knew the name was supposed to ring a bell, but it didn't.

"Throgmorton?" Mrs. Jeffries repeated.

"Of Throgmorton's Carriages. They're up Nottingham way, surely you've heard of them. One of the wealthiest families in the Midlands."

"Oh yes, of course. Please go on."

"A couple of years after they was married, Dorothy Hodges went off by herself to the Lake District. She drowned when the skiff she were in overturned."

"Presumably, then. Mr. Hodges had a substantial amount of his own money when he married his second wife. He probably inherited quite a bit from his first wife's death," Mrs. Jeffries mused.

"Not a penny," Mrs. Goodge said smugly. "He probably thought he were going to, but them that's got money knows how to hang on to it. When she drowned, her people made sure that Hodges got nothing. All of her money was tied up in trusts and such."

"Were you able to find out where Leonard Hodges was when his first wife died?"

"He was in Scotland—he worked for Dorothy's father. Old Mr. Throgmorton had sent Hodges to Edinburgh." Mrs. Goodge shrugged. "But peculiar as it is—I mean, Mr. Hodges losin' both wives in strange ways and him not even forty yet—there weren't no hints of foul play attached to Dorothy Hodges's death. And from what I've heard of the Throgmortons, if they'da thought that Hodges had anything to do with the drowning, they wouldn't have let it go."

"Coincidences do happen," Mrs. Jeffries said thoughtfully.

"Yoo-hoo," shouted a familiar voice from the top of the stairs. "Anyone home?"

"What's Luty doin' here this time of day?" Mrs. Goodge asked as they waited for the elderly American woman to make her way down the stairs. "She and Betsy aren't going out until this evening."

"Afternoon, Hepzibah, Mrs. Goodge," Luty Belle Crookshank said as she came into the kitchen.

They both gaped. Luty Belle, who favored bright colors despite her advanced years, had outdone herself. Today she wore an emerald-green-and-white-striped day dress with a heavily draped apron over a kilted skirt. A velvet hat with a bottle-green feather was perched jauntily on her white hair.

"Are you two gonna gape at me all day or ask me to sit down?" Luty asked with a grin.

"Oh please, sit down, Luty," Mrs. Jeffries said hastily. "You know you're always welcome here."

"I come by to offer ya some help," Luty said eagerly. "Heard ya was workin' on another one of the inspector's murders."

Mrs. Jeffries was taken aback. "Gracious, how on earth did you learn we're working on a case?"

Luty chuckled. "Stop frettin', Hepzibah. It ain't common knowledge if that's what you're a-thinkin'. But I was shopping on Regent Street today and I happened to run into Wiggins."

"What's Wiggins doin' on Regent Street?" Mrs. Goodge muttered. "I thought he was supposed to be gettin' that footman at the Hodgeses' to chat a bit."

Mrs. Jeffries brushed that aside. "How much did Wiggins tell you?"

"About Abigail Hodges?" Luty pursed her lips. "Not much, just what little he knowed. But once he mentioned the word 'murder,' I knew you'd be wantin' my help."

"That's very kind of you, Luty," Mrs. Jeffries began cautiously. "But so far—"

"I'da been here earlier only I was already promised to go over to Stockwell to the orphanage." She frowned. "They's a-havin' prizes' day and 'course I had to go. Without me all those pious old biddies that show up for that kinda folderol woulda had some of them young'uns thinkin' they ought to be grateful for the very air they breathe." Luty shook her head in disgust. "Land's sake, why can't people just give generously outta the kindness of their hearts instead of makin' them puir young'uns put on a show fer 'em. But that's enough about that. I'm here now and rarin' to get started."

Mrs. Jeffries stared at her helplessly. Though Luty Belle Crookshank was fully aware of their activities in helping the inspector, she wasn't sure if including her in every investigation was a wise idea. Despite her liveliness and energy, Luty was no longer young. And on their last case, it had been Luty herself who'd come to them for help. But as she gazed at the elderly American's sharp brown eyes and determined expression, she knew she didn't have the heart to turn her away.

Besides, Luty could be very useful.

"What time are you and Betsy meeting Edmund Kessler this evening?" Mrs. Jeffries asked.

"Seven. Why?"

"Because the spiritualist Edmund is taking you to visit may know something about one of the other persons in this case." At Luty's puzzled frown she broke off and smiled. "Let's get you a cup of tea while I explain everything we've learned so far."

Half an hour later Mrs. Jeffries had finished telling Luty everything when the backdoor opened and Betsy stepped inside.

The maid took off her coat and hat. Her mouth was curved in a dejected frown and her shoulders slumped. "I didn't learn nuthin'," she said disgustedly as she hung up her things on the coat tree.

"You mean none of the shopkeepers would talk about the Hodgeses household?" Mrs. Goodge asked in alarm. The very idea of such tight-lipped discretion filled her with horror.

"Oh, they talked all right," Betsy muttered, "but none of 'em had anything worth 'earin'." She plopped down onto the nearest chair and accepted a cup of tea.

"Now, I'm sure that's not true, Betsy," Mrs. Jeffries said soothingly. "Why don't you tell us what you've heard. As I've said before, at this stage of an investigation, it's very difficult to tell what will or will not be important."

"All right." She sighed dramatically. "The grocer told me the Hodgeses pays the bill regular like and don't haggle none over the prices. Though they was always ready to point out a mistake. I mean, they didn't complain about the prices, but if the bill was added wrong or they was charged for somethin' they didn't get, they'd let the grocer know about it quick enough. The fishmonger and the butcher said the same. Though the boy at the grocer's said that he didn't see how a household the size of the Hodgeses' could be fed properly on the amount of food they bought."

"Now, you see, that's important. There's an indication that the household was stingy with food. They probably underfed the servants," Mrs. Jeffries said, though she wasn't sure she believed it. However, she didn't want Betsy to become discouraged. "Who was in charge of the accounts?"

"The housekeeper, Mrs. Trotter. But sometimes Mrs. Hodges would come in and order things too," Betsy explained. "You'd think that rich people wouldn't be so careful with their money, wouldn't you, seein' as how they have plenty."

"That's how they got rich in the first place," Mrs. Goodge commented. "By watchin' their pennies."

Mrs. Jeffries didn't think watching one's pennies had all that much to do with getting rich, but she wasn't going to pursue the point just now.

"Betsy," she said thoughtfully, "what else makes you think that Mrs. Hodges was overly careful with her money?"

"The girl at the dress shop did tell me that Mrs. Hodges was always complainin' about the cost of her clothes. Not that the cost ever stopped her from buyin', mind you. She even used to complain about the cost of her husband's clothes." Betsy shook her head. "Honestly Mrs. Hodges were in there on the day she died to get an evening dress fitted and she spent the whole time bendin' the poor shop girl's ear about what a fool of a husband she had."

Luty snorted. "Women been complainin' about that fer a long time."

"What precisely had annoyed Mrs. Hodges?" Mrs. Jeffries asked.

"Oh, you know. He spent too much time at his club and he didn't pay enough attention to her. He spent too much money and then he didn't spend enough." She laughed. "First she moaned about all the money he was spendin' at his club and then she whined about him buyin' a ready-made coat and bowler from one of them cheap shops down the East End. I tell ya, there's just no pleasin' some people."

Mrs. Jeffries hid her disappointment well. Betsy hadn't learned anything really useful. She'd picked up a few tidbits of marital gossip, but that was all. "Were you able to learn anything about anyone else in the Hodges household?"

"Not really," she replied dejectedly. She brightened suddenly. "Exceptin' I did hear that Mrs. Hodges's niece just broke off her engagement a while back. That's somethin', isn't it?"

"Of course it is." Mrs. Jeffries forced an enthusiastic smile to her lips.

She'd have to find a way to break it gently to the girl that she'd already picked up that particular item from the conversation she'd overheard at the Hodges house.

"Addie," Betsy continued excitedly, "that's the girl at the dress shop, said that a couple of months ago Felicity Marsden came in an' canceled an order for some clothes she'd ordered for her trousseau. Addie was right annoyed about it too."

"Addie didn't, by any chance, know the name of Felicity's fiancé did she?" Mrs. Jeffries asked eagerly. Thwarted love was sometimes a motive for murder. And the only name she'd overheard this morning had been Benjamin. A surname would be most useful.

"She didn't know his name," Betsy admitted reluctantly. "But she did say that ever since then she 'adn't seen hide nor hair of Felicity. But that don't do us any good. An engagement that ended two months ago isn't goin' to 'elp us find Abigail Hodges's killer." She slumped in her chair. "Sorry. I didn't learn much today, did I?"

"You did fine, Betsy," Mrs. Jeffries assured her.

"I don't know. Smythe has probably already tracked down both them cabbies. . . ."

Mrs. Jeffries pursed her lips. "No, he hasn't. He popped in early this morning. So far he's found nothing."

"Well, one of us better come up with somethin'," Betsy exclaimed. "I've got a feelin' this case is goin' to be real difficult."

Luty Belle reached across the table and patted Betsy's hand. "It ain't gonna be any more difficult than any of the other cases. Now stop frettin', girl. It's early days yet."

"It's a rather sordid story, inspector, and not one that I'd care to repeat." Esme Popejoy smiled sadly as she handed Witherspoon his cup of tea. "But I do understand that you're investigating a terrible crime, and therefore you need to know."

"Er, actually, all I wanted to know was whether or not Mr. or Mrs. Hodges had mentioned their house being unattended," Witherspoon sputtered. Really, this interview wasn't going at all well. He knew he should have taken Barnes's advice and gone on home, leaving the interviewing of Mrs. Esme Popejoy until tomorrow. But dash it all, he'd wanted to get it over and done with.

"That's all you wanted to ask me? But surely you don't believe Mrs.

Hodges was killed in a robbery?" Mrs. Popejoy exclaimed. "Surely you can see that she was murdered. You're not having much success tracing the jewelry, are you?"

Inspector Witherspoon was so startled his hand jerked, slopping tea into his saucer and rattling the cup. "Oh dear," he groaned. "How on earth do you know that!" He caught himself abruptly, realizing he really shouldn't be admitting such a thing to one of the principals in this case. "Really, Mrs. Popejoy, I've no idea what you're talking about."

This, his last interview of the day, was turning out to be his worst.

Women like Esme Popejoy made him fidgety. With her delicate features, slim womanly figure, dark auburn hair and lovely blue eyes, she made him nervous. Very nervous indeed. He was never precisely sure how to talk to such creatures. They were so very different from men. When they smiled and laughed and raised their perfectly shaped eyebrows, well, a fellow practically became tongue-tied.

Embarrassed by his thoughts, the inspector quickly looked away and focused his attention on his surroundings. He stared fixedly at the voluminous folds of the elegant blue silk drapes before dropping his eyes to the royal-blue carpet. The settee and other furniture in Mrs. Popejoy's drawing room was white damask and he was terrified he was going to spill his tea all over the cloth and leave a horrid stain if that woman didn't stop staring at him. Drat it all, he really should have let Barnes handle this interview.

"Come now, Inspector," Esme Popejoy replied. "You needn't pretend with me." She leaned forward and looked Witherspoon directly in the eye. "You see, I *know*. I know it wasn't a simple robbery gone wrong. It was cold-blooded murder."

"But how could you possibly know such a thing!"

She gave him a slow, wise smile. "You wouldn't understand," she said softly. "Men so rarely do. But then again, perhaps you're not like other men. I've heard you're exceptionally intelligent."

"Oh, well," Witherspoon murmured modestly. Perhaps it was just as well that he hadn't let Barnes interview this lady. Why, talking to her was getting easier by the minute. Gracious, she was such a perceptive woman. He was surprised to find that his nervousness had almost completely gone. "I have had some modest success. . . ."

"But of course you have," she agreed, reaching over and patting him gently on the arm. "And it's because you're so brilliant, so much more broad-minded than the average person, that I'm willing to speak so openly with you. You see, I know it was murder because Lady Lucia warned Mrs. Hodges."

"Lady Lucia?" Witherspoon repeated. "Who's she?" He felt a flutter of apprehension.

"My spirit guide." Esme gave him another dazzling smile. "She almost didn't come that evening, you see. I'd told Mrs. Hodges that Lady Lucia really only likes to come at dusk, when one lights the gas lamps, but Abigail was late, so Lady Lucia was, well, annoyed. That's why the warning was so muddled. She's generally much clearer than that."

The inspector felt as if he was losing control of the conversation. He decided to try to tactfully ignore this rather peculiar digression and backtrack. "Er, yes, I'm sure she was annoyed. Now, if you'll recall, I did ask if Mr. or Mrs. Hodges had mentioned that their home would be empty. Not only were the servants not home, but their niece was out as well."

Mrs. Popejoy stared at him for a long moment before answering. Her voice, when she finally replied, was rather cool. "Yes, Inspector, you did. To answer you, Abigail had told me Felicity was out for the evening, but she hadn't mentioned the servants being gone."

"I see."

"Do you?" Mrs. Popejoy raised one perfect eyebrow. "I don't think so. You see, Abigail was rather concerned about Felicity. She didn't trust the girl. That's what I was trying to tell you earlier, but you insisted upon digressing."

Witherspoon would have liked to have told Mrs. Popejoy that he wasn't the one who'd digressed, she was. But naturally one didn't like to contradict a lady. "I'm dreadfully sorry," he murmured. "Please do go on."

He might as well listen. Not that he thought for a moment that Mrs. Popejoy had anything but gossip to tell him. And as for her assertion that Mrs. Hodges was murdered and that the robbery wasn't real, well, that was sheer dramatics on the woman's part.

"As I said before," she began, "it's rather sordid. Felicity Marsden got herself engaged. But her fiancé was most unsuitable. He was a fortune hunter by the name of Benjamin Vogel. A nobody. Abigail loathed the man. But as Felicity was of age and threatened to elope, she knew there was nothing she could do about it. Abigail finally decided to pay Vogel off, and the dreadful creature took the money and broke his engagement to Felicity." Mrs. Popejoy laughed harshly. "But do you think the girl was grateful? No, she blamed her poor aunt for Vogel's disgusting character. Abigail was beside herself. She confided in me. Told me how worried she was, how desperate she was to have her niece love her again. That's one of the reasons she wanted to come to me on the night she was killed. She was going to ask Lady Lucia for advice. But as I told you, she got a warning instead. And the warning, though it was muddled and unclear at the time, has become very clear to me now. Lady Lucia was warning her to be careful of her niece."

"Did Lady Lucia actually say that?" Witherspoon asked before he realized how ridiculous the question sounded.

"Not in so many words," Mrs. Popejoy stated. "But Abigail had just asked her a question about Felicity's future and Lady Lucia's only answer was to tell Abigail she was surrounded by darkness, death and despair."

"But that could mean anything."

"Only to those who don't understand," Mrs. Popejoy cried passionately. "Don't you see? Sometimes the veil between the flesh and the spirit is so strong we only receive part of their message. But I know Lady Lucia. She was warning Abigail Hodges to be careful of her niece."

"Really, Mrs. Popejoy," the inspector warned, "you mustn't say such things. We've accounted for Miss Marsden's whereabouts on the night of the . . . er, robbery and she couldn't possibly have done it. Furthermore, where would a young woman like that get hold of a firearm?"

"From her former fiancé, Benjamin Vogel. He had a gun. Why don't you ask him what he was doing that night!"

Mrs. Jeffries glanced at the clock and then back at the impatient faces sitting around the kitchen table. They were waiting for Betsy and Luty Belle. Smythe was glaring at the floor, Mrs. Goodge was nursing a last cup of cocoa and Wiggins was yawning.

The inspector had finally gone to bed. He'd come home in an awful state and Mrs. Jeffries had spent the evening listening to him recount every detail of his day. She'd learned quite a bit. Now they seemed to have several suspects. Why, even the inspector was almost convinced that the robbery hadn't been genuine, though he'd been loath to admit it at first.

"Cor, what's takin' 'em so bloomin' long?" Smythe snarled as he scowled at the clock for the twentieth time. "Don't that silly girl realize we've all got a lot to do tomorrow? We can't hang about all night waitin' for her to get herself home."

"It's not that late," Wiggins soothed.

Just then they heard the rumble of carriage wheels and the clip-clops of horses' hooves as Luty Belle's coach pulled up at the front door. As Betsy had her own key, it took only a few moments before the two excited women came hurrying into the kitchen.

"It's about time," Smythe said.

"Land's sake," Luty exclaimed as she sank into the chair next to Mrs. Jeffries, "what a folderol. I tell ya, tonight was better than a Barbary Coast saloon on payday. Yes indeedy . . . that woman puts on quite a show."

"I take it you're referring to your evening with Madame Natalia." Mrs. Jeffries smiled, delighted to see that her friends had enjoyed themselves.

"It were ever so excitin'." Betsy giggled. " 'Course no one would believe it for a moment. There were six of us, countin' Luty Belle and Edmund and me. We all sat around this tiny little table and held hands. Madame Natalia went into a trance, sort of like bein' asleep only you're really awake, and then she called up her guide. His name was Soaring Eagle."

Luty snorted. "Soaring Eagle, stupid name. Knew a few Indians, none of 'em had names that silly."

"Well, go on," Wiggins said eagerly. "What happened then?"

Betsy giggled again. "Everyone started askin' questions—some of them were really funny too. That Mrs. Parnell, she were there with her husband, she wanted to know what cemetery she ought to be buried in."

"Yes, well, I'm delighted to see it was so entertaining for you," Mrs. Jeffries began.

"That's about all it was," Luty interjected. "If that woman was really talking to a dead Indian named Soaring Eagle, then I'm the Queen of Sheba. But what was really important was that we got an earful about Esme Popejoy."

"Why, that's wonderful," Mrs. Jeffries said, glad that neither Betsy nor Luty Belle was taking this spiritualism business too seriously. "The rest of us have had a fairly good day with our inquiries too. Before any of you begin, why don't I tell everyone what I've learned and, more importantly, what the inspector's learned."

For the next half hour they sipped cocoa and listened as the housekeeper recounted her experiences at the Hodges home. Then she told them about Inspector Witherspoon's interviews with Thomasina Trotter, Jonathan Felcher and Esme Popejoy.

"Sounds like Mrs. Popejoy's puttin' a flea in the inspector's ear about Miss Marsden," Smythe said when she'd concluded. "From what I found out at the pubs, no one believes Mrs. Hodges was killed by a robber. For one thing, there ain't been no burglaries in that neighborhood in months, and for another, one of the footmen from the house next door to the Hodgeses' told me he were out on the street fer half the evenin'. Lookin' for the family cat, he was, and he didn't see no one comin' and goin' to the Hodges house. All he saw was Mrs. Hodges's hansom drive up and her havin' a go at the driver before she flounced into the house."

"What were she goin' on at the poor driver about?" Mrs. Goodge asked.

Smythe shrugged. "I don't know, the footman was too far away to make out what she was sayin', alls he could tell was that she were madder than a crazy cat. 'Course, he says she were always yellin' at somebody. I didn't have much luck findin' the driver that drove her cab."

"Did you have any luck finding the driver that took Mr. Hodges and Mrs. Popejoy to the station?" Mrs. Jeffries asked hopefully.

"Yeah, I found 'im," Smythe admitted, "but he weren't much 'elp. He just said he picked the two of 'em up and took 'em to the station."

"What about the gun?" Wiggins said. "Is the inspector going to ask this Mr. Vogel about his gun?"

" 'Course he is," Smythe snapped. " 'E's duty bound to at least have a chat with the bloke, even if he did get his information from that Mrs. Popejoy."

"I don't think the niece had anything to do with it," Luty declared. "Seems to me if she was goin' to shoot someone, it would be her ex-fiancé. He's the one that took the money not to marry her. Besides, from what we found out about Esme Popejoy, I wouldn't credit much of what she says."

"Here, wait a minute before you start in about this Mrs. Popejoy," Mrs. Goodge said tartly. "I've got my bit to say about Mr. Hodges." She then spent the next ten minutes telling everyone at the table exactly what she'd already told Mrs. Jeffries. By the time she'd finished, they were all shaking their heads.

"This is gettin' real confusin'," Wiggins muttered.

"Kin I tell what we learned about Mrs. Popejoy now?" Luty Belle asked.

"Yes, please," Mrs. Jeffries soothed. She didn't know what to make of anything she'd heard this evening, but as was her habit, she tucked all the information safely in the back of her mind. She wouldn't think about it until she had the peace and quiet of her bedroom.

Luty cleared her throat. "Well, fer starters, Madame Natalia says that Mrs. Popejoy ain't no medium. Claims the woman used to work in the music halls, did some singin' and dancin' and some kind of mind-readin' act."

"And she charges an arm and a leg too," Betsy chimed in.

"But the best part is that we heard she don't just charge people fer a readin', that's what they call goin' and watchin' a medium try all that mumbo jumbo. She keeps *on* chargin' them."

Mrs. Jeffries stared at Luty quizzically. "Whatever do you mean?"

"I mean, according to Madame Natalia, Esme Popejoy don't charge people fer puttin' 'em in touch with the dead, she charges them from then on." Luty shook her head in disgust. "After she gets her spirit guide to find someone's dear departed relative, she starts givin' 'em warnings. Pretendin' the warnin's is from the great beyond, from a relative they loved and trusted. Then she tells 'em if they don't come back the next week to find out what's goin' to happen next, that she can't be responsible for what befalls them."

CHAPTER 5

"What a perfectly appalling way to behave," Mrs. Jeffries exclaimed. "You don't mean to say that every time some poor unfortunate soul gets one of Mrs. Popejoy's warnings, she then keeps them coming *back* in order to avoid disaster?"

"And she charges them a pretty penny for the advice too," Betsy said.

"Doesn't this Madame Natalia charge too?" Smythe asked.

"Sure," Luty agreed. "But Madame Natalia gives ya yer money's worth. There ain't a bunch of spirits moanin' gloom and doom at her seances. Soaring Eagle, fer whatever he's worth, jawed out more advice than a preacher on a rainy Sunday. You wouldn't have to go back to git yer answers. And accordin' to what Madame Natalia said, that's jus' what you'd have to do if Esme Popejoy got her hooks into ya. Not only that, but this Popejoy woman won't sit fer jus' anyone, no sirree. Ya gotta be well-off before she'll even let ya through the door. Ya gotta be recommended by someone."

"Sounds to me like Mrs. Popejoy isn't much more than a refined sharper," said Smythe, referring to the class of professional tricksters that induced unwary innocents into card games or skittles for money and then cheated them ruthlessly before disappearing.

"Or maybe the *madame*," Smythe continued thoughtfully, "may be just tryin' to cut out the competition. 'Ow do we know she's not makin' up tales. I don't expect this Natalia woman likes losin' customers to Mrs. Popejoy, especially if Mrs. Popejoy's gettin' all the people with fat purses."

"You may have a point there, Smythe," Mrs. Jeffries said earnestly. "And there's something else we need to consider. Mrs. Popejoy was on her way to the station or on a train to Southend when the murder was committed. She may well be an unprincipled person or a trickster, but if what Madame Natalia told us is true, she'd be the last person to want Abigail Hodges dead. One can't extort money from a corpse."

No one had an answer to that. They sat silently, all of them trying to understand the separate pieces of the puzzle they'd each brought to the table.

"Hmmph," Luty finally said. "I was lookin' forward to havin' Edmund fix us up a séance with Mrs. Popejoy. Be fun to let her try her tricks on me. But you're right, Hepzibah. She wouldn't have no reason fer wantin' Abigail Hodges dead, so I expect we'd better concentrate on someone who would." Birdlike, she cocked her head to one side. "Who's gonna git her money?"

"Well, from the conversation I overheard this morning between Jonathan Felcher and Felicity Marsden, I think we can assume Mrs. Hodges's estate is going to be divided between her husband and her niece."

"I know what you overheard, but jus' because someone thinks they're gonna inherit somethin' don't make it a fact. I remember ol' Cyrus Plummer back home, he was always tellin' everyone he was gonna get his great-aunt Polly's farm, but when Polly died, she'd up and left the farm to Norman Heckler. Made ol' Cyrus madder than hell, but weren't nothin' he could do about it. No one knows who's gonna get what until the will is read."

"Hmmm," Mrs. Jeffries murmured. "You may be right. But we won't know who stands to benefit financially from Mrs. Hodges's death unless the inspector speaks to her solicitor. And until the inspector determines that this case is murder and not robbery, I don't suppose he'll pursue that line of inquiry."

"You mean he's still thinkin' this was just a robbery?" Smythe asked incredulously.

Mrs. Jeffries sighed. "I'm afraid so, even though they haven't had any success in tracing the stolen jewelry." She paused and drummed her fingers on the tabletop. "You know," she finally said, addressing the group at large, "the more I think about it, the more I realize Luty's right. It's imperative we find out who benefits from Abigail Hodges's will."

"'Ow can we do that?" Wiggins said as he stifled another yawn. "Mrs. Hodges's solicitor in'n likely to tell us."

"But that shouldn't stop us from tryin'," Smythe argued. "Seems to me if we start askin' around, we can at least find out who was likely to inherit. Maybe it really is Mr. Hodges and Miss Marsden."

"That's precisely what I had in mind," Mrs. Jeffries said. "From what

I've heard of Mrs. Hodges's character, it wouldn't surprise me if she wasn't one of those persons who is quite vocal about the intended disbursement of her worldly goods."

Wiggins frowned. "Huh?"

"She means the old woman might be one of them that's always threatenin' their nearest and dearest with bein' disinherited," Luty explained.

"Exactly," Mrs. Jeffries said. "But that isn't all we must do. We've also got to ascertain if Jonathan Felcher, Felicity Marsden and Thomasina Trotter were where they said they were when Mrs. Hodges was murdered."

"Why the housekeeper?" Betsy asked. "Why not the rest of the servants too?"

"Because none of them had gone to school with Mrs. Hodges. According to the inspector, Thomasina Trotter was once of the same social class as her employer. Then she ended up working for her. Something about that doesn't seem right. So it's very important we confirm her whereabouts," Mrs. Jeffries explained. She wasn't sure what she was after here, but she knew they still didn't have near enough information. "Now, Wiggins, did you have any luck with Peter the footman today?"

Wiggins shook his head. "No, I hung about the 'ouse for the better part of the day, but 'e didn't come out."

"You didn't happen to notice anything else interesting, did you?" Mrs. Jeffries asked kindly. She didn't want him to feel as though he'd failed.

"I didn't see anything," Wiggins said eagerly, "but I 'eard somethin' that might be useful. One of the housemaids from across the road from the Hodges place told me the lights was lit at the Hodges house." He leaned forward eagerly, putting his elbows on the table. "But the funny part is—and Nellie saw this with her own eyes; she's got a room on the top floor and she could see right across the road to the house—that around ten o'clock, all the lamps started goin' out. One by one. She watched it go from room to room, candles and lamps and even the gaslights were put out."

"All right," Mrs. Goodge put in, "so the killer turned off the lights. That doesn't tell us anything."

Wiggins looked crestfallen. Mrs. Jeffries hastily intervened. "Thank you, Wiggins. That particular fact may be very important eventually." She rather agreed with Mrs. Goodge, but she didn't want to say so. "Are you up to more footwork tomorrow, lad?"

" 'Course I am. What do you want me to do?"

"I want you to keep an eye on Felicity Marsden tomorrow. Keep watch on the house, and if she leaves, be sure and follow her." Mrs. Jeffries thought that was a safe enough task for the boy. She'd send Betsy to have another go at talking with the Hodgeses' footman.

"Is she pretty?" Wiggins asked hopefully.

"What difference does it make what she looks like?" Smythe snapped. "She might be a murderess, so make sure she don't spot you."

The coachman looked at Mrs. Jeffries. "Do you still want me to try and find the driver that brought Mrs. Hodges 'ome that night?"

"Yes, I'd like to know why she was so angry with him." Mrs. Jeffries cocked her head to one side. "But I'd also like you to see if you can find out any information about Jonathan Felcher. Double-check his whereabouts the night of the murder and find out as much as you can about his character." Mrs. Jeffries turned her attention to Betsy and Luty Belle. "Betsy, I think you need to try to make contact with someone from the Hodges household. A maid or a footman, perhaps you can find that young boy Peter. Find out anything you can about Felicity Marsden's broken engagement and also whether or not it's true that Mrs. Hodges paid Benjamin Vogel not to marry her niece."

"What about me?" Luty asked.

Mrs. Jeffries gazed at her helplessly. The others were young and strong and could easily take care of themselves. But she didn't want Luty Belle Crookshank lurking in passageways or trying to pry a few words out of servants. She was too old for that. Yet she couldn't come right out and say so. Luty would be mortally offended.

"Come now, Hepzibah," Luty said tartly. "I ain't askin' to follow anyone or some such foolishness as that, I knows what I'm capable of doin'. But surely I can do somethin'?"

"Of course you can," Mrs. Jeffries assured her. "You're a valuable asset to our inquiries." She broke off, still trying to think of something for Luty to do, when inspiration struck. "I've just the thing. Gracious, why didn't I think of it before? Felicity Marsden was allegedly with the Plimptons on the night of the murder. Try to find out if she actually was at Sadler's Wells watching the ballet. And more importantly, can you find someone who will confirm that Felicity Marsden was with them all evening?"

Luty nodded eagerly, her dark eyes flashing with enthusiasm. "That oughta be easier than shootin' fish in a barrel. I know plenty of folks who's always goin' off to the ballet. I can find someone who was there that night."

Mrs. Jeffries heaved a silent sigh of relief. Luty's chore wasn't really needed. The inspector had already confirmed that the Plimptons had taken Felicity out that evening. But it was important that she be made to feel wanted and useful.

"Now, I believe we'd all better get some rest." Mrs. Jeffries stood up. "Tomorrow is going to be a very busy day."

Jonathan Vogel lived in a ground-floor room in a run-down lodging house in Paddington. Inspector Witherspoon and Constable Barnes arrived before nine in the morning, hoping to catch the young man before he left for his employment.

Barnes rapped lightly on the door and it was opened a moment later by a tall, blond-haired young man dressed in a white shirt, tie and brown trousers.

"Yes," he asked cautiously, eyeing Barnes's police uniform warily. "What do you want?"

Despite the man's careful diction, the inspector could faintly hear the flat, nasal accent of east London working class. The young man might be respectably dressed and well educated, but he wasn't all that many years out of Whitechapel.

"Are you Mr. Benjamin Vogel?" the inspector asked.

"I am, and who might you be?"

"Inspector Witherspoon of Scotland Yard. This is Constable Barnes. We'd like to have a word with you, sir."

Vogel opened the door wider and motioned for them to step inside. The room was small, ugly and crowded with mismatched furniture. There was a bed covered with a mustard-colored bedspread, a wardrobe with two of the knobs missing from the bottom drawers, a threadbare green-and-brown carpet and a pair of limp-looking dull brown curtains at the one dirty window. Opposite the bed was a cracked leather divan and next to that a scarred table and a single cane-back chair. On the floor beside the table were several stacks of books.

"Now, what's all this about, inspector?" Vogel asked. He didn't invite either man to sit down. "I'm a bit short on time. I don't want to be late for work."

Witherspoon could understand that. "We won't keep you long, Mr. Vogel. Could you please tell us where you were on the night of January fourth?"

Vogel's light eyebrows drew together in a puzzled frown. "January fourth? Well, let me see. I'm not all that sure I can remember."

"It was only three days ago, sir," Constable Barnes stated.

Vogel drew a deep breath. "Oh? Well, I was probably right here. Where else would I be? Yes, that's right. I came straight home from work and spent the evening reading."

"Are you acquainted with Mrs. Abigail Hodges and Miss Felicity Marsden?" Witherspoon asked. He could see Vogel stiffen.

"Yes."

The inspector watched him carefully. "Were you aware that Mrs. Hodges was murdered on January fourth?"

Vogel's eyes widened. "Good Lord. Really, no, I must say I hadn't heard."

Witherspoon didn't believe the man. There was something very theatrical about Vogel's reaction, he thought. The inspector was quite pleased with himself. "Theatrical" was a word he'd heard his chief use more than once when he was describing a suspect's expression.

"You didn't read about it in the papers, sir?" Barnes said softly.

"Newspapers are useless," Vogel declared firmly. "I never waste my time on them. How was Mrs. Hodges killed?"

The inspector glanced at the constable. Barnes shook his head ever so slightly, indicating that he didn't believe one word Benjamin Vogel was saying.

Witherspoon sighed silently. Really, Vogel was a terrible actor. The man's tone, his manner, his expression. Goodness, his act was so patently false a two-year-old could see through it.

"She was shot," the inspector replied slowly. "Twice. Once in the head and once in the heart. It happened during the course of a robbery."

"That's dreadful." The Adam's apple in Vogel's throat bobbed up and down as he swallowed. "Appalling."

"Were you engaged to Miss Felicity Marsden?" Witherspoon cocked his head to one side.

"I was," Vogel admitted. A dull red crept up his cheeks. "But Miss Marsden and I ended our engagement over two months ago. I haven't heard from or seen her or anyone else in her family since then."

The inspector hoped the next question would take the man by surprise. Really, he so hated it when people tried to lie to the police. "Didn't Mrs. Hodges help to end that engagement? Didn't she pay you a great deal of money not to marry her niece?"

"That's a lie," Vogel snapped. He clenched both his hands into fists. "A filthy disgusting lie. I love Fliss, I wouldn't have taken all the money in the world to break our engagement."

Startled, Witherspoon blinked. Benjamin Vogel sounded like he was telling the truth.

"But we have it on good authority that Mrs. Hodges did pay you to break your engagement to her niece." The inspector phrased his question carefully. "Are you denying it's true?"

Vogel laughed harshly. "Of course I'm denying it. No doubt you've heard all sorts of nasty gossip about me. Mrs. Hodges made sure that everyone including Fliss would believe the worst about my character. The old harridan even tried to get me sacked. Oh, I don't deny that she came around here offering me money, but I refused to take it. I threw her out. Somehow, though, she convinced Fliss that I had taken money not to see her anymore. She sent the ring back."

"So you've had nothing to do with the Hodges household since Miss Marsden returned your engagement ring?" Witherspoon asked.

"That's right," Vogel answered.

"Where's the engagement ring that Miss Hodges returned?" Witherspoon asked. He was quite proud of that question. Surely if Mr. Vogel were telling the truth about his association with Felicity Marsden, he'd be able to produce the evidence of his broken engagement.

"I didn't keep it," Vogel replied harshly. "I'm not a rich man. When Fliss sent the ring back, I sold it. What did you expect, that I'd keep it for sentimental reasons?" He laughed bitterly. "Between Abigail Hodges and Felicity they managed to kill any tender feelings I might have once had. If you want to see that ring, Inspector, you can take yourself down to Webster's on the Kensington High Street and buy it yourself."

The inspector was suddenly embarrassed. The anger and pain in Vogel's voice were real. "I, er, don't think that will be necessary." He would, however, send a constable to check Vogel's story.

"So you've had nothing to do with anyone in the Hodges household in two months?" Barnes persisted.

"As I've already told you, no." Vogel sighed deeply. "Now, if you don't mind, I'd like to finish dressing for work."

"Just one more thing, sir." The inspector had suddenly remembered Mrs. Popejoy's wild assertion. Naturally he didn't believe much of what she'd told him. Certainly he didn't for one moment believe in gaslight spirits warning victims of their intended deaths, but he couldn't in good conscience ignore the one fact that might be of importance.

"Please, Inspector," Vogel replied, heading for the wardrobe. "Do make it quick. I mustn't be late."

"Do you have a gun?"

Vogel stopped in his tracks and whirled around. "A gun? Why on earth do you think I've a gun?"

"Never mind why, sir," Constable Barnes interjected. "Just answer the question."

Vogel cleared his throat and cast one quick, nervous glance towards the wardrobe. He looked like he was trying to decide whether or not to tell the truth. "Yes. I do. It's a—"

Witherspoon cut him off. "May we see it, sir?"

Constable Barnes had put his notebook away and now watched Benjamin Vogel carefully as the man hesitated.

"Yes, of course." Vogel went to the wardrobe, pulled open the door and yanked a small, square case off the top shelf.

Taking the case to the table, he slammed it down and turned to stare belligerently at the two policemen who were right behind him.

"You've not got a warrant, have you?" Vogel said. His voice cracked ever so slightly.

"No, Mr. Vogel," the inspector replied. "We haven't. You'd be well within your rights to refuse to show us the gun." Actually Witherspoon wasn't terribly sure about that; he'd dozed off during the lecture on legal search procedures.

Vogel took a deep breath and shook his head. "I do want it noted that I'm cooperating with the police of my own free will."

"That'll be noted, sir," Barnes assured him dryly.

He unlatched the clasp and lifted the lid. "My God," he exclaimed. "What on earth . . ."

Witherspoon and Barnes looked into the case.

The gun was gone.

"But of course I was at the ballet," Miss Myrtle Buxton exclaimed. "Why, everyone was there that night."

Luty hid her satisfied smile by taking a sip of the fine Indian tea Miss Buxton had so thoughtfully provided. Myrtle Buxton, wealthy, single and well past sixty, lived across the road from Luty's own Knightsbridge home. Myrtle wore a pale rose day dress that blended perfectly with the pink overstuffed settee and dark burgundy carpet. Her silver-gray hair was arranged in tight curls, her eyes were a vivid blue and Luty was sure the woman had on a bit of rouge. No one Myrtle's age had cheeks that bright. Not that Luty cared. If she wanted to paint her face, it was her business.

The important thing was, Myrtle devoted practically every waking moment to her social life. A notorious gossip, Myrtle Buxton had developed an eagle eye for noting who was where and with whom. Luty knew she'd come to the right woman.

"Too bad I missed goin'," Luty replied. "But I've been kinda busy lately. Some friends of mine was there that night, though—the Plimptons. Did ya happen to see 'em?"

Myrtle waggled her ring-bedecked fingers coquettishly. "I saw *everybody*," she declared proudly. "Of course I saw the Plimptons. But I didn't know they were friends of yours. Gracious, I wouldn't have thought you'd know that family. They are a very stuffy bunch."

"Er, uh, I met 'em at a party last month," Luty lied.

"Rather conventional people," Myrtle mused. "Not your sort at all, Luty. They've a box at the theatre, you know."

"Was the whole family there?"

"Goodness no! Horace Plimpton wouldn't go near the ballet if his life depended on it and Henrietta Plimpton's one of those women who continually fancy themselves as ill. No doubt she'd taken to her bed for the evening. It's old Mrs. Plimpton, Georgianna, who's the social one in that family. She, her granddaughter and another young woman were in the box that night." She paused and shook her head. "Not that I understand why Georgianna bothers. She fell asleep the minute she sat down. Dreadful habit, falling asleep in public. Her mouth actually *gaped* open. It stayed that way through the whole performance. I must say, she makes a spectacle of herself. Still, if it wasn't for Georgianna, I don't suppose poor Ada Plimpton would have any social life at all." Myrtle broke off and gazed at her friend curiously. "Why are you asking?"

"No particular reason," Luty replied with a casual shrug. "I just happened to hear they was all there that night and I wondered how that could be? Ya see, I had an argument with a friend of mine who claimed that I was gettin' so old I couldn't see straight. I thought fer sure I saw Miss Plimpton and another young woman leavin' the theatre before the ballet even started. Well, Hepzibah—that's my friend—she claimed I was seein' things and that a decent young girl wouldn't be out on the streets at that time of night gettin' into hansom cabs." She paused and smiled apologetically. "I reckon she must be right, I couldn't of seen her if they was sittin' in the Plimpton box. Guess I'll have to tell Hepzibah she was right. I tell ya, Myrtle, it's hard gettin' old." She lowered her head and sniffled pathetically.

"Nonsense." Myrtle was instantly sympathetic. She reached across and patted Luty on the hand. "You're not old at all and you most certainly could have seen Miss Plimpton and another young lady outside the theatre. Though I must agree with your friend, it isn't the sort of behavior decent young women should indulge in. But that's becoming the way of the world these days. Women wanting the vote, wanting equality and even going out to work . . . shocking. Not at all like in my day."

Luty bit her tongue to keep from telling Myrtle that she thought women should vote, work and do anything else they danged well pleased. "But I thought you just said you saw the girls sittin' with Mrs. Plimpton?"

"Only at the beginning," Myrtle explained. "You see, I happened to notice that as soon as Georgianna Plimpton fell asleep, both young ladies slipped out of the box. Ada Plimpton came back a few minutes later. But the other girl didn't come back until the last curtain call."

Luty tried to appear unconcerned. "Reckon the girl must have gone and sat with someone else," she replied casually.

"She most certainly did not," Myrtle said archly. "I looked. I tell you that young woman left the theatre. She was gone for at least two hours."

Remembering she was supposed to be playing a pitiful elderly lady, Luty pretended to be shocked. "Goodness gracious, where on earth do you think a young girl would be at that time of the evening?"

"Hmmph." Myrtle snorted indelicately. "Where do you think she'd be? She was probably off meeting some man."

"Get off with ya," Wiggins whispered. He stared in exasperation at the shaggy, skinny, long-haired brown-and-black dog who gazed back at him with adoration. "You've served yer purpose, you silly hound, and I've given you a bit of bun, so scarper off."

The dog sat down and rested his head on Wiggins's foot.

"Blimey, it seemed a good idea at the time," he muttered.

Upon arriving at Camden Street, Wiggins had been dismayed to find the quiet residential road devoid of traffic. And he couldn't get to his usual hiding place because the butler from the house next to the Hodgeses' was standing outside his ruddy door.

Wiggins hadn't known what to do. Then, out of nowhere, this silly mutt showed up. The animal was very friendly, and took to the footman like a duck to water. He decided to pretend the dog was his. He'd spent the next ten minutes walking up and down the road with the dog trotting obediently at his heels. He hadn't had the Hodges house out of his sight in all that time, either.

Wiggins stamped his feet and pulled his coat tighter against the chill.

The dog shivered. Wiggins sighed. Poor thing, you could see its ribs. When the butler finally disappeared, Wiggins had been able to dart into his usual hiding place, a narrow passageway between the two homes opposite the Hodges house. The dog had come with him.

"Look, boy," he tried again, squatting down and patting the animal's head. "Run along home now, I've got to keep watch and I don't have any more currant buns."

The dog whined and nudged his nose against Wiggins's coat pocket.

"Oh, you're still hungry, aren't ya?" he said sympathetically. He wished now he'd given the poor animal all the currant buns and not just half of them.

Sighing, Wiggins glanced up just as the door of the Hodges house opened and Felicity Marsden stepped outside. She paused at the top of the stairs and turned her head quickly one way and then another before darting down the stairs. Under one arm she had a dark fur muff and she carried a small brown paper parcel.

Wiggins straightened up and dashed into the road behind the girl. The dog followed.

Felicity hurried up the quiet street, her high heels tapping rapidly against the paving stones. At the corner, she turned towards the Queens Road.

"Go on home," Wiggins hissed at the dog again as he quickened his steps to avoid losing sight of his quarry. The dog woofed softly and bounced around his ankles, almost tripping him.

"This ina' game." He tried to push the furry bundle to one side without hurting the animal. "And if I lose 'er, you'll never get another crumb out of me, you silly cur."

The dog wasn't in the least intimidated. He continued to trail Wiggins as they moved rapidly up one street and down another. Several times Wiggins and the dog had to hide behind a tree or a postbox to avoid being spotted, for Felicity Marsden frequently stopped and looked behind her.

Breathing hard, Wiggins tried to keep the young woman's slim back in sight. As they turned onto the Uxbridge Road he almost lost her in the now crowded street, then he spotted her crossing to the opposite corner in front of the Uxbridge Road station.

Darting in front of an omnibus, Wiggins spared a worried glance at the dog and was relieved to see it keeping pace with him.

Felicity Marsden had turned onto Holland Road. Wiggins and friend followed. He wasn't worried about getting lost. He knew this area well.

She stopped suddenly, turned to glance behind her and then slipped through a gate. Wiggins waited for a moment and hurried after her.

He frowned as he reached the spot where she'd disappeared. Felicity Marsden had gone into St. John's Church. For a moment he wondered what to do, whether or not he should go in after her. The dog woofed softly. Wiggins made up his mind. He pushed open the gate and went into the churchyard.

"I 'eard that Mrs. Hodges broke up her poor niece's engagement," Betsy said to the young man. He was the footman from the Hodges household.

Peter Applegate smiled shyly and deftly plucked off his rather soiled porkpie hat. He dusted the park bench carefully and then motioned Betsy to sit down.

"Aye, that she did," he said as he sat down beside her. "She didn't think Mr. Vogel were good enough for Miss Fliss. But she were wrong. He's a nice man, he is."

Betsy gazed around the small park where the two of them were resting and stifled a twinge of conscience. She was investigating a murder here, she told herself sternly. All's fair. But she felt bad about shamelessly flirting with the lad in order to loosen his tongue. He'd practically fallen over his feet when she'd suggested a stroll in the park. And he was only a child. He couldn't be more than fourteen.

"But being nice weren't all that important, at least not to one like Mrs. Hodges," Peter declared. "Look how she's treated poor old Mrs. Trotter all these years and them two went to school together!"

"Really?" Betsy said, though she already knew that information. "You mean she weren't very good to her servants?"

"Good!" He laughed harshly. "Mrs. Hodges didn't know the meaning of the word. Worked us like dogs, she did."

"Even Mrs. Trotter?" Betsy decided to pursue that line of inquiry.

"Especially Mrs. Trotter," he declared. "Had her fetchin' and carryin' and doing all sorts of things no housekeeper I ever saw did."

"Why did Mrs. Trotter put up with her? Surely she could have gotten a position somewhere else?" Betsy shrugged nonchalantly. "I once worked in a miserable place, but I didn't put up with it. I took myself right off and got another position."

Peter eyed Betsy slyly. "You're askin' an awful lot of questions. Why? What's it to do with you?"

She racked her brain to come up with a reasonable excuse. Then she gave him a brilliant smile. "Well, if you must know, I work close by here"—she giggled—"and the truth is, my mistress is as nosy as all get-out. She sent me over here to learn what I could about the murder. I didn't want to do it, mind you. But, well . . ." She broke off and dropped her gaze, fluttering her eyelashes in the process. "I'd seen you about and I figured comin' 'round would be a good excuse to talk to you."

Peter stared at her incredulously for a moment and then he smiled. "Oh, well, that's allright, then."

She silently drew a long, breath of relief. Mrs. Goodge was right, she thought, a few honeyed words and a bit of battin' the eyelashes and a man will believe any load of old rubbish you tell 'im.

"Anyways," she said shyly, "we was talkin' about Mrs. Trotter. It's real interestin', I mean 'earin' about others and 'ow they live." She deliberately began dropping her *h*s. "You never said why the woman was putting up with Mrs. Hodges."

"Oh, that. Mrs. Trotter was hangin' on because she wanted something from Mrs. Hodges."

"What?"

"Don't know. But I 'eard 'em talkin' about it a few times. Once when I was takin' coal to one of the upstairs fireplaces, I 'eard Mrs. Trotter beggin' the old witch to tell her where someone was."

"Who was she talkin' about?" Betsy said, leaning closer.

"Never 'eard no name. Just Mrs. Trotter saying over and over, 'Tell me where she is, tell me where she is.' " He shook his head. "It were right pitiful, old straitlaced Trotter begging like that."

"Poor Mrs. Trotter." Betsy shook her head sympathetically. "I reckon she's right upset, what with Mrs. Hodges gettin' 'erself done in that way."

"Upset!" Peter laughed. "Not bloomin' likely. I don't know who Trotter was on about that day, but I do know that since the old witch's death, Mrs. Trotter's been happier than I've ever seen her. Walks about the house hummin' and smilin' and talkin' to herself. Barmy, if you ask me."

Betsy wondered what to ask next. Then she wondered how on earth she was going to get rid of Peter. "Is Mr. Hodges a nice master, then?"

"He's all right," Peter replied. "Nicer than she was. Bit of a dandy, but other than always brushin' lint off his sleeve or havin' me put more polish on his boots, he's not too bad."

"I suppose Mr. Hodges wasn't too happy about Mrs. Hodges wanting to go to séances?"

"Where'd you hear that?" Peter's brows drew together.

"You mean it isn't true?"

" 'Course it's not true. Goin' and tryin' to talk to the spirit of Mrs. Hodges's dead son were Mr. Hodges's idea. He started talkin' about it right after he and Mrs. Hodges got married. Mind you, that caused a bit of a stir."

"Are you sayin' it were Mr. Hodges that believes in spiritualism, then?" Betsy asked, just to be sure she understood him correctly.

"'Course it were him. Mrs. Hodges didn't believe in all that silly stuff."

"How did Mrs. Hodges meet up with Mrs. Popejoy then?" Betsy asked.

Peter stared at her suspiciously and she quickly added, "I read about her in the papers. Caught me eye, it did. I'm interested in spiritualism myself. You never know, do you? Could be there's lots the dead could tell us. And that Mrs. Popejoy did claim some spirit tried to warn poor Mrs. Hodges to be careful."

"Yeah," he muttered. "She did say that, din't she. But I don't believe a word of it."

"Well, Mrs. Hodges must of, she kept goin' to see the woman."

"Only because Mr. Hodges wanted 'er to," Peter declared. "Mr. Hodges claimed it would give Mrs. Hodges a bit o' peace."

"You never answered me question. 'Ow did Mrs. Hodges meet up with Mrs. Popejoy?" Betsy asked quickly, now that she'd finally loosened Peter's tongue again.

The boy gave her a slow, sly grin. "It were Mr. Hodges that introduced them. Fact of the matter is, I reckons Mr. Hodges knows Mrs. Popejoy from way back. They was old friends. Good friends too. If you get my meanin'."

CHAPTER 6

Mrs. Jeffries spent the afternoon sorting linens. The task freed her mind to concentrate on the case. She was convinced that the death of Abigail Hodges wasn't a simple robbery gone wrong. It was murder. Premeditated murder. She could feel it in her bones. But there were still far too many unanswered questions for her to make any assumptions as to the identity of the killer.

Picking up an armload of tablecloths and napkins, she made her way downstairs to the kitchen.

"Hello, Mrs. Goodge," she said brightly as she opened the door to the cupboard and slipped the linens inside.

"Good afternoon. Miserable day out, isn't it." The cook was standing at the table next to a large earthenware bowl filled with ground meat. Beside the bowl was a silver cast-iron sausage maker and a tin of sausage casings.

"Yes, it is. I do hope all this rain isn't hampering the others in the investigation. Are we having sausages for dinner?"

"No, I thought I'd do these for a late-night nibble—it's chicken tonight for all of us. But sausages can come in handy when we're all 'round the table givin' our news."

"What a good idea," Mrs. Jeffries said. "And you do make such lovely sausages, so much better than the ones available at the butcher's."

"I should hope so," Mrs. Goodge exclaimed. "Lord knows what goes into those others. Wouldn't have them in the house." She finished grinding the last of the meat and wiped her hands on a towel. Mrs. Jeffries noticed her stretching her fingers and flexing them before she reached for the tin of sausage casings.

"Your rheumatism is bothering you today, isn't it?" Mrs. Jeffries said, watching as the cook fumbled with the lid on the tin.

"Always does when it rains. But at least in this house a body can sit a spell when the pain gets too bad." Mrs. Goodge put the tin down and plopped into a chair. "Not like some houses I've worked in. Now, that reminds me, I found out a bit about Mrs. Hodges and how she runs her house." She gave an inelegant snort. "Real strict, she was. Made the servants pay for their tea and sugar every month, prayer gong every morning before breakfast, with the housekeeper leadin' the prayers because Mr. and Mrs. Hodges couldn't bother to stir themselves out of bed that early. And cold meat from the day before for the servants' dinner at one o'clock. Sounds a right miserable place, doesn't it?"

Surprised, Mrs. Jeffries gazed at the cook curiously. When she'd first taken up her post here, her own unorthodox way of running the household had caused Mrs. Goodge much alarm. She'd put an end to any silly divisions between the upper and lower servants, insisting that Smythe, Wiggins and Betsy be treated in the same manner as herself and the cook. She'd eliminated morning prayers with the comment that anyone who wanted could worship the Almighty in the privacy of their own room, and she'd informed them that as long as their duties were carried out, she had no need to supervise them directly. Meals were taken together with everyone waiting on themselves instead of expecting the lowest kitchen maid to do it all (not that they had a kitchen maid, but that onerous burden would normally have fallen to Betsy) and what was done on one's own free time was one's own business. Mrs. Jeffries was well aware that her way of managing a household was unusual, but as long as the inspector was satisfied, she wasn't concerned.

"Mrs. Hodges certainly seems to have run her household very strictly," Mrs. Jeffries finally agreed, "but that's not so unusual. Most households function in much the same manner."

"More's the pity," Mrs. Goodge muttered. She stared off into the distance for a moment and then shook herself out of her reverie. "Well, we've not got all day, have we? I did just like you asked and found out a bit about that Mrs. Trotter."

Mrs. Jeffries gazed at her in admiration. "Goodness, Mrs. Goodge, that's very quick."

"You might say I had a bit of luck. The grocer's boy come by this mornin'. He delivers to the Hodges house too and he gave me a right earful about Thomasina Trotter." Mrs. Goodge leaned forward on her elbow. "She's a real strange one, she is."

"Strange? How do you mean?"

Mrs. Goodge tapped her finger gently against her temple. "Up here," she said, her voice hushed. "She's touched. Not right in the head. The woman spends her free time out walking the streets."

Mrs. Jeffries stared at the cook in bewilderment. "Are you implying that Thomasina Trotter is a . . . a . . . prostitute?"

"No, no," Mrs. Goodge said impatiently. "She's not lookin' for men, she's lookin' for women. She stares at young girls. Accosts them in the street. Goes right up and looks into their faces, studyin' 'em like. Why, she's gone as far as Whitechapel—and even worse, she's done it at night. Can you imagine that? Being on the streets in the East End after dark. I tell you, the woman's daft. Completely daft."

"Goodness, that is most odd," Mrs. Jeffries replied. "Were you able to find out why she does it?"

"No. I wasn't. But I'll keep at it. Just give us a few more days. I've got me sources askin' around."

"You know," Mrs. Jeffries said thoughtfully, "from what you've just told me about Mrs. Hodges having been so very strict with her servants, I'm amazed she allowed her housekeeper to do such a thing. Surely she must have known Mrs. Trotter was behaving rather oddly?"

"But she didn't know about it." Mrs. Goodge laughed. "For goodness' sake, who'd tell Mrs. Hodges anything? The servants didn't like her much and I'm sure she weren't the kind to sit and natter with the tradespeople who delivered to the house. And for all her daft ways, Thomasina Trotter's a bit of a sharp one. She obviously used to tell Mrs. Hodges she were goin' to visit her old nanny." She broke off and frowned. "Now, what was the woman's name? Oh yes, Miss Bush. Anyways, after the grocer's boy left this mornin', I sent young Willie Spencer, the lad that works over the garden for Colonel Norcross, over to Fulham to have a gander at Mrs. Trotter's nanny."

"Why how very intelligent, Mrs. Goodge," Mrs. Jeffries said. "How did Willie do?"

"The boy did well enough, I reckon." Mrs. Goodge smiled smugly. "He spoke to Mrs. Bush herself. Mind you, nothin' she said made any sense. Willie says the poor thing's half out of her mind. She's old, you know. Sometimes they get that way. So the way I figure is that Mrs. Trotter used to tell her mistress she was visiting with Miss Bush, who wouldn't even know what day it was, let alone whether or not anyone had come calling, and then instead of actually goin' to see her, Mrs. Trotter would wander the streets starin' at young girls." She shuddered. "Horrible, isn't it?"

"If you're right," Mrs. Jeffries mused, "and there's no reason to believe you aren't, then that means Thomasina Trotter doesn't have an alibi for the time of the murder."

"That's what I'm thinkin' too."

"Gracious, this sheds a whole new light on the situation."

"But why would Mrs. Trotter want to kill her mistress?" Mrs. Goodge shook her head. "That's the part I can't understand. The woman might be a bit daft, but a murderess?"

"We don't know that she did kill Mrs. Hodges, but then again, we don't know that she didn't," Mrs. Jeffries murmured thoughtfully. After a moment she smiled at the cook. "Keep digging, Mrs. Goodge. I think we might be onto something here. Tell the others we'll meet back here after the inspector's gone to bed this evening. Perhaps we'll have even more pieces to add to this puzzle."

As Mrs. Jeffries went back up the stairs to finish her linens, she made a mental note to urge the inspector to double-check Thomasina Trotter's alibi. And just to make sure, she thought, I'll send Betsy or Smythe around to talk to Miss Bush and her neighbors.

"Now, Constable Barnes," Inspector Witherspoon said patiently, "we didn't really have any grounds to arrest Mr. Vogel. A missing gun isn't reason enough to take him down to the station to help us with our inquiries."

Barnes pulled the door of the hansom shut. "Ladbroke Road Police Station," he called to the driver before turning to the inspector. "Yes, sir, I know that. But what about his landlady? She claimed she never saw him come in that night."

"Yes, but she also told us she doesn't see him come in most evenings. Her rooms are at the back of the house," the inspector replied tiredly. "Furthermore, we've no idea if his gun has anything at all to do with Mrs. Hodges."

"She was shot with a revolver," Barnes insisted. "And his revolver's missin'. We know he needs money and we know he hated Abigail Hodges for interferin' in his relationship with Miss Marsden. He knew the layout of the house, he could have found out that the Hodgeses was goin' to be out that evening and he could have broke in just plannin' on robbin' them when Mrs. Hodges surprised him. That would explain why she was shot. Vogel knew she could identify him."

"Then where is the jewelry?" Witherspoon asked. "As far as we know, it hasn't turned up at any of the usual places and we know it wasn't in his room. Mr. Vogel was quite within his rights to refuse to let us search, but he didn't and the jewelry wasn't there."

"He could have hidden it somewhere," Barnes suggested, but he didn't sound very sure of himself. "I expect you're right, sir. We didn't have all that much evidence against the man."

"Vogel's not the only man in London who owns a revolver," the inspector said.

"True, but most of them that owns guns can probably produce them," Barnes muttered. "Still, I'm sure you know what you're doin', sir."

Witherspoon hoped the constable was right. At this point he wasn't all that sure he did know what he was doing. Perhaps he should have brought Mr. Vogel in—but then again, he hated making an arrest unless he was absolutely certain.

"But it's still hard for me to believe it was professionals that broke into the Hodges house and killed that poor woman," Barnes continued thoughtfully. "It just didn't have the right feel, if you know what I mean, sir."

"I do indeed, Constable. As a matter of fact, I've recently come to the same conclusion myself," Witherspoon admitted. "There are simply too many peculiar circumstances in this case. I think we'll just have to keep at it. Did the lads come up with anything useful from the neighbors?"

"Not really, sir." Barnes reached for the door latch as the hansom pulled up in front of the station. As soon as the horses stopped, he opened the door and leaped out. The rain, which had started out as a drizzle when they'd left Vogel's rooms in Paddington, was now a downpour. "Better make a run for it, Inspector," Barnes called as he took care of the driver.

The Ladbroke Road Police Station was a large brick building with a paved yard in front. The larger and more conspicuous of the two doors led into the front office with its constables behind the counter and the charge room, while the other, smaller door led to a main staircase, which in turn led to offices and the canteen.

It was this smaller door that Witherspoon made a dash for. Inside, he stopped and shook the water off his bowler. He was reaching for his spectacles when a uniformed constable appeared at the top of the staircase.

"Good afternoon, sir," the young policeman called down. "The station officer would like to see you. He says it's urgent. He's in the charge room, if you'd care to go in."

Witherspoon, who'd hoped to get a cup of tea, stifled a sigh. He went through the connecting door into the front office. After nodding politely at the constable on duty behind the counter, he entered the charge room.

Witherspoon grimaced as he stepped inside. He hated this bleak place. There were no windows and the walls were painted a dull, ugly green. The hardwood floor was scarred and stained from years of heavy, weary feet. There was a plain wooden bench alongside one wall for the prisoners to sit on, a wooden table for them to turn out their usually meager personal effects and a tall desk for the station officer to sit at as he listed the charges against the prisoners in the crime book. At the end of the room was another door, which led to the detention room. All in all, Witherspoon found the whole place dreadfully depressing. Not at all like the records room at CID headquarters at Scotland Yard. He sighed wistfully at the thought of his former position and then straightened his shoulders, remembering his duty.

The door from the detention room opened and the station officer stepped inside. "Oh, good day, sir. I see you got my message. Sorry I wasn't here," he said politely, "but we've had a busy day. Two in lockup in the last hour."

"That's quite all right, Constable, er . . ."

"Kent, sir. Constable Kent. I was on my way in today when I was stopped by Constable Griffith. He's got a message for you about the Hodges case. They've found the stolen jewelry."

"Really?" Witherspoon was genuinely surprised. He'd never expected those jewels to turn up.

"Yes, sir. Constable Griffith wanted me to make sure you stayed here until he arrived. He should be here anytime now." Kent hurried over and stuck his head out of the door. "Can't imagine what's keeping him."

"Goodness, did he say where the jewels were found?" Witherspoon fervently hoped the stolen items had been found at one of the shops in Shoreditch or St. Giles that the police knew solicited stolen merchandise.

"No, sir, he didn't," Kent said. "But here he is now, sir. Griffith," he called across the front office. "Inspector Witherspoon's in here."

The inspector would have liked to have left this miserable room for the front office or, better yet, for the canteen, but he didn't get the opportunity. Constable Griffith, all six feet two inches of him, was already inside the charge room. Barnes was right behind him.

"Sir," Griffith exclaimed. "We've found the jewels." He handed the inspector a black cloth bag.

Witherspoon opened the bag and spilled its contents onto the table. "Where did you find them, Constable?"

"At the Hodges house," Griffith replied. "In Felicity Marsden's bedroom. The bag was pinned to one of the folds in the curtains, up along the upper rails."

"Looks like you were right, sir," Barnes said. "This wasn't a bloomin' robbery. No thief in his right mind leaves the goods behind."

Witherspoon's spirits sank. Drat. The murderer was far too clever for his liking.

"Took us a while to find them," Griffith continued proudly. "I almost missed them too, but then I noticed one of the curtain rings was angled crooked and there was a funny bulge in the fabric right below it."

Witherspoon dragged his gaze from the jewels and stared at Constable Griffith. "Why on earth did you search Miss Marsden's bedroom?" he asked.

Constable Griffith's bright smile faded. "But, sir, you told me to. At least you sent me a note."

"I most certainly did not," the inspector protested. He thought back on everything he'd done that day and he was absolutely sure he hadn't sent Constable Griffith a message to search the Hodges home. Witherspoon knew perfectly well that he occasionally got a bit muddled, but even he'd remember writing a note.

"But, sir," Griffiths pleaded. He stared at his superior in panic. "I've got the note right here." He reached into the pocket of his jacket and pulled out a piece of paper, which he immediately thrust into Witherspoon's outstretched hand.

Opening the folded paper, Witherspoon frowned as he scanned the contents. "My apologies, Constable," he said, looking up. "This is indeed instructions from me authorizing you to search the house."

Griffith sighed in relief.

"But I didn't write it. How was it delivered?"

"A young lad brought it to me as I was leaving the house across from the Hodges home," Griffith explained slowly. He looked terribly confused by this turn of events. "We were finishin' up the house-to-house, trying to talk to all the neighbors. The boy, he was just one of them street arabs, sir, couldn't have been more than eight or nine, he told me it had been given to him by Inspector Witherspoon."

"I do believe, sir, that I really should get you a headache powder," Mrs. Jeffries said to the inspector. The poor man looked positively dreadful. He'd come home with his shoulders slumped and rain pouring off the rim of his hat. She'd immediately ushered him into the drawing room, put him in his favorite chair and poured a nice glass of sherry. She'd then sat down and listened to his tale of woe.

"That won't be necessary, Mrs. Jeffries. As soon as I've had a bite to eat, I'm sure I'll feel much better." He took another sip of his drink. "It's just, well, one gets embarrassed when one's been made to look a fool."

"Now, sir. Don't be ridiculous. How could you possibly have been made to look foolish?" She clucked her tongue. "It's hardly your fault that someone forged your signature onto a note."

"It's good of you to say so, but that's not the only reason I feel badly," he confessed. He stared morosely at his sherry. "I think perhaps I should have listened to Constable Barnes. He wanted to bring Mr. Vogel into the station for questioning and I didn't think we had sufficient evidence."

Mrs. Jeffries clucked her tongue again. "Now, now, sir. I'm sure you made the right decision. Why don't you tell me everything that happened today. It'll do you good to get it off your chest."

She straightened as she heard a harsh, muffled rumble that sounded like it was coming from belowstairs. The inspector heard it too.

"I say, did you hear that?" he asked.

"Yes. It was probably something falling off the back of a cart." She didn't care what the sound was. Unless the house was on fire, she wanted nothing to distract the inspector from telling her what had transpired that day.

"Thought it sounded like a dog," he murmured. Then he took a deep breath and told his dear housekeeper all about his utterly dreadful day.

Mrs. Jeffries listened very carefully.

The inspector retired early that night. Mrs. Jeffries waited until he'd disappeared up the stairs and she heard his bedroom door close before she hurried down to the kitchen.

For once, everyone was there. Even Luty Belle had managed to come.

"Hatchet said he'll be back fer me in an hour," Luty said, referring to her butler. "His nose is out of joint on account of havin' to go out in the wet, but he'll git over it. I couldn't wait till tomorrow. I've found out some information that's gonna set your hair on fire."

There was another muffled rumble sound and everyone started in surprise.

"What was that?" Betsy asked.

"Sounded like a dog," Mrs. Goodge replied.

"I heard the same sound a while ago," Mrs. Jeffries said.

"It's thunder," Wiggins put in.

"Thunder?" Smythe exclaimed. "It weren't a bit like thunder. You'd better get the muck out of yer ears, boy."

"And I'd better get them sausages," Mrs. Goodge said as she stood up and bustled down the hallway towards the cooling pantry. "Don't anyone start until I get back."

They all waited patiently, sipping at the cocoa the cook had put in a pot on the table. Mrs. Jeffries could tell from their faces that each of them had something to report.

"Arrg!" Mrs. Goodge screamed. Despite her rheumatism, she fairly flew down the hall, clutching an empty platter in her hands.

Alarmed, Mrs. Jeffries and Smythe both jumped to their feet. Betsy scooted back from the table to get a better view, Wiggins sank into his chair and Luty pulled a pistol out of her fur muff.

"For goodness' sakes, Luty," Mrs. Jeffries cried when she saw the gun, "put that thing away before you shoot someone."

"I'll put this away when I know why Mrs. Goodge is howling her head off," Luty retorted.

"Me sausages," the cook yelped. She slammed the empty platter onto the table. "They're gone."

"Is that what all the shoutin's about?" Smythe said in disgust. "For pity sakes, Mrs. Goodge, someone probably ate them."

"But they was there less than ten minutes ago," Mrs. Goodge insisted. "And I've been hearin' strange noises all evenin'. I tell you somethin's in the house."

Another rumble exploded from the back of the hall.

"Now I know that weren't thunder," Luty said. She aimed the pistol at the dimly lit passage and got to her feet.

Wiggins leaped up. "Don't shoot," he shouted. "'E's only a puppy." He threw himself in front of Luty. "Please, put that gun away. 'E was hungry. 'E followed me home and I didn't have the heart to turn 'im out. He's a good dog, Fred is."

Wiggins turned and rushed down the hallway towards the small, rarely used storage room. A few moments later he returned with the dog in tow.

"Fred's sorry 'e ate the sausages," Wiggins said apologetically to Mrs. Goodge. The animal looked at Mrs. Goodge and licked his chops. "But it were an accident. The door to the cooling pantry was open when I was bringin' 'im down the hall and the poor mite was so hungry that when 'e smelled that meat, 'e couldn't 'elp hisself."

Surprised by this turn of events, they all stared at the footman and the dog. Fred wagged his tail.

Mrs. Jeffries cleared her throat, Smythe chuckled, Mrs. Goodge snorted, Betsy grinned and Luty put her gun away.

"Can 'e stay?" Wiggins asked as he knelt by the animal and started stroking his rather mangy coat. " 'E's got nowheres to go and we can't just turn 'im out. 'E'll starve."

"But, Wiggins," Mrs. Jeffries said gently, "what will the inspector say?"

Still wagging his tail, Fred stepped closer to the table. Smythe tentatively put his hand out and the dog licked it. Then he went to Betsy and nuzzled his head against her chair.

"We can talk 'im into it," Wiggins insisted. "Our inspector's a kind'earted gentleman, 'e wouldn't want to see the poor little pup turned out in the cold."

"Let's have a go at it," the coachman put in. "I don't mind sharing me room with a dog. As long as Wiggins agrees to keep 'im clean."

"I don't know," Mrs. Jeffries said hesitantly.

"Oh please." Betsy added her voice to the chorus. "I like dogs and this one looks like he's right friendly." Fred bumped his nose against her knee.

Mrs. Jeffries didn't believe in dithering. She made a decision. "All right, we'll ask the inspector if we can keep the dog. But, Wiggins, the animal will be your responsibility. You must treat him kindly, keep him clean and ensure that he's walked properly."

"You won't regret it, Mrs. Jeffries," the footman promised. " 'E's a good dog, is Fred. 'E'll even come in 'andy on our investigations. Why, with proper trainin' and such 'e can probably learn to pick up the scent and follow the trail."

Fred chose that moment to flop down flat on the floor and go to sleep. Everyone laughed.

"Mind you keep his nose off the trail of my sausages in the future," Mrs. Goodge muttered. But she smiled at the animal as she said it.

"Now that that's settled," Mrs. Jeffries said with a worried glance at Fred, "let's find out what each of us has learned today. Luty, why don't you go first. We don't want to annoy Hatchet any more than necessary."

Luty told them all about her visit to Myrtle Buxton. She was a good storyteller, and when she got to the part about Felicity Marsden leaving the ballet, everyone was leaning towards her, their faces alight with interest.

"Cor," Smythe said when she'd finished. "That means that Miss Marsden don't have an alibi."

"True," Mrs. Jeffries said, "but it doesn't mean she murdered her aunt. It could just as easily mean she wanted a chance to see her young man."

"Thomasina Trotter don't really have an alibi either," Mrs. Goodge interjected. She told them what she'd heard from her sources that day as well.

"Well, I've learned something important too," Betsy said when the cook had finished. She told them about her conversation with Peter Applegate.

"Are you tellin' us that it were Mr. Hodges that introduced Mrs. Popejoy to his wife?" Luty asked.

Betsy nodded. "And that's not the half of it, accordin' to Peter. He thinks that Mr. Hodges and Mrs. Popejoy knew each other from a long time ago."

"Was he just guessing or does he know that for a fact?" Mrs. Jeffries asked.

"He weren't really sure," Betsy said cautiously. "But a couple of months back, right after Mrs. Popejoy had been 'round the Hodges house the first time, Peter claims he saw Mrs. Popejoy and Mr. Hodges together driving in a carriage down Oxford Street. But when Peter happened to mention it to Mr. Hodges, Mr. Hodges acted like he didn't know what he was on about."

"I'm gettin' confused," Wiggins said. "Was the man Mr. Hodges, then?"

"Hold yer horses, boy," Luty interjected. "She's gettin' to it. Go on, Betsy, what happened then?"

"Peter says he didn't think much about it, he just thought he'd made a mistake. But the very next day Mr. Hodges left the house and forgot his walkin' stick. Well, Mrs. Hodges gives Peter the stick and tells him he can probably catch up with her husband at Holland Park." Betsy paused dramatically. "But when Peter reached the park, he didn't just find Mr. Hodges. He saw Mr. Hodges and Mrs. Popejoy together and they was huddlin' under a tree. They didn't hear Peter comin', so they weren't careful with what they were sayin' to one another."

"What did Peter hear?" Mrs. Jeffries asked quickly.

"He heard Mr. Hodges sayin' that Mrs. Popejoy had better be careful, that they wouldn't like it to be like the last time. Then he laughed like and said, 'Remember what happened three years ago.' "

Wiggins shook his head. "I still don't get it."

"Neither do I," mumbled Mrs. Goodge.

"Don't you see, if he's referrin' to something that happened three years ago, something they both knew about, that proves he knew Mrs. Popejoy three years ago."

"Hmmm," Mrs. Jeffries said. "Perhaps, or perhaps not. Mr. Hodges could have been referring to a social or political event that *everyone* knew about. Something that was in the papers and was common knowledge, or he could have been chatting about something like last winter's weather. We've all commented that 1886 was the coldest winter anyone could remember. Mr. Hodges could just as easily have been having a polite conversation with Mrs. Popejoy." She shook her head. "Mr. Hodges just isn't a reasonable suspect in this case. When Inspector Witherspoon was interviewing Mrs. Popejoy yesterday, she mentioned a friend of hers, Harriet Trainer, was sitting in the ladies' waiting room when she arrived at the station with Mr. Hodges. The inspector told me today that they'd confirmed Mrs. Popejoy's story. Harriet Trainer positively identified Leonard Hodges as the man who accompanied Mrs. Popejoy to the station. And several witnesses saw him at his club not long after."

"So it doesn't matter if they knew each other or not before Mr. Hodges married Mrs. Hodges," Betsy said glumly. "And Peter were ever so sure they did. Said it wasn't just that incident in the park, it were other things too. Like the way they look at each other."

"Huh?" Wiggins scratched his head.

"Like the way you look at Sarah Trippett, lad," Smythe said, and Wiggins blushed.

Mrs. Jeffries tapped her fingers against the table. They'd learned much so far. Felicity Marsden didn't have an alibi, Mrs. Popejoy may have known Mr. Hodges longer than anyone had thought and he'd been the one to encourage his wife to go to a spiritualist. But she still didn't have enough information. She smiled at Smythe. "I believe it's your turn now."

The coachman shrugged. "My news isn't all that interestin'," he confessed. "But I did track down the hansom driver that brought Mrs. Hodges home. He claims she were angry because he'd driven her home by way of the Strand instead of the quieter streets. Said the woman was shoutin' so loud he never got a word in edgewise, otherwise 'e'd of told 'er it were 'er own husband who'd instructed him to take the long route."

"You mean Mr. Hodges told the driver to go down the Strand?" Luty asked.

"Indeed, Mr. Hodges told the bloke exactly how to go. Told the driver he and the missus had words and 'e wanted to give 'er time to get over her temper."

"That's very interesting," Mrs. Jeffries said. "And quite possibly true." She then told them what the inspector had confided to her. She told them about Benjamin Vogel's now vanished gun, the jewels being found in Felicity Marsden's room, the note to Constable Griffith that the inspector hadn't written and the fact that Vogel's landlady couldn't confirm his alibi.

"That's it then," Mrs. Goodge muttered darkly. "They did it together. Felicity Marsden and Benjamin Vogel. Mark my words, they're the killers."

"Now, we mustn't jump to conclusions," Mrs. Jeffries warned. "We don't know that Mr. Vogel and Miss Marsden were even together that night, and even if they were, I hardly think that proves them guilty of murder."

"But they both got a motive! 'Is gun's missing, and the jewels was found in 'er room," Smythe protested. "Sounds to me like that's pretty good evidence."

"On the surface it may well be," Mrs. Jeffries replied. "However, the inspector mentioned that he didn't think Mr. Vogel was stupid. Hiding jewels you've conspired to steal in one of the other conspirators' rooms strikes me as the mark of a very stupid man."

"Maybe he's going to blame it on her," Luty suggested. "Wouldn't be the first time a man's taken advantage of a woman's love. I once knowed a woman, good woman too, right smart. She up and helped her feller rob a bank. When the law caught up with 'em, he left her holding the money and hightailed it down to Mexico."

"That's terrible," Wiggins mumbled.

"But why would he do that? The jewels weren't worth much," Betsy said. "Seems to me the object was to get rid of Mrs. Hodges so he could marry her niece. With Mrs. Hodges dead, Miss Marsden probably stands to inherit a tidy sum. Lots more money than those piddly pearls were worth."

"Maybe all he wanted was vengeance," Luty insisted. "Lots of men have done that. Spent a lifetime trackin' someone down who'd done 'em wrong. Why, I knew a feller once who spent twenty years—" She broke off as Wiggins moaned. "Land's sake, boy. What's ailing you? My stories ain't *that* bad."

Wiggins moaned again and buried his face in his hands. Everybody stared at him, their expressions concerned.

"Wiggins?" Mrs. Jeffries prompted gently. "What's wrong? What is it?"

The boy looked up, his face a mask of misery. "You 'aven't 'eard what I've got to say, and when you do, you'll all be wantin' to put the noose around poor Miss Marsden's neck for sure. And I know she couldn't have done it, I just know it."

"You're only sayin' that 'cause you think she's pretty," Smythe mumbled.

"Don't be ridiculous, Wiggins. We're hardly likely to want to put the noose around anyone's neck at this point in our investigation." Mrs. Jeffries didn't add that she personally didn't see the point of hanging criminals in any case. The criminal justice system in England had been doing that for years and she didn't see that it had done all that much good. There were still plenty of criminals about. But this was hardly the time to enter into a debate over one of her more radical views. That could wait.

"You will when I tell ya," he moaned.

"Oh, go on and tell us, lad," Smythe snapped. "We're 'ardly like to grab a rope and go get the woman to string her up tonight."

"Please," Mrs. Jeffries said quietly. "Tell us what you know."

Wiggins nodded and told them about following Felicity Marsden to St. John's Church. "When I was standin' in the churchyard, I saw the vicar come out the front door, so I nipped 'round the corner to the back and what do you think I saw?"

Luty rolled her eyes. "Hurry up, boy. Hatchet'll be here any minute and I want to hear this."

"Miss Marsden. They's a graveyard behind the church and she were dartin' from one 'eadstone to another," Wiggins continued. "Well, as I 'ad Fred with me, it were kind of 'ard to keep 'er from spottin' me, so we finally 'unkered down in some bushes. Then I saw 'er stop beside a newly dug grave. She kneeled down like she were goin' to pray, only instead of prayin' she started diggin'. When she stood up again, the little brown parcel she were carryin' weren't in 'er 'ands." He paused again. "She'd buried it."

"Did you go dig it up?" Smythe asked.

Wiggins blushed. "Er, I were goin' to."

"What do ya mean, you was goin' to?" Luty slapped her hand against the tabletop. "What stopped you, boy?"

"It were gettin' dark," Wiggins said defensively. "And I didn't want to be late gettin' 'ome. I tell you, the place was right 'orrible. Startin' to rain, and Fred here was hungry and then it got black as night, and what with all this talk of spirits and communicatin' with the dead, well, I weren't goin' to 'ang about there diggin' in some grave on me own."

"Oh, Wiggins," Betsy teased, "are you tellin' us you was scared?"

"I didn't say I was scared!"

Luty was shaking her head in disgust. "What a greenhorn," she muttered.

"Blast, boy," Smythe snapped. "The dead is dead. They'll do you no 'arm. You should have seen what Miss Marsden was buryin'. It might be too late now."

" 'Ow do you know the dead is dead?" Wiggins argued.

"Silly goose," Mrs. Goodge muttered.

"Now, now," Mrs. Jeffries said firmly. "Stop picking on Wiggins. I hardly think Felicity Marsden would bury something in St. John's churchyard this afternoon just to go back and dig it up this evening."

"True," Smythe agreed, "but someone else might."

CHAPTER 7

Naturally, after Smythe's pronouncement, everyone had an opinion concerning the best course of action. Wiggins wanted to go to bed and worry about someone digging up Felicity Marsden's cache in the morning. Smythe, Betsy and Luty Belle wanted to dash off to St. John's instantly, and Mrs. Goodge, who wouldn't have gone in any case, tended to side with Wiggins.

Undecided, Mrs. Jeffries gazed at the footman thoughtfully. "You weren't followed today, were you?"

" 'Course not. Even if someone did spot me, unless they was faster than Snyder's hounds, they couldna kept up with me and Fred. We barely kept Miss Marsden in sight ourselves."

Satisfied, the housekeeper nodded. "I believe then that as you're the only one who knows about Miss Marsden's trip to the churchyard, no one else could possibly get to it before we do."

"Reckon you're probably right," Smythe said. "Wiggins and I can go do a bit of diggin' ourselves tomorrow morning. If we get to the church right after dawn, we can get in and out without anyone seein' us."

"Go on with you, man," Betsy snapped. "Why should you and Wiggins get to do all the nice things? I want to go too."

"Nice!" Smythe stared at the girl incredulously. "I was only tryin' to be considerate. Diggin' about in a damp, cold churchyard at this time o' the year isn't exactly what I'd call nice."

Luty yawned widely. "Quit yer squabblin', if it's all the same to everyone, Hatchet and I'll be 'round tomorrow mornin' before yer inspector's stirrin'. We'll bring the carriage, that way we can all go."

"That sounds like a fine idea," Mrs. Jeffries said quickly.

• • •

True to her word, Luty, with a grumpy butler in tow, called for them in her carriage at half past six the next morning. As there was little traffic at such an early hour, they made excellent time to St. John's.

Dawn was breaking as they piled out of the carriage. Luty had directed Hatchet to bring them to the back of the church.

The churchyard was enclosed by a low stone wall capped by a thick iron railing. A small, locked gate was the only entry.

"Nells bells," Luty exclaimed as she glared at the heavy black lock. "How come you people lock up yer dead tighter than a bank vault? I ain't seen a cemetery yet in this country that wasn't surrounded by bars. What're ya expectin' them bodies to do? Come back and haunt ya?"

"Actually," Mrs. Jeffries explained cheerfully, "the railings were erected around most cemeteries and churchyards early this century. It was an attempt to keep the bodies from being stolen."

"Pardon the interruption," Smythe hissed softly, "but Wiggins and I'll have a hunt 'round the other side to see if we can't find a way in. If we can't, we'll climb the fence."

"Good idea." Mrs. Jeffries said.

Luty tugged on her sleeve. "Who the dickens would want to steal corpses?"

"Hmmm, oh, professional body snatchers," Mrs. Jeffries replied absently as she anxiously watched Smythe and Wiggins disappear around the corner. Then she turned to gaze at the back entrance of the church; she wanted to be able to call out a warning in case a vicar or someone else came out into the yard.

"Body snatchers," Luty muttered. "Why the dickens would anyone want a bunch of dead bodies?"

"To sell to medical schools," Mrs. Jeffries said, still keeping her gaze on the church. "The students need them for dissection."

Betsy winced. "That's disgustin'."

"There weren't enough bodies, you see," Mrs. Jeffries continued. She thought she might as well satisfy Luty's curiosity while they waited for Smythe and Wiggins. "The problem was most prevalent in Edinburgh—they simply didn't have enough bodies for the students to dissect. Medical schools, which, from what I've heard, didn't ask too many questions about how the bodies were procured, would pay between seven and ten pounds per corpse. Surely you've heard of that dreadful Burke and

Hare—they actually used to murder their victims in order to keep the supply available. Well, with that kind of money in the offing, body snatchers began to prey upon recent burials. Naturally this upset the relatives, and so they started standing guard for a number of days after the loved one was buried."

"Givin' the body time to rot, huh?" Luty asked with relish.

Betsy moaned softly. "If you two are goin' to be so gruesome at this time of the mornin', I'm going to sit with Hatchet."

Luty looked offended. "We're not bein' gruesome. Hepzibah is just tellin' me some of the more interestin' bits about you English." She grinned at the housekeeper. "How come they put up the gates then, if relatives was standin' guard?"

"They wanted to be doubly sure." She pointed to the spiked points on the top of the railings. "The railings were designed to make it difficult to get a body over the gate. But the newest churchyards don't have them."

Luty, who obviously found the subject fascinating, said, "How come?"

"After the passage of the Anatomy Act of 1832 it became much easier for medical schools to acquire bodies legally. That, of course, took the profit out of stealing from graves and that particular crime has virtually died out. It was rather distasteful, I'll admit, but if you keep in mind the dreadful poverty so many people are forced to endure, you can understand why it happened."

Smythe, with a panting Wiggins trailing him, appeared from around the corner. He waved them over.

"There's another gate on the side," he whispered. "We've got it open. But we'd better be quick, there's a few lamps coming on across the road."

Leaving Hatchet to keep watch for patrolling constables, they went into the yard. Wiggins led them to the spot where Miss Marsden had buried the parcel. It was just beneath the headstone of one Percival Pratt, who departed this world only a week ago.

Sinking to his knees, Smythe took a trowel from beneath his coat and began to dig. "I've hit somethin'," he muttered as he tossed the trowel to one side and brushed some dirt off the package with his fingers. He brought out the parcel and handed it to Mrs. Jeffries.

Everyone gathered closer as she carefully eased off the string and unwrapped the paper. "Oh dear," she murmured softly. "It's a gun. Probably the one that killed Mrs. Hodges."

Wiggins made a sound of distress. "Poor Miss Marsden. This'll put a noose 'round 'er neck for sure."

"Not necessarily," Mrs. Jeffries replied. "Just because she buried the gun isn't evidence that she did the shooting."

"But who else could of done it?" Betsy asked. "And if it weren't Felicity Marsden, then why did she come all the way over here to get rid of the gun?"

"That's a very interesting question," Mrs. Jeffries answered quickly, "and one we'd better discuss thoroughly before we take any action." She hastily rewrapped the weapon. "Here, Smythe, hold this while I retie the string."

"What'dya doin' that fer?" Luty asked. "Ain't we gonna take the gun to the inspector?"

"No, we're going to put it back right where we found it and go back to Upper Edmonton Gardens," Mrs. Jeffries declared. "We've much to discuss before we tell the inspector anything."

"Cor, Mrs. J," Smythe said with a shake of his head. "Are you sure? I mean, this is hidin' evidence."

"It most certainly is not." Mrs. Jeffries cast a quick glance to the back of the church. "We're not hiding anything, we're replacing it. And we must hurry. It's getting late. I don't want to have to explain our presence here to the vicar. Now stop worrying, all of you," she said earnestly as she looked from one concerned face to another. "Believe me, I know what I'm doing."

"We're going to have another little chat with that Mr. Vogel today," Inspector Witherspoon declared. He reached for another slice of toast from the rack and liberally smeared it with butter and marmalade. "Then we're going to ask Miss Felicity Marsden to explain how that jewelry got into her room."

"Perhaps Miss Marsden doesn't know," Mrs. Jeffries suggested. "You know, it is possible the jewels were put there to throw suspicion on the young lady. After all, Miss Marsden was at the ballet that night."

"Hmmm, I'm not so sure of that. I'm going to send Barnes around to the Plimpton house today to double-check Miss Marsden's statement."

"Really? Why?"

"Actually," the inspector replied, "it was something you said that got me to thinking we'd better have another look at Miss Marsden's alleged movements on the night in question."

"Something I said," Mrs. Jeffries repeated innocently, though she was much relieved. She'd been dropping hints that everyone's statements as to their whereabouts on the night of the murder should be double-checked.

"Certainly. You stated that once one was seated in a crowded dark theatre, it was jolly easy to slip out without anyone being any the wiser. Especially if one was seated next to an elderly woman who probably fell asleep as soon as the curtain came up."

"Oh that," she replied airily. "Well, I only said it because I remembered how my great-aunt Matilda used to doze off when we took her to the theatre in Yorkshire." She laughed gaily. "But I must say, I'm very flattered that you took my little observations seriously."

Witherspoon smiled. "You mustn't be so modest, Mrs. Jeffries," he said as soon as he'd swallowed his toast. "Why, you said it yourself, one of my characteristics as a detective is to take everything I hear seriously. Why, hearing your little bits about human nature seems to spark something in my own thoughts. Jolly good too; otherwise I'd never have been able to solve some of the difficult cases I've been given."

"Are you going to examine Jonathan Felcher's and Mr. Hodges's movements as well?"

Witherspoon shrugged. "We've already double-checked Mr. Hodges. As I told you last night, Barnes got a statement from Miss Trainer that she'd seen Mr. Hodges escort Mrs. Popejoy to the door of the ladies' waiting room."

"So you did," Mrs. Jeffries murmured. "How silly of me to forget."

"You're not in the least silly," the inspector declared. "But I do believe we'll double-check Mr. Felcher's whereabouts and perhaps even that housekeeper, Mrs. Trotter. She's an odd sort of person. Constable Barnes repeated the most peculiar rumor about her yesterday." He then proceeded to tell her what she'd already learned about Thomasina Trotter's excursions into the streets of London.

"How very unusual," she commented, when the inspector finished.

"Yes, isn't it." Witherspoon sighed. "But then lots of people have eccentric habits. It doesn't necessarily make them murderers."

Mrs. Jeffries waited until the inspector left before pouring herself another cup of tea. The house was very quiet. After they'd come back from St. John's this morning, she had hastily given everyone another assignment and they were all out gathering information.

Betsy had gone to make contact with someone in Mrs. Popejoy's establishment, though Mrs. Jeffries didn't see that course of action as being particularly fruitful. Mrs. Popejoy and Leonard Hodges were the only two people involved in the case who had unshakable alibis. Smythe had gone to have another word with the driver who'd taken Mrs. Popejoy and Mr. Hodges to the train station, though again, that was probably a waste of time. Luty had decided to try to ferret out any gossip she could find about Mrs. Trotter, and Wiggins had announced he was off to find evidence that Miss Marsden was innocent.

Mrs. Jeffries sighed. This whole case was so muddled. No one was where they were supposed to be that night. Everyone seemed to loathe the victim, so there was no shortage of suspects, and now it looked like the evidence was pointing directly to the one suspect who had the most to gain by Abigail Hodges's death. Felicity Marsden.

Or did she? The housekeeper tapped the side of her teacup. They still didn't know for sure that Miss Marsden was going to inherit a large portion of the estate, and until the inspector got around to questioning the woman's solicitor, they wouldn't know. And Mrs. Jeffries didn't like the manner in which this new evidence against the girl was being discovered. It was too tidy. Too neat. Almost as though someone were directing the action from behind the scenes.

Someone who had sent Constable Griffith that note about searching the house. Someone who had wanted those jewels found. Someone who, if Benjamin Vogel were to be believed, had taken the gun out of his room without his knowledge. Someone who wanted to implicate Felicity Marsden and her former fiancé. Or maybe, she thought, they had done the murder and staged the robbery. But surely, she argued silently, no one is stupid enough to have made all those mistakes.

Or were they? Mrs. Jeffries put her cup down.

She shook her head and decided to go over the reasons someone would want Abigail Hodges dead.

Felicity Marsden hated her aunt because she'd thwarted her relationship with Benjamin Vogel. But if that engagement was truly over, the two of them would hardly have conspired to fake a robbery and stage the murder. Mr. Vogel deeply resented Mrs. Hodges's lies; that could be his motive. But if it were, it was pretty weak. And what about the nephew, Jonathan Felcher? He hated the woman because he wanted control of his own money and she wouldn't give it to him. Then there was the housekeeper. Mrs. Jeffries shrugged. Who knew what on earth possessed Mrs. Trotter.

Mrs. Jeffries knew she needed to do something. But what? Suddenly she leaped to her feet.

Jonathan Felcher. No one had really taken a good look at him. She hurried to the backstairs and called to Mrs. Goodge that she was going out.

It was time to take a closer look at Abigail Hodges's nephew. And after that, it was time to have a chat with Felicity Marsden.

"We'd like to speak to Miss Marsden, if you don't mind," Inspector Witherspoon said to Leonard Hodges.

"Felicity? But she's resting now," Hodges replied. "Look, Inspector, I hardly think you need disturb the girl. She's told you everything she knows."

Witherspoon stared at him curiously. "But I'm afraid she hasn't. You realize, of course, that finding the jewelry here in this house—more specifically, in Miss Marsden's room—changes the entire nature of this investigation. We really must speak to her."

Hodges nodded slightly in acknowledgment. "I can understand your reasoning, Inspector, but I'm not certain I entirely agree with it. Couldn't the thieves have panicked when they murdered my wife and hidden the jewelry themselves?"

"If that were the case, I hardly think the miscreants would have bothered to hide the jewels! Why not simply take them along with them as they left?" Witherspoon suggested. "And even if you're correct, pray remember where they were found, pinned inside the upper folds of the curtains. Hardly the actions of a person in an agitated state of mind, sir."

Hodges sighed. "Yes, I see your point." He stepped over to the bellpull and yanked the cord. When the maid appeared, he instructed her to fetch Miss Marsden.

Without being asked, Witherspoon sat down. "Mr. Hodges, I presume your late wife made a will?"

Hodges slowly turned his head and stared at the inspector. "Yes, she did."

"Do you, by any chance, happen to have any idea as to how her estate was divided?"

"As a matter of fact, I do," Hodges stated calmly. "Abigail wasn't reticent about her plans. Everything she owned is divided equally between myself and Felicity."

"What about Mr. Felcher?"

"He has his own property. Now that Abigail is gone, he'll obtain control of his holdings." Hodges brushed a piece of lint off the collar of his elegant black mourning coat. "Unlike most women, Abigail controlled her own property."

"That's most unusual, isn't it?" the inspector asked. He wasn't sure, but he'd always thought that once a woman married, her husband legally became the possessor of everything she owned. Of course he could be mistaken, there was something going on in Parliament about a Married Woman's Property Act, but he wasn't sure it had passed. Or had it? Yes, by golly, he thought, he did remember reading about that in the newspapers. Something about a woman owning two hundred pounds of her own money . . . no, that didn't sound right. Wasn't there another act in the offing? One that entitled them to keep all their own money? Oh dear, he thought, politics were such a muddle, one couldn't be expected to keep every little thing straight.

"Abigail was an unusual woman." Hodges smiled sadly. "And as to the laws and customs of our great nation, they had no influence on her. Her money and holdings were in the United States and the laws and customs of that land are far different than here. Interesting place, actually. Women are accorded a great deal more freedom, I believe."

The inspector immediately thought of Luty Belle Crookshank. "Er, yes," he said with a smile. "You're quite correct."

"Abigail inherited substantial real-estate holdings in both New York and Baltimore from her first husband," Hodges explained. "The property is administered by an American law firm and quarterly funds are drawn on bank drafts through the Bank of New York."

The inspector wondered what was keeping Miss Marsden. He was most impressed by Mr. Hodges's openness. Quite grateful, as a matter of fact. Now he wouldn't have to have one of those tiresome conversations with Mrs. Hodges's solicitor. He suddenly realized there was something very important he must ask. "Mr. Hodges," he said cautiously, "did Miss Marsden know she was going to inherit half of her aunt's fortune?"

"He drinks like a bloody fish, he does, and gambles too," Elspeth Blodgett exclaimed. "I say, it's right nice of you to bring me here. I've never been in one of these places. Tea shops, that's what they call 'em. I know 'cause one of me lodgers is always meetin' her young feller at the one in Piccadilly Circus. She's one of them typewriter girls, has her own Remington, she does, claims she makes twenty-five shillings a week."

Mrs. Jeffries waited patiently for Jonathan Felcher's landlady to pause for a breath. It had taken only the barest hint that she was inquiring into Mr. Felcher's character on behalf of the family of a young lady to loosen Elspeth Blodgett's tongue. The woman certainly liked to talk.

Immediately Mrs. Jeffries had known that if she could get a cup of tea in front of the landlady, she'd have a veritable gold mine of information. As Mrs. Blodgett was on her way to do the shopping, it was quite easy to convince her to make a quick detour into a very convenient ABC Tea Shop.

A waiter pushing a trolley topped with seedcake, currant buns, digestive biscuits and meringues stopped beside their table.

Mrs. Blodgett broke off in midsentence. Her eyes narrowed and she licked her lips as she stared at the tray of sweets.

"Oh please, order anything you like," Mrs. Jeffries said quickly. "On a chilly day like today, a cup of tea just isn't enough. And it's so very good of you to help me in my inquiries."

"Thank you, I don't mind if I do." She pointed a chubby, rather dirty finger at the plate of meringues. "I'll take a couple of those and two of them digestive biscuits as well."

Though she wasn't hungry, Mrs. Jeffries was determined to be sociable and keep the woman talking. She ordered a currant bun and more tea.

"Now," she continued, when the waiter had left, "about Mr. Felcher? You were saying?"

"He's a rotter and a rogue, he is," Mrs. Blodgett said as she dipped a biscuit into her tea. "But that don't keep the ladies away, if you get me meaning. Not much of a worker, always takin' time off in the afternoons and holds on to his job by the skin of his teeth. He ain't above nickin' a few bits and pieces 'ere and there, neither."

"Gracious." Mrs. Jeffries deliberately pretended to be shocked. "Why on earth do you allow such a monster to stay on in your lodging house?"

"I'm no starry-eyed girl. He don't steal from me, I makes sure of that." Mrs. Blodgett cackled. "He may be a rotter, but he pays his rent, and on time too. Besides, it's all the same to me. If that silly aunt of his wants to let him steal her blind, that's her business."

"You mean he steals from his own relatives!"

" 'Course he does. I seen it with me own eyes." Mrs. Blodgett pushed a strand of dirty gray hair out of her eyes and tried to tuck it back beneath an equally dirty gray cap. "I've seen him open her purse and help himself when she ain't lookin'."

"How appalling," Mrs. Jeffries exclaimed. Obviously Mrs. Blodgett didn't think it unethical to spy on her lodgers. "How did you see Mr. Felcher steal? It's rather important. I mean it's my duty to warn Elizabeth's family that the young man who has been paying court to their only daughter isn't to be trusted."

"We've all got to do our duty," Mrs. Blodgett seconded. "Well, like I was sayin', this here aunt of his used to come by occasionally and give

Felcher a dressin'-down. Whenever she'd finish, she'd nip into the back room to put on her hat and coat. Felcher used to open her purse and help himself. Got right quick at it too. Her name was Abigail Hodges."

"The woman who was murdered a few days ago?"

"That's the one, all right. Had lots of money, she did. Felcher was always lickin' her boots and tryin' to get on her good side, but I reckon she had him sussed out well enough." Elspeth smiled slyly. "She never paid no mind to his grovelin' and wheedlin'. But she sure kept him at her beck and call all the time, she did."

"Perhaps Mr. Felcher hoped to eventually inherit something from her estate," Mrs. Jeffries suggested.

Mrs. Blodgett shook her head. "Maybe, or maybe he was always dancin' to her tune 'cause if he didn't she'd tell his employer about Mr. Felcher playin' about with Mr. Macklin's wife."

This time Mrs. Jeffries didn't have to pretend to be shocked. "I'm afraid I don't understand what you're saying?"

"I'm sayin' that Mr. Felcher was playin' about with Mrs. Macklin, his boss's wife. Mrs. Hodges caught 'em together one afternoon. She's had Felcher under her thumb ever since. He's told me more than once 'e wished Mrs. Hodges was dead. Looks like he finally got his wish."

"Jonathan Felcher took them to dinner on the night that the murder occurred," Mrs. Jeffries said thoughtfully.

She spoke too soon, because Elspeth Blodgett suddenly sat back and gazed at her suspiciously. "How do ya know that?"

"It was in the papers," Mrs. Jeffries said quickly, hoping that Mrs. Blodgett hadn't followed the case in the dailies.

"Oh. For once Felcher were tellin' the truth. He did take 'em to dinner that night. Claimed he had a big win at the races." She snorted. "More like one of his women had greased his palm with a bit of cash, if you ask me. Mrs. Macklin wasn't the only rich woman he was spendin' his time with."

"According to the papers, Mr. and Mrs. Hodges then went on to another engagement and Mr. Felcher returned home. I wonder if that's true."

" 'Course it in't true. Felcher never come home that night at all."

Mrs. Jeffries weighed her next words carefully. "Have you told the police that he didn't come home?"

Mrs. Blodgett shrugged. "They haven't asked me. But if they did. I've got no reason to lie to save the likes of him. Why should I? Now that Mrs. Hodges has up and died, he's give his notice. He'll be leavin' at the end of the week. Goin' to America."

• • •

"I think, madam, I really ought to come inside with you." Hatchet helped Luty Belle Crookshank out of the carriage and then turned to survey the area. He arched one silver brow disdainfully at the row of dingy gray houses, the unpaved road, the hordes of ill-kempt children playing in the mud and the unremitting stench from the poultry yard directly across from the home of Mrs. Bush.

"Don't be silly, Hatchet," Luty replied as she brushed off his arm and headed up the broken walkway. "You'll be of a lot more use out here." She jerked her head toward the children, several of whom were eyeing her carriage. "I can handle one old lady. All I want to do is talk to the woman. But if it eases yer mind, stay close to the door and I'll give a shout if I need any help."

Leaving Hatchet muttering under his breath, Luty banged on the door. Several blotches of paint fell off onto the ground. From inside, she heard a shuffling noise, and several moments later the door slowly opened and a quavery voice said, "Who's there? What do you want?"

"My name is Luty Belle Crookshank," she replied. "I'm a friend of Thomasina Trotter's. I'd like to speak to Mrs. Bush." Luty sincerely hoped that Mrs. Bush wouldn't remember this little visit and mention it to Mrs. Trotter.

The opening widened and a shriveled-up woman leaning heavily on a cane appeared. Her white hair had thinned so much there were bald spots on the crown. Her face was a mass of wrinkles and her eyes were dull and glazed. "Tommy?" she said in a singsong voice. "Are you my angel? My Tommy?"

Luty wanted to stamp her foot in frustration. Mrs. Bush wasn't just elderly and a mite forgetful, she was completely loco. Then she was ashamed of herself as she saw the dazed eyes clear.

"Have you come to visit me?" The old woman smiled hopefully.

"Yes, ma'am, I surely have," Luty replied. "May I come in?" she asked, feeling a wave of pity wash over her.

"But of course you can." Mrs. Bush turned and shuffled down a darkened hallway, leaving Luty to follow after her. "I don't get so many visitors these days. Gets lonely, you know. I'd offer you tea, but . . . but"—she broke off as they came into the parlor.

Luty, who wasn't fussy about cleanliness, resisted the urge to hold her nose. The room smelled as though something had died in it. There were huge patches of damp on the walls and ceiling, the wallpaper was gone in spots and the furniture was moth-eaten and covered in dust.

Mrs. Bush lowered herself into a chair and motioned to Luty to take the one opposite her. "Where's Tommy?"

"Well, she's busy right now," Luty explained gently, "but she sent me to visit with you a spell."

"Is she coming soon?" Mrs. Bush asked hopefully. For a moment her gaze sharpened again and she looked at Luty carefully, then her eyes dulled and she sighed. "Did you say you'd stay for tea?"

"That'd be right nice," Luty began, but Mrs. Bush didn't seem to hear her.

"Poor Tommy," she moaned. "She never gets to come and see me anymore."

"I expect she's busy what with her workin' fer Mrs. Hodges and all."

Mrs. Bush paid no attention to her; she rambled on and Luty quickly shut up. She was afraid she'd miss something important.

"She never gets to rest." Mrs. Bush shook her head from side to side. "Day in, day out, she spends every waking moment looking for the girl. Does all the errands for that wicked woman, all of them. Always on the streets, always looking. Never gets to rest. Oh, my poor angel."

"That's right, she never gets to rest," Luty repeated as she decided to change tactics. She reached over and patted Mrs. Bush's hand. "But why don't you tell me a bit about your Tommy?"

A slow, dreamy smile spread across the old woman's face. "She was such a pretty child, such a sweet thing. And she was all mine, practically from the day she was born. Her mother was ill, you know. I raised her." Mrs. Bush suddenly giggled. "But then again, if she hadn't been so pretty, she wouldn't have had all that trouble. I always used to tell her, pretty is as pretty does, but she'd never listen. Willful, that's what she was."

"What kind of trouble did she have?" Luty asked softly.

Mrs. Bush moaned. "Trouble, always trouble. First the money gone and then him!"

"What kind of trouble?" Luty repeated. "What 'him' are you talking about?"

Suddenly Mrs. Bush banged her cane against the floor. Luty jumped.

"There was no Mr. Trotter, you know." Mrs. Bush leaned over and wrapped a clawlike hand around Luty's arm. "He left. But Tommy always pretended there was, always pretended he was coming back to her, and then she'd find the child and the three of them would be together."

"What child?"

Mrs. Bush ignored her. "Tommy could have been happy, you know. But that wicked woman wouldn't let her. They could have come here, but Tommy wouldn't have it, wouldn't have the baby marked like that. She went to her instead. Stole the baby, she did, pretended she was doing it for Tommy, but she wasn't. Wicked she was, so wicked."

"What woman?"

"Told Tommy she was a fool, that kind of wickedness never repents." Mrs. Bush sighed. "But she was always so willful. She insisted, insisted she did, that Abigail would tell her the truth. Now she can't. Gone she is, gone to the dead." Mrs. Bush's eyes flashed fire. "Gone to hell."

"I say, Mr. Hodges," Witherspoon said as he glanced at his watch. "Do you think perhaps you could send one of the servants to see what's taking Miss Marsden so long?"

Hodges looked surprised by the suggestion. "I don't think it's been all that long, Inspector," he said, reaching for the bellpull to summon the parlor maid, "but if you insist, I'll send Hilda up again."

The girl appeared in the doorway.

"Did you tell Miss Marsden we're waiting for her?" Hodges asked.

"I did, sir," the maid replied. "She were in the bathroom when I went up, so I rapped on the door and told her you and the gentleman from Scotland Yard wanted to see her."

"Well, go and see what's taking her so long," Hodges said impatiently. "Perhaps she needs help getting dressed." He turned to the inspector. "You'll be gentle with Felicity, won't you? This whole situation has upset her dreadfully."

"We are not bullies, sir," Witherspoon answered. Really, the way some of these people went on; why, one would think the police were barbaric monsters! "Miss Marsden will be treated with all due courtesy and respect. However, you must be aware that Miss Marsden is in a very precarious position." He broke off as Mrs. Trotter ushered Constable Barnes into the room.

Barnes didn't waste any time. He motioned for the inspector to step closer and then whispered, "You were right, sir. Miss Marsden did leave the theatre. The lady who accompanied Miss Marsden and Miss Plimpton was old and she fell asleep. Miss Plimpton's confessed that her original statement was a lie and she was covering for Miss Marsden."

"Oh dear," the inspector said quietly, "that doesn't look good, does it?"

"Has something happened, Inspector?" Hodges asked. "What's all this whispering about? I demand to know what's happened. I am an interested party; it was my wife that was murdered."

"I'm afraid, sir, I must insist that you bring Miss Marsden down immediately," Witherspoon replied gravely.

"I'll get the girl myself," Hodges said. "Then perhaps we can get this situation straightened out. Whatever information you think you've learned, Inspector, I assure you, my niece is innocent." He turned on his heel and stalked out of the room.

Barnes waited until he heard Mr. Hodges's footsteps going up the stairs. Then he turned to the inspector. "I'm still wonderin' who sent that note. Any ideas, sir?"

The inspector had actually given the matter a great deal of thought. He was rather glad the constable had asked. "Actually I've already deduced who it must have been."

Barnes looked appropriately impressed.

"Obviously"—Witherspoon lowered his voice—"it was one of the Hodgeses' servants."

"Really, sir?"

"But of course, who else could it have been? It was someone in the household who didn't want to risk losing their position by coming forward and telling the police what they'd learned, but on the other hand, they didn't want justice to be thwarted either."

They heard the sound of pounding footsteps on the staircase. Alarmed, both men hurried into the hall.

Leonard Hodges, breathing hard and looking very agitated, stopped on the bottom step. "I'm not really sure what to make of this," he began. "Honestly I'm certain there's a reasonable explanation, but I don't know what it could possibly be."

"Please calm yourself, Mr. Hodges," the inspector said. "Just tell us what's wrong."

"It's Felicity."

"Yes, what about her?" Barnes asked as he began edging towards the staircase. "Is she refusing to speak to us?"

"She's gone."

CHAPTER 8

Mrs. Jeffries paused across the road from the Hodges home. She pursed her lips, wondering what approach to take with Felicity Marsden. Perhaps she should slip around to the back of the house and wait and see if the girl came out into the garden, that would ensure them privacy. But then she glanced at the gray, darkening sky and realized that with the weather so bleak and cold, her quarry was hardly likely to come into the garden at all. Yet Mrs. Jeffries didn't want to run into the police! For all she knew, Inspector Witherspoon might be inside the Hodges house at this very minute.

Suddenly the front door opened and the object of her thoughts appeared on the front steps. The inspector stood there, waving his hands and talking earnestly to Constable Barnes. His bowler was askew, as though he'd tossed it on his head without proper care, and his coat was undone. Mrs. Jeffries could see he was extremely agitated. Something must have happened. But what? She had to know.

She saw the inspector point to his left, in the direction of the Queens Road, and then Constable Barnes nodded and hurried away. Mrs. Jeffries decided to take the bull by the horns. She waited until Barnes was out of earshot and quickly crossed the road.

"Oh, Inspector," she called gaily as she came up behind him, "how very nice to see you, sir."

Witherspoon jumped in surprise and whirled around. "Why, Mrs. Jeffries, what are you doing here?"

"I'm just on my way to Fitzchurch's," she explained. "They've such lovely linens and we've quite a few sheets that need replacing. Well, as I had to pass here to get to there, I thought I'd just have a peek at the"—she broke off and pretended to be embarrassed—"scene of the crime. Oh dear, sir, I'm afraid you'll think me such a busybody, but I was so terribly curious."

"That's quite all right, Mrs. Jeffries," the inspector said quickly, seeing his housekeeper's obvious discomfort. "I understand completely. Naturally you would be curious."

"How very understanding you are, sir," she replied. "But then, that's why you are such a brilliant detective. You understand people."

Witherspoon's chest swelled with pride for a brief moment before he remembered the latest development in this baffling case. "It's jolly good of you to say so," he said. "But I'm afraid this case has even me a bit flummoxed."

"Nonsense, sir," Mrs. Jeffries said briskly. "I've absolute confidence in your abilities. Whatever has happened is, I'm sure, only a temporary delay."

"Do you really think so?" he asked hopefully.

"Of course. Now, tell me, sir. What has you so agitated?"

"I fear my prime suspect has flown," he confessed on a sigh.

"Oh dear, how very tiresome for you."

"It most certainly is. Really, young people these days! No respect for the law. I tell you, Mrs. Jeffries, as difficult as it is to imagine such a thing, that young woman has something to hide."

"I take it you're referring to Miss Marsden?" Mrs. Jeffries asked. She was rather surprised by this new development. "Did she know you were waiting to see her?"

"Yes. The maid told her we were downstairs waiting to speak with her," the inspector replied, "but when Mr. Hodges went up to fetch the young lady, he found her gone. She'd also taken her carpetbag and some clothes."

"Oh dear, sir." Mrs. Jeffries clucked sympathetically. "That's most annoying, I'm sure. But not to worry, you'll soon catch up with her."

"I've sent Barnes to get us a hansom," Witherspoon continued, glad of the chance to unburden himself. "We're going to see Benjamin Vogel. If he's gone as well, we'll know the two of them are our murderers."

Mrs. Jeffries almost bit her tongue to keep from telling the inspector he shouldn't jump to conclusions. Instead she said, "But I thought Miss Marsden had broken her engagement to Mr. Vogel?"

"That's just what they wanted everyone to think. But one of the housemaids has admitted that Miss Marsden and Mr. Vogel have been secretly meeting with one another." Witherspoon's eyes narrowed. "Hilda Brown has been acting as their go-between. The supposed breakup of the engagement was just a ruse. No doubt they didn't want Mrs. Hodges cutting Miss Marsden out of her will."

"So you think that Miss Marsden and Mr. Vogel conspired together?" Mrs. Jeffries's mind was racing furiously. "But why?"

"Because Miss Marsden stands to inherit a great deal of money upon her aunt's death, that's why."

"She's the sole beneficiary to Abigail Hodges's estate?" Mrs. Jeffries wanted to be absolutely clear on this point.

"Not the sole beneficiary," Witherspoon said cautiously as he peered up the road for Barnes. "Mr. Hodges gets the other half. The estate's worth over a million pounds."

"Gracious, sir, that is a lot of money."

"Many would kill for such an amount," Witherspoon replied, "and I'm almost certain that Miss Marsden and Mr. Vogel did."

A cold blast of wind slammed into them, rattling the branches of the trees. Mrs. Jeffries drew her cloak tighter as she saw a hansom cab turn into the road and come towards them. She was running out of time, but there was one last important point she needed to impress upon the inspector.

"But, sir," she said softly, "who sent the note to Constable Griffith?"

"Note?" Witherspoon stared at her blankly.

"The one purportedly from you, sir," she explained. "Constable Griffith searched the house and found the jewels because he thought you'd instructed him to do so, but you hadn't."

"Oh that. Well, obviously, it was one of the Hodgeses' servants. Possibly even young Hilda Brown herself." Witherspoon brightened perceptibly. "Yes, I'm sure that's who sent the note. No doubt the girl realized what Miss Marsden had done. She probably felt very guilty for being a party, even an innocent party, to such wickedness."

Mrs. Jeffries thought that a possibly illiterate maid having the gumption to forge an inspector's name on a note was about as likely as pigs flying. She had to do something. She was sure that note hadn't been written by Hilda Brown, just as she was becoming more and more certain that Felicity Marsden and Benjamin Vogel weren't the killers.

The hansom drew up next to them. Mrs. Jeffries smiled and patted the inspector on the arm. "I'm sure you're right, sir. It probably was the maid. Mind you, the girl must be better educated than most servants." She broke off and laughed gaily. "Why, so many of them can barely read or write. The girl's obviously clever too, if she had the foresight to forge your name. Apparently Miss Brown knew exactly what to do to get the uniformed lads to make such a quick and thorough search. My thinking that perhaps someone was deliberately trying to lay the blame for this heinous crime at an innocent woman's feet is simply silly. Why, you're far too just a man to arrest someone for a crime merely because it's the easiest course of action."

Her words had the effect she'd hoped. The inspector's face fell and she could tell he was truly unsettled. For the truth of the matter was that the inspector *was* a just man. Now that she'd hinted that Felicity Marsden might be an innocent victim instead of a heartless killer, she knew Witherspoon wouldn't rest until he got at the truth.

"Yes, well, I'll just be off," the inspector said as he reached for the latch and opened the door. Constable Barnes caught sight of Mrs. Jeffries and smiled. "Hello, Mrs. Jeffries," he called. "What are you doin' over this way?"

"I'm just on my way to Fitzchurch's," she replied.

"Perhaps I'll give this whole situation a bit more thought," Witherspoon muttered as his housekeeper and constable exchanged pleasantries. He was still muttering to himself when Barnes closed the hansom door and the horses clip-clopped briskly away.

Mrs. Jeffries started walking. She thought about the various pieces of information she'd learned. It could well be that someone was indeed trying to make the police think that Felicity Marsden and possibly Benjamin Vogel were the killers. But then again, there was the chance that Inspector Witherspoon was correct and the note had been written by a servant or someone else who didn't wish to come forward. But that was rather farfetched. Again, she had the feeling that some unknown hand was moving the pieces of the puzzle to and fro. The note, the jewels, the ease with which Miss Marsden's and Mr. Vogel's alibis had been shattered, it was all too neat and tidy.

She turned the corner onto Princes Road. Felicity Marsden and Leonard Hodges were the two who stood to benefit the most from Abigail Hodges's death and Felicity was the one without an alibi. But what about Jonathan Felcher, she thought. Didn't he benefit as well? He might not inherit anything directly from his aunt, but now that she was dead, he'd have control over his own money.

And, she reminded herself, Felcher was planning on leaving the country in a few days. That certainly bore thinking about.

She stopped at the corner of the Uxbridge Road and waited for several moments before there was a break in the traffic. But if Felicity Marsden was innocent, she thought as she darted behind an omnibus, why had she buried a gun in St. John's churchyard? Mrs. Jeffries had a twinge of conscience at this thought.

So far she'd done nothing to lead Inspector Witherspoon to that gun and she knew she really should. Yet she couldn't help but feel that even with the inspector's passion for justice, with the kind of evidence that gun suggested, he'd have no choice but to arrest Miss Marsden and Mr. Vogel for the crime.

And Mrs. Jeffries didn't want that. Something was seriously wrong with this case. The evidence against Felicity Marsden and Benjamin Vogel had seemed to happen in the twinkling of an eye. It had all come about too quickly.

Mrs. Jeffries stopped and stood still. Of course. Why hadn't she realized it before? Shaking her head at her own stupidity, she quickened her pace. Someone was indeed trying to make it appear that Miss Marsden and Mr. Vogel were the perpetrators of this terrible murder and now she understood why. The real killer had only started planting the evidence against the young lovers when it had become obvious the police weren't convinced Mrs. Hodges had been killed by a burglar. When the burglary plan fell apart, she thought, whoever was behind this had switched to another plan. That was the way it must have happened. Nothing else made any sense.

With an increasing sense of urgency, Mrs. Jeffries decided on a course of action. But first, she had to find Felicity Marsden and Benjamin Vogel before the police did.

"Can't say that I'm surprised, sir," Constable Barnes said as they came down the steps of Benjamin Vogel's lodging house. "Once we knew she'd run, it were only reasonable that he'd run too."

"Now, now, Constable," Witherspoon replied cautiously. "We mustn't jump to conclusions."

"But, sir, the landlady said that Vogel left with a young woman not more than half an hour ago. It were obviously Miss Marsden he left with and they've obviously decided to make a run for it. Do you want me to have some lads watch the railways and the liveries?"

Witherspoon thought carefully before answering. He couldn't stop thinking about what his housekeeper had said. Despite her assertion that she was just being "silly," he knew that Mrs. Jeffries had a valid point. That wretched note had to have been written by someone. And now that he'd had time to think about it, he didn't think it was Hilda Brown. Drat. But who had written it? And despite the fact that now two of their prime suspects in the case seemed to have disappeared, he didn't think either of them was the author. Why would they have written it?

The note had certainly tightened the noose around Felicity Marsden's throat and that fact, on top of Mr. Vogel's gun being missing, could certainly lead the police into making a good case against the two of them. Especially now that they had evidence that Mr. Vogel had not broken off his relationship with Miss Marsden.

Witherspoon's head began to throb. Drat. Why couldn't it have been a simple burglary? Why did every case he was assigned end up being so complicated?

"Sir?" Barnes said impatiently. "Did you hear me?"

"Er, yes, Constable." Witherspoon made a decision. He wasn't going to chase Miss Marsden and Mr. Vogel. Not yet at any rate. Much as he hated to consider the possibility, it did, indeed, appear as though someone wanted the police to think the two fleeing young people were guilty. But he refused to be manipulated.

"It won't be necessary to send our lads to the liveries or train stations. I'm sure neither Miss Marsden nor Mr. Vogel has left the city." He infused his voice with as much authority as he could. He hadn't the faintest idea whether they'd left the city or not, but if he himself was trying to avoid the police, the last thing he'd do is leave a big, crowded city like London and go somewhere where one stuck out like a sore thumb.

By later that afternoon, Mrs. Jeffries had refined her plan of action. Everyone, except for Wiggins, had gathered back in the kitchen of Upper Edmonton Gardens.

"Have another cup of tea, Hatchet," Luty commanded her butler. "Yer still lookin' a mite blue around the gills."

"Thank you, madam," Hatchet replied. He helped himself to a second cup. "It was rather cold in the carriage and you were gone quite a long time."

"Yup, reckon I was," Luty agreed, "but ya can't rush these things. Specially when yer tryin' to make sense outta the ramblin's of an old woman like Mrs. Bush. Lord A'mighty, I sure hope I don't end up like that poor thing. Unwanted, alone, half-mad and barely able to git around." She shuddered slightly. "I'd rather someone jes' put a gun to my head and put me out of my misery before endin' up like her."

"I take it that means you weren't able to find out anything useful from Mrs. Bush," Mrs. Jeffries said.

"Oh, I found out lots, but I ain't sure if I found out anything that was true," Luty stated. "Mrs. Bush spins a right good yarn, but now whether or not what she told me really happened, or whether or not she's jes' tellin' tales, that's the part I can't figure."

"Why don't you tell us what she said," Mrs. Goodge suggested, "and we'll see if it fits with the other bits and pieces we've picked up."

Luty put down her teacup and leaned forward on her elbows. "From what I could make of what she was sayin', Mrs. Bush claims that Thomasina Trotter had an illegitimate child."

"How long ago?" Mrs. Jeffries asked. The more facts they had, the better.

"Twenty years ago."

There was a gasp of surprise from Betsy, Mrs. Goodge's jaw dropped, Smythe raised his eyebrows and even Mrs. Jeffries looked stunned.

"Yup, that's right, twenty years," Luty continued with a wide grin. "That means Mrs. Trotter weren't no young girl when she got into trouble. She's close to the same age as Mrs. Hodges was, so that would put her about fifty-two now."

"But that means she had the baby when she was thirty-two," Betsy said with a shake of her head.

"That's right," Luty said. "Her family disowned her when they discovered she was with child and the man responsible did like a lot of men—he run like a scared rabbit rather than own up to what he'd done. Mrs. Trotter had no one to turn to 'ceptin' her old friend Abigail. Anyhow, Abigail took her in, took care of her doctor bills and arranged for the baby to be adopted out."

"So Mrs. Trotter has been working for Mrs. Hodges ever since?" Smythe asked.

Luty shook her head. "No, after she had the baby, her daddy died and she went back and lived with her mother. A few years later the mother died. But Thomasina didn't inherit one dime, wasn't nothing left. So then she went to work for Abigail."

Betsy sighed. "It's a good story, but I don't see how it has anything to do with Mrs. Hodges's murder."

"Now hold yer horses, girl, I ain't finished," Luty said impatiently. "There's a few things I ain't told ya yet. Seems like Mrs. Trotter began to think she made a mistake in givin' her baby up just a few months after she'd had the child. She got some idea in her head that if she could find the baby, she could get her back and take her away somewhere's like Canada or the United States. Only Mrs. Hodges wouldn't hear of it, told Mrs. Trotter she was a fool and a dreamer and she wouldn't tell her where the girl was." Luty paused and took a deep breath. "Then, after

Mrs. Trotter's mother died, Mrs. Hodges changed her tune a bit, started saying that maybe it wouldn't be so bad if Mrs. Trotter did find her daughter. Strung the poor woman on fer years, promising to tell her and promising to leave her some money in her will so she and the girl could go off and start a new life. But she never did. Never told her." Luty broke off and sighed. "Then, a few years ago, Mrs. Trotter started walkin' the streets—lookin' for the girl, she was. It was a mad thing to do, but I think that by then, the poor woman was mad." She smiled sadly.

"But how can she be so . . . so . . . lunatic and still keep workin' for the Hodgeses?" Betsy interjected. "Didn't they notice there was somethin' not right with the woman?"

"There's all kinds of madness," Luty said softly. "It ain't all rantin' and ravin'."

"So with Mrs. Hodges dead, Mrs. Trotter will never have any hopes of finding the girl," Mrs. Goodge interrupted.

"Poor thing," Betsy murmured.

"I wish you'd all give me a chance to finish," Luty complained.

"Perhaps they would, madam," Hatchet said quickly, "if you didn't stop speaking at the more melodramatic points in the story."

"That's the best way to tell a tale." Luty exclaimed indignantly. She glared at her butler.

"True, madam," he replied smoothly, "but as I understand it, you ought not to be telling tales here, you ought to be stating facts."

"Oh, don't be such a stuffed shirt, Hatchet," Luty snorted. "What's the good of a bunch of dry old facts when you can string 'em out into a right good story."

"That's true, Luty," Mrs. Jeffries said hastily. "But perhaps you'd better conclude, we've an awful lot of information to pass along here this afternoon."

"Oh, all right. The point is, Mrs. Trotter is going to find out who adopted her child." Luty surveyed their stunned expressions with satisfaction. "Abigail left a letter with the solicitor. Upon her death the letter is to be given to Thomasina Trotter and it contains the name of the couple who adopted her child."

"Cor," Smythe said thoughtfully, "that's a pretty good motive."

"Yes, but why now?" Mrs. Jeffries mused. "Why wait twenty years to kill someone?"

Again Luty smirked in satisfaction. "Because Mrs. Hodges only recently told Mrs. Trotter about the letter. That's right, it was after she started goin' to them séances that her conscience seemed to start workin'.

Mrs. Bush told me that it wasn't more than a month ago that Mrs. Trotter come in all excited like and said that Mrs. Hodges had written this letter and given it to her lawyer."

Mrs. Jeffries cocked her head to one side. "Do you think Mrs. Bush was telling the truth?"

"She's got no reason to lie," Luty replied thoughtfully. "I don't think she really knew who I was or what I was doin' there, but once she started on about Mrs. Hodges and Mrs. Trotter, she sounded right sure of herself." She made a sweeping gesture with her hands. "But I reckon it could jes' be a story. The poor old thing's not right in the head."

"Well, we'll just have to see how your information fits in with other facts as we go along, won't we?" Mrs. Jeffries gave Luty a wide smile. "You've done a remarkably good job."

"Better than I have," Betsy chimed in. "I didn't learn nothing today."

Mrs. Jeffries patted the girl on the arm. "That's all right, dear. You've certainly done more than your fair share in the past. By the way, does anyone know what's keeping Wiggins?"

Mrs. Goodge frowned darkly. "He's probably out chasin' after that Sarah Trippett and forgettin' he was supposed to be back here."

"If not Miss Trippett," Betsy said, "then some other girl. Honestly sometimes that lad gets his head turned by nothing more than a hint of a smile."

Smythe snorted. " 'E's not the only one."

"What do you mean by that?" Betsy demanded, crossing her arms over her chest and glaring at the coachman.

"I expect my meanin's clear enough," he replied. "You've got no call to always be on about Wiggins when you're no better than 'e is. All that Edmund has to do is crook 'is little finger and you go runnin'."

"That's a bloomin' lie." Betsy leaped to her feet, her blue eyes blazing fire.

"Now, now, you two," Mrs. Jeffries interrupted. "Stop it this instant. We've enough problems on our plate just now without the two of you quarreling." She turned her head and gazed sternly at Smythe. "I do believe you owe Betsy an apology for that last remark," she said firmly.

Smythe's lips flattened to a thin, mutinous line.

"And," Mrs. Jeffries continued, turning her gaze to the maid, "I believe Smythe does have a point. None of us has the right to constantly assume Wiggins shirks his duty because of a pretty face."

Betsy dropped her gaze and slipped back into her chair. "All right, I'm sorry for what I said about the lad."

"Sorry, Betsy," Smythe mumbled.

Everyone turned and looked at Mrs. Goodge. She sighed. "Oh, all right, I shouldn't have said what I did either. Now, is everyone happy? Can we get on with this?"

"Indeed we can," Mrs. Jeffries stated firmly. She told them all about her visit with Elspeth Blodgett, stressing the fact that Mrs. Blodgett claimed the police had never bothered to ask her whether or not Jonathan Felcher had been home on the night of the murder.

"That don't sound right," Mrs. Goodge said. She sliced off another slab of seedcake and put it onto her plate.

"I know," Mrs. Jeffries agreed. "It certainly is peculiar. The police are generally very thorough in their investigations."

"Do you think this Mrs. Blodgett could be lyin'?" Smythe asked.

Mrs. Jeffries thought about it for a moment. "I don't think she's necessarily lying, but I do think it's possible she's made a mistake."

"Mistake?" Luty asked. "Hepzibah, no offense meant, but the way the law dresses in this country, it's purty danged hard to mistake them for anything other than what they are."

"I quite understand your point, Luty," Mrs. Jeffries explained, "but what I'm saying is that I don't think that the police neglected to go 'round to Mr. Felcher's lodging house and ask about his whereabouts, but I do think it's likely that they didn't speak to Mrs. Blodgett. They probably spoke to her hired girl. Mrs. Blodgett seems to spend a good deal of her day out of the house."

"But why would the hired girl lie for Mr. Felcher?" Betsy asked.

"I don't think she did. But she's Russian. Mrs. Blodgett told me herself that the girl can barely speak English." Mrs. Jeffries stared thoughtfully at Luty. "With all your connections, Luty, do you happen to know anyone who speaks Russian?"

"Russian, huh?" Luty's eyes narrowed and she shook her head. "Don't think I can help you much there. Now, if you were lookin' for some Germans, I could find you a couple of them faster than hot beer down a hog's gullet."

"I know some Russians," Hatchet announced.

They all stared at him in surprise.

"I've several acquaintances from Russia," he continued, ignoring their incredulous expressions. "And if it would be helpful, I'll be happy to take one to Mrs. Blodgett's lodging house and see if the girl did indeed speak to the police."

"Why, thank you, Hatchet," Mrs. Jeffries said. "That would be very helpful indeed."

"Why?" Luty asked. "What difference does it make? We already know that Mrs. Blodgett said Felcher wasn't there that night."

"True, but I'd like to know why the police have given up their investigation into Mr. Felcher's movements," Mrs. Jeffries explained. "And furthermore, Mrs. Blodgett has a bit of a grudge against Mr. Felcher. She seems most put out that he's leaving the country next week. I don't think she'd be above trying to get him into a bit of trouble by spreading the rumor that he wasn't where he claimed to be that night. And we do need to know for certain."

"You've found out quite a lot today," Betsy said in admiration.

"More than you know, my dear," Mrs. Jeffries replied. She then went on to tell them about her meeting with Inspector Witherspoon in front of the Hodges home. She told them about Miss Marsden's disappearance and about both the girl and Leonard Hodges being the sole beneficiaries to Abigail Hodges's will.

"Then it's got to be Miss Marsden that done it," Mrs. Goodge said. "She were the one that buried that gun, she's the one that's gettin' the money and she's the one that's disappeared."

"Mr. Hodges inherits half the estate," Mrs. Jeffries reminded them. "And with Abigail Hodges gone, Thomasina Trotter will learn the whereabouts of the child she gave up and Jonathan Felcher will gain control of his own property. So Miss Marsden isn't the only one with a motive."

"My money's on Thomasina Trotter," Luty declared. "I think that findin' out about that letter finally pushed her mind too far. She decided she didn't want to wait anymore, so she killed the old girl."

"I reckon it were that Mr. Felcher," Mrs. Goodge said.

"Drinkin' and gamblin', they always lead to trouble. Besides, makin' it look like a robbery is the kind of silly theatrics a man would come up with. Women's got more sense."

"Truth is," Smythe added, "we don't know who done it. Mr. Hodges has got just as much motive as the rest of them."

"But he's a nice man," Betsy protested. "I'm sure he's not the killer. Why, today he took a bundle of clothes over to St. James Church to give to the vicar. They was newish things too, a good coat and hat that look like they'd never been worn. I know 'cause I followed him. Besides, 'e's the only one who couldn't have done it—he's the only one with an alibi."

"I thought you were going to make contact with someone from the Popejoy household," Mrs. Jeffries asked Betsy.

"Oh, I did," she replied. "But after I finished, I thought I'd nip over to the Hodges house and see if I could find out anythin'. Mr. Hodges was comin' out the front door when I got there, so I followed him. Didn't have much else to do, the only thing I heard over at the Popejoy house was that some old admirer of Mrs. Popejoy's was pesterin' her again. But I reckoned that didn't have nothin' to do with the murder. Mrs. Popejoy stopped seein' this Mr. Phipps months ago." Betsy shrugged and laughed. "From what Peter tells me, Mrs. Popejoy's a bit of a flirt, always has been. She kept this poor Mr. Phipps dancin' to her tune for months before she got tired of him."

"We know it weren't her," Mrs. Goodge said impatiently. "What I want to know is how come this Mr. Felcher's up and leavin' the country all of a sudden."

" 'Cause his aunt's dead, that's why," Luty said tartly. "I think one of us ought to keep watch on Mrs. Trotter. No tellin' what she'll do next."

They all began arguing for their various candidates in the role of murderer. Hoping the free flow of ideas would spark something in her own mind, Mrs. Jeffries didn't interrupt. She listened. But after a few moments she realized they were doing nothing but going over every detail they'd already learned. She glanced up at the window and noticed that night was falling even though it was barely five o'clock.

"I say," Mrs. Jeffries said loudly, "did Wiggins happen to mention precisely what he would be doing this afternoon?"

"I can't think what's keepin' the boy," Mrs. Goodge said, "but I'll save him a bit of cake. He'll be hungry when he gets home."

"I'd hoped he'd be here by now," Mrs. Jeffries murmured. "For you see, there's something else we must do and we must do it quickly. We've got to locate Felicity Marsden before the police do."

"Why?" Betsy asked.

"Because I don't think she's guilty. If the police find her and Mr. Vogel, they'll arrest them. You've all forgotten one of the most important clues in this investigation. The note. Someone wrote that note to Constable Griffith ordering him to search the Hodges home. That someone is probably the person who planned and executed the plot to murder Mrs. Hodges."

"How can we find the girl?" Mrs. Goodge asked cautiously.

"Come now, Mrs. Goodge," Mrs. Jeffries said. "With your sources of information, you can probably find anyone in London. But for the rest of us, we'll have to rely on our feet and our good sense."

"You mean you want us to wander the streets searchin' for the lass?"

Smythe asked. He looked horrified. "But we don't even know what she looks like."

"Besides, if the girl's got any sense, she's long gone by now. What if she's left the city?" Luty added.

"It'll take days," Betsy complained.

"Of course it won't," Mrs. Jeffries declared. "You're all forgetting yourselves. You're all forgetting just how good you are once you set your mind to a task. Betsy, you can easily keep an eye on Miss Plimpton. She's a friend of Miss Marsden's. She actually lied to protect her, so it's safe to assume that if Miss Marsden is in difficulties, she might try to contact Miss Plimpton. Smythe, you can talk to the liveries and cabbies around the area. Someone must have picked up Miss Marsden and Mr. Vogel. Remember, they were in a hurry. They wouldn't have hung about the neighborhood waiting for a tram or an omnibus. Luty, you've acquaintances all over the city, many of whom travel in the same social circles as Miss Marsden. You can ask about and see if anyone's spotted her."

There was a general murmur of agreement around the table. Mrs. Jeffries leaned back and smiled. "Good, then it's all settled. Our first priority is to find Felicity Marsden."

"You don't have to do that," Wiggins's voice piped in. Everyone turned and looked. Wiggins and a tail-wagging Fred were standing in the doorway.

"It's about time the two of you come home," Mrs. Goodge said. She stood up and headed for the cooling pantry. "Poor Fred hasn't had a bite to eat all day."

"What about me, then?" Wiggins exclaimed. "I haven't 'ad me tea, either."

Mrs. Goodge returned with a plateful of scraps, and Fred, who'd been butting his head against Betsy's knees, deserted her instantly.

"Sit down and have something," Mrs. Jeffries told the boy. "And then tell us what on earth you meant by that provocative statement."

Wiggins poured himself a mug of tea and cut a huge slice of cake. "Huh?" He stuffed a huge bite into his mouth.

"She means what did you mean when you said we didn't have to do that," Betsy explained. "What were you on about?"

"Felicity Marsden." While they all waited he picked up his mug and downed a mouthful of the strong brew. "You don't have to go huntin' for her."

"Oh dear," Mrs. Jeffries said, "does that mean the police have found her?" She thought perhaps Wiggins had run into the inspector.

Wiggins started to reach for his fork, but Luty snatched it out from under his fingers. "Boy," she said tartly, "some of us ain't as young as you are. I'd sure as shootin' like to know what you was talkin' about before I die of old age."

"I'm trying to tell you I've found Felicity Marsden." Wiggins grinned triumphantly. "You'll never guess where she is. Me and Fred were ever so clever. I told you I'd find out she weren't guilty. I just knew a pretty lass like her couldn't have done such a terrible thing."

As the footman rambled on, Luty rolled her eyes, Mrs. Goodge sighed, Smythe scowled and even Hatchet pursed his lips together.

Wiggins's cocky grin faded as he stared at the faces surrounding him. "She's staying at Jonathan Felcher's lodging house," he blurted. "And so is Mr. Vogel."

CHAPTER 9

"How on earth did you manage to find out where Felicity Marsden went?" Luty exclaimed. "We only jes' found out she'd flown the coop."

"I followed the lass," Wiggins announced. "Fred and me was walkin' in the road 'round the corner, tryin' to suss out who to talk to next. All of a sudden this gate opens and Miss Marsden comes flyin' out like the 'ounds from 'ell was on her 'eels. I could see she had a carpetbag with 'er, so I figured she weren't doing her shoppin'. As soon as she walks past, me and Fred were right behind 'er."

"Did she see you?" Smythe asked.

Wiggins shook his head. "No, the lass were in such a state she wouldn't 'ave noticed a bloomin' elephant doggin' her footsteps. She were right upset. White as a sheet she was, movin' so fast she kept trippin' over her own feet. Why she almost ran in front of an omnibus. I trailed her to a lodgin' 'ouse and then she and this bloke come out. There was a boy sweepin' in front of the 'ouse next door, so I asked the lad who the bloke was. He told me it were Benjamin Vogel. So naturally I took off after the two of 'em."

"You've done very well, Wiggins," Mrs. Jeffries said. "Knowing Miss Marsden's whereabouts will certainly make our investigation easier."

"What are we going to do, then?" Betsy asked eagerly.

"Tomorrow morning we're going to confront Miss Marsden and Mr. Vogel." Mrs. Jeffries stated firmly, "and then we're going to get to the bottom of this case once and for all."

"Tatty-lookin' place, isn't it?" Wiggins clucked his tongue. "Imagine a lady like Miss Marsden hidin' out in a miserable hole like this."

"Perhaps it's cleaner on the inside than on the outside," Mrs. Jeffries said doubtfully.

"I wouldn't bet on it," Smythe muttered.

They stood on the pavement outside Mrs. Blodgett's lodging house and eyed the place warily. The building had once been white, but was now a uniformly dirty, dingy gray, matching perfectly the leaden dull skies overhead. The walkway leading to the porch was broken and uneven, the windows were dirty and there was black peeling paint on the doors and ledges. A gang of noisy boys ran back and forth across the road, chasing a ball, and in the house next door to Mrs. Blodgett's a slovenly man with red, watery eyes watched them apathetically.

"How very sad this place is," Mrs. Jeffries said as she led the way to the house. She pursed her lips, knowing this neighborhood was actually far better than many areas of London. At least here the children didn't look as though they were starving, the windows weren't broken and the road wasn't littered with garbage and trash.

Gingerly she banged the green-scaled brass knocker and then waited. A few moments later the door was opened by a stocky, dark-haired young woman who stared at them with a blank, incurious expression on her face.

Mrs. Jeffries was grateful that Elspeth Blodgett hadn't answered the door. She smiled at the girl and said, "Good morning."

The girl bobbed a brief curtsy and nodded.

"We'd like to see"—she hesitated for a moment—"the young couple who arrived yesterday." She was fairly certain Vogel hadn't given his real name when renting the lodgings.

The maid frowned in confusion.

Mrs. Jeffries held up her hand and pointed to her wedding ring. "Yesterday," she said slowly, "the new lodgers. A man and woman."

"Ah." A smile crossed the girl's face, transforming her blank features and making her rather pretty. "The Mr. and Mrs. Brown. They come. *Da, da.*" She opened the door and pointed to a narrow, dark staircase. "Room is at the high of the stairs."

"Huh?" Wiggins whispered. "What'd she say?"

"She means the top of the stairs," Smythe explained. He darted ahead of Mrs. Jeffries. "Let me go first, these stairs don't look all that safe."

The stairs didn't sound particularly safe either. The banister was rickety and covered in a layer of dust. And the stairs creaked and groaned as the three of them made their way to the top-floor landing.

"Why would someone like Miss Marsden want to come to a place like this?" Wiggins asked again, shaking his head in disgust.

" 'Cause it's the kind of 'ouse where no one asks any questions as long as you can pay the price of a room," Smythe replied. He looked at Mrs. Jeffries. "You want me to knock?"

She nodded and the coachman rapped lightly against the thin wood.

The door opened a crack. "Yes, who is it?"

Smythe wedged the toe of his boot into the crack. Mrs. Jeffries summoned her most charming smile. "Mr. Vogel, my name is Hepzibah Jeffries and I must speak with you."

"You've got the wrong man, the name's Brown. I've never heard of this Mr. Vogel. Go away and don't bother us."

He tried to close the door but couldn't. "Now see here," he sputtered angrily, glaring at Smythe's toe.

"Listen, Mr. Vogel," Mrs. Jeffries said quickly. "If you don't speak to me, you'll find yourself under arrest. If I could find you so quickly, then the police can't be far behind."

Slowly the door opened, revealing a grim-faced young man and an equally worried-looking young woman standing behind him.

"Who are you?" Benjamin Vogel said flatly. "A blackmailer? How much will it take to buy your silence? Be warned, though, we've not much money."

"I'm afraid you don't understand, Mr. Vogel," Mrs. Jeffries said. "I'm not here to blackmail you, I'm here to help you."

"Why should you want to help me?" Vogel said suspiciously. "I'm nothing to you."

Mrs. Jeffries decided to take a firmer line. Standing out on the landing trying to convince this young man she was solely interested in justice was simply taking too much time. "That's correct, I don't know you from Adam. However, I do know that the gun used to kill Abigail Hodges is buried in St. John's churchyard, the stolen jewels were found in Miss Marsden's room at the Hodges house and that neither you nor Miss Marsden has an alibi worth two shillings."

Vogel's jaw dropped and the color drained from his cheeks.

"Now," she continued firmly, "if you'll let me and my friends inside, perhaps we can help you extricate yourselves from this terrible mess."

Silently Vogel opened the door wider.

Mrs. Jeffries, with Smythe and Wiggins right behind her, rushed into the room. "As I've told you, my name is Mrs. Jeffries and this is Smythe and Wiggins."

"I still don't understand why you should want to help us?" Vogel put his arm protectively around the woman.

"Because if I don't, you're going to be arrested for murder, a murder I'm not all that certain that you or Miss Marsden had anything to do with."

Felicity stepped forward. "How do you know who I am? I've never seen you before."

"But I've seen you," Mrs. Jeffries replied. "Now, we don't have much time. I suggest you answer my questions as quickly and completely as you can."

Felicity Marsden looked at Benjamin Vogel and he nodded slightly. "Would you like to sit down?" he asked. He grimaced as his glance took in the shoddy, scratched table and chairs and the lumpy settee that made up the furniture. "It's fairly dirty, but Fliss and I managed to spend the night here without having to fend off anything worse than the cold and damp."

Mrs. Jeffries shook her head. "No, thank you. First of all, I must know where the two of you were on the night Abigail Hodges was murdered. The police already know that neither of you have alibis."

"We were together," Felicity Marsden replied. She lifted her chin defiantly. "And I'll tell the whole world if it's necessary. I don't care what anyone thinks of us or our morals. We were together and no one can prove otherwise."

"Be careful, Fliss," Vogel said gently. "You're making it sound as though we were doing something wrong. But we weren't." He looked at Mrs. Jeffries and said, "It's not what you think. We weren't doing anything improper. Fliss and I arranged to meet at the theatre, then we spent the next two hours walking about, just talking. That's the only way we've managed to see each other since Abigail started interfering in our lives."

"So you've been seeing each other all along," Mrs. Jeffries said, confirming what she already knew. "And breaking off your engagement was merely a pretense. Is that correct?"

Vogel dropped his gaze. "Yes. We had no choice. Abigail didn't think I was good enough for her niece. She tried buying me off, and when that didn't work, she told Fliss a packet of lies."

"I never believed her," Felicity declared. "Never, not for one moment."

Mrs. Jeffries studied the girl shrewdly. "But you pretended you did, didn't you?"

"There was no choice." Felicity shrugged her shoulders. "I knew what Abigail was capable of. I knew how very ruthless she could be."

"Excuse me," Smythe interrupted, "beggin' your pardon, miss, but you're of age. Why didn't you just tell Abigail to sod off and marry Mr. Vogel. Why sneak about?"

The two lovers exchanged glances. Then Vogel cleared his throat. "We were trying to wait her out. My company has agreed to send me to Canada. It's a promotion." He smiled proudly. "But that's not going to happen till next month. I was going to go on to Toronto and Fliss was going to make arrangements to join me there as soon as possible."

"But short of tossin' Miss Marsden out on 'er ear," Wiggins asked, "what could Mrs. Hodges 'ave done to you if she knew you was still seein' each other?"

Vogel laughed bitterly. "She could have ruined our entire future. My new position will ensure Fliss and I can marry. I'll easily be able to support a wife once I'm in Toronto. But if Abigail had known we were still seeing each other, she'd have gotten me sacked. She was a rich, powerful woman. I work for Tellcher's, they're a rather conservative merchant bank. If she'd had any idea I was still engaged to Fliss, she'd have been 'round there like a shot. One word from Abigail Hodges would have been enough to have me tossed in the street with no references and no prospects."

"But instead Mrs. Hodges is dead, you've still got your employment and Miss Marsden stands to inherit a great deal of money," Mrs. Jeffries said thoughtfully.

"But we didn't have anything to do with her murder," Felicity cried.

"Perhaps," Mrs. Jeffries replied. "But you can't deny that you both had good reason to wish Abigail Hodges was out of the way."

Felicity waved her hand impatiently. "Of course we did, she made our lives miserable. We had to sneak around like two children hiding from their nanny. Wouldn't you loathe having to behave in such an undignified fashion? But we didn't kill her. The night Abigail was murdered we were walking around trying to keep warm. It was a horrid night out, cold and damp and foggy. And that wasn't the first time we'd had to spend what few hours we had together on a public street." She closed her eyes briefly and shuddered. "But I didn't mind that part of it so much. I could easily put up with the cold and the wind and the rain. What I hated was the constant worry that someone, some friend of Abigail's, would see us."

"Well, if you've been sneakin' around for two months without gettin' caught, you've been pretty lucky," Wiggins said cheerfully.

"Lucky!" Felicity Marsden snapped. "We weren't in the least bit lucky. We were almost discovered several times." She turned to her fiancé. "Remember when we saw Mrs. Popejoy? That was a close call. She'd have gone running to Abigail like a shot."

"Mrs. Popejoy," Mrs. Jeffries interrupted quickly. "What about her? Did she happen to see you that night?"

"Not that night, but one other time we were together. It was a fortnight or so ago." Felicity laughed nervously. "And it wasn't just Mrs. Popejoy we almost ran into either. We thought Uncle Leonard was with the woman. That would have been utterly disastrous. Leonard wouldn't have kept silent. He knows what side his bread is buttered on."

"Now, Fliss, don't upset yourself," Vogel said gently. "Everything turned out all right in the end. Mrs. Popejoy didn't see us and the man she was with wasn't your uncle. In the dark and the fog, you just thought he looked like Leonard."

"I know," Fliss replied. "But it was still a very close thing. When I think of how Aunt Abigail could have ruined—would have ruined you without a second thought, it makes my blood run cold."

"If I was you, Miss Marsden," Smythe said, "I'd keep them feelin's to myself when the police start talkin' to you."

"The police! Why should I talk to the police? We're innocent." Felicity began wringing her hands together. "As much as I loathed my aunt's interference in my life, I wouldn't have killed her and neither would Benjamin."

"Then why did you run?" Mrs. Jeffries asked.

"I was scared. First I found that wretched gun and then last night Uncle Leonard told me that Abigail's jewels had been found in my room. Today, when the maid told me that the police were downstairs waiting for me, I couldn't think of what to do, so I tossed a few things in my bag and slipped out the back door. I went straight to Benjamin's."

"Who, luckily for you, hadn't gone in to work today," Mrs. Jeffries said, turning her attention to Mr. Vogel. "Could you tell me why you didn't go in this morning, please?"

Vogel shifted uneasily. "I sent a note there, telling them I was ill and that I wouldn't be in for a few days." He jerked his chin up defiantly. "Well, why shouldn't I take some time off? I've an excellent record, and after I saw my gun had been taken, I decided perhaps it would be best to . . . to . . ."

"Be prepared to make a run for it?" Mrs. Jeffries finished for him. She felt a wave of sympathy for them, but she had to make sure their flight hadn't been prearranged. "Now, Miss Marsden. Can you tell me where exactly in the house you found the gun, and more importantly, why you didn't give it to the police right away?"

"I found it in my drawer yesterday morning. As soon as I saw it, I knew I couldn't give it to the police. It was Benjamin's." She swallowed painfully. "Even worse, the gun had been fired recently. The barrel still smelled of powder. But as God is my witness, I've no idea how it got into my drawer. I was terrified. All I could think of was getting rid of the obscene thing."

" 'Ow come you buried it in a bloomin' churchyard?" Smythe asked. "If I was goin' to get rid of a gun, I'd throw it into the Thames."

Felicity gave Vogel a shamefaced glance. "Because it was Benjamin's and I knew he wanted to have it with him when he travels. He couldn't afford to buy another one—and he's going to Canada soon. I didn't dare hide the gun in the house or bury it in the garden. Then I remembered Abigail and Leonard had gone to a funeral at St. John's just last week. I knew the earth would still be soft enough to dig in, so I took the gun and buried it there." She paused and gazed at Mrs. Jeffries curiously. "How did you find out where the gun was?"

"You were followed, Miss Marsden," Mrs. Jeffries replied honestly. "But what makes you so certain Mr. Vogel's gun is the one that was used to murder your aunt? Are you familiar with weapons—are you absolutely positive it had been fired recently?"

"Yes, I am," Felicity declared. "My father taught me how to handle guns when I was a girl. He hunted. And also I'm sure that whoever really did the killing is trying to make it look as though Benjamin and I were responsible. I began to suspect yesterday that someone wants us to take the blame. Benjamin sent me a note telling me his gun had gone missing. Then when the jewels were found in my room, I knew for certain."

"Mr. Vogel," Mrs. Jeffries said, "assuming it was your gun that murdered Mrs. Hodges, how do you explain someone being able to steal it from your room?"

Vogel stroked his chin. "I think it was stolen on one of those nights that Fliss and I were out together."

"You leave your rooms unlocked then?" Smythe asked.

"No, of course not. But half the time my landlady is drunk and the lock on my door is so flimsy a child could open it," Vogel replied earnestly.

"I suppose it's possible," Mrs. Jeffries murmured. She wasn't sure she believed him, but then again, she wasn't sure she didn't either. "Were you planning on giving up your employment? Surely you realize that the police will be around there fairly quickly."

Vogel shrugged. "Losing my job is better than hanging, Mrs. Jeffries.

You see, the police already knew my gun was gone. Once Fliss told me about the jewels being found in her room, I knew we had to get away. I don't know who was responsible for killing Abigail Hodges, but I do know that whoever it was is planning on making sure that Felicity and I take the blame."

"That certainly appears to be the case," Mrs. Jeffries said. "However, it may not come to that. Miss Marsden, who else had a reason to want your aunt dead?"

"Well, Jonathan, my cousin, wasn't overly fond of her. She's had control of his inheritance for years now." Felicity tilted her head and looked sadly around the room. "Abigail's kept him on a pittance of an allowance, otherwise he wouldn't be living in a hovel like this lodging house. She was always trying to get him to move into her house. She liked controlling people. But he refused, preferring instead to eke out a living working for that shipping company and living in a place like this."

Mrs. Jeffries was curious. "Why did you and Mr. Vogel come here? Was it because of your cousin? Were you hoping he'd help you?"

"We came here," Vogel replied, "because we knew Jonathan's landlady wouldn't ask any questions. We were afraid to go to a hotel. We thought that would be the first place the police would start looking. We didn't come here to involve Felicity's cousin in our trouble."

"Besides, Jonathan's gone." Felicity smiled grimly. "He's gone to Leicestershire to take care of some business. It appears as though he'll have the last laugh after all, now that he's gained control of his inheritance. I don't think he's even planning on staying for Abigail's funeral or the reading of the will. He told me he's sailing next week for America."

" 'Ow come everybody leaves this country?" Wiggins asked.

Much as Mrs. Jeffries would have liked to stop and give the footman a short, concise lesson on surplus population, improved opportunities for advancement and a pioneering spirit, she refrained. This was hardly the time or place.

"His property is in America," Vogel explained, taking Wiggins's question seriously.

"Exactly 'ow much money does Mr. Felcher get control over now that Mrs. 'odges is gone?" Smythe asked.

"I'm not certain of the exact amount," Felicity replied, "but I think it's close to fifty thousand pounds."

"Cor, that's a lot of money." Smythe glanced at Mrs. Jeffries. "Lots would kill to get their 'ands on that amount."

Felicity shook her head impatiently. "Jonathan's no more capable of murder than I am. I know he drank a little and perhaps gambled more than he should, but he's no murderer."

Mrs. Jeffries heard the shuffle of footsteps on the stairs. She held her breath, hoping it wasn't Inspector Witherspoon. Everyone else heard the noise too, for the room fell silent until the steps faded down the corridor.

Sighing with relief, Mrs. Jeffries decided to hurry matters along. Time was getting on. "Is there anyone else connected with Mrs. Hodges who might have reason to wish her dead?"

"Mrs. Trotter wasn't overly fond of my aunt," Felicity admitted. "I think the woman's half-mad, I don't know why Abigail kept her on or why Mrs. Trotter stayed. They quarreled quite frequently. And Leonard wasn't the best of husbands. I can't prove it, of course, but I suspect that he only married my aunt for her money."

"Careful, my love," Vogel said softly. "People may one day say the same of me."

"That's ridiculous," Felicity declared.

"Why do you think that Mr. Hodges wasn't in love with his wife?" Mrs. Jeffries didn't think this was a particularly fruitful line of inquiry, but she might as well listen.

"Oh, he acted devoted to Abigail whenever they were together. But I used to watch his face when he thought I wasn't looking." She shivered delicately. "Sometimes he stared at her as though he hated her and it was so awful. She was besotted with him."

"How long had they been married?"

"Let me see, not all that long. About eighteen months. Yes, that's right. They were married in July of eighty-five. Abigail was determined they wed, even though it was barely a year to the day from his first wife's death. She even married him against the advice of her solicitors."

"Goodness, Mr. Hodges seems a respectable enough man," Mrs. Jeffries commented. "Why would Mrs. Hodges's solicitors object to him?"

Felicity smiled wryly. "They weren't keen on his background. Leonard hadn't much money of his own. His investments weren't doing all that well. He had only a small income from some property up north. But I gather it wasn't doing all that well—there were only some tenement flats, a shop or two and a theatre, I believe. But it didn't bring in much, all of the property was in the very poorest section of Leeds. And there was something to do with Leonard's first wife. She died under very mysterious circumstances. Drowned, I believe, in a boating accident in the Lake District. I can't remember all the details, but Mr. Drummond, that's Abigail's solicitor, claimed that Leonard's former father-in-law, a man named

Harry Throgmorton, had tried to get the police to bring a case against Leonard after she died."

"What'd 'e do?" Wiggins asked eagerly. "Push 'er over the side?"

"No. Leonard wasn't there when the accident happened. He was miles away, but you know how people are, there was some ugly gossip." Felicity frowned. "I'm sorry. I simply can't remember any more details. But I do know that Abigail instructed Mr. Drummond to threaten Mr. Throgmorton with legal action if he said another word about Leonard."

Mrs. Jeffries was very disappointed. "Well, if you do remember any more details, please let me know at once." She reached into her cloak and drew out a scrap of paper. "If you think of anything, anything at all that's pertinent to your late aunt, please send word to this address."

"You mean, you want us to stay here?" Vogel asked in disbelief.

"Yes, I believe that by the time the police get 'round to looking for you here, we'll have found out who the real killer is."

As they'd arranged earlier, they met Hatchet at an ABC Tea Shop. The butler, looking extremely dapper in a formal old-fashioned morning coat and top hat, met them at the entrance and ushered them inside to a waiting table.

"I've taken the liberty of ordering tea, madam," he announced to Mrs. Jeffries. "And of course"—he glanced at Wiggins and Smythe—"an assortment of buns and cakes."

"Thank you, Hatchet," Mrs. Jeffries replied. "That was most thoughtful. May I ask if your inquiries were successful this morning?"

Hatchet grinned. "Extremely, madam. So successful that I and my associate had to duck behind a letter box to avoid meeting the landlady of the establishment from which you've just come."

"In other words," Smythe said, "Mrs. Blodgett almost caught you."

"Precisely. However, as you'd clearly surmised earlier, Mrs. Blodgett left to do her shopping early, and after your good selves had gone inside in pursuit of your own inquiries, my associate and I were able to make the acquaintance of Miss Kuznetzov."

"Excellent, Hatchet." Mrs. Jeffries smiled in delight. "You seem to have developed a real talent for this sort of thing."

Hatchet acknowledged the compliment with a dignified nod. "I'm glad you think so, but one isn't sure one really wants to develop this particular skill. Questioning the lower classes and immigrants from the less enlightened nations isn't something one would care to do on a daily basis.

Especially this young woman. Miss Kuznetzov has a very suspicious nature."

She reached over and patted his arm. "I'm sure it was most difficult."

"That it was, madam, but we managed." Hatchet coughed delicately. "After my friend—speaking in Miss Kuznetzov's native tongue, of course—had convinced her we weren't from Her Majesty's secret police—"

"The what!" Smythe exclaimed. He looked truly shocked.

"The secret police," Mrs. Jeffries explained quickly. "An institution which is common in other parts of the world. Especially that part which is ruled by the Czar of Russia."

"Quite, madam," Hatchet said. "Now, if I may continue. After we'd convinced the young lady that no such institution existed in this nation—"

"I should bloomin well 'ope not," Smythe put in.

Hatchet ignored him. "We, of course, being a free people. She was very cooperative in answering our questions. She told us that Mr. Jonathan Felcher had, indeed, been gone the night Mrs. Hodges was murdered. She hadn't meant to mislead our police, of course. But Miss Kuznetzov's English isn't very good. She said that whenever one was dealing with a uniformed official, she'd learned to agree to whatever they said. The truth is, the poor girl didn't have a clue what she was being asked. She simply kept hearing Mr. Felcher's name, and not wanting to get him into any sort of difficulties, she kept nodding in the affirmative whenever the police asked her a question."

"Cor, you mean she just kept sayin' yes because she were scared to say no?" Smythe looked really disgusted now. "That's the daftest thing I ever 'eard."

Tempted as she was to take this opportunity to further educate Smythe, Wiggins and Hatchet on the evils of unrestricted monarchies and their attendant institutions, Mrs. Jeffries forced herself to stick to the matter at hand.

"Gracious. Then Mr. Felcher doesn't have an alibi for the night Mrs. Hodges was killed," Mrs. Jeffries said softly. "And neither does Thomasina Trotter, Felicity Marsden or Benjamin Vogel."

"But Miss Marsden and Mr. Vogel were together that night," Wiggins protested.

"That's what they've said," Mrs. Jeffries replied. "And they may very well be telling the truth."

"You think they might have done it, then?" Smythe asked.

"I don't know," she admitted honestly. "I'm tempted to believe their story, but I don't know for sure. Not yet at any rate."

Mrs. Jeffries was silent on the trip home. Smythe and Wiggins were still talking about the horrifying conditions one must find in places like Russia, but she'd deliberately stopped listening to them.

She closed her eyes and let her mind wander, trying for that free flow of concentration that seemed to come from nowhere, but that could actually serve to point her rational thoughts in the right direction.

Mrs. Trotter might be mad, but was she a murderess? Jonathan Felcher hated his aunt and now had control of fifty thousand pounds. But did the murderer steal Mr. Vogel's gun from his bedroom? And why go to such silly lengths to try to make the murder look as though Mrs. Hodges had interrupted a robbery and then bungle the job so badly? And who had written the note? Mrs. Jeffries sighed and picked up on the conversation.

"I wonder if you could get arrested for arguin' with a tram driver?" Wiggins said. "They wears uniforms. Or maybe a train conductor or even a vicar. Could you get nicked for arguin' with a vicar in Russia?"

"In Russia they're known as priests," she murmured. Vicars, priests, Mrs. Jeffries thought. Churches. Yes, of course. Why hadn't she considered it before? The footman's last words triggered something in the back of her mind. She sat bolt upright and stared straight ahead as the snippets of information and hard facts came together in her head and formed a true straight course.

As they descended from the omnibus near Holland Park, Mrs. Jeffries suddenly turned to Smythe. "I need you to do something and I need you to do it right away."

" 'Course, Mrs. J," Smythe said, looking concerned. "What is it?"

"That driver, the one who drove Mr. Hodges and Mrs. Popejoy to the train station, do you think you can find him again?"

"Yes, but it may take a bit o' time."

"We don't have time, Smythe," she said earnestly. "You must find him quickly."

"All right." The coachman shook his head doubtfully. "But he's already confirmed he took 'em to the station. I don't know what else 'e can tell us."

"Find out if the hansom stopped anywhere on the way. If it did, ask the driver to take you to that very spot." She reached into her cloak and pulled out some coins. "Give him a guinea if you must, but it's imperative that if they stopped, he must take you to the precise spot."

Puzzled, Smythe pocketed the coins and pulled his coat tighter against the suddenly chill wind. "All right, I'll be off then."

"Can you be back late this afternoon?" Mrs. Jeffries's voice stopped him.

He frowned and pulled out his pocket watch. "It's already gone eleven. But I'll do me best. Would three o'clock do you? There's a few lads that owe me a favor or two. Maybe I ought to get them to give me a 'and on this one. I reckon from the way you're actin' that it's important."

"Excellent." She turned to Wiggins. "And I want you to get over to Luty's. Tell her and Hatchet to come 'round to see us this afternoon at three. Tell her it's imperative she be there."

"You want me to go now?" Wiggins wailed. "But I 'aven't 'ad me lunch."

"Gracious, Wiggins, you've just had a huge tea. Three currant buns and two tea cakes should be enough to keep even someone of your prodigious appetite from starving to death."

He gave her a shamefaced smile. "All right, but while I'm gone, could you look in on Fred?"

"Yes, of course I will," she promised. Her brows drew together in concern. "The dog's not ill, I hope."

"'E's right as rain, Mrs. Jeffries. But 'e gets a bit lonely without me, you see, and I promised him I'd be back by noon."

CHAPTER 10

Mrs. Jeffries glanced at the clock. It was five past three and there was still no sign of Smythe. "Oh dear," she said apologetically, "perhaps Smythe was unable to accomplish his task."

"Give him a few more minutes, Hepzibah," Luty said. She absently reached down and patted Fred on the head.

"Madam," Hatchet said, "am I to understand that our presence here implies we won't be attending Mrs. Mettlesham's at-home? We're due there at precisely five o'clock. You accepted the invitation last week."

"Well, we'll jus' have to unaccept it, won't we?" Luty said impatiently. "I ain't budging from here until I find out what Hepzibah's got up her sleeve. Besides, them at-homes is nothing more than fancy tea parties fer a bunch of gossipin' biddies."

"Oh Luty," Mrs. Jeffries said, "I know I told you it was important that you be here, but I certainly didn't mean for you to cancel your engagement. Gracious, I'm afraid I've acted prematurely. Without Smythe's confirmation of a very important piece of information, I'm afraid—" She broke off at the sound of the backdoor opening.

" 'E's 'ere," Wiggins cried. He sprang to his feet and Fred, who probably thought it was time to go for a walk, leaped up as well.

"Sorry I'm late," Smythe said, reaching down to pet Fred, "but it took a bit o' time to track that driver down. I found 'im, though, and I did just like you said, Mrs. Jeffries. You was right, you know."

Mrs. Jeffries closed her eyes briefly in relief. This was the first real confirmation of what had been nothing more than a rather farfetched theory on her part. Yet if one looked at the matter rationally, it was the only sequence of events that made sense. "So the driver did make a stop that night."

"Yup, I 'ad the bloke take me to the exact spot too," Smythe explained. "That's what took us so long, you see. The driver 'ad a bit of trouble backtrackin' the route he took to the train station. It were so foggy that night the poor feller could barely see the backside of his 'orse."

"But he was able to find the place again?" Betsy asked anxiously.

The coachman grinned. "He remembered just fine once we were on our way." His smile faded and his expression sobered as he turned his attention to Mrs. Jeffries. "And he's prepared to swear to it in court too, if that's of any importance."

"It is, Smythe," Mrs. Jeffries replied fervently. "It's of the utmost importance. Now tell us all the details."

"Like I said, it were foggy that night and the driver was thinkin' of haulin' in and quittin' for the evenin' when he gets this fare from Mr. Hodges and Mrs. Popejoy. They get in the cab and direct 'im to take them to the railway station, but they hadn't been movin' for more than ten minutes before Mr. Hodges is shoutin' at him to go another way. Said he wanted to make a quick stop." Smythe made a wry face. "This didn't set too well with the driver, I can tell you that. He was right narked about it. But they was payin' good money, so 'e did as 'e was told. Mr. Hodges finally called for him to halt just as they were goin' down Lewis Road. Then Mr. Hodges and Mrs. Popejoy nips out of the hansom, tells the driver to wait and disappears into the fog. A few minutes later they was back. They climbed in and Mrs. Popejoy shouted for 'im to drive on."

"Let me make sure I've got this correct," Mrs. Jeffries said. "When they entered the hansom the second time, it was Mrs. Popejoy who spoke to the driver, not Mr. Hodges."

"That's what 'e said."

"Hmmm," she murmured softly as they all stared at her. "That certainly makes sense." Mrs. Jeffries gazed at Smythe. "Now tell me exactly what you saw when the driver took you to the spot he'd stopped at on the night of the murder."

"Just a minute, Hepzibah," Luty interjected. "I've got a question. How long did they stay stopped?"

"'Course the driver couldn't be too certain about that, 'e weren't lookin' at 'is watch. But as close as 'e can figure, it were about five minutes," Smythe replied.

"Five minutes isn't enough time for 'im to have nipped 'ome and done in 'is missus," Wiggins put in. "Not unless this Lewis Road is just around the corner from the Hodges 'ouse. Was it?"

"No, the road's a good distance away," Smythe admitted. He turned to

Mrs. Jeffries. "Despite the fog bein' thicker than clotted cream, once we was in the neighborhood, the driver remembered everythin'. He'd stopped in front of a pub, a place called the Red Lion. 'E pulled up right under the sign and waited. Now, next to this pub is a couple of shops—"

"What kind of shops?" Mrs. Jeffries asked quickly. She needed details.

"A Frieman's Butcher Shop and the Lewis Road Fishmongers. Across the road is Phipps Chemists, and next to that a small hotel called Billson's." He tilted his head to one side. "Funny, though, the name on the chemist's shop was right familiar to me. I know I've 'eard it before."

"It sounds familiar to me too," Mrs. Goodge muttered.

Smythe frowned. "I wish I could remember where I'd heard it before."

"I can," Mrs. Jeffries said. She stood up and pulled a small black purse out of the pocket of her dress. "But before I explain, you've all got pressing matters to attend to immediately, before the inspector gets home for dinner tonight. If my assumptions about this murder are correct—and after hearing Smythe's information, I'm sure they are—then we'll have this murder solved within the next twenty-four hours."

"Who done it then?" Luty asked eagerly.

"I'm sorry, I can't tell you, not just yet. I need a bit more evidence. And if everyone is successful with their tasks this evening, I'll know for sure." Mrs. Jeffries wasn't being coy, but before she accused anyone of murder, even here in the privacy of the kitchen, she wanted to make absolutely certain she was right.

Not giving those around the table time to do anything but look surprised, she began issuing instructions.

"Wiggins," she ordered briskly, "you've got to get to St. James Church. According to what Betsy told us, Mr. Hodges gave a bundle of clothes to the vicar to be distributed to the poor."

"What now?" Wiggins moaned. "Ahh. It's bad enough you won't tell us who the killer is, but if I nip all the way over to that church, I'll miss me supper."

"Stop yer moanin', boy," Luty said kindly. "If you're hungry, you kin chew on a bun as you go, but this here's more important than missin' a meal or two."

Wiggins blushed. "Sorry," he mumbled. "Guess you're right. Now, what do you want me to do, Mrs. Jeffries?"

She drew out a pound note and handed it to the footman. "It's imperative we get our hands on those clothes. If you have to, buy them." She glanced anxiously towards the window, frowning at the darkening sky, and then looked at Luty. "I hate to interfere with your plans for this afternoon. . . ."

"Don't worry about that, madam," Hatchet said cheerfully. "The plans are of no importance. Mrs. Crookshank and I are always delighted to be of service to the cause of justice. What do you want us to do?"

"That's mighty good of you, Hatchet," Luty muttered dryly. "But I thought you was frettin' over me missin' that tea party."

"Not at all, madam," he replied smoothly. "I was merely reminding you of the engagement. It's hardly my place to interfere in your decisions."

Luty snorted. "All right, Hepzibah, give us our orders and we'll get to it."

"I want you to contact Edmund Kessler," she said. "Betsy can give you his address. Supposedly that young man is well known in spiritualist circles. You must get him to arrange a séance at Mrs. Popejoy's for tomorrow night." She started to open the purse again.

"Don't bother reachin' fer any money," Luty commanded. "I'll take care of greasin' any palms that's needed to git that woman to see us."

"Really, Luty," Mrs. Jeffries said, feeling her cheeks turn pink. "That's not necessary. . . ."

"Don't be silly, Hepzibah, I've got more money than I'll ever spend—"

"That she does, madam," Hatchet interrupted, "that she does."

"Pipe down, man," Luty said, exasperated. "And I don't mind spendin' some of it to catch a killer. Besides, I owe you all."

Mrs. Jeffries gave in. She knew that Luty Belle Crookshank could be one stubborn woman. "Thank you, Luty."

"What if Kessler's full of hot air?" Smythe suggested, carefully avoiding Betsy's eye. "What if he can't make the arrangements? Didn't we 'ear that this Mrs. Popejoy don't just see anybody?"

"Edmund's not full of hot air," Betsy said defensively. "You just wait, he'll be able to fix it up."

Seeing another argument in the making, Mrs. Jeffries quickly intervened. "I'm sure that if Mr. Kessler fails us, Luty will be quite able to use her considerable connections to ensure Mrs. Popejoy is amenable to our plans."

"Yup, much as I hate to admit it, money can jus' about buy anything," Luty said.

"Will you be wantin' me to do anything?" Mrs. Goodge asked. She tried to sound unconcerned, but Mrs. Jeffries could hear the hopeful note in her voice.

"Of course I do," the housekeeper assured her. "But it might be very difficult."

"You just tell me what you need, I'll take care of it." The cook's ample bosom swelled with pride. "I've never run from difficulties in my life and I don't intend to start now."

"It's rather old gossip, I'm afraid," Mrs. Jeffries began. "But I'm confident that if anyone can dig up the information we need, you can. Find out exactly how long Mr. Hodges and Mrs. Popejoy have known each other, and most importantly, find out if Mrs. Popejoy was anywhere near the Lake District when the first Mrs. Hodges accidentally drowned."

"Hmmm," the cook mused, then her broad face broke into a wide grin. "It won't be easy, but it should be fun. I always did love a bit of a challenge. I'll get you somethin'. How much time have I got?"

"Not much, I'm afraid. If my plan's going to work, I'll need some answers by tomorrow, the earlier in the day, the better." Mrs. Jeffries turned her attention to Betsy. "I've a task for you, of course, but I'm not certain you can do it this evening."

"Why couldn't I do it now?" Betsy asked. "It's not gone four o'clock yet."

"Yes, but it's getting dark outside. Dreadful, these winter evenings, the night falls so early. I'm not sure it's safe for you to be out and about."

"Can I go with the lass?" Smythe asked. He carefully avoided looking at Betsy.

Mrs. Jeffries shook her head. "No, I'm afraid I need you for another task." She glanced uncertainly at the maid. "Oh dear, I really don't want you out alone. . . ."

"Come on, Mrs. Jeffries," Betsy pleaded. "I know how to take care of myself. I'll be very careful. If Smythe can't go with me, maybe we can get one of his cabbie friends to drive me. Where do you want me to go?"

Mrs. Jeffries thought about it for a moment. "That's a good idea. Now, I want your word of honor that if you aren't successful in getting the information we need by nine o'clock, you'll come right home. Furthermore, you're to use a hansom cab and not be walking about on the streets. Smythe can take you out when he leaves, and make sure he puts you in a cab with someone he trusts." Mrs. Jeffries then spent ten minutes giving Betsy her instructions.

As the housekeeper told the maid what she wanted her to do, Smythe's mouth flattened into a grim, disapproving line. "Hey, now. I don't rightly think the lass is up to all that," he objected, when Mrs. Jeffries had finished. "This feller might be in cahoots with the murderers."

"I quite agree, Smythe. He may well be," Mrs. Jeffries said kindly, "but if Betsy is driven there by your friend Jeremiah and he keeps her in sight the whole time, I do believe she'll be all right."

"I will, I promise," Betsy said. "And you've said yourself, Smythe, Jeremiah's a good bloke. He'll keep an eye on me."

"I don't see why I can't take her," Smythe insisted. He scowled at Mrs. Jeffries. "Whatever you've got in mind for me, can't it wait till later?"

"I'm afraid not," Mrs. Jeffries answered. "You need to leave right away. You'll be gone most of the night."

"Cor, all night?" Smythe's eyebrows drew together. "Where ya sendin' me? Scotland?"

"Not quite that far," she said kindly. She knew the coachman wasn't trying to shirk his duty. His objections to going out this evening were solely because he was worried about Betsy. Mrs. Jeffries understood his concern. She was worried herself, but she had to have more information. And Betsy was the best person available to obtain it. Smythe's special talents were needed for another purpose.

"Then where am I goin'?" he said impatiently.

"You're going to Southend."

"I say," Inspector Witherspoon said as he glanced around the dining room, "it's jolly quiet tonight. Where is everybody?"

Mrs. Jeffries laid a second pork chop on the inspector's plate and put it in front of him. "Mrs. Goodge is where she always is—the kitchen. I didn't think you'd mind, but I sent Betsy over to Mrs. Crookshank's for the evening. Everyone's got the flu and they needed an extra hand."

"Of course I don't mind," Witherspoon replied. "I was merely curious. It's not often the house is this quiet. I say, did you tell me this morning that we'd got a dog?"

"Yes, a stray. Wiggins found the poor thing in the street. He's out walking it now. Again"—she smiled brightly—"knowing how kindhearted you are and how much you love animals, I didn't think you'd object if we kept the animal. Dogs do help keep the rodents away."

"That's all right then. Have Wiggins bring the dog in when he gets back. I'd like to meet him. What's his name?"

"Fred," Mrs. Jeffries murmured. "Now, sir, how is the investigation going?"

"Not well." He sighed and began cutting his chop. "As I told you earlier, our chief suspects have disappeared."

"Miss Marsden and Mr. Vogel?" Mrs. Jeffries said innocently. She knew perfectly well who the suspects were, but she knew they were innocent. Now she had to concentrate on getting the inspector to learn the same thing. "You know, sir, this morning you told me about Mrs. Trotter."

"Yes, I remember. What about her?"

"Well, after you left, I heard the most extraordinary gossip about her. I wonder if it has any bearing on your case?"

Witherspoon's fork halted halfway to his mouth.

"You know how I abhor gossip, sir," Mrs. Jeffries continued quickly, "but I really felt it was my duty to listen, seeing as how you're investigating this terrible crime."

"By all means, Mrs. Jeffries," he said, hastily putting his fork down next to his plate. "Do tell."

"Supposedly Mrs. Trotter has been walking the streets of London looking for her daughter." She gave an embarrassed smile. "Twenty years ago Mrs. Trotter had an illegitimate child. Mrs. Hodges helped to adopt the child out. I've heard that Mrs. Trotter wanted the child back. But Mrs. Hodges refused to tell her where the girl was. She promised Mrs. Trotter that upon her death, she'd leave a letter naming the adoptive parents of the child."

Witherspoon looked shocked. "How very strange." He started eating again.

Mrs. Jeffries stared at him. "But, sir," she finally said, when he continued shoving peas in his mouth, "don't you see, that means Mrs. Trotter had a motive for Mrs. Hodges's death."

"Oh yes," the inspector replied. "No doubt Mrs. Trotter is a tad peculiar in her habits, but as it happens, we know she had nothing to do with the murder."

Now it was Mrs. Jeffries's turn to be surprised. "How do you know?"

"Because of her habit of walking the streets." He smiled knowingly. "She's known to many of our lads, you see. She was seen on the night of the murder by one of our constables. Mrs. Trotter was hanging about Waterloo Bridge for hours that night. She was seen getting into a hansom cab around eleven. Another constable saw her in the area near Mrs. Bush's house less than half an hour later, so whatever motive she may have had, however odd the woman is, she couldn't have committed the murder. She hadn't time."

"I see," Mrs. Jeffries commented. "Your constables have obviously been very busy." She knew perfectly well Thomasina Trotter wasn't the killer, but she had hoped to muddy the waters a bit and get the inspector's mind off Felicity Marsden and Benjamin Vogel.

"We do our best," he replied proudly. "I say, is there any pudding tonight?"

"There's a Royal Victoria."

"Ah, delightful. Her Majesty's favorite." He chuckled. "And mine too. Will you share some with me?"

"No, thank you, I've already eaten." Mrs. Jeffries decided to try a different approach. "You know, sir, I've been thinking about something you said. You once told me that appearances are often deceiving."

"Really? I said that?"

"Yes, sir. It was during those horrible Kensington High Street Murders. . . ."

The inspector shuddered. "Please, Mrs. Jeffries, not while I'm eating. That case was absolutely dreadful."

"I know, sir, but you solved it."

"Of course I solved it," he said, "but to be perfectly honest, I can't quite remember how."

"You did it by not being deceived by appearances, sir," she replied.

"You've a remarkable memory, Mrs. Jeffries."

"Not as good as yours, sir," she shot back quickly. "Well, I was thinking about something else you mentioned about the Hodges case, and naturally the two ideas began to flow into one in my mind."

He gazed at her quizzically. "I don't believe I understand what you're getting at. What specifically are you referring to about the Hodges murder?"

Mrs. Jeffries knew she had to tread carefully here. "Appearances, sir. That's what I'm getting at. Mr. Hodges and Mrs. Popejoy appear to have an alibi. . . ."

"But of course they do," he protested. "We double-checked with Mrs. Popejoy's friend. She saw them together at the train station."

"Yes, but did she really see them, or did she only think she saw Mr. Hodges? You've said it yourself, sir. Sometimes eyewitness evidence is the least reliable. Ten people will see the same incident, and if you ask them to describe what they saw, they'll each describe something different. And what about Mr. Felcher? Was he really in his rooms, or did he only make it look like he was there in order to fool his landlady into saying he was?" She spoke quickly, earnestly; she had to get the inspector to start looking beyond the obvious.

He frowned in confusion. "I'm not really sure I understand."

She forced herself to laugh. "Now, sir, you know very well what I'm doing. You're just up to your old tricks and teasing me a bit. Why I'm repeating your own advice to you and you're sitting there letting me go on and on."

Witherspoon laughed as well. But she could still see the uncertainty in his eyes. He really had no idea what she was getting at. "Perhaps I am, Mrs. Jeffries. Er, what do you think I'm going to do next?"

"That's an easy one." She smiled smugly. "You're going to do what you always do and double-check everyone's alibi. You're going to send some constables out to have a word with the hansom drivers in the area and see what else you can discover. You're going to continue searching for Miss Marsden and Mr. Vogel, and once you find them, you're going to ascertain if their flight was caused by panic or by guilt. And last but not least, you're going to confirm that Mr. Felcher really was in his rooms." She sat back and folded her hands in her lap. "You can't fool me, sir. I know how that brilliant brain of yours works. You've been planning on doing this all along."

The inspector didn't retire for the night until after 9:30. Mrs. Jeffries, who'd been keeping an eye on the clock, hurried down to the kitchen.

She was greatly relieved to see Betsy sitting safely next to Mrs. Goodge. "Thank goodness, you're back. Has Wiggins come back yet?"

"He come in a half hour ago, dropped that bundle of clothes on the floor," Mrs. Goodge replied, pointing to a paper-wrapped parcel lying by the dish cupboard, "and then he went up to bed."

"Good." Mrs. Jeffries walked over and picked up the parcel. She came back to the table, sat down and turned to Betsy. "Were you successful?"

"Everything went right as rain," Betsy announced. "I did just like you said. The shop was still open when I got there, so I went in and got a good look at him. Then I waited for him to come out. I saw him wearin' his hat and coat."

Mrs. Jeffries untied the string and pushed the brown paper aside. Standing up, she shook out a man's coat. "Now, think carefully," she instructed Betsy, "was the coat Mr. Phipps was wearing like this one?"

"That's it, all right." Betsy pointed to the slightly flattened bowler. "And he had on a hat like that one too. I also got friendly with a girl who works for Mr. Phipps. She's a right little chatterbox, too. Told me all sorts of things about Mr. Phipps."

" 'Ere, don't I get a turn?" Mrs. Goodge chimed in. "It's gettin' late and I've got to be up early if I'm going to have a word with the milkman."

"Let Mrs. Goodge go ahead," Betsy said magnanimously. "The rest of what I've found out isn't much more than gossip. It can wait a bit."

"Thank you," Mrs. Goodge said. "I found out a bit of what you wanted. I wasn't able to learn if Mrs. Popejoy was anywhere near the Lake District when the first Mrs. Hodges drowned, but I did find out that she and Mr. Hodges have known each other a lot longer than they let on."

"Peter was right, then," Betsy interjected.

Mrs. Goodge nodded. "He certainly was." She gazed at Mrs. Jeffries. "Remember when we heard that Madame Natalia claimed that Mrs. Popejoy weren't a real medium and had probably worked in the music halls?"

Mrs. Jeffries nodded.

"As luck would have it, my sister's husband's cousin works in one of them music halls, has for years. Knows everyone and everything that goes on. Well, I sent him a note as soon as we were finished this afternoon, and while you and the inspector was at dinner, Ernest—that's the cousin—he dropped 'round. He told me that Esme Popejoy used to work in a theatre in Leeds. A real ratty place, didn't do much business and had the worst acts you've ever seen. Mrs. Popejoy used to do a mind-readin' act. But you'll never guess who owned the theatre."

"Leonard Hodges?" Mrs. Jeffries replied.

"That's right. It were one of his investments." Mrs. Goodge smiled triumphantly. "Now can you tell us who the killer is?"

"Not yet, Mrs. Goodge," Mrs. Jeffries replied. "I really need to speak to Smythe before I make an accusation. Betsy, did Mr. Phipps remind you of anyone?" She wanted to make sure she didn't plant the suggestion in the girl's mind. If her theory was correct, there was only one person that Ashley Phipps could resemble.

Betsy hesitated. Mrs. Jeffries's heart plummeted to her toes. Oh dear, what if she was wrong?

"He didn't act like him much, Mr. Phipps is a right nervous, rabbity sort of feller, but from a distance he looks an awful lot like Leonard Hodges."

Mrs. Jeffries didn't get much sleep that night. She was absolutely sure she knew what had happened on the night of the murder, but she was having a difficult time thinking of a way to get Inspector Witherspoon to come to the same conclusion. She wasn't so terribly sure that sending Luty Belle to a séance at the Popejoy house was going to accomplish her goal.

By five o'clock, she decided that trying to sleep was pointless. She got up, lit a lamp and walked over to her desk. She might as well write everything out—perhaps putting pen to paper would help her tune the finer points of her plan.

Sitting down, she reached for her letter box. She reached in to get some paper when suddenly her fingers stilled. Of course, she thought, notes. Why, it would fit right in. It would work perfectly if the timing were right. And, of course, if Smythe confirmed the last bit of evidence she had to have.

Luty Belle and Hatchet arrived just after the inspector had left for the morning. Mrs. Jeffries hurried them into the kitchen. Smythe, Betsy, Mrs. Goodge, Wiggins and Fred were waiting.

Smythe gave them a bleary-eyed glance and then rubbed his hand across the stubble on his cheek. "Cor, it's been a long night. Let me say my piece so I can get a bit of sleep."

"By all means, Smythe," Mrs. Jeffries said quickly, "speak right up. You'll need a bit of rest. We're not through with this case yet and I fear I shall have you running about even more before today's over."

He yawned. "Right. I went to Southend, just like you told me. Miss Trainer's 'ouse is just down from a pub, so I tried there first. But I didn't have much luck, none of her servants was in that night and no one knew much about 'er. Spinster lady, keeps to 'erself mostly."

"Oh dear," Mrs. Jeffries said.

"Don't fret, Mrs. J. I didn't let that stop me." He suddenly grinned. "There's more than one pub in Southend. The third one I tried, I got lucky. There was a lad in there that does odd jobs for the lady. He knows all about 'er. Said she were a silly, nervous woman it'd be dead easy to fool. He also told me she's very shortsighted, but she won't wear her spectacles."

"Excellent, Smythe." Mrs. Jeffries turned to Luty. "Were you able to arrange things for tonight?"

"Edmund's goin' 'round to see Mrs. Popejoy this mornin'. I told him to fix it for seven o'clock." Luty cocked her head to one side. "Are you gonna tell us who done it?"

"In good time, madam," Hatchet interrupted, "in good time. We haven't heard what Miss Betsy has to say yet."

"Thank you, Hatchet," Mrs. Jeffries said. She smiled at Betsy. "I believe it's your turn now."

"Like I told Mrs. Jeffries and Mrs. Goodge last night, I saw this Ashley Phipps fellow," Betsy began. "And I also did a spot of diggin' about him.

He was gone on the night of the murder, and even better, he's been in love with Mrs. Esme Popejoy for ages."

"Mrs. Popejoy!" Mrs. Goodge snorted. "Well somehow, I'm not surprised. That one sounds like she's been around the park a few times."

"Do go on, Betsy," Mrs. Jeffries said.

"What? Oh yes, as I was sayin', about six months ago Mrs. Popejoy up and tells Mr. Phipps she don't want to see him no more," Betsy continued. "He were ever so upset. Went 'round with a long face for weeks, at least that's what Gertie—that's the girl who cleans for him—told me. Then, less than two weeks ago, he gets a note from Mrs. Popejoy saying she wants to see him. Cheered him right up, that did."

"Why don't you tell everyone who Mr. Phipps resembles," Mrs. Jeffries suggested.

Betsy smiled proudly. "Ashley Phipps looks very much like Leonard Hodges."

For a moment they all looked puzzled, then one by one, their expressions changed.

"So that's 'ow they did it," Smythe muttered.

"Clever, wasn't it," Betsy agreed.

"Diabolical, that's what it was," Mrs. Goodge muttered.

"Brilliant plan," Hatchet said, "but rather risky."

"I'll be danged," Luty exclaimed. "If that don't beat all."

"Huh?" Wiggins scratched his head.

"Now." Mrs. Jeffries reached into her pockets and drew out the notes she'd written earlier. "We've much to do today if we're going to bring this case to a successful conclusion."

"I don't understand," Wiggins wailed.

"I'll explain it to you later," Mrs. Jeffries said. "But for right now you must get busy." She handed him a note. "I want you to take this note to Phipps Chemists on Lewis Road. Don't let anyone see you, but make sure that Ashley Phipps himself reads it."

"But 'ow can I do that? What if 'e isn't there?" Wiggins asked.

"If he isn't there," Mrs. Jeffries said patiently, "then track him down. But it is imperative he receive that note and that he receive it today." She pulled another note out of her pocket and handed it to Betsy. "Take this one to Mr. Hodges, but make sure he doesn't receive it until six o'clock this evening. Do you understand?"

"I understand," Betsy replied, reaching for the paper and tucking it carefully into her pocket.

" 'Ow about me?" Smythe asked.

"Well," Mrs. Jeffries hesitated. "I know you're awfully tired. . . ."

He grinned. "I ain't that tired. What is it?"

She told him. Then she gave Luty and Hatchet some instructions. "Be sure and be there right at seven o'clock. Do whatever you must to get Mrs. Popejoy to start the séance on time."

"Do I get to go to this one?" Betsy asked hopefully.

"No, I'll need you with me," Mrs. Jeffries replied. "Besides, Peter might be there, and if he sees you, it could ruin everything. Mrs. Popejoy mustn't suspect."

She spent the next ten minutes going over the fine points of her plan and looking for flaws. The others picked at it, but couldn't pull it apart.

"Everything should work perfectly if nothing untoward or unexpected happens," she said.

"Something unexpected always happens," Luty warned. "That's the nature of life. But in this case, if everyone does like they're supposed to, them varmints that murdered Mrs. Hodges should be locked up before the day is out."

CHAPTER 11

"Come in. Sit down. Let Madame Natalia help you with your troubles." She smiled sympathetically and gestured towards a round table covered with a spotless white cloth. A crystal ball rested in the center of the table.

"Thanks, don't mind if I do." Luty plopped down in a chair and motioned for Mrs. Jeffries to do the same. "But we didn't come for no séance, not that I didn't enjoy it the last time I was here."

Mrs. Jeffries dragged her gaze from Madame Natalia's "study" and took the chair next to Luty. The room was most extraordinary. The blinds were drawn and the windows were covered in layers of pale mauve and blue gauzy fabric that seemed to float mysteriously of its own accord, for she couldn't feel a draft. In front of the fireplace was a painted octagonal screen etched with the golden script of some unknown language. Over the mantel, there was a huge black-and-silver drawing of the zodiac and at each end of the mantel stood a brass brazier wafting up delicate-scented smoke rings.

Mrs. Jeffries took a deep breath and inhaled the exotic scent of sandalwood. She blinked and fixed her gaze on the portrait of an ethereal young woman with long flowing hair. She blinked again, trying to force her eyes to adjust to the dimness. The only light in the room came from dozens of candles scattered about on the tops of tables and highboys. Then she turned to the medium.

Madame Natalia was staring at Luty. She was dressed in a full bright red skirt with a white sash around the waist. Her blouse was emerald green, high-necked and had wide, flouncy sleeves. On her head was a turban the same color as her skirt. Tiny black curls escaped from around the top and sides.

"If you are not here for a reading," Madame Natalia asked archly, "then I do not understand why you've come."

"Actually," Mrs. Jeffries replied, "we're here for a bit of professional advice."

"Advice?" Madame Natalia laughed. "But I do not give advice, Mrs. Jeffries. The spirits do. I'm merely the channel for the voice from the other side."

Mrs. Jeffries noticed that the more the woman spoke, the thicker and more exotic her accent became. "Yes, well, I'm sure you're probably quite good at being a channel, but we were thinking of engaging your services for a rather different matter."

"I do not perform parlor tricks," the medium replied haughtily.

"We wouldn't dream of asking you to do such a thing," Mrs. Jeffries assured the woman quickly. "However, you do have certain, er . . ."

"We want to know how you fake that Indian's voice," Luty stated bluntly.

Madame Natalia swelled with indignation. "I do not fake this voice. It is real, as real as you or I. How dare you, madam. How dare you insult me and the spirits."

"Now don't git on yer high horse. You put on a right good show for people," Luty retorted. She plonked her purse down on the table. "You do a danged good job. We wouldn't be here if you didn't."

"I don't know what you're talking about," Madame Natalia replied. But she seemed to have lost most of her righteous indignation and her eyes were locked on Luty's purse.

"Please, madam," Mrs. Jeffries said quickly. "We've the highest respect for your abilities and we really do need your help."

"Let's start talkin' turkey," Luty interrupted. "We know you ain't talkin' to the other side, whatever in tarnation that is, but we think you're right good at soundin' like Soarin' Eagle." She broke off and opened her purse. Taking out a wad of notes big enough to make Madame Natalia's eyes widen, she plonked them on the table right under the madame's nose. "Now, do we talk business or do I pick up my money and skedaddle?"

The medium hesitated briefly, reached over and snatched the bills. She tucked the money into her sash, grinned and extended her hand. "The real name's Nessie Spittlesham. The feller out front is my husband, Bert." She leaned forward on her elbows and pushed the crystal ball to one side. "Now, as you say, let's talk turkey. Exactly what do you ladies want?"

"Can you teach one of us to do what you do?" Mrs. Jeffries wasn't sure how to explain what she wanted. But if her plan were to be successful, she needed this woman's help. "With your voice, I mean. Luty says that when you're speaking as Soaring Eagle, it sounds very authentic."

" 'Course it sounds authentic," Nessie said proudly. "All my voices sound good. I've been workin' on them for years. Let me see if I've got this right. You want me to show one of you how to sound like Soaring Eagle?"

"Not Soaring Eagle," Luty said. "We want you to teach us how to sound like someone else, like someone from the other side, like a ghost."

Nessie regarded them thoughtfully. She didn't seem overly upset by the unusual request. "What kind of accent does your ghost have?" she asked.

"Upper-class English," Mrs. Jeffries replied promptly. "But actually, we'll need you to help us learn to do two separate voices. Oh yes, and we'll need to know how to do this by tonight."

"Two voices," Nessie yelped. "By tonight? That's bloody impossible." She jerked her chin towards Luty. "And with that flat twang of hers, it'd take me a bloomin' year to teach 'er to sound like a toff."

Luty snorted.

"Well, how about me?" Mrs. Jeffries asked. "Could you show me? It's dreadfully important, you see."

Nessie drummed her fingers on the tabletop. "How come you two want to learn something like this anyway? You thinkin' of goin' into the business? 'Cause if you are, I can tell you now, it's a bleedin' 'ard way to make a livin'."

Mrs. Jeffries studied the woman for a moment before answering. She decided to tell her the truth. "We've no wish to go into this professionally," she explained. "We only need this particular skill for one night. If you can't teach us, are you available for hire tonight?"

"Lord, Hepzibah," Luty exclaimed. "What are you doin'? We can't get her into the Popejoy house. What do you expect me to do, hide her in my muff?"

"Did you say Popejoy?" Nessie snapped.

"Don't be absurd, of course we can get her in," Mrs. Jeffries replied. "And yes, I did say Popejoy. You see, Nessie, we're trying to catch a murderer. To do that, we're going to need your help."

"Now, Constable," Inspector Witherspoon asked for the third time, "you did say this driver was prepared to testify in court?"

"Yes, sir," Barnes replied patiently. "The driver is fully prepared to testify to the truth. The cab stopped on the way to the train station that night. Mr. Hodges and Mrs. Popejoy both got out. But I don't see what good it's goin' to do us, they were only gone five minutes."

Witherspoon didn't see what good it was going to do either. But somehow he felt it was important. He sighed. His head ached, he'd missed his lunch, and despite having found the cab driver, he was still no closer to a resolution on this wretched case. On top of that it was starting to rain again.

"Excuse me, sir." A middle-aged constable stuck his head into the office. "But there's a Mr. Phipps to see you, sir."

"What about? I don't know any Mr. Phipps."

"He says he's got a note from you, sir. Says it's about the Hodges murder."

"A note! From me?" Witherspoon couldn't believe his ears. Egads, was there a whole army of people out there sending notes with his name on them? By golly, he was going to get to the bottom of this. "Send him in."

A moment later there were impatient footsteps in the hall and a man in a bowler hat and heavy topcoat stepped into the inspector's office.

"Why, it's Mr. Hodges, sir," Barnes began. "No, it's not. Beggin' your pardon, sir, but you look very much like another gentleman."

"My name is not Hodges," the man snapped as he advanced towards Witherspoon's desk. He had a high-pitched very feminine voice. "It's Phipps. Ashley Phipps. And I demand to know the meaning of this." He flung the note onto the inspector's desk.

Witherspoon opened the paper. He scowled as he read its contents. "Barnes, what do you make of this? 'Dear Sir,' " he read. " 'You are in possession of vital information concerning the murder of Mrs. Abigail Hodges on the night of January fourth. Kindly come into my office at the Ladbroke Grove Police Station to help us with our inquiries. Signed, Inspector Gerald Witherspoon.' "

"Did you write it, sir?" Barnes asked.

"Of course I didn't write it," the inspector replied.

"Then why does it have your name on it, Inspector?" Phipps said angrily. "And furthermore, I've no idea what this is all about. I've never even heard of this Abigail Hodges."

"You didn't read about the murder in the newspapers?" the inspector asked.

"No, I did not," Phipps retorted. "Are you claiming you know nothing about this note, sir?"

"I didn't send it, Mr. Phipps. I've no idea who did."

"If this is someone's idea of a joke," Phipps sputtered, "well, I must say it's in dreadfully bad taste. If you didn't write this, sir, then I take it I'm free to go?" He began edging towards the door.

"Just a minute, sir," Barnes said. "You don't, by any chance, happen to remember what you were doing on the night of the fourth, do you, sir?"

Phipps stopped. "As a matter of fact, I know precisely what I was doing. I was at home with my mother—we live just over my shop in Lewis Road." He faltered as he saw the inspector and Barnes exchange glances.

"I was there until half past nine," he continued. "Then I escorted a lady friend to the train station. Both ladies will be quite happy to confirm my whereabouts on the night in question, I'm sure."

"What's the name of your lady friend, sir?" Witherspoon asked. He held his breath.

"Mrs. Popejoy." Phipps smiled proudly. "Esme Popejoy. A lady who I hope will soon do me the honor of consenting to be my wife."

Betsy pounded on the door knocker and then scurried quickly into the shadows. She saw the door open and the maid appeared. Hilda Brown frowned and stepped outside. She glanced up and down the road.

Betsy held her breath as the girl shrugged her shoulders and turned to go back inside. Suddenly she stopped, knelt down and picked up the envelope that was lying at her feet.

Betsy let her breath out as the maid went back into the house.

It was exactly six o'clock.

Silently Betsy stepped out of the shadows and hurried down the road to the waiting carriage.

"Cor, it took you long enough," Smythe growled as he opened the door and helped her inside. He climbed in behind her.

"Well, I had to wait and make sure she saw it," she responded. "Mr. Hodges is due home soon. Let's hope she gives it to him right away. If this is goin' to work, he's got to make his move in the next hour."

"When you requested a private reading," Esme Popejoy said, glancing from Luty to Hatchet and then to their heavily veiled companion, "I assumed you meant you'd be alone."

Luty waved one diamond-bedecked hand negligently. "Does it make a difference whether there's one or two of us? I didn't think you'd mind, considerin' what I'm payin'." She gestured to her companion with her large fur muff. "This here's my sister, she ain't never been to one of these here séances. But if my bringin' her troubles you, I'll be glad to ante up with a little more cash."

"That won't be necessary," Mrs. Popejoy said. "Your sister's presence doesn't bother me, but then, I'm not the one who matters." She smiled and turned to the table in the center of the room. "It's Lady Lucia who occasionally gets temperamental. She doesn't like surprises. Please, come over and sit down."

"If it's all the same to you, madam," Hatchet said, edging quietly towards the window behind the table, "I'd prefer to stand over here, out of harm's way, so to speak."

Mrs. Popejoy raised one delicate eyebrow and cocked her head prettily to one side. Dressed in an elegant peacock-blue evening dress and matching velvet ribbons in her upswept auburn hair, she was the very picture of the lady of the manor.

"I'm afraid that's impossible," she stated firmly. "I don't allow anyone to stand away from the circle during my séances. It upsets the balance."

Hatchet tripped over a footstool and stumbled backward, catching himself on the window ledge.

"Are you all right?" Luty cried. She grinned at Mrs. Popejoy. "Clumsy feller, always trippin' over his own feet."

"I'm quite all right, madam," Hatchet replied tartly. He leaned against the window for a brief moment, his hand resting on the lock. "Just give me a minute to recover."

"If you'll be seated," Mrs. Popejoy prompted, "we'll get started."

As soon as the butler had sat down, she clapped her hands together and a maid appeared. The girl began turning off the lamps as Mrs. Popejoy lit one large white candle and pushed it into the center of the table.

From outside the window, three people crouched quietly in the bushes. Mrs. Jeffries and Betsy stood on one side and Smythe on the other. Keeping low, they all cocked their heads as close as they dared to the small opening. Luckily Hatchet had been able to get the French window cracked enough for them to hear some of what was going on in the room. If they were really lucky, Mrs. Jeffries decided as she stared at the narrow opening between the small panes of glass, an unwanted blast of wind wouldn't give them away.

"Please join hands and close your eyes," Mrs. Popejoy ordered. Save for the one flickering candle, the room was now in darkness.

Luty held her breath as she saw the candle flame twist and jump as though it were being chased by the wind, which, she knew, it was. Hatchet's little stumble had accomplished their goal. Now she only hoped that this daring plan would actually work. If it didn't, she was going to end up with a lot of explaining to do.

Luty extended her hands. Hatchet sat to her right and Nessie to her left. Then she waited for the séance to begin.

Mrs. Popejoy began to breathe deeply and evenly. Luty saw the flame jump again and she felt like spitting. The medium's chest began to move up and down as she took in long and large breaths of air. Suddenly a low, eerie keening sound issued from the woman's throat.

The keening turned into a moan and then a wail. "Darkness," the medium finally whispered, "darkness everywhere."

From Luty's left, there was a low groan.

Mrs. Popejoy didn't open her eyes, but her mouth moved. "Death, despair. I must tell you . . . I must warn you."

"Water," came a voice from out of nowhere. "Drowning. No, no, murder!"

Mrs. Popejoy's eyes and mouth popped open at the same time.

But the voice continued. "They killed me. Killed me. Murder, murder."

"Who the dickens are ya?" Luty blurted when it looked like Mrs. Popejoy was going to say something.

"My name is Dorothy." The voice was a piteous wail.

As instructed, Luty kept her eyes on Mrs. Popejoy, who was rapidly turning white. "What do ya want?"

"Justice," the voice screeched.

Hatchet jumped and the veiled lady jumped too.

"Is that Lady Lucia?" the butler asked Mrs. Popejoy quickly.

Mrs. Popejoy blinked in confusion. Luty almost laughed out loud. They had the woman between a rock and a hard place. The medium could hardly admit she hadn't the faintest idea what was going on.

"Dead." This voice was decidedly different from the first. "Murder."

"Who the blazes is this one?" Luty asked. "Lady Lucia? Yoo-hoo, are you Lady Lucia?"

"Abigail . . ." The voice trailed off. "Murdered."

Mrs. Popejoy was slowly rising from her chair, her face a mask of shock.

Suddenly the door to the drawing room burst open. Inspector Witherspoon, Constable Barnes and Ashley Phipps entered.

"You can't go in there, sir," yelled the maid. She rushed after them. "Mrs. Popejoy is having a séance."

The bright light from the hallway spilled into the darkened drawing room. Mrs. Popejoy, her hand at her throat, her eyes wide with fear, stared at Ashley Phipps as if she'd seen a ghost.

"Dreadfully sorry, Mrs. Popejoy," the inspector began. "I say, it's awfully dark in here, do you think we could have some light?"

The maid looked at Mrs. Popejoy, but the woman wasn't paying any attention to her. Her eyes were fixed on Ashley Phipps. The girl hesitated for a second and then began to light the lamps.

"So sorry to interrupt you, Esme dear," Phipps said, "but this police inspector here seems to think I've something to do with some murder."

"Egads," the inspector cried as he caught sight of Luty Belle. "It's Mrs. Crookshank. What are you doing here?"

"I've come fer a séance," she said tartly. "And we were gettin' a right earful before you interrupted. Some women named Dorothy and Abigail was comin' through from the other side. They claimed they was murdered. Maybe it's a good thing you showed up after all."

Mrs. Popejoy suddenly gasped and they all turned as Leonard Hodges came stalking into the drawing room.

"Leonard," she yelped, "what are you doing here?"

He pulled a note out of his pocket. "You sent me a note, you said it was urgent."

"I did no such thing," she said earnestly, glancing quickly at the inspector. "I think you'd better leave," she continued in a weak voice. "We're rather busy right now."

"Please don't go, Mr. Hodges," the inspector put in hastily. "It's just as well you dropped in. The constable and I have a few questions for you."

"Just a minute," Phipps chimed in. He stared at Hodges. "Who are you?"

Hodges seemed to notice Phipps for the first time. He started in surprise and then glanced quickly at Mrs. Popejoy.

No one spoke. There was only the sound of Hatchet's chair as he quietly got to his feet.

"I don't know what the meaning of this is," Mrs. Popejoy began.

Witherspoon decided to take control of the situation. "Mr. Hodges. You stated that you escorted Mrs. Popejoy to the train station on the night your wife was murdered, is that correct?"

"Of course." Hodges looked nervously from Phipps to Mrs. Popejoy.

"But Mr. Phipps here claims he was the one who escorted Mrs. Popejoy on the night of January fourth."

"He's mistaken. Tell him, Esme, tell him he's wrong."

"I most certainly am not mistaken," Phipps insisted. "For goodness' sakes, Esme. My mother and Mrs. Cravit both saw you when you came to the door. This is ridiculous. Just tell this policeman the truth."

"The truth," she whispered.

"Don't say another word, Esme," Hodges ordered.

"Esme," Phipps exclaimed. "What on earth is going on here? You know yourself we made arrangements for me to take you to the station weeks ago."

"Is it Dorothy who got herself murdered?" Luty asked innocently. "Or was it someone named Abigail?"

The inspector shot Luty a puzzled frown. Constable Barnes cleared his throat and Hatchet moved over to stand by the door.

"Mr. Hodges, I'm afraid I'll have to ask you to come down to the station to help with our inquiries," Witherspoon said.

"Based on what?" Hodges snapped. He pointed at Phipps. "This man's word. I don't see why you should believe him."

"It's not just Mr. Phipps's word. You see, we've also found the driver of the hansom you and Mrs. Popejoy took that night. He's prepared to swear that he stopped in Lewis Road. That's where you obviously slipped off, and Mrs. Popejoy then allowed Mr. Phipps to accompany her. What we'd like to know, sir, is where did you go when you left Mrs. Hodges?"

Hodges looked wild. "This is absurd. Why, Esme can confirm that I never left her side that evening."

Witherspoon turned to stare at Mrs. Popejoy. "Is that correct?"

"I—I—I'm not really certain," Mrs. Popejoy muttered.

"Mrs. Popejoy," the inspector said sternly, "I'm afraid I must insist that you come down to the station also. There's something very much amiss here. I think, perhaps, you know more about Mrs. Hodges's death than we've been led to believe."

"Now see here," Phipps sputtered. "The only thing Mrs. Popejoy did that night was go to Southend to visit a friend. That's hardly a crime."

"No, but conspiracy to murder is," Barnes put in softly.

"Murder!" Mrs. Popejoy exclaimed. "I didn't kill anyone. And I'm not going to take the blame."

Outside the window, Mrs. Jeffries and Betsy huddled closer to the window, straining to hear everything that was being said. The housekeeper felt a surge of relief as she heard the uncertainty in Mrs. Popejoy's voice. Their plan was working. Esme Popejoy had become so unhinged during the séance that she didn't realize what she was saying.

"It was his idea, his plan," Mrs. Popejoy insisted. Her voice had a high-pitched hysterical ring to it. "He killed them both. He bungled the first one and now he's trying to pin this one on me. But I won't have it. I'm not going to face the hangman for the likes of him."

"Shut up, you stupid fool," Hodges hissed. He glared at her. "She doesn't know what she's talking about. She's a silly, hysterical woman and you can't believe a word she says."

"They'll believe me, all right," Mrs. Popejoy yelled. "I'm not the one that pulled that trigger. I'm not the one that's going to hang."

"I think we'd better get to the station," the inspector said. "We'll need complete statements from both of you."

"We're not going to accompany you anywhere," Hodges stated flatly.

"I'm afraid you are, sir," Witherspoon began. He broke off suddenly and his eyes widened. Beside him, he heard Constable Barnes's sharp hiss of breath.

Hodges had pulled out a gun.

Witherspoon fought off a surge of panic as he stared down into the barrel of a revolver. "Now, Mr. Hodges, sir. Put that thing away before someone gets hurt."

"Put this gun down?" Hodges laughed. "And let you arrest me. I hardly think so, Inspector."

"But I wasn't going to arrest you," Witherspoon replied. He swallowed heavily. "I was merely going to have you and Mrs. Popejoy accompany me to the station."

"To help with your inquiries." Hodges sneered and jerked his head towards Mrs. Popejoy. "She wouldn't last an hour under police interrogation. I should never have trusted her. Silly, stupid cow. I should have known how weak she was when she started believing in this spiritualism nonsense. Go to the station with you? Do you think I'm a fool?"

"No, of course you're not a fool," the inspector said. He forced himself to stay calm. Egads, here he was in a whole roomful of people facing a madman with a gun.

A chill blast of wind slammed into the room, rattling the partially open window. Hodges started and whirled towards the window.

Suddenly a hand sliced down on Hodges's arm and with a cry of rage he dropped the gun. It clattered to the floor and skittered across the room.

Barnes rushed to Hodges, twisted his arms behind his back and slapped him in a pair of handcuffs.

There was a loud commotion in the hallway and everyone turned. Three police constables burst into the room. "We heard you needed some help, sir," the first one said.

Witherspoon blinked in confusion. Where the devil had these fellows come from? But he wasn't one to look a gift horse in the mouth. "Quite right, we can use a hand here." He pointed to Mrs. Popejoy, who was staring blankly into space. "Please apprehend that lady." Then he turned to Leonard Hodges. "I'm arresting you for the murder of Abigail Hodges."

The inspector cautioned both his prisoners and a moment later they were led away.

Hatchet knelt down and picked the weapon up. He handed it to Witherspoon. "I believe you should take charge of this, sir."

"Thank you, er, ah . . . Mister . . ."

"Hatchet, sir. I'm Mrs. Crookshank's butler."

"Well, good work, Mr. Hatchet." Witherspoon stared at him curiously. "I must say, that was a rather nice trick. Wherever did you learn how to disarm a man in that fashion?"

"Now will someone please tell me 'ow you knew it were Mr. Hodges and Mrs. Popejoy?" Wiggins pleaded.

They were sitting in the drawing room at Upper Edmonton Gardens, for Mrs. Jeffries insisted they might all as well be comfortable. The inspector was likely to be tied up for hours at the police station.

Mrs. Goodge had brought in a tray of cocoa and a Battenberg cake. "You mean you haven't figured it out yet?" she asked as she sliced the cake.

"If I'd figured it out, I wouldn't be askin' now, would I?" Wiggins replied. He nodded his thanks as the cook handed him a plate.

"Well," Mrs. Jeffries began, "I can't say it all came to me in a blinding flash, but once all of you began bringing in your various items of information and gossip, I realized the murder could only have been committed by the two of them. There were so many little things that didn't add up." She shrugged. "And once I began to really examine everyone's motive, the suspect who had the most to gain was Mr. Hodges."

"Excuse me, madam," Hatchet said. "But I don't quite follow that line of reasoning. Surely Mr. Felcher, Mrs. Trotter and Miss Marsden all benefited by Mrs. Hodges's death."

"True. But how much, enough to risk being convicted of murder?" Mrs. Jeffries stated. "You see, Miss Marsden and Mr. Vogel had no reason to kill her; they already had made plans to go to Canada."

"What about Mr. Felcher?" Betsy asked.

"True. He gained control of his inheritance, but why kill Mrs. Hodges now? He'd been putting up with his aunt for years. Besides, he had no idea what time the séance was going to end that night and he certainly didn't know that Mr. Hodges wasn't going to be bringing Mrs. Hodges home." Mrs. Jeffries reached for her cocoa. "The same can be said of

Mrs. Trotter. No, when you looked at the murder rationally, when you examined all the pieces of the puzzle, there was really only one solution. But of course I didn't begin seeing the pattern until the note."

"Which note?" Wiggins wiped a cake crumb off his cheek. "The ones you sent tonight?"

"No, the one instructing the police to search the Hodges house," she said. "You see, that was a deliberate attempt to point the finger of guilt at Miss Marsden. Once I realized that, there was only one person who had reason to want Miss Marsden and Mr. Vogel convicted of this crime."

"What reason?" Luty asked. "I figured whoever sent that note was just tryin' to save his own skin."

Mrs. Jeffries shook her head. "Oh no, that note led to the discovery of the jewels in Miss Marsden's room. There was only one person who would benefit if Miss Marsden were convicted of murder. That person was Leonard Hodges. You see, you can't profit from a crime, so if she'd been convicted of murdering her aunt, Mr. Hodges would have received the whole of Mrs. Hodges's fortune. I think that at first they really tried to make the murder look like a burglary gone bad. But when they bungled it so badly, they had to fall back on another plan. In one sense it was an even better plan. Getting Miss Marsden arrested would have given Mr. Hodges the whole of his wife's fortune."

"But how did they do it?" Wiggins persisted. "I know it 'ad somethin' to do with that hansom and stoppin' on the way to the station. I know that Mr. Hodges got out and nipped off to kill his wife and Mrs. Popejoy got that Phipps feller to ride off with her. But didn't the driver notice he were a different bloke than the one she started out with?"

"No, Mr. Hodges had deliberately worn the same kind of coat and hat that Mr. Phipps habitually wore," Mrs. Jeffries said. "Remember when Betsy told us that Mrs. Hodges had gotten angry at her husband for buying some cheap clothes from a ready-wear shop in the East End? Well, then when Betsy mentioned that she'd followed Mr. Hodges to St. James Church and watched him give an almost new coat and hat away, I realized that Hodges had deliberately tried to disguise himself that night and now he wanted to get rid of the evidence."

"How do you think he got Vogel's gun?" Smythe asked.

"Probably exactly like Mr. Vogel himself said. He stole it."

"Well, it was a fine piece of work, Hepzibah," Luty said earnestly.

"Oh please, don't give me all the credit." She gestured around the room. "All of you deserve to take a bow. Smythe's tracking down that coachman and confirming they'd stopped so the switch could take place,

Betsy's information about the coat and hat, Wiggins following Miss Marsden and of course you and Hatchet were invaluable."

"Do you think Phipps was in on the plot?" Betsy asked.

"No. I think he's an innocent pawn." Mrs. Jeffries took a sip of cocoa. "Remember, Mrs. Popejoy hadn't had a thing to do with the man for months. Until, that is, they were ready to do murder. Then she up and asks him to escort her to the train station. It was really a very simple plot. Mr. Hodges and Mrs. Popejoy drive off in a hansom, providing the both of them with an ironclad alibi for the murder of his wife. They make a stop, Hodges gets out, goes home, commits murder and then saunters off to his club. Mrs. Popejoy lets Mr. Phipps escort her to the train station and goes off to visit a friend. Clever, but not quite clever enough."

"Well, it was jolly clever of you two to take that Madame Natalia along with you tonight." Mrs. Goodge clucked her tongue. "Imagine bein' able to do all that fancy stuff with her voice."

Luty chuckled. "She's good. Her father was a ventriloquist. And it sure helped to move things along. Mrs. Popejoy was so rattled by all them voices from the grave she give herself away."

"Do you think they really did murder his first wife?" Smythe asked, his expression sober.

"Yes," Mrs. Jeffries replied slowly, "but I'm not sure the police will ever prove it. And, of course, Hodges didn't gain anything. Dorothy Throgmorton's family saw to that. I suspect that's why he married Mrs. Hodges. He and Mrs. Popejoy planned it from the beginning. We know they've known each other for years. He married Abigail Hodges, acted the devoted husband, introduced her to spiritualism and Mrs. Popejoy and then murdered her."

Hatchet clucked his tongue. "Disgusting. Murdering innocent women for money."

Mrs. Jeffries nodded and then looked at Hatchet curiously. "I must say, Hatchet, you certainly saved the day, disarming a man with a gun. You were quite brave tonight."

"Hatchet's right good at some things," Luty agreed with a wide grin.

The butler glowered at his mistress. "Bravery had nothing to do with it. I assure you, I disarmed Mr. Hodges for the sole purpose of inhibiting Mrs. Crookshank from pulling out her own weapon. The last time she pulled a gun out of her muff, we were repairing holes in the ceilings for weeks."